BODIE & BROCK THOENE

SHILOH AUTUMN

THOMAS NELSON PUBLISHERS
Nashville • Atlanta • London • Vancouver

Published in association with the literary agency of Alive Communications, 1465 Kelly Johnson Blvd. Suite #320, Colorado Springs, CO 80920.

Published in Nashville, Tennessee, by Thomas Nelson, Inc., Publishers, and distributed in Canada by Word Communications, Ltd., Richmond, British Columbia, and in the United Kingdom by Word (UK), Ltd., Milton Keynes, England.

Unless otherwise noted, all Scripture quotations are from the NEW KING JAMES VERSION OF THE BIBLE, © 1979, 1980, 1982, by Thomas Nelson, Inc., Publishers.

"Brother Can You Spare a Dime?" words by E. Y. Harburg, music by Jay Gorney. Copyright ©1932 by Harms, Inc.

Except for recognized historical figures and family members, all characters are fictional, and any resemblance to persons living or dead is strictly coincidental.

Library of Congress Cataloging-in-Publication Data

Thoene, Bodie, 1951–
   Shiloh autumn / Bodie and Brock Thoene.
     p. cm.
   ISBN 0-7852-8066-9
   I. Thoene, Brock, 1952– . II. Title.
PS3570.H46S48   1996
813'.54–dc20   96-12341
                                        CIP

Printed in the United States of America

1 2 3 4 5 6 7 — 00 99 98 97 96

To Tom and Bettie Turner
on your Golden Wedding Anniversary
July 13, 1996

We have written these stories down so your children and children's children will remember where we come from and where we are all going!

One day we will meet beside the river and our Lord will dry every tear.

For now, we must live in the joy of that promise and recall that for every generation Life is hard, but God is faithful.

Other Books by Bodie and Brock Thoene

Where are the songs of Spring? Ay, where are they?
Think not of them. Autumn has its music too . . .
Hedge crickets sing; and now with treble soft
The red-breast whistles from a garden croft;
And gathering swallow twitter in the skies.

—adapted from *To Autumn* by John Keats

PROLOGUE

No one in Shiloh saw it coming. Not even Grandma Amos—and it was rare for something that big to escape the old woman's prophetic vision.

Not one woman in all of Shiloh got up that morning, whipped up a batch of biscuits and gravy, and remarked to her man over coffee, "I've got me a feelin' the whole world's gonna come crashin' down 'round our ears."

No groups of men gathered at the barbershop or the livery stable to discuss hard times a-coming—as far as anyone knew, hard times were the regular order of business. No women talked worriedly over afternoon cups of coffee. No families gathered in the Baptist church and the Methodist church to pray for special strength and courage.

It did not happen that way.

Instead, life just went on as it always had.

By the first of October in 1931, most of the cotton had been picked and trucked in to Hooper's Cotton Gin. After that, most folks had turned to worrying about things other than getting their cotton harvested before Mr. Boll Weevil came up from Texas to have his supper in western Arkansas. Now that the bales were made and Hooper had said that all was going to be fine for another year, Shiloh could begin fretting over regular things once again. Young'uns. Too quiet in school. Too rowdy. Too skinny. Growing too fast to keep in shoes. Husband down with a bad back. Sore knee. Toothache. Bellyache. Wife down with a headache. Pregnant again. Oh, Lord, another mouth to feed. Still not pregnant. Oh Lord, send us a child! Mule with a bowed tendon. Cow gone dry. Barren sow. Prize hen stopped laying.

The failure of ten banks in a city in Illinois had made the newspapers, but such matters carried little weight in Shiloh. Shiloh folks had wised up and stopped using banks altogether after Wall Street went bust in 1929 and took a mess of bankers with it. Those who had cash money (not many did) stuffed it into a mattress or hid it in a tin box under a loose plank in the floor.

So there was no inkling that a crisis in distant Tennessee could spin off like a tornado and slam down with a fury against the red earth of a little town in Arkansas.

No inkling at all that so much could change from one Shiloh autumn to the next. . . .

PART I

The Farmer Is the Man

The farmer is the man, the farmer is the man
Lives on credit till the fall.
His pants are wearing thin,
His condition, it's a sin.
They've forgot that it's the farmer feeds us all.

—Nineteenth-century folk song, author unknown

C H A P T E R 1

Shiloh was not an easy place to locate, even with a road map.

To find it, you either had to be from Shiloh or really lost. But it was there on the map all right: smack between Hartford to the west and Mansfield to the east. Four miles either direction.

Railroad men and hoboes knew the town by the water tower and the trestle that crossed James Fork Creek. The Baptist circuit preacher knew it for James Fork Baptist Church and cemetery. The Methodist circuit preacher knew it for Shiloh Methodist Church and cemetery.

The congregation of the Baptist denomination was made up of farmers who lived mostly on the north side of the creek. Methodist farmers lived on the opposite bank. Neither group thought more highly of the other than it ought.

When drought hit western Arkansas, Baptists took to immersing their new converts inside a large, round, corrugated stock tank, which was tediously filled by hand from a deep well. Methodists adapted more readily to the crisis by wading midcalf into the stream and pouring a cupful of water over the head of the penitent.

It was generally believed by the Methodists that if the drought did not break soon and the wells went dry, their Baptist neighbors would have to pull up stakes and push on to a moister climate.

The Baptists, on the other hand, believed that the searing heat of summer was merely a hint of what the Methodists had to look forward to in the hereafter.

As for the effect of the drought on the farmland itself, citizens on both sides of the creek had been forced to adopt the Methodist form of crop irrigation. Water was doled out to the thirsty cotton fields one cupful at a time.

There were two places in Shiloh where the discussion of doctrine was off-limits. The first was Shiloh Grammar School, a small, one-room structure where sixty children attended first through eighth grades. Students from both sides of the James Fork were united by a mutual dislike of the schoolteacher.

Neutral territory for the adults was Shiloh General Store, a dusty old log building that sagged and leaned into the slope of the hill it topped. The interior smelled of leather and camphor and peppermint and tobacco, and every inch of space was crammed with the necessities of life. Wall pegs supported plow collars and plow lines, trace chains, harnesses and hames. Rows of shelves held cans of kerosene, boxes of chewing tobacco, patent medicines and all varieties of canned goods, bib overalls, thread, and calico material for dresses and curtains and tablecloths. At the ends of shelves and against the walls stood barrels of crackers, kegs of molasses and flour and nails, sacks of chicken feed. Glass jars crowding the counters were filled with hard candy, pickled pigs' feet, pickled eggs, and pickled pickles.

In the back corner of the store was Shiloh's post office—a small caged cubicle with fifty numbered pigeonhole slots on the wall. Nearby was a counter with the cash register, an enormous brass contraption with bells that clanged like a fire engine to announce the purchase of even a penny's worth of candy. Directly behind the register was a curtained alcove that housed the only telephone.

In the summer, the iceman made a delivery three times a week to leave fifty pounds of ice in the square Nehi soda cooler that stood on the porch beside the door. Those who could afford it bought a soda to sip as they sat on the long benches outside the store and talked over their crops or bargained over the price of a mule or worried aloud about the weather. Those who could not afford a soda dipped into the cooler and took a chunk of ice to suck on.

This summer, fewer Nehi sodas had been sold, and more chunks of free ice had disappeared into the mouths of worried men and sweaty children who did not have a penny for the hard candy on the counter.

But now summer was long gone, although the heat still lingered, and October 1, 1931, was just about over. All the customers had collected their mail and their purchases and gone home. Two old women moved in separate directions through rows of cracker barrels, canning jars, sacks of flour and sugar, and stacks of everything that a tiny country store could hold and not bust its seams.

Then the telephone began to ring.

Grandma Amos, who owned the Shiloh General Store, was something over eighty years old. Withered and bent, with skin like parchment paper, she walked with little mincing steps toward the insistent telephone.

Eight rings. Nine rings. Ten rings.

Willa Mae Canfield looked up from her work, planted a plump hand on a massive hip and waited, a look of exasperation and bemusement on her round ebony-colored face. Willa Mae was something past sixty and the size and shape of the enormous potbellied stove in the center of the room. A few inches movement to the right or left as she swept the dust from the floor and her hips would have swept away the row of peach tins from the shelf.

Although the Confederacy had fallen nearly seventy years before, Grandma Amos still insisted that the South would rise again. She had witnessed the burning of Atlanta and cheered the assassination of President Lincoln. She did not like Yankees in any form.

Willa Mae, on the other hand, was the granddaughter of a Cherokee Indian and a former slave. She was in no hurry for the old south to reappear.

And yet the two women got on well. Age had made Grandma Amos dependent on Willa Mae. And the years had given Willa Mae tolerance for a cantankerous old woman like Grandma Amos whose mind was firmly planted in the soil of the last century and whose conversation was at its best when the subject turned to the good old days before the war—meaning the War of Northern Aggression, Mister Lincoln's War.

In exchange for her work at the store three days a week, Willa Mae and her husband, Hock, were allowed the use of a cabin not far from the farm of their son, Jefferson. Willa Mae cleaned and cooked meals, opened the boxes of merchandise, and kept things in good order. Her ability to organize Shiloh General Store was considered a kind of miracle by most residents in this corner of Sebastian County. For the first time in living memory, spools of thread were not mixed with penny nails, and horse laxative was not stored in the Nehi cooler with soda pop.

This evening, Willa Mae wondered whether the caller would hang up before Grandma Amos reached the telephone.

Nineteen rings. Twenty. Twenty-one. Whoever was on the other end knew it always took Grandma Amos a long time to get there.

Willa Mae's thick arms were full of merchandise. A stack of overalls. A half-dozen home canned jars of plum jelly from Missus Faraby, the schoolteacher. Two boxes of Beechnut chewing tobacco.

Twenty-three. Twenty-four . . .

"You gonna get that thing, Gramma Amos?" Willa Mae halted beside the heap of denim work clothes.

Twenty-five.

"I'll get it! Durn thang! Ain't had no peace since they put 'er in here!"

Twenty-six.

"Well then, pick it up an' say howdy, Gramma! It don' make such a racket when y' picks it up an' talks in it!"

Twenty-seven. "How-do! We're all closed up till mornin'. But who's this a-callin'? Gramma Amos here on this end. . . ."

Willa Mae sighed with relief and went on about her business while Grandma hollered into the mouthpiece that the caller should speak up because she was half deaf.

"Is'at you, Brother Williams?" The old woman's voice shrilled until Willa Mae was sure everyone in Shiloh and beyond could hear. "You was just here t'day a-bringin' the mail from Hartford. What y' callin' so soon fer, Brother? Ever'body's gone home by now."

Brother William's words crackled and buzzed from the receiver into the store. Willa Mae could not understand all of what he was saying, but his voice was plenty loud enough all the same. Miraculous things these telephones. Brother Williams calling from four miles away in Hartford. Sometimes Willa Mae suspected that Brother just liked to use the telephone because he did telephone at odd hours and with insignificant news.

"What's that? What y'all hear from Memphis? . . . Brother, I don't know nobody from Memphis who's still alive. Used t' have some folks up Memphis way. Second cousins on my mama's side. Good people, too. Owned themselves a cotton plantation . . ."

"Gramma! That's 'xactly . . ." Brother's voice was mostly clear as anything.

Grandma continued. "Those Memphis cousins're all passed on now. . . . What y' babblin' 'bout, Brother? . . . Memphis . . . what? . . . Speak plain or I'm a-gonna hang this contraption up an' go have me some supper.... Yessir. Willa Mae's still here.... No, you cain't. She's a-fixin' my supper...."

Hearing her name mentioned, Willa Mae stood up from where she stooped in front of the shelf of jams and jellies. "Does Brother Williams want t' talk to me, Gramma? 'Cause if'n he do, you gimme that telephone. I gots work t' do, an' then I gots t' get on home. Hock was feelin' real poorly this afternoon, an' I don' want t' be gone long from him."

The old woman shouted back. "Why would Brother want t' talk t' you, Willa Mae? Who's gonna have news for you from Memphis?"

The buzz of Brother's voice became more urgent. Willa Mae pondered the deep purple of the schoolteacher's plum jelly. "I don' know nobody from Memphis," she agreed.

Grandma Amos, who had lost the thread of Brother's conversation, answered Willa Mae. "I *know* that! I *said* that! Who'd be a-callin' you from Memphis?"

A word or two from Brother became clear. "Never seen . . . Memphis . . . sky done fell . . ."

Grandma Amos lowered the earpiece and glared at it.

"A twister, was it?" she asked.

"Nothin' like it! Listen . . . I gotta . . . ol' woman . . . will you . . . ?"

Grandma scratched her chin and plucked at the long whisker on her cheek. "I cain't figger what this crazy fool is a-talkin' 'bout," she said to Willa Mae. "Blah. Blah. Blah. Sky done fell on Memphis."

She stood on tiptoe and shouted into the telephone. "Brother Williams! Shut your trap! Ain't nothin' happen in Memphis I care 'bout nohow! Ain't no news from Memphis cain't wait till t'morrow t' hear when you bring the mail. Lawd! When them dirty Yankees took Richmond we didn't hear 'bout it till it come out in the papers. Atlanta was somethin' else agin. I seen the smoke with mine own eyes. Wish I hadn't, but I did. Bad news can wait, my mama always said. There's some bad news I just shushed up 'fore it come outta the mouths of those who wished t' tell me. Some bad news I still ain't heard, I reckon."

"Well . . . got word . . . Mister Tedrow . . . Western Union . . . fifteen thousand . . ."

"Now Brother, me an' Willa Mae's got work t' do. My bones is achin' an' I want my supper 'fore it's breakfast time. I'm an old woman. Tell me quick. Have the Yankees captured Memphis?"

"Gramma . . . tryin' t' tell . . ."

"Brother, is anybody dead from Shiloh?"

"No, ma'am. But Gramma . . ."

"Any of our folks here in Shiloh got folks from Memphis that've up an' passed on?"

"No, but . . . ain't what I'm . . ."

"Well then, honey, that bein' the case, I'm a-gonna go set an' rock an' smoke a spell, an' you can ex-plain this Memphis thing come mornin'." With that she replaced the receiver with a firm hand.

"That was Brother Williams," Willa Mae stated flatly.

"Yes, t'was."

"You ain't gonna tell me what he wanted?"

"Don't know what he wanted. You got the corn bread in the oven?"

"Cain't you smell it?"

"I can't smell nothin' no more, Willa Mae. Snuff done burned my smeller away." Grandma Amos inhaled deeply to demonstrate. "Don't matter. What I mean is, have you got the liver and onions fried?"

"Well, if'n you cain't smell liver an' onions, Gramma, I don' know what to say. Yes'm. It's fried, all right. Cooked up an' in the warmer."

Grandma Amos lived in a single room, a lean-to at the back of the store. She sniffed again, hard. "I don't smell liver nor onions neither. Lawd. Well, I guess it don't matter. I didn't smell that dead squirrel under the floor till you pointed it out."

"Stunk up the whole place."

"Sometimes it's worth it, not havin' a smeller."

"Supper's in the warmer," Willa Mae repeated. "Mind you eat it. Don't let it dry out in there. I gots to get home t' Hock."

"Well, then. Get on." Grandma Amos turned her back and toddled toward her room. Stopping beside the harnesses, she looked up at the rafters as though some thought had penetrated her brain like a shaft of light. "Lawd? 'Pears t' me, if what Brother Williams says is so, it's a-gonna ruin a lot of folks hereabouts. Fifteen thousand bales in one day? Never heared tell of such a thing. Not since Sherman marched through Georgia! I s'pose Hooper'll be the first t' go. I pity the rest. S'pose folks ain't gonna be able t' pay me what they owe in the ledger?"

Willa Mae studied her a moment and thought what a crazy old woman Grandma Amos was at times. Tetched was the only word for it. Her mind would clear up when she ate something.

"Gramma? What you sayin'? The crop's done made. Hooper's gon' settle up in a few weeks, an' you'll get paid by ever'one who owes you. Which is all of Shiloh. You'll have t' get yourself another ledger after the settle. Now, you quit frettin'.'"

Grandma Amos shrugged. "It don't matter. I'm a-gettin' too old for all this anyhow."

"What you gabbin' on for, Gramma?" Willa Mae paused in the doorway as Grandma Amos disappeared into her room. "Gramma Amos?" Willa Mae called louder. "What's this Brother Williams thing all about?"

A wizened head poked out to reply. "I'll study on it t'night whilst I eat supper. Mebbe I can tell you in the mornin' if'n it comes t' me. Don' know how I missed this one, Willa Mae. The word of knowledge 'scaped me entire. I thought this drought was trouble enough for Job himself. Not so bad as the war of the Yankee invasion, I reckon. But the South may not rise again after this one." The door slammed shut.

The discussion ended on that cryptic note. Willa Mae left the place shaking her head in puzzlement as she hurried home to her husband.

C H A P T E R   2

I
t was time to say goodbye.

Hock Canfield knew it. So did Willa Mae, although after a lifetime together she did not want to admit it.

"Open up the winder, ol' woman," the little man whispered from his bed. "Lemme see the day."

She did as he asked, flooding the one-room cabin with light.

Mist and wood smoke hovered just above the thick stand of oak and hickory trees that bordered the cane and cotton fields of Shiloh. The gold and rust and flame-red shades of the autumn morning reflected in the winding ribbon of the James Fork Creek. Puffs of steam rose in exclamation points above the treetops as the Rock Island train rattled over the trestle.

The baying of hounds and the shouts of small boys echoed across the valley between Sugarloaf Mountain and the hazy blue range of the Poteaus. War whoops and yelps and cries of exultation blended with the long wail of the locomotive.

"Wonder if'n them boys is ever gonna catch that possum critter." Willa Mae stepped aside so Hock could see the colors of the day. "Been chasin' it mos' the night now." She sat in the rocker beside him and took his bony hand in her own.

"I been listenin'," Hock croaked, and nodded as if the sounds of the hunt gave him great pleasure. "Hounds is music to a boy." He closed his eyes as if remembering the music of his own boyhood and tried to hum some old song, but his lungs failed him.

"Possum don' like it much, I reckon." Willa Mae raised her husband's fingers to her lips. His hand was light and dry and brittle, a leaf waiting for the breeze.

"Finished soon."

Did he mean the hunt? Hock drifted off for a moment until the howl of pursuit became the sharp yapping that meant the possum was most likely cornered.

Hock's eyes snapped open again. "Up the p'simmon tree. Not long now."

Willa Mae did not want the hunt to end. The commotion that had begun last night had pulled her husband back to consciousness. Doc Brown had told her Hock had spoken his last, that he would not see the morning light. But it was dawn. From three o'clock this morning, Hock's thoughts had run with the boys. He had wagged his head on the pillow, and his feet had twitched beneath the quilt as their voices carried from the creek and through the woods then up the ridge. For these few hours Hock had remained with Willa Mae. It was as if he had to keep breathing long enough to catch the possum critter, toss it in a sack, bring it home for supper.

And so Willa Mae talked about other nights when Hock had hunted in the woods near their cabin. "I remembers back in Pisgah when you an' the young'uns . . ."

"Through the p'simmon patch."

"Do you remember, Hock? Y'all chased that possum . . . the big'un. . . . All night it were. Like these young'uns. . . . An' then Jefferson clumb the tree in Cody's yard, and the branch . . ."

Hock's mahogany face puckered in a grin. His words wheezed out. "Jeff! Get on down! Branch ain't strong enough. . . ."

"Down come Jefferson, and that possum got clean away."

Once again the old man tried to croak out the music he had heard in his mind through the night.

Possum up a 'simmon tree
Rabbit on the ground . . .

Willa Mae gave a laugh and joined him soft and low. Like she was singing a lullaby to her babies.

Lawd, Lawd, possum,
Shake them 'simmons down . . .
Tell me, does you love me now?

Hock's eyes locked on hers. So many years they had loved each other! He reached up and tried to say something. The words dissolved into a fit of coughing.

Willa Mae patted his back. "That's enough, I reckon. . . . I *knows*, Hock, honey . . . I knows *ever'*thing. Don' try t' say no more. . . ."

The two were silent for a time, listening to the morning and thinking of mornings long ago. Then thoughts of tomorrow morning crept into Willa Mae's mind.

Lawd, Lawd! It always is harder to be left behind than to be the one to go!

Then she prayed to be strong and shook off the ache of tomorrow. "It's still today, ain't it?" she said aloud. "And Jeff be comin' by for breakfast this mornin', Hock."

He squeezed her hand. Found his breath. "Home . . . Thinkin' 'bout goin' home, old woman . . . done wore me out."

"Lawdy, Hock! Mount Pisgah's a long way off from here even if you was able."

He did not reply. Was it Mount Pisgah he was thinking of—the home where they had brought fourteen children into the world and laid five of them to rest?

"Be glad to see the chilluns."

"Jeff be comin' by this mornin'." Of all nine living children, only Jefferson was nearby.

"I is thinkin' 'bout Widdie."

Willa Mae nodded and patted his arm. Little Widdie had passed on some years back when the flu epidemic had carried off so many.

So Hock was thinking of Widdie and those other Canfield young'uns all laid out beneath the row of ragged crosses in the colored cemetery there in Mount Pisgah.

"Reckon little Widdie will be right glad. . . ." She could not finish. She raised her eyes to the rafters, and the faces of five children, long since dust, came to her mind. Strange how all her world had grown up and grown old, but the young'uns she and Hock had buried were just the same in her memory. Always the same. She could not see the crosses on the hill in Pisgah. Not the colors of the flowers in the valley. Only the faces of her sweet babies, alive and smiling.

Now she imagined Hock holding each child in his scrawny arms again. And in the vision Hock was young, too.

"Real soon, honey." She stroked his cheek. "Real soon. I won't hold on too tight."

Hock sighed with relief at the thought of reunion.

"Can you eat somethin'?" she asked.

"They done got the . . . possum treed."

"That's right, honey."

"Them Tucker . . . boys."

"That's right, honey. Birch and Trudy's young'uns and little Davey Meyer with 'em."

The frantic yipping slowed. A slight breeze rustled the blue-checked curtain.

She sang the old tune again. It was the tune her grandpap had sung going out to the cotton patch way before daylight in the slave days. It was the tune she had sung to her babies as she rocked them to sleep.

Rabbit up a gum stump,
Possum up a holler.
Git him out, little boy,
And I gives you half a dollar,
I'll tell you how I loves you now . . .

The song pleasured Hock. Content, he closed his eyes.

Willa Mae kissed his cheek, then got up to check the corn bread. Hock always was fond of hot corn bread and buttermilk in the morning. Lately he would eat nothing else no matter how she scolded. He had been a small man all his life. Now he weighed no more than a child.

A whisper. "He'p me t' the winder."

Willa Mae's shoulders were as broad as a man's. In her younger days she could pick four hundred pounds of cotton a day. Now she moved slow, but she was still strong.

Shoving the bed across the floor, she plumped the pillows up so Hock could see down the slope to where the Tucker boys had the possum cornered.

Shiloh was waking up. The day was singing.

Saturday night and Sunday too
The old times on my mind,
Monday mornin' 'way 'fore day

Gots to leave old times behind.

Tell me who will love me now. . . .

It was the ol' granddaddy of all possums up that hickory tree. Maybe the biggest possum ever treed in Shiloh. The boys got one good look at it when it scrambled up the trunk. Practically the size of a coon dog, it was; a legend of a possum! The kind of critter men would talk about for years down at Dee Brown's barbershop.

The truth of it was that eleven-year-old Tom Tucker didn't much like the looks of any possum, be it big or small. He thought the little ones looked like big rats and the bigger ones like *giant* rats: beady eyes . . . pointy noses . . . fat, hairy bodies . . . long, hairless tails.

Nor did Tom like the way a possum played possum, rolling its eyes back, twitching and foaming and pretending to be dead when it was cornered or scared . . . playacting so's a dog or a feller didn't know if the thing was really dead or not, so's a feller had to kill the thing twice to make sure it really was genuinely dead. Gave him the creeps.

He did not enjoy eating possums for supper much either. They were greasy, gamy-tasting things even when baked up with sweet 'taters. Usually he took a bite or two, just because he had hunted it and caught it, but that didn't mean he liked the flavor of it.

But the hide! Now that was something else again. A good possum hide would fetch two bits from Brother Williams down at the livery stable, and this was going to be a good one, a real big one. Maybe worth more than two bits. The hide of a legend ought to be worth more than usual, oughtn't it?

The redbone coonhound sat panting and slathering and smiling up at the limbs of the hickory tree.

Tom put his hand on the young dog's head. "You're just wore out, but you won't give it up, will you, Rosey?"

Rosey blinked three times but did not look away from where she knew the possum to be. The slobber of anticipation dripped from her jowls. To Rosey's way of thinking, dining on possum grease was like slurping up an ice cream soda at Mr. Winters's drugstore or sucking on an all-day sucker or licking frosting out of a bowl. And chasing critters through the woods all night was like going to a Tom Mix double-feature Saturday matinee down at the Hartford Bijou.

Little Bobby, who was nine, wiped his nose on the red-checked flannel of his shirtsleeve, then tossed a hickory nut up at the trunk. "Shoot. Rosey ain't wore out. It's all the rest of us who's wore out. I'm wore out."

Not much more than a pup, Rosey was proving herself to be a great coon dog just like her mama, Emmaline. Tom had his suspicions, however, that they may have followed the trails of a dozen different critters before Rosey finally treed this one.

The three boys had not intended to hunt. They only meant to sleep out—to have one last night together before their cousin David Meyer said goodbye and boarded the Rock Island train to head west with his daddy and mama. But then, after the campfire died down, the possum had blundered through the bushes at the edge of camp, and Rosey had taken over. One sniff and she had leapt, baying, from among the bedrolls, jerking the boys awake. Her excitement had pulled them along all night as surely as if they were tied to a leash.

"How we gonna get it down?" Bobby pitched another hickory nut at the trunk.

"Too bad Rosey can't climb a tree," Davey Meyer added, sitting wearily on a stump. "That thing's up there, all right. Two bits for its hide. I'd sure like one-third share of that two bits in my pocket to take along on the train with me."

"How do we split twenty-five cents even? Three guys into two bits? Three ways? It don't go." Bobby screwed up his face as if the division hurt his brain.

"We don't have no hide to sell . . . yet," Tom warned. His voice was hoarse from hollering all night. "Rosey did her stuff. The catching and skinning is up to us."

"Yeah," Davey agreed. "Well, we better do something. Been running all night. Better have something to show for it."

"I'm hungry." Bobby leaned against the tree and crossed his arms. "Real hungry."

"Then go home," Tom snapped at his brother. "If you can't think of something, just go."

There was silence for a minute or so as all three of the boys tried hard to think of something. But what? Tom stared at Davey, who was walking around the tree, looking up.

"See anything?"

Davey squinted into the shadowed branches. The sun had not yet risen over the Poteau range, and it was still too dim to spot exactly where the possum was hiding.

"Nope."

Codfish, Davey's big black Newfoundland retriever, had given up entirely. Codfish was not much of a hunting dog. All night he had galloped along behind Rosey for the fellowship of it, howling because Rosey howled, sniffing where Rosey sniffed, and finally stopping at the base of the hickory tree because Rosey stopped here. But now, sniffing the trunk, Codfish lifted his leg to widdle on the bark in disdain, then scratched his ear and plopped down. Actually catching a critter at the end of the chase had never occurred to Codfish. Now that the romp had finally come to an end, the bearlike canine lay curled and snoring at the feet of his young master.

That instant the corona of daybreak topped the peak. Light flowed like water, chasing shadows down the slope to wash Shiloh with the morning.

Through the gnarled limbs a shaft of light struck the east-facing side of the trunk to reveal a hole hidden in the center of a knotted swell of bark, impossible to see unless the light was just right.

"There!" Bobby hollered. "Just under the big branch!"

Rosey yapped three times. She had known it was there all along. Codfish raised his head. Suddenly awake, suddenly no longer hungry, the trio of boys jumped up and danced a jig at the foot of the mammoth hickory.

Then the shifting illumination swept past the hollow, and the spot was hidden in the shadow again. Just that quick, their glimpse of the old possum's secret vanished completely from sight.

"We got him now!" Davey whooped and thumped Tom on the back.

The grin on Tom's face faded. "But we ain't got him. That hole is ten feet up there. Or more. We ain't got him."

"We'll climb 'er!"

"You ain't nothing but a knee-high man!" Tom scoffed. "That's the biggest hickory in the woods. Daddy wouldn't cut it down 'cause it's so big. Got no branches low enough even for Jefferson to catch hold of! So how we gonna climb 'er?"

"We'll smoke the thing out!" Davey cried.

"Too high up." Tom leaned against the tree as if to push it down. "Smart possum. Old, smart possum."

Bobby, who was little but quick of mind, scanned the distance from the ground to the possum's door. It was almost exactly three boys high.

"We'll do like them circus fellers!" he announced. The others glared at him for a moment until the suggestion took hold.

"That's right!" Davey pounded the tree with joy. "Stand on one another's shoulders, reach in, and pow! We catch hold of him, pull him out, and wallop him senseless!"

But who would do the reaching in? And who the pulling out?

This was briefly discussed. Tom and Bobby knew something about the teeth of possums. Big yellow teeth, this old feller would have. Sharp teeth. They mentioned this concern to Davey.

"Don't matter!" Davey paced as he talked. His hands flapped against his dungarees like he was trying to fly. "I'll climb up, yell, and yodel into his hole and scare him so bad he'll faint away with terror that we found him! You know the way possums do. And while he's playing dead, I'll snatch him by the tail, throw him down, you guys clobber him, and we'll be rich!"

There was still the matter of how to divide twenty-five cents three ways. Eight cents each with one penny left over. It was decided that the boy who climbed to the top, reached in, and pulled granddaddy possum out got the extra penny. Davey, who was born a city boy and therefore part fool, eagerly accepted the task. The bargain was sealed with spit and a handshake.

Being biggest and strongest, Tom was on the bottom. He pressed himself against the tree and helped Bobby climb up to stand on his shoulders. Nothing to it. The rough hickory bark provided good hand-holds. Getting Davey to the top of Bobby's shoulders was only slightly more difficult.

A human ladder, the three grunted and huffed and warned one another about leaning too far this way or that. An ant climbed from a crevice in the bark and crawled across Tom's hand. Bobby's shoes dug into his shoulders.

"Hurry it up!" Tom shouted at Davey.

"Can you reach it?" Bobby called up.

"There it is!" Davey was giddy. "I see the dadgum thing's eyes." Then he began to wail. His voice rose and fell like something out of a spook story. He yipped and shrieked a piercing scream that would have made any human critter cringe with fright. No doubt a possum, even an old experienced possum, would keel over from the terror of such a sound. It would roll its beady eyes back and froth at the mouth and look so horrible and dead that nothing would want to touch it . . . except for three boys.

Davey left off the banshee wail.

"Has it sulled yet?" By this Tom was asking if it had passed out.

Davey's voice carried down. "Don't know. Lemme . . ." The hand went in the hole. "I feel something! It ain't moving. There's its tail. Hold on! I'll have it in a . . ."

An instant later the banshee wail started up again. This time it was louder than the first time. It was about the worst hollering that Tom had ever heard. Great screams like something dying a terrible death. Davey began a kind of tap dance on Bobby's shoulders.

"Hold still!" There was fear in Bobby's voice. It was a long way to fall.

Two more ants crept up Tom's fingers to the cuff of his shirt.

The shrieking continued from the top.

"Ain't you done up there yet?" Tom called to Davey.

Bobby shifted on Tom's collarbone to brace himself against the struggle on his upper levels and added to the urgency. "Hurry it up, Davey! The thing's out cold by now."

"Get him!" Tom ordered. "Hurry it up!"

Silence. A pitiful whine from Davey. "I can't. He's got me, boys!" A choked cry. "He's bit me clean through the . . . meat 'tween my thumb and finger!" More shouts; curses to turn the face of a dockhand red. But not even curses had any effect on the legend. Now the begging began. "Lemme *go*! Pleeeease. Lemme loose! Turn loose!"

This was a very bad situation. Davey could not pull his hand out of the possum's hole because the possum was all swelled up like a toad. The possum would not turn loose. No matter how Davey Meyer screamed for mercy, old granddaddy possum would give no quarter. Below decks, where Tom and Bobby clung to the tree for dear life, the bark was suddenly alive with a tribe of red ants being warmed by the sun and excited by the rubbing, bumping, and jostling of their little roads and trails.

"Go, Rosey." Tom's words were barely a whisper. "Get Mama. Get help, girl!"

Jefferson Canfield walked barefoot up the dusty lane. Worn-out work boots, their frayed laces tied together, were slung over his broad shoulder. This was not so much to preserve the shoes, although that should have been a consideration in such hard times. But Jefferson, being Jeff, did not often dwell on hard times or saving the soles of such things as shoes.

Truth was, in spite of being five inches past six feet in height, with the visage of a battered hickory tree, Jefferson Canfield had never really grown up inside. He had never much liked leather pinching his big feet. He liked summer under his heels—the feel of grass between his toes. He would rather wade home through the cool current of the James Fork than step across the creek from rock to rock.

Home. Shiloh had become more than home to him. He called his cabin Dreamland.

Last night, sitting out on the porch with the stars winking bright from horizon to horizon, he had said to his wife, Lily, and the young'uns: "Shiloh be a magic place. The Lord talk all 'bout it in the Good Book. Settled by wanderin' folk that seen such sorrow in their time they had no voice lef' to speak even a word. When they firs' come over the mountain they look down at the Promised Land. They seen the sky an' the valleys an' the fields an' cricks. The sight make 'em so happy they begun t' sing out to the Lord and name ever' place they lay eyes on. And there they stay forever more."

He wasn't just talking about the children of Israel. He was talking about himself, too, and about Lily. Of course, the young'uns were too little to know much, but they listened with big eyes to the deep, mellow tone of their daddy's voice. They had come into the world after the grieving and sorrowing times were over. Jeff supposed they never would hear all the story about their mama and daddy. It was better that way.

This morning Jefferson hummed the words in rhythm with the retreating Rock Island locomotive as he walked beside the tracks.

Sugarloaf. Poteau. Goin' to the moun-tain!
Pine Grove. Prairie Grove. Goin' home! Goin' home!
Buggy Hill. Fox Hill. B'side still wa-ter.
Rock Island. Red Yard. See my Lord . . .
Nail Crick. Riddle Crick. Home, my Je-sus.
Petty John. James Fork. My daddy goin' home.

Sing the names out loud, and Shiloh was a song. His mama had always said that Thomas Jefferson Canfield could set anything to a tune.

Put it all together with the corn and cotton and bright orange pumpkins on the fields; add the persimmons and the sweet gum and the oaks and hickory and sycamore, and Shiloh was his Promised Land.

It was almost, but not quite, heaven. Jeff figured it would do just fine till he went home to the genuine article.

Jefferson turned his eyes up toward the purple banner of a morning cloud. He fixed his mind on all these pleasant things . . . these good things . . . as he hurried along the lane toward the cabin where his mama and daddy lived.

The road sloped downward, gently rounding the small white structure of Shiloh Methodist Church and the cemetery beside it. The pastels of early morn reflected on the tall rippled windowpanes, giving the small white clapboard building an ethereal glow as if the Lord had dropped in for a visit. Another day, Jeff might have stopped by to say howdy, but not today. He thought of his daddy and quickened his stride.

Cutting across the field, Jefferson's gaze lingered a moment on the open gate of the wrought-iron fence and the old tombstones covered with lichen and the new ones carved with old familiar names. These were the silent members of Shiloh Church.

All around the field, thin fingers of smoke from the cookstoves marked the spots where the rest of the congregation was waking up in their farmhouses and getting on with the day.

But just over the low hill, where Jeff's daddy and mama lived, no smoke rose this day. The sky was empty above the cabin of Hock and Willa Mae; the embers of his mama's cookstove had been allowed to go out. There was only one reason his mama would neglect to rekindle the fire.

A lonesome feeling swept over Jeff, crowding out every other thought and emotion.

So the fire had died.

He stopped midfield. His big hands hung limp at his sides. He had known it was coming, but he had not expected that the world would feel so empty for it.

"You done lef' us, Daddy," he whispered with certainty. "I hoped you'd wait a while, leastwise till Lily have the baby."

In the distance, where the smoke should have been, a slight breeze skittered over the treetops as if a hand had brushed the highest branches. It moved toward him, dropping low at the edge of the woods to ripple across the tall grass of the pasture. Jeff stretched out his arms as if to embrace it. Warm and fragrant, it touched him softly, then swept by. He traced the ripple with his eyes to the big oak in the churchyard. Dry leaves rattled in the branches above the green-shingled roof and then were silent.

There followed a flash of blinding sunlight, burnished copper, gold, and blue. He shielded his eyes. It faded in an instant as the sun shifted from the mirrored panes into shadow. Shiloh Church was just the small white clapboard structure once again . . . windows dark . . . doors closed . . . leaves blowing across the stone steps. Silent. Empty and dull.

Maybe it was not the sun. Maybe not the wind.

Jeff raised his hand in farewell.

For a time, he stood rooted there. Insects buzzed in his ears, bringing him around. His mama would be needing him, he knew. He set out again.

Rosey was not the kind of dog that would get herself written about in a Jack London novel.

When Tom told her to get help, she wagged obediently and sauntered over to Codfish. She sniffed him and whined, but Codfish was not Mama. Codfish was no help. He lay sleeping on his back in a patch of sunlight. His huge paws hung motionless in the air, and he snored like a drunk wearing out a hangover. Rosey lay down beside him and solemnly contemplated her boys. Her patient demeanor demonstrated complete trust that they would get her possum down sooner or later. Until then, she would wait at their feet.

Their voices gone now, the boys stood like a totem pole of misery against the old hickory tree. Twenty minutes had passed since granddaddy possum had latched on to Davey's hand.

An occasional moan drifted down from the top, letting Tom and Bobby know the possum had not changed its mind. After all, they had ruined its entire night. Now that it had them prisoner, old possum was not inclined to show mercy.

At the sound of approaching footsteps Rosey leapt up. Codfish opened his eyes reluctantly and rolled over, but did not rouse himself further. Rosey wagged and sidled away.

Tom tried to say the word "Help," but the cry came out like the squeak of a hinge.

"Is 'at you, Rosey gal?" It was Jefferson Canfield.

In an instant the three captives began croaking and fidgeting and thrashing their arms.

"Lord! . . . Lord a-mercy! What you young'uns? . . ."

Jeff grasped the situation instantly, and reached his mighty arm up to support Davey's seat in the palm of his hand.

Suddenly relieved of their burden, Tom and Bobby collapsed in a heap at the big man's bare feet.

"Didn' your daddy teach you better'n that? Go stickin' your hand through ol' possum's front door!" He nudged Tom with his toe. "Git on up here, chil'! Tom! You gots to he'p your friend get shed of that critter."

Jeff snatched Tom by the back of his denim coveralls and slung him through the air to perch on his shoulder.

It was plain to Tom that Davey was in a bad way. To the elbow, his right arm had disappeared into the hole. Altogether, his face looked as if someone had taken hold of his ears and stretched everything back. He was white as a sheet. Turned down lips were pinched with a trace of blue at the corners. Eyes were wide and helpless.

"Can't get him out. Too heavy," Davey managed.

"What . . . do I do?" Tom asked.

Jeff hollered, "Grab holt of that critter an' pull 'im out!"

Tom did not express his fear that the thing would let go of Davey and latch on to him. Gritting his teeth he made a nervous sound something like the buzzing of bees. Reaching into the dark hollow, he groped for the tail of the possum. It was there, limp like a dead snake against the smooth inside wall of the trunk. He grasped the hairless thing and pulled it to the opening. Davey huffed and squeezed his eyes tight shut.

Tail first, the possum emerged. Then fat haunches and back legs extended over Davey's outstretched arm. It was a tight squeeze, like a cork in a bottle. The animal was heavy.

"Pull 'im hard! Dadgum!" Jefferson shouted. "He's sulled for certain now. Cain't do no more harm than he's done 'less he wakes up." A quick glance at Rosey and Codfish identified a potential danger. The dogs were alert now and snuffling around the base of the hickory. One clear look at the possum, and there would be no holding them back. Jeff ordered Bobby, "Catch them dawgs 'fore they make this worse'n it already is! Take 'em on up to my folks' place. Lock 'em in the barn. Do as I say, now!"

Bobby obeyed, reluctantly leading Codfish and Rosey from the scene, across the meadow and up the hill in the direction of the Canfield cabin. Tom didn't watch him go. He was too occupied with imagining what would happen if that possum woke up. He grimaced and renewed his grip on the hairless tail.

One final tug brought out the possum's head, jaws locked on the fleshy part of Davey's hand between thumb and forefinger. Sure enough, old possum was playing possum. Limp as a rag, it lay in Tom's arms. Looked dead as anything; teeth sunk in deep. Davey's blood dripped from its mouth and down the fur beneath its chin. Gently lowered to the ground, Davey took one look at the possum and his hand and promptly swooned. Possum and boy lay side by side, still attached and unconscious in a cradle of hickory roots.

"Biggest tick I ever did see." Jefferson shook his head in admiration of the size of the animal. "Fetch me a stick, Tom. I'm gonna have to break its neck."

Tom balked. He had seen the killing done a dozen times. A heavy stick laid across the critter's neck, then a quick jerk of the tail, and it would be all over. But this possum was different. He was smart and old.

Tom hesitated. "That possum . . . he beat us fair and square, too. I kinda feel for it." And Tom did feel regret that their valiant opponent had to die such an ignoble death. A stick across its neck . . . it seemed a shame to kill something that had been dodging humans, dogs, and bullets for so many years.

"Fetch me a stick, I says!" Jeff was gruff.

Davey's eyes fluttered open. He moaned and cussed his captor. Jeff frowned and glared down at Davey. Jeff did not hold with blasphemy. Davey Meyer was adept at it.

"Mebbe oughta leave this boy 'tached till he learn t' speak with respec' 'bout ol' possum. T'ain't the critter's fault y'all be so dumb." He nudged the hairy back of the animal with his big toe, then cast a sideways glance at the stock pond one hundred yards across the clearing.

Jefferson placed the limp animal across Davey's chest then scooped up possum and boy together. "Come on then, Tom. Y'all gots a thing or two t' learn, I reckon." They trudged along the berm of the pond, then across the crusted mud to the murky brown water.

"You's a good swimmer, ain't y', chil'?" Jeff asked Tom.

"Reckon . . ." The word was barely out of Tom's mouth before Jeff grabbed him with one hand and tossed him high into the middle of the pond.

With a wail of protest Tom splashed down, sending a geyser of muck and slime into the air. Once his feet found the bottom, the water was chest high, and it was real cold. Cold enough to wake the dead. "What'd you do that for?"

Jefferson, pleased with his plan, hooted approval. "Stay where you is, boy."

"How come you throw'd me in here? I got no possum hooked on me."

"Just had t' know. It ain't too deep, is it, Tom?" Jefferson called.

Tom pulled a thick piece of water grass and a patch of green slime off his face. He was angry and embarrassed. "No, it ain't, but—"

"Good. Don' want nobody gettin' hurt. Ain't no cottonmouths swimmin' 'round out there?"

Tom froze. He searched the area around him to see if a viper had been disturbed by his noisy intrusion. "No, sir."

"That's real good. Jus' stay there till I says come out." Now Jefferson glanced down at the possum and muttered. "Well, ol' man, looks like you's 'bout to be free agin." Jefferson waded in until he stood midcalf in the mud and muck. Stretching out his giant arms, he held Davey and the possum out over the deep water and let go.

The result of this total immersion? Revival. Resurrection. Suddenly released from the jaws of his tormentor, Davey hollered and flailed. Old granddaddy possum sprang instantly to life. After a brief moment of confusion, the thing paddled once around the sputtering hunters and headed for the far bank.

Davey struggled in the opposite direction. Coughing and cussing and waving his punctured hand, he splashed over to Jefferson, who snatched him out of the water, lifted him up, and threw him once again to land a dozen yards beyond Tom.

"Y'all wouldn't know it to look at 'em, but possums takes to water like they was fish," Jefferson remarked. The animal reached the far side of the bank, waddled out, shook himself, glanced backward, then trundled off into the woods.

Jeff shaded his eyes and looked after it, then without another word to Tom and Davey, he turned to gaze for a long moment in the direction of the Canfield cabin. Tom saw some grim thought strike Jeff just as plain as if the man had been hit on the head with a board. The bright gold-capped smile faded. Brow furrowed. Sorrow filled his brown eyes. It was an expression rarely seen on the face of one so affable as Jefferson.

An instant later, like ol' possum, Jeff had clearly forgotten all about the two hunters up to their necks in the pond. Without a backward glance, he left them to struggle out alone.

Tom wrapped an arm around Davey's waist and helped him reach the shore.

Davey's hand displayed a perfect pattern of possum teeth, uppers and lowers. Swollen twice its normal size, it was a big balloon, or the udder of a milk cow in need of milking. It looked to Tom like it was blown up almost to popping.

"You're in a bad way," Tom said.

Davey gulped air and gaped with horror at his wounds. "My pitching hand!" he wailed as the two stumbled and fell forward in the mud. Davey gasped and groaned and retched. Ten seconds of silence followed as he lay there in the mud and considered the contents of his stomach. Then, weakly, "I feel better now," he told Tom, who at the first gurgle had leapt out of range. "Help me up." Davey extended his left hand, and Tom tugged him to his feet.

"Where's Jeff got off to in such a hurry?" Tom mumbled.

By now, Jeff's long stride had gobbled up the distance across the field. He was at the base of the hill and, not slowed by the steep terrain, was moving toward the cabin.

Tom eyed Jeff's back with resentment. Jeff had not only pitched them in the pond, he had left them to fend for themselves. They were cold and wet and covered with mud and green stuff. Davey was injured, and there wasn't even a possum to show for it.

"You won't tell I puked, will you?"

"Shoot. Anybody'd puke."

"You won't tell the guys, will you?"

"'Course not." They were friends and second cousins, after all. "You up to fetchin' the dogs home?" Tom patted Davey gently, as if he was trying to comfort a little kid.

Davey nodded his assent. Slowly, they struck out after Jeff. Water squished in their shoes. Wet denim overalls clung to their skin. Underwear bunched in their crotches. Teeth chattered in the cold morning air.

By and by, like shipwrecked sailors fetching up on dry land, they came to the Canfield yard. They leaned on one another and stood swaying outside the picket fence. The place was strangely silent except for a dozen chickens that crooned and pecked bugs in the garden.

Beyond the fence, nobody moved. It was hard to tell if the people in the yard were breathing.

Bobby sat on the top rail of the hog pen. Chin in hand, he appeared to be intent on the snoozing Duroc hogs.

Jefferson, head cradled in his crossed arms, sat hunched on the top step of the porch. Willa Mae, her massive form perched on the edge of a tree stump a dozen yards from Jeff, was simply staring away off into the sky. Her back was ramrod straight. The navy blue serge dress with the white collar was the old woman's Sunday go-to-church dress.

"What's wrong with everybody?" Davey whispered, forgetting his injury for a moment.

The whisper sounded like a shout. With a sigh of resignation at the interruption, Willa Mae turned her eyes toward the latecomers, but did not speak or ask them to come in.

She had a peculiar smile on her face. Tom had seen her look just the same way when he met her on the road one morning last May after the black circuit rider had preached a revival all night down in Frogtown. On that day Tom had asked Willa Mae if she was sick or something. She had explained that she had gotten filled with the Holy Ghost at the meeting and worn herself out singing and shouting hallelujah all night.

But Tom didn't think the circuit rider had been around anytime recently. Last Sunday, Jeff and Willa Mae had been there in the back of the Shiloh Church as usual.

Jefferson raised his head. He did not seem to notice the boys at first.

Then, "Y'all come on into the yard, boys. . . . My daddy's done gone home to be with Jesus." A long pause as the fact of Hock Canfield's death settled in and became real. Had a dying ever been announced in such a matter-of-fact way?

Tom stared in disbelief at the darkness of the open door of the house. He expected that any minute old Hock Canfield would come out and slap his knee and ask the boys about the possum. But he did not. Then Tom knew for certain that Hock had flown away and that the husk of him remained behind in the cabin. It left Tom with a strangely detached feeling. Willa Mae had gotten herself all spiffed up for the occasion of Hock's departure and in expectation that folks would come calling when the word got out around Shiloh.

Bedraggled and weary, the boys were the first visitors.

Jeff stood and called to Willa Mae. "Mama, get the iodine. Young Davey done got his hand bit real bad by that possum."

Willa Mae nodded and muttered, "Lawd, Lawd. Well, such things will happen. They will. Hock know'd 'bout such things. Loved a good possum hunt, that man did. Leastwise he waited to cross over that river into Gloryland till he know'd y'all got it treed."

She called to Bobby and motioned with her thick arm for him to get down off the hog pen. "I needs you t' fetch me some wood, honey." Another shooing gesture to her son. Jeff stepped to the side as she passed. "Jeff, honey . . . kindle the fire, would y'. I done let it go out." She lumbered slowly up the steps. "Draw some clean water from the well, Tom, and set it on t' bile. Reckon y'all be needin' some breakfast, too."

And then, "My, my. Davey, come on up t' the porch then, honey; I'll tend t' that hand. Here, baby, let ol' Willa Mae see what that possum done."

C H A P T E R 3

The hinges of the gate groaned as Trudy Tucker entered her garden. She held the gate open for three-year-old Joe, who toddled in clutching his beat-up old spoon and tugging a galvanized bucket behind him. Even at this young age it was plain that the child had inherited his mama's love of making things grow. He pushed past a tomato plant and made his way to the radish patch, which was his responsibility.

Framed by two-by-fours and sheathed in chicken wire, the fence around the garden had been built high to keep deer and other critters from jumping in and helping themselves to the bounty of beans and greens, yellow squash, eggplant, okra, tomatoes, and rows of sweet corn. Of course, this restriction did not apply to Joey's pet Rhode Island Red hen, who followed him serenely through the gate before stopping to pluck a bug from the rich red dirt.

The gate, held by a stiff metal spring, slammed tightly shut as soon as Trudy pushed the wheelbarrow past it. It shrieked and banged against the frame with a terrific clatter, sending a flock of pouting sparrows flying up in a cloud from the hickory tree outside in the yard.

Trudy's husband, Birch, had offered a dozen times to fix the racket. Just one little drop of oil would put an end to the squeak, he said. Birch resented even the slightest implication of rust and neglect on his farm. The thick-planked barn doors swung back without complaint whenever Birch led out the mules and the wagon. The screen door on the porch did not peep when children and dogs came booming through. Even the hinges of the outhouse door were well oiled and respectful.

But the garden, sloping down a gentle hill toward the James Fork Creek, was Trudy's domain, and she insisted that the rusty voice of the gate remain intact. Unoiled hinges were better than a watchdog, she told Birch. What if some hungry tramp were to sneak in at night to steal her tomatoes and her beans or pick the purple eggplant clean? How would she know unless the hinges warned her?

Trudy parked her barrow at the end of a row of cabbages, straightened, and breathed her satisfaction with the garden and the newly awakening day.

Early morning, after the cow was milked, was the best time for harvesting. This was fact. The apples were cool and crisp, ready to store in barrels and lug down to the root cellar to last the season. The best cider was pressed from morning apples. Corn picked just after dawn was sweetest. Morning squash and tomatoes were firmest and juiciest when the light was pale blue and the ground was still cool. Green beans had more flavor and snap before the sun got high enough to warm them on the vines.

On Sunday afternoons at a Shiloh Church potluck, Trudy could tell from the first taste of a covered dish who had harvested their garden late in the day and who had been up and working before the sun. Most folks who coaxed their supper from soil to canning jar to cookstove to table had the same acute sense of what was good and what was best upon the palate. Trudy would not have her produce become the object of discussion at a social event unless it was judged to be the best. She was sensitive about such things, and so, this morning, as every morning, the work began early.

Beyond the rows of ripening corn, Joe jabbed the dirt with his spoon and held up a radish for his mama to see. Henny, the auburn-feathered chicken, cocked her head sideways and studied the root for a moment. The hen scratched the ground twice in imitation of Joey's spade work, uncovering an earthworm to devour.

"A radish!" the little boy shouted, as if this was a great discovery. It was always a sort of miracle to him that his mama's promises were true, that something had really grown from a seed he planted and watered, that there really was something edible under the ground.

The radish was a scraggly little thing, but Trudy congratulated him on its red color and told him that he would make a fine farmer when he grew up big like his daddy. With a serious expression, the child stooped over the bucket and dipped the radish in clean water. Then, after a long moment of grave contemplation, he crammed it whole into his mouth. Joe always ate the first radish he pulled—a matter of pride. It made his eyes water. After that one, Trudy knew he would not eat another until tomorrow. Still chewing, he began to irrigate his crop by scooping one spoonful of water on each green top.

At the far end of the enclosure, bits of tin and old canning jar lids fluttered from the gnarled limbs of the apple tree, winking in the early morning light. Even a slight breath of wind discouraged red-winged blackbirds and sparrows from trespassing. But something other than the wind was shaking the little pieces of metal now. A tall ladder leaned against the trunk, and the faded denim of a pair of pant legs showed beneath the leaves.

"Be careful!" Trudy called to her husband.

"You worry too much, woman!" came a disembodied voice from the heart of the tree. "I been climbin' trees since I was Joe's size. . . ." The tin on the tree trembled fiercely with his motions.

"Be careful, Birch! You'll knock the apples down!" She had a rule that any apple that hit the ground, bruised or not, would end up on the cider press. Not a bad ending, but second rate at best.

She shook her head and spread her apron toward the long, tall rows of beanpoles. Dewdrops clung to perfect pods. Stretching her hands to the harplike twine that supported the vines, she began to pluck the beans and hum a tune.

Trudy Tucker, at thirty-four, was still somewhat of an enigma to the folks of Shiloh. Tall and strong, with chestnut hair and warm brown eyes, she had come to this place two years before when her husband had inherited his father's farm.

It was plain from her way of speaking that she was born and bred a city gal. A former teacher, her speech was something straight from *McGuffy's Grammar.* Her boys did not dare say *ain't* when she was within earshot, though they said it plenty when she was not around.

Another thing about Trudy Tucker: She was Jewish. Daughter of a former Fort Smith dry-goods merchant, she had gone north to get a regular Yankee college degree in New York City—a truly foreign land! Although few Shiloh citizens knew the details of how she had come to fall in love with such an unlikely fellow as Birch Tucker, it was generally known that they had met on the train when he came back from the Great War.

And here was something else a little strange. . . . Trudy Tucker loved books. There was invariably some volume of something open on her lap when the buckboard rattled down the road to Hartford. When the Shiloh Ladies Sewing Circle came to the Tucker house to quilt, there were always sly winks about the fact that one whole wall of the parlor was taken up with bookshelves crammed with books.

"Now when Birch's mama, God rest her, lived in that house, it were china from the Jewel Tea peddler on them shelves . . . real nice they was. Birch's cousin Maybelle took ever' cup and plate. Lost 'em all in the tornado—Lordy, what a mess! But books in a parlor? Ain't seen so many books in the li-bary down to Fort Smith . . . t'aint natural."

Although she loved the verse of Whitman, Keats, and Browning, she was careful not to mention poetry in public. Folks thought such conversation was uppity, and perhaps it was. This she had learned early on.

But often, in her garden, poems came to Trudy's mind. Like Walt Whitman, she had come to believe that the creation of one perfect, living leaf was as much a miracle as the making of far-off galaxies.

For Trudy, life was a close-up thing. Happiness was never a distant yearning, not a remote thing to seek after. She could hold love in her hands as she kneaded the bread, hear it in the echoing hills around her, see it in the faces of her husband and her children at the supper table. Miracles grew on the beanpoles here in her garden. Here. At home.

As for all those leatherbound volumes? Books defined those things she saw close up and felt and knew to be true about her life. Black print on white paper gave a voice to her inner self, asked questions she had not known to ask, held up a mirror to reflect her soul.

And the soul of Trudy Tucker was a large soul, and deep. It was for this reason that the bookshelves in her parlor were crammed full and still there was not room enough to hold it all.

The near perfect peace of that Shiloh morning was interrupted by an approaching rattle that sounded something like the snare drums in a marching band: chookuh-shish-shish-shish, chookuh-chookuh-shish-shish, punctuated by the syncopated crack of an automobile backfire.

Birch Tucker stuck his blond head out from the branches of the apple tree to listen. Trudy paused in her labor as three loud bangs and a mechanical shudder confirmed the identity of the vehicle.

"There's only one thing on the road sounds like that," Birch called to her as he made his way down the ladder, his long legs covering two rungs at a time. "Somebody's died. It's the hearse from Smith's Mortuary."

Birch might well have emphasized the word *the*. There was no mistaking the 1919 vehicle that sobbed and shook as it carried departing residents of Sebastian County to their final resting places. The Smith Mortuary hearse was a sort of bad news telegraph whenever it took to the roads. Just the sound of its motor was enough to make the folks of Shiloh and Hartford start brushing off their funeral duds and begin figuring what to bake for the potluck after services. The hearse was loud enough, some said, to wake the dead.

"Wonder who?" Trudy muttered under her breath. She glanced down the hill toward the roof of Jeff and Lily Canfield's house across the James Fork. Could this mean that old Hock was gone?

"Can't be old Hock," Birch said, as if he had read her mind. "The hearse wouldn't be coming for him. Jeff told me that when the time came he'd just like to borrow our wagon to fetch his daddy."

Joe played heedlessly in the dirt while Trudy and Birch stepped out of the garden and stood together watching dust rise from the road. If the hearse turned to the right, it could be going to the house of any of a half-dozen good friends and neighbors. To the right were houses full of young families—families with children. Trudy hoped the vehicle would turn left at the fork, cross the creek, and head toward the coal mines where she did not know folks quite so well.

"Maybe Grandma Amos?" Trudy questioned.

"Must be Gramma Amos," Birch agreed as the hearse turned right at the fork. "Practically a landmark, she was. That old woman's sure gonna be missed."

They contemplated her passing for a few moments longer as the hearse drew nearer, slowed, then turned up the lane that led directly toward Birch and Trudy.

"Well, he's come to the wrong house this time." Birch gave a friendly wave.

Clouds of dust billowed up, obscuring the identity of the two figures crammed into the cab. Brown film coated the black finish as well as the windshield, but through the glass partitions in the back Trudy could see a dark pine coffin.

Brother Williams stuck his head out the side window and gave a shout. "Good mornin', Birch! Howdy, Trudy! Don't worry none! This ain't here for y'all. I just caught me a ride with Mister Smith."

It was a mighty cheerful greeting, considering the method of transportation. Brother Williams owned the livery stable and garage in Hartford. Five days a week he rode horseback from Hartford to Grandma Amos's Shiloh store to deliver and collect the day's mail.

The hearse moaned and trembled as it climbed the hill. Coughing once, it died in front of the barn and rolled to a stop.

Birch and Trudy walked slowly toward it, as if they did not want to get too near.

"Is it Grandma Amos?" Birch asked as Brother Williams and the undertaker unfolded themselves from the hearse.

"Lord, no." Brother rubbed the stubble on his face and spit a stream of tobacco juice at a red hen. He hitched up his faded denim overalls, frayed at the heels and suspended precariously by one strap. Tall and gaunt, stoop-shouldered like a big buzzard, if he had been dressed in a black suit he would have looked more the part of the undertaker than Mr. Smith.

"Are you picking up or dropping off?" Birch inclined his head at the coffin and directed his curiosity to the undertaker.

A jolly faced, round little man in a long, black frock coat, Hubert R. Smith looked like something out of another century. A seller of patent medicines, Trudy thought, not an undertaker.

"Dropping off." The mortician jerked his stubby thumb at the pine box. "Old Hock Canfield has gone to his rest."

Birch and Trudy exchanged a look. The news was not unexpected, but it was still hard to imagine the world without the little man.

The undertaker mopped his brow and squinted toward the sun. "I supposed, wrongly, that Jefferson Canfield would be wanting his daddy buried down at the Nigra cemetery in Frogtown. I thought to drive the deceased there while the day was still cool. But Jefferson called from Grandma Amos's store and said his daddy was gone and he wanted him buried on the farm, and would I bring out that nice pine coffin I have been keeping in reserve for just such an occasion." Palm open, the undertaker gestured proudly at the grim item. "A fine coffin. Brass handles. Our seven-dollar model. Jefferson has been paying it off in labor. Digging graves, as you know. Two more to go, and it's free and clear."

Trudy could not help but wonder whether the undertaker would repossess the coffin if Jefferson failed to complete the contract.

Brother leaned against the fender of the hearse. "I just hitched a ride is all."

"I don't hold with home burials." The undertaker's smile faded a bit. "But being as the deceased is a Nigra and Frogtown cemetery is a far piece for the relations of the deceased to travel, I can see the reason of it."

Jeff had spoken of the matter to Birch and Trudy some weeks before. He would bury his daddy on the little knoll just above the James Fork, if they did not mind.

"We had a word with Jeff about it a while back," Birch said.

"That's what I wanted to check." The undertaker flexed his hands and popped the knuckle of his right index finger. "Seeing as you still hold the mortgage on that piece of land, I didn't want to leave off a coffin and drive all the way back to Hartford, then get another call saying that I have to get back out here and deliver the deceased down to Frogtown in the heat of the day. Just wanted to make sure you didn't object to a Nigra being buried on your land is all."

"It's Jeff's land. His daddy." It was plain that Birch did not like the tone of the conversation. "His business. Frogtown's a mean little place to bury a man. I told Jeff it didn't make no difference to me and Trudy. Does it, True?"

She shook her head, wishing the business was finished.

"There won't be ice or embalming needed if he's to be buried here."

Birch swallowed hard. "Well, then. You best get on out and drop it off. I'll hitch up the team and take the wagon over yonder after 'while."

Brother, who had been staring at the mules in the corral, broke in. "No. No, Birch. You'd best get on inta Hartford."

"Hartford?"

"That's why I come by—and then I almost forgot. You sold all your crop of cotton down at Hooper's gin in Hartford, didn't you?"

"Most all. We've still got mebbe a bale left to go in the north field."

"You won't want to take it to Hooper's. You been paid?"

"Not yet."

"Well, then, you best get on down there. There's fixin' to be a riot at Hooper's gin, and you don't want to miss it. Not even for a funeral."

Brother's face was uncharacteristically serious. Birch was puzzled. "Quit driving around the barn, Brother. What're you talking about?"

"Cotton market done gone belly up. Less'n five cents a pound. Ain't been that low since America was a colony. That's what Doc Brown says, anyway. Hooper promised you better'n five cents a pound, I reckon."

As the color drained from Birch's face, Trudy felt as though she was being suffocated. They had been promised twice that for their cotton crop.

"I sure could use a cup of coffee, Trudy," Brother said. She did not move, and so he shrugged and continued. "This is the way it is, Birch. Cotton's gone down the flume. So has Hooper's Cotton Gin. If you aim to get anything at all out of your crop this year, you'd best load your weapon and get into town like every other farmer in Sebastian County. See?"

The wheels of the wagon churned up a cloud of red dust from the parched dry clay of the road into Hartford. From Trudy's vantage point on the spring seat, it seemed that the little town was a magnet, drawing to itself hundreds of wagons, trucks, and automobiles. As Birch whipped up the team, she could see that every road and lane for miles around was marked by a broad column of crimson and orange, like the biblical pillars of fire and cloud.

Birch was in such a hurry to find out the truth of Brother Williams's ominous news that he barely stopped the wagon long enough for Davey Meyer and Codfish to bail off outside Doc Brown's home where his father and stepmother were staying. "Tell them we'll stop by later," Trudy called before her words were whirled away by the wind. She saw Davey standing beside Doc Brown's gate, forlornly waving his bandaged fingers, before the dust swallowed him.

Trudy had insisted on going to Hartford with Birch. And since Jeff and Lily had enough to deal with, what with grief and the needful things around Hock's passing, there was no one to watch the children or baby Joe. So the whole Tucker family was descending like the wrath of God on Hartford. Or, more correctly, on Hooper's Cotton Gin.

They were far from being the first ones there. When Birch slapped the reins on the mules' rumps and spun the wagon into the drive leading to the gin, the gravel-surfaced yard was already full of buckboards and Model-T Fords. On the porch of the white-painted wooden building that was the office stood Mr. Hooper himself. He was dressed in his usual white overalls and wide-brimmed straw hat, but beneath it his normally cheerful face was an ashen gray and his arms hung limply at his sides. Just to look at him made Trudy feel cold all over. There was no mistake. Something was terribly, terribly wrong.

Outside the circle of concerned cotton growers was an outer ring of interested townsfolk. Trudy saw Dee Brown, the barber; Boomer from the livery; Mr. Winters, the pharmacist. . . . It was as if the entire community was holding its collective breath. Cotton was the source of income for the whole county, the lifeblood of everyone's financial well-being.

Dan Faraby and five of his nine children were in the buckboard closest to the porch. He was standing upright and shaking a buggy whip at the sweating figure of Mr. Hooper. "Quit stalling!" Faraby snarled. "What are you trying to pull here, Hooper? Explain yourself!"

Hooper retrieved an enormous red bandanna out of his overalls and mopped his face. He did this several times, as if he could wipe off the grayness, but he did not succeed. At last the noisy arrivals of all the latecomers slowed, and Hooper motioned for silence.

"My friends," he began. "You know that we have done business here for close to fifty years. Why, my daddy . . ."

"Get to the point!" Arley Palmer demanded, hammering his fist on the hood of his Ford pickup. Inside the cab, on the tattered seat, his wide-eyed wife jumped at the sharp noise. "Are we gonna get paid what's owed us or not?"

"You know that the price of cotton dropped to six cents a pound last week," Hooper explained.

"What's that got to do with us?" Amos Grier shouted. "We all made deals with you a long time before that!"

"You promised me eleven cents a pound," Birch called out. "All my figures is based on it."

The roar of "That's right! Me too! I was promised twelve! Ten for me! Does he think we'll take less? How we gonna live?" overwhelmed Hooper's attempt to reply.

When the babble subsided again, the gin owner tried to continue, but his voice cracked with strain and emotion. Trudy felt sick with worry, but sorry for the man at the same time. "I say, you know that cotton dropped to six cents. But what you don't know is that the Memphis market . . . our market . . . took in fifteen thousand bales yesterday." He paused to let the number sink in. It was a huge amount to be dumped on the market at one time—more than ten times any other market in the country for one day's trading. "And," he continued slowly, taking a big gulp of air. "And they paid four cents a pound." His voice trailed off.

"But you . . . So what? . . . How about . . . ?"

"Please!" Hooper implored. "I'm trying to explain. I'm wiped out, too!" Trudy shuddered at the horribly embracing sound of his words. "The Memphis buyers won't honor any of their contracts over five cents a pound. I paid out good money, every cent that was owed, up to the day before yesterday. But now I'm bust. I can't even keep the gin. Don't you understand? The bank owns it all now!"

"But four cents a pound won't even pay for the seed," Birch yelled. "You mean after all the harvest is in, I'll still *owe* money?"

"I got eleven mouths to feed," Dan Faraby shouted, waving the tip of his buggy whip under Hooper's nose. "What about that? We demand satisfaction!"

Mr. Hooper drew himself upright and wiped his face again with the bandanna, which he then let slip unnoticed through his fingers. In a small, exhausted voice, barely heard over the angry rumble of the crowd, he said, "And you shall have it."

He turned and pushed open the screen door of the office, disappearing inside. The buzz of the farmers rose again, speculating that Hooper had the money to pay all right. If he suffered because of Memphis, what was that to the growers? They were owed what they had been promised. Hooper would bring out his cash box, Trudy heard someone say. The Hooper family had gotten rich on the sweat of others for long enough.

Trudy was struck with a sudden sense of foreboding. "Let's go, Birch," she urged.

"What, now? We can't leave. What about our money?"

"Let's go," she said again, urgently. "Now!"

Their discussion was interrupted by the single, loud report from inside the Hooper ginning company office. The wavy panes of glass in the front window jumped and rattled in their frames. The explosion rolled out through the screen door, extinguishing the conversation in the crowd. Everyone heard a metallic clatter from the office, followed by a heavy thump like a bale of cotton falling down.

There was a moment's frozen horror in the mob, then the men in the front rank rushed toward the door. As each entered the office, they stepped over the bandanna lying on the planks of the porch. It looked to Trudy as if each farmer was forced to cross a thin pool of blood.

Brother Williams and the undertaker related the news of the cotton disaster to Jefferson as they unloaded Hock Canfield's coffin onto the front porch of the cabin.

Hat in hand, Brother expressed his condolences, but Jeff was left wondering if Brother was sorry about Hock or the price of cotton.

After that, nobody came. All morning, dressed in his Sunday suit, Hock Canfield lay in the satin-lined casket propped between two chairs in the center of the room, awaiting the visitation of friends and neighbors. But hours ticked past, and only Grandma Amos stopped to pay her respects. Black bonnet shielding her withered face, the old woman peered down at Hock.

"He don't look half bad for one who's passed," she said. "Y'all can remember him lookin' all peaceful there on that satin cushion . . . sleepin'-like. Very lifelike, if'n y'all ask me. There's the difference 'tween black folk and white folk. Black folks keep much better lookin' after they've passed on than white folks do."

Jefferson did not know if he should thank her. Everyone knew that Grandma Amos was so old she did not know what she was saying half the time.

Then the old woman tapped her pipe on the edge of the casket as if to call for attention and said in a loud voice to Hock, "You cain't expect much of a wake. All of Sebastian County is in mournin' for Old Man Cotton, who up and died in Memphis."

Moments later, fearful she might miss some news, Grandma Amos lit her pipe and tottered back down the hill to the store.

"She's tetched," Jeff said to his mama.

"Yes, she is," Willa Mae agreed. "If speakin' the truth makes a person tetched, then Grandma Amos done went 'round the bend a long time ago." Willa Mae tugged at the strap of Jefferson's overalls. "You get on back home now. I'll be all right. Don' mind bein' alone with Hock for a time. And you gots somethin' to tend to for your daddy that won't wait."

CHAPTER 4

There was a natural order to life and death that determined the degree of solemnity at a funeral and wake in Shiloh.

The death of a child or of a woman in childbirth was invariably an occasion where voices were not raised above a whisper and the food on the long table remained nearly untouched.

A man leaving a widow and children behind ranked next in grief and concern. In such a case the question simmered beneath the surface: How could a woman alone raise her children and keep the farm?

The circumstance of a wife leaving behind husband and small children was less grim because of the probability that the husband could and would readily remarry. The woods were full of women in the market for a man.

And the potluck meals that commemorated the passing of one as old and black as Hock Canfield were normally lively gatherings punctuated by laughter and pleasant discussion. At such affairs, bargains were struck and conversation ran the gamut from the price of mules to the question of which widower was about to marry what local spinster lady. In ordinary times it would be difficult for an outsider to tell that such an occasion was a time of mourning.

But the day of Hock's burial was anything but ordinary.

He was laid out to rest on the gentle knoll just opposite the James Fork Creek from the Tucker home, in a grave his son had dug the day before. Jefferson gave his daddy's eulogy and preached a fine sermon that was interrupted only briefly when Rosey chased a rabbit and fell into the grave. This and the sermon should have been the object of much discussion afterwards, but it was not.

Folks crossed the creek on the footbridge and trudged silently up the hill to the feast that waited at the home of Birch and Trudy.

When the wake of Hock Canfield finally began, one observer noted that it was the most solemn Shiloh function in many years. Not since the death of Guy and Nelda Hardy's nine-year-old daughter two years before had the guests at a funeral potluck remained so grim.

Birch Tucker had brought long planks and two sawhorses from the barn and set up a table outside next to the well. Trudy had laid out a large honey-cured ham from the smokehouse, and every visitor brought some covered dish created from a family recipe that had been passed along for generations to be served at just such an event.

The table was packed with Shiloh's bounty, with more than enough for everyone. It was a feast meant to remind the living that life went on. But today, men with plates of heaped-up food stood quietly among their neighbors and stared out across the cotton fields or down at the dust on their boots.

Ida Grier said to Trudy, "They told Amos that since Hooper's gone under we owe the bank money. That bank feller, Mister Smith? He come to the farm an' looked over everything we own, and he put it on a list. Mister Smith told Amos they aim to take the mules and our plow, too, to pay off the debt. 'How we gonna farm without mules?' Amos asked him. He didn't explain that. What's Mister Smith down at the bank a-gonna do with mules and plows?"

Trudy started to reply, but at that same instant a dark-green 1931 Dodge pulled onto the lane that led to the Tucker farmhouse.

Ida Grier blanched and put down her plate. "Why that's him a-comin' yonder! That's Mister Smith, Trudy! Leastwise that's his car. What's he doin' a-comin' here?" Ida chewed her lip as the thought exploded in her mind that perhaps they were not the only folks in Shiloh about to lose their mules.

Trudy cast a grim glance toward Willa Mae, who was seated in the midst of a gaggle of children on the porch. "I would presume he has not come to offer condolences to Willa Mae Canfield." Excusing herself, Trudy hurried off to find Birch.

"Gone down to the creek with the boys to look over some coon tracks," said Brother Williams. "Too bad he ain't here, and with a big gun, too. That's Henry V. Smith a-comin' yonder."

Trudy thanked Brother, squared her shoulders, and hiked down the center of the gravel drive to meet the automobile.

The driver was Delbert Simpson, a nervous, unhappy-looking little man who long ago had traded any possibility of local friendship to become the assistant manager in Smith's bank. This title meant that Delbert swept up, turned down loan requests, foreclosed mortgages, chauffeured Henry V. Smith on his forays out to assess his wealth, and other unpleasantness.

Trudy, seventy-five yards from the crowd in her yard, held up her hands to stop the progress of the bank president's car. She did not move, except to lift her chin defiantly and place a hand on the silver hood ornament.

Delbert poked his worried face out the side window. He was sweating, sunburned, and rumpled. "Missus Tucker? Mister Henry V. Smith, President of Hartford Federal Bank, has come to pay a business call on Mister Tucker."

"I have heard about Mister Smith's recent visits to other farms. You are intruding. We have guests. No doubt you have made the rounds of Shiloh today whilst we have all been gathered here?"

Trudy could see Smith through a partially open curtain that divided the driver's seat from the passenger compartment. If Greed ever had a name or a face, Henry V. Smith fit the picture. Old, pale, and corpulent, he gazed at the world from beneath the brim of his panama hat. His face drooped until his eyes were nearly lost behind folds of skin, and his lips barely moved when he spoke.

Henry V. Smith hated Birch Tucker for several reasons, all of that were well known in Sebastian County. Not only did Birch refuse to do business with Hartford Federal Bank, he also spoke openly of his mistrust of him and warned prospective customers away. Once he had publicly called the bank president a cross between a vulture and a worm-eaten hog.

All true, Trudy thought, wishing Birch was there.

"You are not welcome here, Delbert," she added firmly. "Even in the best of times. And today is not the best of times."

Delbert disappeared to explain this to the dim shape in the back-seat. Popping out again a moment later, he said firmly, "Mister Smith has every right to be here, Missus Tucker. There are inventories to be made, you know. Y'all know what this is about. Mister Smith has a responsibility to see that . . . well he owns Hooper's Cotton Gin outright, which means that he has every right to collect what is owed to the gin."

"Tell Mister Smith he may come back tomorrow, and we shall discuss this matter then. There has just been a funeral here."

Smith leaned forward and muttered emphatic instructions to Delbert.

Delbert nodded and repeated the command. "The list needs to be made immediately. Before things . . . assets have a way of disappearing when a dirty business like this is in the works."

Still clutching the hood ornament, Trudy drew her breath to speak but was interrupted by the deep voice of Doc Brown behind her.

"Delbert!" Doc Brown barked. He and his brothers, Dee and James, stood shoulder to shoulder with an even dozen men to block the road ten feet from where Trudy stood. "Delbert Simpson, I'd say y'all are settin' on trouble unless you turn this thing around and head out of here."

"Now, Doc!" Smith's protest from the car was loud enough to be heard.

"You'll be saying 'Now, Doc,' when I'm plucking buckshot out of your assets. You may be the only bank president in town, but I'm the only doctor."

Dee Brown added, "When Mister Smith's assets are in my barber chair—well, my straight razor has never slipped yet, but there might be a first time if he runs off all my steady customers."

From the backseat Henry Smith hollered, "Is that a threat, Dee Brown? Doc Brown?"

"Don't forget me," shouted the third brother, James, who was known for his strength at the forge as well as for his temper. "I'd say that hot iron, well placed, is what Mister Smith needs in his assets. And I'm the man to do it."

Smith, bright red with rage, screamed out the window as more of the funeral guests moved toward his car. "I'll call the po-leece! I'll call Sheriff Potts and have y'all . . ."

At that, Sheriff Potts stepped through the crowd with his shotgun cradled in his arms. "Y'all are trespassing on private property, Delbert. You're disturbin' the peace, too. This here is a private gatherin' of a peaceable nature. We done had us one funeral already t'day. If y'all stick around, Delbert, Mister Smith? There might be one or two more in the works."

Delbert's eyebrows went up. He mopped sweat from his brow. Without turning to Smith for further instructions, he threw the Dodge into reverse, then backed out more rapidly than he had come.

Jefferson Canfield buried his daddy in the morning. He earned another dollar against the price of the coffin by digging Hooper's grave at the Baptist cemetery that afternoon. At night, he lay in bed thinking about fifteen thousand worthless bales of cotton rotting on the docks of Memphis.

Three of those bales were his. From these fields. He had gotten up every morning, looked out the window to the dark green of the cotton stalks. Through every day he had hoed and watered and with tender prayers had caressed the blossoms, buds, and bolls. At night he had laid himself down to sleep in Dreamland and asked mercy on his crop just the same as if cotton was a child or a member of his family. He had prayed for rain, and when rain had not come he had carried water to the plants in buckets. He had prayed that the boll worm would not come, and it had stayed away. Then he and Lily had dragged the cotton sacks down the rows themselves and picked the field clean.

Three bales among the thousands. The work of one entire year—sunrise to sunset, seed to cotton sack—those bales had represented his hope for the next twelve months. Jeff had figured ten cents a pound on his bales, plus seed for next season's crop. Five hundred pounds per bale. That should have been one hundred and fifty dollars paid out from Hooper's gin. With odd jobs, maybe work at the coal mines or building roads, it might have been enough to live on for the next year, even after paying Birch Tucker his share.

Well, all that was lost now, rotting beside the river. Waiting for a river barge that would never come. Most likely the cotton would be burned—Jeff's three bales along with all the other bales from Shiloh. Fifteen thousand bales up in smoke. Thousands of dreams just like the dreams of Jefferson Canfield. What a fire that would make!

Jeff wrapped his arms around Lily and went to sleep whispering his worries to the Lord and wondering how his daddy had managed to raise up nine children in such a hard world.

He woke long before the sky began to lighten, with thoughts of his daddy and the nearness of Lily's time flooding his mind. The ending of one life and then the beginning of another. The way of things. All sweet and fine and bitter and sad mixed together.

Jeff lay unmoving beside Lily a long time. They fit like two spoons together. She faced the rough-hewn log wall. He tucked his cheek against the nape of her neck and breathed in the sweetness of her skin. His big hand rested on her swollen belly, and even as she slept, he felt the baby stirring in her womb.

"Mornin'," Jeff whispered.

Soon now there would be another little life placed in Jefferson's care. It was hard to believe it had been nearly two years since the twins were born. They were a pair, those two—Little Bill and Mamie, named after Willa Mae. Now they lay at opposite ends of the crib in the corner of the cabin. Mamie, who was the stronger of the two and sassy, slept holding on to Little Bill's foot. When Little Bill was awake, he smiled most times. He stayed happy long as he could suck his thumb and clutch a worn-out piece of blanket for comfort.

Those babies had come into the world on the night of the last great thunderstorm to sweep across the Poteau range and flood the James Fork.

Time had whooshed by as Jeff and Lily watched the young'uns take root in life. But when he thought of the rain, it seemed like it had been a mighty long time since that night.

The twins had grown strong and healthy over the last two years while the land had shrunk and shriveled in the drought. His rejoicing in their lives had increased even while hope for the fields and crops had diminished.

But here was Hope again, tapping out a message beneath his hand, wasn't it? This morning he could not help thinking about it—remembering. Somehow putting birthing and rain clouds together was a natural thing in his mind. The harvest moon, big and yellow and misty-like. A new baby. Wasn't that a portent of stormy nights and the creek flooded so Doc Brown couldn't cross over in time?

Lily stirred and sighed. "You 'wake, Jeff?"

He patted her stomach in reply.

"Thinkin' 'bout yo' daddy?" she asked.

"Some. How he use t' lay 'wake in that ol' cabin in the deep of night. Hock Canfield, he never worry out loud in the daylight. Jus' at night. I use t' hear 'im worry 'bout all kinds things to the Lord. Use t' lay there in the dark and whisper prayers. Never a night go by in that cabin that I ain't heard his whisper. Strong man, my daddy. Had no fears of dyin'. . . . World gon' be a sorrier place since he gone on home t' Jesus."

"His time, I reckons. Cain' change it by stewin' over it."

"I know it, gal. I give it over to the Lord. Daddy's in his hands. . . ." A long pause.

"We gon' lose this place, Jeff?"

"Don' rightly know. Las' night I was thinkin' 'bout goin' on up to the coal mines. Seein' if I couldn't get work up there."

"I never had nothin' so sweet as this place, Jeff. I'd purely hate t' leave it. But long as we still had us . . ."

"Then I was thinkin' 'bout y'all. You, Lily. An' Little Bill and sweet Mamie. Then the new one a-comin' at such a time. Worl' be a hard place nowadays."

"Always was." She turned to face him. "I been thinkin', too." She intertwined her fingers with his. "Thinkin' 'bout your mama. Thinkin' if'n it was me an' if'n I had to live without you."

"She done face that. Long time ago she says to me, 'Jeff, honey, we ain't all come inta this world at the same time, and we ain't all gon' leave at the same time.'" He said this in a voice and inflection that sounded just like Willa Mae. It made Lily laugh in spite of the topic.

"Well, I ain't so strong as she is. Lovin' you done melted me down inside. Cain' think no more 'bout livin' alone." Lily sighed and rolled over to face him. She lay her hand on the course stubble of his beard.

"Don' want to take the chance I might lose you, gal. Don' want nothin' like last time, Doc Brown not able to come for so long. You know how it is. Once a mare have one foal, she has the next one double quick. Won't take you no time for that baby to get here. I wants the Doc close by."

"Las' time was a flood. Ain' been no rain since then. The James Fork ain't but a foot deep at the ford. 'Sides, your mama birthed lots of babies."

"Might come another storm. There's a new way of things. I wants this chil' borned by Doc Brown."

"Your mama, she make a fine midwife. She had enough young'uns of her own t' know 'bout such things. And we ain' got money t' pay Doc Brown."

Jeff was silent for a time. Lily was right. There was no cash to pay Doc Brown's five-dollar fee for delivering a baby.

"I got t' think on this."

"Ast yo' mama t' come stay a spell. She's delivered more babies than Doc Brown an' Jesus put t'gether."

That was a fact. In her day, Willa Mae had not only attended the births of most of the young'uns on the Pisgah cotton plantation, she had also pulled breeched calves from straining cows, slapped the pink backsides of newborn piglets, breathed the first breath into the lungs of prize coonhound puppies. She had lifted newborn colts to stand and guided them to the mare's teats for the first time. Mares, sows, cows, and womenfolk all seemed soothed to have Willa Mae on hand when the hour of need came. Lily wanted her there.

"Me an' Birch pickin' cotton in the north field today. You ripe as a melon, gal. I don' want you out there in the heat. Don' want you alone, neither. I'll go talk t' mama. Ask if she's up t' comin' over so soon after Daddy leavin'."

Trudy opened her eyes to the song of the thrush calling daylight to the garden. The big red rooster crowed from his coop and was answered by ten others from across the hills.

Trudy turned her face from the soft light of the window. Birch was not there. Stretching out her hand, she brushed her fingers over the sheets. They were cool. How long had he been up? She had gone to bed ahead of him last night. For a long time she had lain awake, needing the comfort of his arms around her. He had promised to wake her when he came to bed, but this morning there was no indentation on his pillow.

The house was quiet except for the soft clink of a coffee cup against a saucer. Had Birch slept at all? Or had he stayed awake all night worrying and pacing and figuring? They had not yet spoken about the cotton crop or Hooper's death, what it all meant to them, what they were to do now.

This morning, Trudy knew, Birch would be ready to talk about it. She got up quietly, not wanting to wake the boys. The floor creaked beneath her feet as she made her way to the kitchen. Birch sat at the round oak table. The cash box, a tarnished blue tin cracker container normally stored beneath a loose plank in the flooring, was open. Birch's inheritance from his Grandpa Sinnickson, a gold pocket watch with a twenty-dollar gold piece as its fob, was all that remained inside. Invoices were sorted and carefully placed on the surface of the quartersawn oak like a deck of cards in a game of solitaire. Coins and dollar bills were neatly arranged on top of each slip of paper.

Birch heard her enter, but he did not look away from the window or the line of tall birch trees his grandfather had planted the day he was born.

Unshaven and haggard, he only glanced up when Trudy was beside him and the soft white fabric of her cotton nightgown brushed his arm. He leaned his head against her stomach and sighed.

"You didn't come to bed last night," she said softly, cradling his head in her hands.

"You smell so sweet," he said, kissing her through the fabric. "I should have. It would have been better if I had."

"Is it that bad?" She looked at the watch, the neat piles of coins, the slips of paper, each reckoning with a sum at the bottom of a column, each written by a different yet familiar hand.

Birch looked up and leaned back in the chair. "Not so bad as for other folks, from what I hear. Jonas Hocott. The Woods, Dan Faraby. Families with more debt than us . . . real bad shape, most of 'em. Jeff and Lily only stand to get fifty dollars, and I know he owes the store." He reached out for her again and put his arm around her hips, pulling her close. "At least we can pay our debts. After that . . ."

Trudy looked out the window. Sunlight topped the white-barked branches of the trees. She let Birch bury his face against her. Stroking his hair, she tried to comfort him, although she felt in need of comfort herself.

"We'll make it," she said, thinking of the garden and the shelves of canned food in the root cellar.

"We've got seventy-five dollars and Grandpa's watch left. The gold piece on the watch chain . . ."

"Not that. . . . We can make it without that." She lifted his chin with her finger, then stooped to kiss his lips. His beard was coarse against her cheek.

He said in a halting voice, "I can't figure out the *why* of it all, Trudy. Everything was so fine . . . I thought."

She kissed him again. "Don't think for a while. Come to bed, Birch. Things will look better if you rest with me a while."

He stood and gathered her into his arms. "Only you!" he whispered against her neck. "You and the kids, True. But I wanted more for you than hard times."

She did not speak, but took his hand and guided him to the bed as the thrush sang outside the window.

CHAPTER 5

"Tie Rosey to the tree stump, Tom, and make it quick." Trudy was already perched on the seat of the wagon beside Birch.

Rosey didn't go to the stump willingly. Tail tucked between her legs, she planted her backside on the hard ground and braced her front paws as Tom grabbed the hide at her neck and dragged her toward the dreaded rope.

"You brought this on yourself, Rosey gal," Tom explained to the resisting hound. "Chased that rabbit right into Hock's grave. Mama says you got no dignity nor a lick of sense about manners."

Trudy called to Tom. "Thomas! We shall be late. I promised Missus Faraby I would arrive early to have this cake there for the cakewalk!"

Rosey fought against Tom, her loose pelt stretching out like bread dough as he inched her toward the stump. ". . . and then . . . you up and stole . . . the ham off the preacher's plate when he wasn't lookin'. Mama don't trust you to come to the dance."

Rosey replied with a series of mournful yips as the rough rope was threaded through her leather collar and tied off tight. As Tom walked away she ran after, lunging against the end of her line and falling backward in a flailing heap.

Tom felt sorry for her, but it couldn't be helped. Truth was, the incident at Hock Canfield's graveside wasn't the real reason Tom had been leaving Rosey tied up in the yard lately. Her presence served as a reminder to every man and boy in Shiloh and Hartford that Tom had been recently hunting possum.

David Meyer, his hand still bandaged, had waved farewell last week from the Rock Island train in Hartford. Tom envied his cousin's quick escape from Sebastian County. Davey's departure with his parents left Tom to face the humiliation of the great possum debacle alone.

Lucky Davey: off to China where people didn't even know what a possum was! When a Chinaman asked him how he got those holes in his hand, he could say he got bit by a wild opossum in the forests of America. Wild opossum might mean anything to a Chinaman—a bear maybe, or maybe a tiger. A Chinaman might think anything. There was no reason for ridicule if a guy got bit by a tiger.

Tom, however, wasn't so fortunate as to melt into the obscurity of the Orient. The same morning Davey left, Mr. Dee Brown, proprietor of the Hartford barbershop, had stepped out on the sidewalk with shears in hand to hail Tom.

"Well, if it isn't the great opossum stalker come to town! Did you skin that monster yet? Or did he skin you? Need the use of my shears?"

Brother Williams from the livery stable overheard the jibe. Brother mentioned Tom's new moniker to Boomer, the stablehand.

". . . then Dee called Tom Tucker Ol' Possum Killer!"

Everyone in the county knew that Boomer was a few bricks shy of a load when it came to brains. Always true to his name and equally so to his occupation as manure shoveler, Boomer spread the word to everyone within earshot. From there it was only a matter of minutes before everyone in Hartford was greeting Tom as Ol' Possum Killer—quickly shortened to Possum. In that variation, the name stuck to Tom like fresh cow dung on a new shoe.

Wesley Oak had called him Possum at school. Tom thought to settle the matter quietly with Wesley on the way home. Unfortunately, Wesley was twice as big as any kid in his class, owing to the fact that it took him two years to get through each grade. Wesley thrashed Tom good, leaving him with a black eye and his dungarees torn off and thrown up a tree.

"Lookee here boys! I done skinned Possum Tucker!"

Now, with Wesley Oak to back them up, even worthless little kids were calling him Possum all day long.

It had been altogether a bad week.

Tom's mama had tried to soothe his ruffled pride by explaining that soon folks would forget about the whole thing.

"Let them talk, Tom, honey. It means they are giving someone else's reputation a rest."

But somehow, the disgrace didn't go away. Whenever little Rosey trotted behind him, Tom noticed that the smirks were more common, and the jokes about possum hunting more frequent.

"Where'd you git that shiner, Possum? You been huntin' agin?"

Until Tom and Rosey lived down their failure by bringing in the biggest possum hide ever seen, Tom didn't want to remind anyone that granddaddy possum had outsmarted them.

This evening, baby Joe and Bobby sat against the toolbox in the back of the wagon. Fried chicken and three rhubarb pies were packed in the hamper for the annual Shiloh School harvest dance. In a shallow basket perched on the toolbox was the most glorious and beautiful chocolate cake ever seen in these parts. Trudy had worked on it most of the day. Emerging from the kitchen, she had to admit that this was one of the finest chocolate cakes she had ever seen or tasted. She knew this for a fact because she had nibbled crumbs from the cake pan and licked the icing from the bowl herself while the boys were away at school.

Rosey yapping and howling behind him, Tom climbed into the wagon and hung his head in gloomy anticipation of the ribbing he would take at the gathering.

"What's wrong with you?" Bobby asked Tom as Birch clucked to the team and the wagon lurched forward.

"None of your business." Involuntarily Tom put his hand to his eye.

"Possum . . ." Bobby smirked.

"You call me that again, I'm gonna snatch you baldheaded!"

Trudy, ramrod straight in front of them, settled the matter. "One more word and you shall both be back sitting on the stump beside Rosey."

"It ain't fair. . . ." Tom blustered.

Trudy replied regally, "It *isn't* fair."

"That's what I said. Bobby was . . . he was there, too! Why should I be the one? Why do I have to get called Possum?"

"'Cause you're older and supposed to be smart enough to know better than to—" Bobby began, crossing his arms.

"Bobby was closer to that fool Davey Meyer than I was! Davey was . . . on his shoulders."

"Sure! You're the one sent him up there. And him a dumb city kid! How's he supposed to know a guy can't stick his finger at a possum?"

"Bobby was the middle guy, and I was on the bottom!"

"With that shiner you look more like a raccoon."

Tom replied to the insult with the hard whack of his knuckle against Bobby's thigh. Bobby howled louder than Rosey.

Trudy, who was not a mother to be taken lightly, whirled on the seat and grabbed the hair of both brothers. Years of wrestling reluctant livestock had given Trudy a grip like a champion arm wrestler. Lifting the boys up from sitting positions to an awkward, helpless crouch, she pressed their faces together, cheek against cheek, until Tom's nose pointed off sideways. In crisp, distinct tones, Trudy threatened them with instant banishment—and no supper at what promised to be the best potluck of the year.

"One more unpleasant word, and you shall have no cake!"

As if to support her dire threat, Trudy's now-famous, much vaunted, most wonderful chocolate cake leapt up and did a back flip off the toolbox. It landed with a dull thud, half in the bed of the wagon and half on Tom's shoe.

In shock and horror at the sight of the devastation, Trudy released her grip on the brothers. This momentarily gave Tom and Bobby time to scramble to the back of the rig and out of her reach.

They were instantly friends again. United by dread at the sight of the cake smashed all over the wagon bed, they linked arms and huddled while Trudy clapped her hands in anguish, rolled her eyes toward heaven, and made little gasping noises. A moment later she demanded that Birch halt the wagon.

Birch obeyed, as he always did when he was too close to ignore the command. Still grasping the lines, he took a long look at his gold pocket watch, then turned and cocked an eye at the mess.

"Well, True," Birch remarked dryly, "your cake is smashed to pieces. No sense foolin' ourselves. All that fuss in the kitchen today . . . it's hog fodder now."

This led to another outburst of gasps and squeaks. Trudy closed her eyes and tapped her fingers rapidly over her heart as if it might pound out of her chest.

"It'll still taste good, Mama," Tom offered timidly.

Trudy's eyes snapped open. Ashen-faced, she held up both hands in admonition. "Not . . . another . . . word," she breathed. "Not . . . one . . . word . . . from any of you. Or I shall not be accountable . . ."

"You best take Joe up front here with us, before he's all over that cake." Birch hefted the little boy up, putting him in Trudy's lap.

Tom suspected that it was this move on his father's part that saved the two older brothers from getting walloped.

Trudy rode in grim silence all the way to the Shiloh School dance. She did not look back, or she would have seen Bobby and Tom eating chunks of the broken cake. It was delicious.

"We're late," Trudy said, sounding like the white rabbit in *Alice in Wonderland*. "Terribly, terribly, late!"

And so they were. It was dark, and the field was already filled with a jumble of buckboards and Model-T Fords by the time the Tucker family arrived.

The Shiloh School dance was held three times each year to raise the salary for the schoolteacher. The event had moved to Darrell Oak's place about eighteen months earlier, when the previous location had burned down with no money available to rebuild.

Before the 1929 Wall Street Crash, when cotton was at its peak and Shiloh farmers were flush, admission to the event had been the princely sum of two bits. For the last two years, however, the entrance fee had been lowered to ten cents for the head of a household plus one jar of canned goods per family member.

This change of policy had been enacted for two reasons. First of all, very few Shiloh residents had two bits to spare. Secondly, the school-marm, Miss Price, had married Dan Faraby, a widower with nine children. Since she was no longer a spinster lady and had a husband to care for her, it was assumed that she did not need school housing and required less salary.

On particularly difficult days at school the students still called her Ol' Miz Half-Price behind her back. Somehow the name seemed even more fitting since her stipend had been lowered from thirty dollars a month to eighteen.

Marriage had wrought other changes for Miz Half-Price Faraby. She had bobbed her gray-streaked hair so it was stylish just like the ladies in the magazine ads. And Tom had recently noticed that Mrs. Faraby no longer sported a moustache. Little Darnly Faraby had explained this wonder by describing in detail how her new stepmother had taken to smearing hot paraffin wax on her upper lip, then jerking it off until her eyes watered and the moustache disappeared. She did the same where her eyebrows grew together above the bridge of her nose. Now she had two eyebrows instead of one long one.

Then last spring Mrs. Faraby had gotten filled with the Holy Ghost at a tent revival over in Booneville, and now everything about her had changed. These days she smiled frequently and held hands with her husband in public. Having gained about forty pounds, she no longer looked thin, grim, or wicked like the hairy wolf spider that lived in the woodpile. The transformation had been something of a miracle. Even the nine children of Dan Faraby had begun to warm up to their stepmother. No one dared speak ill of her in front of the Faraby tribe for fear of being reported to Half-Price Faraby. And it seemed this fear was increased by her new strategy of calling an errant pupil in after school for a "heart-to-heart," as she referred to her disciplinary chats. Personally, Tom would rather get paddled than have a heart-to-heart with Mrs. Faraby. Tom had liked her much better when he had reason to hate her.

Now there was Half-Price Faraby, just like always, sitting at the little ticket table at the entrance to Darrell Oak's barn. Fiddle music filled the air, courtesy of Mr. McClung of the Hartford Music Company, and Mrs. Faraby's foot tapped in time. She shook hands with Arley and Nina Palmer, the Hocott family, and Brother Williams and Boomer, who were escorting Grandma Amos. Mrs. Faraby nodded and listened carefully as Grandma Amos stopped to deposit her dime with a cackle. The old woman waved her cane around the dance floor to recount a cotillion in Atlanta, when she had been a southern belle and her beau had been a Confederate officer.

The air smelled sweet, the familiar sweetness of Shiloh autumn. Tom inhaled the aroma of newly mown hay. A cool breeze wafted up from the bottomland to push away the searing heat of summer. Light radiated out from the cracks between the boards, making the exterior of the barn shine in the night like a cage of golden bars.

From his place at the end of the line, Tom could see the raffle quilt hanging behind the stage. It was made in a pattern like a hundred little American flags—red, white, and blue, with stars around the border. From the rafters above the pine-plank dance floor hung a banner proclaiming the words *God Bless America*. This and the patriotic bunting that decorated the interior of the barn were part of the Hartford Fourth of July decorations, on loan from the Hartford City Council.

To the right of the punch bowl was a table loaded with jams and jellies, cakes and pies. Next to these stood the rows of box social suppers prepared by the single women of Shiloh to be auctioned to the young men. It was all very grand, Tom thought, forgetting for a few moments his humiliation and apprehension.

Then a small treble voice behind him spoke. "Howdy, Possum."

Fists doubled, Tom whirled around, ready to defend his honor. He was face-to-face with Sally Grier, the prettiest girl in sixth grade. Her blonde hair was bobbed in flapper fashion and tied back at the side by a yellow hair ribbon. Tom recognized her pale-blue cotton dress as the same one her older sister, Louanne, had worn to many dances over the last two years. It had been cut down to fit Sally's delicate frame.

Sally's luminous blue eyes gazed right into Tom's face. She always had a sort of surprised look about her. She blinked as if she was not expecting to see Tom here.

"Hullo, Sally." He half turned, pretending to look into the barn so she wouldn't see his black eye. "How come you called me Possum?"

"I like it. It's friendly-like, don't you think?"

He certainly didn't think so, but he would not argue with a girl as pretty as Sally Grier. "I guess. I didn't much like it."

"There's lots of Toms in the world, but I reckon I only met one boy named Possum."

He shrugged. Sally could call him a Duroc hog if she thought it was original and fine. He changed the topic. "Looks like there's a lot of good stuff to eat in there. Last time there was ice cream. Mama's cake fell and smashed in the wagon on the way over, but me and Bobby had some anyway. Where's Louanne?" He said this last part because the dress reminded him of Louanne.

"She didn't come."

"How come?" The line inched forward.

"Didn't feel like it, I guess."

"Where's your folks?" Tom scanned the parking area, but there was no sign of the Grier family.

"Didn't feel like it neither."

Tom's mama glanced down at Sally. What was that pained look Tom noticed in his mother's eyes? "Sally, you look lovely. What a beautiful dress."

"Thank you, Miz Tucker, ma'am." Sally offered a small curtsy.

Tom knew his mama liked the Grier children's manners. Trudy had often remarked that Ida and Amos Grier may have been poor sharecroppers trying to scrape out a living on the meanest land in Sebastian County, but they had real treasures in their children. Tom had to agree with his mama. Even homely Louanne had fine manners.

"Where are your father and mother?" Trudy asked Sally.

"Didn't feel like . . . they couldn't . . ." the girl stammered, as if repeating the words were too much.

"I am pleased you could come as a representative of your family," Trudy told her.

"Thank you kindly, ma'am. Well, but I . . . can't stay." Sally looked away in the direction of her home. Her daddy sharecropped a rocky farm just over the far hill and split the profit with Darrell Oak. Three days ago on the porch of Grandma Amos's store, Darrell had commented within Tom's hearing that the soil of the Grier place was too pitiful for any man to work unless he was crazy or desperate.

Sally continued, "I just seen . . . saw . . . the light over here. So I come out for a walk to see. But I can't stay."

Sally couldn't stay? Then why the dress? Why the ribbon in her hair? She was sure brushed down and curried up for a gal who was just out for a walk.

"I wish you would stay. Most everybody's inside already. We were late," Tom replied, forgetting completely that she had called him Possum.

"I didn't bring my ticket money." She frowned at his shiner. "I was just out walking, so I stopped."

Trudy rummaged in her hamper and extended a quart jar jammed with green beans. "Here's an extra. Give it to Missus Faraby at the table, and that is all the ticket you need."

"Thank you kindly, Ma'am. But I couldn't take your green beans when I have forgot my own."

"The boys will tell you they are not overly fond of beans. I intended to leave this on the canned-goods table anyway. You may as well use the jar for admission, lest it go to waste."

With a curtsy and a thank-you-ma'am, Sally Grier accepted the quart Mason jar as if Trudy had offered her as much as a dollar bill.

"Y'all's mama is sure nice," she said to Tom and Bobby.

Tom noticed the heads of his daddy and mama lean together as Birch whispered something to Trudy.

Bobby, who had been playing Paper, Rock, and Scissors with Othar Hocott, shrugged. "We got ourselves more beans down in our cellar than we can eat in a hundred years. That's why Mama brung 'em. You should see all the beets, too. Like to make me throw up."

This seemed to relieve Sally. Her brow furrowed as she pondered the jar and said, "Our garden didn't fare well. The whole county over yonder shriveled up. We're not so close to the crick as y'all. Our well went dry the end of June. Me and Louanne spent all summer fetchin' water for the garden from the crick. Buckets and buckets. Didn't do much good anyhow."

Sally Grier lived two miles from the James Fork, and two miles was a long way to haul water, Tom knew. Her hands showed evidence of half-healed blisters and calluses and bloody cracks around the nails. As if she felt his curious gaze on her fingers, Sally shifted the container behind her back and held it there out of sight until they reached Half-Price Faraby at the ticket table. Sally stood swaying slightly before the teacher and then hesitantly placed the quart glass among the others on the table as if she half expected Mrs. Faraby to challenge her right to admission with a jar of borrowed green beans.

Mrs. Faraby, who had surely witnessed the exchange of the green beans and knew their source, simply smiled and thanked Sally for the offering as if the girl had toted the beans from her own home.

Another curtsy and a thank-you, and Sally slipped off to perch on the hay bales with the other schoolgirls. Tom, as was fitting, walked to the far side of the barn where the boys were congregated.

"Hey, Possum!" Alvin Palmer greeted Tom with the much hated name, aiming to get a rise out of him. An expectant silence fell over the group as Tom climbed up on the top rail of the stall.

Alvin tried again. "I called you *Possum*. . . ."

"Hey Alvin, sorry. Didn't mean to ignore you," Tom apologized, as though Possum was his given name.

Othar Hocott considered Tom suspiciously. "Well, ain't you gonna beat the tar out of 'im? Alvin ain't half so big as Wesley. You could whup him easy."

"Don't want to," Tom answered.

"How come?" Bobby asked. "You was gonna whup me for calling you Possum on the way over, and I'm your brother."

Tom plucked a bit of straw and placed it in his mouth. "I like Possum."

"Like it?" Alvin exclaimed. "Yesterday you got the daylights thumped out of you by Wesley Oak because of it."

"That was yesterday." Tom glanced toward Sally, who was sipping punch and laughing with the other girls. "There are lots of Toms around. I don't know nobody else named Possum. Except me. It's original. Besides, me and Bobby mean to catch that old possum out there. Ask Jefferson Canfield. That's the biggest possum anybody ever saw. Big and old and smart. He just won the first battle, that's all. Me and Bobby and Rosey'll get him. We've got us a plan."

Bobby looked worried at this revelation. They had not discussed any such plan. As a matter of fact, after taking one look at David Meyer's possum-bit hand, Bobby had more or less decided he would never get closer than ten feet to a possum.

Tom's calm demeanor defused the bomb, sucked all the joy out of the jibe. His friends brooded on the matter for a few moments, and then the discussion turned to possum catching, hunting dogs, and traps for everything from wild ducks to rats to bears.

An hour into the evening, with the music playing and the boys spitting into the hay as they spoke of manly things, Tom half suspected that his friends had grown envious of his new name. Alvin expressed the thought that if he could choose a new handle for himself, he would go by Bear. He was hooted off the stall rail and shoved down to be buried in the hay.

"Cub is more like it!" shouted Othar.

And so, Alvin Palmer, with his wild shock of red hair and smattering of freckles, became Cub.

Bobby was renamed Mutt. No one knew why. It just seemed to fit.

Jim Pierce, who was half Indian, accepted the moniker of Catfish. This seemed fitting since he was the most skilled fisherman of the group.

Towheaded and nervous, Othar Hocott, who had gotten used to being ridiculed for his first name, asked to be dubbed Bull. More howls of laughter until Tom fell off the fence backward and tears streamed down his cheeks. Othar Hocott was the younger brother of Barney Hocott, who was big and mean. But Othar was nothing like his brother. He was dubbed Cotton, which everyone knew was soft and worthless.

But Cotton Hocott was not sure about this new name.

"My daddy got nothin' from old man Hooper at the settle. Not a cent to pay off nobody. You know, he bought last year's seed on credit, too. Borrowed against the crop to buy our truck and build the new barn. I heard Daddy say cotton has cost us everything we put up for coll—, something, I ain't sure what the word is. Means he pledged every stick of furniture and the mules for the loan. I don't know what he'll say having a kid named Cotton. Wish y'all would think of somethin' else. Any ol' critter will do."

Tom, feeling sympathetic, nodded. "How does your daddy feel about squirrels?"

Othar considered the change for a long moment and nodded. "I reckon Squirrel is almost as good as being named Possum. Sure. I'll go by Squirrel. But what're we gonna call my brother?"

In absentia the fellows christened Wesley Oak "Stumpy," and renamed his boon companion, Squirrel's brother Barney, "Pigpen." Tom thought these two were especially clever—"Stump" for Oak and "Pigpen" for Barn. Besides, the corruption of his enemies' Christian names was a sweet revenge that made him forget the black eye and the humiliation of the previous week.

"There's Pigpen and Stumpy now," Squirrel remarked, pointing to the entrance. "Bet they been out smokin' and drinkin' too."

Tom knew this was probably a fact. After all, Wesley's father owned the barn where the dance was held, and Wesley was mostly allowed to go his own way as long as he didn't get caught or bring shame on his family. But shame meant different things to different families. For instance, Wesley could fight all he wanted so long as he didn't get beaten.

Wesley spotted Tom across the room. The larger boy's mouth curved down, as if he resented the fact that Tom was in his barn and smiling. Cutting across the dance floor, Stumpy Wesley made a beeline toward Tom.

"Don't let's call them Stumpy and Pigpen to their faces," Bobby suggested.

Tom was still smiling when Wesley, hands on his hips, planted himself in front of the group. "Well, if it ain't Possum Tucker."

"Hey, Wesley." Tom had trouble not laughing as the label Stumpy flitted through his mind.

Wesley spit on the floor. "I didn't think you'd have the guts t' show up."

"Yeah," agreed Barney, who did smell something like a pigpen. Catfish and Squirrel chuckled.

Wesley assumed their mirth was in response to his bluster. He drew himself up and crossed his arms, daring Tom to defy him. "What're you doin' in my barn, Possum?"

"Better a barn than a pigpen!" Tom replied, and all the boys began to laugh. "Better here than doin' a tap dance on an ol' stump!" This brought hoots from the group.

Eyes narrowed, Wesley looked from one boy to another with belligerent suspicion. Mirth confused him. He wiped his mouth on the sleeve of his shirt. "Just watch yourself, Possum!" he growled.

For a moment Tom thought Wesley would slink off to some corner and sip another jar of hooch without incident, but it was not to be. Wesley turned as Sally Grier, punch in hand, took a seat beside Martha Milburn.

"It's that cracker, Sally Grier!" Wesley muttered. "How'd she get in? Them white trash claim they don't got no money. Her pa owes my pa plenty, I can tell you. That liar claims they don't have nothin' but dust in their root cellar! Pa said Amos Grier better not show his face around here till every penny gets paid back. So how'd Sally Grier get in here?"

With that announcement, Wesley stomped toward Sally to challenge her right to be at the dance. She saw him coming. Her joy faded. Wide blue eyes blinked in horror at his approach but she stood frozen, unable to move, like a rabbit caught in headlights on a dark road.

Tom leapt from the stall rail and hurried after Wesley as the fiddler struck up "O, My Darling Clementine." Tom brushed past his mama and daddy as they waltzed. Barney Hocott ran after Tom, clutching his shirt and telling Tom to mind his own business. Tom whirled and shoved Barney back, then plunged ahead through the dense crowd.

Wesley reached Sally in a few short strides. He took his usual belligerent stance—legs apart and hands on hips. Tom heard him say, "Well, now. If it ain't Sally Grier. Where's your daddy? Where's your . . ."

Tom jumped onto a hay bale and shouted at the top of his lungs, "Wesley Oak! Call me Possum, will you? Well, I'll tell you what you are! A dirty stinkin' skunk!" With that, Tom flew from the bale, slamming hard against Wesley. The girls screamed and scattered.

The unexpected fury of Tom's assault caught the bigger boy completely off guard. Wesley had pivoted sharply toward the sound of someone calling him a dirty skunk. So it was that his wide open mouth caught the full force of Tom's fist.

Wesley made a futile grab to keep himself upright and came away with a handful of bunting from the decorations. Arms flailing, Wesley staggered backwards, bumping into a table of grown-ups. He collided with Brother Williams's elbow just as Brother was raising a glass of pink lemonade to his lips. The resulting jostle slopped the sticky, rose-colored beverage all over Brother's shirtfront and flooded the other guests at the table as well.

Before Wesley could say 'scuse me, or even recover from his stumble, Brother's wiry arm fetched him a shove from behind that propelled him back toward the advancing Tom. At that same moment, Wesley's feet tangled in the spiral strand of patriotic trimmings that he still held clutched in his fist.

Body flying forward and feet trapped beneath, Wesley lunged directly into the whipping path of Tom's right hand. Wesley's height advantage was no help to him once his chin was at the level of Tom's belt buckle; the roundhouse swing clobbered him just over his left eye.

Wesley was already on his knees when Tom barreled into him, and both boys ended up on the ground with Tom astride Wesley's chest. "He's gone crazy!" Wesley hollered. "Get him off me!"

The two boys continued to exchange blows, though both noses were already bloody. Through the rush of blood in his ears, Tom could barely make out the fact that the musicians had stopped abruptly and that the scraping of the fiddle had suddenly been replaced by the sound of his mother's voice yelling his name. An instant later, Tom found himself being hoisted up by his collar and the seat of his britches.

Wesley Oak, whose left eye had acquired the makings of a shiner to match Tom's, still threw punches at his now defenseless opponent. But Boomer and Brother Williams grabbed an arm apiece and dragged him back.

Tom squirmed in the undignified pose and managed a look over his shoulder. His father was the one holding him suspended above the dance floor. "Let's go outside, son," Birch said. "I think you have some explainin' to do."

CHAPTER 6

The smell of grits and scrambled eggs awakened the Tucker brothers early, despite the fact that the school dance had kept them up until after midnight the night before. Tom was hungry until he opened his eyes to see his father framed in the doorway of the bedroom.

"Get up, Tom," Birch said in a solemn voice. "Fetch a switch from a birch tree and wait for me in the woodshed like we talked about last night."

Birch turned on his heel, leaving Tom to consider his fate. Appetite fled as he remembered the dance and the fight and the assurance from his father that there would be a reckoning come morning.

"It's mornin'," Bobby said from his pillow.

"Shut up," Tom replied glumly as he wondered if he should choose a thick switch or a skinny one.

Bobby read his mind. "Thicker switch won't sting so bad."

"Yeah." Tom slipped out of bed and pulled on his overalls.

"Leastwise you'll get it over before breakfast."

"It was worth it."

"Why don't you tell Daddy why you punched Wesley? 'Bout Sally Grier an' all. Damsel . . . in a dress . . . like in *Ivanhoe*. You know, like Mama read to us. . . ."

"Wouldn't do no good. You know he's givin' me a lickin' 'cause Mama don't like it when we fight. He's gotta do it; otherwise she'll be after him."

Bobby agreed that this was true. Both brothers had heard stories at the barbershop of their father's youthful battles. He had been handy with his fists. In fact, Doc Brown said that Birch Tucker would have made a fine professional pugilist if the Great War had not come along. Tom suspected that Birch was secretly proud that Tom had thrashed Stumpy Oaks last night. He dared not express that pride where Trudy could hear it, however, lest she box his ears.

Trudy often remarked that fisticuffs were barbaric and on par with backwoods cockfights, pit bull matches, and throwing people to the lions in the Roman Colosseum. She based much of her opinion on the fact that Jefferson Canfield had been forced to fight other convicts in prison contests. The big man had a face full of scars, cauliflower ears, a bent nose, and capped teeth to show for it. Trudy held that for anyone to profit from another man's blood was an abomination. She insisted that there were better ways to settle disagreements. But she had yet to come up with one that worked consistently in every disagreeable situation.

Tom had just cut a switch of medium thickness and was heading for the woodshed when Jefferson came jogging up the hill toward the house. He was out of breath—stuttering and sweating.

"Get your mama, boy," he gulped. "Lily's time has come an' my mama say, if your mama would be so kind, my mama needs her on down to Dreamland to help out with the baby."

And so Tom's appointment in the woodshed was postponed, his fight with Wesley forgotten, as Trudy gathered supplies and hurried off to help Willa Mae deliver the child.

Birch led Jefferson to the north field with the manly declaration that they needed to finish gleaning the cotton field before the rains came. There was precious little cotton left to pick, and no sign of rain. But Willa Mae had told them to go make some use of themselves because there never was anything so worthless as a man around the house when babies came into the world.

This left Tom and Bobby to watch after Joey and the Canfield twins. "I'd rather pick cotton," Tom said.

"Least you didn't get whupped."

"Dad'll get back 'round to it. Mama won't let him forget."

Bobby eyed the three young'uns. "What will we do with them? We were goin' down to the spook house today for the meetin' with Squirrel and Catfish. How can we take a bunch of little kids out to the spook house?"

The spook house was the deserted farmhouse two miles down the road past Shiloh Church. The land had belonged to the family of Sully Faulk for as long as there had been white men in Arkansas. But in 1927 Mr. Faulk, who was an educated man with grand ideas, had mortgaged the farm in order to invest the cash in the stock market. Every day on the porch of Grandma Amos's store, Mr. Faulk had read the stock market report and declared to all that soon he would get rich and retire from farming forevermore. He had advised that others should follow his example.

Those who had heeded Sully Faulk's advice had lost everything but their skins when Wall Street crashed. After one payment was missed, the Faulk farm had been repossessed by Jenson Consolidated of Meribah City, along with fifty other farms over three counties in western Arkansas, and the owners evicted. Now those houses stood deserted while the land was farmed with tractors in a fraction of the time and with a minimum of manpower.

Two years of neglect had left the Sully Faulk spook house a windowless wreck standing in the center of Jenson Consolidated cotton fields. Posted as strictly OFF LIMITS, it had become a favorite meeting place for Tom, Bobby, and their friends.

Bobby suggested depositing Joey, Mamie, and Little Bill in the Tucker garden for a while.

Images of Mama's prize vegetables uprooted and devoured discouraged the idea. "Can't leave 'em in there," Tom remonstrated. "Joey would be all right, but not the babies. Willa Mae says when they're that age they eat anything. They're like goats; that's why we call 'em kids. When you were little you swallowed a penny and it came out t'other end all colored like a rainbow. I wanted to keep it, but Mama threw it away. A whole penny down the hole. Still coulda spent it on hard candy. Nobody had to know where it'd been. . . . And then, remember that time Joey et Daddy's fishing bait? Worms."

"Yeah," big-eyed Joey agreed. "Worms. Take me with you, Bobby!"

This fact established, Tom fetched the old wood-wheeled pony cart out of the shed and loaded up the three younger children. Rosey was not big enough to be hitched to the cart, so Tom decided he would pull it to the spook house and Bobby would pull it back.

"You get all downhill," Bobby protested.

Tom put a chunk of firewood in his brother's hands. "You keep watch at the rear for mad dogs." This meant Bobby had to walk backward all the way to the spook house.

"Why do I always . . . ?"

"Either keep guard or stay home with the kids. What would Mama say if we was to take them all the way to the spook house?"

"We ain't s'posed to go there 'tall. She'd whup us anyway if she knowed we're goin'."

"Exactly. And just think if we not only went to the spook house, but the babies got jumped by a stray dog with hydrophoby, too."

"She'd whup us double."

"She'd kill us, is what she'd do. So you stand guard. It's easier walking backward downhill. If you see any dog frothing at the mouth and such, you beat it senseless."

Bobby peered doubtfully at his weapon and considered the wrath of his mama if the young'uns came to harm. Then he imagined hand-to-hand combat with a frothing, snarling stray. "Okay," he agreed, shouldering the stick.

For fear of Rosey encountering rabid dogs, the hound was locked in a stall in the barn, where she wailed and whined and yapped to be released.

The five travelers set out: Tom pulling, Bobby walking backward with the stick at ready, and the three little ones perched happily in the cart. They passed Birch and Jefferson in the north field. The men sat talking together on the back of Birch's green-enameled buckboard with the big letters FAMOUS on the side. Jeff looked nervous. Without smiling he waved to the children, snatched off his hat, mopped his brow, and looked away off toward Dreamland where his baby was being born. Neither man asked where the boy-drawn pony cart full of young'uns was headed, nor did Birch demand that they be back at any certain time.

Even hitched to the pony cart and hauling three small children, Tom felt exaltation and relief. The men had barely even noticed them. For the first time he began to think that with Lily giving birth, his punishment might be forgotten.

The road to the spook house turned off the main highway just beyond Shiloh School. Along the way there was a half-section of farmland marked with a weathered sign:

PROPERTY OF JENSON CONSOLIDATED
KEEP OUT!
TRESPASSERS WILL BE PROSECUTED.

This second patch of three hundred twenty acres had been repossessed so long ago that the farmhouse had disappeared completely. Tom knew the name of the family who once lived there. Birch had told him stories about the sons of Farmer Norton, who had both perished in France during the Great War. The farm had been taken over shortly afterward. Norton moved away to St. Louis and died in the poorhouse.

Whenever they passed the old Norton farm, Birch would snort and tell them, "You boys stay away from Jenson land. It's cursed, I tell you. Prosperity bought by treachery against others is a curse. Remember that."

Tom remembered it even though he did not understand it. Birch never offered more explanation.

His father's vehemence against Garrick Jenson made Tom look hard at the old Norton fields as they trundled by them today. He often tried to imagine what it was that made Birch so angry. The fields gave no answer. Jenson tractors plowed straight furrows. Jenson cotton grew tall. There was plenty to harvest every year.

Had the land been better somehow when old man Norton and his two sons lived in the house that was vanished now? Were the fields viewed more kindly by God when the Nortons plowed with mules and picked their cotton by hand?

Just beyond the old Norton place was the Sully Faulk farm. The split-rail fence dividing the properties had been removed, and now both fields were farmed as one. The Faulk's barn had been torn down. Trees around the house had been cut and the stumps pulled. Every foot of bare land right up to the house was planted in cotton. Now the cotton had all been picked, and the rolling fields surrounding the house were crowded with dead stalks and empty bolls. Stray shreds of cotton still clung to the spiky stalks.

The boys had often speculated on why the old house was left standing. Maybe the Jensons planned to use it for storage sometime. Or maybe they figured to fix it up and rent it out for extra income.

It had once been a decent house. Four rooms downstairs and a porch. A lean-to with a kitchen in the back. One big dormitory-style room on the upper floor. But it had not had a coat of paint in years. The shingles were rotten now. Tin cans and tin buckets had been flattened out and hammered over the holes in the roof to keep the rain out. Only there wasn't any rain. The porch leaned, and the front steps were broken. Somebody had kicked in the front door. A single plank nailed across the entrance warned intruders to KEEP OUT. Every window had been rocked. The floor inside was littered with glass shards, dust, leaves, and piles of trash left by the hoboes and bums who camped there sometimes. The eerie glow of occasional fires built in the fireplace by these vagrants had given the old structure its name: the spook house.

It was a perfect place, in other words, for club meetings. Tom and the others had brought canned peaches and applesauce and such from the root cellars of their homes and stored them away beneath a rotten plank beside the stone fireplace.

Within the same secret compartment, wrapped up in waxed paper and placed in a biscuit tin, Tom kept his precious copy of *The American Boy's Handy Book*. The volume was subtitled, *What to Do and How to Do It*. In all projects from building lean-tos, boats, traps, or kites to the finer points of party games and dog training, The Book, as it was called, was the ultimate authority.

Squirrel Hocott and Catfish Pierce were already waiting beneath the oak tree beside the lane. They sat with their backs against the tree, and their eyes stared angrily toward the spook house. They looked up sullenly when Tom called howdy. Their expressions darkened even more when they spotted the young'uns in the pony cart.

Catfish, who had a Cherokee disdain for all things not manly and warriorlike, stood up and brushed off the seat of his pants. "Well I'll be a suck-egg mule! Y'all brought the whole nursery, too."

Tom halted. Bobby came around from behind the cart and rested his stick of firewood on the wheel.

"Lily Canfield's havin' her baby," Tom explained.

Squirrel asked, "What's that got to do with anything?"

Bobby replied, "We got to keep the kids because of it."

Catfish sucked his teeth and directed his gaze to Tom. "Did you get whupped?"

"Not yet," Tom answered truthfully. "Prob'ly later."

Squirrel stood up and stretched. "Boy, it was sure worth it to see you get ol' Wesley—I mean, Stumpy."

For a moment the memory of the previous night's glory obscured the reality that there was a cart full of young'uns beneath the tree.

Then Catfish shrugged. "We thought y'all weren't comin'. Thought Possum prob'ly got beat so's he couldn't sit down. But no matter. We ain't gonna get our meetin' anyhow today. Look yonder. . . ." He raised his brown arm and pointed toward the spook house with a grimy finger.

Tom shaded his eyes against the glare. In front of the derelict building was a decrepit wagon loaded with heaps of junk. It was hemmed in by a stake-bed truck on one side and a brand-new Studebaker on the other.

Catfish, who lived just over the rise, explained the odd gathering. "Some poor folk stayed at the spook house yesterday an' last night. Jus' passin' through, saw the place were empty, so they moved in to sleep, I reckon. I seen the light from their lantern last night. Gimme the creeps. But they ain't staying. "

"Whose Studebaker?" Bobby asked, impressed.

"Don't know," Squirrel Hocott said. "But I was at Gramma Amos's store when that big guy came in. Made a phone call to somebody 'bout the squatters in the house. Says the lady is sick, asks what he should do. Should he let 'em stay or what? Because the man says he don't want to leave. First he's beggin', then he says he'll fight."

Catfish took over. "They'll move on all right. Look yonder."

Tom turned his head just as a thin scarecrow of a man came flying from the front porch of the house. He pitched through the rail and tumbled to the ground among the cotton plants. The distant sound of wailing and a sharp scream accompanied the scene. A moment later, two husky men carried out a woman and loaded her onto the old wagon. Three others followed bearing children in their arms and dumping them like half-full feed sacks onto the mattress tied on the back of the buckboard.

The light was bright behind them. "Look yonder what they're a-doin'," Squirrel Hocott said in a hushed voice as the three men turned and each gave the vagrant man a kick in the belly. Then as the children wept loudly, the raggedy man was lifted up and tossed onto the spring seat beside his wife.

A moment later, a tall slim man in suit coat and tie emerged from the house and stood with arms crossed on the top step of the porch, his thinning blond hair lifting in the breeze. A well-dressed woman, short and stocky, followed him. She wore a blue floral dress and a small hat with flowers on it.

"Jenson," remarked Catfish with disdain. "An' his wife, Carol-ine."

The couple on the steps did not move as the spavined mule was hitched to the wagon and then led to point away from the house and down the dirt lane that had once been a driveway. One of the stocky workmen retrieved a whip from the back of the truck. He beat the mule hard across its boney rump, sending it down the lane at a halting trot.

The raggedy man raised himself from a hunched position and grabbed for the reins. Still bent, he managed to guide the mule down the road, turning just beyond where the boys watched. A cloud of big blue flies rode on the mule's face, making its ancient eyes weep as it jogged away from the Faulk house.

Tom caught a glimpse of the dirty faces of the three vagabond children. They were not much different in age than those he lugged in the pony cart. But they were gaunt, their faces puffy from hunger. Clothes were ill-fitting and their feet bare. The man's face was covered with blood from the beating he had received. His wife had arms like toothpicks, although her belly was watermelon sized, and she was close to her time. Her face was white and sick.

"Where they goin'?" Bobby mumbled.

"Folks like that don't have no place to go. They just go from place to place." Catfish sniffed and stuck out his lower lip in an angry pout.

Squirrel stepped forward from beneath the tree. "Now look what they're a-doin'." He spat into the rutted road and wiped his mouth on the back of his hand. "Look there!"

Torches were lit as the Jensons stepped off the porch of the spook house and took their places beside the dark blue Studebaker.

"Oh no!" Bobby wailed. "They're gonna burn 'er!"

"My book," Tom said in quiet despair, knowing that there was nothing to be done to save The American Boy's Handy Book.

The torches were tossed into the old farmhouse. Those on the hill stepped back as the old boards and rotten shingles erupted in flame with a roar.

"Blast! There goes our spook house." Squirrel shook his head from side to side as the entire place was consumed in flame within minutes.

Tom watched as the family of outcasts looked back at the pillar of smoke. The wagon retreated down the road. He forgot about The Book for a moment and wondered what harm could have come if the poor folks had been allowed to stay for just a while in the old windowless house.

Just before noon, Tom and Bobby returned to the house with the young'uns. Birch was hammering a new board on the corral gate where the mule had kicked it in. Trudy was hanging out wash. She sang softly and slightly off-key to Henny, Joey's pet Rhode Island Red, who perched attentively on the clothesline pole.

"Lord, woman!" Birch exclaimed before he saw the boys and the wagon. "It's just a chicken!"

Trudy interrupted herself long enough to reply to his admonition. "I was not singing to Henny," she defended. "However, if I had been so inclined, Willa Mae says Henny will lay twice as many eggs if she is sung to. She swears by it, and so far I'm a believer."

"Well, if Willa Mae says . . ."

Tom and Bobby exchanged wry glances. Their mother was no songbird, but Joey's feathered friend was an exceptional hen.

A sheet flapped in the dry wind. The hen flapped her wings in a kind of chicken greeting. When Joey and the twins ran toward her, she clucked and ruffed up her feathers, a sure sign that she was pleased at the return of her flock. Trudy, reading the hen's signals, looked up and waved broadly.

"Jefferson and Lily have a baby girl!" she called. It seemed to Tom by her cheerful demeanor that she had altogether forgotten about the fight and the woodshed. Tom wanted to tell her and Birch about the Sully Faulk spook house and the vagrants and the Jensons, but he knew such an admission would lead Trudy to ask why they had been there and what they had gotten into. He nudged Bobby with his elbow. "Remember. Keep quiet."

"Bring the babies into the house. I shall bathe and feed them before you take them home. I promised Lily and Jefferson and Willa Mae I would send a meal along tonight."

Birch placed the hammer on the fence post. "How-do, boys. Where y'all been so long?"

Bobby blurted, "Up the Sully Faulk road. Mister Jenson done set fire to that old spook house. He had three guys with him and his wife, and they ran off some poor folks from the place. First they beat up the man and . . ." He clamped his hand over his mouth. His eyes grew wide.

Tom groaned. "Now you done it. . . ."

"I didn't say . . ." Bobby protested, but it was plain that the damage was done. The hand over the mouth and the crouched-down posture, like a turtle drawing into his shell, gave the truth away.

Birch's brow furrowed. He wiped his hands on the front of his bibs.

Trudy gathered Henny under her arm and came toward them. "What were you about to say?"

Bobby made a rubber face the way he often did when he was afraid that what was in his brain was about to come out of his mouth. Usually it did.

"What was it you wanted to say? Just tell the truth," Trudy asked again, gentle and coaxing. This was an unfair way to wheedle out information, because she made her voice sound like she would not wallop them if they told the truth.

"Yes'm," Bobby replied dumbly, like a dog rolling over on its back and wagging its paws in surrender.

"Say it then."

Bobby said it. "Tom's *Handy Book* got burned up, too."

Birch inhaled deeply. "Y'all been *inside* the spook house, have you?"

Too late to stop it now. In a few minutes, the whole thing had come rolling out into the open. The club meetings. The canned food beneath the plank. The Book, which was now ashes in the rubble.

Later, after Birch whipped the two brothers with medium-sized birch switches in the woodshed, they were set to cleaning the coop of Trudy's prize Rhode Island Red chickens.

They worked without speaking for a long time. Autumn light, a gold color, leaked through the old boards of the coop and dropped in bright pools on the floor. It was an image Tom remembered reading about once. Something about soft light in the chicken coop and a clutch of eggs in the nest looking all golden . . . something like that. What was it?

Up in the attic Tom had found letters about Shiloh written by his grandma to Birch when he was away in the war. She mentioned the neighbors often: church potlucks, who had a baby, who died, and such as that. The Faulks were a family she had written about. There had been an after-church sing at their house one Christmas. Mrs. Faulk had a piano in the parlor and had laid the table with all sorts of good food . . . honey-cured hams and a turkey. Folks had sung half the night and it had begun to snow, so some slept over.

It came to Tom that there were still folks living in Shiloh who would look at the ashes of the Sully Faulk farmhouse and remember that holiday outing. He wondered how older people could bear the passing of the happy times and the empty places left by change and grief. He thought about old Hock and how it would have been better if the old man had lived to see that new baby. Could joy be as deep if it went unshared?

All these things ran through Tom's mind, before his thoughts settled down at last to the fire and the poor folks turned out of that old wrecked house. Had there ever been happy times for them? Or was it true what Catfish had said, that such people have no place to go, they just go from place to place?

It was too much to hold in his head. Such questions made him melancholy, like the echo of his own voice calling back across the valley, never giving an answer. . . .

"Next time I'll try a skinny switch." Bobby broke Tom's reverie.

"You didn't have to get switched at all." Tom's rear end was still stinging as he shoveled old straw into the wheelbarrow. "If Mama didn't go on so much about the intelligence of these hens of hers, I'd say you got the brains of a chicken."

"You were gonna get whupped anyway." Bobby shrugged and scrubbed the perches with a wire brush.

"You weren't."

"I feel better about it all the same. I felt bad all day about you gonna get a whippin' for defendin' Sally. But this is somethin' different."

"Same old woodshed to me."

Bobby worked in silence for a time, singing off-key to the hens like his mama. And like her, his keen sense of justice finally took form in words. "Naw. This was different. Gettin' thrashed by Daddy for beatin' Stumpy Oaks just didn't set right. I figure if a guy's gonna get whupped, he oughta deserve it."

"Is that why you told? Birdbrain. Got yourself a lickin' same as me."

Bobby did not reply for a while. "Don't matter if they know now anyway. The place is burned down. The *Handy Book* is gone. Brother Williams says a feller might as well get hung for stealin' a racehorse as a chicken."

Tom considered the wisdom of Brother Williams's words, cocked his head in a very fowl-like stance, and scratched his cheek. From her roost, Henny clucked her agreement in an almost human voice and imitated his gesture. "Maybe so." Tom nodded. "Something like that, anyhow."

CHAPTER 7

Aday or so later, armed with a court order and a beefy, sour-faced bodyguard hired out of Fayetteville, Henry V. Smith and Delbert Simpson returned to the Tucker farm. Greeted cheerfully by Rosey, who knew no better, Smith patted the dog on the head.

"Write that down on the inventory, Delbert," Smith instructed. "Redbone hound."

Trudy called the dog to her as Birch stepped out to block Smith's progress. "I've got till January to pay off Hooper's note." Birch spat angrily into the dirt. "You got no right to come onto my place!"

Smith raised the court injunction over his head like Moses on Sinai throwing down the Ten Commandments. "I got *every* right! Here is my right! You stand in my way and I'll bring the law down on you. You'll wake up in jail tomorrow, Birch Tucker! Law of the land is what gives me the right to inventory what you have as collateral . . . in case you don't pay me what you owe!"

As if the place was already the possession of Hartford Federal Bank, Smith made a list of each piece of farming equipment from the FAMOUS wagon to the mules. While Trudy and Birch looked on in silence, Smith counted every cup and saucer, every pot and pan, every chicken and rooster—all creatures great and small, including Rosey.

Then Henry V. Smith, cane in hand, walked the boundaries of the cotton fields. He stayed for a long time at the corner of the north field. He scooped up the soil in his hand and rubbed it between his fingers. He seemed pleased with what he found there. Before climbing back into the Dodge, Smith shaded his eyes against the sun, stared at the grim couple on the porch of the farmhouse, and almost smiled. Like the soil of the north field, he now had most of Sebastian County in his palm. He knew it. He believed that the farm of Birch Tucker was finally within his reach.

Smith did not often say much, but today he seemed happy to speak. "Bankruptcy settlement against Hooper's gin says you have until the first of January to pay back the cash the late Mister Hooper advanced. Ever play dominoes? Hooper's gin owed Hartford Federal. You owe Hooper's gin. I'm head of the line. That's the law. That's how it works." Smith held up the inventory. "Best be making plans to move on. And plan on traveling light, Birch Tucker."

Birch did not reply. His arm around Trudy's shoulders, he watched the sleek automobile drive away, its cloud of red dust rolling on toward the farm of Dan Faraby.

"Go get the cash box, True. We've got things to tend to." Birch said after a time, "He'll keep that dog on his list over my dead body. We got till January, but I'll pay him off tomorrow."

Old habits were hard to break in Sebastian County. Every Saturday morning since before the War of Northern Aggression, local farmers had brought their surplus into Hartford for the townsfolk to swap or purchase.

This autumn there was no surplus to swap and no cash to buy as much as one eggplant or a single jar of jam. Pickup trucks and buckboards were empty. Even so, Hartford was packed with menfolk come Saturday morning. Horses and mules stood rump to rump at the hitching posts beside Model-T pickups.

There was some business transacted for the sake of tradition. Woody Woods brought his wife's persimmon pudding to swap with Mr. Winters, the pharmacist, for a jar of aspirin. Arley Palmer toted in three pint jars of blackberry jam. And so it went. Every man brought something to Hartford to barter. No matter how small and pitiful the offering, each was determined to return home carrying something different in his poke. This morning deals were made without the pretense or the bother of setting up produce stands. Farmers leaned against the support posts along the boardwalk or sat on the long wood benches and whittled sticks as small bargains were struck: two jars of peaches for four jars of green beans, three live hens for a sack of cornmeal . . .

Birch and Jefferson gravitated toward Dee Brown's barbershop.

Last year, apples had filled Birch's bushel basket. Today, a mere three dozen were stashed in the small wicker hamper he carried. Jefferson brought sixteen of Willa Mae's late-harvest tomatoes for Doc Brown in a paper bag. Hardly anyone had tomatoes these days. Doc Brown had told him when he pulled Willa Mae's bad tooth last week that he would rather be paid for the dental work with tomatoes than cash money.

Of all the business establishments in Hartford, Jefferson felt the most welcome at the barbershop. Dee Brown and his brothers were grandsons of old John Brown, the very same John Brown who had gotten himself hung and started the Civil War for the cause of emancipating the slaves. The brothers were mostly forgiven for being related to John Brown and were generally accepted by folks in Sebastian County because they were indispensable. Doctor. Barber. Blacksmith.

Like the old patriarch, however, the brothers differed from many of their neighbors in their attitudes on race. They simply did not notice the color of a man's skin, and they objected when anyone else did. Dee Brown would sooner throw a Kluxer out on his head as collect two bits for shaving him. Jim Crow laws did not apply in the Hartford barbershop. Dee was fond of telling Jefferson to sit wherever he liked. The Kluxers in the county knew that it was Dee Brown alone who set the policy in his establishment. After all, Dee was the man holding the straight razor to their Ku Klux throats, so they better watch their attitudes.

Through the gold arch of letters on the plateglass window, Jefferson could see the three Browns involved in a serious discussion with Brother Williams. Doc Brown, draped in a white cloth, sat in his brother's barber chair. Jim Brown, a blacksmith by trade and the largest and most fierce of the three Browns, was hammering the wooden arm of the waiting bench with his open palm and expounding as Jeff and Birch entered. The bell above the door rang as if to announce the end of round one.

Jim Brown, tall, lean, and sunburned, was wild-eyed and redder than usual in the face. "If President Hoover is the Chief Executor, it seems to me he ought to find a quicker way to execute us here in Arkansas than starving us to death!"

Jim seemed to Jefferson a perfect likeness of his infamous grandfather. A fire-eating prophet of the Lord, a crusader against wrongs, a wielder of the broadsword against injustice! The blacksmith looked up, startled by the arrival of the newcomers. "How-do, Birch. Jefferson . . . We're just discussin' the overthrow of the government."

"The usual treason and sedition," Doc added.

Dee snipped his shears rapidly in the air. "Jim thinks we ought to render all government officials incapable of producing offspring."

"I'd use something more than barber shears on 'em." Jim spat a stream of tobacco juice, hitting the spittoon with a clang.

Brother Williams blew his nose forcefully into his kerchief and stuffed it back into his pocket. "How-do, Birch. Jefferson. How y'all?"

"Fair to middlin', Brother. How's ever'body?"

The greetings were made and the standard replies were given. Jefferson took a seat beside Jim Brown, who peeked in at the tomatoes and gave a low whistle.

"I brung your tomatoes from Mama, Doc."

"That Willa Mae!" Doc reached for Jefferson's bag and looked in at the miracle of sixteen tomatoes. "That woman can coax whipped cream out of a dead heifer."

Jeff said, "Mama says to tell you she's much better now that you took that tooth, although she spits some now when she talks too fast. She is much obliged."

Birch held up the basket of apples and gestured at his shaving mug on the shelf. "Would you take these for a shave and a haircut, Dee?"

The barber scratched the back of his head. "No. But if Trudy will bake me two apple pies next week, I'll give you two weeks' worth."

"Done." Birch grinned.

"Sit down," Dee instructed. "You're at the back of the line, which means you'll have to listen to Jim expound about President Hoover for thirty minutes or so."

"I can talk about other things." Jim sniffed indignantly. "Lawyers, for instance." He was revving up again. "We wouldn't be in the fix we're in if it wasn't for those fancy, moneygrubbin' lawyers up in Washington. . . ."

The morning rocked along pleasantly this way until at last the bell above the door rang again and Dan Faraby entered, looking pale and shaken.

"I'm done up, fellers," he said. "Altogether done up." At that he pulled out a white sheet of paper and extended it to Doc. "I was hopin' you could ex-plain this here bank letter t' me, Doc. I dunno . . ."

Doc frowned and read the document, which was signed by Henry V. Smith, as well as a judge named Armstrong from Huntington.

"Seems Mister Smith, the esteemed president of Hartford Bank here, claims you owe the bank money," Doc said quietly.

"Who don't?" Brother Williams hooked his thumb on the strap of his bibs and bit off a chaw. "Ever'body owes that ol' skinflint money." He nudged Jim. "Let's us get off lawyers an' talk 'bout bank presidents. . . ."

"The ruin of us all," Jim agreed. "Over two thousand banks gone bust this year. I think the weasels who run the things have just stolen the workingman's savings and sailed off to Tahiti."

Faraby seemed not to hear. "What is this, Doc? Judgment for Deficiency? This says they can auction off all my stuff to pay the Hartford Bank what I owed to Hooper. It don't make no sense to me, Doc."

"How much credit did Hooper give you against your crop?"

Faraby mentally calculated, gazing up at the ceiling. "I got me a buzzard-wing sweep mowin' machine. I got me a windrow rake with spring tines. I got me a new wagon with a patented manure spreader. Borrowed three hundred and sixty-five dollars from Hooper for the lot, thinkin' I could pay him back when the cotton crop settled. Then cotton went bust and Hooper went bust and I went bust. . . . But the bank already repossessed ever'thing I borrowed for when they took over Hooper's gin."

Doc nodded. "Hartford Bank . . . meaning Henry Smith . . . resold your equipment for one hundred and ten dollars. The court says you still owe a balance of two hundred and fifty-five dollars to Henry V. Smith and the bank."

"And now Smith intends to auction off everything that ain't nailed down on my place next Saturday to pay what I owe. Includin' Missus Faraby's furniture that she brung with her when we was married. Her inheritance. Can they do that, Doc?" Faraby, who was a small man, seemed to shrink even smaller before Jefferson's eyes.

"I'm afraid so," Doc Brown said quietly. "All your livestock and belongings. But not your land, Dan. The court judgment does not allow Smith to take your land to settle the debt."

"How'm I gonna work my land if I ain't got a team an' a cultivator an' a plow? What good's the farm if I can't farm? What's the Missus gonna say? She sets great store by that furniture of hers. What am I a-gonna do with nine kids and no beds in the house nor even a chair t' sit upon?" Faraby tucked the letter back into his pocket. With a despairing wave of his hand, he left the men in the shop.

"Well, that's a bank for you," Brother Williams muttered. "King Henry Smith and that little rat Delbert Simpson runnin' 'round the county an' repossessin' . . ."

"Delbert ain't so little no more," Jefferson commented.

"That is true," Jim Brown agreed. "He's growing broader every year he feeds at the trough of Henry V. Smith. That is a fact."

"Speak of the devil." Birch pointed across the street as Delbert Simpson hurried from one post to the next tacking up auction notices.

Like a stray dog marking trees, Jefferson thought.

"He's headed this way," Dee said, sprinkling talcum powder on Doc's neck. "Looks like ol' Delbert's in need of a close shave, fellers. He's a talkative little jaybird, always telling everyone's business. Mind if we move him to the head of the line?"

Jefferson purely admired Dee Brown. He could shave the fuzz off a peach and never break the skin. And he could get a fella so comfortable in his barber chair that it was something like being mesmerized.

Sweating and huffing, Delbert cut across the street as Woody Woods read an auction notice and spit just behind the bank assistant's run-down heels. Delbert seemed unaware of the black looks that followed him toward the barbershop.

"Do your stuff, Dee." Doc patted his brother on the shoulder and took a seat to listen.

The bell above the door announced the arrival of pudgy little Delbert Simpson and the beginning of round three.

"How-do, Delbert," Birch said in a friendly enough tone.

Delbert gave him a do-you-mean-me? look and replied cautiously, "How-do . . . uh . . . Birch."

Then the others greeted him politely, although Jefferson could almost hear the silent thoughts whirring in the minds of the other customers. If the truth had been spoken, it would have gone something like this:

"How-do, Delbert, you bootlicking toad. How's it feel to have sold your soul to the likes of Henry V. Smith? How's it feel to earn your living emptying out the chamber pot of that rancid bag of hog guts?"

But for the sake of acquiring information, every man held his peace. Even Jim Brown, who had not said how-do to Delbert Simpson in three years, said, "How-do, Delbert, how's your mama?"

"She's fine. Except a little gouty. . . ."

At the mention of gout, Doc broke in. "Tell her to lay off the rich foods, Delbert. . . ."

"I'll tell her, Doc, but you know Mama. Comes of bein' married to a butcher all these years."

Delbert looked like the son of a butcher. He was the perfect image of his daddy. Chin disappeared into his neck; belly extended over his belt and strained the buttons of his shirt. He was knock-kneed and his trouser legs rode up the inside of his round thighs when he walked. Birch often commented that from the rear Delbert's backside looked like two hogs fighting under a blanket. His eyes were pale and watery, and his mouth was continually open in a stupefied grin as if he could not breathe out of his nose. On top of that, no matter what the weather, he smelled like an onion field. The aroma of Delbert Simpson made many a strong man weep.

Dee opened the bottle of bay rum aftershave and poured a little on his hand. "Plenty hot out there, isn't it, Delbert?" He slapped his scented hand against Delbert's shoulder in a friendly way. It helped some.

"It is. A scorcher. 'Specially for October."

Pleased by the sudden interest, Delbert snatched off his hat, loosened his tie and collar, and looked for a seat. His eyes fixed directly on Jefferson because it was customary, after all, for a colored man to give up his place to a white man. But this was Dee Brown's place, and Jefferson did not budge.

Dee, noticing Delbert's silent expectation, snapped his towel loudly against the seat of the barber chair as if to brush away the snips of hair, but it was plain to Jefferson that Dee would prefer to snap the towel against Delbert's ample rump. Dee Brown smiled at Delbert, but only with his mouth, not his eyes.

"Well, Delbert, I can see you're a busy man. How about I shave you first? You could use a haircut, too, boy. You're looking like a sheepdog 'round the ears."

Delbert did not have much hair on top, but it was true that he was shaggy on the fringes.

"Sure 'nuff?" Delbert looked to the others for assent.

To a man, they encouraged the bank assistant to go first. After all, they told him, no one else was in a hurry. No one else had much going on.

Grinning in a moony sort of way and touched by their courtesy, Delbert took his seat. Dee took his time with Delbert and talked in soothing tones about the weather and such while he clipped the thin paper collar around the banker's neck and draped the sheet over him. Dee Brown had a voice that could lull a wild bronc to sleep.

"Why Delbert, you're tight as a wire." Dee rubbed Delbert's shoulders and Delbert went more slack-jawed than usual. "Something bothering you, boy?"

Delbert's eyes were half closed and out of focus like he was trying to look at the end of his nose. "It's this . . . auction. . . ."

Delbert did not seem to notice the sudden stirring among the audience.

"Auction?"

"Deficiency notice . . . Faraby's place . . . a little to the right . . . uh-huh. That's a big house. Mister Smith's got big plans."

"Auctions all over these days, I suppose." Dee worked the back of Delbert's head until the fringe of hair stood out like he had stuck his finger in a light socket.

"Uh-huh. That's real nice. . . . Mister Smith's hired Mister Steuben, the auctioneer out of Oklahoma City, to handle it."

This raised eyebrows. Everyone had heard of Augustus Steuben, who by reputation was capable of selling ice to Eskimos.

Dee stirred the shaving cream in Delbert's mug. The company sat in expectant silence and waited for the next question as the click, click, click of the shaving brush against the cup filled the room.

Dee slathered the white foam onto Delbert's jowls, then laid the straight razor against the strop. "Steuben, huh? Expensive, isn't he?"

"Yes, siree. His fee is a third of the take, but Mister Smith expects a good return. Court's given the bank everything on the Faraby's inventory—dishes, furniture, chickens, mules, you name it. The bank expects to make a good profit on the judgment, maybe four or five times the amount of the debt, on account of the court allows expenses to be included in the take. And you know how good Mister Smith is at thinkin' of fees to charge."

To a man the entire audience nodded their agreement, but the unity of assent went unnoted by Delbert.

"Who's Steuben going to sell to? Nobody 'round here can buy anything." Dee checked the razor for sharpness and then continued to strop it in spite of the fact that it could have cut through steel by then.

Delbert jabbered on. "Notices goin' up as far away as Fayetteville. Already got a call from the biggest wholesaler in the Midwest. . . . Mellon's the name. He's been over in Scott County. Lots of farm auctions . . . foreclosures . . . in Scott County . . . Anyways, Mellon already bought the farm equipment Hartford Federal repossessed, but he says he's ready for more."

Birch and Jefferson exchanged looks. Chester Mellon's wholesale business was known by farmers far and wide as the Bone Yard, and Mellon was called the Buzzard. He publicly called the depression his golden opportunity. He had gotten rich by buying below value at distress sales and reselling everything from household goods to livestock for a few pennies more than his cost.

"Mellon figures t' do even better when the auction gets rollin'. He'll outbid everybody and still make a profit. . . . Mister Mellon . . . I purely do admire that automobile of his. A 1929 Chandler, dark blue it is, and Mellon keeps it waxed so it shines like a mirror. . . ."

Dee commenced to shaving Delbert only after the most critical information had been gotten out of him. So there it was: City merchants were expected to drive down from Fort Smith. They might buy the furniture. It was pretty good furniture, too. Lots of it. Fine stuff that the schoolteacher, Mrs. Faraby, had inherited from her rich parents. The Hartford Bank stood to come out way ahead on the deal. And as for Mr. Steuben, the famous auctioneer, he would be coming into Hartford on Friday before the auction and would be staying at Miss Zelda Brown's boardinghouse.

Polished like a new apple and smelling of bay rum, Delbert Simpson paid his two bits. The bell above the door pinged the end of round three. Delbert waddled back across the main street of Hartford. He snubbed up his tie and threw back his shoulders. There was nothing like a close shave to make a man feel swell and clever and optimistic about life.

Had Delbert looked back through the plate glass of the barber shop, he would have seen the three Brown brothers, Birch, Jefferson, and Brother Williams standing in a row behind the gold letters, watching him.

"You're a master, Dee," Jim Brown said solemnly.

Doc added, "I only wish I could extract a tooth or remove a corn so effortlessly."

"Candy from a baby," Birch remarked, patting Dee on the shoulder.

Brother Williams spit into the spittoon. "Whooowhee, Dee Brown, that was somethin' t' behold."

Jefferson wagged his head in amazement. "He don't even know what a close shave he got." Dee sucked his teeth in a satisfied way and accepted the adulation of his friends and siblings.

Doc's eyes narrowed as he thought over the terms of the court document. "That writ says when all the movables have been auctioned, the judgment has been fulfilled, no matter what the take was. So . . ."

"So," Dee echoed, "the question is, what will we do to gum up the works?"

The assembly watched Delbert recommence distributing the auction notices. "Sedition," Doc said.

"Treason." Jim raised a finger and jabbed at the air.

"The usual," Brother Williams said in a satisfied tone.

The old bay horse snorted nervously and craned his neck around from the hayrack. A matched team of Missouri mules likewise left off feeding to prick up their ears at the unexpected groan of the livery's rear door. It was late, way past time for any normal activity.

Even Brother Williams's lazy old yellow cat, Stonewall, abruptly stopped his grooming. When low, murmuring voices came from the back of the stable, Stonewall disappeared into a crevice between two boards.

The first figure that crept into the dim yellow circle of lamplight was stripped to the waist and wore a flour sack painted like a Halloween jack-o'-lantern as a mask over his face. On his arm he sported a black crepe ribbon, and in his hand he brandished a two-foot-long dagger known locally as a toothpick.

The sinister shape revolved slowly, checking to see that no one else was inside the barn. "Come on in," the voice of Brother Williams hissed from inside the flour sack. "It's all clear."

Three more men wearing black armbands crowded through the back door. Doc, Dee, and Jim Brown stood grinning in the center of the straw-covered floor. "Of course, it's all clear," Doc teased. "It's your own stable, Brother. Who did you expect?"

Brother grumbled, "Just bein' cautious is all. Anyways, here's the axle grease and the whitewash." He retrieved two tin cans from a shelf and set them on the floor.

"What, no red?" Dee Brown complained. "How'm I gonna be Red Hand, the bloodthirsty renegade, if there's no red paint?"

"This ain't no costume party," Brother scolded. "There ain't no prizes nor trophies."

"We mean to do it up right," Jim explained. He stripped off his shirt and proceeded to stripe his cheeks and his pale chest with alternating bands of grease and paint. His arms, face, and the vee of his shirt collar were already burned dark brown by his smithing occupation, so that his body appeared to have been decorated all over.

When the rear door opened again, the four men froze until they recognized Birch and Jeff. Birch had a hatchet in his hand, and Jeff carried a bundle under one arm.

"Howdy Birch, Jeff," Brother intoned as the unofficial leader of the savage band. "Jeff, I cain't figger how we're a-gonna make you out to be no red Indian."

"That's all right, Brother," Jeff said, unfolding a bedsheet and showing the two eyeholes cut in the middle. "I done had practice bein' a ghost before this."

"Is this all of us?" Doc asked, blacking out his eye sockets with grease and helpfully applying white dots to his brother Dee's back. "Who are we missing?"

"JUST ME!" roared a voice from over the heads of the men. A wild-eyed shape with a shock of bushy hair stood erect in the hayloft and rattled a pair of trace chains. "WHOOOEEE!" All the men jumped, and Birch's intended arrowhead shape on his chest turned into an unplanned lightning bolt.

Brother Williams shuddered, and goose bumps popped out along the line of his bony spine. "Durn it, Boomer!" he scolded. "I told you not to do thataway! You ain't s'posed to scare *us*. Get on down here and leave off jangling them chains!"

"BEEN PRACTICIN'," Boomer explained at his normal volume of speech. "PUT THE FEAR OF GOD INTO THAT AUCTION MAN, YOU SAID, I CAN DO THAT, SURE ENOUGH!"

"*You* ain't coming!" all three brothers Brown vowed in a single voice.

"OH, YES I AM!" Boomer pledged.

"We got to let him," Brother pleaded, spreading his hands to placate the angry looks. "He overheard me talkin' to Dee about it. An', well, y'all know how he runs off at the mouth. Ever'body in town'll be in on it if we don't take Boomer and swear him to secrecy."

The other conspirators exchanged frustrated looks and then agreed to the necessity of letting Boomer join up.

"You listen to me an' listen good," Brother instructed. "You don't say nothin', understand? Not tonight and not ever after. You keep your mouth closed all the time, less'n you want the whole town to jump outta bed. And don't wave them chains till I tell you to." Boomer nodded his understanding, his eyebrows puckered together as if the additional pressure on his face was necessary to keep his mouth shut. "An' stop clankin' 'em when I says to stop, got it?" Another scowling nod.

"All right then, Boomer of the Screaming Eagle tribe," Doc Brown said with a laugh. "Come here and get into your war paint. It's time to go attack the fort and scalp us an auctioneer."

The creaking of the steps that led to the landing outside the upstairs bedrooms at the rear of Miss Zelda Brown's boardinghouse might have been caused by the wind. But the air in Shiloh that night was remarkably still and calm.

The rustling noises that came from near the wall at the side of the old wooden structure might have been cats playing in the moonlight or chasing mice around the woodpile. But the cats had already been frightened into seeking shelter themselves. They peered watchfully out of the neatly stacked rows of split oak.

The murmuring voices that a wakeful person might have detected rising up into the night sky went unheard. Despite the occasional clank of chains followed by harsh shushing and ironic demands for silence, no one in Miss Zelda's rooming establishment noticed anything amiss. Of course, Miss Zelda herself, proper spinster lady that she was, and no relation to the brothers Brown, heard every one of the noises, but she had been advised by Doc to ignore them. Which she did.

Had Mr. Augustus Steuben suffered from insomnia, he would have heard all these things, as well as a grunt of pain and a mild epithet when the knee of the figure masked in a flour sack collided sharply with an unnoticed wheelbarrow in the yard. But Mister

Steuben, having consumed nearly a gallon of chicken soup and dumplings beyond counting, to say nothing of half an apple pie, was well into his third hour of deep slumber. The substantial feed and the half-empty bottle of Scotch whiskey on the nightstand pretty much ensured that he would not awaken when five disguised forms crept across the planks of the landing and entered his room. Nor did he.

"Bottled in bond," Doc said, indicating the liquor. "Must be a wealthy man to drink imported hooch in the middle of Prohibition. And just look at the grin on his face. Prob'ly dreamin' of the state fair. Thinks he just knocked down the highest price per pound ever for a prize Duroc hog."

"Shoot fire," Brother Williams returned. "He could win the prize hisself, only he'd be a Chester white." The livery owner pointed to the expansive heap of Steuben's stomach covered by an insufficient length of undershirt.

"We're not here to judge his bacon," Jim Brown growled. "Get on with it. Wake him up."

Doc grabbed the sagging flesh of the ponderous left arm and shook it. There was no response except a widening of the smile on Steuben's face. "Dreaming he's on stage next to the Hog Queen," Dee surmised. "Pinch him." The beam on Steuben's face was replaced by a pouting frown. It seemed he was not ready to leave the pleasant scene in his mind.

Doc intensified the squeeze on the elbow and shook more violently. Steuben tried to yank his limb free, but Doc kept it tightly gripped. Brother pinched the auctioneer's right earlobe, then did it again harder.

Steuben swatted at the annoyance with his right hand. His wild swing brought him into contact, not with the expected biting insect, but with the knotted cords of a wiry arm.

Steuben's eyes snapped open and he looked up into a pair of hideous faces! The head of a painted scarecrow leered at him from one side, and a skull with hollow eye sockets smirked on the other. The auctioneer screamed, but his yell for help was cut short by a hand clamped over his mouth. The taste and smell of axle grease flooded his senses, mixing vilely with the stale booze in his mouth.

"Augustus Steuben?" a sepulchral tone queried from the foot of the bed. Steuben's pop eyes craned anxiously past the mound of his trembling belly, and he shook his head, trying futilely to clear his fuddled brain. Another apparition stood there in the moonlight, brandishing a hand ax. It was flanked by two more, equally hideous creatures, who had firm grasp of Steuben's legs.

The question was repeated, and now the auctioneer nodded his head, jowls quivering. "This is your only warning," the specter pronounced. "You have been party to deprivin' folks of their property for the benefit of moneygrubbin' skinflints. You have taken advantage of the misery of others. You . . ." the spokesman paused and seemed to grope for words. "You done been weighed in the balances and found wanting. Do you admit your guilt?"

The palm over Steuben's mouth was withdrawn far enough to let him breathe and reply, but held in readiness to press down if he screamed. The auctioneer felt suddenly very sober. "I see what your game is," he said, mustering up the remnants of his courage. "This is illegal," he wheezed. "You can't do this; it's against the law."

Jim Brown, whose face and brawny arms merged with the darkness while his white chest seemed to float unsupported, plucked up the Arkansas toothpick and waved it around the turned posts of the footboard. "In a pig's eye," he said. "Illegal like the Boston Tea Party was illegal. There's law that's bought and paid for, and then there's right and wrong. Got it?"

Steuben nodded again, as if acquiescing. The pressure on his arms and legs lessened.

In a move that was remarkably quick for so much tonnage, Steuben rolled to his left and threw his bulk into Doc's legs, carrying them both to the floor. Scrambling upright in his flowered boxer shorts, the auctioneer put his shoulder into Dee, knocking the barber aside in a wild rush to gain the door to the hall.

Just as Steuben's hand touched the knob, it opened toward him. The biggest phantom of all, covered from head to toe in a white sheet, reached out to grab him. "Beware!" it wailed. "Beware!"

The balding man stumbled backward, right into the waiting arms of a trio of savages. "Just as we thought," Birch declared. "He don't yet see the error of his ways." So saying, Birch yanked on Steuben's arm, and the others each added their tugs and shoves, till the auctioneer was spinning like a top. The inertia of his massive stomach kept him rotating until he fetched up against the door that led out onto the landing. Steuben seized the latch with renewed hope of escape.

On the platform just in front of Steuben appeared still another frightening vision. Clanking chains with both hands, Boomer screeched

at the top of his lungs, "BEWARE! BE . . . WARE! YOU AIN'T TOO
BALANCED, AND AIN'T NOBODY WANTS YOU!"

Steuben threw up both arms to ward off the metal links and backed
clumsily away. A pair of Indians holding a shovel handle behind his
knees tripped him, and the auctioneer sprawled across the coil rug at
the foot of the bed.

"BE-WARE!" the outside ghost continued to shout. "BEWARE OF
THE ARROWS BEIN' WEIGHED!"

"PSSST," Brother whistled. "That's enough now!"

"BE–!" the balcony spirit yelled defiantly, and then stopped
abruptly.

"Now, brothers," Birch said shaking the hatchet. "He ain't convinced. What shall we do with him?"

"NO! No, wait!" Steuben pleaded. "I am convinced! Don't hurt me!
I got a wife an' kids. I won't even go to the blamed auction. Just let me
go!"

Birch and Doc smiled at each other above the prostrate form. "Do
you see these black bands?" Doc asked in a grave tone. "Do you want
your family to be wearing them?"

"No, no!"

"Then you will not recognize any bidder who is not wearing one of
these."

Steuben raised up on one elbow and ran a fleshy palm over the
fringe of hair that encircled the shiny dome of his head. "I don't get it,"
he said. "You *want* me to go to the auction?"

"'Course we do," Jim answered, waving a skinning knife under
Steuben's nose. "We just want it to run smooth. And that will happen
provided you don't even see any bidders unless they're wearin' one of
these." He touched the tip of the blade to the crepe. "And you'll see
plenty of these as reminders. Savvy?"

The auctioneer swallowed hard, his eyes bulging as he looked from
one grim face to another. Then he nodded again and held up his hands
in token that this time he really meant it.

"Leave him the proof that this was no dream!"

Steuben looked in horrified expectancy from knife to dagger to
hatchet. The tall wraith clad in the sheet closed in and, swooping down,
wrapped the auctioneer from head to middle in the bed linen, rolling
him over a few times for good measure.

By the time Steuben had untangled himself and peered cautiously around, all the night callers had fled. But from the fringe of cottonwoods that encircled the rear of the boardinghouse he could still hear the rattle of chains and the occasional distant call of "BE-WARE!"

CHAPTER 8

Bobby twisted the road sign around so that the arrow toward Hartford pointed to Mansfield and vice versa. "Look, Tom," he said, "how about this?"

His older brother shook his head. "Won't work," he said. "Anybody comin' to the sale will have passed through either Hartford or Mansfield before gettin' this far. Might even tip 'em off that something's up. Daddy says old mellon-head is a crafty one."

Bobby looked disappointed. "Oh," he said, cranking the wooden post back around. "Then what?"

"Don't feel bad," Tom urged. "It's the right idea. Now listen," he said to Trent Faraby. "How does your pa tell folks how to find your place?"

Trent sniffed, scrubbing his nose on his shirtsleeve. "Pa always says to turn sharp to the right after you pass the church, keep goin' 'til the ford of the Jim Fork, then right at the lane with our name on the sign."

Tom nodded thoughtfully. "Ain't there a road to the left 'bout a half mile before your place?"

Trent agreed. "But that's a dead end. They'll figger it out."

Tom's grin spread across his face. "Not with us helpin'," he said.

When Delbert Simpson drove past in his Model-T, the boys hid in the culvert. It would not pay to let the enemy know there was a plan under way. Besides, Tom explained, the henchmen of Henry V. Smith already knew how to locate the Faraby farm.

Minutes later, the Faraby children had all been dispatched to different roads, lanes, and intersections surrounding their place. The sheer number of Faraby siblings made it easy to cover all the approaches. Tom, Bobby, and two more conspirators took their station near the spot where the road swung around a bend of the creek. On the grassy verge they sat down, baited hooks with worms for catfish, and awaited the arrival of other, bigger fish.

The first automobile driven by city folks looking for the Faraby place was a dust-covered Chevrolet. The man behind the wheel was easily discouraged from searching too hard. He was already sweaty and looked fed up with the washboard roads.

Tom merely said, "Faraby's? Not hereabouts, I don't guess. There was a family name of Farley over in Scott County . . . in Abbott, mebbe . . . or was it Waldron?" He politely offered directions to the county line some five miles away, but the man in the straw hat and string tie accelerated away in a cloud of sputtering exhaust. "Didn't even say thank you," Tom mused.

The second and the third arrivals were similarly treated to generous assistance. At one point the driver of a dark red pickup truck leaned out of his cab and spat a stream of tobacco juice between Tom's feet. "You wouldn't be funnin' me, would ya, son?"

"No, sir," Tom said solemnly. "Who was it you said you wanted?"

When the man had repeated his request, Tom, Bobby, Squirrel Hocott, and his older brother, Barney, obligingly indicated all four cardinal points of the compass. The red pickup departed with a clash of gears and a stream of profanity, but headed directly away from the Faraby place.

The elder Hocott brother stuck out his hand toward Tom. "Shake," he said. "Tucker, you're all right. I ain't gonna believe what Stumpy Oaks says about you no more. He ain't here helpin' neighbors, and you are. That so-and-so even said folks what has troubles with the bank just don't know how to do business, says they deserve what they get. You ain't like that."

"Thanks, Pigpen . . . I mean Barney."

"It's okay." Barney Hocott grinned. "Possum."

The sun was climbing toward midmorning when a glimmer reflecting off an approaching windshield alerted the troops to another arrival. The oncoming car was the expected dark blue Chandler, a few years old, but shining with chrome bumpers and grill. The man behind the wheel, who wore his dark suit and tie stoically despite the heat, was more canny than any so far. Reaching into his jacket pocket, he withdrew a quarter and held it out so it caught the light. "Name's Mellon," he said. Tom was half afraid Bobby would admit that they already knew the name, but his little brother stayed still and serious. "This is yours to share if y'all will ride along and show me the way. I got a lead on some farm equipment I can pick up cheap. I already got a buyer waiting in Little Rock, so I need to get to that auction. If you'll help me out, the money's yours."

"Yessir," Tom agreed. "Pigpen, you and Squirrel stay here while me an' Bobby help this gentleman out." Tom hopped onto the running board on the driver's side, and Bobby scrambled onto the other. "Okay," Tom urged. "Let 'er rip."

The breeze stirred by the thirty-mile-per-hour speed felt good on Tom's face. He was sorry to see the turnoff approach so quickly. "There it is," he said, indicating the narrow dirt lane to the left.

A sudden application of the brakes almost stood the Chandler on the wings of its gleaming chrome hood ornament. "I thought the turn was to the right," the dark-haired man with the pencil-line mustache argued suspiciously. "The bank notice said to the right."

Tom shrugged. "Must of heard wrong," he replied, "see?" Tom pointed to a slab of pine nailed to a fence post. The painted letters clearly spelled out FARABY.

The Chandler pulled off the road, both front wheels dropping into deep ruts. The rear tires thumped on another pine plank that lay facedown in the parallel tracks that were almost deep enough to be called ditches. The grass and the weeds between the rows had grown to hang over the center of the trail. The first time that the Chandler whined above five miles an hour, the right front tire banged over a hidden rock, slamming the auto down onto its frame and jolting Bobby off the running board. "You kids walk in front of me," Mr. Mellon demanded after he finished inspecting the undercarriage for damage. "Warn me about those rocks. I don't want to knock the bejeebers out of my car."

The route ahead ascended a steep incline. For the first fifty feet the Chandler climbed like a champ. Then its rear wheels spun on a patch of loose shale, spraying gravel behind with machine-gun force as Mellon gunned the engine. The car lurched forward, then slid down again farther than it had gained. "Maybe you should reverse her back and take a run at it," Tom offered.

"That's a good idea," Mellon agreed, wiping his sweat-drenched forehead with a white pocket handkerchief that was quickly becoming the red of the Shiloh countryside. Backing down the hillside was part steering and part controlled skid. At the bottom, Mellon threw in the clutch, revved the engine, jammed the Chandler into gear, and roared up the grade as Tom and Bobby jumped aside.

The auto sped upward, past the halfway point, bounced heavily on another boulder like a horse rearing, smashed down again, and stalled, high-centered between the ruts. There was a loud screech and a scraping noise as the axles slid free of the granite ridge on which they were impaled.

Tom thought that Mr. Mellon must certainly have had enough by now, but the man was persistent. Backing all the way down the hill again, Mellon aimed the car to ride on the ridges instead of between them and ground his way successfully to the top.

At the crest of the knob, Mellon alighted from the auto and looked down the reverse of the incline, a grade every bit as steep as the one just climbed. What was more, the route led directly into the water of the James Fork Creek. "Hold on a minute," he protested. "How deep is that water? I won't be able to stop at the bottom of this hill before going into the stream."

Tom shook his head. "The depth ain't nothin' to worry about, mister. It ain't but six inches or so out in the middle."

"You're sure?" Mellon inquired again.

"Absolutely," Tom agreed. "See where the tracks climb out on the other side? You're almost there now. Can we please have our quarter?"

"Sure, kid." Mellon tossed Tom the coin. Then to himself he muttered, "I won't have to worry about any competition at this auction."

The Chandler gathered speed as it rolled downward. The road was smoother, and aside from needing to steer quickly between two tree stumps, Mellon guided the car safely off the grade and into the ford of the creek. The water level, as Tom had predicted, came less than halfway up the wire-spoked wheels.

As Tom and Bobby watched from the hilltop, the auto moved smoothly, engine purring, to the midpoint of the stream. Then it seemed to hesitate, as if grabbed from beneath by some unseen force. It bucked twice, coughed, and settled awkwardly, one side lower than the other.

Mellon was out and perched on the running board. "Hey," he yelled upward. "What goes on here?"

"Don't get down, mister," Tom warned. "That's quicksand. We'll go get somebody with a team to pull you out."

"Quicksand?!" was the anxious reply. "How long is this gonna take?"

"Set tight," Tom instructed. "We won't be more'n two or three hours at most."

On the way back to the main road, Tom picked up the board over which the Chandler had driven and tossed it into the elderberry bushes. *DEAD END*, it read. *QUICKSAND AHEAD*.

Jefferson Canfield and Jim Brown waved the steady flow of traffic into the pasture from the tree-canopied lane that led to the Faraby farmhouse. So far the boys down the main highway had done a fine job of redirecting unwanted bidders toward the border of Mexico.

Thanks to Boomer, who had stolen the carburetor out of Henry V. Smith's touring car, the bank president was not expected to attend the auction.

Midway through the parking of the vehicles, Jim Brown wiggled his index finger in his ear and called to Jefferson, "Heads up! Here comes that son-of-a-butcher . . . Delbert Simpson. Lemme handle him, Jeff."

With utmost courtesy and neighborliness, Jim Brown directed Delbert to park his convertible Model-T beneath the mulberry tree where Jefferson had noticed a flock of wild pigeons roosted.

"A few deposits for the assistant banker," Jim said with satisfaction.

Aside from Delbert, only a few hostiles had managed to run the blockade. Jefferson and Jim Brown allowed the strangers to park; there was no way to turn them back once they made it this far. The two men smiled stoically and welcomed them to the Faraby auction, but did not give them black armbands. The black mourning ribbons were reserved for some three dozen trusted friends and neighbors who slipped them over shirtsleeves with broad winks and passed extras to wives and daughters who would bid on dishes, pots and pans, and furniture— womany stuff.

Grandma Amos remarked that she recalled wearing such a ribbon on the day of the sack of Atlanta. Of course, in Grandma's case, the crepe hardly showed, since she dressed all in black all the time anyhow.

But the head-to-toe expression of bereavement made her sort of the unofficial head of the conspiracy.

The Faraby yard was cluttered with tagged and numbered furniture, boxes of china, crates of chickens, and farm machinery. A mare and weanling colt stamped and whinnied in one corral. Two milk cows bawled through the fence rails to their calves. A team of huge bay mules stood nose to tail in the round pen, and Dan Faraby's prize boar snuffled loudly in his enclosure.

"Dan's countin' on takin' first prize in the fair with that hog," Trudy heard Birch remark to Doc Brown.

"Still will," Doc replied gruffly. Then to Joey, who perched on Birch's shoulders, he added, "You taking your Henny to the fair, young Joe?"

"Sure," bubbled Joey. "Gonna win first prize!"

"Shoot." Doc chuckled. "Now my hen has no chance at all."

The smallest Faraby children sat glumly in the dining room chairs, which were scattered among headboards, footboards, bureau drawers, highboys, lowboys, the dining room table, a camelhair sofa, and an ebony grand piano.

Appropriately clad for a funeral, Mrs. Faraby wore a black, high-collared dress. Ashen-faced but stoic, she stood beside Trudy and gazed over the scene like the wife of Job might have done. Wringing her linen handkerchief in her thin hands, she leaned against an enormous Victorian sideboard crafted from Hawaiian koa wood. Her grandfather had won it off a retired sea captain in a New Orleans poker game, and it had been a treasured family possession ever since. "Losing that," the schoolteacher had told Trudy, "is what I regret most."

On the advice of Sheriff Potts, the Faraby clan was not a party to the plot against the Hartford Bank president and Mr. Augustus Steuben. Dan Faraby and his wife remained completely unaware of the nocturnal visit to the auctioneer.

Steuben had made a call on Sheriff Potts before sunup, informing him about the threats and asking for advice. Sheriff Potts had warned Steuben that Sebastian County was full of desperate characters and told him he had better be careful of his very life. It was wise, Sheriff Potts told the auctioneer, to keep his mouth shut because he could not tell who, among the many, had come calling the night before.

"If'n I was you," Potts informed him, "I'd believe every word them hoodlums uttered. Carry on the auction in a proper fashion, of course.

A feller like you can't do otherwise. But carry a big gun, Mister Steuben, t' defend yourself when it's over. You'll need it."

After alerting Doc Brown to Steuben's complaint, Sheriff Potts, a black armband tucked inside his hip pocket, had promptly left the county to visit his elderly mother over in Charleston.

The auctioneer took his place on top of a flatbed wagon and held up his hands for silence. "Welcome, friends," he said in a voice that sounded unusually high and strained. "No bids are too small," he encouraged, looking around at all the black ribbons that were in evidence, "and no offer refused. Let's get this show on the road with this fine brace of mules." He indicated the matched pair of mules, which were widely admired around the county for their strength and stamina.

"Tell you what I'm gonna do," he said. "It'd be a shame to break up the team, so bid for one and get both. What d'ya say? Who'll give me ten?"

"What? What'd he say? Both for one price?" Delbert Simpson frantically questioned a stoic Doc Brown. Doc patted the strip of crepe that encircled his biceps and nodded with satisfaction, but said nothing.

A thicket of black armbands shot up, and a few sleeves without the identifying marks were also raised. "I'll give ten," Birch offered. "Ten cents."

"Ten cents," agreed Joey's piping voice over Birch's head.

Steuben's eyes bulged more than before, but he continued as if the proposition were exactly what he expected. "Thank you. I have ten. Who'll make it twenty?"

The men with the upraised armbands dropped them to their sides, their mouths pinched tight shut and their expressions stony. The uninitiated looked around with surprise. A small, bookish fellow in round spectacles who had driven all the way from St. Louis called out loudly, "I'll make it a dollar!"

A lean, hawk-featured man, whose straight black hair and saddle-leather skin tone suggested Cherokee blood, offered two dollars. Steuben looked down at the gavel as if he had not heard either man. "I have ten cents. Who'll make it twenty?"

"Wait." Delbert waved. "There's a bid over here."

"Going once, going twice."

"Make it five dollars then," the St. Louis buyer suggested. "Did you hear that?"

"Sold for ten cents," Steuben announced, banging the gavel and wiping his face with a handkerchief.

"What?" Delbert fairly screamed. "Did he just sell both mules for ten cents? Mister Smith expected them to go for fifty dollars apiece."

Jim Brown and his brother Dee closed in on the St. Louis bidder from opposite sides. In a friendly tone, Dee explained that the Missourian was probably wasting his time and that he might find more of interest at a different location, like back in Missouri. Looking from the determined face of Dee to the thick neck and broad shoulders of Jim, the stranger from St. Louis readily agreed and departed in his Ford.

"Don't bother tellin' me," the brown-complected bidder with the hook nose said when approached by Dee. "You don't hafta set on a flagpole to see which way the wind's blowin'. I'll be leavin', too."

The hot rays of the late afternoon sun were blocked by the spreading limbs of the giant pepper tree that stood just to the west of the rambling Faraby home. The exact location for the house, Mrs. Faraby had explained to Trudy, had been chosen by her husband's grandfather, precisely because of the huge tree.

The two women sat on the porch that spanned the entire front of the place. A steady stream of armbanded neighbors, women, and children—approached the steps as Trudy looked on. Grandma Amos had led the parade, handing over a blue silk parasol with a snort and a cackle for having outfoxed that Yankee bandit Henry V. Smith.

Like a file of supplicants approaching an oriental monarch, every single person in the line presented a household object for Mrs. Faraby's instruction as to where it should be replaced. Beside the schoolteacher stood two of the Faraby children, who interpreted their stepmother's emotion-choked words for the patient helpers.

"Ma says the Victrola goes in the parlor on the square oak table," Missy Faraby reported to Sarah Hocott. "And Ma says thank you so, so much."

Across the yard at the entrance to the barn, Trudy could see that a cluster of men were doing the same thing with Dan Faraby's farm equipment. Jeff carried a scythe, and if that were not weight enough, had slung two mule collars over his shoulders. He disappeared into the shadow of the stable's doorway and returned a moment later to help

Brother Williams and a dazed-looking Dan Faraby move a chicken coop back into place.

In the pasture, under a tree, Delbert Simpson sat on the bumper of his Model-T, his flushed and sagging face following each piece of property as it was returned to the Farabys. Trudy could not hear him fretting to himself, but she thought she could read his lips. He was saying over and over again, "What will Mister Smith say? How could this happen? What will Mister Smith do now?"

"'Scuse me, Missus Faraby," Lily said at her turn to ask directions. "Where does these canaries belong?" Inside the gilded wire cage, a pair of yellow birds hopped and fluttered from perch to perch, trilling loudly. "They shore sings nice."

"Oh, bless you, Lily," the schoolteacher said in a tight squeak. "They do so brighten life, don't they? You'll find a stand for the cage in the dining room . . . that is, if it is not still outside on the auction block."

"No, ma'am," Lily said. "I seen your boy Trent and Miz Trudy's Bobby carry it in the side door 'bout ten minutes ago."

Trudy scanned the yard again. It seemed that everyone from Shiloh was there. All were engaged in busy scurrying, like ants storing up provisions. Besides Delbert, the only static group was the small knot of men around Augustus Steuben—Birch and the three Browns. Trudy could hear the clink of coins as Birch counted money into Steuben's outstretched hand. "Twenty-two ninety-nine, twenty-three dollars. Twenty-three and ten, fifteen, forty, fifty . . ."

Trudy smiled again and felt the same glow inside as she had experienced when she watched the auction take place. Every single neighbor, from youngest to oldest, had brought out their precious pennies, nickels, and dimes. Each had made an undisputed purchase, handed the money to Birch for accounting, and then proceeded to present the belonging back to the Farabys. Except for Delbert and Steuben, there were no sleeves left that did not sport the identifying bands.

"Twenty-five seventy-six, twenty-five eighty-six . . ."

Willa Mae stumped heavily up onto the porch, carrying a drawer from the koa wood sideboard. "I hears you set great store by this," she said with a gentle smile. "Thought you might like to hold it." Willa Mae placed the wooden tray into Mrs. Faraby's outstretched arms as if handing over an infant.

Too overcome to speak, the schoolteacher bit her lip and nodded vigorously. Silent tears rolled down her cheeks, and the two children closest wrapped their arms around her neck.

"If'n you don't mind," Willa Mae offered, "I's gon' see to your kitchen. I reckon these chillun and me can re-place it all where it goes. Come on, young'uns." Willa Mae led a dignified parade of Faraby, Hocott, and Grier children into the house. Each child proudly carried a single cup, spoon, or plate.

"Twenty-seven thirty-three, thirty-eight . . ."

From inside the house came the discordant pinging of someone pounding on the grand piano, someone who clearly had no talent for playing the instrument at all. Trudy half rose from the porch chair, wondering if she should go see which child was messing about and shirking his or her work.

"It's all right." Willa Mae's deep chuckle reached Trudy. "It's just Boomer playin' his piany." Trudy sat back down.

"Twenty-nine dollars and fifty-seven cents," Trudy heard Birch report, "an' that's the lot. Does that figure match your tally, mister auctioneer?"

The sweating face of Augustus Steuben looked around the circle of Shiloh men, again took in the armbands, and allowed that the total did agree with his calculations. Steuben studied the double handful of coins, then dropped a fistful of change into his pants pocket. Trudy saw Doc and Dee Brown step apart just enough to give Steuben an avenue of escape, and he scooted through the opening toward Delbert Simpson.

The auctioneer announced to the assistant banker the total of the take and then the bank's two-thirds share. In a voice loud enough for all in the farmyard to hear, Delbert wailed, "What's Mister Smith gonna say?"

The screen door behind Trudy and Mrs. Faraby banged open, and Boomer came out onto the porch. "I SURELY DO ADMIRE THAT THERE PIANY," he screeched. "IT SOUNDS REAL PRETTY. AND ONLY COST FIFTEEN CENTS, TOO. BUT I AIN'T GOT SPACE FOR IT IN MY ROOM AT THE STABLE. RECKON I'LL LEAVE IT HERE WITH YOU, IF'N YOU DON'T MIND."

Mrs. Faraby allowed that Boomer could come over and play his piano any time he wanted.

"The jig is up." Sheriff Potts hitched up his trousers and sat down heavily in the barber chair while Doc, Jim, Brother Williams, Birch, and Jefferson waited for the final results of what had come to be known as the Penny Auction Rebellion. "Take a little off around the ears, Dee."

"What'd the federal marshall say?" Doc thoughtfully scrubbed the stubble on his chin and leaned forward to hear Potts's reply.

"He's got a list from Henry Smith of every man, woman, and infant who wore an armband or placed a bid," the sheriff harrumphed loudly. "But he can't arrest nobody because nobody knows who them wild red Indians was who waylaid the auction man in his bed and sabotaged the sale."

Jefferson said in a serious tone, "Ask me, I'd say Steuben was drunk."

"He had a bottle of . . ." Doc's voice trailed off.

"That's right," Jim Brown interjected too quickly. "It wasn't bootleg . . . uh . . . whiskey . . . uh . . ."

"On his night table . . . hmmm . . . Miz Brown noticed the smell of it. . . . There weren't no Injuns," Brother Williams tugged his earlobe thoughtfully.

"Nor chains clankin'," Birch agreed.

"He was dreaming." Dee shook out the white drape and Jefferson looked hard at it, then turned away.

"No ghosts neither!" Brother Williams was quick to add.

Sheriff Potts screwed up his pudgy face, working his mouth over to one side and puffing out his cheek as if Dee was already shaving him. "I can't tell this to just anybody. Official business. Understand?"

Nods all around.

"This is the way it stacks up, boys," Potts continued. "Whoever done this is gonna get away with it. . . ."

Sighs of relief. A sudden shifting in their seats. The mopping of brows.

"Leastwise . . ." Potts raised his hand in a pontifical fashion. "This time I figger the guilty parties will get away with it. Providin' . . ." He glared directly at Brother Williams. "Providin' that whoever was a-clankin' them chains will stop jumpin' out from behind bales of hay at the livery stable and rattlin' the traces at the customers. . . ."

"Boomer's just . . ." Brother Williams rolled his eyes.

"Boomer!" Potts boomed the name. "Lord a'mighty! Of all the . . ." His hand went up again to stop himself. "What's done is done. But this is what's comin': Smith has hired Pinkerton men. Private bodyguards. He's aimin' to start foreclosin' on ever' piece of property he's got a line on."

The group exchanged looks as if to say they had only begun to fight.

Potts lowered his chin like a bull about to charge. "It worked once, but it ain't gonna work again. Whoever . . . WHOEVER . . . done this . . . has got away with it one time, but it ain't gonna work again, boys!"

Doc raised one shoulder and sucked on his teeth. "Well, then. If ever we hear who was involved, we will tell them what you said, Sheriff."

Potts settled back in the chair and closed his eyes. "I'd have arrested Steuben and throw'd him in the jailhouse if somebody'd told me about the whiskey."

CHAPTER 9

The Penny Auction Rebellion was only one small battle in the war that now threatened all of Sebastian County.

After his disgrace, Henry V. Smith was stepping up his timetable for the ruination of every farmer in Shiloh. Day after day he made the rounds of local farms and added to his inventory lists.

Smith's car roared past Tom and Bobby on their way home from school. Birch and Trudy were unusually grim and silent when the boys banged through the screen door of the back porch and into the kitchen. Trudy did not ask how class had gone or if they had homework to do. Birch looked angry as he chopped kindling in the yard.

The brothers took advantage of this preoccupation by dumping their schoolbooks on the bed and taking off down the hill to the creek. Gathering handfuls of late season blackberries, they circled around and returned to the barn where they kept a stack of dime novels hidden in the hayloft.

They read for a while until Birch and Trudy entered the barn together. Tom put a finger to his lips and shoved the dime novels into the hay. Then the two boys sat silently in the loft of the barn while their mama milked the little Jersey cow and their daddy trimmed the mule's hooves.

"He'll work somethin' out, Trudy," Birch mumbled. "Two months he's got. There's other ways to get cash. Coal minin' and such. Hocott ain't gonna lose his place, True. . . ."

"Where have the boys gotten off to?" Trudy asked Birch in the sort of voice that indicated she did not wish to discuss this if Tom and Bobby might overhear.

Milk pinged a few beats against the bottom of the tin bucket before Birch answered.

"Last I saw"—the rasp of file against hoof punctuated his words—"they hauled off yonder toward the creek. Whoa up, there. Huntin' for coon tracks, I reckon."

Bobby nudged Tom. They exchanged grim looks. So the Hocott farm was next on Smith's list. What would happen to Othar and Barney Hocott?

The mule stomped his foot impatiently. "Easy now." Birch slapped its rump in warning. "I'll speak to Tom and Bobby. They've run off without doing their chores."

"Let it go, Birch." The milk pail was filling up rapidly. The ping became a rhythmic splash. "Let them just be children today. Such a dreadful day. Othar and Tom are such pals.

"These boys will catch on soon enough what's happening to everybody all right. Now we're broke, too, but at least Smith's got nothin' on us."

"It means we tighten our belts is all."

"I promised 'em we'd get that surplus army tent down at Gramma Amos's store when the settle came."

Bobby grimaced. Did this mean they would not get the tent?

Trudy replied after a long moment. "They have made do without a tent this long. It's shoes I'm concerned about. Tom has already worn out the toes of his shoes playing marbles. I told him to take off his shoes when he plays, but . . . Well . . . it was new shoes I was hoping for . . . Bobby is growing so fast. . . ."

There was a rustle of straw as Birch moved to the rear of the mule, patted its flank, and spoke in soothing tones as he hefted the mule's hind leg and resumed work.

For a while neither Birch nor Trudy spoke. Tom looked down at the toes of his shoes. The leather was almost worn through. He wondered if all the important stuff had been talked about already. Every kid in Shiloh needed new shoes.

Birch finished the near hind hoof and moved to the off side before he continued. "Woody Woods asked Judge Flowers about it. . . ."

Bobby sighed and rolled his eyes at Tom in disappointment. They were trapped in the hayloft now. Mama would take a switch to them both if she knew they were eavesdropping, and this conversation had yet to mention anything exciting. Tom put a finger to his lips, urging Bobby to be patient.

Birch continued methodically. "We got bad drought here, hit us worse than Oklahoma. Maybe it ain't just a matter of everybody finding the cash to pay off Smith . . . which will take a miracle. I don't know . . . prayin', beggin' God for rain, and there ain't rain. . . ." The rasping file and the milk jetting into the bucket filled the silence.

"What did Judge Flowers have to say about it?"

"Woody asked if Smith and the bank had the legal right to do this—claim farms and assets and auction everything off to settle the debt even though Hooper promised us eleven cents or more. Judge Flowers said a handshake ain't worth the paper it's written on." Birch gave a short, bitter laugh. "Woody says the judge said the handshake of a dead man won't stand up in court until Judgment Day comes, and then maybe we'll get justice but not before. Should've had a contract."

"Where does that leave everyone else?"

"Busted, most of 'em. Owing Hartford Federal. New corrals, plow, harness. We all lived last year on the promise of this year's crop. But we're better off than most 'cause we had enough to pay off Smith. We can sell off the stock a little at a time to make it. The sow. Your chickens. . . ."

Tom's mama replied with a long sigh. She loved those chickens, Tom knew. And she doted on the sow as much as if it was a good hunting dog or something. This was a hard thing.

Trudy said in a soft voice, "I heard from Willa Mae that Grandma Amos talked to Brother Williams about Mister Hooper's son."

"Buck Hooper? Crazy as a loon. I'd rather share a soda with a copperhead snake than meet up with him. Last I heard he was across the Oklahoma border making moonshine and drinking half of every jug he distilled."

Trudy's tone was pleasant as she shared the gossip. "Brother Williams heard that Buck is mad enough at Mister Smith that he says he's coming to Hartford to burn down the bank and shoot Henry V. Smith on sight."

"That would be one way for our prayers to be answered."

Tom and Bobby leaned forward and grinned. This was good stuff. Potential arson. Possible murder. Information worth hearing. Something to tell at school.

"He might do it."

"Buck'll have to stand in line, I reckon," Birch said. "How'd Brother Williams get hold of such news?"

"He has a cousin in Ione who regularly buys moonshine from Buck. Buck was really upset about his father but dared not come to the funeral for fear of being arrested."

"Buck's plain crazy," Birch said. "It runs in the family. His uncle was hung in Missouri for killing a Chinese waiter who spilled chop suey on his suit coat."

As if to punctuate the story, the clatter of an arriving Model-T Ford was accompanied by an engine backfire that sounded like a rifle shot.

"Woody Woods is here," Birch remarked dryly, as he straightened beside the mule.

Milk bucket full, Trudy went to meet the neighbor. She stood in a shaft of late afternoon light and waved. "We're in here, Woody!"

Tom and Bobby crept to the edge of the loft and peered down as Woody Woods strode excitedly into the barn. Without so much as a howdy, he started talking with a rush. "Henry Smith and his goons was out to our place, Birch, and I was ready to get a gun and do him in, too. Then I thought about my children and the disgrace of it and I turned coward. Someone's bound to do it, though."

"Hey, Woody." Birch greeted his neighbor in a calm voice, as if murder was not on everyone's mind. "I was just trimmin' the mule."

Woody paused, came to his senses, and tipped his hat to Trudy. "How-do, Trudy. Birch. How are y'all?"

"Fair to middlin'," Birch replied.

An awkward pause, and then Woody rushed on. "The Lord has answered our prayers! I come to see if y'all heard about Garrick Jenson? Out Meribah way?"

"Why?" Trudy asked. "Is he out to kill Henry Smith also?"

Woody's answer was surprising. "In a manner of speakin', yes. I reckon he is, in a way. Kill Smith's back-stabbin' deals, you might say. The Jenson Consolidated cotton gin is givin' advances and credit to us farmers against next year's cotton harvest, Birch!"

"Well, Jenson Consolidated's the company can do it," Birch said. "Lord. They own the cattle on a thousand hills, as the song goes."

"Cotton seed, too. He's figgered in the cotton seed. He's got somethin' goin' with the government, I hear. Farmer's Drought Relief, he calls it. You hear me, Birch?" Woody was laughing as he spoke. He wrung his beat-up hat in his hands. "Jenson is givin' advances so's we can pay off what we owe Smith. So's folks in Shiloh can hold on for another year!"

"We have no choice but to take the cotton in to Meribah and see what Mister Jenson has to offer." Trudy crossed her arms defiantly as Birch climbed reluctantly onto the spring seat beside Jefferson.

Birch nodded and bent to kiss her cheek. "You're right. No choice. Don't wait supper on me." He gave a small wave of farewell.

The Tucker wagon was heaped high with the last cotton gleaned from the north field. Five hundred pounds; the cargo would make one bale of high-grade cotton. Birch knew he would be lucky to get twenty dollars out of the entire load.

"Gooberpeas," Birch said to Jefferson as the iron wheels jolted over the ruts toward the town of Meribah. "Peanuts. That's the ticket. I should've listened to Trudy's cousin Max. He told us cotton was on the way down. Plant goobers, he told me."

Jefferson held the reins of the mules firmly in his hands. Out of habit, the team tried to turn on the road toward Hartford. They had seldom traveled beyond the crossroads to Meribah. They perked their ears and swung their big heads back as if to look over their shoulders and ask if Jefferson had not made some mistake. But after a while they quit thinking about where they were going and listened to Jefferson's mellow voice. "Git on, mules. Git on up there. . . ."

Jeff said to Birch, "Boll weevil ain't gonna 'preciate it if everybody in Sebastian County plant gooberpeas. Boll weevil's a-movin' this way from Texas fixin' t' dine on Arkansas cotton in the next year or so. He ain't gonna like it when he gets here."

"Trudy said none of this would've happened if I'd planted peanuts last year like Max said I ought."

"Reckon she's right. "

"She ain't happy with me that I didn't listen. She ain't said much 'bout it yet, but she'll get 'round to it. . . . Old habits. Been plantin' cotton as long as I can remember."

"Gals don't think 'bout how it always was down here. . . . Cotton. 'Fore I was born that's been the way of it down here. I use t' sit top my mama's cotton sack whilst she pull it through the rows. First thing I know'd, I had myself a little sack on my shoulder. By the time I'm nine I'm pullin' my own weight. Twelve years old, I'm pickin' three hundret pound a day like any growed man."

"Them days're gone, Jeff."

"I ain't gonna miss 'em."

"Goober peas, that's the ticket. The whole north field, that's what."

Jefferson agreed. "Roast 'em. Salt 'em. Mash 'em up an' make peanut butter. My mama makes the best peanut butter! Leastwise a man can eat gooberpeas if the world goes sour."

". . . Replant the south field in cotton, though, just in case the price goes up. It's sure to go up next year. Couldn't go lower." The clop of hooves beat a rhythm on the packed road.

"When I was bustin' rock, buildin' roads on the chain gang, I used t' dream 'bout eatin' goobers all day long." Jeff droned on like a man half asleep in the warm morning sun. The mules cocked their ears to listen. They were good mules who liked Jeff's stories. He clucked his tongue and urged them on. Their big heads bobbed in unison with each step.

Birch, his mind on business, rubbed his chin thoughtfully. "Woody Woods says Mister Jenson's givin' away cotton seed. Be a waste not to plant it. Jenson figgers it's goin' back up. . . ."

"Salty peanuts chased down with a glass of cold cider sounds sooooo good. . . . Boss man used t' eat peanuts front of us convic's. There we was a-sweatin' an' a-sufferin' in that hot sun. He'd swig down a soda pop. . . . kep' his soda pops in a wood tub this high with ice. . . . Rub that ice all on his face, then eat more peanuts. . . ."

"A guy can feed peanuts to his stock if there's nothin' else."

"Sometimes that boss man'd eat ice-cold melon, too. With salt on it. Bust it open right there. Bright red, it was. He'd jus' eat the heart. Throw the res' in the dirt. Spit the seeds out an' juice run all down his chin an' his shirt. . . . Oh, man! I know'd how ol' Dives felt in hell longin' for a drop of water on his lips. . . . I'd a-been happy jus' eatin' the rind! Meaner than the lash on my back that was. . . ."

"Man can't live on cotton alone. Goober peas. That's the ticket."

The whirring of the Jenson Consolidated cotton gin could be heard before Birch spotted the Meribah water tower and the tall brick church steeple of Meribah Fellowship of Abounding Holiness looming above the trees. Two more wagonloads of cotton and a Model-T truck with a bale on its flatbed followed them as they turned onto the main street.

At first glance, Meribah was more prosperous than Hartford. Just across the border from Oklahoma, the town had gotten its start as a jumping-off place from Arkansas into the Indian Territory before Oklahoma was a state. Wheelwrights, blacksmiths, coopers, hotels, saloons, eating places, and merchants of all varieties had built the town. It had burned down several times and on each occasion had built itself back grander than the time before. When statehood was declared for Oklahoma, Meribah had survived by providing the necessities of life for the coal miners who came down from the mountains. It had shrunk in size but remained prosperous.

Over the past half-century, most of Meribah and the surrounding farmland had gradually come under the ownership of Granddaddy Morris C. Jenson and from him to his descendants. The two thousand seven hundred residents of Meribah were like people everywhere, some good, some not, most somewhere in between. But all owed some allegiance to the Jenson Consolidated company.

Nearly everyone in Meribah, of every creed, claimed kinship back to Granddaddy Morris. Birch remembered the old man well. He had lived to the ripe old age of one hundred and five and had perished by throwing himself down a well in a fit of anger because his three grandchildren had plotted together to put him in a home.

The youngest grandchild, Garrick L'roy Jenson, was most like his old Granddaddy Morris. He even looked like the old man. At forty-five, he was tall and thin with abruptly sloping shoulders, a receding chin, large nose, and wide mouth shaded by a thick blond mustache. Hair was pale and wispy and rapidly disappearing. Forehead was high, and his head seemed entirely too big for his pencil neck and frame. But it was a fine head when it came to making bargains that were beneficial to the company. As a child Garrick's mama had taken him to visit a phrenologist to read his cranial bumps. The conclusion of the reading was that Garrick L'roy was the most clever and brightest of his siblings and would certainly go far.

An astute businessman, as the phrenologist had predicted, he was also mostly likable—very likable as long as he got his way, which was most of the time. He smiled often, laughed with a jolly guffaw, and greeted folks he met on the street as if they were family. Garrick managed the managers of the Jenson farmlands, the stock sale yards, the cotton gin, the grist mill where farmers brought their grain to be ground to flour, and a textile mill.

The hooves of the mules clopped hollowly against the pavement as they pulled the load toward the tin roof of the cotton gin at the other side of town.

"This sure ain't Hartford," Jefferson said under his breath as he felt the eyes of the populace follow their progress past the movie theater.

"Too many cars," Birch agreed. All sorts of automobiles were pulled in at the curb in front of shops and businesses like cattle to a trough.

"Lots of brick." Jefferson turned his eyes to the astounding steeple.

"Practically Oklahoma City."

"Not enough dust for that."

"Company town. Jenson Consolidated don't allow dust in Meribah unless there's profit in it. Ain't you heard?"

"Seems to me that ain't all they don't allow in this place." Jefferson gestured without looking up. Signs in every store window, park bench, and drinking fountain stated plainly, WHITES ONLY.

"This must be where Jim Crow lives," Birch replied with a curt nod. He muttered under his breath, "We'll get our business done and get on home."

The large sign of Jenson Consolidated arched over the main gate of the compound. The noise was deafening. Cotton fibers swirled in the air. The place was alive with activity, like the old times. Jeff pulled up the mules beneath the metal awning that covered the scales. Tractors, trucks, and wagons moved in all directions around the place. Mountains of seed were heaped beyond the gin. Freight cars on a siding were loaded with bales.

A few familiar faces stood out among the men and machinery. Some, like Birch and Jefferson, had come all the way in from Shiloh. Woody Woods perched smiling on the running board of his Model-T. Sharing a twist of tobacco with Arley Palmer, he laughed the way a man laughs when he's got good money from the settle and can buy his young'uns shoes and his wife a hat.

Birch waved and hollered. Woods stood up, spit, and strode toward the wagon. He held up a long, white envelope and smacked it triumphantly against the palm of his hand. Arley followed after.

"I got it!" Woods shouted out over the racket. "Garrick L'roy Jenson! He's our man! He loaned me ever' cent I owed to pay off Smith's bank and then advanced enough credit at the stores here in Meribah t' get us through next season, too! Says Meribah can use the business whilst ever' other town is blowin' away."

"Tell 'em about the picture show." Arley Palmer, following behind, poked at the white envelope with his dirt-blackened finger. "Tell 'em what Garr Jenson done for the kids."

"Free tickets to the picture show." Woods announced. "Not just a couple, either. He said we'd had a heck of a time of it, me an' the missus, an' we oughta bring all the young'uns in to Meribah to see the William Powell picture this Saturday night."

"He done the same for me." Arley produced his envelope and wagged it under Birch's nose. "Said he hated t' see every kid in western Arkansas starvin' on account of some other man's bad business like Hooper. He said we all oughta be friends, seein' as we was neighbors now. Lord a'mighty! If he was a-runnin' for president of these United States, he'd have my vote."

Jefferson quietly nudged Birch and nodded in another direction. Birch followed his gaze to a familiar beat-up old wagon, without paint and mostly held together by baling wire. Amos Grier was beside it, watering the two skinny mules from a bucket. His manner lacked the enthusiasm of Woods and Palmer. Amos Grier was a sharecropper. He did not own the land he worked. Maybe things had not gone as well for him in the meeting.

"What about Grier?" Birch asked.

Palmer shrugged, uncomfortable at the question. "What's he got for collateral? Couldn't get a dollar each on them mules at the glue factory. He don't even own the wagon. Cain't blame Garr Jenson. Grier ain't a good risk."

"Grier said he'll be movin' on when he figgers out where to go," Woods added. "His daddy was on that land before him. Too bad. But I reckon things change."

Birch didn't answer, just climbed down from the wagon and headed across the compound. It was understood that Jefferson would stay with the wagon, water the mules, and be seen but not heard. The only safe thing to do was to keep his eyes to the ground and play dumb. Meribah was just that kind of place. Jefferson pulled his red kerchief over his nose and mouth and his hat brim lower on his brow. He crossed his arms and stared at the back of the mule's ears.

The first thing Birch noticed about Garrick Jenson was the perfectly formed necktie. Every time Birch had met Jenson, the knot that completed his business costume had been precisely tied and exactly straight.

The second thought, which always accompanied the first, was how the man's tie and his prominent Adam's apple made an upside-down exclamation point. It was a symbolic representation of his hearty manner.

This afternoon, Jenson extended his hand to Birch and laughed in a robust guffaw that in no way fit with his thin frame and narrow shoulders. "Birch Tucker! How nice to see you. Been hoping for a chance to welcome you to Jenson Consolidated. Come in, come in!" Jenson held open the swinging wooden gate that separated the front office from the inner sanctum behind. It reminded Birch of the front of a courtroom.

Birch was uncertain how to respond to Jenson's jovial greeting. After all, it was a string of tragedies and misfortunes that caused his presence in Meribah; otherwise he would never have been there at all. Fortunately, Jenson did all the talking. "Caro-line," he called, pointing his receding chin toward a frosted-glass doorway. "Caro-line, come and say hello to Mister Tucker."

When the indicated passage opened, Birch recognized the blonde woman, who emerged in an off-white linen jacket and skirt, as Garrick's wife. Caro-line, the two halves of her name distinctly pronounced and never, ever run together, was Jenson Consolidated's right-hand man, so to speak.

"The brains of the outfit," Garrick announced. "My boss." Then he guffawed again, although there was truth in his jest. Birch knew that Caro-line managed the accounting of the firm, as well as overseeing the company store, the hotel, the cafe, and the other mercantile ventures in which Jenson Consolidated had a role.

"How-do, Miz Jenson," Birch said politely.

"Well," she said, her small mouth puckering. Caro-line's thin-lipped smile turned down at the corners rather than up. "Well, Mister Tucker, welcome." Mrs. Jenson looked at Birch's shoes and then past him toward the entryway. Her gaze never quite rose to the level of his eyes. "Garrick," she said abruptly to her husband, her duty to Birch already discharged. "There are some matters about which I need to see you."

"Very soon," Jenson agreed. "We won't be long."

The short, plump woman pivoted on her heel and disappeared into her office, closing the door behind her. Garrick draped his long, bony arm familiarly across Birch's shoulders and led him through a portal identical to his wife's.

"Have a seat," Jenson offered, indicating a stiff oak chair in front of a massive flat-topped desk. The seat Birch took was too low for the desk; it made him feel short when across from Jenson, even though Birch was the taller of the two men. "Got some cotton to sell, have you? Of course, of course."

"Just one wagonload. Five hundred and ten pounds," Birch said.

"Too bad. But perhaps we can do business for your whole crop next year. What do you have there?" Jenson asked, reaching for the weight affidavit and the paper twist that contained the sample of Birch's cotton. Jenson gave the fibers a quick glance. He never held it up to the light, never stretched out the strands to look at the length of the staple. "Fair grade," he said, tossing the sample onto his desk.

Birch indignantly retrieved the specimen cone. "Not just fair," he said, "nor even middlin'. High grade. I know cotton. Best cotton in these parts."

Jenson laughed too loudly, leaning not back but rather sideways in his chair. The top half of his skinny body hung over the arm, as if the line of his necktie kept him from falling out. Birch had called his bluff. "Of course, of course. Now, how much do you need to satisfy your debts? We've been helping out quite a few of your neighbors. No doubt you've heard. Jenson Consolidated will take over your obligations, even advance you enough—"

Birch's interruption caused a fleeting sour expression to cross Garrick's face. "No debts, thank the Lord," Birch said. "We don't owe nobody a penny, and we can make it through another year on our own, God willin'. I'll find extra work, an' we'll get by. So, I just got the one wagonload to sell."

Jenson's eyebrows shot up. "Well then," he murmured, jotting something on a notepad on his desk. "Well, well, well." Garrick laid down his pencil, bent his body across to the opposite tack, and opened his center desk drawer. He extracted a crisp bill and two dimes and handed them to Birch. "There you are."

Birch unfolded the note and stared at it. Alexander Hamilton gazed back at him. He had expected to see Andrew Jackson. "This is only ten dollars," he said, extending the currency back over the desk. "Two cents a pound?"

Garrick Jenson's arms were folded across his chest. "That's right," he said, refusing to take back the bill.

"But that cotton's worth at least four cents a pound right now," Birch argued. "Twenty dollars a bale. Memphis quote yesterday was back up to four and an eighth."

"Ahhh," Jenson hummed. "In Memphis. But your cotton is still in Arkansas. What about shipping and handling costs? Rail freight and delivery? We have to make something, don't we? After all, I have a responsibility to the property."

Birch chewed on this a minute. He hated the idea of going home with only half what he had expected. How could that be fair? Of course, if cotton had been twelve cents, then maybe two cents a pound for the cost of doing business would have seemed correct. Then the thought that had nagged the back of Birch's mind rose to the surface. "But you won't be shippin' to Memphis," he said. "Jenson Consolidated has a cloth mill. That cotton'll stay here in your own factory."

"Yeahhhhh," Jenson drawled, stretching out the word. "But you've got to see it from our point of view. We are in competition with the big mills, like up north, that can afford to buy in much larger quantities. I'm afraid that's the best we can do." He nodded at the ten-dollar bill still in Birch's fist. "You won't find a better offer anywhere right now. Of course, we could gin the cotton for you and then return the bale for you to sell wherever you like."

"What would you charge for the ginning?" Birch asked quietly.

"Two cents a pound" was the shrugging reply.

Looking at the cash and thinking about having to pay ten dollars to Jenson, then still having to freight one single bale somewhere else, Birch conceded. "All right," he said. "The cotton's yours."

"Good, good," Jenson exulted, bounding upright with all his former energy and enthusiasm. "A pleasure to do business with you. I remember that land from your father's time," Garrick said. "Good to see it back in production. Caro-line," he called out. "Mister Tucker is just leaving. Come and write him up his receipt." He adjusted the knot on his tie.

"Ten dollars and twenty cents. Five hundred and ten pounds. High grade did we say? We've got to keep this proper."

Without comment, Caro-line entered the office and presented Birch with the receipt. Birch thanked her, and she responded with a sour look and a sigh, as if even two cents a pound was more than high-grade cotton was worth.

"Oh," Garrick said, turning back to his desk. "Almost forgot your theater tickets."

Birch walked slowly out to the wagon, where Jeff was watering the mules. Birch looked down at the ten-dollar bill clutched in his fist, then extended the money to Jefferson. "Your share," he said quietly.

CHAPTER 10

The easy credit advanced by Jenson Consolidated, though sweetened by theater tickets, was not free of conditions. Shiloh families were instructed to do their credit shopping only at Meribah stores or their accounts would be closed. And since no one had any cash with which to buy, the flow of customers into Shiloh General Store all but dried up like the James Fork.

"Barter! That's the answer!" Grandma Amos declared to Willa Mae. "Just like in the last days of the glorious South. Confederate scrip weren't good for anything 'cept mebbe wipin' a baby's behind. Barter. That's what saved us then, an' it'll save us now. . . ."

This new economic policy resulted in the return of old customers. As a result there was a large chicken coop filled with chickens of every size and variety behind Shiloh General Store. More fowl and livestock were added daily to the pens of the establishment.

"There ain't a matched pair in the bunch," Grandma Amos said to Willa Mae. "Ever'thing from Rhode Island Reds to White Leg'orns."

Willa Mae pointed at a diminutive rooster standing alone in a small cage beside the water pump. "Where'd that'n come from?"

"Lettle Fred Woods brung in that banty fightin' cock. Says he found it peckin' bugs all alone 'longside the road just outside Meribah when he was a-comin' home from the picture show."

"You figger it's the one Miz Caro-line Jenson has the re-ward out on?"

Grandma Amos shrugged. "Fred brung it in the crate an' traded me for a bag of lemon drops. It's the only thing I know I can get anything for. I cain't even pick me up two eggs the same size out there. Lawdy!"

Willa Mae eyed the assortment in the crowded coop and nodded. "We got us enough fryers t' feed Gen'ral Lee's army, Gramma Amos."

"Cain't get a nickel apiece at the Jenson sale yard for 'em. Jenson says it costs more t' feed stock than it can be sold for in Fort Smith."

Willa Mae clucked her tongue in disgust. "He say they cain't make a profit?"

"I know what they're up to. Steal livestock for pennies at the Meribah sale yard. Then Garrick turns the critters over t' Miz Caro-line Jenson, an' he sets her butcher to work right there. Then they hang the meat in the butcher shop cold box or cook it up an' sell it for two bits a meal at the Meribah Hotel restaurant. They're the regular U.S. Mint."

Willa Mae shook her head. "Tell a workin' man what he's got is worthless, then turn 'round an' get rich off'n what he's raised with his own hands. Lawd don't 'prove of such things."

"Well, the Almighty's kep' awful quiet about it." Grandma Amos pointed at a tall white rooster strutting majestically inside the chicken-wire pen. "I give Ida Grier two dollars' credit for that big feller yonder 'cause she needed a sack of flour an' beans or them little girls was gonna go hungry. I know why Ida wanted shed of him, too. He commences to crowin' 'round three in the mornin'."

"Reckon he wants t' get started 'fore all the other roosters wake up."

"I'm ready to get my gun an' blow his head off."

"You do that. He'll make a fine supper if'n he ain't too tough."

"Two dollars for that thing."

"Yes'm. It's a lot for a rooster."

"A lot for my supper, too."

"That ol' gentleman Leg'orn is more'n three feet high. He'd feed ten men." Willa Mae cocked an eye at him and imagined half in the frying pan and the other half in the stewpot for dumplings.

"Think I'll have young Tom Tucker carry 'im over t' Meribah. He can slip it real quiet-like into Miz Jenson's coop full of prize hens since her banty rooster's gone missin'."

"Ha! Like breedin' a draft horse to a Mexican chee-wa-wa." Willa Mae hooted at the image. "Banty hens do like roosters!"

"That ol' Leg'orn could take on Miz Jenson's whole henhouse. Crow at three in the mornin' an' have the entire bunch wore out by the time the sun come up."

"A big rooster like that'd add a lot to a flock of banties. Eggs so big their eyes'd pop. I never did know why anybody'd have them little banty hens when they could just as easy raise somethin' as good in the skillet as it is to look at."

Grandma Amos took a pinch of snuff and sneezed three times into her kerchief. "Miz Jenson likes 'em cause they're lettle an' mean like she is herself."

"Banties was always fightin' stock where I come from. Seems an odd thing for Miz Jenson t' raise."

"First it was the money, I s'pect. But I think Caro-line Jenson is hooked on cockfightin' on the sly, like that husband of hers. They still sell all the mean'uns 'cross the line in Oklahoma, I hear. The feller at the blacksmith shop over in Meribah makes cockspurs out of razors. Strap 'em on, an' those roosters goes t' fightin'."

Willa Mae did not like banties, nor folks who bet on cockfights. Chickens were meant to lay eggs, and those that didn't were meant for Sunday dinner. "I won't have a banty. Just in the coop a banty'll peck the eyes out of a weaker chicken. But they *are* as pretty as a lady's Sunday hat in the Sears an' Roebuck wish book!"

Grandma turned away from the coop and shuffled back toward the store. She waved her cane as she spoke. "I heard from Brother Williams that Miz Jenson paid twenty-five dollars for a banty rooster from Vermont, so's she could take him to the fair. Had him shipped all the way from Vermont. That's the same one she's a-lookin' for now." Grandma Amos hung the cane over her arm and blew her nose like a bugle. The leghorn drew himself up and crowed in response.

"What's the re-ward?"

"Five dollars. Huh! Never heard anything like it. She's so cheap she don't usually give more'n pennies for a critter. Buys the best for peanuts, then puts her name on what other folks raised and hauls the whole shebang to the county fair. Likes to win, too—mebbe that's why she's put out the reward, with the fair next week an' all. But payin' so much ain't her usual style. Must be a talkin' banty. . . ."

On cue, the captive banty rooster flapped his wings and crowed. Willa Mae flapped her big arms back at him. "Sings and dances, too."

"Well, I'd purely like t' see what kinda critters we'd get if that big white Leg'orn got in an' mixed it up with her little foofy hens."

Willa Mae studied the bantam rooster and considered the sort of money Caro-line Jenson must have stashed away to be able to pay twenty-five dollars for a little feathered thing like that. And five dollars more for a reward!

"Just so's she can win a blue ribbon?"

"To my way of thinkin', it's the chicken farmer in Vermont deserves the prize."

The whole thing struck Willa Mae as altogether wrong. "Gramma, do you want me t' fix this big ol' Leg'orn for your supper or not?"

"Leave 'im be. He ain't worth two cents, but I give Ida Grier two dollars' credit for him, an' I ain't ever paid that much for a chicken. Prob'ly too tough t' eat anyway." She turned and pointed her stick at the crate containing the scrappy bantam rooster. "I'll have this'un for my supper instead. He'll make just enough to fry up for me, an' he only cost me a bag of lemon drops."

Opening day of the Sebastian County Fair took place in Huntington on October 21, 1931. The Ferris wheel, hauled all the way from Little Rock, topped the trees and loomed larger than the water tower beside the Huntington grist mill. Calliope music hooted over the town, drawing people to its laughter. Horses whinnied, mules brayed, Model-Ts chattered along with the excited voices of Sebastian County citizens. The aroma of the stock barns and barbecue and hot dogs filled the air. Lemonade sloshed in the huge clear-glass vats that the carnival barkers toted from county fair to county fair. Here, if only for a little while, the depression and the drought could almost be forgotten, although the unseasonable heat and the dust were hard to ignore.

Even the sad news that Thomas Edison had died the week before had been translated into a local celebration. In tribute to the inventor, the entire fairgrounds had been hastily rigged for an enormous display of electric lights, and the Ferris wheel had been strung with lights that spelled out Edison's name.

Tom and Bobby Tucker had one goal in mind as the Tucker buckboard rolled beneath the arched gate of the fairgrounds. That was to be on board the Ferris wheel when all the electric lights went on. But the Grand Illumination would not take place until eight o'clock that evening, and there was plenty to do and see before then.

When they pulled up beside the poultry barn at eleven that morning, the temperature was already near ninety degrees in the shade. Doc

Brown stood in the entrance, wiping his forehead with a big white handkerchief. He cast a wary eye at Joey and then at Henny as Birch lifted the crate from the wagon.

"Well, I might as well take my hen home," he remarked with a wink at Trudy. "Joey is here with Henny, and my chances are lost."

This comment brought a confident grin to Joey's round face. "You can hold my ribbon," he promised the doctor.

"Well, then," the doctor bantered back. "I guess I'll have to let you in." He stepped aside and gestured down the long central aisle of the structure. Cages of hens, pullets, and roosters filled long shelves stretching from one end of the barn to the other. White placards marked each class and breed. Joey's Rhode Island Red entry would share a position in the American Class with Doc's White Plymouth Rock. The English, Mediterranean, and Asiatic entries followed up and down the rows. Cages were filled with oddities of the poultry world—sprouting crests, beards, and feathered shanks.

Halfway down the aisle marked "Special Classes," Caro-line Jenson stood peering in at a line of cages containing bantam hens and two roosters. Her entries were practically the only birds entered in their class—sure to win a ribbon. While every other fowl simply suffered patiently in the heat, Caro-line Jenson had recruited a small black child to stand behind a block of ice in a wheelbarrow, waving a large fan to cool the caged birds.

"This is one time I could wish I was a chicken," Birch said.

Trudy batted her eyes at him. "Not if you were one of her birds, you wouldn't."

Doc rubbed his hand over his mouth and mumbled, "Must be a substitute rooster. Grandma Amos invited the other one to supper, I hear tell."

Trudy turned away in disgust. "There's always another prize chicken to be had if a lady's got enough cash."

Doc cleared his throat and abruptly changed the topic. "Can't remember it ever being quite this hot this late in the year. They're having all sorts of trouble over at the swine barn; that tin roof just soaks up the heat. I heard that three or four hogs got overheated, and poor ol' Dan Faraby lost his boar—kept pouring on buckets of water to cool the critter down, but it died anyway. I tell you, it's just too dadgum hot for a county fair. . . ."

As Doc droned on about the miseries of the weather and then its effect on human health, Tom peered out beneath the eves of the poultry barn at the Ferris wheel.

"It's only a penny to ride in the daylight," Doc explained. "I've gone up twice already. Thanks to Mister Edison dying on us, the price goes up considerably after dark. It'll be a nickel each."

"I'll remember to thank him if ever I meet him," Tom remarked dryly as he and Bobby headed out to explore. He and Bobby only had a nickel each to spend the entire day.

Beneath the shadow of the Ferris wheel, barkers hocked their wares and proclaimed such wonders as the Two-headed Albino Calf from Paducah and the Fattest Fat Lady this side of the Mississippi and Strongman McCoy, who could lift a draft horse clean off the ground. But business was slow along carnival row. Folks had few nickels to waste on peep shows and second-rate circus oddities.

Trudy had told her sons that the best things at the fair were free. Of course she had not considered the Ferris wheel. Nor had she wandered down Pork Chop Alley, a long corridor of steaming, grilling, boiling, baking, barbecuing food booths set up by at least fifty various auxiliaries, clubs, and church groups.

It was not quite lunchtime, and yet the alley was doing a brisk business. Tom fingered his nickel in his pocket and perused the vast array of goods on display.

Freemasons from Mansfield sold corn on the cob two for a penny. Lots of butter and salt.

Methodists from Midland proclaimed that true greatness had been achieved within their simmering vats of chili beans. One nickel per bowl with corn bread.

Baptists from Patterson sold all manner of cakes and pies at two pennies apiece. They competed for business against the German Lutherans across the row, who were famous for their pastries.

Midway between the Boy Scouts' baked potatoes and the chunks of watermelon sold by the Brotherhood of Coal Miners was the reason Sebastian County Fair had remained primarily a gathering of white citizens.

Half a dozen grim-faced fellows worked a booth decorated with a mural of a night rider on his steed. The KKK meal sold for two bits a plateful with plain white bread on the side. There were many who bought one plate to share while they discussed the real reason behind the troubles of America.

Bobby nudged Tom, inclined his head toward a florid-faced, pale-eyed man who was grilling chicken parts over a large portable barbecue grill. "That guy flippin' the chicken over the fire is the same guy that helped burn down the Sully Faulk house."

"Yeah." Tom's eyes narrowed with resentment at the memory of that day. "Figures he'd be a Kluxer, don't it?" This was the big man who had kicked the vagrant hard in the stomach as he lay in the dirt beside the broken porch of the old house.

Bobby added, "And right over there is Garrick Jenson, too."

Sure enough, sleeves rolled up, necktie perfectly in place, Garrick Jenson sat at the picnic table, eating a heaping plate of barbecue chicken in the company of another, younger man.

"Who's the feller with him?" Tom was disturbed by a vague familiarity of the man with Jenson. Well muscled, with a thick, bull-like neck and a few days' stubble on his face, he seemed the exact opposite of thin and dapper Garrick Jenson.

"I dunno. But I think I seen him somewhere. . . ." Bobby's brow furrowed, then he whirled. "Crikey, Tom! That's Buck Hooper! Ol' dead Mister Hooper's kid!"

Tom made a face at the thought of Mr. Hooper's brains all over the office. Involuntarily, he wondered who had cleaned up the mess.

Bobby sat quietly. "Uh-oh. That Buck Hooper's lookin' at us."

Sure enough, Hooper's bloodshot eyes were staring hard at the brothers. He leaned in and said something to Jenson, who gave a quick glance and then a short laugh.

"Well, Buck's told Jenson that Mama's Jewish." Bobby shrugged. "We ain't eatin' there today."

"Don't want to anyway," Tom said as they turned away. "We only got a nickel each. Just enough to eat or for one ride on the giant wheel tonight. You do what you want, but I'm gonna ride!"

It had been a very bad afternoon for Squirrel Hocott. He never seemed to have any luck when it came to showing hogs. Last year, his barrow had broken loose from his chute and run the judge down. This year it had been too hot for hogs even to think about running away.

But the one-hundred-fifty-pound market hog he had entered in the showmanship event had still managed to ruin his day.

White shirt drenched with sweat, green tie cocked off, and beads of perspiration streaming down his flushed face, Squirrel had herded his black-and-white Hampshire around the large show ring by tapping the hog on one side and then the other with a cane. This contest was more about the ability of the owner to show his hog than it was about the quality of the animal.

The trick to winning was to keep a sharp eye on the judge and never get between him and the hog. A really fine showman knew always to position his hog so the official could get the very best view of it from snout to tail. This was not as easy as it sounded. Hogs were not dogs. They often did whatever came into their minds—and this one evidently decided the weather was just too hot for any more walking.

Three steps away from the judge, the Hocott Hampshire had given a snort, nosed the soft dirt, and plopped down contentedly in the middle of the ring. It had stretched out and wallowed. It had passed gas in a long and sonorous raspberry that was heard distinctly in the back row of the stands. It had blinked languidly up at Squirrel as he worked to get it back on its feet.

The judge had immediately waved Squirrel out of the contest, but there was no getting the critter to budge. Squirrel had tapped it, nudged it, pushed it, pleaded with it, but the hog had remained where it flopped. Squirrel Hocott may have been the first thrown out of the running, but he had been last to leave the ring. It had taken three men pushing with hog panels and a child leading the way with a bucket of feed to finally move the animal back to the stalls. Needless to say, Squirrel had not placed in the competition.

Now that the prodigal pig was finally secure in its pen, Squirrel loosened his tie and flung his 4-H hat at the sleeping animal. He was perched miserably on the top rail when Tom and Bobby found him.

"Don't say anything," Squirrel demanded.

"Okay," Tom agreed.

"Did you see?" Squirrel asked after a long pause.

"Yep," Tom answered.

Squirrel moaned and cradled his head in his hands. "Lord. I don't even like hogs. Hate this. Only do it 'cause my pa says I ought."

"Joey's got that chicken of his entered in poultry," Bobby offered in an attempt to change the subject. "Missus Jenson is over at the poultry barn with a little kid wavin' a fan over a big block of ice to keep her banties cool."

This information snapped Squirrel out of his morose mood for a moment. "Say what? Keep *what* cool?"

"Banty chickens," Tom answered, sliding up next to Squirrel to look down at the Hampshire.

"Oh. Banties. Thought you said . . . well, it would've been somethin' to see." Squirrel cast a wry look at Tom. "My pa calls Caro-line Jenson the Ice Lady. That would explain it."

Tom, Bobby, and Squirrel arrived back at the poultry barn just as the judging of the English Class of chickens was drawing to a conclusion.

Tom spotted Ice Lady Jenson standing proudly beside the cages of her black banty chickens. A profusion of blue, red, and yellow prize ribbons fluttered from the wire mesh of each Jenson crate. Caro-line Jenson's chickens had won a prize for every entry. One hen had gone on to take the large purple rosette, indicating that it had won best in the Asiatic Class of poultry. This meant, as usual, that Caro-line would have a banty hen competing in the Best of Show event at the end of the festivities.

Squirrel nudged Tom. Tom nudged Bobby, then inclined his head toward the small cake of ice remaining in the wheelbarrow. Squirrel snorted and pointed to the puddle that the Ice Lady was standing in. The boys burst into gales of laughter.

Caro-line, smiling in a motherly, misty way at her banties, somehow sensed she was the target of their laughter. The tight smile faded, and her look returned to the usual icy glare.

Across the tops of the crates, Tom spotted Joey riding high on the shoulders of his father. A giant purple ribbon was pinned to his pint-sized overalls.

"Look yonder!" Tom directed the gaze of his companions to Joey.

"Crikey, Tom!" Bobby shouted. "Henny's won the American Class!"

Tom just stared in amazement. Folks who knew about chickens— Doc Brown, Willa Mae, and Jefferson, for instance—had said all along that Henny was a really good hen, sure to win best of the Rhode Island Red breed. Tom had thought they were just saying so because it made

Joey smile. But now! For Henny to go and win the American Class was a sort of miracle!

"I didn't know she was *that* good!" Bobby said, echoing his thoughts.

Tom gave an incredulous laugh. "Joey said the angels told him last night that Henny would win everything."

"Joey's always talkin' to angels. Talks to that chicken, too. Says she talks back. He got it right out of Mama readin' the Oz book, if you ask me." Bobby shrugged and twirled his finger at his temple.

Tom agreed. "Him and Gramma Amos always hearin' voices. All the same, Henny's won this far. Wish some angel'd whisper to Joey how we could get up on the Ferris wheel when the Edison lights get switched on."

"Holy smokes," Squirrel breathed in an awed tone. "He's just a kid. An' that chicken of his . . . that chicken! It beat Doc Brown's White Plymouth Rock! Nobody ever beat Doc Brown's White Plymouth Rock in the American Class b'fore this. 'Course the Ice Lady's banties win Best of Show every year." This revelation brought a renewed outburst of glee from the boys. An old man in a sweat-stained fedora cranked himself around and glowered down at them for silence.

Tom apologized. With difficulty he restrained himself from further laughter by concentrating his attention on Joey, Mama, and Daddy across the way.

Doc Brown, beaming proudly on behalf of Joey's win, flanked Birch and Joey on one side. Trudy, her face all wistful and weary and happy at the same time, stood holding on to the child's small foot as they watched the final judging of the English Class. Her gaze moved from Joey's face to the enormous ribbon draped down his front and then back to grin happily at Birch and Doc. It made Tom glad to see them there. He knew Mama was more pleased and relieved by the outcome than Joey was. Shoot, Joey had said all along that Henny would win. The kid had been so confident that even if Henny had taken second, he would have claimed the red ribbon was best and Henny was champion. There would have been no talking him out of it.

Tom shoved his cap back on his head and strained to see the English Class birds now being judged in order to get a line on which hens Henny would be competing against in the final round.

The English Class was primarily for meat-producing fowl. First-place winners from several breeds were being examined by a trio of judges while the anxious owners looked on hopefully.

Heads nodded together as the judges wrote marks on a clipboard containing the standards of breed perfection. At last the chief official held up his hand and called for attention.

The judge, a man with the color and jerky demeanor of a stalking marsh heron, bobbed his head forward on his skinny neck and proceeded to recite the admirable traits of the Dorking Hen. Tom knew this was a sure sign that the bird had come in last. Judges always told first what was wonderful about the losers.

Ten minutes later the official had worked his way through the fine qualities of the Redcap, Sussex, and Orpington breeds. At last his gaze alighted fondly on the little White Cornish hen. And thus, to the patter of polite applause from a crowd of one hundred onlookers, the winner of the English Poultry Class was chosen.

In front of Tom, the old man in the sweaty fedora gave a whoop, tossed his hat into the air, and rushed forward to congratulate his wife, who owned the bird. She was as gnarled as Grandma Amos and bent over so she was half the size of her lanky husband. The old couple cradled the little Cornish hen and accepted the rosette. All three blinked in unison as their photograph was snapped. The old woman wept and kissed the little bird on its feathered noggin.

And now the officials were moving into the final competition, the one to determine Best of Show. A bespectacled announcer read out the list of competitors: Henny, the Cornish hen, Caro-line Jenson's banty, and an enormous White Leghorn hen from the Mediterranean class that belonged to a tall, pleasant Scotsman with brown grizzled hair and a thick mustache. Then the announcer held up the prizes for the event. The winner would receive a round brass medal hanging from a red, white, and blue ribbon, a small silver-plated loving cup, and a bright copper weathervane with the likeness of a rooster perched on top.

"Mama would purely love to have that copper rooster on top of the house," Bobby said in a reverent tone.

"Ain't gonna happen," Squirrel said authoritatively. "My aunt in Meribah was inside the parlor of the Ice Lady once when my cousin was deliverin' some ironin'. That Jenson house is crammed full of trophies and medals from them little banty chickens. Caro-line Jenson always wins."

"What you mean . . . always?" Tom challenged as he considered how fine the copper rooster would look on the roof. It would catch the first rays of the morning and shine like a beacon. It would spin in the Shiloh wind and crow to the points of the compass.

Squirrel shrugged. "Caro-line Jenson won't have it no other way. She has to win. Her an' Garrick have final say on poultry judges. My uncle works with the Sebastian County Fair committee, an' he says they only hire judges that like banties better'n all the others. That's the way Garrick and Caro-line Jenson win stuff. They donated that copper weathervane as the prize 'cause Ice Lady knows she's gonna win it back.

"B'sides," he went on, "my uncle says Jensons are the only ones with real power 'round here. My uncle knows plenty 'bout them two that he can't say since he works at Consolidated an' goes to the same church as Jensons, and Garrick Jenson runs the church an' all the people in it, too. My uncle says it's better to act dumb and pretend not to see how they do business. Anybody don't agree with the Jensons or dares to say the truth out loud about how they cheat folks gets this." Squirrel drew his finger slowly across his neck, illustrating the penalty for disloyalty to the Jenson couple. "Garrick's mighty proud of his righteousness, my uncle says. He don't like nobody pointin' out the truth. He's real nice, too, long as you don't let on you're on to him. Anyway, my uncle says little folks don't stand a chance competin' against folks like them. Joey's 'bout as little as they come. So Joey's Rhode Island Red can't win the medal or the copper rooster, see?"

Tom eyed the Ice Lady with a sense of resentment. He figured Squirrel was chattering back the facts as faithfully as his Meribah relatives had presented them in private at some family gathering. Squirrel was good at repeating information picked up at the dining table from grown-ups who did not know he was listening.

The heronlike official made his way toward the prize table, stopping for a moment in front of Birch and Joey. The judge reached his thin hand up to pat Joey on the arm. Joey flicked the purple rosette and pointed at Henny, saying something in a voice too quiet for Tom to hear. Smiling, the judge moved on to take his place behind the prize table.

Tom caught the alarm in Caro-line Jenson's cold eyes as she witnessed the pleasant exchange. She sucked her teeth suspiciously and said loudly enough to be heard by the small crowd of cronies flocked around her, "Are we judging poultry or children here?"

At that moment, Garrick L'roy Jenson ambled up to the group, grinned at the banties, and acted very pleased, flattered, and amazed that all his wife's chickens were decorated. She responded by whispering into his sloping shoulder and casting dark looks toward the other finalists.

Garrick Jenson frowned and extended his overbite in consternation. He chewed his lower lip and craned his neck sideways to cock his ear toward her words as she spoke. His expression seemed to admit that it might be possible Caro-line's banty hen did not have this one in the bag. Glancing meaningfully toward Birch and Joey, Garrick then scowled at the judge, who beamed at the copper rooster and called for the finalists in the Best of Show competition to bring their birds to the judging stand.

There were no chairs for the spectators, so the crowd formed a semicircle as the contestants carried their hens forward. First Caro-line and her black banty, then the old woman and her Cornish White, then the Scot and his handsome Leghorn, and finally Joey, Henny, and Trudy faced the crowd. Joey, a bit abashed by the crowd, had lost his grin, but he stood straight and hugged his hen determinedly.

The judge stepped to the front and bobbed his head as he looked down the line. He praised the diligence of each owner and remarked that never had he seen better examples of all the breeds gathered together in one show. Would each of the contestants care to offer advice about the raising of such fine poultry?

Caro-line Jenson, being first in line, began by humbly thanking the judge for the honor of being chosen as a finalist in the competition. "Precise planning is everything," she said. "Pedigree . . . Only breeding the finest rooster with the finest hens can . . ."

Squirrel intoned under his breath, "Uncle says this batch comes from Missouri. Somebody else does the work; she gets the glory."

The attention upon her, the Ice Lady continued. ". . . best chicken feed . . . temperature-controlled coop . . . create the surroundings that let our chicks blossom and . . ."

And so the advice flowed on until it was clear to all that there was no authority on the hatching and nurturing of chickens like Caro-line Jenson. Her facilities were state of the art, her knowledge exceeded that of all others in the state.

The old lady with the Cornish White was humbled. She mumbled something about just picking out the best chicks from her flock and hoping one might make it that far. The Scotsman told how this hen had caught his eye and so he had taken a chance. And then it was time for Trudy to speak. Joey stood proudly at attention at her knee. He cradled Henny in his arms.

Well modulated and distinctly northern in accent, Trudy Tucker's voice sounded very different from everyone else's in the poultry barn.

"Our Rhode Island Red hen is eleven months old. She was hatched in our coop but raised by our son Joey." Joey shuffled his feet and ducked his head in embarrassment at the mention of his name. Trudy continued, "But as you can see, Joey has asked that I speak on his behalf." She paused and patted the boy who looked up at her appreciatively.

"The brood hen who hatched Henny was carried off by a fox when the chick was a day old, so we brought her and three other chicks into our kitchen. With a little guidance, Joey hand-raised them in a box beside the cookstove. This one . . . is just special. A pet, really. We had not thought to enter her in this event until Doctor Brown, who has lovely White Plymouth Rock chickens often entered in this competition, suggested Henny might have a chance to win something." Joey looked down at the bird, who fluffed her feathers in contentment. "The judge has asked why we are partial to Rhode Island Reds. Honestly, we chose to raise this breed because I like the color of the sun on their wings." A titter of laughter rippled through the crowd. Tom rubbed his hand over his flushed face. Mama sounded like she was teaching a class in poetry instead of talking about the finer points of chickens. He wished his father, who understood farmers and critters, had spoken instead of his mother.

Trudy continued, "My husband later informed me that Rhode Island Reds are sweet-tempered and good egg layers. We find this to be very true. So . . . we are learning more about them as we go along. This much I am sure of from watching Joey. Sometimes love is enough to make little things grow and flourish into perfection. A dream, when cherished and nurtured, can become a lovely reality. This is the fulfillment of my child's dream. Even if Henny were not a lovely creature, she is still special to us. Joey is honored to have his small friend represent the American poultry breeds as a finalist in this Best of Show competition. Joey?" She stooped and addressed the child. "Do you have anything to add?"

Joey shook his head violently. It was all too much—simply too much attention for one little boy.

"Who'da thought that the Ice Lady could be so mad?" Squirrel Hocott exclaimed as the trio made their way through the midway crowd toward the Ferris wheel. "My daddy'll never believe she could get steamed up!"

"Guess she ain't much used to losin'," Bobby remarked blithely.

Tom nodded his head. "She ain't used to bein' beat, but she didn't really get boilin' til she heard that the chicken that whupped her fancy feather duster was owned by a three-year-old kid. Lotta good it did her to keep her banties cool!"

The friends snickered till they chuckled, chuckled till they chortled, and wound up to a fit of hee-haws that wore them out completely, their shoulders shaking with wheezing laughter. Then one of the three would just say the word *banties* and it would start all over.

"Say, men," called the guess-your-weight barker. "What tent did y'all get that laughin' gas in? I need me some."

That set them off again. It took a supreme effort of will to gather the control required to get down to serious business—the careful study of people waiting to ride the Ferris wheel.

"How about the lady in the blue bonnet?" Bobby suggested.

"Naw, it might blow off and we'd have to start all over," Tom said.

As human markers, they settled on a couple where the wife was a good foot taller than the husband and outweighed him by a hundred pounds as well.

"And his pants is hitched up high enough for Noah's flood," Squirrel observed, pointing to several inches of bare shank below the hem of the man's trousers.

"Perfect!"

Some revolutions of the steel structure later, the tagged pair came out of the exit and the time for calculations had come.

"Didn't you kids just ask me the time a little bit ago?" demanded the cotton-candy salesman, looking between the fluffy mounds of spun sugar. "You got a train to catch or somethin'?"

"Please, mister," Tom repeated the request. "It's important."

Moments later Tom, Bobby, and Squirrel were huddled together completing their reckoning. "Now the illumination is set for exactly eight o'clock," Tom reminded the group, "and we want to be on board when it happens. What with loadin' and unloadin', the time on that contraption is six minutes."

Bobby was already counting back places in the line. "Fifteen, sixteen, seventeen . . . I make it right by the hot-dog stand."

"An extra minute to make sure we are up in the air . . ." Squirrel mused.

"Got it!"

At precisely the right moment, the three friends meshed smoothly into the line and pestered everyone around for the correct time. They even let two sets of surprised teenagers go ahead of them in order that the timing would be perfect.

As they neared the platform where the loading of the swinging metal cars took place, Bobby fretted that they were too early still. "What if they're late throwin' the switch?" he worried aloud. "What if we're done already?"

Before Tom and Squirrel had time to consider the problem, the issue was resolved with the crash of drums and the rattle of a marching cadence. The flourish and buzz of the snares announced the progress of the official procession toward the platform and the magic switch, which was located just across an open square from the Ferris wheel. The boys would have a perfect view of the ceremony as well as its effect.

They were whisked aloft to the combined efforts of two trombones, three trumpets, and a valiant piccolo soaring into "Stars and Stripes Forever." "Is this swell!" Tom grinned as the wheel revolved another notch upward and his stomach dropped toward his toes.

"The best," Bobby agreed as the dancing high notes chased each other through the evening sky. "And just gettin' dark enough, too."

Familiar landmarks grew small as the wheel whooshed upward and around. People became doll-like and voices echoed hollowly beneath the rush of the cool evening air in Tom's ears. There was one sublime moment when the basket was poised at the highest arch of the orbit, then it swooped downward toward earth again. The band's rendition of the Sousa favorite finished with such a crash that the hairs on the back of Tom's neck stood up and a delicious shiver ran along his spine. The gondola swept past the man at the control stick and then rose again.

An instant later they again reached the exact peak of the wheel and hung rocking over the crowd and the dark grounds as if floating on air.

"Ladies and gentlemen," the loudspeaker blared into the sudden silence. "The moment you have been waiting for has arrived. The Grand Illumination in honor of Thomas A. Edison, the Wizard of Menlo Park, is about to take place. Throwing the switch will be Honorary Marshall Henry V. Smith, president of Hartford Federal Bank."

The smattering of polite applause was matched by a few hisses and boos and an amused titter that ran through the audience. Standing on the raised platform, in the only lighted area to be seen, the bank president approached an oversized black-handled switch and prepared to send the electric current surging through the proclaimed thousands of electric bulbs.

Bobby grasped Tom's arm and pointed toward the edge of the stage at Smith's back. "Tom," he gasped. "Look there!"

The bucket swayed as Tom and Squirrel leaned forward for a better view. "What?" Tom began. "I don't see . . ."

Emerging from the shadows, weaving from side to side and waving a sawed-off shotgun, was Buck Hooper, son of the cotton-gin owner driven to suicide by Smith and his bank. "Henry Smith!" Hooper bellowed, his voice a drunken slur of anger.

Smith turned around, the look of irritation on his features melting into one of fear and horror. He staggered backward, bumping solidly into Delbert Simpson and pushing the chubby assistant into a sign that announced: "See the Wild Man of Borneo—Alive and Untamed!" Delbert fell, sprawling. Those in the crowd nearest the platform screamed and shoved backward into the other onlookers as shouts of "Look out! Get back!" erupted from the mob.

"Golly, Moses!" Bobby shouted. "A ringside seat at a killing!"

"Duck down!" Tom ordered. "The way Buck's waving that scatter-gun, he's as likely to hit us as Henry V." The three crouched lower in the car, but still peered eagerly over the rim.

"Henry Smith!" Hooper roared again. "It's time to settle accounts, and I aim to do it!" So saying, he thrust the weapon forward toward the bank president. Smith clutched his chest and stumbled back again, tripping over and falling across the unfortunate Delbert. In an effort to catch himself, Henry V. reached and grabbed the light switch. His weight pulled the handle downward to the closed position and the promised illumination blazed forth. The president of Hartford Federal slumped on the stage in the glaring brightness.

Buck lowered the shotgun in consternation. "Get up!" he ordered. "I ain't finished tellin' you why you need to be kilt, you fat slug. Get up, I say!"

Tom saw Jim Brown tackle Hooper from behind. The sawed-off double-barrel flew from Buck's grasp and slid across the stage, where Sheriff Potts pounced on it. Forgotten in the excitement, the Ferris wheel did not revolve, and Tom, Bobby, and Squirrel kept their ringside seat during the pandemonium that exploded.

"Get Doc Brown!" Potts yelled. "Smith is dead!"

"I didn't shoot him," Buck protested. "The gun ain't even loaded! I just wanted to scare the old goat!"

Buck Hooper had accomplished his goal. Bank President Henry V. Smith was literally scared to death. For nearly three-quarters of an hour, Tom, Bobby, and Squirrel Hocott perched at the peak of the giant wheel while folks rushed around like ants.

The whole experience was like sitting in the balcony and watching the exciting part of a movie. Blessed, glorious luck! This would give the threesome a tale to tell for weeks!

Handcuffed and struggling, Buck Hooper got hauled off to the local jail in the back of a pickup truck.

"He'll get out," Bobby predicted. "Can't hang a guy for scarin' somebody t' death, can you?"

"Woulda been better if Buck had shot him," Squirrel concluded.

After a time a woman on the lower branches of their perch began to holler that she wanted let off. Her protests evolved into hysterics, which finally drew the motorman back to his post. He emptied the bucket of the hysterical lady and her beau first of all. For a moment it looked as if there might be a brawl.

"Leave us up there half the night . . ."

"Forced t' witness such a disgustin' . . ."

"Want my money back! T'weren't a ride! We just set up there!"

Then the impossible happened. The owner of the carnival ride passed by. Hearing the ruckus, he reached deep into his pocket and pulled out a handful of nickels. As each seat was vacated, the nickels were slapped into outstretched hands with a grave apology.

Tom, Bobby, and Squirrel received their nickel refund. All that excitement and cash enough left for a bowl of Methodist chili and corn bread . . . or another ride on the wheel! They chose to go up again for another turn.

That night the Tucker family slept out beneath the wagon in a wide field by the river like a hundred other families who had come too far to go back on the same night. Mama had packed a big meal in a hamper. Tom and Bobby ate twice as much as usual, but there was plenty left over for the trip home in the morning. Joey slept with the enormous loving cup at the head of his bedroll and the copper rooster weathervane propped against the spokes of the wagon wheel.

Long after the Edison Illumination had been turned off, Tom lay awake and looked up at the white mist of stars. The clear, bell-like voice of a young woman sang "Home, Sweet Home" as a guitar strummed.

"Tom?" Bobby's voice was drowsy.

"Uh-huh?"

"Jeff's gonna be mighty pleased about what happened tonight, ain't he? What I mean is . . . ol' Henry Smith keelin' over like he done."

"How's that?"

"Jeff had only one grave left to dig 'fore ol' Hock's fancy coffin is all paid off. Guess he won't mind that it's King Henry dyin' that helps him out. Guess this clears the debt, and it's nobody Jeff'll mind buryin'."

C H A P T E R   1 1

The most terrible day in Tom Tucker's life started off really fine.

It was Saturday and still hot, in spite of the fact November had arrived. The sun was well up by the time Tom finished feeding the chickens and Bobby gathered all the eggs.

"Twenty-two," Bobby said, latching the gate of the chicken coop. He was sweating and looked tired, even though the day was just beginning. "Mama said whatever eggs we gather this morning, we can take 'em all into Hartford and trade 'em for ice cream at Mr. Winters's drugstore after the picture show."

Twenty-two eggs would be enough for ice cream and a soda and maybe an all-day sucker apiece.

To combat the steady drain of business away from Hartford into Meribah, Pop Lyle, who owned the Hartford Bijou, was offering a special Saturday matinee. For the price of one admission ticket, two people could get in to see Norma Shearer and Clark Gable in the movie *A Free Soul*. Pop Lyle called it "Free Soul Day." In addition, there was to be live music at the intermission; a quartet led by Mr. McClung of Hartford Music Company would be singing gospel songs and other popular tunes as well. The show would be topped off by a young people's singing contest, the winners to be awarded ten free passes to the Hartford Bijou. Like every other child in school, the Tucker brothers had been practicing all week and were planning a duet rendering of "The Ballad of Jesse James." They were pretty good at it, too.

The entire family had planned to attend, but the previous night Joey had taken sick. He was fevered and cranky, so Mama allowed that after chores Tom and Bobby could ride the mules alone into Hartford.

Overalls freshly laundered and pressed, Sunday shirts starched and clean, shoes brushed and hair brushed, they caught the mules in the pasture, threw gunnysacks over the bony backs, rigged the bits and bridles with cotton rope reins, and set out to ride four miles into town. Tom carried the basket of eggs on his arm. Rosey trotted along beside. Her tongue hung out and dripped slobber because it was so hot.

But even the heat felt good to Tom. It seemed like summer, like old times. The mules' hides glistened in the sun and smelled warm and earthy like mules do when they move and sweat. Tom wanted to practice for the singing contest, but Bobby said he did not feel like it. Tom cussed him for being a spoilsport and sang the alto harmony part alone. The ears of his mule cocked to listen, and the hooves kept time on the gravel road.

They did not go fast along the lane, but a mile out they began to spot other rigs, buckboards, and the Faraby's Model-T pickup jammed with children. Tom did not want to practice his singing in front of them because they had an entire routine worked out and Mrs. Faraby was going to play the organ to accompany them.

"Let's take the shortcut," Tom said when they came to the gate of the Hocott pasture.

"It ain't shorter," Bobby said, looking done in. "And we have to ford the creek with the mules. I don't want to get wet. You know ol' Bob likes to lay down and roll in the water when he gets hot."

"He won't." Tom tried to open the gate without dismounting, but could not manage it. "Get down and open that blasted gate!"

Bobby sighed heavily. "Do it yourself."

"I got to hold the eggs. I'll do it on the other side. Open it. Open it or you ain't goin'. I got the nickel."

Bobby grimaced and slid down. No argument. This was not like Bobby. The burlap blanket slipped off and landed on his head. He did not get angry or throw it down and stomp it like he might have done some other day. He let it go, then looked at it lying in the road. He seemed too worn out to care.

"Mama said you'll get your overalls dirty if you ride him bareback. Put the burlap on up there," Tom instructed.

Bobby picked it up as if it was heavy and pushed it slowly onto the mule's back.

Clumsily, he fiddled with the latch on the gate, working it open finally after Tom told him four times how to do it. It was not that Bobby did not know how to open a gate; he just had trouble with it this morning.

And then the strangest thing of all: Bobby could not get back up on that mule. He tried to jump up, led the critter alongside the fence and climbed the rails, but he just could not make that final leap from the fence onto the mule.

"What's wrong with you?" Tom asked. "Are you sick or somethin'?"

Bobby did not answer. He held the cotton rope reins and perched there on the rail staring across the gulf. It was not more than three feet from the fence onto the patch of burlap where his backside was supposed to be.

"Somethin's wrong," he said in a slurring voice. "I can't."

"You want to go home? You want to miss Free Soul Day? And the singin' contest? And the quartet?"

"No. I just . . . feel funny."

With an exasperated sigh, Tom dismounted and helped his brother up onto the mule. He eyed the pasture and considered the fording of the creek. If ol' Bob took it into his head to lie down and roll in the water, Bobby would not be in shape to stop him. He was just sitting up there, kind of slumped over the mule's high withers.

"You think you oughta go home?"

"I don't . . . want . . . to miss it."

"You're sick, ain't you, Bobby? You've gone and got sick and didn't tell Mama about it."

Bobby nodded. "I don't want to miss . . ."

"So now we got out here, and I gotta take you all the way back home. Then I gotta put up your mule, and maybe I'll be late."

"Sorry."

"Sorry don't cut it. Well, you ain't goin'."

"Sorry," Bobby said again. He did not argue. "You go on ahead. I'll get back home."

Tom was worried some, but he was more angry than worried. He mounted Jake with a hop and glared at Bobby. "Now how am I gonna sing in the contest?"

"Sorry."

"You shoulda said something before. Now I have to take you all the way back."

"No, you don't. . . . Go on. Before I make you late."

Tom considered the offer and accepted. "Get on straight home. Along the road. . . . You sure you'll make it back all right? Because I don't want to get whupped for not takin' care of you."

"Yeah. I'm okay. Get goin'."

Tom jerked his head once in agreement and ordered the dog. "Rosey, go home with Bobby. See you later." The dog obeyed, and Bobby and his mule turned homeward. That was the thing about a mule. Ol' Bob did not need anyone to tell him which way to the barn.

Tom urged his mule the other direction and kicked him into a jackhammer trot. They covered the distance to Hartford in half the usual time. Tom was not late to Free Soul Day yet. Folks were just beginning to pair up at the box office for their two-for-one tickets. Every kid from school was there, and all the ones from the Hartford school, too. Everyone hollered, "Hey, Possum!" And there, not in line, but beside the line, at the edge of the plank sidewalk, was Sally Grier. She was staring at the sandwich board sign with the pictures of Clark Gable and Norma Shearer. She wore her blue dress. Golden hair had a ribbon in it, just the same as when she had come to the school dance.

Tom knew she did not have the money for admission. Nobody with a nickel or a two-for-one partner would be staring at the sign. He patted the nickel in his pocket. "Good ol' Bobby," he said as he rode up to Sally.

She stood with her back to the shadow of the big mule. Her gaze was riveted on the movie poster on the board. The mule peered over her head as if he was taking in an eyeful of Norma Shearer.

"Hey, Sally!"

She smiled over her shoulder at Tom, squinting her eyes against the glare of the sun at his back. "Hey, Possum!"

He held up the basket of eggs. "Mama said me and Bobby could trade these eggs for a soda and stuff after the picture show."

"That's nice." She tilted her head and turned back to the poster as if to study it from a different angle.

"Bobby got sick as a dog on the way to Hartford."

"That's too bad."

"Guess we can't sing 'The Ballad of Jesse James' in the contest together after all."

"I heard y'all singing when you went by the house. I thought sure y'all would win, too, Possum."

"Oh, well. I'm going to the movie all the same. It's too bad I don't have anybody to partner up with. I got this entire nickel and it's two-for-one. . . ."

Sally's expression brightened as if some idea had lit up her brain. She tossed her blonde hair and waved away a fly. "I don't have a partner, either . . . but I didn't bring a nickel." She stroked the nose of the mule.

"I can share. If you want to."

"It'd be a shame to waste, wouldn't it?"

They both agreed that it would be a terrible pity not to take advantage of such a bargain. So Sally took the eggs and held the place in line while Tom hurried to the ticket office to purchase two for one.

It was five in the afternoon, maybe later, when Hartford began to empty out. Buggies, Model-Ts, buckboards, and mules rattled out of town while contented passengers hummed the songs sung by the Hartford Music Company quartet.

Sally, who had sat beside Tom the whole day and shared ice cream at the drugstore, thanked him kindly and told him that if there was ever again a Free Soul Day she would like to partner up with him. He couldn't think how to reply to such a fine compliment, so he just said goodbye. After that she caught a ride home with the Faraby family.

Four boys shared the back of Tom's mule as they headed home toward Shiloh. Tom held the reins, Catfish Pierce was behind him, Cub Palmer came third, and Squirrel Hocott perched on the rump.

Wesley Oak, still a little green beneath the left eye from where Tom had hit him, snarled at the mounted group from the front of Winters's drugstore.

Tom lifted his hat. "Hey there, Stumpy!"

At this insult, Wesley glared and spit and tugged at his cap. But he did not go for Tom because Sheriff Potts was standing right there in front of the barbershop talking to Dee Brown.

"Half the county's lookin' on or I'd stomp your head."

Catfish Pierce hooted. "Even with half the county lookin' on, 'pears t' me Possum Tucker left you stumped."

"He jumped me when I wasn't lookin'. He knows it and so does everybody else."

Catfish said, "He could beat you any time."

"Yeah?" Wesley challenged. "Name the time and the place and I'll . . ."

Mr. Winters stepped out of his drugstore and interrupted the confrontation. "Haven't you boys had enough excitement for the day?"

Squirrel Hocott wiped his nose on his sleeve. "Wesley's got a chip on his shoulder big as a house."

"Tryin' t' start somethin'," Catfish agreed. "He ain't content that Possum give him a shiner. Tryin' t' start somethin' . . ."

"Possum Tucker." Wesley spat. "You and that pitiful mutt of yourn couldn't catch a real possum if it jumped up and bit you. Proof is what that possum done to that cousin of yourn."

Tom felt himself color and the humiliation of that morning returned. "Wasn't me or Bobby that stuck our hand in there. And Rosey did her part. She treed . . ."

Brother Williams sauntered up to join Mr. Winters on the sidewalk. "What's this? Y'all talkin' about that pup of my Emmaline's?"

"That's right." Wesley snickered. "Worthless thing she is, too. I got the best of that litter. My Boone. Now that's a huntin' dog."

Brother Williams was followed by Boomer, who scratched his head and joined the conversation. "BOONE DOG AND ROSEY! TWO GOOD PUPS, ALL RIGHT! I KNOW'D 'EM BOTH SINCE THE DAY EMMALINE HAD 'EM! I'D OF SAID ROSEY WAS THE BEST, BUT SHE—" he boomed.

"Shut up, Boomer." Brother Williams sniffed impatiently. "We ain't int'rested in—"

"—THAT ROSEY AIN'T BEEN—"

Brother Williams nudged Boomer to silence. "They're both good as their mama."

Wesley gave a hearty laugh. "Boomer's right for once. Rosey AIN'T. . . ."

Mr. Winters held up his hands like a referee. "It can be settled. Without fists. Y'all both have your permanent teeth. It would be a pity for you to knock them out when a possum hunt could settle the matter."

"By doggies!" Brother Williams snapped his finger. "I'll put up a dollar to see that! A huntin' contest between two of Emmaline's pups."

"Sounds fair to me. I'll put up another dollar," Mr. Winters agreed. "We'll take up a subscription for the prize money. What do you say, boys? We'll start a week from next Friday night at seven at Shiloh schoolhouse. Twelve hours you'll have. Bring your possum into Hartford Saturday morning for the prize."

"I'm game," Tom agreed, but a momentary doubt rose in his mind. Boone dog was bigger and more aggressive than Rosey, even though she was the smarter of the two.

"Now, here's the code." Brother Williams gazed up at the sky as he thought it through. "You two boys is under a peace bond. If'n either of you fights t'other before, durin', or after the contest, you lose."

Wesley looked doubtful about this part of it. He rubbed his cheek unconsciously as he remembered getting walloped by Tom. "What do you mean by fighting?"

Mr. Winters glared at him. "I mean disturbing the peace of the rest of us. I mean keep your hands to yourself and your mouth shut. Plain enough?"

"I reckon," Wesley agreed grudgingly.

Tom nodded. "Sure."

"All right, then." Brother Williams put up his hand to silence Boomer, whose mouth was working as if he wanted to speak. "Don't interrupt me, Boomer, or I'll smack you good! I'm talkin' about a bond of peace here!"

Boomer's face stretched back as he raised his hands to protect himself from a blow that never came.

Brother Williams continued. "Well now, what was I . . . ? Right. The victor'll be decided by who catches the biggest possum next Friday night week. That's full of the moon, ain't it?"

Mr. Winters allowed that it was.

"Y'all remain peaceable in word and deed, and then we'll see who's got the best dog. Fair enough?"

Wesley grinned. "And no backing out for no reason or the contest is forfeit. If we miss the next moon there won't be another 'fore possum season's over." Wesley added, "I know I'll be there. We'll see if you got the guts, Tucker. Me an' Boone dog are gonna eat you an' your mutt alive."

The threat had no effect. Tom and the three passengers behind him nearly fell off the mule from laughing. They were still laughing as one by one the boys jumped off at their farms and waved goodbye.

Tom took the long way home, riding the last mile alone through the Hocott field and across the creek.

He reached the gate that opened into the Tucker pasture and leaned down from the mule's back to open it without dismounting. He could see his house and the barn, but he did not want to look because he did not want to think about evening chores. He was still smiling, still laughing at nothing at all and savoring the day.

"Bobby missed a good one," he said, slipping the headstall off the long head to set the mule loose. Slinging the bridle over his shoulder, he walked slowly up the hill, brushing the tops of wild grass with his hand.

Rosey heard him coming and galloped down the slope to greet him. Tom stooped to accept her sloppy kisses. "We're gonna catch us the biggest possum in the county. You up to whuppin' your brother, Rosey girl?"

Only then did he raise his eyes and see his father sitting on the front steps of the house, staring down at his boots.

Birch wore his hat pushed back the way he did when he was tired and his head ached so much that the weight of a hat brim was almost too heavy to bear. His elbows were on his knees, his hands clenched together.

The happy feeling fled. The grin vanished. Tom felt suddenly afraid. But what was there to be afraid of? Had he left something undone this morning? He mentally ticked off all the chores accomplished before breakfast and could not think of one he had forgotten.

"Hey, Dad!" he shouted and gave a broad wave. But Birch did not acknowledge him.

At first glance everything seemed the same as always. Tom looked over his shoulder and spotted Bobby's mule grazing beneath the cool shade of the oak tree. Then Esmerelda bawled from her stall in the barn. She needed milking. The chickens had not been fed. They clucked and strutted aimlessly in the coop. The sow grunted and stood up expectantly in the pen as Tom walked by. The fence Birch had intended to mend today was still a pile of boards beside the corral. Mama's washing was only half hung on the line. Three bedsheets and two shirts were stiff and dry. The rest was still jumbled in the basket, like Mama had left off in a hurry.

Then Tom noticed that Doc Brown's beat-up old car was parked beside the barn.

Tom looped the bridle over the fence post and walked slowly toward the house.

"Dad?" Tom stood on the slate stones of the walkway.

"Hullo, Tom." Birch glanced up, then quickly down again. He rested his chin in his hands.

"What's wrong? Why is Doc Brown here? Is Joey . . ."

"Both of your brothers are real sick."

"Are they gonna be okay?"

Birch ran his fingers through his hair and his hat fell off, but he did not notice. Inhaling as if it was hard to breathe, he stammered, "I . . . don't . . . know."

"What's . . . ?"

"I thought Bobby . . . was . . . with you."

"He didn't feel good, so he went home."

"I was workin' on the gate. Rosey came up to me. Then I heard somethin', and the mule was standin' there by the barn. Bobby wasn't on 'im. The reins were draggin'. Mule stepped on the reins. Bobby wasn't in the house. Wasn't anywhere . . ." Birch raised his head and looked way off down the lane. "I thought he was with you, see? Thought y'all were together. . . ."

"He didn't feel good." The glory of the day evaporated. The afternoon in Hartford was not even a memory. Instead, Tom's mind was filled with the vivid image of Bobby trying to get on the back of that mule. "He was sick, so he left."

". . . Then Jefferson come walkin' up the lane carryin' Bobby home in his arms. Limp like a dishrag. He must've fell off . . . . I don't know . . ."

"I thought he'd be all right.. . . . I didn't mean to . . ."

"Doc is in there with both the boys."

"Bobby said he could make it back fine."

"Doc's doin' what he can, but . . ."

"I wouldn't have let him if I'd known he wouldn't . . ."

". . . He just don't know what can be done."

Tom sank to the step at his father's feet. "I thought he'd be okay. I didn't know." He felt shaky and light-headed. Why had he let Bobby come back alone? Why hadn't he stuck with him and seen to it he made it back to the house?

The screen door groaned open. Doc Brown said in a serious voice, "Birch?"

Birch stood up. "Will they make it?"

For a long moment Doc did not reply. "Infantile paralysis. I'm pretty sure of it. This is far more than I can deal with here. Trudy is packing a few things. We've got time to get the boys on the evening train to Fort Smith."

Something inside Tom went stone cold. Was it his fault? If he hadn't let Bobby come back alone, would his brother be so sick?

Birch's tone had an angry edge to it as he instructed Tom, "You'll have to tend things here. Be responsible."

Tom had not been responsible. He had left Bobby. "Dad, I'm sorry. . . ."

Birch seemed not to hear. "Do the milkin' and feedin' with nobody to tell you to."

"Yessir."

"Get down to Jefferson's place and tell him what's happened. Ask if Willa Mae can stay here with you."

"Yessir." Tom cradled his head in his hands. Did this mean Bobby and Joey might die? How long would everyone be in Fort Smith?

Doc interjected. "I'm going to drive over to the store to use Grandma Amos's telephone. I've got to call the station at Hartford and have them hold the Rock Island for us, then the hospital in Fort Smith for an ambulance to meet us when we get there. Be right ready to go when I get back." Doc clambered down the steps, tapping Tom on the shoulder as he passed by.

Tom followed after to crank the engine on the doctor's old Ford. The automobile lurched forward and Tom trotted alongside, keeping pace. "Is Bobby and Joe gonna be okay?" he shouted over the rattle of the motor.

"I just can't say, Tom." Doc did not slow to answer.

Tom pleaded, "I didn't know he was so sick or I wouldn't . . ."

"Get on back to the house now. You'll have to be a man. Your mama and daddy are going to need your help."

With a spurt of speed, Doc ended the conversation, leaving Tom standing alone in the red dust of the road.

Infantile paralysis. Polio.

Telephone calls to the hospitals in Fort Smith revealed that twenty-four cases had been admitted to St. Edward's Charity Hospital in the last two weeks. Doc Brown came back with the news that there were no more beds available at St. Edwards. Privately owned and expensive, Sparks Memorial Hospital was the only option remaining.

"The best facility for the care the boys will need," Doc Brown explained to Birch and Trudy as they carried the boys out to his car for the ride to the depot. "There is a specialist who will meet us at the hospital." He looked down at his hands in a gesture of helplessness. "They would not admit them without a commitment of a thousand dollars, Birch. I told them you were good for it."

Trudy put her hand on Joey's fevered brow and stroked his face. "It doesn't matter," she said grimly.

Birch glanced at Trudy in the backseat, cradling Joey in her arms. There was nothing in the world that mattered when stacked up against Bobby and Joe. He said slowly, deliberately, "We want to bring them home again, Doc. We want our boys well. We'll do what we have to."

"They'll get the best care there is," Doc assured them, throwing the Ford into gear. "I know Doctor Harding. A young fella. Trained at Johns Hopkins. Knows his business. They'll have the papers drawn up and ready. I told them it would take you a few days to come up with the cash. But they'll admit the boys on my promise that you're good for it."

Doc Brown tended the Tucker brothers all the way to the hospital in Fort Smith and then, when Dr. Harding took over, he hurried back to Sebastian County where babies were about to be born and other emergencies lurked.

Trudy felt frightened and very alone when he was gone.

Birch and Trudy waited three hours in the pale green waiting room of Fort Smith's Sparks Memorial Hospital before Dr. Harding emerged from a door at the far end of the corridor. The dim light from the ceiling fixtures cast his face in shadow. His head was bowed, gait slow and weary.

Trudy put her hand on Birch's arm, looked toward the doctor, then deliberately stood to face the news.

"Mister and Missus Tucker."

Birch extended his hand in a grim handshake. The doctor did not meet their anxious eyes. He looked first at the clipboard and then toward the lamp at the nurses' station and back at the clipboard. His gaze remained fixed on his own scrawl as he spoke almost in a whisper.

"You are aware of the spread of infantile paralysis . . . poliomyelitis . . . in western Arkansas and Oklahoma?"

Birch had not been aware. Trudy nodded.

"Infantile paralysis," the physician continued. "In most cases there are no clinical signs or only mild symptoms: headache, sore throat, fever. Recovery in one to three days. This unusually hot weather has extended the hazardous season."

"Come on, Doc," Birch pleaded. "We know our boys got more'n that. Just spill it."

Trudy clutched Birch's hand. She felt sick. The walls of the room seemed to close in around her.

Polio.

"All right, then." The eyes of Dr. Harding met Birch's. "If you want it straight. You may wish to take a seat, Missus Tucker."

Trudy did not move. "No. Thank you."

"Your sons . . . in both cases . . . have developed alarming complications. I mean that the disease has invaded the nervous system. At this moment the legs of your older son . . ."

"Bobby," Trudy choked.

"Yes. . . ." The eyebrows of Dr. Harding arched. Gaze returned to the records as if he could not bear to see the reaction as he told the full story. "Bobby is . . . still able to breathe on his own. However, the three year-old . . ."

"Joey," Birch said hoarsely.

"Joey is in a deep coma. There is marked paralysis in the muscles of his throat. Breathing is extremely labored. He has bulbar poliomyelitis with complications of encephalitis. Do you understand what I am saying?"

"You're sayin' Joe has the sleepin' sickness on top of this other."

"His prognosis is not hopeful. It would be cruel of me to lead you to believe otherwise. Bulbar poliomyelitis often causes respiratory failure. . . ."

Trudy felt as though she was walking through a nightmare. The words of the doctor receded to an echo. Details of the chipped linoleum tiles and paint flaking from the walls came into sharp focus. The scent of antiseptic made her stomach churn. The sound of her heartbeat rushed in her ears. She heard a woman's voice repeating Joe's name. It was her own.

"You gotta do something." Birch clasped the doctor's arm with both hands.

The physician nodded, gently pulled himself free, and led Trudy to the long wooden bench. Groping for the arm of the seat, she sank down and leaned her head heavily back against the wall. She closed her eyes and prayed that she would wake up from the terrible dream, but it still played out before her. Yesterday she had worried about losing the farm. What did that matter compared to Bobby and Joe?

". . . Iron lungs . . ."

Land and plows and seed and mules all receded to a faint echo. Everything important in life had come down to this pinpoint of survival, the next hour, the next breath.

". . . breathe for the victims when they cannot breathe for themselves. . . ."

"Then use it!" Birch insisted.

"This is not Kansas City. We have only one unit available. very expensive . . ."

"But both boys. . . ."

Dr. Harding paused and took a deep breath. He laid his hand on Trudy's shoulder.

"You must listen to me. There is only one unit open in Fort Smith—room for one child only. Bobby is still in the early stages, but his breathing is becoming more labored. He might make it if we put him in the iron lung immediately."

"But Joey!"

"I must be blunt, Mister Tucker. Joe has sustained extensive brain damage. It is my opinion that your younger child will not survive through the night."

Trudy reeled forward, covering her face with her hands. *Joe? Not survive the night? Then the sun would not rise! There would be no more mornings.*

Birch begged the doctor as if he could change something. "But if he's in that iron lung thing! If it's breathing for him!"

"If we give Joey the aid of the iron lung, then you may well lose both your sons within the week, Mister Tucker."

"But ain't there some chance we can take 'em both home? I gotta know if there's a chance."

"A miracle, perhaps."

"A miracle! You're tellin' me . . . us . . . that we gotta choose b'tween the two? You sayin' that we gotta stand by tonight and let our little baby die or maybe Bobby will die, too?"

After a long moment of contemplation, Harding replied. "We have only one unit and two very sick little boys. I am saying that there is a chance Bobby will survive if he gets the assistance he needs immediately."

"What can we do?" Birch blurted, then turned to the wall with a choked sob. His words became a barely audible whisper. "Let Joey go without a fight? I ain't ready for this. Not now, dear God!"

"No one is ever prepared for something like this, Mister Tucker. I placed calls to the hospitals in Fayetteville and Hot Springs, thinking perhaps we might be able to borrow another unit. Every iron lung in the South is in use. It is remarkable that we have one available. I cannot tell you what to do. I can only tell you the facts and await your decision. If we get him in the unit, Bobby has a chance. . . ."

He did not finish the thought, but Trudy heard the truth ringing clearly in her heart. *Joey will be gone by morning. . . .*

Trudy's eyes were dry. She spoke in a quiet voice. "I . . . we . . . need to see our babies."

Dr. Harding nodded, touched Birch's elbow, and led the way to an isolation ward.

The room was dimly lit. It smelled of antiseptic. The hiss of oxygen masked the sound of labored breathing. A clear tent was draped over Joey's crib. Through it, Trudy could see that his blue eyes were half open, yet he did not see her. His limp body was propped into a partial sitting position to prevent him from choking. Skin was ashen; lips were tinged with blue.

"Joey?" Trudy said his name. "It's Mama and Daddy . . . Joey?" She glanced at the doctor. "May I touch him?"

Dr. Harding nodded and guided her hands through the folds of the covering.

Trudy stroked his forehead. He was cold as ice, as if life had already gone from him. "Joey? Honey? Mama is . . ." Words failed. She stood over him a long time and smoothed his hair back and stroked his cheek. "Joey? Please . . ." She pleaded, "Mama's here. Daddy's . . ."

There was no response, not the flutter of an eyelid nor the twitch of a finger on his still, small hand. The child's breathing was shallow and irregular.

Was it only yesterday? Joey had run across the yard, shouting for her to come see some new and wondrous discovery. What was it he had wanted? She had only glanced through the kitchen window as she washed the morning dishes. Her mind had been on other things.

Yesterday's laughter had been a holy sacrament. The last hour of joy was worship he would have shared with her. . . . *If only I had known.* . . .

His eyes stared vacantly upward. The piping voice diminished to a tiny wheeze. She knew there would never be another moment of recognition or tenderness, no chance to say goodbye. He was beyond her reach now.

"Lord!" Birch put his arms around Trudy's waist and leaned his head against her back. "Trudy! We're gonna lose him! Oh, True!"

Dr. Harding stood at the foot of the crib in silent acknowledgment of the terrible fact. "You still have Bobby." Then he pulled the curtain back that separated the two brothers.

Also in an oxygen tent, Bobby turned his eyes toward the light. There was a flicker of recognition when he saw Trudy and Birch. His lips moved slightly, breathing out the single, exhausted, syllable, "Ma. . ."

"Please," Trudy said to Dr. Harding. "Do what you must." Arms outstretched, she bridged the gap between the two brothers. The fingers of her right hand rested in Joey's open palm in a gesture of farewell. Her left hand grasped Bobby's clenched fist, holding tightly to his life.

"Fight, Bobby," she said. Then, "Doctor Harding says . . . he says he's going to help you breathe easier, honey. But you cannot give up. Do you hear me? Don't be afraid. We'll stay right here. You're going to make it, Bobby."

CHAPTER 12

Book open on his lap, Tom leaned against the arm of the sofa in the circle of light and pretended to read *Uncle Tom's Cabin*. Willa Mae darned the socks in the basket. Chapter fourteen, where Mama had left off reading last night, was marked with an oak leaf pressed between sheets of waxed paper. Tom did not read ahead, but turned back to the very beginning—back to the page where Mama had first opened the book and Daddy had held Joey on his lap while Tom and Bobby had lain down on the floor to listen to her read.

Chapter I: In which the reader is introduced to a man of humanity.

Two weeks ago they had all been together in the room, listening to that page. Tom touched the print, and he could see them all as plain as anything.

Mama's foot tapped as she rocked and her words carried them far away from Shiloh. Little Joey sucked his thumb, and he leaned against Daddy's chest until Mama's voice lulled them both to sleep. Bobby lay on his back with his hands beneath his head and stared at the shadows on the ceiling as if he was watching clouds go by. And Tom lay beside Rosey and scratched her belly until her hind leg danced a jig. . . .

So it had been every evening: one chapter each night, until tonight.

Rosey was mournful. Her head cradled in her paws, she stared at the place where Bobby should have been and sighed a deep hound-dog sigh. Tom put his bare foot against her back and kneaded her stiff, short coat with his toes. "It's okay, Rosey," he said softly, even though it was not okay and he was miserable, too. She thumped her tail once, then closed her eyes. It was awfully lonesome in the parlor this evening.

Tom stroked the words and paragraphs of page one. He would not read beyond chapter fourteen until the entire family was here with him again. Then they would pick up where they left off and finish the book together.

The question popped out of his mouth. "When are they coming home?"

"Soon as they can, I reckon," Willa Mae replied, taking tiny stitches in the toe of Bobby's sock. The wick of the lamp was too high, and it began to smoke. Glancing up from her needlework, she adjusted the flame down. "Lawd!" she said, biting off the thread and fishing a black sock from the sewing basket. "These ol' eyes. . . . He'p me with this, will you, Tom? Come over here t' the light, honey."

He laid the book facedown, stepped over Rosey, and stood beside the arm of her chair while Willa Mae chose the navy blue spool from the sewing basket.

"Is that blue or is it black? I cain't see color good no more."

"It's blue."

"Is this sock blue or is it black? Cain't tell the difference. . . ."

"It's black."

"Well, it won't do. Blue thread an' a black sock. Your mama would skin me if'n I darn all these socks with the wrong color thread."

"Yes'm."

She fussed in the basket and retrieved the black spool, holding it up for Tom's inspection. He gave a nod. "Yes'm."

Willa Mae wrapped the thread in the sock and laid it aside on the lamp table among photographs of Mama and Daddy and Bobby, Joey, and Tom all together. Then the old woman leaned forward as if she was only just seeing the little picture gallery for the first time.

Tom did not move away. He remained beside her, his fingers touching the wooden arm of the chair. His gaze was riveted on the black-and-white images of faces tucked and smiling against the glare of the sun. All in a row they stood: the same people, different ages, different days, different sizes, all smiling likenesses in black and white and gray. The pictures had been arranged on the table since they had moved to Shiloh. Mama had put them out the first day, and Tom had picked them up once a week to dust beneath them. More pictures had been added to the collection, but Tom had not ever stopped to look at them before. Not really seen them . . .

Willa Mae picked up the largest photograph, the one taken at the photographer's studio in Oklahoma City when Daddy had worked in the oil fields. Joey was tiny then, sitting on his mama's lap. Mama dressed him in a white bonnet and a baby gown with lace.

"Joey looks like a girl in that one," Tom said.

Willa Mae smiled. Faded eyes reflected deep sorrow as if she saw the future in the picture. "Pretty baby, ain't he?"

"He's gonna hate this when he gets big enough to know." He tried not to think the thought that came next.

Willa Mae hummed a moment like she always did when she was thinking hard and had something important on her mind. But she did not say it, whatever it was. She pressed her lips together tightly and replaced the picture frame beside the lamp and murmured, "Sweet Jesus knows. Only Jesus knows. . . ."

Tom wiped his nose and blurted something he had read in the dime novel stashed out in the barn. "Ol' Indians say gettin' your picture took steals a piece of your soul."

"Hmmm. Y'all . . . you an' Bobby been readin' them penny dreadfuls again, ain't you?"

"Yes'm."

"Best not let your mama catch you. . . ."

"No'm." He did not want to talk about the penny dreadfuls. He wanted to talk . . . needed to know something about . . . "What if they don't come back?"

Willa Mae nodded, and the nod acknowledged the possibility of *What if.* "Honey, we gots to leave the ones we love in Jesus' hands. Tha's all. Jesus knows."

Tom knelt down beside her chair. The old woman's broad shadow blocked the light. "I'm scared," he said quietly.

She placed her hand on his head and smoothed his hair. "It's all right t' be scared, I reckon. I been scared lots of times. Tell it to Jesus, baby. He don't mind when we're scared."

"I want everything to be all right again. Like it was last night. Bobby and Joey, you know?" He turned his eyes up to the photographs. . . . *Dad, Mama, Joey, Bobby, Tom, on the porch . . . Smiling faces. Heads turned slightly against the glare. Eyes squinted against the brightness.* Would the next family photograph be missing someone?

"Cain't hold on to yesterday, Tom, honey. Cain't be scared of tomorrow. Just gotta believe when dark times come Jesus gonna carry us right on through the night till the sun shine on us again. And it *is* gonna shine again. . . ."

Willa Mae prayed a long time, running her fingers through his hair, until Tom was tired out. She said Amen and got him a glass of cold buttermilk to drink before she tucked him in. Willa Mae let Rosey sleep beside him on the bed where Bobby should have been. He was comforted by the sound of her breathing. The lamps were put out, and Tom began to pray again that in the morning he would be glad to see the sun come up. Outside, a mockingbird trilled a night song from the low branches of the hickory tree. Through the window, the moon was a faint heelprint against the sky. The whistle of the night train sounded shrill and lonesome in the distance.

Tom woke once in the middle of the night. His pillow was wet, so he figured he had been crying in his sleep for a long time. The moon was gone. The mockingbird had stopped singing.

Early morning light glowed behind the pale yellow window shade and tinged the bedroom with an amber cast. Outside, jays were scolding and swooping down to steal the feed from the hens in the chicken coop.

Tom lay on the bed for a moment and tried to remember what was wrong. Had he been dreaming? A nightmare? He put his hand out to nudge Bobby awake and touched Rosey instead. It came to him then. Everyone sick and gone to Fort Smith.

There were voices in the kitchen. Who was it?

Willa Mae and a man.

Jefferson. "Doc Brown . . . called up Gramma Amos. . . . I come soon as . . . You want me to . . ."

"Lawd, Lawd! Po' little fella. . . ."

"Should we wake 'im, Mama?"

"It can wait. Let 'im sleep a while, I reckon."

Tom sat up suddenly and kicked the sheets back. Rosey gave him a sideways look from her pillow as if to say she did not want to be awake yet. He nudged her off the bed, then stepped out onto the plank floor in his bare feet. The boards squeaked beneath him, giving him away. The voices in the kitchen fell silent.

Before he reached the door, it opened. Jefferson blocked the frame. His face was all in shadow and he stood there, neither moving to the side nor speaking as Tom grasped the turned post of the footboard. Rosey sidled past Jeff, her nails clicking against the floor. Jefferson did not seem to notice.

"Mornin'," Tom said.

"Mornin'."

Tom knew something terrible had happened from that one word. There was no light in it, no greeting, no intimation that Jefferson was glad to see the daylight.

Rosey whined and scratched at the back door to be let out. Willa Mae spoke nonsense to her, asking the dog if she slept well, as if Rosey could answer. The kitchen door opened and closed.

"You need to use the necessary, Tom? I got somethin' t' tell you," Jeff said in a sorrowful way.

"Tell me first." Tom did not want to wait. He had to hear it all and now. His stomach was churning, and he felt like he would throw up.

"Sit down." Jeff stepped into the room.

Tom did not sit. He clung to the footboard and put one foot on top of the other, balancing on one leg. "Just say it."

Jeff sat down on the bed. It sagged beneath his weight. Now Tom saw his eyes. Sorrow reflected in the deep brown. They were tinged with red at the corners as if the big man had been crying. Tom watched the large calloused hands reach out to him. He felt Jeff's fingers gently grasp his shoulders and release and grasp again as if the hands had a mind of their own and did not know if it was best to hold Tom like a child or let him stand alone like a man. Then the hands moved reluctantly up and held Tom's face between them.

"Just tell me," Tom said fiercely, knowing.

"All right. It's Joey."

Tom blinked back in disbelief at Jefferson's broad black face. Every detail became distinct. The bent nose. The scar that ran through his lip. The notch in his ear where another convict had bit it through. Scars everywhere . . . everywhere! Jefferson's wounds no longer bled and yet they were still visible. What sort of wound was left inside when love got ripped away, Tom wondered? He felt the tearing; the finality of death struck him like a blow.

"Joey died," Tom said flatly, and his own words surprised him. His voice was so calm. How could he speak in such an even tone when everything was breaking up inside?

"Your baby brother's done gone to be with Jesus, boy."

"But yesterday morning . . . just . . . yesterday . . ." Tears streamed down his face. He lay his cheek against Jeff's shoulder for a moment and then rage filled him up. He pushed himself away and ran from the bedroom into Daddy and Mama's room, where they had moved Joey's cot yesterday afternoon. The sheets were mussed. The pillow held the indentation of his head. A small, pale blue sock lay on the floor beside the tiny bib overalls Mama had stitched so Joey would look like Daddy, like a farmer. On a chest stood the photo taken at the fair: a beaming Joey clutching a ribbon in one hand while under his other arm nestled Henny, equally proud and half as large as her owner. The ribbon itself lay draped over the small loving cup beside the picture.

Everything was just the same, looked the same, was just as he had left it. Joey gone? How could it be?

Jefferson waited outside the room as Tom stared at the things that had belonged to Joey and yet . . . Joey was gone.

From one morning to the next. It had happened that quick, and now nothing would ever be entirely right again.

CHAPTER 13

They brought Joey back from Fort Smith in a white, child-sized pine coffin.

Trudy held it across her lap all the way home to Shiloh in the backseat of Doc Brown's automobile.

She sent word ahead that Joey had loved his garden, and she would have her baby buried within sight of the place he most liked to spend his days. Beneath the broken rope swing, the message said.

And so Jefferson took his shovel and went down across the creek to where the scarred earth had not yet healed above Hock's grave. There, Jefferson climbed the well-shaded knoll above the stream.

It was a place that Birch had told him about.

"You know the place, Jeff. Look up into the branches of the old oak tree. There's the frayed end of a rope still there where me and my little brother used t' swing out over the water and jump in."

Jeff dug a small but deep grave beneath the spreading limbs of the water oak. It was the hardest digging he had ever done, he later told Lily. All the while, as the dirt flew up, Jeff kept looking at the strong branches of that tree and the frayed end of happy memories. As if it was his own memory, he thought about brothers skinny-dipping in a swimming hole and swinging far over the water with a whoop as they plunged in. It came to Jeff that he was turning over the very earth where Birch had laughed and launched himself. It must seem to Birch like ten thousand summers ago now, Jefferson reasoned. Yet somehow it didn't seem right that the same ground upon which joy had danced should now be displaced by such sorrow.

Jeff figured by the measure of his own days that life was mostly like that—layer upon layer of happy and sad all mixed up with ordinary days. Each day passed away, happy, sad, ordinary . . . hours and minutes, words and looks spent without thought until finally the days ran out.

Then, Jesus! We'd call it all back again if'n we could. Live one day over again if'n that could be! An' how we all wish we ain't wasted so much worry on stuff that don't matter nohow. . . .

These things came to his mind in a jumble as he finished his task and looked up at the copper rooster on the roof, then at Joey's patch of garden—the radish tops still green and alive in the sunlight.

There was no way to put it off. After the funeral, Birch borrowed Doc's car and set out to do what was required.

It was late afternoon, and the sun hung over the top of Sugarloaf Mountain when Birch, still dressed in his funeral clothes, reached Meribah. Doc Brown's car backfired and gave a shudder as Birch made the turn beneath the arched metal letters of Jenson Consolidated.

The machinery was silent today. Through the open doors of the warehouse Birch saw mountainous bales of cotton stacked and waiting to be transported to Jenson's Meribah Textile Mill. A flash of resentment rose in him at the thought of his own ten-dollar bale among those in the Jenson Consolidated warehouse.

Garrick and Caro-line Jenson had made a profit of at least five hundred percent on that one bale. This was accomplished by paying Birch rock-bottom price, bypassing wholesalers and middlemen, manufacturing textiles in the Jenson plant, paying workers slave wages, and selling the product directly to the merchants. Multiply such business practices by several thousand bales a year, and it was clear why the coffers of Garrick and Caro-line Jenson's business enterprises were overflowing and their profit margins were increasing.

An enormous new company building and warehouse had just been completed, and new looms purchased and installed at the mill. All this had been proudly accomplished as working folks lay down each night and asked God how they could make it through another season. What would it take to buy the kids' new shoes this year? How could a man come back when he was so far behind?

Work harder?

Stay longer in the fields or the factory?

Take a second job?

Those employed by Jenson Consolidated already labored from "can see to can't see"—from sunrise till after dark. Advances against wages were made and were deducted from every paycheck with interest. Credit at the company store and exorbitant prices assured that workers would remain in debt and therefore in the service of Jenson Consolidated.

From the sharecroppers who plowed, planted, and harvested on Jenson land to those who ginned the cotton or worked the looms in the textile mill, getting ahead was a long-forgotten dream. Life had all come down to the pinpoint of simple survival.

And yet . . . like every man who had come with a proposal for Garrick Jenson and his wife to consider, desperation, grief, and fear tempered Birch's resentment.

What if the Jenson's would not accept the farm as collateral? Surely people with so many resources would be able to advance cash for Bobby's hospital costs. The sum needed was small compared to the value of the land, Birch thought as he set the brake and shut off the motor.

The door to the Jenson Consolidated office opened on well-oiled, respectful hinges. Caro-line Jenson, the Ice Lady, turned around from a filing cabinet and said to Birch's collar button, "Well, well, Mister Tucker. What brings you back to Meribah? Do you have another bale of cotton to sell?" The way she leaned on the word bale underscored a dismissal of Birch as hardly worth the bother of talking to.

"I need to see Garrick," Birch said.

"Mister Jenson is in a meeting," Caro-line said, indicating the closed door to the inner office. "You may wait if you wish." She nodded coolly toward a wooden bench in the corner under the front window and returned to her filing without another word.

Loud chortles reached Birch's ears from behind the frosted glass. Birch recognized Jenson's belly laugh, but also heard the sound of Garrick's mirth echoed by a high, reedy snicker.

There were many times in the next hour and a quarter that Birch considered getting up and walking out—out of the office, away from Jenson Consolidated and away from Meribah. But each time he thought his patience was exhausted, Birch thought of Bobby, remembered the iron lung and the specialist, and forced himself to remain seated.

When Garrick's door finally opened, the first figure to emerge was a fat man whose high-pitched whinny should have belonged to Jenson. "We sure got 'em!" the obese man exulted. "Them strikes up north played right into our hands, yessir. Charge whatever we want for fabric an' no mistake. They either deal with us or shut down, eh, Mister Jenson?"

Garrick laughed again, clapping his visitor on the back. "Only the beginning," he said. "You're about to be the wealthiest textile whole-saler in the South."

"Garrick," Caro-line interrupted. "Mister Tucker wishes to speak with you."

Noticing Birch for the first time, Garrick nodded, drawing his chin back into his neck like a turtle pulling in its head. "We'll talk again soon," he said to the portly salesman. The fat man pulled together the sides of his white shirt to ease the strain on the buttons and left.

"What is it?" Garrick said to Birch without preface. No greeting, no invitation to enter the private office.

"My boy's sick . . . bad sick . . . in the hospital in Fort Smith. I need money." The pent-up words tumbled from Birch's mouth. He was a man who never talked about his personal concerns, but the mental rehearsal of the last ninety minutes made the story gush out.

"How tragic, how awful," Garrick murmured in suitably sympathetic tones. Birch never saw that while saying the words, Jenson was looking at his wife and not at Birch at all. "Come in and sit down. How can we help?"

Birch explained about the polio and the equipment needed and the guarantee of payment required by Sparks Memorial. "I'll mortgage my place," he said at last. "Best bottomland in all of western Arkansas. Worth ten thousand dollars with buildin's and machinery."

Garrick put on a long face. "I see," he said doubtfully. "But this is way outside our customary dealings. What is your proposal exactly?"

"I need twelve hundred dollars," Birch said, "and I got seventy acres to put up as collateral."

Garrick Jenson pounced on Birch's words like a cat on a mouse. "I thought your farm was eighty acres."

Birch nodded. "It is, but I've already struck a bargain about ten acres on the west side. They can't be included in what we do here."

"Is it subject to a contract?" Garrick inquired, glancing again toward Caro-line. "You aren't trying to use the same property for more than one loan, are you, Mister Tucker?"

"Nothin' like that," Birch said. "Just an agreement between me and a friend."

"Well," Garrick said, leaning sideways in his chair and glancing toward Caro-line. Some unspoken communication passed between the man and wife. Birch saw it, but could not decipher the meaning.

Caro-line took over. Not meeting Birch's steady gaze, she said in a tone that let him know she did not believe any business with him was worth the risk. "Arkansas is not the Promised Land, now is it? Farms are drying up and blowing away everyday in these parts. How can Jenson Consolidated be certain you can meet the service on the debt?"

Swallowing a dozen angry replies, Birch thought again about Bobby. Bobby with a chance to make it because of the mechanical lung. Bobby who, without the money, would be transported across town to St. Edward's Charity Hospital. Then there was the memory of Joey and the vision of Bobby lying very still.

"Part of the money I need is to seed the north acreage in peanuts," Birch explained. "Money will be in gooberpeas next season no matter what happens to cotton."

Once again Garrick Jenson entered the conversation. "No!" he insisted. "It must be all in cotton or there can be no deal." Then in a quieter tone he continued, "You must understand our position, our responsibility to the property. We understand cotton; our business is cotton. We would not care to speculate in the unknown."

Birch considered the words, wondered why it was anybody's business what he planted if he made the payments on time, and then thought again of Bobby. "All right," he said.

"Now as to the amount of the loan," Jenson continued smoothly. "Land isn't worth anything anymore; you know that. The boss and I will have to talk it over, right, Boss?" Here Garrick looked at Caro-line and smiled and received her puckered, downturned smile back. "But perhaps we could allow twelve hundred dollars on the Tucker place?" It was a question, not a promise. They would talk about it, the two of them, and decide how much, if anything, they could give on a farm worth ten thousand dollars.

Birch felt helpless, sick, and somehow ashamed. "I'm good for it. God is my witness. I'll pay you back every penny," he said quietly. Even as he spoke the words, he sensed that his promise to repay was not at issue. There was something else again: making deals, turning profits, running Jenson Consolidated. Even kindness was a form of control.

These thoughts tumbled through Birch's mind as he contemplated her raised eyebrow and his almost imperceptible shrug. Circumstances had given them power over his life and the lives of those he loved. He wanted to run from their presence, but he did not. His need was too great, and they knew it.

Jenson grinned and opened the desk drawer and withdrew a slip of paper on which he scribbled a note. "Here's a voucher for a sandwich. Take it on over to the cafe and get something to eat—on us. Come back in an hour and we'll let you know. Go on now and don't worry about a thing. Sorry about your boy . . . these things happen. . . . Glad you came to see us . . . see what we can do . . . perhaps we can come to some terms that work for us. . . ."

Birch found himself on the pavement outside the Jenson Consolidated office with a meal ticket in his hand. The close of the door in his face cut off the flow of kindly, understanding phrases.

The cheese on Birch's sandwich was as dry and tasteless as candle wax. At that, it was no worse than the bread. The uneaten meal lay in front of him like the well-preserved artifact of an ancient civilization. The squinty-eyed waitress who had tossed the plate in front of Birch forty-five minutes earlier told him that the voucher paid for one cup of coffee only; refills were a nickel each. When Birch declined, she shrugged and wiped her hands on the tail of a grimy apron, then proceeded to use the same grease-stained cloth to idly smear circles on the adjoining tables.

Looking at his pocket watch for the third time in as many minutes, Birch decided he could wait no longer. He pushed the chair back and returned to the Jenson office.

Caro-line met him at the swinging gate and barred his progress. As if confronting a defendant at the bar of justice, she appeared ready to read his sentence from the paper she lifted from the top of the file cabinet. But where was the judge? Where was Garrick Jenson? Through the open door into the back office, Birch could see no evidence that Garrick was present.

"Mister Jenson has already left for the day," Caro-line stated flatly, looking past Birch's left shoulder. "I will go over the papers with you and conclude the transaction today, or you may come back and review it with him."

"When?" Birch asked. "I need to know today if you're gonna help, and I need to let the hospital know."

"Very well." She sniffed. "We'll proceed. But we are very near closing, so this cannot take much time. It is, after all, a standard contract. Nothing much to it, really."

"You mean you'll let me have the money?"

Managing to look skeptical even while agreeing, Caro-line replied, "We've decided that your property is adequate security . . . barely. I've already obtained the legal description from the county clerk's office and entered it here on the documents. Here is the check, already made out to Sparks Memorial Hospital, in the amount of one thousand dollars."

"Wait a minute," Birch said, holding up his hand. "What I asked for was twelve hundred."

"The loan amount *is* twelve hundred," Caro-line confirmed with a quick arch of her eyebrows. "But naturally we have deducted our processing fees and the recording fees and the appraisal fees and the cost of the cotton seed."

Birch looked and felt shaken. "You mean I'm to repay twelve hundred, but you're only gonna give me a thousand? That ain't right!"

Caro-line sniffed and turned away without any regard for Birch's pained expression and replaced the papers on top of the file. "Oh well, if you want to quibble over the details, you can make an appointment to see Mister Jenson. Now he'll be out of town on business; come back a week from tomorrow."

"No, wait," Birch urged. "It won't keep that long. Go on with what you were saying."

"You must not keep interrupting." Caro-line sniffed. "I am staying late myself just to be neighborly, but we must get this business concluded."

Only nodding because he did not think he could trust himself to speak, Birch urged her to continue.

"As I was saying, this is our standard form of credit contract. It requires you to, of course, make all your purchases at Jenson Consolidated businesses."

"All our—"

"All *credit* purchases," she clarified smoothly. "Cash purchases can be made anywhere, but you can't expect Jenson Consolidated to allow you to receive credit from other merchants on top of your obligation here. If you buy on a charge anywhere else for the duration of the loan, the entire balance becomes due and payable at once."

Birch was so busy absorbing the fact that he and Trudy would have to do most all their shopping in Meribah that he missed the next two standard provisions and only rejoined what Caro-line was saying to hear the words, ". . . standard split of the profits. Here is the paragraph that explains how the market value of your crop will be figured. This is the loan calculation. The rate is 20 percent, with the first payment of four hundred and eighty dollars due on November first of next year."

"Ain't 20 percent a mite steep?" The words were blurted out before Birch could prevent it. Then he feared she would really fold everything up and send him packing, but apparently this exception was expected.

"There are establishments charging 40 percent," she said with a downward twitch of her mouth. "And remember, you did come to us and not the other way around. Sound business practices and good management require us to be careful with the resources of Jenson Consolidated. We have an obligation . . ."

"To the property," Birch concluded wearily. "Yes, I know. Go on."

"That's really the lot," Caro-line said. "Mister Jenson anticipated that you would want this matter concluded right away and so he has already signed both copies. If you will just initial each page and sign beneath his name, I'll be happy to take the hospital's payment to the post office for you on my way home."

Birch's head was spinning. She seemed to imply that only people who could afford it should ever get sick and, further, that if given the money directly he would spend it on booze or something. And that payment . . . it was two hundred dollars more than the total value of this year's yield. What if . . . ?

Then he thought once more about his son. He thought about Bobby fighting, hanging on, and nothing else mattered. "Show me where to sign," he said.

Caro-line folded one copy of the contract, creased it sharply with a thumbnail, and inserted the papers into an envelope before handing it to Birch. "There you are," she said. "I hope your boy pulls through all right. Goodbye."

In a daze, Birch stumbled out toward Doc Brown's car. When his hand touched the door handle, it suddenly came to him that he did not know the length of the loan. How long had he signed up for? Turning around, he saw the last of the window shades being pulled down in the Jenson Consolidated office. The shape of the figure Birch glimpsed just before the blinds were drawn looked like Garrick Jenson. But no one answered Birch's knock on the door, and after ten minutes of futile waiting for someone to emerge, he gave up and headed home.

C H A P T E R   1 4

His arm around Rosey, Tom sat on the front step and looked at the rubber tire hanging from the hickory tree in the yard. Then his gaze wandered over the creek where the small mound that was Joey's grave stood beside the bigger mound belonging to Hock.

Everyone but Willa Mae had gone home now, leaving the house lonely and empty feeling. Tom could hear the clank of dishes in the washpan as the old woman cleaned up. After a time there followed a low murmuring of two voices. Tom could not make out what was said, but there was Mama, sounding stricken and out of breath, as if her words had to fight their way up to the surface from a great depth. Then Willa Mae, mellow and soothing and oh, so sorry about everything! For everything!

". . . Only Jesus, honey . . . hurt so bad . . . Lawd know all about it, honey. . . ."

Presently, Willa Mae came out on the porch and said back to Trudy, "Y'all know where I'll be t'night. Gramma Amos is feelin' poorly an' ask me t' come sleep over, tend all them chickens. But I'll come 'round early in the mornin' 'fore you leave back to Fort Smith, honey. An' you know I'll do a heap of prayin'."

"Thank you . . . Willa . . . Mae."

Tom did not turn around, but he knew the women were embracing.

"There now . . . there, there, honey . . . it's all right . . . it's . . . let it all out. . . ."

Another breathless thank-you from Mama. Then the screen door squeaked and she went inside, closing a series of doors behind her so she could cry and cry, thinking Tom would not know.

Willa Mae, smelling of gravy and wood smoke and dish soap, stood quietly behind Tom.

He hoped she would not speak kindly to him now because he did not want to break. Not again. Maybe not ever again. Why didn't she just go on back to Grandma Amos's place and leave him sitting here, unnoticed, unmoving, like a stone.

"I'm goin' on now, Tom."

She had said his name, and it was impossible to pretend he had not heard.

"Yes'm." His voice sounded puny and childish to his ears.

"I got your daddy's supper in the warmer. You fetch it for him when he come home from Meribah."

"Yes'm." A slight breeze stirred the tire swing like invisible children were playing on it. Or maybe his memories were rocking it.

"Kitchen's all clean. Neither your Mama nor Daddy gonna be thinkin' 'bout doin' the dishes after your daddy eats. You clean up after."

"Yes'm." The last sunlight illuminated the heap of pine boughs on Joey's grave. No flowers anywhere in Shiloh, but the pine boughs smelled like Christmas.

"Well, then." She bent forward and kissed the top of his head. "Sometime the only way t' keep goin' is t' keep goin'."

"Yes'm. I'll help."

"You're a good boy. Lawd Jesus keep you close, chil'!"

In the corner of his vision he could see her big flat feet busting out of her shoes as she walked past him down the steps, but he did not look up into her face when he said goodbye. He feared the look of her sorrowing, holy eyes and the way they saw right into his soul and drew out his grief and made him want to be rocked in her arms!

Only when the crunch of gravel beneath her footsteps receded did Tom dare to raise his eyes. Then, in the deepening twilight, he saw the dust of Doc Brown's borrowed Model-T on the road.

Dad was back. Tom stood up, not wanting his father to see him hunched down and useless on the porch. He went inside and laid the table as the rattle of the motor came nearer and finally, with a backfire like a gunshot, fell silent. Taking the plate from the warmer, Tom stood in the doorway as Birch climbed wearily up the steps.

The screen door was like a gray veil softening his father's form, but the dark lines were plainly visible beneath his eyes. A long white envelope protruded from the chest pocket of his suit. His eyes seemed incapable of seeing past whatever thoughts were in the front of his mind. He moved slowly, like a very old man. Hand on the door latch, he paused a moment, touched the envelope, furrowed his brow in a frown, and then came in.

"Hullo, Dad," Tom said, uncertain of how he should sound.

"Evenin', Tom." Birch raised his eyes to the closed bedroom door. "Your mama?"

"She went in there. . . ." Tom inclined his head toward the bedroom. ". . . a while ago. Sleepin', I think."

"Good. . . . That's good." Birch hung his beat-up fedora on the hat rack.

"I set your place at the table." Tom stepped aside, giving his father room to pass, but Birch did not. Tom saw the inside thought take over his father for a moment.

"What's that you said?"

"I got your supper on the table. Willa Mae said . . . well, the food's warm if you're hungry."

Birch was pale beneath his tan; it gave his skin a grayish cast. "That's thoughtful of you, Tom." He walked into the kitchen and scraped the chair across the floor, then sat down carefully like he had done the time his back was hurt. Staring at the plate of food, he managed a near smile by way of thanks. "Looks good," he said. "But I—I ate somethin' over in Meribah. A sandwich. Maybe later."

Tom put the heaping plate of food back in the warmer and waited for his father to say something—anything at all. Instead, Birch took out the long white envelope and removed its contents. He smoothed the document out between the knife and fork and spoon as if it was his meal. Tracing each line with his finger, he began to read, looking up only when Trudy came into the room.

"Hullo, Birch." Her eyes were swollen and red-rimmed, her normally tidy hair mussed. One strand hung down over the side of her face. She pushed it back as she stooped to embrace Birch, but it fell again.

"We got it," he told her. "A thousand. In the mail to the hospital already." Birch indicated the document.

"Thank God." Trudy glanced up at Tom as if she noticed him for the first time. Then, "Do you have chores, Tom?"

He nodded but explained his presence. "Willa Mae told me to get Dad's supper."

"I'm not hungry," Birch said in a miserable tone. "Thanks anyways, Tom. It'd be a help if you'd do the feedin' for me tonight."

"Sure," Tom agreed and left his parents to talk about those inside things that kept them from seeing him or anything else.

He was grateful to have work to do. It made him feel better somehow, and he understood what Willa Mae had told him about keeping going. He took his time at the chores, stroking the noses of the mules and speaking in dulcet tones to the milk cow.

It was past dark by the time he finished the feeding, and he felt some better.

He used the necessary and washed his hands at the pump. When he looked up toward the house he could see the lamp was lit in the kitchen. In the circle of light he saw his mama and his daddy sitting across the kitchen from one another. The white papers from the envelope were spread out between them. Birch's eyes were closed and his head was cocked back, face toward the ceiling as if he was praying.

Trudy pored over the document. She clamped her hand over her mouth, as if to keep herself from speaking. Every few lines on the page she took away her hand and blurted a question: "But. . . how can they . . . 20 percent interest over five years?"

"Standard contract, she said."

"But Birch," Trudy moaned. "It means we'll pay them back twelve hundred . . . no, *fourteen* hundred dollars more than the loan. How can we manage it?"

"We already knew I'd have to have another job, True," Birch said softly. "What other choice did we have?"

But Trudy was not listening. She was reading the next provision. "The first two years' payments are nothing but interest," she sighed. "And part of the third, before we ever start paying their blood money. And even if we had the cash to pay Jenson's off early, we have to pay all the interest anyway. This is the worst thing I've ever seen. Didn't you even read it before you signed it?"

Tom heard the panic in his mother's voice, like she was winding up toward hysteria. He wanted to put his hands over his ears, to block out the sound. He did not want Mama to be frightened. What could he hang on to if she got scared?

"And this . . . look at this!" Trudy's breath was coming in short gasps, as if the paper had somehow hit her in the pit of the stomach. "This says that *they* will tell *us* what the cotton is worth, and then they get to keep half—half!—of the value."

Tom's gaze shifted to his father hoping for calm, solid confidence; silently pleading with his father to explain it all away, to say it was all right. But Birch's face was ashen. He seemed frozen. His shoulders slumped in an attitude of defeat, in the posture of a boy who has just cried *Uncle! Don't hit me again!*

And all Birch could say, over and over, was, "What else could we do? What choice did we have?"

"You know . . . *you know* . . . nothing matters but Bobby. I don't care if they take everything we own. But how could you let them do this? What about your promise to Jefferson?" Trudy asked, scanning the contract again. "How could you tie his ten acres into this wickedness?"

Tom saw a wild light come into his father's eyes, and Birch jumped up. "It ain't supposed to say that!" he protested loudly. "I told 'em they could only touch seventy."

Trudy held out the paper like an accusation and pointed to something Tom could not read. Whatever it was, it galvanized his father into action.

"I got to go to Gramma Amos's place!" Birch shouted. "I got to use the phone and call Garrick Jenson right now!"

There was no reply to the hammering on the front door of the store, even though Birch had thrown back the screen so hard that it rattled the wavy glass of the front window. He pounded on the faded and weathered panels that had once been painted pale green but were now a sun-bleached gray. Grandma Amos was partially deaf, he knew, but the thunder of his banging was enough to wake the dead.

Presently, in between staccato bursts of his fist, Birch noticed the first evidence that someone had heard his desperation. The musical creaking of the floorboards was given rhythm by a weary shuffle and harmonized by the soft complaint of vexed groans. "Lawd, lawd," Birch heard Willa Mae mutter. "What's the matter now? Who's'at knockin'?"

"It's me, Willa Mae," Birch called. "Lemme in. I gotta use Gramma's phone. It's important."

"Birch? You been home? You got bad news?"

Impatiently Birch urged her to open up. "I can't explain through the door," he said. "But I'll tell it all to you right after I make a call!"

The bolt on the inside slid back with a thin clink, making Birch suddenly aware that he could have lowered his shoulder and broken the panels down. This reflection slowed him just enough to avoid running over Willa Mae in his haste to get to the telephone. As it was, he swung his body sharply around her bulk and sprinted to the little enclosure that sheltered the instrument.

He drummed his fingers on the tin of the Bull Durham tobacco sign as he waited for the operator to respond. There was still more waiting and more fretting as she contacted the Meribah exchange and requested the Garrick Jenson residence.

The voice of Caro-line Jenson, faint and with a tinny ring, as if coming through a drainpipe, answered. "I need to talk to Garrick," Birch blurted. "There's been a mistake. The papers ain't right."

"What is the nature of the mistake?" she asked in haughty tones. "Besides," she added as an afterthought, "Garrick is away."

"I told you only seventy acres of the place could be used for collateral. I told you about the promise made on the other ten."

"Well." She sniffed. "That was never clear . . . not clear at all. You do own all eighty acres, do you not? That's what the clerk's office says."

"Yes, but . . ."

"I fail to see what you think is in error."

Birch almost screamed at her over the phone, realizing only barely in time that she would just hang up. "Please," he said through gritted teeth. "Let me talk to Garrick. Otherwise I'll just have to drive back to Meribah and see him in person."

There was a space of silence on the line. Birch knew that Caro-line was pondering what to do next and that by now she had heard enough fierceness in his voice to know he would in fact show up on their doorstep.

Caro-line did not come back to repeat the lie. The next voice Birch heard was Garrick's. "What is it, Mister Tucker? Why are you disturbing us at home and annoying my wife?"

"I told you that I already had an obligation on ten acres of my property," Birch said evenly. "You can cheat and swindle me all you want on the rest, but you can't make me break my word to someone else."

His voice light and flip, Garrick replied, "What do you expect us to do about it?"

"Change it!"

"Oh, no." Jenson laughed. "No one forced you to sign. No one but you was in such an all-fired hurry to get his hands on money. If you did not take the time to read the contract fully . . ." Garrick's voice became snide. ". . . or have it explained to you, then it's nobody's fault but your own. You signed and the money was paid and there's an end. And if you think we won't foreclose on the whole eighty acres, you're sadly mistaken."

It was on the tip of Birch's tongue to damn Garrick Jenson and his wife to hell forever. Instead, choosing his words with care, he said, "Garrick, you set out to cheat me. You took advantage of my need, and you took advantage of my nature. If you'll swindle me, you've done it to others. You are a liar and a thief, and someday your chickens will all come home to roost."

Birch drove back from the store, parked at the barn and, ignoring the fact that Trudy still sat in the lighted kitchen, walked down the hill and across the creek to Jefferson's cabin. Afraid to knock, he stood outside the gate and called to the dim glow of a lantern in the window.

"Jefferson! Jeff! It's Birch. I've got to talk to you!"

"Come in then," Jeff returned as if the late arrival did not surprise him.

Birch would not enter the cabin.

"Leave the lantern," he requested as Jefferson tugged up the strap of his overalls and stepped barefoot out onto the porch. "What I got to say to you I can't bear to say in the light."

Jeff could not see Birch's face in the darkness of Dreamland's front porch, did not need to read the eyes to know that the troubles of Job had visited his friend. Birch told him about Bobby and the thousand dollars and then all the provisions in the Jenson contract—what it meant to both of them, to their wives and children and farms. It was as if Birch was all alone, talking to himself, talking to God, pleading for answers to questions that had no explanation this side of eternity.

Jeff let him talk on and on, the bitterness and grief pouring out.

". . . When first I heard what Garrick Jenson had done . . . Lord! And this, on the day we've laid Joey to rest. For myself, I could bear it, but how will Trudy? . . . And now this ten acres I promised y'all is . . . I thought it was enough that I told Jenson, but he . . . It's my fault; I shoulda read it. Why didn't I read it?"

At last Jefferson spoke. His voice was rusty from being quiet for so long. "You didn't read it 'cause all that matters is your young'un . . . sweet Bobby . . . an' you figgered Jenson's word was good enough."

"Caro-line said I didn't make it clear about your ten acres. Wasn't clear? I been playin' it back over and over, and I told 'em. . . ."

"Don't matter that you told 'em, Birch," Jefferson said gently. "Them two ain't right-hearted, that's all. I heard t'day, well, at the funeral potluck . . . Woody Woods an' Arley Palmer an' a couple of the others, they signed a Jenson contract just like you done. They didn't really study on what all them fancy legal words might mean till later, and then—hit 'em like a lightnin' bolt! Garrick an' Caro-line Jenson cheated ever'one that put his name on Jenson papers. Some folks knows it, others gonna figger it out when all they get for their hard work is an empty sack an' a kick in the behind."

"This is your place, Jeff, but on accounta my . . . carelessness . . . it's beholden to those who care more about property than folks."

"It's a fine place, too. But it's jus' a place. This ain't about what's mine and what's yours. Me an' Lily loves y'all, Birch. We loves them young'uns, too. You know if some man come up t' me an' said, gimme what you have or I'll blast them Tucker kids . . . why, I'd give up Dreamland. Yes. I'd give up ever'thing so's Bobby could have a chance. An' if'n I could bring back your baby boy . . . ."

"I know, Jeff . . . I know, I know." It was good that the lantern was still inside. At last, after days of strain, Birch let down. He cradled his head in his hands and Jeff knew he was crying.

"I am laid low, Jeff. Everything I ever feared has come upon me in one day, and I can't figger what I done to bring it on. Tried to be honest. Kept my word. Paid my debts. Work hard as I can and do good by Jesus. . . ."

"You done as good as any man I know, Birch."

"Look back at where I was last week. I was thankful to God. Sweet Jesus! Sleepin' in my own bed with a good wife. Our three boys safe under the roof of our home. Owned no man anything. And now . . ."

Birch was played out. His words wound down, faded away into an exhausted silence. Only then did Jefferson speak in a quiet voice.

"You was there that night when the Klan killed my Tisha. They shot her down when they meant t' kill me. Far as I know, those men still walkin' 'round free."

"I know. You suffered more than we ever . . . I know that, and I . . ."

"I ain't makin' out that your burden ain't as hard t' bear as mine! Lawd, no! What I mean is . . . we all gots us a burden, Birch. I done spent ten years in prison for somethin' I didn' do."

"It don't seem fair. None of it." There was an edge of anger in Birch's voice.

"That's jus' what I said. All that time I was studyin' on my suff'rin', on what's fair an' such as that, wonderin' why God let it all happen! Good Book say, Fret not thyself because of evildoers. But why'd He let evil men go an' kill my gal an' lock me away? I hated ever' man who done me wrong! They stole my life, an' I hated 'em deep inside and fierce as a fire! Until it come t' me one day that t'weren't suff'rin' eatin' me up inside. T'weren't loneliness. T'wer hate. Ever' day hate stole my life from me. Hate done locked me up, put leg-irons on my soul! Hate didn't hurt the evildoers that stole my life. They jus' went on their way doin' evil, sayin' what they done was right an' God was their God. Nawsir!" He let his words sink in. "You think it matters t' Garrick Jenson how you feel? Think he's a-gonna change his ways 'cause Birch Tucker call him a liar? Don't make no difference t' him. He spits in God's eye even while he's a-singin' his hymns on Sunday."

"I can't let go of it, Jefferson."

"Let the Lord deal with him, Birch. Y'all got enough trouble."

"I can't let him get away with it."

"Fight him, sure. But leave his soul for Jesus t' deal with. My daddy used t' say that ever' word a man speaks is like a bright speck shinin' in a river bottom. Jesus catch those words in a bottle. He holds a man's promises up to the light to see what's fool's gold an' what ain't. Jesus gonna dump Jenson's promises in the trash heap come Judgment Day, I reckon."

"I can't wait that long."

"It ain't as long as you think. Life travels by mighty quick. Shame t' waste even one hour on what cain't be changed."

"I won't forget what he did to me, to all of us. Today, of all days! How can I leave that behind me?"

"Then today gonna be what you carry with you ever' day. Hate for that man an' his connivin' ways gonna be your load to bear until you lay your burden down, Birch."

He turned, and a ray of lamplight from the window caught on the scars and creases of his battered face. "You lay it down, Birch," he said softly. "Lay it down at Jesus' feet 'fore it crush the life right out of you."

The school bell was already ringing when the borrowed Model-T topped the rise of the hill. From his high perspective, Tom saw the girls' jump rope swing over once, twice, and three times, then fall limp to the ground. Wesley Oaks's football arched upward in one final kick and tumbled down.

Tom was late. He had missed the half hour in the schoolyard before school when kids eased themselves into the day.

"I'm late," he said, anxious to get away from his parents' strained silence.

"You exaggerate, Tom." Trudy stared straight ahead through the windscreen. Her normally straight posture was slumped a bit.

"But I missed the—" His argument halted by a withering look from Birch, Tom finished with a docile "Yes'm."

"I have also been a schoolteacher, and I know that Missus Faraby will not mark you tardy if you are in your seat when she begins the roll."

"Yes'm." Tom agreed because he had no choice. Mrs. Faraby marked tardy if a feller was not standing beside his desk when she opened the roll book.

"We shall telephone Grandma's store from Fort Smith at three-thirty sharp this afternoon," Trudy instructed, "so be on time."

"Yes'm. I will be." His friends were lined up by twos on the front steps. Mrs. Faraby faced them at the head of the column. Fifty-eight heads pivoted in unison as the Ford backfired. Eyebrows lifted as the simultaneous thought penetrated their brains that this was Doc Brown's Ford carrying the Tucker family who had buried little Joey only yesterday. Tom saw this on the faces of his friends and knew exactly what they were thinking because there had been days when he had been on the other side. He hated the fact that grief somehow separated him from everyone else. Most of them would spend the day wondering what to say to him and how to say it. If he played football or marbles like usual, the girls would whisper in amazement that he could be so unfeeling. If he hid out in the classroom and read during recess, Mrs. Faraby would stroll past and pat him on the shoulder or, worse yet, say something to console him. He did not want to be consoled. He did not want sympathy. He wanted . . . what? He wanted it to be last Friday.

"They're looking at us," Tom said. "I told you I should walk."

Mrs. Faraby clapped her hands and pulled the eyes of the students back around to the front. Averting her own gaze, as if the three Tuckers had driven up stark naked, Mrs. Faraby marched her students more quickly than usual into the building.

Suddenly Trudy turned in her seat and grabbed Tom's hand, leaning her cheek upon it. "I know this will be a hard day for you, Tom." Her eyes grazed the band of black mourning crepe on his sleeve. She pulled him close in an awkward embrace over the seat back. "I wish it were not so. I wish we could be here with you." She kissed his forehead and mussed his hair. He was glad everyone had gone inside.

He touched the armband. "It's okay, Mama. I'll pretend it's Penny Auction Day again," he said, trying to call up something cheerful.

Birch did not hug him. He extended his hand. "You'll be the man of the place for a while. Do your work. Mind Willa Mae and Jefferson. We'll get back home with your brother soon as we can."

"Yessir." The school door slammed shut. Tom looked anxiously at the structure. "I . . . tell Bobby . . . I miss him."

"Say your prayers." Trudy's eyes were brimming. If she blinked there would be tears.

"Yes'm." Tom looked away, not wanting her to blink. "Can I go in now?"

He scrambled out of the car and up the steps as the Ford sighed and rattled off. Tom turned just long enough for his mind to take a picture of his mama and daddy. Staring straight forward, they were, off to return Doc's car and catch the ten o'clock train back to Fort Smith.

Mama was dressed in a navy blue skirt and blouse because she had spilled sweet 'taters on her black clothes at the funeral yesterday, and she had nothing else to wear. Strands of chestnut hair tumbled in wisps on the back of her neck from beneath her hat. Birch wore his brown felt fedora and his black suit. Though Mama had brushed it and brushed it, the fabric of his coat was still dusty from the ride out to Meribah.

Another loud backfire, then the Model-T rounded the bend and disappeared behind a screen of pine trees. Tom chewed his lip and briefly considered taking off in the opposite direction, finding a quiet place to sit beside the James Fork. But he did not yield to his instinct for flight. Inside he heard the roll being called. He was T for Tucker, and Mrs. Faraby was only at G for Grier. Sally's voice said, "Present." Tom entered the classroom. Heads swiveled at the groaning of the hinges and the creak of the floorboards.

"Eyes forward," Mrs. Faraby barked in her old, not-to-be-messed-with voice. Then, tender and sympathetic, "Welcome Thomas. Please take your seat."

If only she would have called him tardy and told him to write his crime of lateness a thousand times on the chalkboard!

He sat in his seat. Second seat from the front behind Catfish Pierce. Sally Grier to his right, and Wesley Oaks directly behind him.

"Thomas Tucker?" Mrs. Faraby called his name after hesitating to skip over Bobby.

"Present, Missus Faraby."

"We are glad to have you with us. . . ." Why was she being so nice?

From the corner of his eye, Tom caught sight of Sally looking mournfully at him.

He wanted to jump up and run out. Then, a miracle. The blunt end of a pencil jabbed at his back. *Wesley!* This was not a friendly jab, but the kind of poke, poke, poke, that served warning. *Enjoy the sweetness now, 'cause I'm gonna chew you up!*

Something boiled up inside Tom. He was glad for the pencil in his back, glad for Wesley's disdain. It made him angry, and he much preferred anger to everything else he had felt the last few days. He cast a fierce look over his shoulder at his enemy. *Come on, you green lump of pond scum,* Tom's look said. *Do your worst. . . .*

Roll call completed, they stood for the flag salute.

"I pledge allegiance . . ."

Wesley's harsh whisper substituted a different sort of vow for the patriotic oath.

"Your brother dyin'? It don't change nuthin'!"

"Of the United States of Ameri . . ."

"One week from Friday, Possum killer . . ."

"And to the republic for which . . ."
"Me an' my Boone dog . . ."
"One nation . . ."
"We gonna run y'all inta the ground!"

C H A P T E R   1 5

The aroma of freshly baked bread drifted into the open window of the Fort Smith boardinghouse from the Shipley Baking Company three blocks away. The scent was tantalizing to Trudy and Birch, who had subsisted for a week on one meager meal a day served in the dining room of Miller's Rooming House. Since Trudy's family had moved away, they knew no one in Fort Smith who could help.

"This is the way it is, True." Birch placed his grandfather's pocket watch on the sagging mattress. "Widow Miller charges five dollars a week for each of us, room and breakfast." He stretched out the heavy chain and turned over the twenty-dollar California-minted gold piece the old patriarch had soldered onto the chain. "That's ten dollars a week for both. And we're broke."

"We'll look for less expensive lodgings."

"Won't find cheaper than this unless we go out to the Hooverville and build a cardboard shack like the rest." He tapped the gold coin. "I won't have it."

"Not your grandfather's watch, Birch."

"The double eagle. Just the coin, not the watch. Widow Miller says she'll take it in exchange for four weeks' room and board. . . ."

"Four weeks! For both of us?"

Birch shifted uneasily in his chair. "I told her I had work across the river in Van Buren."

"Birch! You're not going to leave me here?" Tears welled in her eyes.

He grasped her hand. "Four weeks' room and board for you. That's a whole month, Trudy. Maybe Bobby can come home after a month. Widow Miller says you can move in with the old woman, says she'll take Granddaddy's watch fob in payment."

Trudy, beaten, shook her head in dismay. "But where will you go?"

"Man can sleep anyplace long as it's out of the rain. And there ain't been any rain in Arkansas, so I ain't got nothing to worry about."

"Birch . . . give her the watch fob for two weeks for both of us. By then, something will turn up."

"Bobby needs you here. Needs to look up from that tin can he's stuffed into and see his mama's face lookin' down at him. I'll hunt work meantime."

"Then leave me and go home to Shiloh if you must. Sleep in your own bed at least. Eat what I've got canned in the root cellar. I'll stay on here."

He shook his head in disagreement. "Jefferson can handle the place with Tom's help. Look, True, I got to find extra work. I met a guy this morning at the Coca-Cola plant. All of us at the gates lookin' for work. Nothing available down there. Supervisor come out and said he was sorry they weren't hirin'. I told him my boy was in the hospital here and that I needed work real bad. He said they're buildin' a new road over in Van Buren. Told me to give his name to the foreman. Mister Bourne. Ten dollars a week they're payin'. If I can get it, they'll feed me, too. They've got army tents set up and a regular chow wagon. I can maybe come over on weekends."

It was Friday night, and there was a youth sing in Hartford led by Mr. McClung. From the hill, Tom watched the Faraby pickup, crammed fuller than usual, as it made its way toward town. No one had asked Tom to go along because it was still too soon, according to the calendar of grief, for him to have any fun.

He pretended not to care, did not let on how much he envied the other kids squashed into the back of the Model-T. But inside he knew what a rat he was. How could he want to sing while Bobby was in the hospital and Joey so lately gone?

Tom watched the red dust of the road billow up and heard the laughter of his friends and wished beyond anything that he was going to Hartford, too. What kind of person was he anyway to want such a thing at such a time? Selfish. Mean-spirited. Ill-tempered. Rotten to the core. Tom named himself all these things and knew in his heart that Bobby would not be so bad off right now if he had not been left alone on the road.

It had been days since Tom looked anyone straight in the eye. At night when he said his prayers with Willa Mae, the words came out stiff and stilted. From the "Our Father Who Arts" to the "God Blesses," he recited the formula by rote and without feeling. He prayed aloud only because it was expected of him. But he no longer believed God heard him. After all, even the prayers of Mama and Daddy, Willa Mae, Jefferson, and Lily had gone unanswered in the matter of Joey. Why then, would the Almighty listen to Tom, who would rather be singing in Hartford than praying on his knees?

Later that night, as Tom rose up from the cool floor beside his bed, he could feel Willa Mae's gaze, pitying, sorrowful, locked on him. There was a question in those faded old eyes that he could not answer. He avoided looking back at her, choosing to stare instead at his reflection in the windowpane.

Was that really him, he wondered? Or maybe he was seeing the image of his soul, pale and sad and so much younger than he felt. His soul was in need of a haircut, Tom thought. A long pause followed before Willa Mae brushed her calloused hand over his head.

"Anything' you needs to talk over, honey?"

"No'm."

"All right, then. If you needs anythin' in the night, chil', ol' Willa Mae's just yonder in the next room." She asked him the usual things about brushing his teeth and washing his neck and such. When he replied to each query properly, she kissed him good night and tucked him into the cold sheets as if he was still a little boy and not eleven years old. Turning down the lamp, she left him alone with his thoughts. He was glad of the darkness, glad that she could not hear when he began to whisper to God the things that were on his mind.

The secret thoughts were not prayers really. He did not ask for divine guidance with the possum hunt next Friday night nor beg God to let Rosey pick up the scent of the biggest critter in the hills. The matter of the hunt had been on his mind some, but it was of small importance compared to everything else. Tom had no list of requests for the

Almighty, only regrets, just bad feelings and wishes that things had turned out different.

"I shouldn't have left Bobby to come home alone. My fault . . . I know it. I done wrong. Daddy thinks it's my fault. He thought I was takin' care of Bobby. But I went to the picture show instead and . . . If only it was me 'steada him. . . ."

Finally, he closed his eyes and tried to feel his legs getting weaker and his breath coming short and difficult. "It shoulda been me. I'm stronger. Oh, Jesus, lemme trade places. . . ."

For a time he thought his legs really were getting weaker. He imagined Willa Mae coming in to rouse him in the morning and finding him limp like a dishrag, past help, while Bobby, in Fort Smith, jumped up out of that iron lung thing and asked Mama for hoecakes and grits for breakfast. Wouldn't that be some kind of miracle? Wouldn't the doctors be surprised? And maybe Daddy and Mama could get a refund on all they paid the hospital and they could pay back the Jenson blood money right away and come home, stay home in Shiloh forever. . . .

But then Tom felt the necessity to pee and his legs, still strong, carried him to the outhouse. Betrayal.

Wide awake now, he sat on the porch step to gaze up at the thick band of the Milky Way and wonder what little Joey was doing up there. And what was old Hock Canfield doing now that he wasn't old anymore? Probably teaching Joey to hunt possum angels. They wouldn't kill a possum in heaven, Tom figured, only catch it for fun and turn it loose afterward in the branches of some great, golden hickory tree.

In the cool night Tom heard the distant backfire of the Faraby pickup as it returned from Hartford. Snatches of happy melody drifted across the hills of Shiloh. He pretended it was Joey and Hock and a flock of angels singing to him.

I've got a home in Glory land
That outshines the sun . . .

Tom laid his head on his knees and croaked out the last of the verse as the voices echoed in the valley, then rose up and passed beyond his hearing.

Look away beyond the blue.

Jefferson had picked up the hammer right where Birch had laid it down the week before. The sound of its hard crack against the new boards of the corral gate made the Tucker place sound alive again. Half expecting to see his father at work on the fence, Tom emerged from the house. Jefferson paused a moment as the screen door slammed.

Sunlight glinted on the auburn feathers of Joey's chicken. Jefferson had placed the hen on an upright post of the fence where she now cocked her head and blinked down at the big man with interest.

"Mornin'," Jefferson said around a mouthful of nails and wagged the hammer in greeting.

"You got Henny out of the coop." Tom plunged his hands into the pockets of his overalls and walked slowly toward the gate.

Jeff plucked the nails from his lips and stood to scratch the chicken's neck. "Mama says this hen's pinin' for comp'ny." He shook his head in wonder. "Never seen the like in no other chicken 'fore this. You'd think she was a dawg with feathers. Your mama sure do make ever' critter into some kinda pet."

"She does," Tom agreed, reaching up to stroke Henny.

"That milk cow, Esmerelda? Bawls ever' time your mama come near the barn. And the sow. What's she call the sow?"

"Miss Lucy."

"Never heard of a sow named that."

"Mama says it reminds her of her third-grade teacher, Miss Lucy. They look alike or something."

Jefferson peered doubtfully toward the hog pen and scratched behind his ear as if he was trying to fathom a third-grade teacher with the looks and personality of a white Chester hog.

"Sunburn real easy, did she? This schoolteacher? Miz Lucy?" Jeff asked.

"I guess so." Tom shrugged.

"Remin' me t' ask your mama when she come home." Jeff grinned.

Tom did not want to talk about how much he wished his mama was home, about how much he missed her. "Henny'll be glad to see her."

"I reckon even little pea-brain chickens can miss somebody as good as your mama is. And your mama sets great store by this bird. Hate t' see her stop layin' 'cause of neglect." Jefferson leaned against the rails and put his hand on his back as if it pained him.

Tom blurted. "She was Joey's chicken."

"So she was."

"I don't think she misses Joey, though. Don't think she even knows . . . he's gone . . . really."

"Critters knows such things. Dawgs. Cats. Cows. Mules. Even chickens, I reckon. Stuff comes to 'em outta the blue. Sometimes they just sit there, an' a fella can see some thought strike their little brains. They jus' look off kinda dreamy-like an' . . . see there?" He jerked a thumb at the chicken.

Henny, her head cocked curiously, peered up toward a single passing cloud.

"Mama says critters see things folks don't see," Tom remarked quietly.

"Angels an' such," Jefferson agreed. "My mama always say so, too. Like Balaam's ass in the Good Book. I do believe it. Mebbe that's why they don' grieve so fierce as human critters."

Silence. Tom heaved a sigh. "Wish I could see."

Jeff put a big hand on Tom's shoulder. "Lawd give human critters different kind of sight, I reckon. He call it faith. Good Book say we have hope not 'cause we see with our eyes, but . . . we see the truth . . . *in here*. . . ." He tapped his thumb over Tom's heart.

"I'd rather see stuff with my eyes."

"Only thing Jesus ask of us is to trust God even when things is tough."

"Don't know what I'm supposed t' trust no more, Jeff."

"Just that God ain't stopped lovin' y'all. Your mama. Daddy. Bobby.

"What about Joey?"

"God must love little Joey special, 'cause he done call that little baby home to glory an' right outta this hard world. Think of it, Tom!" Jefferson gazed up at the cloud and for a moment his face was transfigured with longing and joy. "God done let Joey *see*! Let that chil' see all the things we're still down here *wantin'* t' see! Now your baby brother know ever'thing you don't know! He won't never have t' grieve. Never have t' hurt inside nor wonder 'bout t'morrow! No, don't you worry none 'bout God lovin' your baby brother! Why, Jesus be holdin' Joey in His arms."

"I sat out most the night. Lookin' at the stars and wishin' something would show itself. Or some voice would . . . explain, you know?"

Jefferson hummed his understanding. "We gots t' wait for that. That's what *hope* means. Someday we all gonna understand. Good Book says on that great day the Lawd gonna wipe away *ever'* tear."

"But . . . I want to know *now!* I prayed last night that it'd be *me* 'stead of Bobby. That I could die an' everything'd be all right for everybody else."

"Like Joey, huh? I know that prayer. Uh-huh. I know what you mean. Sometime, sometime it seem too hard t' bear. We stay here whilst others leave. . . . Oh, yes. It is hard."

"Maybe too hard."

"Not ever that hard. Too much good all mix in with the hard. . . . Gotta let your life play out to the end, boy. Be like Jesus. Love folks like Jesus did. Jesus change ever'thing for the whole worl' but one person at a time. . . . Who knows? Mebbe jus' by livin', keepin' on, we can make things better too. . . ."

"Can't make things like they was. Can't make Bobby walk. Bring Joey back."

"I know you gonna see that brother of yours again one day. I gots folks over yonder I'm just longin' t' see again, too. Someday . . . well, I know it's gonna happen. Goodbye ain't forever. I see that truth inside here." He tapped his own broad chest. "Life is mighty hard sometime, Tom, but it's good, too, ain't it? Us that believe, we're all bound for Gloryland. But we're goin' there one at a time! An' Tom, even if you an' me lives t' be ol' mens like my daddy was? We gonna come t' the end of our long journey, an' we gonna say, 'Jesus? How'd it get by so fast?'"

Jefferson grinned. "Meantime, we all jus' gotta trust Jesus! Trust is all the Lawd ask. And there ain't no other way t' get through trials an' come out better for it."

Jefferson picked up the hammer after that and turned his attention back to the corral. Tom helped him mend the broken boards of the gate and in the simple act felt somehow mended. Not altogether mended, but better, anyhow.

No angels had spoken to him from heaven. Just Jefferson, who was walking through this hard old world just like Tom. Fixing broken things. Jefferson, with his cauliflower ears and his skinned knuckles and his bib overalls hitched up by one strap. Not anything like an angel.

Suddenly, it was possible again for Tom to talk of hounds and possum hunts and Wesley Oaks and the full moon next Friday night.

It was the duty of Grandma Amos to sort through the mail as it arrived at the Shiloh General Store. There was seldom much in the delivery. Plenty of bills came these days, and there was sometimes a letter from someone's far-off relation, like Willa Mae's children or her sister in Washington, D.C., or Trudy's cousin Max. But never had anyone in these parts received the volume that arrived for Thomas Tucker. This being the case, Grandma made much of holding Trudy's daily correspondence up to the light and wondering aloud who would be writing little Tom Tucker so regularly.

Willa Mae did not know if Grandma Amos truly forgot from one day to the next who sent the letters or if she just delighted in announcing in a offhanded way that yet another item with news from the big city had arrived in the post for young Tom.

As the gnarled hands slipped Trudy Tucker's plain envelopes into the numbered pigeonhole also labeled with spidery letters, S. Tucker, Grandma announced, "Did you know, Willa Mae, the S. stands for old Sam Tucker, who was Birch's daddy? Now, that was a man that liked his likker. A mean'un when he was in his cups." She shook her head. "Someday I'm a-gonna change the name on that box. Mebbe change it to T. for Tom. Mebbe P. for Possum. 'Deed I am." But she never got around to changing it.

Letters for Tom arrived from Fort Smith each day at the Shiloh Store post office by way of Brother Williams's mail pouch. Willa Mae could have easily carried the messages back to the Tucker farmhouse since she was spending every night there with Tom, but Tom liked to come by the store each afternoon when school let out. It was his custom to stand at the mail counter and stare at his box through the bars of the cage at his box and ask, "Is there anything for me?"

Then Grandma Amos would tell the boy to be patient, that her eyes weren't what they used to be and her legs didn't travel fast no more and she could only do one thing at a time. . . .

It was a sort of game they played, a game that drew out the suspense and enabled Tom to savor the moment of holding his mama's letter in his hands and carefully opening the seal and finally reading the latest news. And knowing the news was probably not bad. A letter was a safe thing to get, whereas a phone call or a telegram would have been expensive, and such expense would have been justified only by delivering bad news.

Today, the Thursday before the great possum hunt, the news was mostly good. Bobby was holding his own. His spirits were up since getting Tom's letter and all the other letters and pictures the kids at school had drawn. They were stuck up all over the iron lung and pinned to the curtains of his room.

Mama stayed with Bobby at the hospital every day. Daddy was off in Van Buren working on paving a new road there. Two weeks' work, it was, but the Lord was providing. They had been able to cash Grandpa's gold coin, the one on the watch chain, to pay an entire four weeks' lodging. Trudy had read Tom's letter to Bobby about the great possum hunt to take place come Friday. She wrote that, upon hearing the news, Bobby had smiled for the first time since he got sick and said in a loud voice, "I'm gonna pray Jesus that Tom and Rosey kick Wesley Oaks's a—!"

Bobby had said the forbidden word right out, in front of the doctor and nurses, although Trudy did not spell it in the letter because it was one of those words she thought ought to be stricken from the *Webster's*.

Then Bobby looked at Trudy and said, "You can't whup me, 'cause I'm in this tin can."

At this remark the doctor had stated to everyone that he believed Bobby Tucker would be out hunting possum himself by next autumn and that Trudy would have a devil of a time keeping up.

Tom read the letter to himself first, then he read it aloud to Grandma Amos, Willa Mae, Jefferson, Lily, and the babies and finally to Brother Williams, who carried the story back to Hartford and Dee Brown's barbershop. From there it spread to who-knows-where. By Friday morning everyone was talking about Bobby and Tom and the great possum hunt.

CHAPTER 16

Rosey felt it, too: the tension of the night, the pent-up excitement that preceded the hunt. She jumped when Tom's fingers brushed the nape of her neck, and she quivered all over like a watch spring about to bust. "Easy, girl," he murmured, knowing he was speaking as much for his own benefit as for the dog's.

"You all right, Tom?" Jeff asked.

"Nerved up some, I reckon," Tom replied.

"Don't hurt nothin'. Keep you sharp. You remember all what we talked about?"

"Yessir, I think so." Tom patted the hatchet that hung from the tool loop on the waist of his overalls.

Though it was not yet seven in the evening, a dark stillness flowed out from under the trees, filling the dirt lane the way rising waters engulf a riverbank. The flood of night gathered down in the rift of the James Fork, swelled upward to swamp Buggy Hill on the east, and then lapped against Sugarloaf to the west. Stars popped out, little challenged by thin, wispy mare's-tail clouds.

"Gonna be a grand night for possum huntin'," Tom said. Rosey wagged an uneasy wiggle of agreement. "Wish you could go with me, Jeff."

"Wouldn't be right," Jeff said. "I couldn't keep still no way. 'Sides, best you do this on your own. You an' Rosey is ready, sure enough."

Ahead and off to the side, Tom saw lanterns being lit at the schoolyard. A match flared, multiplied itself to become the orange glow of a lamp, then jumped to a second and a third before being waved out. The glow of the three lanterns brightened to yellow and steadied. So he and Rosey were not early, as he had planned. Others were there ahead of them. "C'mon," he urged, and they doubled their pace toward the meeting.

Jim Brown, Mister Winters, and Brother Williams stood within a circle of lamplight, waiting for the contestants. Wesley and his dog Boone had not yet arrived; for that, Tom was grateful.

"Howdy, Tom, Jeff," Brother said. "You an' Rosey ready?" Tom acknowledged that he was indeed prepared for the competition. "Well. . . ." Brother squinted at a pocket watch the size and shape of one of Willa Mae's biscuits. "It lacks five minutes of the hour, so we cain't say yet that the other team is a no-show."

"Who's a no-show?" Wesley Oaks growled, strutting into the circle from the opposite side. "Me an' Boone been here an hour already. We run a rabbit just to get warmed up."

If this information was meant to intimidate Tom, Wesley's dog seemed to have a similar purpose. Stiff-legged and bristling, and twenty pounds heavier, the bluetick hound advanced on his sister, who promptly cowered and lowered her head. Wesley laughed a coarse, ugly snicker. "Both of 'em are yeller. She wants to give up right now, see?"

Tom kicked Boone away from Rosey and doubled up his fists. "Wanta see yeller?" he challenged.

Jim Brown's hand yanked him back as Brother scolded, "Now, remember the bond!" Brother glared at both boys, the rays of the lamps on the ground stretching the shadow of his bushy eyebrows up across his forehead and making him appear much meaner than he sounded. "Let's get the formalities done and get this show on the road. First, to the matter of witnesses."

"Witnesses?" Wesley drawled. "What for?"

Brother gave him a withering glance. "On accounta there's been contests where some scalawag had him a critter already cotched and waitin' in a cage. For this here hunt, it's only what you nab between now and sunup and bring back to this spot counts."

Brother peered sternly at Tom to see if he understood the terms and continued after Tom's nod. "I," he said archly, "cain't be a witness, seein' as how my Emmaline spawned both pups and I might unmeaning give assistance. Witnesses are strictly prohibited from helpin' in any way," Brother warned, flashing his bushy brows around the circle, "less'n the contestant gets hisself lost or hurt and says he gives up."

Brother extended a cupped hand from which protruded two matchsticks. "Tom, you first. Short straw draws Mister Winters as witness. Other contestant goes with Jim."

Tom plucked a matchstick and held it up for inspection. It was full length. Brother opened his palm to show the other broken off short. So Tom would be accompanied on the hunt by the blacksmith and Wesley by the pharmacist.

"Now to the other matter: bound'ries," Brother said, but his instructions were disturbed by the arrival of an audience. Rumbling in from town in the barber's Oldsmobile were Dee and Doc Brown. At about the same time, Squirrel and Pigpen Hocott and Cub Palmer materialized from the shadows. Tom had not expected there to be onlookers. All the newcomers pledged to wait all night at the finish so as to greet the winner.

"Where's Boomer?" Doc wanted to know.

"Too noisy," Brother said. "Left him back at the stable. We got too much jawin' an' carryin' on as it is."

Doc grew quiet, but Tom saw him hide a smile behind his hand.

"All you spectators will keep still! As I was sayin'," Brother resumed in an impatient, official voice. "Bound'ries. North confine is the highway betwixt Hartford and Mansfield. You can range as far south as your legs can carry you, keepin' in mind the deadline o'course. We draw again for east and west, the dividin' line bein' the Jim Fork. West is short straw. Wesley, you choose."

This was by far the more critical decision. The land west of the creek sloped across bottomland, through gooseberry thickets, and then rapidly climbed a ridge of oak and pine that stretched for two miles: perfect mixed cover for possums.

East of the streambed lay similar bottomland, but the only grove big enough to have the hollow trees favored by critters was a little knob that covered three-quarters of a mile. The eastern territory also included the Ouachita Hills, but hunting there would mean crossing miles of open, scrubby ground and being much farther away from the finish line.

Wesley chewed his lower lip, his brow furrowed with concentration. Tom, his fingers crossed on the hand he held behind his back, jumped suddenly when Rosey licked that hand.

Making his selection, Wesley drew out the chosen match with painful slowness. "Ha!" he snorted with triumph. "Short straw again. Wanna give up now, Possum Tucker?"

Tom's sigh of relief was covered by Brother's remonstrance against fightin' words. Tom was pleased that he had drawn the same side of the creek where he and Bobby and David had run ol' granddaddy possum; he just didn't want Wesley to know that he had been hoping for the east side all along. For the tenth time he jingled the sixteenpenny nails that filled the back pocket of his overalls and then bent over to speak words of encouragement to Rosey.

At the word "Go!" shouted by Brother Williams, Wesley and Boone sprang away into the darkness. They set out at a fast trot, forcing the short-legged pharmacist to run to keep up.

Tom started off at a much more studied gait. He aimed Rosey northeast toward a place he had been thinking of all week. Although he had a likely beginning point in mind, Tom did not want to rush Rosey. He wanted her to settle into the rhythm of the hunt. Tom imagined his hound inhaling the night and the scent of its inhabitants, then drawing a kind of picture in her canine brain of the whereabouts of all the critters. He did not want to make her miss something by forcing her to hurry.

Jim kept pace, the lantern swinging with his easy stride as if he were signaling a train. Behind them a bonfire flared as the rooters lit a pile of brush and prepared to spend the night camped on the school grounds.

Answering blaze with blaze, the orange disk of the rising moon crept above the rim of the surrounding hills. It looked like an enormous forest fire on the horizon. And as if propelled by the force of the moon's appearance, a cool, fragrant breeze swept over Shiloh. "Let me tell you," Jim Brown said, thumping his free hand on his chest. "A night like tonight makes a man glad to be alive."

Words of agreement were ready to tumble out of Tom's mouth, and he checked them just an instant before they did. Glad to be alive? Was it right for him to feel that way with his baby brother so lately buried and his other brother still in the hospital? Tom felt instantly ashamed that he had forgotten both grief and worry so easily. What would the blacksmith have thought if Tom had returned his intended offhand remark? But he had to make some acknowledgement of Jim's words. What should he say?

But then the need to respond was relieved by the baying of Wesley's dog, Boone. Although they had been parted only a few minutes, it appeared that the other side already had the advantage. Tom called Rosey back and made her sit beside him. Together they listened to the sounds of the chase. Presently they heard Wesley's angry voice shouting at Boone.

The glow of the lantern held aloft showed a grin on Jim's face, but still he waited for Tom to speak. "Boone must've took out after another rabbit." Tom laughed.

"That's just the way I figure it," Jim agreed. "That Wesley should have known better. Having Boone practice on rabbits made that hound think rabbits were what was wanted. Maybe Wesley isn't the great possum killer he thinks he is."

The pleasure of this shared revelation eased Tom's guilt. He thought that Bobby would also like to hear what a blunder Wesley had made. 'Course, it was now more important than ever that Tom and Rosey win. Any other result was unthinkable. It would be a victory in which Bobby could share, especially if the win included revenge on ol' granddaddy possum.

And striking the trail of granddaddy possum was exactly what Tom had in mind. It was not enough to catch just any possum. Winning depended on bringing in the biggest animal, and Tom was certain there were none larger in those parts than the critter that had given him his nickname.

The moon had risen high enough above the horizon to have shrunk in size and turned more silvery before Rosey struck her first hint of possum aroma. They had reached the antique apple trees on the swell of Cherokee Hill. The tangle of almost bare branches, the small, knobby fruit mostly devoured or fallen and rotted, did not look like a promising spot. The ancient orchard, planted long before the recollection of living men, was mute testimony that some frontiersman had settled here long enough to call the spot home and to encircle his cabin with fruit trees. But now the pioneer, his family, his home, and his memory were long gone. Only this patch of gnarled trees remained.

But this location was Tom's ace in the hole. With the persimmons that possums favored almost all gone for the season, Tom counted on the lumbering granddaddy critter's being bright enough to have substituted another spot to dine.

Sniffing among the damp places where apples had dropped and decayed, Rosey stiffened and barked once. It was her way of announcing that she had located what was wanted, but she did not go charging off into the brush.

Asking Jim to bring the lantern, Tom praised Rosey, then pushed her aside as he bent low and studied the tracks in the dark earth. Possum tracks, to be sure, but too small to be *the* possum. Taking Rosey firmly by the collar, Tom led her away, circling to the other side of the grove. "Aren't you afraid of wasting—" Jim began, then stopped talking abruptly as Brother's warning about not giving assistance came to his mind.

"It's all right," Tom answered. Then he explained his plan. "If we don't cut granddaddy's trail, then we'll come back here. But not yet."

From far off, on the other side of the James Fork Creek, Boone dog yapped again. The sound was eager, anxious. From the hilltop, Tom could see Mr. Winters's lantern race forward along a ridgeline before flicking out as Wesley and his witness plunged into a ravine.

"I admire your assurance, son," Jim said. "But it looks to me like your competition has warmed up some."

It was on the far side of the hill and on the downward slope that Rosey barked another time. The grade was all dried grass and tumbled rocks, and for a time no readable prints could be found. A possum again, sure enough, but was it the right one this time?

No tracks at all could Tom find. The smoothly polished surface of a fallen oak's trunk gave no clues, nor did the rounded nubs of granite boulders that glimmered in the moonlight. Should he put Rosey on this trail now or continue searching for proof? Tom adjusted the burlap sack that was tied around his waist like a sash, turning the knot back to the front. He called for the lantern again, looking intently at the soil just below each lump of stone.

It was beneath the edge of the fourth boulder that Tom found what he sought: in the bare earth between the rock and the grass, a single track. It was clearly a possum's footprint and a big one. Granddaddy possum had been clever, jumping from rock to stump, but he had slipped up once and left this one clue to his passing. "This is it," Tom whooped. "And it's fresh. Let's go, Rosey!"

The chase was on. Rosey, pleased at being allowed to follow the scent, launched out ahead as if she had been shot from a gun. Ranging out of sight in the darkness, each time she circled back to ask the humans if they couldn't travel faster and move a little more quickly. Ignoring the baying and howling that still reached Tom's ears from the other pursuit, Rosey contented herself with brief, businesslike yips.

The trail led due north. In half an hour, Tom came to the first sign that the possum knew he was being followed. Rosey led the way to a rotten log beside a spring from which the granddaddy critter had been scratching a meal of grubs. Interrupted by the sounds of the hunt coming along his back trail, old possum had gotten careless and left a flurry of skittering tracks. Immediately Tom climbed a nearby cottonwood and took his bearings. Just over a mile away was the high ground along which ran the Hartford road. Tom shinnied down and, dragging Rosey away from the scent, set off at a run along the slender trace of an old trail.

"Tom," the blacksmith puffed, startled at the sudden sprint. "I still can't give you any advice, but would you mind telling me what you're up to?"

Over his shoulder Tom called back, "He's headed straight for the road. If we don't get ahead of him and turn him, he'll cross the boundary and we'll lose him for sure."

"But how do you know he won't turn off?"

"Because I know where he's going . . . if we just don't give him no other choice!"

Most of the next hour was spent jumping over deadfalls, dodging around gooseberry brambles, and losing scraps of clothing and skin on unexpected wire fences. Once Tom caught his foot in a trailing vine and sprawled full length, only to jump up immediately and race on. Another time there was a delay while Tom set Rosey free from a branch on which she had caught her collar. But mostly the boy and the dog ranged easily side by side, their witness panting along behind.

When they reached the grade of the Rock Island line running parallel to the highway, Tom declared that they had come far enough. "We're ahead of him now," he declared. "Okay, Rosey. Let's pick up his trail again."

The moonlight painted the swale in silver and black, as if the real world had been replaced by a newspaper photo of the same scene. An owl hooted and rushed off in a flurry of rustling wings. Mice skittered under the fallen leaves where they rummaged for hickory nuts. Over the knife edge of a bare rise, the full orb of the moon floated in a pond.

And just ahead, on the inner slope of the bowl containing the small lake was the rapidly bumbling form of granddaddy possum. He looked like a furry gray bowling ball rolling downhill in the shimmering, dollar-bright glow. "After him, Rosey!" Tom shouted. "Don't let him get to the water."

Racing forward again, Rosey was no longer silent. Barking and yelping for all she was worth, she and granddaddy appeared to be on a collision course. Tom had a moment's worry about whether the animal would actually tackle his dog head-on. But the possum was not a 'coon or bear. Sensing that his retreat by water was cut off, he reversed himself, lumbering up the slope and back into the darkness.

Tom and Rosey followed the spoor directly to the base of the old hickory tree where granddaddy had taken shelter before. Looking to see if Rosey agreed, Tom noted that the redbone hound was stretched up the trunk of the tree, confirming what he expected. Jim Brown arrived a minute later, wheezing and out of breath. "I tell you, I am about done up," he said between gasps. "Did you lose him?"

Tom shook his head. "He's in that hole up yonder," he said, pointing up into the shadows.

"Where?" Jim asked in disbelief. "I can't see anything. Those limbs are as bare as can be, and there's no possum up there."

Tom tried to explain where the hollow in the trunk was located, but no matter how high Jim held the lantern, he could not make out the opening. "Well," he said at last. "Even if there is a den up there, how are you going to reach it? There's no limb low enough, I can't help you, and you can't drag a ladder all the way out here. Now what?"

"Want a sandwich?" Tom answered without explaining a thing. "I got a bottle of coffee, too."

"Tom Tucker, have you lost your senses? You don't even know if that animal's up there, or how you can get to him if he is, and you want to sit down and have a picnic?"

Tom shrugged and unwrapped the burlap potato sack from around his waist. From it he produced a folded waxed-paper heap of Willa Mae's brown-sugar and butter sandwiches and the jug of coffee. As he munched the sweet, crunchy sandwiches, he gathered fallen limbs and branches, testing them for soundness and rejecting several that were either too big or too small.

When he had collected a sizable pile of sticks, he sat down on the ground and, using the hatchet, trimmed a flat place in the center of each. Rosey lay on the earth nearby, watching the proceedings with interest and wagging as Tom tossed her crusts of bread sticky with butter and sugar.

"Look there," Jim exclaimed, pointing to the west. The pinpoint of yellow light, which was Wesley's lantern, had blossomed to become a dark red blaze on the farthest ridge. "Boone dog must have treed one," the blacksmith reported. "Looks like Wesley built a fire beside the tree to smoke him out. Is that what you're doing with all these branches? It would have been easier just to gather brush."

"I don't aim to cook him before I skin him," Tom retorted, and he carried the trimmed boughs to the trunk of the tree. Dipping into his hip pocket for the spikes, Tom nailed a waist-high crosspiece and then another as far up as he could reach. "There's more coffee left," he said, climbing up to nail another limb still higher on the trunk before swarming back down and returning with two more.

"Well, I'll be . . ."

It was the work of only a few minutes to reach the level of the hole in the trunk. An ominous rustling like a coiled snake let Tom know that the occupant was indeed home, watchful, and not willing to be trespassed on. Remembering only too well what had happened to Davey, he knew this was the trickiest part.

Once more back down the improvised ladder, Tom selected two of the stoutest sticks, round like broom handles, and tied them against his waist with the now-empty sack. He asked for the lantern and carried it up, hanging it on a nail in the trunk above the possum's lair. Looking in at a furry mass in which two beady eyes shone and a pair of yellow fangs snicked together, Tom saw his adversary face-to-face.

Keeping a cautious distance back from the hole, Tom poked the first stick into the opening . . . and almost had it wrenched out of his hands. Granddaddy possum grabbed the branch in his teeth and locked his jaws down tight. Swinging his head from side to side, the critter seemed almost human, using the limb as a club to bat Tom off his perch. This was the point at which Tom had to trust Jeff's advice the most. *He won't let go once he's catched hold,* Jeff had said, *long as he thinks he's chewin' on you. Do what you gotta do.*

Tom whipped out the other trimmed stick as if he were drawing a sword. He jabbed the possum in the throat and whacked him over the head. But not to make him let go, oh, no. If Jeff was wrong, if the possum decided to charge the attacker and not the weapon, if he came snapping out of the hole right at Tom's face, Tom would have no choice but to jump.

The animal snarled angrily and made ratlike grinding noises with its teeth, but it never let go of the stick in its mouth. Presently, prodded in it's flanks and struck on its backbone, the creature swelled up, frothed at the mouth, and rolled its eyes back in its head. It had sulled.

Tom released his hold on the sticks so he could wield his hand axe. "How're you doin' up there?" Jim called.

"All right," Tom yelled down. He hoped his voice did not sound as quaky to the blacksmith as it did in his own ears.

"Wesley must be having a time of it," Jim reported. "There's a blaze big enough to light up half the country."

It was difficult for Tom to pay attention to the blacksmith or to anything except the business at hand, because the hardest part of this whole operation was starting. Chopping around the edges of the hollow, Tom set out to enlarge the opening so the possum could be pulled out. *Don't let him wake up,* Jeff had cautioned. *He'll come for the hand holdin' the hatchet just sure as you're born.*

The awkward moment arrived when Tom, unable to swing the blade left-handed, was leaning out to the side of the tree trunk in order to expand the far side of the hole. Before the boy was able to separate the noise he was making from a renewed scratching inside the lair, the possum rushed the opening. With a panicked cry, Tom flung the hatchet into the air, missed his handhold, and dangled from one grip, his feet scrabbling against the rough bark of the tree.

The possum lunged for Tom's hand, its teeth snapping in the air just a fraction of an inch away from the boy's fingers. Then Tom's feet regained the rungs and his left hand closed around the club. Frantically he pounded the possum around the whiskers and between the shiny black eyes. With an exasperated sigh, the fat rodentlike body collapsed in imitation of death throes once more.

"Do you need the ax again?" Jim asked. "'Cause if you do, you'll have to come down for it. The rules won't let me fetch it to you."

Tom studied the size of the cleft in the tree trunk. "I think it's big enough now," he announced, hoping he was correct. He did not want to even think about climbing down to retrieve the ax, then having to face a newly revived possum again.

Experimentally tapping granddaddy brought no response. A flurry of whacks and thumps all around the den produced nothing more threatening than a drip of slobber and the possum equivalent of a snore. The moment of truth had arrived. *You gotta hold him secure,* Jeff advised. *Like any critter, he'll wake up if he thinks he's gonna fall.*

For at least the tenth time, it crossed Tom's mind that maybe he should reclaim the hatchet after all and use it to bash the possum in the head. Once more, he rejected the notion in favor of his original plan.

Taking a deep breath and holding it, Tom reached both arms into the hole and threw the opening of the gunnysack over the puffed-up animal. Tom pulled the bag like a net, scooping up the critter, then dragged his catch toward the crack that was now large enough to pass the bloated body. A shudder ran all down Tom's spine when he was nose-to-nose with the beast, a sense that the slightest bobble would find a snarling, snapping nightmare scrambling out of the trap right at the level of his eyes.

Tom eased the weight of the sack outside the hole, hunching his body up on the tree trunk to support the descent. He hugged the possum in a tight embrace, and when he had to breathe at last, he drew in a lungful of possum smell: rotten fruit, damp earth, and a heavy, oily, musky stench.

Then, abruptly, it was done. Granddaddy possum was safely inside the sack and the mouth tied shut. Whether he thought he was resting inside a possum-sized hammock, Tom could not say, but the animal made no protest as the boy slung the coarse bag over his shoulder and carefully descended the hickory tree.

Jim had not even been watching the end of the drama. "Good Lord," he said, staring off toward the west. "It looks like Wesley and Mister Winters have set the whole woods on fire over there. What a time they'll have keeping that from spreading into McCaskill's hay. Say! Are you done? Is that him?" Jim gingerly prodded the lumpy sack with a boot toe.

Nodding wearily, Tom sank down on the ground. "Is there any of that coffee left?" he asked. "I could use some."

The sky was graying toward dawn before Tom heard the noise of the returning men. He had been drowsing on the ground, leaning against the schoolhouse wall. Rosey dreamed at his side, her twitching feet showing that she was replaying the chase in her mind. Tom opened one eye and watched Doc and Dee Brown sway into view, supporting Mister Winters between them. "You aren't having a heart attack, Louis, nor apoplexy either," Doc was reassuring the drooping pharmacist. "It's just good, old-fashioned exhaustion. We are all of us getting too old to be gallivanting around the countryside all night. Add to that the chopping and shoveling of the past few hours, and it's a wonder any of us are still standing."

Tom's view of those who had rushed to fight the brushfire accidentally set by Wesley confirmed Doc's words. Their clothes were streaked with dirt and soot and torn in places that looked painful to the wearers. Dee Brown's face was bright pink beneath the layer of smoke smudges, as if he had been sunburned.

"What a night!" Brother Williams exclaimed as he joined the group. He looked altered somehow, and as Tom studied the pointed features, he realized that the livery owner's eyebrows had been singed off. The fire did not seem to have damaged his mood, however. "Somebody did oughta write a song about it. Yessir, the great possum hunt and fire of thirty-one. It'd be a humdinger."

Jefferson spotted Tom and came over. Jeff seemed unharmed by the night's festivities. The faded blue of his overalls was masked by black and earth-colored stripes, but otherwise he was unchanged from the night before. He smiled as he saw the bulging sack by Tom's feet and widened his eyes in question. Tom gave an answering grin. "Where's Stumpy?"

Before Jeff could reply, Brother Williams continued his call for a musical tribute to the event. "Yessir, biggest possum I ever seen! Biggest in these parts!"

That comment shook the last drowsiness from Tom. How could they know? The gunnysack was still tied securely, granddaddy possum still tucked away. Jim Brown had promised not to tell. Had he broken his word?

The crunching of the weeds coming toward the school from the creek bottom announced another returnee. Wesley Oaks plodded slowly up the hill, dragging something behind him. In many respects the boy doing the hauling and the load he pulled could have been interchanged: Both were overgrown; both were covered with grime, soot, and brambles; and both were missing patches of hair. But the form being towed into camp was unquestionably dead; it was a big possum. Boone dog ranged alongside his master and their quarry. The hound's head was down, his tongue hung out, and he limped on one foreleg, but he wagged his way into the circle of men to receive their praise.

"The way that possum jumped and ran down that tree with his hair all smoking, he looked like a flaming meteor."

"And Boone dog got right in his face and turned him ever which way till Wesley pounded him senseless."

"Too bad about your aim, Wesley. I reckon Boone's leg ain't broke. He'll be all right in a week or so."

"I can taste that ice cream right now," Wesley said to nobody in particular.

"What ice cream?" Brother Williams wanted to know.

"All the ice cream that five-dollar prize is gonna buy me," Wesley crowed.

Jeff spoke up. "'Pears to me you might be celebratin' a touch early. This contest did have two entries, right?"

"What?"

"What's he mean?"

"Cain't be nothin' like . . ."

"Jim, how come you didn't tell us?" Doc demanded of his brother, who had rejoined the circle last of all.

"Because Tom asked me not to, till it was official. Besides," the blacksmith continued, "just what part of the forest fire did you want me to interrupt with the news?"

"All right, all right," Brother Williams scolded in his best official voice, though it squeaked and cracked from all the smoke he had inhaled. "Let's see this other animal."

Through the sack, Tom poked granddaddy possum real hard to make certain the animal was still sulled, then he untied the string and let the mouth of the burlap bag fall open.

"Well, I'll be a suck-egg mule."

"Did you ever . . . ?"

"How could there be two so big? Twins, maybe?"

The whine of Wesley's voice came over the exclamations. "But mine is still bigger, ain't it? Ain't it?"

"This calls for an official weigh-in, wouldn't you say?" Doc inquired of a stupefied Brother Williams.

"Yep. Yes, indeedy. We gotta go to town to Mister Winters's for the weighin'," Brother agreed.

"Wait just a minute," Wesley protested. "How come his possum is still breathin'? How'd he catch somethin' so big and bring it back alive? Maybe he had this one hid out."

"Wesley," Jim Brown said sternly. "I was there, and I saw him take it. Are you calling me a liar?"

Wesley backed away from the brawny blacksmith's scowling face. "No sir, I just . . . Boone and me . . . ours is still bigger," he concluded lamely.

"That'll be for the scales to decide," Brother opined. "Ain't nothin' in the rules says the critter gotta be dead to count. Let's take 'em to town."

The crowd gathered around the front porch of Mr. Winters's pharmacy in Hartford was much larger than the group that had witnessed the hunt from the school grounds, although none of those participants would miss the finale either. The audience that speculated on the wooden porch and around the yellow-painted curbstone and atop the hitching rail and balanced on the water trough rim included Hocotts and Palmers, Canfields, Browns, Turners, and a host of Farabys. Sally Grier was there, beaming at Tom every time he glanced her way. The McCaskills showed up in force to see for themselves the cause of the ruckus that had first threatened and thereafter saved their hay. Pop Lyle, unable to imagine why there was no line in front of his ticket booth the morning of a Harry Carey western double feature, had hung out a "back in ten minutes" sign and joined the official weigh-in as well.

"Friends," Brother Williams croaked. It sounded as if he and a bullfrog were doing a ventriloquism act. He cleared his throat, downed a swig of ninety-proof Echols' Catarrh Cure thoughtfully provided by Mr. Winters, and tried again. "Friends," he said with more of his customary strength, "we have had the most stunnin' possum hunt ever seen in these parts. And you are about to witness the official conclusion."

"AWFUL CONFUSION!" Boomer echoed. It had not been possible to keep him away from the prize ceremony, although Brother had tried.

"Keep still, Boomer! As I was sayin', a triumph of man an' hound workin' as a team."

"HOW'D BOONE DOG GET HIS LEG HURT?" Boomer wanted to know.

Wesley Oaks ducked his head, and Brother lost his train of thought. "Boomer, I'm not a-gonna tell you agin . . . uh . . ."

Doc Brown smoothly took over. "The contest was for the largest possum caught between seven o'clock last night and daybreak this morning. The two contestants were Wesley Oaks and his dog, Boone, and Tom Tucker and his hound, Rosey. Now, since both entrants have captured possums, both of them enormous, it falls to Mister Winters and the weighing of the two animals to settle the matter. The winner will receive a five-dollar prize, courtesy of Mister Louis Winters. . . ." Winters limped forward and bobbed his head, giving the audience a clear view of Merthiolate-painted scratches and a large sticking plaster on one ear. ". . . and other Hartford shopkeepers, such as my brother Dee." Dee's rose-colored face beamed through the thick layer of greasy Bag Balm cream with which his cheeks were slathered.

Brother Williams angrily straightened his slouch hat. It was already too low on his head, owing to his singed hair, but it still did not ride low enough to hide his missing eyebrows. "I was gonna say all that," he growled. "Now for the scales."

The weighing device to be used was a heavy-duty one borrowed from the feed-and-grain instead of the slight capacity scale Mister Winters used for measuring out candy. The big dial hung suspended just below the rafters of the porch overhang, and the large galvanized, scoop-shaped pan dangled inches above the boardwalk.

"Wesley," Brother commanded. "You bring your critter on up here first."

Wesley sneered at Tom, grinned around at the circle of young ladies, and dragged the possum carcass up the steps to the scales. He and Jim Brown hoisted the body up into the pan, and the needle of the dial jumped halfway around the scale. "The of-ficial weight is," Brother proclaimed unnecessarily, since everyone could read the verdict: "seventeen pounds, eight and one-half ounces."

Scoffing again at Tom's unopened gunnysack, Wesley hauled the remains of his critter back down the wooden steps. "What with the prize money an' the dollar for the hide, I'll be eatin' ice cream for a week."

"Huh." Brother snickered, unable to keep his impartial character. "Where you gonna find somebody to give you a dollar for that pelt? It looks like one of Dee's Saturday victims after he spent all Friday night at his brother's poker game." Everyone laughed at that except Wesley, who grimaced, and Dee, who turned even brighter red.

The moment of truth had come. Tom felt more nervous than he had at any time since the beginning of the hunt. To have captured granddaddy possum, even braved sticking his hands in that terrible cleft in the tree . . . What if it was not enough? The sack was hoisted onto the pan, and there was a collective gasp from the crowd. The black arrow on the dial pointed to seventeen pounds, fifteen ounces. The two measures differed by less than half a pound!

"Tom Tucker, you. . ."

But that was as far as Doc got in his message of congratulations. "Hold on!" Wesley called, swearing under his breath. "It ain't fair. What about the bag? It ain't fair. You gotta weigh the possum without the sack. 'Sides," he added in a skeptical, slighting voice, "how d'ya know he didn't slip somethin' else in there with the possum?"

Jim Brown threw Wesley a black look.

"Now, keep still, everyone!" Brother Williams demanded. "Fair is fair. With the difference so slight, we gotta put 'em even up. Tom'll have to take away the sack."

Tom looked around for support. Were they really going to make him put the live animal up on the scales, surrounded by dogs and people, and expect it to lie still? What if it chose that moment to seize its chance to escape?

"You gotta do it, Tom," Jefferson said. "Go on, like I told you."

With the potato sack on the sidewalk, Tom once again drew out the hatchet.

"What's he gonna do?"

"Is he gonna kill it now?"

"Safest way. Might run off or bite folks or both."

Everyone in the crowd jumped as Tom rained a flurry of blows with the hammerhead of the ax onto the planks on either side of the catch bag. The impacts sounded like gunshots, and the timbers quivered until the heads of several nails were bounced loose to stand up above the lumber. Then Tom tossed aside the hatchet, ripped open the tie, and scooped granddaddy possum up and onto the scales.

"Seventeen and ten! Tom Tucker is still the winner!" The roly-poly rat body was back inside the knotted pouch before that possum even had time to collect his wits, if he had ever even awakened at all.

Wesley Oaks stared in disbelief, then, muttering about liars and cheats, headed off down the dusty road, dragging the possum carcass and cussing at Boone for not finding a bigger catch.

"Tom," Mister Winters said, calling the boy up onto the porch. "We of the prize committee take great pride in presenting you the award of five dollars cash. What are you gonna do with it? New baseball mitt, perhaps? Ice cream?"

Quietly, as if embarrassed, and looking to Jeff to see if it was all right to say what they had already talked over, Tom said, "I'm gonna send it to my folks in Fort Smith, so my ma can spend another week near my brother Bobby."

The silence was as loud as the cheering had been a moment earlier. Jeff beamed and nodded to say, *You done good.*

Then Brother Williams swept off his slouch hat, flinging it upside down on the steps of the pharmacy. "You know," he said to Mr. Winters, "I didn't have a chance to contribute to the prize money before. I reckon it'd be all right if I did it now." So saying, he dropped a dollar into the hat, then stepped back to clear a space next to the battered felt.

A hail of nickels, dimes, and pennies filled the hat halfway up to its brim. Pop Lyle said that since everybody had donated all their spare change to the prize fund, and he had not yet contributed, he had best run the Harry Carey double feature for free.

When all was totaled up, the money in the hat came to over sixteen dollars.

The screen door slammed behind Tom as he entered Shiloh General Store. There as a welcoming committee were Grandma Amos and Willa Mae, neither of whom had made the trip into Hartford for the official weigh-in. Tom had snagged a chunk of ice from the soda cooler and licked it as he listened to more praise.

"What're you gonna do with the skin?" Grandma Amos asked when the congratulations were done. "Hide that big'll fetch another two dollars, plus havin' the braggin' rights in these parts."

Tom looked back out through the mesh to where Rosey lay on the porch, keeping an uneasy eye on the heap of gunnysack. "Ummm," Tom said. "I'm not sure yet what I'm gonna do with it." His voice trailed off in some consternation. Then he cleared his throat, and in an adult manner said, "But I need to do some business with you, Gramma. I want to send a U.S. Post Office money order to my mama in Fort Smith."

Grandma waved her walking stick and nodded. "Certainly, young Mister Tucker. Come to the office."

Despite the manly nature of Tom's actions, Willa Mae could not help seizing him as he passed in the aisle to give him a big hug. "Your mama and daddy sure got somethin' to be proud of," she said.

Tom shrugged and managed to look even more embarrassed than he had already. Released from Willa Mae's embrace, Tom found Grandma Amos had the book of money orders open on the counter below the pigeonholes. "How much did you mean to send?"

From the bloused-out front of his overalls, Tom extracted a sack made from the tied-up corners of a large, dark blue bandanna. It was as big as Tom could hold in two outspread hands and made a satisfying heavy clunking noise when he set it on the counter. "Money orders cost a quarter, includin' the postage?" he asked.

"Correct," Grandma agreed. "An' I'll throw in an envelope and paper if you need to write a note to go with it."

Unknotting the ends of the kerchief, Tom displayed a heap of coins and a single five-dollar bill. "Then," he said, recalculating one more time, "fifteen dollars buys Ma three weeks' stay in the rooming house. I want to send sixteen dollars. After I pay the two-bit fee, that'll leave me ten cents over."

He stopped and reflected a moment before continuing. "Enough for Jeff and me to have a Nehi and a sack of molasses popcorn each. If . . ." Here the grown-up slipped and the eleven-year-old boy reappeared. ". . . ,if y'all think it's all right for me to keep back the dime."

"Honey," Willa Mae boomed. "I think I can speak for your mama. She says you go on an' eat up that corn and drink that soda. You shore earned it. Fact is, you spend that extra dollar on yourself if you've a mind. Nobody gonna think the less of you."

"No," Tom said forcefully, reaching for the notepad and pencil. "I want Mama to spend the extra dollar on Bobby. Whatever he wants, he can have. He was in on the first hunt for granddaddy possum, and he's got a share of the reward comin', too."

The sun had not dropped far toward the first sunset after the great Shiloh possum hunt when Tom and Rosey were again on the bank of the stock pond. Stretched out on the berm of red earth, Tom munched a handful of molasses popcorn and took a swig of grape soda. He was studying the mouth of the bag, which had been untied ever since he and Jeff had reached the spot. The old possum still had not emerged. "You don't 'spose he really up and died, do you, Jeff?" Tom worried aloud.

"Naw," Jeff said, tipping his head sideways to observe the gunnysack. "If you was the one chased all to thunder, hauled out in the middle of the night, throwed in a bag, dragged all over creation, and then had to listen to folks speculatin' on how much your hide was worth, you wouldn't be in no big hurry to come out neither." Reminded once again that the possum skin was valuable, Tom turned to Jeff with a question on his lips. "You doin' right," he said with approval. "Granddaddy possum done earned a peaceful old age. We don't need his meat for the pot nor his hide for coverin'. Seems like him and God met a need for you; now you lettin' him go is like not bein' greedy."

There was a small movement in the sack, no more than a ripple really, but it made Rosey sit up and cock her head sideways as if imitating Jeff. "Rosey," Tom hissed. "Leave him be."

The mouth of the pouch widened from within, and the snout of granddaddy possum emerged. He stiffened at the sight of the trio watching him from twenty yards away.

"It's all right," Tom called softly. "I'm much obliged to you. You can go now.

"Oh," he added as the big critter started to amble away, "I'm sorry about choppin' the whey outta your house."

Granddaddy lumbered off up the slope and disappeared into the brambles.

"Don't you worry 'bout his house," Jeff urged. "His home may be gone, but he still got his skin. Sometimes in this world, that's what you got to be thankful for."

PART II

Dreamland

Once in khaki suits,
Gee we looked swell,
Full of that Yankee Doodle-de-dum.
Half a million boots went sloggin' through Hell,
I was the kid with the drum.
Say, don't you remember me, they called me Al—
   It was Al all the time.
Say, don't you remember I'm your pal—
   Brother can you spare a dime?

C H A P T E R   1 7

On the afternoon of February 23, 1932, two dozen citizens of Shiloh huddled together beneath the water tower that stood beside the Rock Island railroad tracks. Bobby Tucker was finally coming home, and they were waiting to greet him.

The morning was cold and wet, raining a slow drizzle that clung to strands of hair, dripped down collars, soaked through trousers, and dampened socks from the top all the way to the toes. The crowd danced the slow, shivery jig of folks who had been waiting outside too long. They shifted from one foot to the other, shoved hands deep into pockets, ducked heads down between shoulders. Words rose up in steamy vapors from behind mufflers.

But no one complained about the damp. Rain, even this bone-pene-trating drizzle, was considered an answer to prayers, a sign that the Lord had not entirely abandoned this desperate corner of the world after all.

There were few umbrellas among the crowd; it had not rained in so long that people had lost the habit. Only Doc Brown and Mr. Winters had thought to bring the things along. Doc passed his to Willa Mae, who held it over Grandma Amos, lest the old woman take a chill and Shiloh lose a national treasure. Mr. Winters left his unopened, declaring that he would put it to use when Bobby Tucker got off the train and not before.

Tom stood beside Jefferson, who held the bridle of the mule team. At the first hint of a cloud, Jeff had rigged a canvas tarp over the back of the buckboard to protect Bobby on the ride home. The big man did not own a heavy coat, but Lily had stitched him a canvas duster that shed the rain nearly as well as a rich man's oiled slicker. His battered felt hat drooped beneath the weight of the water. He could only see by lifting his chin every few seconds and peering out from beneath the dripping brim.

"Your mama and daddy gon' be mighty pleased to see these folks when the train come," Jeff said.

Tom glanced around the group. Older folks, mostly. He wondered if Bobby would be disappointed that his friends had not been allowed to come. Squirrel Hocott's mom had pitched a fit when he told her he was going to greet Bobby. Catfish Pierce's dad had told him that if he came he'd get sick and end up just like Bobby, a helpless cripple his whole life long. People were scared plenty of infantile paralysis, and no one was really certain how catching it was. People were taking no chances with their young'uns until it was known that Bobby's illness could not be passed along.

Word was around that Bobby had left the Fort Smith hospital not because he was well enough to do so, but because money had run out. And that was partially true. Even though Bobby had been removed from the iron lung the week before Christmas, he still spiked an occasional fever and lapsed into delirium. He still needed extensive care and a vigorous program of treatment.

And the Tucker's funds were indeed exhausted. Trudy had worked part-time in the hospital laundry, earning enough to pay her room and board for the past few months. But the cold spell had put an end to Birch's road work, and there were no jobs to be found in Fort Smith or across the river in Van Buren either. Hundreds of unemployed men ate their meals at the charity soup kitchens and slept in the shelter of cardboard boxes down by the river. Starvation was no longer rumor, but fact, in western Arkansas and on into Oklahoma.

But here in Shiloh the shelves of the Tucker root cellar were full. Corn, beans, okra, and applesauce in pale blue glass canning jars were neatly organized on the musty shelves. Jefferson had butchered a hog in December, so ham and bacon hung in the smokehouse and milk and fresh eggs were there for breakfast, buttermilk and corn bread for supper at night.

Depression or not, there was still food on the table at the Tucker farm. This was reason enough to come home as soon as Bobby was declared fit to travel.

On Tuesday the doctor in Fort Smith had announced that Bobby was strong enough to be transferred to the children's polio ward at St. Francis Charity Hospital across town. Trudy asked if, instead, the short train trip to Shiloh might be possible if he was kept warm. Could they not bring Bobby home?

The physician replied with the question of the necessary months of ongoing treatment: hot baths morning and night, deep massage, and the slow, painful task of working to regain some use of muscles.

Trudy insisted that she was perfectly capable of doing whatever it took to get Bobby back in the pink again. Could she not give him better care at home, where he would be the center of her attention?

The doctor shrugged and shook his head, expressing the opinion that it would be better for Bobby to be in a ward among other children with similar disabilities to prepare him mentally and emotionally to face the world as a cripple.

This comment made her draw in her breath as if the good doctor had kicked her in the stomach instead of offering advice. She squared her shoulders and admitted that there was no longer any hope that she and Birch could stay on in the city. How could they leave Bobby behind in Fort Smith? His spirit would break. (She did not mention her own spirit.) All the professional care in the world could not substitute for home and familiar faces all around. Only love could prepare him to face the world not as a cripple, but as one determined to walk again.

And so the doctor reluctantly agreed that Bobby Tucker could be released for home convalescence. He wrote out a strict regimen of therapy for Trudy to follow. The next day, with Birch's last paycheck, the Tuckers had purchased tickets on the Rock Island line.

This afternoon the distant trill of the locomotive seemed more insistent than usual.

To Tom's ears the shrill cry sang out: "COMIIIING HOOOOOME!"

The hair on the back of Tom's neck prickled. The collection of friends exchanged looks, shifted positions, then trooped twenty yards along the berm to the place on the line where experience said the passenger car would slide to a stop.

It was then that Tom saw Sally Grier and her mother standing on the opposite side of the tracks. Sally wore the one blue cotton dress she put on for special occasions. She did not smile at Tom, but waited motionless with her hands clasped in front of her as if the iron rails were a barrier she could not cross no matter how she wished to. Mrs. Grier was a tall, gaunt woman, worn far beyond her years, as tattered as the navy blue serge dress and the old-fashioned hightop black shoes she wore. She fluttered a small white envelope at Tom.

Tom waved at Sally and gave her a big halloo. Her lips were pressed tightly together, her gaze turned northward to where the Rock Island would soon appear.

The chugging of the engine became distinct. Mrs. Grier said something quietly to her daughter. Tom assumed that the woman meant for Sally to stay put, that like every other mother in Shiloh she was warning Sally against getting too close. Tom understood.

The whistle shrilled again. Two billows of smoke rose above the trees. The ground quivered a bit. Tom felt the earth tremble through the worn leather soles of his shoes. His stomach jumped. He felt suddenly wide awake, something like being scared, as if he should run and holler.

"She wants you to come get that letter, Tom," Jefferson said, giving Tom a nudge forward. "Go on. Hurry up. Train's a-comin'."

Tom scrambled up the gravel berm, careful not to step on the rails because of the pulsing vibrations they conducted, as if the fearsome vitality of the train's approach was deadly electricity.

Mrs. Grier extended him the envelope from the other side. "This is for your mama," she said.

"Yes'm. It's good for y'all t' come down for Bobby."

The lean, joyless woman stepped back. "Sally an' me wanted t' thank y'all. Tell your mama we was prayin', an' we will . . ."

Now the whistle drowned out her words. The treetops around the bend were obscured in the black cloud of smoke. Tom felt the rumble of the earth. He stepped back from the tracks as the pit of his stomach quivered from the bigness of the train and the excitement of the homecoming.

Mrs. Grier retreated a few paces on her side. Sally, her thin sweater soaked, hugged herself and mouthed the word *goodbye*.

"I hope your brother recovers altogether," Mrs. Grier called as the whistle faded.

"Thank you, ma'am. Bobby will be able to receive vis'tors soon, I'm told. Maybe then Sally can . . ."

The locomotive made a shout like a trumpet. The bell clanged jubilation, chopping off Tom's thoughts and jerking him to attention.

Fifty yards from the water tower, the engineer stuck his upper body out the side window of the cab and waved his big gloved hand. Tom waved back at him, then shouted at Jefferson to look also. When Tom turned his eyes back toward Sally and Mrs. Grier, they were walking slowly away toward the road.

Tom pocketed the envelope and scrambled into position beside Jefferson. Conversations were shouted over the racket.

The cowcatcher cut off Tom's view of the departing girl and her mother. The massive drivers slipped and churned, then revolved half-reverse, and the great iron machine sighed and shuddered and halted where all knew it would.

The engineer, John Catherwood, swung out on the step and held himself by one hand above them. Many were the summer days that Catherwood pulled the chain of his whistle and waved his cap as he passed the Tucker brothers walking beside the tracks. A hero to all the boys along the route, he had taken a personal interest in the middle Tucker boy over the past months, even delivering a striped railroader's cap to the hospital. Now he seemed to take a personal pride in delivering young Bobby home.

"Howdy! Hey, Tom Tucker!" he shouted. "That brother of yourn is there in the second car!" He jerked his thumb, and Tom found himself suddenly running toward the gap where the conductor had just stepped out. The men followed in a herd. All were ready to lift the ailing child and bear him above their heads to the wagon.

The womenfolk hung back. Beneath the canopy of the umbrella, Grandma Amos and Willa Mae proceeded slowly, carefully, over the slick gravel.

Tom saw Birch push past the conductor. How thin his father looked! How worn. Three months had aged him ten years.

"Here we are!" Birch cried. His voice was the same. Tom reached the car first. Birch extended his hand and pulled Tom up, lifting him bodily over three steep steps.

"My boy! My boy!" Birch cried. "Your mama is in there with Bobby." He laughed and kissed Tom on the cheek, then set him on the ground again. "Ho, Jefferson! Howdy, Jim! Doc Brown! Brother Williams! Mighty glad y'all come to meet us. We'll need a hand gettin' Bobby off the train."

Mr. Winters popped open his umbrella in anticipation as ten strong men clambered up to help. One or two would have done as well, but every man in Shiloh wanted to bear the returning hero home from his great battle.

In the end, it was Jefferson and Birch who carried him off. But they let him down to the welcoming arms of the folks of Shiloh.

Mr. McClung of the Hartford Music Company broke into song:

We shall know Him, we shall know Him,
And redeemed by His side we shall stand.

The voices of the crowd, hesitant at first, took up the refrain of praise and thanksgiving. At the same time, they looked with curiosity and sadness at the boy who was being bundled toward the buckboard.

How small Bobby Tucker looked, pale and shrunken. He was a shadow of the boy he had been on those long hot days last summer when the brothers had chased the Rock Island as she roared by.

And then he smiled. Wasn't that a smile? Everyone saw it as the familiar faces crowded around him and laid their rough farmer's hands on his ashen forehead.

The boys were all tucked in—Bobby in the bedroom with Rosey by his side, Tom in a cot on the closed porch. Prayers of thanksgiving had been said. It was almost ten o'clock, but Trudy did not want to go to bed. For the first time in more than three months, Trudy and Birch were alone together in the parlor of their own house.

"They say it is the smell of a place you remember best." Trudy watched as Birch poked another short log into the open mouth of the parlor stove.

"Nobody cuts wood for a stove like Jefferson." Birch blew on the embers, then watched with satisfaction as the dry bark caught a spark and ignited.

Trudy closed her eyes, laid her head back on the lace doily on the sofa, and inhaled deeply. "It's true, I think. The aroma of wood smoke, something about the scent of this old house. It breathes the word *peace*."

"Those poor Fort Smith fellers standing out on Garrison Avenue right now, all warming their hands over an oil drum with scraps of wood for fuel, if they could see me now. . . ." Birch was grinning when he turned to Trudy. She raised her head to look at him.

Then between them some unspoken thought passed. Their eyes caught and held. The joy died away, and realization took hold.

Trudy's eyes brimmed. The homecoming was not all wonderful. There were other things to remember, cold realities that the aroma and the surroundings had reawakened.

"We've had no time to think about . . . anything . . . have we, Birch?" she asked, looking down at her clasped hands. *No time to grieve for Joey,* is what she meant to say.

He remained crouched by the glowing stove, a stick of wood in his hand. His glance flitted to the end table where the photographs were grouped in a semicircle around the base of the lamp. He stared at one. The last one. Last autumn . . . boys healthy and strong . . . clustered in a group on the top step of the porch. Joey on Birch's shoulders. Sunlight on their faces. Bobby with one eye squinted against the brightness. Joey's eyes closed tight even though he smiled broadly. How long ago? Four months?

"I don't want to think about it." He tucked his chin as if a pain had gone through his chest.

"Can't we? Together now? I know what you must be feeling."

"Nobody knows. And I don't want to talk about it. Not tonight."

"You never . . . we never have . . . Birch? I keep thinking that if only we can stop long enough to . . ."

"We'll have to get through it," he said gruffly and turned back to the fire, closing the iron door with a clang, just as he had closed himself off from her every day since the beginning of the nightmare.

She needed something more from him. She longed to have him put his arms around her and pull her close and stroke her hair. She longed to comfort him as well. Instead he rose stiffly and looked around with a sort of helpless panic as if he wished now that he were among the men on Garrison Avenue who had only the weather to worry about, whose great concern was where the next meal was coming from.

The worst had already happened to those men. Now only surviving concerned them. Much easier to deal with than coming home.

Things had been strained between Birch and Trudy since the day they buried Joey. Since the day he went to Meribah. Birch put his hand to his head. "Why did you bring it up?"

The first tear spilled over. Her words came from a fierce whisper. She did not want Tom and Bobby to hear her. "Did I? I thought it came to both of us."

"You did. You got that look and . . ."

"Lower your voice."

He did so. "Put the pictures away."

"Oh, Birch! Let me keep his memory at least!"

"Everything's different. I'm different. You are, too. We'll likely lose this place. Maybe it doesn't matter."

"Doesn't matter to whom?" She angrily brushed the tear away with the back of her hand. "You still have two sons. And me."

"I can't think about the way it used to be. I'll go crazy if I do." He walked out of the parlor and into their bedroom, closing the door behind him, shutting her out from his grief and wounding her with his bitterness.

CHAPTER 18

Birch and Jefferson were already gone before Tom awakened the next morning.

"Jeff heard they're hirin' up at the Jenson mine," Willa Mae explained when he came into the kitchen. "Have some corn bread, honey. Pray your daddy an' Jefferson get themselfs some work till plantin' time. I lef' your mama to sleep a while longer. Lawd, she need a year t' catch up after what she been through. Get on with your chores jus' like always."

An hour later, with eggs gathered, cow milked, critters fed, and stalls cleaned, Tom returned to the house.

The kitchen had been transformed. Willa Mae and Trudy labored at the cookstove. The table was covered with a bedsheet and layered with three thick cotton blankets. Stripped to his skivvies, Bobby lay across the table on his stomach. His eyes were nervous, looking anywhere but at Tom.

"Tom, you'll need to learn the routine so you can help when Willa Mae is not here," Trudy instructed over her shoulder.

"Yes'm," he replied, although he wanted to leave the house, take his breakfast out, and eat it in the barn beside Esmerelda's stall.

Bobby saw the revulsion in his eyes.

"It looks really ugly, don't it?" Bobby asked in a choked whisper.

"Naw," Tom lied. "Not so bad."

Bobby's good leg was just the same as always, ready to run across the fields of Shiloh, fit enough to chase possums through the woods or to launch out on the swinging rope and drop with a splash into the swimming hole.

Tom looked at the good leg, the perfect leg, and memories of all those ordinary things flooded his mind. He tried to keep his gaze fixed on the perfect leg because then he could keep smiling. Then his eyes would wander, and he would stare for an instant at the other leg, and his smile would freeze with horror at what was there.

"I know it's ugly. Like a dead thing," Bobby said and turned his face away.

"It'll get better," Tom said, but he did not believe it really would.

Stretched out next to Bobby's perfect leg was a bent shriveled thing that had the appearance of a leg, but it did not match the other. A thigh bone covered with skin, a knot for a knee, more bone without muscle, an ankle and a stub with five toes pointing off at odd angles. It was attached to Bobby, but it did not fit the rest of him.

No one needed to say it: with a leg like this, there would be no possum hunts, no running through the fields or climbing hickory trees. It would be enough if Bobby could walk again. That was what all the fuss was about.

The big copper washtub boiled on the stove, steaming up the windows. Steam condensed into drops of water on the white enamel boards of the ceiling, then dripped down onto the kitchen floor like an irregular rain inside the room.

Willa Mae and Trudy had set up the clothes wringer in the washtub beside the boiling water. Trudy dropped strips of flannel into the bubbling pot.

"This is the worst part," Bobby muttered.

"It'll be okay," Tom said, wanting to put a hand on Bobby's bare arm, but afraid to touch him.

"I want you to go out."

"Mama says I got to watch, so's I can help."

Over her shoulder as she adjusted the clothes wringer, Trudy said, "That's right, Bobby. Tom needs to learn."

Bobby covered his face with his hands. "I don't want him in here!" he shouted.

Stung but relieved, Tom fled the kitchen. He slammed the door behind him and stood just on the other side so he could hear.

"You've hurt your brother's feelings," Trudy's voice scolded as if the issue was Tom's feelings and not the withered leg and the boiling water and the scalding strips of cloth in the kettle.

"I don't want him to see!" Bobby shouted louder than Tom had ever heard him shout before. The shout was shrill and womany. It made Tom feel afraid that the polio had not only shrunk Bobby's leg, but had broken something inside of him, too.

"He's seen your leg at the hospital already," Trudy's voice was soothing, matter of fact, as if this was just an ordinary day. "Nothing to be ashamed of."

"No, Mama! I don't want him to see me cry! Don't you understand? When you put the towels on my leg! I don't want him to see me cry!"

Tom felt all cold. He felt like something was choking off his air. Tears hung in his eyes, and he stared hard at the doorknob.

"All right," Trudy answered. "For now. But he'll have to help me tomorrow. Willa Mae cannot be here tomorrow."

"Why not? I don't want Tom."

Willa Mae answered in a mellow voice. "Baby, I gots to—"

"And . . . don't . . . call . . . me . . . baby!" Bobby screamed. "Joey was the baby, not me! Are you—how come you always talk like I'm too little to understand you?"

"Tha's right. That is right. All right, Bobby, honey. I 'pologize. I reckon anybody's been through what you been through is grow'd up, whether he intended t' be or not."

Quieter now, Bobby begged his mother. "I want Willa Mae to help. Not Tom."

Tom's fists clenched at his sides. He felt like something would shatter if he did not cry out. Why did Bobby hate him now? Why didn't Bobby want him to help with wrapping his leg? And since it was Bobby's leg and the scalding towels against Bobby's skin, why was it that Tom wanted to scream and bawl and cuss?

But Willa Mae forgave Bobby's rage as if it had not happened. "I gots t' work for ol' Gramma Amos tomorrow. You know that crazy ol' woman brought a Hampshire pig in to sleep 'side of her bed two nights ago? She thought it was a dog." Willa Mae chuckled low, then she began to hum.

Except for the melody, all was quiet on the other side of the door. The clank of the long ladle against the side of the kettle. The squeak of the handle on the clothes wringer as the boiling water was wrung out of the first wrapping cloth.

Then Mama's voice quavering like she was angry: "You shall have to bear up, Bobby, if you want to be well again."

Tom wished she would just be quiet!

Silence. Then a slow, agonized moan as the first strip was placed over the shrunken thigh. "Don't want . . . him . . . to see . . . me cry!"

Tom gritted his teeth and leaned his head against the doorjamb. He whispered, "Jesus!" He whispered, "Bobby."

"Don't . . . want . . . Tom . . ."

"Here's another one, honey. Now just breathe in. . . ."

A sharp cry.

"Honey, it ain't gonna hurt for long. Oh Jesus, he'p our little Bobby. Oh, Jesus, You saved his one leg, now he'p us save t'other one."

"Tom'll see me . . . cry . . . oh!"

Tom wiped his cheek with the back of his hand. It was wet. He was crying. Tears and tears, like a flood to break the drought.

He turned the doorknob and swung back the door to the steamy kitchen and stood there gaping at it all. Steam billowed from the pot. Bandages slid through the wringer. Willa Mae, sweating and full of concern, stood over Bobby.

"Tom! Shut the door!" Trudy said sharply, her damp hair falling across her forehead as she cranked the wringer and passed a cloth to Willa Mae.

"Go away, Tom!" Bobby hid his face as Willa Mae placed the searing hot cloth on his calf.

Tom walked to the edge of the table. He put a hand on Bobby's back. "Look at me, Bobby," Tom demanded. "I want you to look at me." The words faltered with emotion.

Bobby turned his head and gazed painfully into his face. "Tom?"

"See? It's okay. You don't have to act strong. Just *be* strong, you know? . . . See, Bobby? I'm cryin', too. . . ."

And so the first morning of Bobby's homecoming passed. Afterward, Bobby was put to bed, where he fell into a deep exhausted sleep. The kitchen was cleaned and scrubbed while Tom sat, pale and shaken by his brother's ordeal. So this was what Bobby's life had been like these many months? And this was what Bobby had to look forward to?

Trudy, who had been living close to Bobby's misery long enough to accept it as fact, broke the heavy silence. "It was lovely to see everyone."

Willa Mae pointed out that Grandma Amos had come out in the rain in spite of a terrible attack of lumbago.

Trudy replied that she must send everyone a note of thanks.

It was only then that Tom remembered the note from Mrs. Grier. He fetched it from the pocket of his jacket and gave it to Trudy.

The envelope had been twice used. Some former address had been crossed out, and Trudy's name penciled in below the California postmark on the stamp. It made sense that Mrs. Grier would only have a secondhand envelope. Everything the Griers owned had belonged to someone else at one time or other. Mrs. Grier had taken a special liking to Trudy because Trudy had given her a secondhand coat and a dress to wear last fall.

The letter was written on the blue-lined notepaper from a school notebook. Trudy read the message through silently, frowned, and looked down at Tom.

She asked curiously, "Did you know the Griers were going?"

It took a moment for him to absorb her meaning. "Goin' where?"

"Missus Grier says that Mister Grier has heard there is work to be had in California."

"California?"

"Yes. Mister Grier hopes to get a job in the oil fields. Kern County. San Joaquin Valley." She waved her hand in a circle and looked up at the ceiling as if there was a map pinned above her. "Somewhere in the central part of the state, I think."

Tom was still trying to comprehend. Sally? Leaving Shiloh? Going away? Heading west where he would never see her again? But Sally had said nothing to him about it at all! She had been more quiet than usual in school, but he had figured it was because of the turn of weather. Everyone got a little blue when the weather turned off cold.

"Po' folks," Willa Mae enjoined. "Drought finally got 'em. Water well dried up some time ago. This rain come too late an' too little. I hear from Gramma Amos they's near t' starvin'. Sharecroppers got no hope for anythin' when times gets this bad. Only mercy is what keeps a sharecropper alive when that happens. Ain't no mercy lef' for the Griers, I reckon. 'Cept maybe out there in California."

"When are they leaving?" Tom asked dully. Who would laugh at his jokes if she was gone? Who would he have to show off for? Who would call him Possum in a voice so sweet that he liked the sound of it better than his own name?

"Leaving . . . this morning." Trudy scanned the letter. "She says here . . ."

Tom was on his feet. "You mean this very morning?"

"Her cousin from Charleston came last night to load up. He is taking the whole family west in his truck and . . ."

"Mama, can I go?" he asked urgently. She blinked at him as if it had never occurred to her how much Tom thought of Sally Grier. "Mama, I got to go tell Sally so long!"

"But I'm certain . . . they've gone already."

"Maybe they ain't left yet!"

Trudy did not correct his grammar. She touched his cheek. He pulled back from her hand, and she considered him with a tender, pitying look.

"Why Tom," she whispered in a surprised voice. "Yes. Hurry then."

Coatless, Tom flew out the door and down the gravel lane with his mother calling after him to come back and put on his jacket. He did not turn back, but jumped the pasture fence and ran through mud and splashed through the shallow puddles until his dungarees were splattered and wet.

He did not slow until the Grier farmhouse came into view. His sides ached. Breathless, he grasped his ribs and stumbled to a halt in the center of the road fifty yards from the house.

He was too late.

The forlorn, unpainted structure on top of the low hill looked as if it had been deserted for a long time. Like the Sully Faulk house, it had a lonely, echoing sort of emptiness about it. No smoke rose from the stovepipe. The front door was wide open, swinging on the slight breeze, hinges groaning in an almost human voice.

Turning away and bending down, he braced his hands on his knees until his breath returned. For an instant he considered continuing up the hill, walking up the steps onto the leaning porch, looking inside. It occurred to him that he had never been in the Grier house.

Straightening, he wiped his mouth on his shirtsleeve and stared up at worn-out shingles patched with flattened tin cans to keep the rain out. When the drought came, had Mr. Grier looked up at that roof and cursed himself for all the work he had put into fixing it? If only there had been rain to leak through the roof, they might have been able to stay. But the rain had not come.

Tom caught the reflection of the Poteau range in clean, sparkling windows that belied the stark poverty of the place. The glass was as spotless as the panes of a rich man's windows.

Tom did not want to see inside. The Griers were proud people. No doubt Sally's mama had left the house clean and swept, inside and out, but it was empty and desolate all the same.

Soon enough, Tom knew, the dust would fill the place just as dust filled the Sully Faulk house. Who would remember that the prettiest girl in Shiloh had once lived there? Who would remember her one blue dress?

Most of the coal mines in western Arkansas had been abandoned after the stock market crashed and the Great Depression clamped down on the country. When suddenly nobody was buying new cars and the auto industry had gone belly-up, there was no demand for large amounts of steel. And with no iron ore to smelt, the demand for coal to fire the furnaces disappeared as well. Most of the miners drifted off to look for work in other parts of the country. But that was before the new strip mine west of Shiloh opened up.

As if the dark green of the oaks and the paler green of the sycamores had been the hide of a beast, the hillside was skinned, the red earth of its flesh stripped and discarded, and the marrow of coal ready to be sucked from the bones of the earth. Steam-driven shovels capable of biting out half a ton of coal at a single scoop were freighted in piecemeal and assembled to begin feasting on the countryside. Donkey engines, hoisting strings of ore cars out of what had shortly before been the vitals of a mountain, drew cheap coal to the surface.

It was no wonder that there was a renewed need for the weakest and puniest component of the labor: men to swing the sledges to break the slabs into liftable boulders, men to shovel and to feed the demanding machines, and men to clean up after the mechanical chewing and swallowing.

Birch and Jefferson approached the white shack that stood guard at the entrance to the Ouachita Mining Company's Pit Number One. They joined a file of men who had heard the mine was hiring.

The sun-browned foreman at the gate waved a clipboard for silence and explained the terms of employment. "You'll work eight-hour shifts," he said, slicking back his curly dark hair. "Eight to four, four to midnight, or graveyard. Pays the same: thirty cents a ton. No meal break, and you show up on time or you're out. We weren't lookin' for you when you came here, just keep that in mind. No union crap, and no agitatin' or you're out."

Slowly the line crept forward. Each man in turn was asked his name and his address. Those accepted were given a slip of paper and told to report to the paymaster for a metal disk engraved with their employee number. "What fer?" asked the tall, raw boned man in front of Birch.

"So's you can draw your gloves," the foreman retorted. "So's we can keep track of how much you owe the company store out of each week's pay."

"Just as I thought," the lean miner snorted. "What'll them gloves set me back? Quarter?"

"Fifty cents," the mine official said without batting an eye. "Shovel or pick needs sharpened, cost you a quarter. Bust one, cost you two bucks."

"I heard it all before," said the tall figure. "Let's get on with it."

"What's your name?"

"Jack Dolan. Monroe, Oklahoma."

The foreman consulted a list of names on his clipboard. "Dolan, Dolan . . . can't use you. Move along."

"How come?"

The ramrod set his hands on his hips. "Do I gotta spell it out for y'? You worked union, you voted union. You ain't wanted here. Now clear off before I set the dogs on y'. Name?"

The demand was repeated again and Birch realized it was his turn to answer. "Birch Tucker. Shiloh," he said. "Worked in a mine 'bout twelve years ago. No union then at all."

"Tucker . . . Shiloh. Can't use you."

"What? I just told you, I ain't never been involved with no union. I really need a job, mister, and I'm a hard worker. What's the problem?"

"Orders," the foreman said shortly. "Anybody else here from Shiloh?" Jeff waved his hand. "Can't use you neither. Big boss says nobody from Shiloh gets hired."

Birch and Jeff looked at each other. "Must be a mistake," Birch said. "Who is this big boss? Lemme talk to him."

"This here mine is part of Jenson Consolidated, and Garrick Jenson don't have time for the likes of you," the overseer scowled. "Clear off, and don't waste no more of my time."

Trudging back down the hill toward Shiloh, Jeff and Birch fell in beside the union miner. "Don't feel too bad," he said. "You ain't missin' much. Union brother of mine lied and got a job here last week. Said the weighmaster don't even look at the scales. If it's piled up higher than he can reach, he calls it a ton. Otherwise he shorts you by half. An' you cain't argue, or out you go."

For the men of Shiloh there was no work to be had at the Jenson Consolidated coal mine, no employment available at Jenson-owned textile mills or at Jenson-controlled factories, feedlots, or farm equipment yards. Not that Birch or Jeff tried all those possibilities. But others from Shiloh did, and they soon discovered that the strands of the web that reached out from the Meribah office of Garrick and Caro-line stretched far and in many directions. Or, as Doc Brown said, the Jenson tentacles were squeezing the life out of Sebastian County.

Which sentiment explained why Doc had suggested the meeting about to take place in Shiloh Methodist Church. The gathering was the outgrowth of debate and discussion started, naturally, in Dee's barbershop, but Doc had made it more official and circulated the word.

The cold, gray morning that confronted Birch as he arrived outside the small, white structure matched his mood, but seeing the world as also oppressed and dull was no consolation. Birch stopped by the graves of his mother and his younger brother, as he always did when passing through the churchyard. The headstones were clean and lately washed, but what grass remained in the fenced enclosure was crushed and brown. It occurred to Birch that another dry summer would spell the end of any lawn in the cemetery; it would all be dirt again.

Doc Brown squeezed Birch's shoulder in friendly greeting. "She was a fine, strong woman," he said, gesturing with hat in hand toward the marker. "Don't we wish we had her counsel now?" Birch shook hands with Doc and with Judge Flowers, who had come with Doc to the meeting.

The interior of the clean, pine-walled single room was already filled with a mixture of Hartford merchants and Shiloh farmers. Arley Palmer spoke softly to Jonas Hocott and Jim Brown over the back of one pew, while Dee Brown, Mr. Winters, Brother Williams, and Jeff were knotted together in a corner. Ten or twelve others nodded and called muffled greetings as Birch entered. Dan Faraby sat alone, his chin sunk on his chest.

Though it was Thursday, not Sunday, and this particular congregation was surely not about to sing any hymns, they all still conversed in quiet, almost reverent tones. Maybe this condition was what Doc had in mind when he suggested the church as a location for the assembly. The barbershop was too public, and the livery stable might have led to riot, arson, and mayhem.

"We all know why we're here," Doc said without preamble. "Jenson Consolidated is a hundred times worse than Henry V. Smith ever was. But the idea is to make certain all of us know all there is to know. Maybe then we can get a handle on what to do. Now, who's first?"

"I had a line on a job breaking mules to harness," Jonas said. "Didn't pay much, but you know, help to get by. Anyways, first day I showed the owner says, 'Sorry, can't use you after all.' When I asked how come, he told me Jenson sent somebody over from their stable. That was it."

"Yeah? Well, that's true clean over in Huntington," Arley reported. "I hired on to repair fences for fifty cents a day . . . an' I don't mind tellin' you folks, we need the cash. But the foreman says Garrick Jenson told him that if he signed anybody from Shiloh, his next load of lumber would cost him double. Nobody can live with that."

"And what about that business of only shopping in Meribah?" Mr. Winters asked. The druggist sounded feisty and ready for battle. "My trade has all but dried up, and it isn't just me. All of Hartford's in trouble. What about that, Judge? Isn't that a restraint of trade or something illegal?"

Judge Flowers spoke into a hopeful silence that awaited his judicial rendering, but when he shook his head there was a collective sigh like a pneumatic auto tire going flat. "As I understand it," he said, "the purchasing restriction only applies to shopping on credit. Since Jenson is extending credit that he is not required to offer, his terms are his terms. Can you make out with barter?"

Now groans succeeded the sighs. "Sorry, Judge," Mister Winters said. "My pantry is so dang full of canned goods I could sell groceries myself, except I can't sell anything to anybody."

Jeff laughed softly in sympathy. "You did oughta see Gramma Amos's place," he said. "She is up past the eyeballs with stock now. Says she can't take no more chickens in trade, less'n doin' business cost her more'n she can afford to feed."

"Shoppin' in Meribah ain't no picnic, let me tell you," Arley declared. "My cow dried up, so we gotta have canned milk for the little ones. Can of Borden's costs, what, ten, twelve cents?" Murmurs of agreement followed. "Yeah, well you, Jonas, and you others who been buyin' in Meribah on credit know what I'm gonna say . . . twenty-five cents a can! Yessir, I ain't lyin'! And everything is priced thataway. Is that right? Is that fair?"

Judge Flowers held up his hand for silence and motioned for everyone to simmer down. "It may not be right or fair," he said, "but it is legal. Jenson can charge whatever he wants; he isn't making you pay it, is he? Now look, let's deal with the contracts you all signed. It's the same thing there. Nobody twisted your arm or held a gun to your head. You are all free, white and—sorry, Jeff, no offense—you all signed of your own free will."

"But what does it all mean?" Doc asked. "If they are trying to keep everyone hungry and beholden to Meribah, that I understand. But what's the point of driving everyone out of business and out of the country entirely? If nobody can afford to live here, who does Jenson sell to then? Does he think he can farm all the land? Even Jenson Consolidated isn't that big."

"It's not the farms they're after," said a small voice from the back of the room.

Birch turned to see who had spoken, but the comment seemed to have come from the pine knots in the walls. Since Dan Faraby's face still pointed toward his boots, it was not until he repeated his words that everyone knew he had spoken.

"What do you mean, Dan?" Doc inquired.

An embarrassed flush spread over Faraby's cheeks. "I got no right to speak here," he said. "Thanks to y'all's help, I ain't beholden to nobody, an' we're gettin' by."

It was true. Since the Penny Auction Rebellion, Faraby's place was clear of debt, and it did not matter that Jenson Consolidated now owned even the Hartford Federal Bank; the Faraby family was in the clear. Dan Faraby's shame that he had received help but had none to offer in return was apparent.

"But I think you should know what I heard," he continued. "You know the Jenson coal mines up in the hills? Well, Jenson hired hisself some geologists, and they told him the seams of coal run all under Shiloh valley . . . right under where we're sittin' right now. Between Jenson credit and the drought, he figgers to own it all and skin the land like takin' the hide off a possum."

CHAPTER 19

The winter weeks passed slowly, moving toward spring. The well at the house dropped lower, and there was little rain to replenish it, so Birch and Jeff began hauling water in oak barrels from the artesian well in the north field. Jeff took half the water home, where he used it to irrigate the long rows of flourishing sweet potatoes, beets, and onions that took up two of his ten acres.

The remainder of the precious liquid was set aside for Bobby's treatments. Boiled and used twice, morning and night, it was then carried out to Trudy's winter garden for irrigating the cold-weather vegetables.

They were more than lucky to have the water well in the north field, Birch remarked again and again. The seemingly endless supply of water from the artesian was a miracle. All around Shiloh the gardens their neighbors had counted on to get them through shriveled and died or produced only stunted reminders of the bounty that had filled Shiloh tables before the drought. But between the dwindling stores in the root cellar, the Canfield produce, and the Tucker greens, there might be enough to see both families through winter and spring until the summer harvest began. If the artesian well continued to produce water through the spring and into summer, then the cotton soon to be planted in the north field would flourish and take care of the debt for this year at least.

"We shall not go hungry," Trudy said to Lily as the two women exchanged spinach and cabbages for yams and beets, "but the children will be awfully weary of eating the same thing every night for supper before we are through this."

It came to the minds of both women in that moment that there were other children in Shiloh who would not be so lucky.

The last day in March, Doc Brown stopped in as he had every week to examine Bobby. It was past the noon hour, and Trudy dished him up a plate of chicken and dumplings. He worried aloud about the malnutrition he had seen among the children in Sebastian County these days. In all his years he had never seen such widespread pellagra nor even one case of rickets till now. The winter of 1932 had changed his perception of common childhood diseases in western Arkansas. He now placed hunger at the top of his list.

But Bobby Tucker? Doc Brown pronounced that he was getting stronger every day. Birch had rigged a trapeze bar above the bed, and Bobby had faithfully done pull-ups until his arms were as strong as ever. But the legs were another story.

"Braces," Doc said to Trudy and Birch through a mouthful of chicken. "I'll be straight with you. He'll have to have leg braces if he's ever going to walk again."

The couple exchanged a worried look. "How much will it cost, Doc?"

Doc screwed up his face in thought. "He'll have to be fitted in Fort Smith. Let me see. There was a child in Barber last year. The Sandburg boy. First fitting cost something in the neighborhood of eighty dollars, I think. Well worth it. The boy is up and around. Uses two canes, but he's walking. With braces on his legs, Bobby'll be up and around in no time. Then as he grows, he'll have to have them refitted periodically."

Silence. The clink of Doc's spoon against his bowl was the only sound in the kitchen for a long moment.

Eighty dollars! Trudy turned to the dry sink and stared out the window with a renewed hopelessness at the pen where Esmerelda nursed a new bull calf. Maybe they could get something for the calf. And then there was the litter of pigs Miss Lucy had produced two months ago. They were coming along fine.

"These leg braces," Birch ventured. "When should Bobby have them?"

"He's strong enough to travel now. It's Trudy's cooking that's done it this far. I'd take him into Fort Smith right away." Doc's voice faltered. He had seen something in Birch's face that erased his cheerfulness. Neither Birch nor Trudy met his searching look.

"Birch? If you don't mind me asking . . . you . . . are you two . . . do you have anything held in reserve for this?"

Birch shrugged. He glanced furtively at Trudy, who wished they did not have to admit that there was nothing at all left in the tin box that had held their savings. "Miz Lucy has a fine litter. Twelve shoats. We had thought to grow 'em up a little bigger before we sold 'em. But I reckon we can get ten dollars apiece for 'em at the Meribah sale yard next Tuesday."

There was a cold wind blowing from the southeast, but the sky was clear. No hint of rain. After breakfast, Birch, Tom, and Jefferson loaded up the litter of shoats for the trip to the Meribah sale yard. Trudy determined she would not look out the window at the squealing troop or the frantic sow, all of whom had become pets.

Willa Mae, who came to watch after Bobby, shook her big head in a chiding fashion. "Trudy, honey, I never know'd no gal who named her hogs and stayed happy on sale day."

"It was just so I could tell them apart."

"Now, I heard you call them little pigs babies! You say, 'Mornin', Wiggles! Come on ovuh here, Happy! Have a little carrot from mama, Fats!' You name all twelve of them, Trudy, and they is all goin' to the sale!"

"I never think that far." Trudy raised her chin defensively.

"Now honey, don't mind me. But I's tellin' you . . . cain't be happy on a farm if'n you baptize and fellowship with the critters the Lawd meant to feed folks."

"They mean nothing to me except as a means to get Bobby's brace, Willa Mae."

"Uh-huh." Willa Mae cocked a disbelieving eyebrow at the leftover bacon cooling after breakfast. "I see. Well, Birch tell me I ought t' have a word with you 'bout the way you be namin' ever' critter on the place. Them Rhode Island Reds f'instant. Birch say 'sides Henny you got all them hens named. He say it's gettin' t' be a struggle jus' decidin' which one you gonna put in the pot."

A large kettle of chicken soup simmered on the stove.

Trudy turned toward the window overlooking the fallow fields. "I admit I'm proud of my chickens."

"Uh-huh. Well, what's the name of the one a-bilin' in that pot?"

"Miz Jenson. She quit laying."

Willa Mae laughed. "You name a chicken Miz Jenson, gal?"

"She reminded me of . . . well, you know. . . ."

"A hen remin' you of a person . . . an' I knows who."

"She sort of . . . lorded over the other hens. No matter how many eggs the other hens laid, she tried to take credit for all of them. Interesting personality, that chicken." Trudy gazed seriously into the swirling broth. "She was not my favorite hen, Willa Mae."

"Woooeee! I hopes y' don't ever get riled at me. I is too fat to name a chicken after. Have t' name a whole beef on the hoof after ol' Willa Mae, honey." A big laugh. "Good thing this hen quit layin'. Y'all wouldn't have nothin' t' feed this young'un if she hadn't. Lots of Shiloh hens goin' in the soup kettle today, I reckon. Needful when the young'uns is sick thisaway with the measles."

Trudy was grateful that the topic changed from naming doomed farm animals to the illness that had swept the valley. "Half the children in Shiloh are down with it, Willa Mae." Trudy gathered her coat and looked in on Bobby one last time before leaving to fill in for Mrs. Faraby at Shiloh School.

"It do come on 'em thataway." Willa Mae shuffled toward the steaming pot of chicken soup. "One chil' in the schoolyard catch somethin' an' then, sure's you're born, ever' chil' that ain't had it's gonna get it jus' the same. But it comes worst when folks don' get enough t' eat."

"How are the twins?"

"Baby Mamie is welts all over. Now, that brother of hers? Little Bill don' look so bad as all that, but his little privates is just covered over with rash. He cry ever' time he wets. Jefferson like to faint dead away ever' time Lily change that baby's drawers." Willa Mae laughed and shook her head. "Menfolk. They's just helpless when it come t' young'uns. My Hock, for 'xample? Ever' time one of the babies used t' get sick, he'd take to swoonin'. I'd end up tendin' him much as the sick chil', an' that's a fact. These babies gets ailin'? They don't remember it one day after. But grown folk? Oh my! We do go on and on 'bout a little pain. Tell ever'body that gots ears 'xactly where we was hurtin' us an' how long it took t' get over, an' how we maybe ain't over it yet."

"Organ recital, my mother used to call it."

"Liver an' spleen, note-by-note! That's a fact!" Willa Mae dipped the wooden ladle into the kettle and tasted the broth and hummed with pleasure. "Good."

Trudy pulled on her gloves. "Miz Jenson soup. Throw a disagreeable woman in the pot and let her stew a while. An old Jewish remedy. My mother swore by it."

"Does wonders for the soul! Don't it?"

"A bully hen, and I shan't miss her."

"There's one in ever' barnyard."

"Birch may say that chicken soup tastes like chicken soup no matter who the chicken is, but I'd never put Henny in the pot!"

"Lawd, no! I can see that . . . well now." Willa Mae puzzled over the sense of it. "What was we . . . ? Soup! That's it. Used t' be an ol' slave remedy, too. My mama tol' me 'bout it. I raise all my young'uns on it, too. That is, when folks could spare a chicken." She flashed a gap-toothed smile. Front teeth gone now, Willa Mae spoke with a bit of a lisp, and when she was thinking hard, she worked her mouth like she was chewing taffy. "Never you mind, honey. Go teach your school now. Ol' Willa Mae'll take good care of your Bobby. Feed 'im up good. Keep 'im from takin' a chill. . . . Them pigs is gonna get them braces on his leg. Reckon Jesus gonna do the rest. Heal your baby up quick."

Bobby hollered from his room. "I ain't a baby!"

Trudy shot back. "You mean *you're not* a baby!"

Willa Mae patted Trudy on the shoulder. "Get on to that school now."

Trudy left the house with Willa Mae's rusty voice ringing in her ears. "I got a home in glo-rrrry land that outshines the sun. . . ."

It was a pleasant sound. Somehow the old woman had taken Trudy's mind off the sale yard. But now the squeals of the litter wrenched her heart again as Birch slammed the crate shut and jumped to the seat of the wagon beside Jefferson. Birch's face was stern as he took up the reins and slapped the lines down harder than usual on the backs of the team. Trudy knew he did not want to go to Meribah, but taking the hogs to the Fort Smith sale yard would occupy two days and there was plowing to do and cotton to think about.

Trudy waved goodbye, but he did not seem to hear her or see her.

The litter of pigs were well on the way up the road in the back of the FAMOUS wagon as Trudy and Tom set out for Shiloh School.

The stockyard in Meribah was, in Jefferson's words, the animal version of the Tower of Babel. Cages of squealing pigs competed for attention with corrals of braying donkeys alongside flatbed trucks heaped six crates high with squawking chickens. In marked contrast to the poor trade going on everywhere else in Sebastian County, Meribah's stock pens were a bustle of activity and sales.

"How do you figger they can do so much business here when the rest of the county is so dead?" Birch muttered to Jeff. The shoats in the wagon bed added their squalls to the uproar.

Scanning the dour faces of the farmers bringing their stock to the yard, Jeff suggested, "Fac' is, if Meribah be buyin' at all, that explains it right enough." He raised his head and pretended to sniff the air. "People smell enough money here to get 'em through hard times. But that don't mean they like it. Some of these folks look so grim they must be partin' with their last pet critters just to keep their heads above Jenson credit."

"Thank the Lord that ain't us," Birch said sharply. "I would have liked to keep these pigs till they were some bigger. But they're prime hogs, worth easy ten bucks each."

Jefferson gestured toward a dusty Ford pickup parked next to a stockade. The bed held three pens of chickens. To the rear bumper was tied the lead rope of a milk cow. "Ain't that Arley Palmer's truck?"

"Sure enough . . . and ever' head of stock he owns, except his mule," Birch agreed. "Wonder what's up."

Jeff clucked to the team and pulled the wagon around beside a vacant stretch of fence, then both men approached Arley's rig. Birch poked his head inside the cab to see if any of the Palmer children were about, while Jeff stroked the face of the Holstein.

"Get away from that cow, boy," snarled a voice from behind Jeff. "That prop-ity just been sold, so you keep your thievin' black hands off it."

The voice belonged to Dudley Steel, a Jenson cousin and a Meribah Klan leader. He was the same pale-eyed thug the boys had seen kicking squatters in the stomach and then serving up chicken at the Sebastian County Fair. Birch had it on good authority that he was none other than the Exalted Cyclops of the Meribah County klavern.

Steel thumped a black wooden cane against his boot top as if daring Jeff to challenge his authority. Beside him walked Arley Palmer, his head down and his runover shoes scuffing idly in the dirt.

"Hey, Arley," Birch said. "Thought this was your rig." Then, to Dudley, "Back off, Steel. We didn't hurt anything. We came to sell some pigs."

"Yeah? Well, have your boy unload 'em in pen four. I'll come take a look directly." The Exalted Cyclops strode importantly away to examine a draft horse tied to a hitching rail.

Arley, Birch, and Jeff watched the retreating form as the immense belly wobbled from side to side like a swaybacked mare. "Prob'ly cain't see down past his gut," Arley observed.

"How's that?"

"Pig poop," Arley said, pointing to Steel's boots. "He got pig poop on his toes same as ever'one else."

"Diff'rence is," Birch said, "Steel's boots have more of it on the inside than the outside. Arley, what're you doing here? Are you selling the whole lot?"

"I'm wore out," Arley said softly. "My old mule up and died two days ago. I can't make a go of it no way. We're pullin' out, Birch. Sold the stock for enough cash to reach California, I hope. Why not," he added bitterly. "My place belongs to Garrick Jenson already. He might as well have the critters, too."

"Hey, Tucker," Steel yelled. "You gonna sell them pigs or not? Get 'em unloaded."

"I expect you can meet my price?" Birch hollered back.

Steel's head pivoted slowly on the rolls of greasy fat that passed for his neck. Birch followed the line of his gaze and glimpsed Garrick Jenson's straw hat and thin face across the horse corral. Steel jerked his head toward Birch as if asking a question.

Birch saw Jenson hold up his index finger, crooked at the first joint. Then Jenson abruptly turned his back and walked off.

"Yeah, we'll take them pigs off your hands," Steel said. "Fifty cents apiece."

The day at school slipped by quickly. Tom had some difficulty calling Trudy "Mrs. Tucker," as was proper in the situation. Other than that, he seemed proud to have his mama teaching ciphers, grammar, and literature from the works of Washington Irving. She forgot about the litter of pigs except to hope they would bring a good price at the sale yard.

"The funnest day at school in a long time, Missus Tucker," Tom said as they walked home together. "It's been lonesome without Bobby there, you know?"

She nodded and he slipped his hand in hers, gave it a squeeze, and pulled it back before anyone could see.

He continued, "I felt bad about the hogs this morning. I'm okay now."

"Me, too." She linked her arm in his and matched his stride as home came into view.

"Been thinking about Bobby getting around. The braces on his leg an' all. Reckon I can pull him most of the way to school in the handcart and then . . ." Tom stopped and raised his chin as a familiar sound drifted down the lane. "Listen, Mama. Something must've happened. They've brought 'em home again."

Sure enough, as they walked up the drive, Trudy could hear the squeal of the pigs. Why had Birch and Jefferson brought the litter back?

Birch and Jefferson were sitting together at the kitchen table when Tom and Trudy came in through the back porch. Trudy knew from the grim look on her husband's face that he had not returned the hogs to their pen out of sentiment.

Birch angrily nursed a cup of coffee as he explained. "Folks were practically givin' away their stock. Jenson offered fifty cents a head for the litter."

Trudy sank down beside him. This was bad news indeed.

"Six dollars for the lot, Miz True," Jeff added. "Why, that leaves nothin'. Worse than nothin'. It don't even pay for that trip out to the sale yard."

Birch did not raise his eyes to meet her gaze. Was he afraid she would see how desperate the situation was? "Gonna have to find another way to pay for Bobby's leg braces. Granddaddy's watch, I reckon. . . ."

Trudy nodded, admitting for the first time that perhaps there was no other choice. Did Willa Mae and Jefferson notice the pain that passed through Birch's eyes at her acceptance?

Willa Mae gave no sign of seeing, just continued washing dishes at the sink. "You boys done the right thing," the old woman intoned. "You brung the litter home. Folks what sold their hogs at that sale? Why, they ain't gonna get enough to buy one load of groceries. So what they gonna eat now they got no stock an' no food in the root cellar neither? They's gonna go hongry. That's all."

"Mama," Jeff added. "Lots of folks from all over two counties was sellin' out altogether. Arley Palmer is pullin' up stakes and movin' out. Maybe the Depression didn't mean so much. But the Jenson Consolidated an' the dust done took 'em out. Folks can't stay another summer. They givin' up."

"Where they gonna go to?" Willa Mae asked.

"West, Mama," Jefferson said. "That's all folks was talkin' 'bout. Ain't that so, Birch? Folks is sellin' out and takin' what they can get. Then they is headin' out West. Promise Land they call it."

Willa Mae scoffed. "This here is the Promise Land. Shiloh. Never seen such fine soil."

"Jenson's gonna peel this fine Shiloh soil back and fling it away like potato skin to get the coal. Just like he's skinned all of us." There was murder in Birch's eyes as he spoke. He thumped his palm down hard on the table, making Tom jump. Then Birch scraped the chair back and charged out of the house. The slam of the door left a vacuum of startled silence.

Trudy broke the unpleasant spell. "I almost believed . . . nothing could rattle him." She put her arm protectively around Tom's shoulder.

"He's got reason t' be riled." Jefferson looked down at his big hands, which were clasped on the table.

"I'd like to kill that Jenson!" Tom broke free from Trudy's side, bursting from the house and running toward the creek.

Jeff stood slowly. "I'll have a word with him."

"With whom?" Trudy's eyes were steely with anger. "Birch or Tom? Tom's learning everything from Birch." She turned away from Willa Mae and Jeff. "I've lost the one, and I do not want to lose the other."

The creek of the screen door hinge signaled that Jeff had gone. Trudy was alone with Willa Mae.

"We could have made it." Trudy did not meet the old woman's pitying eyes.

"Y'all still gonna make it, honey."

"The Depression. Even the drought. We might have made it if only . . . He won't let me near him."

"Trudy, honey . . ." The old woman's voice was thick with compassion. "I seen drought come an' I seen drought go. Done buried five young'uns in my time. Y'all gots a dry spell, sure, but that happens in life. Not jus' to a country or a farm, but in folks' hearts, too. An' I seen enough t' know that sooner or later that dry spell gonna break and there be plenty of water."

"But for now, Willa Mae . . ."

"For now? Pray for him. We all gots us a burden t' bear. Birch has a heavy one, I reckon. An' you can't carry it for him. We womens," she chuckled, "we's always tryin' t' fix ever'thing. Make ever'thing right for our menfolk. For our chillun. We try t' be like God, jus' like that ol' serpent in Eden say we womens would do! But honey, you ain't God! Lay it down! You cain't fix what's hurtin' in your man. He's gotta take it to Jesus. Find his own peace. That's the way of it for ever' soul. You cain't do it for 'im."

"Birch is passing his bitterness on to Tom."

"Then Tom gonna have t' deal with it. Reckon in Tom's young life he gonna have plenty to take t' Jesus, too. You cain't do it for Tom, neither."

"I see what's happening to us, and I can't stop it!"

"T'ain't your place t' fix ever'thing! Pray for your man, Trudy. He gots to find his own way home inside his heart. You jus' s'posed to love him, an' pray! It's the least an' it's the most an' sometime it's the onliest thing a gal can do."

Anger at Birch reared up in Trudy. "But Birch is so . . ." The litany of his every imperfection came to her mind.

Willa Mae closed her eyes and put up her hands as if she would not stand to hear another word. "Let God have His way! He's the teacher an' the Father an' the One that loves your man an' them chilluns even more than you does. There's some things we gals cain't make right!

"The devil whispers worry an' grief in our ear. He say, *'If only that man would do this! How come those chilluns don' listen?'* But you tell that ol' serpent t' get on down the road. I say it again . . . Trudy, honey, you ain't God. No woman is. We might try t' be, but we ain't. Tryin' to be God? That's the first sin an' the first lie an' the terrible burden the first wife and mother carried out of Eden. Now we done inherited that burden, an' we gots t' lay it down at the Cross."

Trudy nodded bleakly and sank into the chair where Birch had been. "Birch had counted so on selling the litter."

Willa Mae was ready to pounce on that topic. "Thank Jesus y'all didn't sell them hogs down the river! Amen an' gloooory be! Now y'all gots a whole litter out there in the pen. You named 'em, Trudy honey. You raised 'em up and fed 'em. Now I say, they gonna feed y'all's fambly, them hogs will."

"But what will we feed the hogs?" Trudy asked as the image of the nearly empty feed sack filled her mind.

Willa Mae snorted. "Trudy, honey, there been razorbacks in this here country since long 'fore the white man come. Hogs don't cut an' run to California ever' time there come a dry spell in Arkansas. Hogs eats what they can. Hogs roots aroun', find they own supper." She shrugged and added, "Seen a sow eat an ol' dead coppermouth once. Didn't hurt her none. Hogs'll eat near anythin'. Rotten p'simmons. Acorns."

Willa Mae dried her hands and then, using the towel, carefully lifted the fresh pan of corn bread out of the oven. "P'simmons. Acorns," she repeated as she slid the pan into the warmer. "Y'all gots plenty of both. Lift up your head, gal. No use t' grumble like the Hebrew chillun in the wilderness."

Trudy managed a laugh. "Fear of hunger when there is nothing in the pantry is one of our Hebrew traditions, I'm afraid."

Willa Mae's hands and eyes were raised momentarily toward heaven as though she was receiving the final authoritative word. "Good Book say the chilluns of the righteous never gonna have t' beg bread! Believe it! Hogs in the bottomland is manna from heaven, my Hock use t' say."

Willa Mae slung her coat over her arm, indicating that it was time for her to go. Trudy rose to walk her out the door. Two steps toward the porch, and the Spirit was upon her again. She turned and put her big hands on Trudy's shoulders.

"Now, I knows, Trudy Tucker . . . bein' Hebrew, your kin never did hold hogs in high regard. But I always said that if Moses had ate my black-eyed peas an' ham hock he would've argued the Almighty out of all that business 'bout folks not eatin' pork an' such. Might've change the en-tire book of Leviticus if'n Moses had ate my cookin'."

Willa Mae paused a moment and closed her eyes to savor the vision. Moses on Mount Sinai and a pot of ham hocks and beans simmering beside the Burning Bush. "Ain't no accidents where the chilluns of the Lawd is concern. He know ever' sparrow that falls! Now listen, gal! Y'all gots some fine ham hocks growin' out there in that pen. Them hogs ain't pets t' be named and coddled. They's manna. They's gonna get y'all through, and that's why they ain't sold. We gonna thank the Lawd A'mighty that they was only four bits a piece at the sale yard an' that y'all brung 'em back here."

CHAPTER 20

The water that flowed from the artesian well in the north field no longer spouted forcefully from the top of the eight-foot-tall standpipe as it had before the drought, but it still reached the surface of its own accord and put out a steady flow of five gallons a minute. Since Grandpa Sinnickson had first dowsed the spot at the confluence of two underground streams, it had never failed. The water was always cold and sweet.

But on this day Birch no longer saw in the abundant water the promise of blessing in hard times or God's provision in trouble. He would not have admitted it, but the water bubbling out of the ground from unseen pressures beneath more closely mirrored the way his loathing of Garrick Jenson spewed out of his heart and ran across everything else in his life.

"It's the last straw," he muttered angrily to Jeff, who was helping him fill barrels from the spring. "Your mama is all for puttin' the best face on that business with the pigs, and she means well, but I'm so mad I can't see straight."

"I notice you seem right 'et up with it," Jeff said quietly.

Birch continued as if Jeff had not spoken, as if he was not really talking to Jeff at all. "I dreamed about tar and feathers last night," he said. "Garrick Jenson looks like a scrawny bird at the best of times. Tarred and covered in feathers, he'd look just like a bony rooster gettin' singed over a slow fire."

"He would at that."

"But that ain't even enough," Birch said with venom in his voice. "Buck Hooper had the right idea, only with a loaded gun. What do you think?" Birch towered over Jeff in the bed of the wagon, and the eyes he turned on Jeff were unnaturally bright.

Jeff forced himself to keep his gaze locked on Birch in the hope that his words would get through. "You don't mean that," he said.

"Why don't I?"

"'Cause you ain't that way, and if that ain't enough, you got a fambly you loves and that loves you. How you gonna take care of 'em when you's in prison? I done hard time an' I know. A man can do the time for his own lookout, but worryin' 'bout his kin eat him up worse'n what is gnawin' on him before."

Birch sat down abruptly on the wagon seat and put his face in his hands. "But I can't take care of 'em now," he groaned. "I signed those papers, and we're caught."

"You didn't have no choice," Jeff reminded him. "You done it for Bobby. What's more, we ain't licked yet. You said yourself we is standin' in the best cotton-growin' land in the state. Ain't that so?"

Birch admitted that it was.

"And this here well of your granddaddy's be puttin' out steady when wells all over is dryin' up and the Jim Fork is droppin' to mud. Ain't that right? What call do you got givin' up now? Shootin' off your mouth like Buck Hooper—you fixin' to crawl inside a bottle like him, too?"

Birch sat up as if Jeff had backhanded him to the face. Images of his father's drunken stupor punctuated by alcoholic rages filled his mind. "No," he said simply.

"Good Book say 'enough for each day is the evil thereof.' So why you hafta go 'round borrowin' tomorrow's trouble?"

Jeff had never spoken to Birch so bluntly before.

Birch turned and stared across the field toward the Tucker home on the ridge and the border of birch trees. When he spoke again his voice was softer and more controlled. "I'm scared, Jeff," he said. "Haven't been this scared but two times . . . first battle I was in over in France and when the boys took sick. But now ever'thing I've worked for all my life is ridin' on this field, the cotton we plant and harvest right here."

"You got manna and you askin' for quail?" Jeff asked him. "You wave your fist in God's face and say it ain't enough?" The big man shook his head. "God done give you your fine fambly and the good land and the good well and the strength to plow and plant and hoe and water and harvest."

Birch heard in the words both a declaration of fact and a prayer as well. "You told me to root out the bitter," he said, "before it took me over. You were right."

The preparation of the north field for the most important cotton crop of Birch's life was proceeding. The dark red soil was cultivated and turned to break up the clods, readied for the planting.

Birch and Jeff stood near the edge of the forty acres, discussing the next day's labor and looking at how the James Fork Creek had fallen. For this time of year, the level was very low indeed. In place of the clear, fast-flowing stream they saw a muddy, sullen flow. As if surrendering to dry ground, the brook had retreated from sandbanks normally under several feet of water and exposed rocks and snags seldom seen.

Jeff pointed to a shallow pool that was now separated from its parent creek by ten feet of bare earth. "Minnows an' tadpoles don't even know they got troubles," he said. "Crick done cast 'em out, and their new home ain't likely to last long. Just like lotta folks these days—"

Jeff's musing was disturbed by the familiar rattling and backfiring of Doc Brown's Model-T. It chugged into view down the Hartford road, and as it drew nearer, Birch noticed that Doc's brother Jim was riding along.

"'Lo Birch, Jeff," Doc called, shutting off his engine with an obstinate clatter. "Glad we found you out like this. Wanted to talk something over with you."

"Sure, Doc," Birch returned. "What's up?"

Doc squinted at the cuffs of his shirtsleeves, coughed, looked at his brother, and then launched in. "You remember what I said about Bobby's progress depending on getting him into braces right away?"

Birch's face fell. "'Course I remember," he said. "But . . ."

Doc hurried to continue. "Heard about the Jenson sale yard," he said. "And I know you were counting on that litter of pigs for the cash for Bobby's treatment."

Birch spread his hands. "We got nothing left, Doc."

"Wait, wait," the doctor protested. "We didn't drive out here and bring this up to make you feel worse. Fact is, my brother has an idea. Go on, Jim," he urged, digging his elbow into Jim's side. "Speak up."

"It's this way," Jim began, obviously ill at ease. Birch had never seen the man tongue-tied before. "Now, I'm just a country blacksmith. But do you recollect Floyd Armitstead's mule—the one that cut his tendon real bad just above the hock? Floyd thought a lot of that mule, but he was so lame that Floyd was going to put him down."

Birch felt confused and looked it.

"Go on," Doc encouraged.

"If you recall, I made up a special shoe with a pair of flanges on the sides. And then I fixed up a pair of steel supports out of buggy springs and welded them to a collar above the next joint. With that collar lined with wool and the metal all covered in leather, that mule was almost good as new. Sound enough for plowing, anyway, just a little stiff. . . . Anyhow, I'm just a blacksmith, not a doctor, but I thought—"

"You could do it for Bobby!" Birch completed.

"I'm just a blacksmith, shoeing horses. . . ." Jim protested, but Birch was already chasing the new thought for all he was worth.

"Jim could do the same for Bobby! Doc, could it work? Could it really?"

"No reason why not," Doc agreed. "Won't be stainless steel, but the principle's the same. Besides, Bobby won't be having to drag a plow behind him anytime soon. It only has to support his weight when he stands."

"How soon can we do it? I mean, how quick can you have 'em ready?"

"Soon as I get a couple of measurements," Jim said. "I'll start today."

Birch was already perched on the car's running board, and he gestured impatiently for Jeff to do the same.

But the scene in Bobby's room was not as cheerful. Just finished with another treatment of scalding hot towels, Bobby was gripping the edges of the bed and biting the pillow in his pain. Worse yet, he did not want anyone else to see his shrunken, toothpick-thin limb.

"Please no, Dad," he begged. "It's bad enough that Doc and Jeff and Willa Mae . . . not nobody else, please, Dad."

Birch struggled with causing his son any more unhappiness, but he swallowed hard and pressed ahead. "You want to walk again, don't you? Here is where you start," and he gestured for Jim to approach Bobby's bedside with his tape measure.

"Hello, Bobby," Jim said with a husky voice. "I just need a minute. Listen, you should have seen your brother and Rosey get after that possum. It was the greatest thing I ever witnessed." His sturdy but gentle hands gauged knee to ankle and diameters around which he could reach with thumb and forefinger. "Almost done," he said. "Next fall you gonna go after a possum yourself?"

Bobby stopped squeezing his eyes tight shut and opened one just a crack. "You think I could?"

"Get you going real soon," Jim promised. "Do my best, anyway. Birch, do you have a pair of sturdy boots that still fit this young man?"

On the way out through the kitchen, Birch stopped Jim with a hand on his arm. "You know I can't pay you," he began.

Jim shrugged and shook his head as if the words were painful in his ears.

"But I want to give you my granddad's pocket watch," Birch continued.

"No, nothing," Jim protested. "I want to do this for Bobby, for nothing. Just let me loose, Birch, I got Boomer keeping the forge hot for me, and if I don't get back soon, he's liable to burn the place down."

Doc and Jim showed up at the Tucker place just after sunup, which meant that they had left Hartford while the stars were still bright. "Worked till after midnight," Doc confided, nodding toward Jim, who was stifling a yawn. "Then he got up again at four, and he's been smoothing and polishing ever since. I tried to tell him he was burnishing shadows, but he just grunted and kept right on."

"Couldn't leave any wickers or rough spots," Jim argued. "Here, Birch, take a look." The blacksmith shyly held open the car door and unfolded a sheepskin-wrapped bundle. There on the fleece lay what looked to be a mechanical leg. It began from a plate across the bottom of Bobby's boot, then two rigid dark-metal rods rose past a circular ankle support. At the top of the column was another round band to go above Bobby's knee. As promised, the places that would touch the boy's leg were covered in fleece. The brace looked sturdy, Birch thought, though the word *heavy* also crossed his mind.

"Already thought of an improved model," Jim said shyly. "I think I can build an ankle hinge that you can pin so it can move either a little or a lot, cut down on the stiffness. But I thought of it too late to get on this time."

"I can't tell you how wonderful this is," Birch said. "Come on, let's show Bobby right now."

Entering Bobby's room, Birch called softly, "Bobby, wake up. Look what Jim made. It's here already, your brace."

Bobby woke from a sound sleep, stared without understanding at his father for a moment, then dropped his gaze to the metal supports dangling from Birch's hand. He took one look and screamed, "No! Leg-irons! Just like they put on Jeff! No, Daddy, take my boot out of that thing. No leg-irons, no! I won't wear those. Take 'em away."

"Easy, Bobby," Birch implored. "Take it easy, son. We'll just put 'em aside for now, all right? Go on back to sleep."

When the three men stood around Doc's car again, Jim's face was creased with sorrow and apology. "I know that old dark steel looks heavy and clumsy," he said. "I didn't have anything else to use. I'm sorry, Birch. Don't be upset with Bobby. He's right; they do look like manacles."

Birch was just as apologetic about Bobby's reaction.

"Nonsense," Doc chided them both. "It looks fine and will work fine. Like any other prosthetic appliance, the wearer has to get used to the idea; he has to see the benefit and not the object itself."

Birch nodded. "Later on, when he's more awake, we'll stand him up. I know he'll like that. I'm sure of it, Jim," he said, thrusting a leather pouch into the blacksmith's hands. "I insist. You take Grandpa Sinnickson's watch. When times get better, maybe you'll let me redeem it back from you."

Politics and tadpoles. It was this unlikely combination that finally awakened Bobby's interest in the leg brace. It had been three weeks since it had first been presented to him.

The presidential campaign of 1932 was an issue that sparked long and loud discussion in the Hartford barbershop and on the porch of Grandma Amos's store in Shiloh. But only one detail caught Trudy's attention as the political debate raged on around her.

"Franklin Delano Roosevelt." Trudy placed the latest copy of *Liberty* magazine across Bobby's lap as he sat up in the bedroom. The leg brace remained where it had been placed in the corner of the room. No combination of reasoning, begging, or threats had convinced Bobby to put on the "leg-irons."

Tom sat on the bed beside his brother and looked at the photograph of the rock-jawed governor of New York. Franklin D. Roosevelt, waving to a crowd of onlookers, stood between two men on the back of a train.

Tom said, "Franklin. His first name sounds like a last name. Just like Jefferson's." Roosevelt's large face seemed friendly beneath the brim of his fedora. Broad shoulders and a powerful upper body gave no hint that what Trudy said was true.

Bobby peered skeptically down at the picture. "He's standing up."

"Yes," Trudy agreed.

Tom stared at Roosevelt's arm, which was linked through the arm of the young man beside him. Perhaps he needed help to balance?

"If he had polio, how can he stand up?" Bobby glanced resentfully at the brace in the corner.

Trudy continued. "He wears braces on his legs like yours."

"I don't see 'em," Bobby argued, studying the image and refusing to believe her.

Trudy explained, "You cannot see Governor Roosevelt's braces because they are beneath his trouser legs, just as your brace will be hidden beneath the leg of your overalls. But he wears steel braces just like the one Jim Brown made for you. And you must wear yours and learn to walk. Then people will not believe you have braces on either."

Silence. Bobby contemplated the big man in the magazine photograph. "Bet he can't go possum hunting."

Trudy countered. "He could if he wished to. He swims well, I have heard. See here." She turned the page to a photograph of the governor in a swimming pool in Warm Springs, Georgia. "And," Trudy continued, "he is running for president of the United States of America."

"Running?" Bobby questioned.

"For president. Against President Hoover and a lot of important men in the Democratic party who have never had polio." Trudy snipped the photograph from the magazine.

Tom did not say so, but from the talk in the barbershop, President Hoover would not be hard to catch and pass this election, even by a challenger running in steel leg braces. If ever there was a president more disagreeable than Hoover, Dee Brown had said, his likes had not been seen since before the time of Abe Lincoln. Beyond that no one, not even Grandma Amos, could remember.

"How far does Roosevelt have to run?" Bobby contemplated the presidential race in literal terms.

Trudy did not dwell on the terminology of national politics. It was enough for Bobby to know that Franklin Roosevelt carried nine pounds of steel on his legs. "Mister Roosevelt must run across the entire country."

Bobby gave a low whistle. At last he was impressed.

Trudy nodded. "Before he could run, first he had to learn to walk again. And in order to walk he had to put braces on his legs." She pinned the photograph of FDR to the blue-checked curtain where Bobby would see it whenever he looked out the window. "And so the first step for you, Bobby, is to put it on."

He did not reply to her statement, but looked past the photo and out the window. "There's Jefferson coming up the lane," he remarked.

Heads pivoted. Approaching the house with purposeful strides, Jefferson carried a large, clear-glass jar in his arms, the kind that pickled pigs' feet came in down at Grandma Amos's store. It was half filled with murky green water.

Rosey sidled up to him in the yard. He stooped and addressed the dog, showing her the container. She wagged as if understanding the purpose of his call.

Tom went to the window and hollered out. "Hey, Jeff! Dad's gone to help paint the church."

"I seen him there." Jefferson held up one of his enormous hands. It was splattered with white paint. "I brung somethin' for Bobby."

"We're all here, talking politics," Trudy returned. "Come ahead."

Jefferson entered with his gift behind his back. He filled the tiny bedroom as he stood at the foot of the bed. "How you comin' with them braces?" He asked this although everyone in Shiloh and Hartford knew that Bobby was not coming along at all.

Bobby shrugged. "Ugly. Like your leg-irons, and I won't put 'em on."

This argument had been heard a hundred times and Jefferson chose to take a detour. "Fine. Well, I brung you somethin' t' keep you comp'ny." The jar swung around. Half a dozen small, fishlike creatures with fat bodies and slim tails wriggled in the water.

"Tadpoles." Bobby seemed pleased.

"They was stranded. Nearly high an' dry. One more day an' they'd of been deader'n doornails. That's a fact. So I was walkin' by this mudhole, an' I hear this little voice." Jefferson cupped his hands around his mouth and in a reedy falsetto repeated what he heard. "'Haaaaaalp! Pleeease, mister! If'n you don't he'p us, we gonna be flybait by noon t'morrow." Jefferson passed the jar to Bobby. "They said other things, too, but that's what 'tracted me to 'em."

Bobby grinned and studied the six tadpoles.

Trudy was less than thrilled. More creatures in the house. Henny already shared a nest with Rosey at the foot of the bed. Now tadpoles? "What do they eat?" she asked.

Tom, Bobby, and Jefferson sniggered at the ignorance of her question. Tom answered, "They eat their tails!"

"What?" Trudy peered through the glass.

Bobby educated her in the mysteries of raising tadpoles. "They're baby frogs, Mama," he instructed. "They swim around like this after they hatch and their tails disappear and they grow legs."

"Ah," she nodded broadly in understanding. Then some thought struck her, and she snapped her head up sharply to gaze with curiosity at Jefferson. He nodded once. They understood some secret that escaped Tom and Bobby.

Jeff added, "When they gets grow'd up, they also talk an' sing."

"Well . . ." Tom cocked his head to one side doubtfully.

Jefferson countered his disbelief. "They does! I been sittin' on the porch of Dreamland an' listenin' ever' night to them bullfrogs down by the crick. They been talkin' to me! Tell me Bobby oughta save their baby tadpoles."

Bobby laughed a delighted snort. He clutched his belly and guffawed at Jeff's story. Nobody could make Bobby laugh like Jefferson.

Bobby asked, "What else they say?"

Jefferson cupped his hand around his ear. "Y'all listen t'night. Y'all gonna hear it, too! Jus' gotta know the language is all!" In a deep bullfrog voice, Jefferson repeated the secret message.

Tadpole gon-na hop! Bobby gon-na walk!
Put 'em on! Put 'em on!
Tadpole gon-na hop! Bobby gon-na walk!
Put 'em on! Put 'em on!

Jefferson repeated the chorus four times until the group in the room was mesmerized by the rhythm of the song. Bobby's eyes grew wide with the wonder of it. His gaze lit on the brace in the corner. Could the bullfrogs mean . . .

Tadpole gon-na hop! Bobby gon-na walk!
Put 'em on! Put 'em on!

Trudy had a soft, faraway expression on her face as if she could clearly comprehend the language.

And it seemed to Tom that he had heard the same refrain sung every night, but he had just not quite understood it until now.

CHAPTER 21

The moon was nothing more than a slice of silver suspended above the Poteau range. It gave off just enough glow to backlight the dark mountains, but not enough to dim the thick band of stars that streaked the sky.

Unable to sleep, Trudy considered the bright crescent from her bed. The fragment of moon was perfectly framed by the window, like a painting, she mused: above the mountains, above the trees, above the valley, above the knoll where Joey slept as the night sang him a lullaby. Bullfrogs croaked beside the slow-moving waters of the James Fork. (Bobby gonna walk!) Crickets chirped in the garden. A whippoorwill called from the stand of birch trees. An owl answered from the old hickory tree in the yard. It was the kind of song that paid no mind to time or human worry.

Each night, as Jefferson had predicted, the bullfrogs sang encouragement to Bobby as little legs began to sprout on the tadpoles in the jar. Bobby had put the brace on. He had stood up, looking something like an umbrella in an umbrella stand, beside the bed. Every day he had showed a little more progress, learning to walk an inch at a time. Today he had taken three steps before he fell. Now it was not a matter of getting Bobby to put the brace on, but how to make him take it off. Jefferson would have to speak to the bullfrogs about changing their tune.

And what of the lameness in Trudy's soul? She recognized it clearly, felt it drag her back from the edge of joy. She wished there was some quiet voice that would teach her soul to stand erect again.

Trudy closed her eyes and tried to focus her mind on the mellow sounds of the night; just to rest a while, to forget about tomorrow and stop yearning for yesterday. But the frantic ticking of the clock on the chest of drawers was louder than the hoot of the owl, more insistent than the crickets. Out in the parlor, the wall clock clucked its tongue, reminding her that their lives and fortunes were still governed by time and that worry was hard to avoid.

As much as she longed to, Trudy could not turn the hours back to happy mornings in the garden with little Joe tending his radish patch. Nor could she, by wishing, slow the rush of the passing weeks until the bills came due. Time was an impatient master, one which could demand everything they owned in the end: the house, the barn, the fields, her garden, the chickens, and the cow. There was nothing that could not be forfeited, including that precious mound of earth where Trudy's heart was buried.

Who will tend his little grave if we are forced to leave this place?

Turning her face from the window, she put her hand on Birch's back. She hoped he was awake, too. She wanted to be held. She needed to cry a while and to be comforted. But he did not stir at her touch, and so she did not cry. The grief remained dry, a hollow, lonely feeling in the pit of her stomach.

Whispered prayer congealed on her lips, *"Dear God. Dear God!"* She could not say more.

The wall clock tocked. A whippoorwill called. God did not answer.

The moon slipped beneath the rim of mountains. Only the stars were out when Trudy finally dozed off. Dreams of soft summer nights played in her mind, and then bright spring mornings with Birch and Joe in the garden.

Warm sun shone on her face. Drops of dew clung to the cornstalks. Chickens clucked and bobbed in search of insects. Little Joe called to her and held up the first radish of the day.

She felt happy again, even though somewhere in her thoughts she was aware that this was only a dream. . . .

And then the garden gate shrieked and groaned as it turned, and a stranger entered. . . .

Trudy's eyes snapped open. Was it a dream? Had she heard the garden hinges? From Tom and Bobby's bedroom the dog growled low and menacing. Night sounds drifted in through the half-open window. Trudy lay very still for a long moment. She heard the click of Rosey's nails against the wood floor as the hound padded into the parlor, then gave a little woof as if wanting to go outside.

Trudy nudged Birch. He groaned and rolled over, then rubbed his face and covered his eyes with his hand.

"Awake?" Trudy asked, her heard pounding. Visions of her garden stripped clean filled her mind.

"Now . . . I am."

"Someone—someone opened the garden gate."

"You're dreamin'," he mumbled and rolled over. "Nobody'd be fool enough . . . enter the holy of holies without your okay. . . ."

Rosey barked and growled as if to emphasize Trudy's suspicion. She reached over and shook her husband.

"I tell you, someone is in the garden, Birch! Stealing our . . . the food right out of our . . . my cabbages."

Another impatient yip interrupted. Trudy fell silent and grasped Birch's arm. He sat up slowly and cocked his head to listen. Nothing but bullfrogs and a mosquito tapping against the window screen. But Rosey growled again.

Convinced of the possibility of a thief, Birch whispered to the dog, "What is it, Rosey girl?"

Reaching down beside the bed, Birch retrieved a single-shot twenty-gauge. Opening the chamber, he slipped in a shell.

"Should I light the lamp?" Trudy whispered hoarsely as Birch stood, put on his boots, and peered out the window.

"No!" he demanded. "I'll have me a look. Stay put."

But Trudy did not want to stay put. "Suppose he comes in through the window while you are outside?"

"Probably just a raccoon. Stay put!"

"No raccoon can open my gate! I am coming with you," she insisted, jumping out of bed and trailing after him in her long white cotton nightgown like a ghost. As was so often the case between them, he had lost the dispute.

"Trudy! Keep back of me, will you!" Birch ordered as she rushed past him into the parlor. He gave her a slight nudge, directing her to remain safe behind him. She obeyed, but clung to the waistband of his boxer shorts as if to hold him back. Rosey brushed against her leg and charged out the door straight to the garden gate, where she commenced to howl at the blackness beyond the chicken wire.

"Something's in there, all right," Birch croaked.

"It's a human something." She pictured her spring garden stripped clean. Stolen spinach. Cauliflower uprooted. Cabbages loaded into a sack and toted off to be boiled and devoured at the hobo jungle. Hollow clay crocks where sauerkraut should have been. Canning jars empty. Hungry children waiting at the table for supper!

Trudy's mouth was dry as she peered around Birch. She could not see anything at all. They shuffled in step through the screen door and onto the porch. Her feet were shoeless. The planks were rough. The night air was cool and fragrant. Trudy shuddered.

Birch whispered urgently, "Turn loose of my shorts, True. I may have to chase him down, and you'll strip me naked if I take off!"

Birch pointed the scatter gun in the general direction of the garden.

Then he shouted his challenge. "Who's there?" His muscles were tense. He was ready for a fight.

No reply. Rosey, concealed by the night, whined.

"Birch!" Trudy warned.

He jumped at her voice and raised the weapon to his shoulder. "*What?* Where is he?"

"Don't shoot the dog." Instinctively she grasped the seat of his shorts again.

"Don't shoot the dog? Turn me loose, woman!" he hissed, wrenching free and jumping off the step. "Now, do as I say, True! Stay here!" Her feet being bare, she obeyed.

He made his way cautiously toward the gate, talking all the while. Trudy could barely see his white undershirt and shorts in the darkness, but she was comforted by the sound of his voice and the crunch of gravel beneath his boots.

"There's one way outta my garden, feller, and I got me a sawed-off, double-barrel, twelve-gauge pointed right at the gate! If that ain't enough to make you give it up, I got me the biggest, meanest hound dog in Sebastian County settin' right where you aim to put your thievin', wanderin', no-good foot! This dog of mine'll chase you down and take your leg right off up to the hip and use your thigh bone as a toothpick! This dog ain't gonna show you mercy 'less I say to. So you best lay down what you aimed to steal and put your hands up high in the air . . . else I'm gonna blow your head clean off and feed the rest of you to the hogs!"

Of course, as far as hounds went, little Rosey did not have a mean bone in her body. No doubt if the thief stooped to pat her head on his way out she would have licked his face and said, "Thank you very much for the visit."

As for the weapon in Birch's hand, it was good for one stinging blast of rock salt, and then maybe Birch could use it as a club. But the story sounded convincing, and Trudy half believed it herself.

Birch's form became a wraithlike apparition that flitted from the gate to the blackberry tangle spiraling along one length of fence. Trudy saw him slink from there to the deep pool of shadows under the persimmon tree. She almost called out to him to be careful, drew breath, changed her mind, then caught the warning halfway out so that a feeble "Birr . . ." escaped her tightened throat.

Still no further noise from the intruder within the garden. Was he a gangster, armed to the teeth with a tommy gun, or a harmless tramp, scared out of his wits? If something did not happen soon, Trudy thought she would scream just to break the tension.

"Get down, dog," she heard Birch grunt. "Outta my way, Rosey."

There was the sound of a slap and Rosey's frightened yip and then everything broke loose at once.

Birch's yell, "Not that way, Rosey!" was accompanied by a wild shaking of the garden fence as if it were caught in the grip of a giant. The roar of the shotgun tore through the silence, intensified by Trudy's pent-up scream and Rosey's now panicked yelps.

In the flare of the muzzle blast, the scene of the confrontation was seared into Trudy's vision. There was Birch tumbled into the arms of the persimmon tree, the barrel of the gun tangled in the fence wire. At the opposite end of the garden patch stood the wide-eyed figure of a man, his mouth frozen in a spasm of terror. All around his head and shoulders, like the photograph of a circus juggler, was a halo of flying cabbages, broccoli, and beets.

The single explosive moment dissolved into a confusion of competing noises and concerns. Trudy's yells, "Birch! Are you hurt? Birch?" were so frenzied that she could not for a time hear that Birch himself was shouting for her to bring a light, fetch the lantern! Rosey skittered past Trudy and up onto the porch, nosing the door open to dive into the house.

An unfamiliar, rasping male voice pleaded, "Don't shoot! I give up! Lord a-mercy, man! Don't shoot!"

"I'm coming, Birch," Trudy called, sweeping off the porch and toward the thrashing heap of vines, leaves, and shotgun barrel that was her husband.

"*No!*" Birch ordered gruffly. "Fetch the lantern, Trudy!" He then directed his growling at the thief. "And you, whoever you are, don't even move. I got the other barrel ready for you."

"Don't worry about me, mister," replied a quaking voice interrupted by dry coughs. "I ain't even gonna breathe till you say it's all right."

Trudy whirled about and screamed again at the sight of another figure that materialized on her porch. It was Tom, with lantern and matches in hand. "What is it, Mama? Did Dad catch a thief in the garden?"

With fingers that trembled so badly it took three tries, Trudy finally got the lantern lit. As the warm orange glow pushed back the darkness, she heard Birch call out, "Okay, Tom. Set the lantern by the gate, then you get back on up to the porch." As soon as this was done, Birch ordered, "Your turn, feller. Walk straight up to that light. Keep your hands way up over your head where I can see 'em."

As the figure in the garden advanced toward the glow, he appeared to shrink in size and grow ever more scruffy with each step. He seemed only about half Birch's size. A scraggly beard covered his cheeks. Ragged trousers protected his bony shanks. It looked to Trudy as though he was wearing the tattered tunic of an army uniform.

Birch kept the barrel of the shotgun pointed at the man's chest as he approached along the fence. "Please aim that somewhere's else, mister," the man pleaded between coughs. "I ain't a bit dangerous, 'cept to myself."

"Come on outta there, then," Birch growled, picking up the lantern with his left hand. "March yourself up to the house whilst I decide what to do with you. Is that a campaign jacket you're wearin'?"

"1918. Argonne," the man hacked out.

"Is it yours?" Birch asked suspiciously.

"It is. And the Purple Heart for eating Heinie mustard gas." His whiskered chin jutted downward toward the medal on his chest.

So the fellow was a veteran of the Great War. The same Great War Birch had fought in. Trudy knew this fact alone changed everything for Birch. No matter that cabbages were scattered all over the ground. No matter that several quarts' worth of beets had been uprooted before they were grown as big as they might have been. For Birch, a campaign jacket and a Purple Heart were something like proof of kinship. A fellow veteran was down on his luck and hungry enough to steal. This was a tragedy, not a crime.

The muzzle of the empty shotgun tipped toward the ground. Birch glanced down at it, then set it aside and leaned it up against the fence. "Come on into the house," he repeated, opening the gate. Trudy shooed Tom into the kitchen ahead of them. There would be time enough in the morning to retrieve the pilfered cabbages and convert them into kraut.

"If you're hungry," Birch said as the man marched past with his arms still in the air, "there's some corn bread in the kitchen and buttermilk. . . ."

The windows of Trudy's kitchen were fogged with the vapors from the boiling coffeepot on the gleaming nickel-plated cookstove. Beyond the red gingham curtains, the first pale hint of dawn over the hills chased the stars away to the west. The morning star, a lone reddish orphan, hung in solitude above the sweet-gum tree.

The stranger's high cheekbones pressed sharply against the taut skin of his face. His brown curly hair was matted and plastered down against his skull above sunken eyes. His hands, even after being washed up in a bucket on the back porch, were still streaked with grease, and the fingernails were broken off short and black with grime. Trudy nudged Tom and Bobby to tell them that it was impolite to stare at the gaunt features, then found herself doing the same thing.

The intruder, now welcomed as a guest, never noticed. His hands cupped the enamel mug of coffee that followed three heaping bowls of corn bread and buttermilk and the leftover chicken drumstick Trudy had intended for Birch's noon meal. Throughout the unplanned middle-of-the-night feeding, the man in the frayed remains of an army uniform had only spoken once, to announce that his name was Will Grove. Nor had anyone interrupted the intense concentration with which he absorbed the simple fare.

After a cautious sip of the steaming brew, he coughed politely into his fist and raised his eyes to the Tucker family seated all around him.

"Much obliged," he said. "I ain't had such fine food in a long while. Maybe not since leavin' home."

"Where is home?" Birch inquired.

Grove got a faraway look in his restless green eyes. "Home?" he repeated, as if the question puzzled him. "Back in '29 I lived in Chi—that's Chicago—me an' the missus and our boy. Lost my job . . . good one, too . . . workin' in the yards. Then the one after that only lasted six months. Then . . . I dunno . . . been on the road now more'n a year. It's the da—" Grove caught the disapproval that had leapt into Trudy's face at the near profanity and amended his speech. "It's the foremen and their capitalist bosses," he concluded. "Cut us back to half hours and then tried to cut our pay, too. But that was before I joined up with the League. Yessir, Worker's Ex-Servicemen's League. Things are gonna change in this country. You just wait and see."

"What about your family?" Trudy blurted out, though Birch shot her a warning look.

Grove shrugged as if the matter was of no consequence. "The bloodsucking leeches who have the money won't hire men with any backbone. But my old lady couldn't understand I had to stand up for my rights . . . principles, don't you see? One day I come home and found a note. Said she couldn't take no more. Took the boy and left me. That was when I started ridin' the rods. Been clean down to New Orleans, lookin' for work. . . . There ain't any. . . . so I started back up north. Another 'bo told me about this Hooverville off the Rock Island spur, said I could get something to eat there. But he was wrong." Grove looked up with a defiant expression. "You folks seem to have plenty and to spare, an' I was desperate, see? In a right world, ever'body has enough, an' nobody lords it over anyone else."

"Does that justify steal—" Trudy reared up ready for a fight, but Birch shot her a look to make her hold her tongue.

"Why didn't you just come up and ask?" Birch wanted to know. "We could have fed you then, same as now, without all the fuss."

Grove shook his head. "Ain't many left as good-hearted as you. Railroad bulls throw hoboes off trains doing fifty, sixty miles an hour. Deputies with big sticks and dogs meet you outside of towns and say, 'Keep movin', bum. Ain't nothing for you here.' Sorta gives you a jaundiced eye, see?"

"And are you heading back to Chi now, Mister Grove?" Trudy asked hopefully, anxious to see the last of the arrogant beggar.

"Nope." Grove shook his grizzled face. "I got the call to meet up with some of my old outfit in St. Louis for the march to Washington." Birch and Trudy looked blank. "You mean you ain't heard tell of the Bonus March? That's why I got my uniform on now. You being a vet and all," he said to Birch, "Belleau Wood, you said? I figgered you already know'd about it. You recollect the extra payment that was voted back eight, ten years?"

Birch vaguely recalled something of the kind. "Dollar a day for every day bein' in the Great War? But that won't be paid till 1945."

Grove shook his head in violent disagreement. "Ain't s'posed to get paid till then," he argued. "But five hundred dollars! Set me on my feet again! If enough of us go to Washington, then them fat-cat Congressmen will get the message. We won't last another thirteen years. We need help now!" He crooked his thumb at the decorations on his chest. "Otherwise, I might could get fifty cents for these. But it won't come to that. The League'll set 'em straight."

"Five hundred dollars, you said?" Birch repeated, his head doing rapid calculations. "That's a good round sum in these times."

"You bet your sweet—, er, life it is," Grove agreed.

"But how long will this take? I mean, you don't expect that Washington will just pony up the money right away, do you? President Hoover says he's against paying direct aid to folks, says it saps the national strength of character."

Grove made a rude noise with buzzing lips that got an interested look from Tom and a scowl of disapproval from Trudy. "Sorry, ma'am," Grove said. "But that President Hoover will just have to come along, if he knows what's what. Ten thousand of us on his doorstep! This ain't just the League, get it? Ever'body who's a vet can go. Why, we won't be gone no time at all—a week, maybe two is all. See, this ain't nothing like a handout. It's our bonus, and we is all entitled to it. Course . . ." He paused to shoot Birch a quick look. "Course, a man's gotta go to Washington to get the payment. Can't just set home and expect something on a silver platter. No sir, man's gotta be there to get his share."

Trudy could see that Birch was deep in thought. "I'll think on it some," he said at last. "And I wish you luck. True," he suggested, "get me a flour sack, will you? I'll bundle up them cabbages and let Mister Grove have 'em. They'll help out a stewpot along the way." Trudy made a small noise of protest but said nothing when she saw the determined set of Birch's jaw.

The wail of an approaching Rock Island freight lent its authority to the announcement that morning had come to Shiloh. "Best be off," Grove said. "Well, Brother Birch, spare us some thought. Course if I had such a fine home and family and farm an' all," he said, half with envy and half with disdain, "I wouldn't be in no rush to leave it, neither."

Trudy watched and listened from the porch as the two men walked out to the dirt lane that led past the front of the house. Birch thrust the cloth pouch of cabbages and beets into Grove's hands. "Good luck," he said again.

"Me and the other boys'll be rolling out of here next day," Grove said. "Then St. Louis. We'll be a week or so gettin' organized. We got men coming from as far away as Oregon. East St. Louis, the rail yard just across the river in Illinois. Just so's you can find us when you make up your mind."

CHAPTER 22

You intend to go, don't you? To Washington?" Trudy brushed past Birch as he mucked the calf pen. He avoided her question, hefting the wheelbarrow and wheeling a load of manure outside the barn. Trudy placed the stool beside Esmerelda and patted the milk cow's sunken flank.

Birch rolled the wheelbarrow by her as he returned, pausing to contemplate the jutting hip bones of the little Jersey. "There's no pasture for her to graze. Don't know how much longer she'll give milk."

"Did you hear me?" Trudy snapped.

"No. What?"

"You heard," she accused, squeezing a teat and letting the metallic buzz of milk against the tin bucket fill up his silence.

"Well then? What if I did?" He turned away from the stall.

Furious, Trudy leapt to her feet, knocking the bucket over and startling Esmerelda. "Then tell me!" she shouted.

He stopped in a shaft of light that beamed down between two planks on the east wall. "I was thinkin' about goin'. Yes. I was."

"Going to Washington with that awful man. That awful man!"

"Is it any worse than sittin' 'round the farm like I done all winter with the walls and the Jensons closing in on us?"

"We've got the well. It's still full of good water. You and Jeff have planted the north field. Birch! You don't have to do this!"

"What chance you think we've got if they've set their minds to strip-minin' Shiloh? I know the type of man Jenson is. And that woman of his! She's worse. Trudy, I got to go. And if Jefferson will come with me, he's got to go, too. It's the only way left."

There was a finality in his voice that convinced her there was no use arguing further. She straightened the stool, picked up the bucket, and returned to the milking.

A half hour passed in silent resentment, Trudy saying nothing and Birch attending his duties with the vigor of a man trying to escape thoughts of other things.

Pulling Bobby in the handcart, Tom came out to the barn to say goodbye before the brothers left for school. He found his parents sullen and preoccupied.

"Hey, Dad?" Bobby called. "Are you goin' to Washington with the soldiers?"

"I do believe I am," Birch aimed his comment at Trudy with the sort of defiant look that indicated even a nine-year-old boy could see the reason of it.

With excited exclamations, Tom and Bobby rolled on toward Shiloh School.

At last Trudy addressed Birch again. "It will be all over the county that you're leaving."

"Good." Birch spat and mopped his brow. "It'll put Jenson on notice that I ain't gonna roll over and play dead."

"It will put him on notice all right."

"What do you want from me, Trudy?" He tossed a pitchfork full of straw into the stall.

"I want . . . you!" Her shoulders sagged. "Oh, Birch!" She tried to choke back the emotion. "I . . . suppose it doesn't matter. Go on, then! Go to Washington! What difference does it make if you leave us? You are here, but you might as well be a thousand miles away! Go!"

He gave his head a shake and leaned against the handle of the pitchfork. "Look . . ."

She whirled on him. "No! You look! Do you think anything matters to us but you? Didn't you learn anything at all from losing Joey? Do you still think it is the land or the house or . . . any *thing* . . . some possession that matters to the boys and me? It's you and it's me and it's us. That's all I care about . . . really . . . anymore."

Shamed by her outburst and the truth of it, he said, "I wouldn't mind so much if only . . . I just hate bein' tricked. I hate that he took advantage of my back bein' against a wall. I hate bein' stole from, Trudy! I want to win this one for once in my life."

"So do I. But . . . I want to have some life to live. Something besides waking up angry every morning and cursing that pack of thieves for what they are doing to us and others legally . . . Oh, Birch! I want . . . you . . . again. No! More than that! I need you more than I have ever needed you in my life!"

"I got to do this one thing." He dropped his chin and gazed down at his worn-out boots. "Forgive me, True, but . . . I can't go down without a fight. Don't mean I don't put you and the boys first, but . . . I just gotta do this one thing." He was pleading for her understanding.

"I am afraid . . . I have some terrible feeling, Birch . . . that you won't come back here to Shiloh. Not ever."

"Please . . ."

She leaned against the rails of the stall as if all strength had left her. She did not reply.

He asked, "Tell me what you're thinkin', True. I got to know."

"I was remembering what Willa Mae said. That I have to let you . . . let you go. That I am not God." She raised her eyes to meet his pained gaze. "I am still right, but I am not God." She shrugged. "So? I give up." Looking up at the rafters of the barn, Trudy sighed. "You hear me, God? Take him to Washington with that awful man. But please . . ." She did not finish.

Birch stepped toward her and put his rough, grimy hand on her cheek. She did not pull back as he wrapped his arms around her. "Thanks," he said. Then, "You put up with a lot from me."

"Yes. I do."

"You do. Yes'm, you do!" He buried his face against her shoulder. "Oh, forgive me, True! I'm selfish and clumsy and . . ."

Leaning heavily against his chest, she closed her eyes and inhaled the mixture of sweat and manure and the faint undertone of lye soap.

"You are everything I want," he whispered.

She turned her face up and kissed him gently. "Come back to us, Birch. I will forgive everything but losing you."

Jefferson saw Birch Tucker coming down the hill and crossing the plank bridge over the creek bottom before Birch had raised his cry of

"Hello the cabin!" It was real early in the morning for Birch to come calling; he must have something mighty important on his mind. Jeff judged the time to be shy of six o'clock, since the shadow of the hickory tree beside the log home still stretched clear down to the streambed.

Not that the hour made any difference to the Canfield household. Jeff had been awake since before sunup. Jeff's mama had come over from her place an hour before, and now she and Lily were gossiping and carrying on while the aroma of baking biscuits filled the cabin. Little Will and Mamie played on the floor, stringing wooden blocks onto a shoelace and pretending they were sewing. The baby was bouncing happily on her grandma's broad lap as Willa Mae rocked in the chair next to the stone fireplace.

Jeff ducked his head through the low doorway to step onto his porch and call out to Birch, "Come on up! You're just in time for breakfast."

"Sorry to be so early," Birch said, following Jeff back inside. "Morning, Willa Mae, Lily. How y'all doing this morning?"

"Heard a gunshot up your way," Willa Mae said. "Critter in the garden?"

"After a manner of speaking," Birch agreed. "That's actually what I come to talk about. It was a man-critter."

"Thievin' from Miss Trudy?" Jeff said in evident disbelief that anyone could be so bold. "Did you shoot him?"

Birch recounted the nocturnal visit with Will Grove and explained about the Bonus March. "Now you can see how he got my attention," Birch said. "Y'all know the fix we're in with Garrick Jenson and the land. We are countin' awful strong on the cotton comin' back and the north field comin' through, but a five-hundred-dollar bonus . . ."

He paused to look around the ancient but solidly chinked and weatherproofed home. "This is your place, Jeff. But like it or not, that snake Jenson has the paper on this land, too. And the way I see it, old man cotton has a grip on us too. What with the seed in the ground and all, we're just waitin' on the rains. If they come, then well and good, and cotton gets us out of this hole. If they don't, then that selfsame seed will strangle us. But if we had close on a thousand dollars between us, why, we could tell Jenson Consolidated where to get off, come rain or shine."

The baby fussed and dug its face into Willa Mae's ample bosom. Lily took the child to nurse it. She went toward the curtain that separated the lean-to containing the bed from the rest of the cabin. "I's still listenin'," she said as she excused herself.

Jeff studied the retreating back of his wife, then let his gaze fall on the twins and his mama. "Washington is pretty far," he mused. "We gonna expect our womenfolk to look after the farm and the chilluns an' all whilst we be gone?"

"And why not?" Lily called from back of the curtain. "Seems t' me you menfolks takes a heapa lookin' after! Feedin' and cleanin' an' all. Does you think, Jefferson Canfield, that we cain' tend t' business whilst you be away a while? You think I cain' chop cotton? An' yo' Tom, Mister Birch. He kin drive team, feed the stock. Why, Jeff, if Birch says y'all needs to go, you go!"

"Easy, Lily." Jeff laughed. "I wasn't bein' disrespectful. Why you so anxious to have us go off to Washington? Did you have a vision?"

"Don't need no vision when somethin' is plain in front of your face. Cotton is in the ground; ain't nothin' to do here 'cept hoe a few weed and pray for the good Lord to send rain. Now, mebbe this bonus business is the Lord's own way to he'p us over these hard times, an' maybe it ain't. But you ain't gonna know if you sets here at home."

Through all of Lily's declaration, Willa Mae had remained silent, neither agreeing nor disagreeing, but with something clearly on her mind. "I need to pray on it," he said to Birch. "I'll give you my answer tonight."

It was quiet when Jeff came to Willa Mae's cabin. His mama sat reading the Good Book beside a large steamer trunk that served as a gallery for family photographs.

"Mornin', Mama," Jeff said. "I been thinkin', an' I got to talk to you."

"I figured you might." She marked her place in the book with a letter from her sister and laid it aside. "Sit down, then."

He sat across from her in a straight-backed pine chair that seemed too small for him. He towered over her, but he still felt like a child as he faced her. "I don't know what t' do, Mama, 'bout this Washington thing," he said quietly.

"Well, then." She paused and waited for him to speak.

"You know what it mean. Jim Crow laws jus' as hard in Washington, D.C., as they is in the heart of the Delta. Don't matter that Mister Lincoln's statue's there. Mister Lincoln's long gone. Just a stony face starin' out on all the poor folk an' the hongry. It's jus' like Aunt Minnie says in her letters."

"I reckon that's right, Jeff."

He nodded once and swallowed hard. "I oughta go, I reckon. Get the army bonus money like the man say. Like Birch wants me to."

"Mebbe you ought."

"But you know what it mean. Mostly white veterans a-goin' to march. White men. Down here there's folks that'd lynch a black man for jus' sayin' he fought in the war."

"That's true, Jeff." So far she had not given any indication of what she really felt about the ex-soldiers going to Washington. She sat with her cheek leaned against her hand and rocked slowly as Jefferson talked on.

"What I mean is, Mama, I's thinkin' if I leaves Dreamland I might not never see it again no more."

"An' if you stay here in Shiloh?"

"Then we ain't gonna get the army bonus."

"An' y'all lose Dreamland all the same."

He nodded and licked his lips. Tapping his fingers lightly against his chest, he added, "There's bound t' be trouble. Not just for me. Not just 'cause I's black, but trouble for ever' man that goes there. You know what Aunt Minnie says in her letters: Mister President Hoover don't think nobody in the whole country is hongry. In the winter he said nobody was cold." He looked down at his hands. "Mama, I fear Birch is chasin' after somethin' . . . somethin' that ain't gonna bring us an answer. An' I owe him ever'thing, so I can't stay behind."

"Then go." Willa Mae wagged her head in agreement. Then she added, "I been savin' somethin' for you, Jeff. There in your daddy's treasure chest." She inclined her head toward the steamer trunk beside her.

The chest had always been a fixture in the Canfield cabin. Jefferson remembered the heavy wooden strongbox from his childhood on the farm at Mount Pisgah. Black pressed metal and scarred oak stays were concealed beneath a scalloped patchwork tablecloth sewn from the fabric of dresses Jefferson could still visualize flapping on the clothesline.

Scraps of memories, the material of that tablecloth had once adorned his sisters and mama as they walked together to Mount Pisgah Missionary Baptist Church. Willa Mae called it her altar cloth; every square was a prayer for the one who had worn it, she said. For Jefferson, the patterns and colors evoked images as clear as the photographs of his family. Images of brighter days, days before the hard times, days when they had all been together.

Willa Mae's attention was riveted on the photographs atop the box. Serene faces in sepia-toned prints smiled silently out at Jeff and Willa Mae. "All our young'uns. I been sittin' here readin' God's Word an' thinkin' how it used to be 'round Christmas. Filled up our lives and our house with laughin', they did," she murmured.

For as far back as Jeff could recollect, his mama had used the chest as a sideboard and spare table during meals. At Christmastime the top of it overflowed with turkey, fried chicken, ham, jam cake, sweet 'tater pie, corn, green beans, and biscuits. As many as six extra guests could be seated around it.

"There they all is, Jefferson. Your fambly . . . sisters an' brothers, nieces and nephews. All lookin' out on us an' smilin'. Some of my babies with your daddy in heaven now. What a reunion that must be! But those of us that're still tied to this ol' worl', well, sometime we gotta go where we don' want to an' do what we don' want to do." Willa Mae ran her finger over the top of the picture frame that held a photograph of Jeff's sisters: Pink, Hattie, and Little Nettie. Then she picked up the photograph of her sister Minnie and husband Ike. "I ain't seen Minnie since we was young'uns. You ain't never seen her."

"No'm."

"You'll like your Aunt Minnie," she said in a tone that conveyed her certainty that they would meet.

"Yes'm." He dropped his head into his hands in misery. "Reckon I is goin', then."

"You got to, Jefferson. Now it's Birch needs your help. Me an' Lily an' Trudy, we're fine strong women. We can tend the fields an' the stock. Y'all have t' go, or the chance'll be gone."

"Yes'm. I know it."

"Well, then. I'll write your Aunt Minnie a letter," Willa Mae offered. "I'll do it tonight. Tell her y'all are comin' t' Washington, D.C., an' bringin' a white boy with you. Tell her y'all need a place t' stay. She'll be right glad of it."

She picked up the photograph and held it to her heart. Patting Jefferson's face, she said, "There's lots of your daddy's things in this here steamer trunk. Special things you'll be needin' since y'all gonna be soldiers again. Hock always called it his treasure chest. We ought to open it up an' have a look, I reckon."

It came to Jefferson that he had never seen inside. There was a lock on the front of it, never unlocked. He had assumed that the key was long lost.

Willa Mae removed the flock of photographs, stacking them neatly on the bed. Pulling away the patchwork cloth, she ran her fingers down one side of a strip of oak and produced a long, thin, iron key. A moment later the hinges groaned as the lid was lifted, revealing the treasures of Hock Canfield.

Carefully folded across the top was an old quilt made of homespun material. "Hock's gramma made this for him," Willa Mae said as she removed the ancient fabric and gently laid it to one side.

Beneath the quilt were several newspapers dating from 1918. Headlines proclaimed the arrival of American troops in France . . . the battle of the Argonne . . . the battle of Belleau Wood . . . finally the armistice and the march of Jefferson's Black Rattlers Division through the streets of New York City.

"Well, I'll be. . . ." Jefferson whistled low at the sight of the yellowed newsprint. Then he laughed out loud at the copy of the French newspaper bearing a photograph of Jefferson as he was awarded the French Legion of Honor on the great field of Champs du Mars in Paris.

"When you sent that French newspaper home with that fine picture, your daddy walked twenty miles to Charleston to find ol' Frenchie LaPin because he figgered Frenchie could read what them fancy French words were. But Frenchie couldn't read a lick of French. Couldn't read English, for that matter, so Hock come on back home. We never did find out what was wrote about you, but your daddy showed it 'round the place all the same and told everybody at Pisgah that you was a hero."

As if to emphasize the point, she reached into a brown paper envelope and pulled out the Legion of Honor medal, which Jeff had presented to his father when he finally made it home from the war.

The memories came flooding back to Jefferson. Not the sounds of military bands or the salutes of the French officers, not the admiration he had felt from the people of Paris or the great parades in New York when he and his men marched up Broadway. "I recollect how good it was to be home again," he said simply, replacing the medal in its envelope. "Seein' y'all in church that first Sunday mornin'."

"We was full of hope in them days," she answered. "Thought the white folks, the Man we sharecropped for, would treat us fair 'cause you fought for your country. Reckon nothin' turns out the way we think it ought." Willa Mae sighed and continued to remove items from the trunk. Mother and son sat down on the clean plank floor beside the trunk and sorted through them.

"There ain't much treasure in Daddy's treasure chest," Jeff said with a shake of his head. "He give everything away that he ever had."

"He used t' say, if you have a closed hand nothing'll come in. If you have an open hand, you give an' you receive. Keep an open hand, he used t' say."

"Give away everything worth anything. . . ." There was no reproach in this assessment; it was simply the truth about Hock Canfield. "But he saved this stuff," Jefferson marveled. "Stuff from when we was kids. Fambly stuff." Jefferson flipped through a stack of old letters. He tapped his finger on his army dog tags, then slipped them around his neck once again and pocketed the Legion of Honor medal, his army paybook, and his army cap.

Willa Mae leaned her head against his arm a moment. "Y'all was his treasures, Jeff. You young'uns is what your daddy treasured mos' in his life. Ever'thing else didn' matter much. Nothin' we had was worth savin' after we lost the farm in Pisgah."

"Yes'm," Jefferson replied as he thought of his own treasures: Lily and the young'uns.

"R'member it. If'n things don't work out the way Birch hopes, y'all r'member what the Lord say about a man's heart bein' where his treasure is."

"I will, Mama."

"Mos' my treasures is in heaven with Jesus. 'Cept y'all. Your sisters. Jefferson, God give you treasures in them babies an' your wife. A place? It ain't worth nothin' without folks to love. Your daddy used t' say, a farm's just dirt an' chickens an' hogs an' such. A house jus' boards an' nails. But fambly! That's our treasure. I is rich as Missus Rockefeller when it comes t' love!"

She sighed and leaned back against the trunk, closed her eyes. "But oh, there is times when I miss Mount Pisgah. Oh Lawd! Yes, I do. Your Aunt Minnie will tell you how t'was when you see her. Me an' Minnie's got us the same memories, only we seen life from different directions."

There were other treasures beneath the letters. A roll of sheepskin recorded in faded black ink, the bill of sale for a male slave in his teens to a plantation in 1856. This was Hock's grandfather. The document had been turned over to Grandfather Canfield by a Yankee captain after the Civil War battle of Devil's Backbone. A well-worn Bible with only remnants of a crumbling leather cover was wrapped in soft calico cloth. In spidery handwriting, its pages contained the names and partial records for two dozen family members who now were only legend in the Canfield family lore.

Willa Mae slid her finger down the page. "This one run off north, got caught and whupped to death by the bounty men. Now this gal, Sally, she was too strong-minded. She got sold on down the river, an' no one ever knew what come of her. This other sister had a young'un and the chil' was sold away from her, so she run off to Indian Territory. . . ."

And so the afternoon passed with Willa Mae beginning with what she knew about the old ones. From there she told how she and Hock had always known one another. They had grown up across the creek on Mount Pisgah plantation, both the children of sharecroppers and the grandchildren of slaves. She spoke of babies being born who did not survive to see their first year, about the sweet fields of home and the soil where those children were buried.

"They're all back there now . . . sisters, brothers, mamas, and daddies, all sleepin' together on that hill, all waitin' together for Jesus t' come an' call 'em to wake up. But me an' Hock, we knowed we wasn't gonna rest beside 'em. We wasn't goin' home to Mount Pisgah ever again."

The shadows were growing long when Willa Mae showed Jefferson the last treasure. At the bottom of the trunk was a Ball canning jar filled with dirt. Willa Mae lifted the jar up to a shaft of sunlight as if it was filled with gold dust. After a moment of contemplation, she placed it on the floor between her and Jefferson.

"What's this, Mama?"

She took Jefferson's arm and struggled to her feet. "Come on, now."

"Where to?"

Willa Mae, carrying the jar full of dirt, led Jefferson outside, down the lanes, over the familiar fields. They stopped when they reached the grave of Hock Canfield.

"Hock always say he wanted to be buried in the good earth of home. After you was gone an' arrested an' on the chain gang, so much happened I ain't spoke about. The Man come and brought in the tractor to do our work. He took our mules and our farm and turned us out. Las' thing your daddy done b'fore we went up north, he walked on down to the knoll where we buried our babies. He scooped up a little ground from each grave and put it in two jars. He brought 'em to me and said that one was for him when his time come an' t'other jar was for me."

Now she was carefully unscrewing the lid to the canning jar. "I done sprinkled Hock's jar out on the day we buried him. Still got mine though."

She took a clean white cotton handkerchief from her pocket. Opening it on the ground, she scooped out some of the soil from the jar with her finger, then gathered up a handful of loose earth from the foot of Hock's grave. This being accomplished, she tied up the cloth until the soil formed a tight ball.

"Now you always have a piece of home with you. Mount Pisgah and Dreamland, too. Home is the place where your loved ones live and where they is buried. But home can be any place where your heart is, too. So take this t' Washington 'long with your medal. This is what y'all fought for, Jefferson—the right t' have a home an' raise your young'uns without fear of them goin' hongry. Go on. Get your army bonus if you can. Save Dreamland if it can be saved. We'll stay here an' pray an' work the bes' we can do. Till Jesus calls us home. . . ."

The khaki duffel bag bearing the name, rank, and serial number of Birch Tucker was packed and placed beside the front door.

Birch sucked in his breath, buttoned his army tunic with difficulty, and turned his profile to Trudy as she ironed the trousers of his old uniform in the parlor.

"Sure been a long time since I had this thing on." Birch patted his stomach and grimaced.

"You don't weigh one pound more than the day I married you."

"You're not living up to your name . . . True . . . sayin' such things. I've got a gut. Never had a gut before. Go on. Admit it."

Trudy grinned. "You have just rearranged yourself a bit."

"My chest slipped to my waist is what you mean."

"There's plenty of room to let out the waist in your trousers. I can move the buttons."

He unbuttoned the jacket and struggled to take it off. "The truth comes out. I've put on a few inches all right. You should have told me what you thought and I'd never got this thing out of the trunk. I'll look a fool marching to Washington in my uniform." He tossed the tunic over the back of the chair and plopped down, stretching his long legs out in front of him.

"Quit pouting." She flicked water on the iron to test its temperature. Too cool. She replaced it on the parlor stove to warm up. "I can fix it," she promised. "You can't pin your campaign medals on your overalls."

"Why not? I'm a farmer. These old bibs are my uniform. Old boots. Old worn-out hat. Don't know what I'm doin' leavin' you and the young'uns anyway to march off to Washington with a bunch of old soldiers. How'll you get along? I put that army suit away a long time ago, and I didn't figger to ever put it on again. It's been thirteen years and my belly has a right to pooch out a little. I'm not goin', True. The uniform don't fit me anymore, and that's the end of it." He stood and paced the length of the room and back, stopping at the window.

Trudy was silent as she considered the unhappy look on Birch's face. He leaned against the window frame and stared off toward the newly planted fields.

"This is not about the uniform, is it?" she asked.

"No, it is not." He crossed his arms and glowered at the tunic as if it was the enemy. "I did my bit in the army. Sharing quarters with a bunch of guys. Like sleeping in the outhouse. I've got used to waking up next to something soft. Smelling lavender in the air when there's not a lavender bush in bloom. Just you . . . I've got used to reaching out in the middle of the night and you putting your leg over mine and . . ."

His words warmed her, made her go soft inside. "I shall miss you, Birch Tucker."

"Oh, shall you now, my little schoolmarm? Well, you seem awfully cheerful about my going. Gonna like having the bed all to yourself? Reading till three in the morning with no one to bother about the light?"

"Nonsense. . . ."

"You're mighty happy about letting out my trousers and packing everything up in my duffel like I was leaving on a deer hunt."

"I *am* hoping you and Jefferson will bring home some bucks, if that's what you mean." She blinked coyly at him, pleased with her pun. She was also pleased that he was missing her so badly already.

"Very cute." He worked at remaining miserable in spite of the fact that she was nearly cheering him up. "You are cute. Why'd you ever marry a guy like me, anyway? You could have married . . . maybe a senator or something."

"You were pretty wonderful in your uniform."

"What about now?" He stepped behind her and wrapped his arms around her waist. Pressing himself against her, he kissed the back of her neck. He whispered in her ear, "You know how much I'm gonna miss you, woman? How hungry I'll be to touch you?"

Turning to face him, she stroked his cheek and smiled up into his eyes. He wanted her now. "You know how dangerous it is for a man to come up behind a woman while she's working? With a hot iron in reach?"

"I'll take my chances. My iron is hot enough to do the job." He kissed her hard and fumbled with the buttons of her blouse. "Give a soldier something to remember on his last . . . day . . . home."

She laughed and took his hands in hers to stop him. "I smell mothballs in that old line, Birch Tucker. And besides, the boys . . ."

"They won't be home from school for an hour. Say yes."

He had her there. She was melting like ice cream in the sun. After a few more moments of struggle, with her help, there was victory over the buttons. Conversation came in staccato bursts between kisses.

". . . school . . . hour-and-a-half . . ."

"Plenty of time."

"One of the reasons . . . I married you . . ."

"More fun than ironing?"

"Yes . . . let me . . . the bedroom . . ."

"Here, Trudy. In the parlor."

He pulled her gently down beside him to the blue coil rug.

Yielded now, she lay on her back. He propped himself on one elbow to drink her in with a look. She felt the blush climb from her throat to warm her face as he touched her. "You are a miracle. My miracle." He sighed and nuzzled the nape of her neck. "And every time the old ladies' sewing circle is over and conversation gets dull, you can look right at this spot and think of our goodbye. Put some color in your cheeks . . . like now. . . ."

She could barely speak. "Shocking, Mister Tucker."

"I aim to please, Missus Tucker."

"That you do, my darling. . . ."

CHAPTER 23

There had been a hobo jungle beside the spur line of the Rock Island railroad for as long as Birch could remember. Usually one or two grizzled tramps were holed up in the hollow during the warmer months of the year. The trestle gave some shelter from the weather, and the James Fork had plenty of water for drinking and cooking. But this spring two things were different: the creek was already low, and twenty men camped in the draw.

A thin trickle of pale blue smoke drifted up into the sky. The same slight breeze that carried the aroma of the wood fire also transported snatches of off-key singing. The words were unfamiliar, but Birch recognized the tune as that of "My Bonnie Lies Over the Ocean":

I'm spending my nights in the flophouse,
I'm spending my nights in the street,
I'm looking for work and I find none
I wish I had something to eat!

Soooo—oup, sooo-oup, they give me a bowl—

A rock rolled under Birch's foot, clattering down into the shallow canyon. The song broke off in midchorus. There was the furious sound of a chicken squawking, then that noise also stopped abruptly.

Birch led the way into the campground, but he and Jeff had not reached the cookfire before being confronted by two large men in torn and greasy overalls. The pair of figures blocked the path. "What you want?" growled the one on the left, a heavyset man a little below Birch's height. His overalls were rolled up halfway to his knees and must have once belonged to a much taller man.

"Will Grove still here?" Birch asked.

"Who wants to know?"

"Name's Birch Tucker. This here's Jefferson Canfield."

The two guards relaxed. "Thought you might be deputies comin' by to roust us," the second man said. The sleeves of his long johns stuck out past the elbows of his denim shirt and his toes protruded from the worn-out ends of his shoes. "Yeah, Grove's here. Hey, Willie the Weasel, come on out. Grove said you might be comin'. He didn't say nothin' about this other feller, though. I'm Slim. This here is Stoney."

Grove emerged from the brush and greeted Birch. To Jefferson he said nothing, but looked him up and down and frowned.

The activity around the campfire resumed. A cast-iron pot of stew simmered over the coals, and an old molasses can served as a makeshift coffeepot. Birch thought that the brew bubbling in the battered silver pail looked darker and stronger than the original contents.

A teenaged boy with a nervous air about him came into view from the middle of an elderberry thicket. He was toting a white-feathered chicken by its recently wrung neck. Skirting the edge of the clearing like a skittish dog, he carried the bird over to a seated knot of men on the far side. No one in this group spoke or acknowledged Birch or Jeff's arrival, but they did not look away either.

"Doc Brown raises White Plymouth Rocks," Birch observed dryly. "I reckon they do run off sometimes."

"Are you the feller what sent over them cabbages?" Stoney asked.

Birch shrugged. He was not looking to get thanked.

"Give me gas something fierce. Next to cucumbers, cabbage is the worst."

"Are y'all goin' to Washington?" Jefferson asked.

Stoney spat noisily on the ground. "What fer? I ain't no vet. Even if I was, I wouldn't go off to no Washington, D.C., on no wild-goose chase."

A quiet, educated voice spoke up from the shade of a cottonwood. "Only Will, Slim, and myself are joining the march from this charming encampment. The rest are either professional railroad inspectors or are traveling for their health."

These words were greeted with hoots of laughter and shouts of "Good one, perfessor." "Fessor, you talk so purty."

The speaker, a tall, thin man with salt-and-pepper hair and gray eyes, rose from the ground and approached Jeff and Birch. "My name is . . . of no particular consequence. You may have heard my handle already. They call me the professor, Fessor for short, although I think it is intended to be a derogatory comment on my grammar rather than a respectful acknowledgment of my former calling. And you, I take it, are headed for Washington."

Birch agreed and mentioned his regiment in France.

"I myself was an ambulance driver," Fessor said. Birch noted that Fessor never met anyone's eyes when he spoke to them. It was, Birch thought, as if the man was embarrassed about something. "Well," the professor continued, "our discipline and training stood us in good stead 'over there.' Perhaps it will come through for us again."

"What's this darkie doin' here, is what I want to know," Grove said. "What did he do in the war? Clean latrines? We don't want niggers with us."

Birch clenched his fists and stepped toward the greasy-haired Grove. Jefferson laid a restraining hand on his arm.

But it was Fessor who spoke up. "What was your regiment, if I may ask?"

"Three sixty-ninth," Jeff said softly.

"Toting toilet paper?" Grove mocked. "Or shining officers' shoes?"

"Be quiet, you ignoramus," Fessor warned. "Didn't you ever hear of the Black Rattlers? Higher casualties and more decorations than almost any other unit. Besides, you Weasels are supposed to be all for integration and racial equality. Don't you know your own group's philosophy?"

"But he's black," Grove protested.

"So's your heart. Come now, Mister Grove. Haven't you heard the expression 'we're all in this boxcar together'? This man has as much a right to join the march as any of us."

"All right," Grove finally muttered. "But I don't like it." He turned his back on Jefferson and squatted by the cookfire, helping himself to a tin cup of stew.

"Weasels?" Birch asked.

Fessor spoke softly to Birch and Jeff. "Worker's Ex-Servicemen's League. Red as Joe Stalin. But Grove is even a bad Commie. Old ways of thinking die hard," he said. "And hatred takes many forms. The regular 'boes, like that group over there in the corner, have no use for the competition of newcomers. And," he added significantly, looking directly at Birch, "those guys have especially no use for farmer types. Many a first-time rail traveler just off the hay wagon has ended up buried in an unmarked grave. Watch yourself."

"The morning freight will lay over on the siding, see, waitin' for the down mail to get past," Grove explained to Birch. "That's our chance. We stay in the willows just beside the bend while she gets rollin'; otherwise a bull might be walking the length and spot us. If we're lucky, we catch us an open box and ride in style."

Birch nodded his understanding, wiping a few drops of nervous sweat from his forehead. Through the screen of branches he saw the truth of Grove's warning: a swarthy, muscular man in dark blue denim strode past where they were concealed. The railroad guard swung a length of pipe in one hand, and he peered into the open cars and under all the rest as he passed by toward the caboose.

"Now when you go to hop her, keep looking forward till after you're up clean," Grove continued. "Otherwise you trip on a tie or bash yourself on a switch like I seen guys do." To Jefferson, Grove said, "And you jump up between cars, on the couplin'. That way we won't crowd each other. Just grab hold of that little lever over the pin and haul yourself on up."

Grove went off to give some instructions to Slim about waiting one more day and then coming along to St. Louis with any late arrivals. Fessor slipped up behind Jefferson and Birch. "If I were you," he said to Jeff, "I would not put any stock in advice handed out by Mister Grove. Grasping the suggested lever would have unpleasant consequences. It . . ."

"Thanks, Perfessor." Jefferson grinned. "But this chil' weren't born yesterday. That thing he's talkin' about is the uncouplin' handle. It would drop the cars and set the brakes. Might even be plumb dangerous to a feller tryin' to swing aboard right then."

Fessor nodded grimly. "I have seen a man lose both legs in just such a fashion," he said. "Give Mister Grove time," he suggested, "and he will grow less hostile as he comes to know you."

"You think I should want to know him better?"

"You make a valid point."

The southbound mail train swept by on the tracks just a few yards away. The thunder of its passing momentarily filled the air with rumble and clatter, and then it was gone.

With a clanking jerk that rattled each car in turn down the line, the northbound train pulled itself into motion. The group that included Birch, Jefferson, Fessor, Grove, and three others emerged from their hiding places and jogged alongside the slowly moving freight. Just at the middle of the curve, out of sight of both ends, was an empty box with its doors latched back.

In a few seconds, all the men were aboard without incident. "How lucky can we get?" Birch remarked, staking his claim to a stretch of wood plank floor with his duffel and his bedroll. "To have one come along wide open in just the right spot."

"It was not luck," Fessor commented from the place where he leaned against an end wall of the car. "There are some brakemen who realize that only one day's notice stands between them and being in the same predicament as we. The guard on this stretch of the line is one of the good guys. He has made a great show of inspecting, but he has also left this opportunity for us."

Birch looked around the dusty wooden interior of the boxcar that would be both home and transportation for a ways. Willie Grove had already built a little fortress for himself in one corner out of bedroll, knapsack, and rain slicker. Curled inside the circle of his belongings, Grove looked like a wild animal all denned up.

The other three who had hopped the same car were talking together in another corner, leaving Jeff and Birch and Fessor to themselves. Crowded together in an area no bigger than a one-room cabin, each group seemed determined to put as much space around themselves as possible.

Jefferson remarked to Birch that the interior smelled faintly of oiled wood and silver polish, like the parlor furnishings of some rich folks. "What do y' think they had in this car before us?" he asked Birch. "Puts me in mind of the table and chairs up to Old Master Howard's house."

Birch stretched out his hand and, from a splinter of wood, plucked a shipping tag that had evidently pulled free of the previous cargo. *Stoddard and Sons*, it read. *Purveyors of fine church furniture and elegant coffins.*

"There you are, Jeff," he commented as he showed off the scrap of paper. "Which do you think it was? Pews or coffins?" As the train picked up speed, a cooling breeze flitted through the cracks in the slats, drying the sweat on Birch's face.

"I ain't superstitious, if that's what you mean."

"Quite right," Fessor agreed. "It doesn't do to see omens and portents in every little thing."

"If it's not impolite to ask," Birch said, "how'd you come to be a hobo? You being educated and all."

"Ah, well, the current economic troubles are no respecter of persons." The man peered intently at the wooden bracing of the ceiling as he spoke. "It seems that a college degree and ten years of service will not guarantee employment if the college itself closes its doors. But you are wrong about one thing."

"Eh? What's that?"

The professor rubbed the stubble on his chin. "Language is useless if it is not precise. I am not a hobo, although I mean nothing critical by the distinction. A hobo is an itinerant laborer, moving about the countryside in search of temporary gainful employment. I, on the other hand, am a tramp."

Birch and Jeff exchanged a look that spoke of their lack of comprehension. "Meaning?" Birch said.

"Tramps and hoboes are both, by nature, wanderers. But I feel no pressure to seek employment."

Jeff grinned. "You a beggar, then?"

"I ain't no beggar!" Grove snapped from his lair in the corner. "What I want is what's owed, what's due me! Workers only get rich folks' scraps. But no more!"

"As the need arises," Fessor said, ignoring Grove's outburst and answering Jeff's question. "Hence this journey to Washington. I see it as a way to aid my fellow man and myself at the same time. A sort of collective begging, if you will."

"Perfessor," Jeff said with one eyelid raised wide and the other squeezed tightly shut. "It's hard to figger when you is pullin' our legs and when you ain't."

Now it was Fessor who grinned as he slid his back down the wall of the boxcar. He folded his long, thin legs comfortably under him and pulled the brim of a weatherbeaten fedora low over his forehead. "I also intend," he said, "to write of my experiences some day."

The same morning Birch and Jefferson left home to join the Bonus Army, a team of surveyors arrived in Shiloh.

Tripods and brass-bound wooden boxes of transits slung over shoulders, they walked along the Rock Island rail line. Pausing to mop their brows, they gazed south in the direction of the Ouachita Mountains, then set out along the back road that led past the general store and on toward the Tucker farm. Around midmorning the heat got to be too much, so they knocked on Trudy's door to beg water from the well. She asked their business as they dipped the gourd into the bucket and guzzled the water. Nothing much, they answered her. The explanation involved something about the county maps and finding right-of-ways for possible electric lines and telephone poles. They asked permission to cross the north cotton field on foot and survey the land that divided farm from farm.

Electric lines? Telephone poles? Trudy agreed to their request and sent Tom down with the watering bucket and fresh peaches before they finished their work and drove away.

The head surveyor, a tall, sunburned man with a sandy beard and a tattered panama hat, stopped at Grandma Amos's store. He chugged down three Nehi sodas and paid extra with silver dollars because the old woman had opened up after hours for him. He telephoned all the way to Fort Smith and spoke with the head man of the Rock Island Railroad. He talked in a normal tone of voice because he thought Grandma too deaf to hear him.

Early evening, as Willa Mae cooked Grandma's supper, she was the first to hear the real purpose of the surveyor's visit. "Yankees!" Grandma Amos tapped her pipe against the porch rail. "Them railroad fellers are the sort that keep the jails and the courthouses of Arkansas in business! The survey man told his boss in Fort Smith that they done surveyed the right-of-way along the road right to Tucker's land. A woman alone on the farm, he said, and he didn't figger Missus Tucker would cause no trouble 'bout it. Her man's gone. Huh! Them Yankees just don't recollect what a southern lady can do when she gets riled."

The old woman rocked furiously in her rocking chair. "They aim to bring convict labor out here to Shiloh to work on another rail spur!" She raised her hand to heaven as though the sky was falling. "Farewell peace an' farewell quiet! More steam engines rumblin' right through the middle of ever'thing! And why anyone needs a rail spur up in them hills I'll never know! Nothin' much up there but bootleggers an' cantankerous hillbillies who'd sooner shoot first and ask questions after."

It was dusk as Willa Mae walked wearily toward Dreamland. Pine stakes topped with red flannel strips lined the gravel lane up to the place the road forked. To the right was Shiloh Church, left was the Tucker farm. The markers stopped abruptly at the corner of the Tucker field.

Willa Mae paused to rest herself against a fence post that was riddled with acorn-stuffed holes drilled by generations of woodpeckers. Even in the half-light she could see that Birch Tucker was a good farmer. Furrows were plowed with unerring symmetry: straight as an arrow, just so deep and only so wide, perfect in height and width and depth for a cotton crop to flourish.

The black bottomland of this forty acres was such that, by July, the field would be crowded with strong, dark green stalks. Come August, bright purple blooms would open to the sun. By the end of September, black, hard bolls would crack open like kernels of popcorn and spill the snowy cotton out.

This evening, the long furrows were topped by small knots of green sprouts. It was plain to Willa Mae that the cotton planted here would make it. The settlement from this crop, taken together with the army bonus money, would pay the Tuckers' debts for another year.

"Lawd A'mighty," Willa Mae whispered. "Bless this here cotton. Bless them as planted an' them as will tend and them as will . . ." She might have stayed there praying in the gathering gloom of twilight, but the flutter of red on the far side caught her eye.

What was it? Willa Mae strained to see just beyond the ancient fencepost in the distant corner. Following a diagonal path across the furrows stood another survey stake. It was as if the railroad crew had drawn an invisible line bisecting the north field.

Willa Mae started out again, circling the south end of the fence. Sure enough, the markers took off from an angle on the opposite side.

Along the rim of bottomland, scarlet banners alternated with the scarred trunks of old white birch trees. Willa Mae had heard that Birch Tucker's granddaddy had planted those trees on the boundary of the farm the very same day Birch was born. Did the railroad men mean to chop those trees down, Willa Mae wondered? From Birch and Trudy's property the markers leapt across the James Fork. Passing within two hundred yards of Jeff and Lily's cabin, the surveyor's trail cut up into the woods and vanished.

The rail yard on the outskirts of Fort Smith where the freight trains were assembled had been, in its own way, as grand as the famed passenger terminal with its domed roof and twenty-foot-tall doors. There had been a time all thirty-two crisscrossing lines and scores of switches, sidings, and spurs had marshaled cars loaded with sugar, cotton, and rice from the South into a supply line of raw materials headed north. The North had responded with automobiles and refrigerators, phonographs and tractors.

The exchange of commerce passing through Fort Smith on the Kansas City Southern had been the shining example of America's prosperity, the twenty-four-hour-a-day representation of a golden future. Stand in one place for less than an hour and you could see cars laden with grapes from California, steel from Pittsburgh, oil from Texas, lumber from the Pacific Northwest. It was like being able to touch the growth of the nation.

But that had been in the twenties—before the Crash, before the Depression, before the slump that left the railroads moving less than half of their previous cargo. When the freight car in which Birch was riding was shunted onto a siding in the Fort Smith yard, he looked out across acres of empty rails and idle cars. He and Jefferson had been dozing when they pulled into Fort Smith. The professor said something about jumping clear when the train slowed, and by the time the two friends from Shiloh were fully awake, all of their companions were gone. The premises seemed so deserted that Birch wondered why anyone had bothered to get off.

A sharp rapping hammered on the wooden side of the boxcar, making both men jump. This was followed by a shrill voice that shouted, "Hey, in there! Get up and get moving! You clear off now, hear? Don't you know better than to stay aboard inside the yard? You all tryin' to get me in bad with the bosses?"

"Sorry, friend," Birch said out of the shadowy corner of the car. "Everybody else hopped off outside of town. We just don't know the rules, bein' new to this business."

"Well I'll be! Birch Tucker, is that you? Trudy kick you out, did she?"

Birch roused himself and beckoned for Jefferson to follow him out of the car. "Howdy, Charlie," he said sheepishly to the short man with the dark brown mustache. "Naw, we're going to Washington with a bunch of other fellers. Seems like maybe we can get Congress to help out us vets."

"That so? I heard something about some march or other; I was in the war, too. But I never thought I'd see Birch Tucker hoppin' a freight."

"The truth, Charlie?" Birch laughed. "Neither did I."

"Now you'd be headin' for St. Louis, if I heard right."

"That's so."

"All right, you just stay put here till 'long about ten tonight. The St. Louis train gets made up then, right over yonder on track three. I'm the only yard bull workin' today, so nobody will bother you none."

"Thanks, Charlie," Birch said. "You are a good man."

"Yeah? Well, here's a word for you. Fenton Pratt works the next length of track. If he ain't the worse there is, then I dunno who else comes close. You mind he don't catch you. Don't ride inside no cars. I seen him lock a feller inside just so's he could set a dog on him later. If you even catch sight of him, get off quick as you can."

Birch looked at Jefferson and shrugged. It seemed that thoughts of how easy this business was had come prematurely. "Thanks, Charlie. We'll be careful."

CHAPTER 24

Tom and Bobby were sleeping over at the Hocott's barn, so all was quiet at the Tucker house tonight.

Brother Williams arrived on Trudy's doorstep at half-past nine in the evening, carrying a Western Union telegram in his mail pouch. He was greeted at the door by Willa Mae, who had stopped to inform Trudy of what she had heard about the survey party. The old woman had stayed for supper and beyond.

Brother entered the parlor and reluctantly extended the official Western Union envelope to Trudy. "I come just as soon as Mister Tedrow at the Western Union office called me. Didn't want to wait till mornin'."

Only bad news came in Western Union envelopes. As Willa Mae stood at her elbow, Trudy accepted the cable with trembling hands. Had something happened to Birch? Or Jefferson? Or perhaps a member of Trudy's family had taken ill or passed on.

"Well, ain't you gonna open 'er?" Brother Williams blurted. He nervously licked his lips and stared intently at the yellow envelope. He had come all this way on muleback, four miles to Shiloh from Hartford, and he was not going back until he knew the nature of the disaster that had befallen the Tucker family.

Trudy nodded. Willa Mae stepped back as Trudy slit the thin paper, removed the message, read it, and then read it again.

Trudy's eyes narrowed. "It is much worse than we suspected, Willa Mae!"

"What?" Brother pleaded. "Trudy Tucker, y'all better let me in on it 'fore I blow a cork. Tedrow don't tell me what's in them telegrams. He just gives the things to me t' carry like I was the Grim Ripper. We got cottonmouth snakes in these parts, an' we got copperheads, and we got telegrams. . . . I gotta know!"

"The railroad, Brother." Trudy passed the telegram to Willa Mae. "Some years ago, it seems the Rock Island Railroad struck a bargain with Birch's father. An option, they call it. This paper says Birch's daddy sold them a right-of-way. They say they have the legal right to cut a path, as the crow flies, straight through our north cotton field. And they intend to do so."

Brother's breath exploded as he fell back into the worn camelhair sofa. "Oh, Lord," he moaned. "All this way, an' I thought somebody up an' died. Right-of-way. Well, that's somethin' Sam Tucker would of done, all right. He didn't plow, nor plant, nor nothin', after Birch left." Brother fanned his face and mopped his brow with relief. "This here farm was all wild oats an' briars an' persimmons 'fore y'all come back an' took over. Right-of-way? Sam Tucker wouldn't of cared none if the whole Rock Island locomotive drove through his parlor long as they give 'im corn likker t' drink. Speakin' of which . . . a man shore gets a thirst when he's all wrought up."

Willa Mae fetched Brother a glass of buttermilk to soothe his nerves. He peered into it for a long moment, then sipped it politely. After a time, Willa Mae escorted him out to the porch and said goodbye. Trudy was too busy pacing to tend to him.

"The news will be all over Hartford by mornin'," Willa Mae said as she came back into the house. "Mebbe this is jus' the railroad talkin' air. Mebbe it don' mean a thing. Jus' tryin' to get 'round y'all."

Trudy did not look at her. She shook her head as if to indicate she believed the information in the telegram. "He was a wretch."

"Who's that, honey?"

"Birch's father. Sold his soul for moonshine. Lived his life in an alcoholic stupor. Mortgaged his farm one jar of whiskey at a time. He disowned Birch because of me, or at least . . . I suppose he might have disowned him anyway."

"A tomcat kill his own kittens if he can. Some mens ain't much better than tomcats."

"I do not doubt he sold a right-of-way to the railroad. What would stop him? But now! The north field is our best land. It's plowed and planted. If we're to have any crop at all this year, it will be from the north field."

"How much land that railroad take?"

"Stakes are laid out to follow the road south, toward our farm, from the main rail line. The road forks at the northeast corner of our land. From there, instead of following the curve of the road, the surveyor marked a diagonal strip across our cotton field. From one corner to the other. Past our place the rails will follow the course of the road again." She smiled grimly. "And that smooth-talking so-and-so promised me he would not disturb the cotton plants. 'Just taking a shortcut,' he told me."

"I seen the markers in among y'all's birch trees, 'longside of the highway. Reckon they mean to take them trees out?"

"I do not doubt it. From what I could see, the crew continued south and surveyed across the creek just about where the West Harmony dumps into the James Fork."

"The waterin' hole?"

"Upstream from it."

"Won't be good for livestock if'n they muddy it up. Only good waterin' hole left in these parts."

Trudy reported that on the south side of the creek the surveyor had trekked along the gravel lane past Jeff and Lily's place.

Willa Mae was silent for a time as she considered the information. Crews of men trampling across the newly sprouted furrows would destroy the entire crop.

"That mean ol' man." Willa clucked her tongue. "He intended the railroad t' mow down them birch trees."

Trudy nodded. "Tomcat. A boozy one at that. Hundred-eighty-proof corn liquor in his saucer."

Willa Mae took a chair at the round oak table. Chin in hand, she considered the situation. "Now, next year it won't matter none to ol' man cotton if a train goes through y'all's field. Next year cotton'll forget the insult of bein' stamped on. Cotton'll cuddle right up t' them tracks next year. Hock used t' say that good cotton seed would sprout in a man's nose if he don't blow it."

"It is good seed. The best."

"But y'all is gonna lose the crop this year. Cain't have big boots trompin' on them little plants. Cain't have mens haulin' rails an' goin' tiptoe through fresh-planted furrows." Willa Mae shook her ponderous head slowly from side to side. "An' them birch trees . . . that's just a shame."

"What am I going to do, Willa Mae? What would Birch do?"

"I reckon he'd get to the bottom of it. If his daddy signed away a part of the farm an' drunk up the money from it. . . ."

"He'd fight them."

"If there's anything that can be fought."

"Birch can't come home to find the north field gone and the birch trees cut down and a train running through the farm."

"Railroad mens is mighty powerful, I reckon. Don' know what can be done. Folks like them drive big automobiles and name locomotives after their mamas. It's hard to fight such folks, Trudy, honey, but we can pray on the matter."

"The telegram says the first crews will arrive in the morning."

"Gonna be an all-night prayer meetin', I reckon. S'pose I best go on down and fetch Lily an' the babies to come on up here."

The view from the catwalk around the gondola car was startling as the Kansas City Southern pulled out of the Fort Smith freight yard and crossed the Arkansas River. The gleam of the rising moon flashed off the water and flickered through the iron lattice of the girders as if the bridge were made of lace. Despite the grime from the coal with which the hopper was filled, the nighttime air was sweet over the stream.

Birch, Jeff, and Fessor were perched on the narrow metal walkway with their bags and bedrolls, enjoying the view and the breeze. "It sure look peaceful enough," Jefferson observed. "Hard to figger how anything be wrong with the world on such a purty night."

Birch nodded. "It seems so, but if everything is so all-fired wonderful, how come we're riding like fleas on this mechanical dog's back instead of home where we belong? Tell me that."

"My daddy always say, a man got to find the sweet in the bitter, the smooth with the rough—find the good in ever'thing what come to him. Otherwise he be always waitin' for things to improve 'stead of seein' what's fine right where he is."

"Your father sounds like he had a large measure of homespun wisdom," Fessor applauded.

"Preach on, Brother Jeff." Birch laughed. "I guess Hock would've said that on this train we don't have to plow or hoe or tinker with broken-down equipment. The view is fine, the grub ain't yet in short supply, and the drink, if it ain't got variety, is sure 'nough available." He gestured down at the river's surface shimmering a hundred feet below them. "Wonder if the rest of the fellers got back aboard after Fort Smith."

"Undoubtedly," Fessor said. "The veterans in this mode of transport, can be no more than the darkest part of a shadow if they wish."

Birch glanced up toward the sky, lit by a lopsided moon. He started to remark to Jefferson about how their wives would be watching the same moon rise back in Shiloh, but stopped at the sudden apparition of a man's form silhouetted briefly against the heavens. "Jeff," he called in a low, tense hiss that was barely audible over the clickety-clack of the wheels. "I saw somebody comin' over the top of that car back there."

"Climbin' over the roof while we's movin'? What for?"

"You could be mistaken," Fessor said.

"Could it be that Pratt feller, trying to sneak up on us?"

"Maybe you was just seein' things," Jeff suggested when minutes passed and no sign of any other human was noted.

Birch shook his head. "My eyes ain't that bad. I saw him plain as day against the moon."

The train rattled over a set of switches, briefly exchanging the rolling, shiplike motion for a short up-and-down pitch. Birch thought the difference was much like a horse going from a canter to a trot and then back to a canter again. Conversation stopped until the extra clatter ceased.

"It is as well to be wary," Fessor said. "Pratt is not to be underestimated when it comes to his capacity for cruelty."

"You alki-stiffs all talk too much," said a harsh voice out of the darkness.

Jeff and Birch both jumped to their feet, clinging to the thin handrail as the train swayed around a curve. Fessor remained seated. "Mister Pratt?" he asked.

The glow from the night sky lit the face of the beefy man who emerged from the shadows holding an ax handle in his gloved hand. A hank of black hair fell over a low forehead, and his nose had been rearranged so many times that Birch thought it resembled a short, fat corkscrew.

"You intend to order us off at the next stop?" Fessor said.

"No." Pratt sneered. The teeth on one side of his crooked mouth were broken off short. "I mean to make you *jump*."

"'Tain't possible," Jeff said, stepping toward the man.

"Back off!" Pratt ordered, swinging the ax handle in a flashing arc. It banged against the hopper of the gondola only a half foot from Jeff's head.

Jeff jumped for the club and, in a sudden move that caught Pratt by surprise, pinned it against the side of the car. Pratt swore violently, trying to twist his weapon free.

The car jostled over another set of switches, throwing the wrestling men from side to side. "Look out, Jeff!" Birch yelled. Though only a couple of feet separated them, Birch was unable to help because Jeff's own bulk blocked the narrow catwalk.

Jeff was tossed against the railing. He lost one hand's grip on the cudgel, and Pratt gave a snort of success with the thought that he had regained control of his weapon. But his delight was short-lived when he discovered that Jeff could still overpower him with just one hand.

Switching tactics, Pratt swung a clumsy left that hit Jeff on the ear.

Jeff wrenched hard on the ax handle and suddenly had the stick all to himself. He poked it straight forward into Pratt's gut. Breath exploded out of the man and he staggered back. The guard knocked the weapon aside as Jeff pressed forward again, but then he over-balanced and fell onto the railing. His middle doubled over the small tubing as his feet left the grid of the ledge and he hung suspended. He screamed in terror.

Jeff flung the club off the train and away into the dark, lunging toward Pratt to drag the man back to safety. Jeff leaned hard on Pratt's shoulders and forced him down onto the catwalk. "Just set there," he ordered.

"Throw him off," Fessor said. "It's the only thing to do."

Jeff shook his head.

"What are we gonna do with him, then?" Birch asked.

"He's gonna leave us alone, ain't you, Mister Pratt?"

In answer, the guard jumped to his feet, spat out a vicious oath, and ran off toward the rear of the train, clambering over iron rungs like a gorilla.

"Now you've done it," Fessor warned. "We'd better get off at the next opportunity."

"You think he'll come back again?" Birch asked.

"With a gun!"

The train was chuffing steadily northward. Birch looked at the telegraph poles swinging past in the moonlight. He knew that you could tell the speed of a racing locomotive by counting the regularly spaced timbers, but at the moment he could not work out the math. All he knew was that they were traveling way too fast to jump off if Fessor was right about Pratt.

"At the very least, we need to change our location," Fessor suggested. "Let's move a few cars further forward." The professor snatched up his knapsack, and Jeff and Birch did likewise.

Something whizzed past Birch's ear like a very large, very angry mosquito. After that he heard the boom of a large-caliber revolver. All three men raced off toward the front of the train. A second bullet pinged off the metal side of the gondola just beside Jefferson's chest.

"Up! Up! GO!" shouted Fessor over his shoulder as he scrambled up the rungs of a boxcar. A third shot planted itself in the wooden siding between his legs. "Stay low, but keep moving!"

Then Birch was on top of the freight, running in a tight crouch along a slim stretch of boards with no handrail at all. The train swung around a bend and he went to his knees, rolling toward the edge. A mere foot from going over the side, he felt Jeff's big hand close around the bedroll and drag him back to the center. The two scrambled farther along the roof.

Behind them came the muzzle flash of another shot and then another. Pratt was on top of the boxcar two cars back, firing across the top of the gondola. Birch hoped that the movement of the train would continue to throw off Pratt's aim.

From up ahead, the engine's whistle screamed as the locomotive reached a crossing. The square body of a Plymouth sedan waited for the train to clear the intersection, its occupants unaware of their front-row seats for the drama just before them.

Another sudden shriek of the whistle made Birch look toward the front of the train. There was inky blackness ahead—a solid mass of dark hillside with an even blacker center into which the train was disappearing.

"Tunnel!" Fessor yelled back. "Hurry!"

The far end of the boxcar had no ladder, no means to climb down to another gondola car just ahead.

"Jump!" cried Fessor's voice from somewhere below. "Into the next car. You can do it!"

Jeff disappeared, flinging himself into the dark.

Birch waited only an instant before following. He hoped that Jefferson had time to get out from under.

Birch hit something soft and immediately sank to his knees as the familiar fragrance of manure rose around him. They had landed in a car loaded with fertilizer. The Kansas City Southern plunged into the tunnel, shutting out all the light. When it emerged from the other side, it immediately began to slow.

"Now we get off," Fessor said, urging them up and over to the side of the hopper. "When you jump, push hard so you get clear."

The three men struggled out of the manure and hoisted themselves over the side at the far limit of the gondola. As the train slowed still further, Fessor studied the swath of grass beside the tracks and pronounced it safe enough, then he dropped away from the freight and tumbled into the bushes beside the rails.

Birch caught Jeff's eye. "Now," he said simply, and the two men landed in a heap of thrashing arms and legs. Jeff's knapsack caught on a branch, spilling his spare clothes and a double handful of corn dodgers. Even with Birch and the Fessor helping, it took ten minutes of scrounging through the turf by the brief light of flickering matches to retrieve his Legion of Honor medal.

CHAPTER 25

The sun had not yet risen above the rim of the mountains. The sky was tinged with blue and violet, the morning cool and sweet. A single star hung just above the horizon. A cow bellowed in the field as an unfamiliar rumble rose up from the northeast.

Trudy could feel the earth tremble beneath her feet. The narrow gravel highway that wound past Shiloh was not meant to carry such an armada of vehicles all at once.

Willa Mae, Trudy, Lily, and the babies stood in a cluster on the porch as the cloud of dust approached the Tucker farm. "Do you think this is Governor Franklin Roosevelt come to ask us for our votes?"

"Oh, Lawd! The chariots of Pharaoh an' all his horsemen, too!" Willa Mae remarked at the sight of dim yellow headlamps strung out for half a mile.

"'Telephone poles,' he said." Trudy's face was set and angry. "'Electricity,' he told me."

"He didn't lie altogether, 'cept he didn't tell the whole truth."

Lily added, "Jes' didn' tell y'all 'bout the railroad."

"'Right-of-way.'" Trudy spat out the phrase as if it had a bad taste. "Every last cent we had is tied up in the seed planted in that field. Every hope of keeping this place."

"These here mens don't have no idea 'bout what kind of woman you is, Miz True. They hear yo' man is gone an' they think a white woman cain' tend no farm." Lily raised her chin in resentment. "Think you cain' do nothin' but cook an' scrub an' sew an' . . . bake yo'self a angel food cake!"

Willa Mae, who knew something about angel food, acknowledged that all hope for such a delicacy was at an end. One clap of a coupling, one blast of a whistle, and the angel food would fall flat as a hoecake.

The lead car, a long, sleek, black Buick with tan panels on the side, passed the north field, then turned on the lane toward the Tucker farmhouse. Following it were flatbed trucks laden with lumber and rails, open lorries filled with laborers, and wagons pulled by mule teams.

Willa Mae shook her head at the approach of the inevitable. "Up north, 'lectric poles sprout like weeds 'long the rails."

Trudy linked her arm with Willa Mae's for support. "All our seed and . . . and . . . my hens will stop laying, too. Listen to this racket!"

Willa Mae nodded at the possibility but tried to put the best face on the situation. "Hens is funny things, honey. They might get used to it. Hock an' me had us some fine chickens in Akron. Factory whistle never 'fected those hens. An easy dozen eggs ever' day. Big eggs, too. But they was White Leg'orns. Y'all got Rhode Island Reds, and them kind is more skittish."

"I'll tell you what they shall not do," Trudy declared. "They shall not chop down Birch's trees nor harm one cotton plant without compensation." With that, she returned to the house and emerged a moment later with Birch's twenty-gauge shotgun in hand.

"What you doin', gal?" Willa Mae put a hand out to stop her.

"What Birch would do."

Lily's eyes were wide at the sight of the weapon; her voice was tremulous. "Miz True . . . mens like these, they does what they wants."

"They won't kill a woman." Trudy frowned and glanced over her shoulder as she reconsidered what they might do. "Not an angel-food-cake-baking white woman, at any rate. But you better go in the house," Trudy ordered. "They are here, trespassing on my property, and I shall not stand idly by and let it happen."

Trudy was off the porch and planted firmly in the center of the yard when the line of vehicles followed the Buick toward the house.

Willa Mae hustled Lily and the young'uns back in the parlor. She closed the door behind them and then, as a witness, she took her place on the top step of the porch to glower at the Buick.

Headlamps fixed on Trudy in her blue cotton dress, the scatter gun cradled in her arms. She hoped it was an unexpected vision. Squinting into the glare, she shifted the gun so the barrel aimed in a lazy way at the windshield. The guttural rumble of the engines challenged her for a long moment. She did not budge or lower the lethal end of the shotgun.

The rear passenger side window cranked down. A hand emerged, palm open, as if to indicate the wish for a parley.

"Well, come on out then," Trudy shouted. "I shall not shoot you. Not without cause, anyway."

The car door swung back and, hands high, Sheriff Potts emerged. In spite of the cool morning, beads of sweat glistened on his face. Sweat stained his khaki shirt.

"Now, Trudy!" he called, but his words were nearly lost beneath the noise. Poking his head back into the vehicle, Sheriff Potts demanded that the engine and the lights be switched off. The driver obeyed him. In a chain reaction, the entire caravan shuddered as motors were turned off. The roar and rumble fell silent until at last Trudy could hear the coughing of a laborer in a truck.

"Now, Trudy . . ." Sheriff Potts began again. He rubbed his cheek nervously, then hitched his trousers up over his belly and hiked up the holster of his revolver.

"That is more like it," Trudy replied. "Silence is what we are used to at this hour of the morning."

"Now, Trudy . . ."

"Is this an official visit, Sheriff, or have you brought friends out for coffee?"

"Official."

"Then call me Missus Tucker and get on with it."

He took a step forward, looked off uneasily toward the hog pen, removed his hat, and cleared his throat into his hand. "Missus Tucker?"

"Yes, Sheriff Potts?"

"Go on now, gal. Put up that scatter gun. Birch wouldn't hold t' you doin' this."

"Would he not? Well, he never would have expected to see you among this rabble, Sheriff Potts. His true friend."

"Trudy . . . Missus Tucker, ma'am . . . they brung me along *b'cause* we're friends an' neighbors an' nobody here wants no trouble."

"Then tell your friends and neighbors to turn their army around and get off my property before my hens quit laying and the cow dries up and I get really angry."

A Yankee-tinged voice shouted from inside the Buick, "Get on with it, Potts! Show her the document!"

Potts replaced his hat and accepted a folded piece of paper from the interior of the Buick. Shaking the paper open, he took a step nearer to Trudy and held it up as if she could see it at that distance. "It's a court order, True," he said. "These fellers brought it on out here just in case. I called Fort Smith. There's no question about it. They got the right. I seen that field. I know what y'all have put into it. But Trudy, they got the law behind 'em. The Rock Island and . . . anyway, y'all didn't know it, and certain folks kept it quiet, but the bottom line is they got ol' Sam Tucker's signature eight year ago. They paid him for that right-of-way when this land of yourn weren't worth a hoot in hell." He walked slowly toward her, the document fluttering in his hand like a white flag. "Lay down that gun. It won't do you no good . . . just cause trouble is all."

She wavered a moment, then let the barrel droop groundward. "What about our cotton seed?"

He shook his head. "It ain't right, but they got the right." Near enough to take the weapon from her, instead he held the paper up, then lowered his voice to a whisper. "It's a lost cause, I tell you, True. I ain't happy 'bout this, neither. Folks in Hartford ain't happy 'bout it. Think it's a dirty underhanded deal."

"Is that supposed to comfort me?"

"Now, some folks out Meribah way are overjoyed with the en-tire project. Jenson Consolidated is gonna get themselves a rail spur up to their coal mine."

Trudy blanched at the mention of Jenson Consolidated. "They're in this too?"

Potts answered with a single downward thrust of his chin. "From the start. And Garr Jenson's Meribah Ho-tel done got itself a contract t' feed this whole stinkin' army. An' they don't care one bit 'bout whose crop is bein' plowed under."

So there is was. The whole truth lit up in Trudy's brain as if electricity had really come to Shiloh!

"Garrick Jenson." Trudy glanced at Willa Mae. A look of comprehension passed between the two women.

No wonder the loan and the seed had been given so readily. Garrick Jenson would be even richer if Birch Tucker had no hope of making his crop this year. Without the cotton from the north field, the entire farm would be forfeited to Jenson Consolidated at the settle come next autumn.

Stunned, Trudy stepped back from the path of the Buick. Sheriff Potts accompanied her to the porch.

"Jenson knew about the right-of-way before Birch planted that field?" Trudy looked Potts straight in the eye.

"I reckon that bunch knew what they was doin' all along, True. His name is on this here court order just the same as the railroad big shots. It's worse 'cause Jenson knew all along this was comin'. I'm sorry." Sheriff Potts stated what he knew was fact and continued. "It's good for y'all that I come out here. Now listen to me. I ain't gonna take y'all's scatter gun 'cause I won't have it on my conscience, the way they're bringin' convicts an' white trash onto y'all's home place t' tear it up. You might need t' use that thing later. If'n you was to find one of these bums sneakin' in your henhouse or . . . or tryin' anything . . . then blow his head off, if it seems the right thing t' do. You got young'uns."

"Thanks, Sheriff."

He put a hand on her arm and raised the volume of his voice again. "Missus Tucker . . . on behalf of Sebastian County and the township of Hartford, I gotta tell you . . . Rock Island Railroad Company of Fort Smith and Jenson Consolidated Coal Mines is layin' tracks to run a coal freight through y'all's north field. They got the law behind 'em. That's a fact. So leave it be, ma'am, an' get on in the house now."

The freight train that pulled onto the siding just outside the East St. Louis rail yard appeared to be without passengers. No hoboes could be seen emerging from the open boxcars. No tramps jumped down from the hoppers of grain or coal. No members of the Bonus Army alighted from the cattle cars.

Then suddenly from under all of these, as well as from below the reefers and the flatcars, a score of men appeared. They crawled swiftly from beneath the cars and rolled out from between the rails to stand grimy, oily, and coughing in the morning sun.

Jefferson sought out Birch, who was doubled over gagging one car length ahead. Birch retched again, then pulled himself half upright and watched his friend's approach through bloodshot and swollen eyes. "Journal box was leakin'," he choked out. "Kept spraying hot oil in my face." He paused to wipe his mouth on his shirttail. "The rest I swallowed. I ain't never riding the rods again."

Fessor joined them. "A rough way to arrive," he said. "But after our little tussle with Mister Pratt, you can bet that all the bulls will be coming down hard for a time. Better safe and greasy than dead. Follow me. I know the layout here."

Birch was still scrubbing his eyes and replacing about as much oil as he was removing when Fessor led them through a hole in a chain-link fence and over a small hill.

Jeff whistled softly, causing Birch to prop one eyelid open with his fingers and peer down the slope. He saw at once why Jeff was reacting in amazement. The hobo jungle near Shiloh had consisted of twenty men living in the brush. That camp could have been a fall hunting party out for deer or wild pigs and roughing it for fun.

But what met Birch's gaze in East St. Louis was an entire settlement—a city of the displaced, the homeless, and the wandering. Fully a thousand men, women, and children lived in tents, scrapwood huts, and old packing crates. Painted on the wall of one cabin, on boards that had once been someone's fence, was the sentiment, "In Hoover we trusted . . . now we're busted."

Fessor had already reached the first line of shacks. He turned to wave for Jeff and Birch to join him. "This the first Hooverville you've seen?" he asked.

"Seen the one outside Fort Smith," Birch said.

"And once we made a trip to Little Rock. One there had maybe forty folks livin' in tents. Nothin' like this!" Jeff pointed toward a row of derelict cars; from the rusted-out body of a 1920 Ford touring car to a wrecked but still shiny 1929 Oldsmobile Viking, each auto carcass housed a family. Birch watched six children crawl in and out the windows and three more bounce on the long hood of a blocked-up Locomobile.

Fessor admitted his surprise at the camp's growth since he had last seen it. "But come on, then. Let's see if we can't find some place to get clean and then rustle up some grub."

They turned down a regular avenue of shanties toward a flagpole that stood at the makeshift crossroads of two dusty lanes. Crudely lettered signposts indicated that Jeff and Birch had arrived at the corner of Affluence Avenue and Prosperity Turnpike. "These folks sure know how to whistle in the graveyard," Jeff commented.

"This is all new to me," Fessor remarked. "Last time this camp was only half its present size. I don't remember the flagpole either."

Fessor was still trying to get his bearings when the three men were approached by a uniformed figure. In full kit, from doughboy hat to sergeant's stripes to polished boots, the short man with the bugle under his arm walked smartly toward them. "Newcomers must report to General Waters," he said.

"Report what?" Birch drawled.

The little sergeant said peevishly, "Report in, of course. Enlist and be assigned to a mess. You are here to join the B.E.F., aren't you?"

The professor worked it out first. "B.E.F. Bonus Expeditionary Force, like the A.E.F. when we went to France. Clever."

"And y'all has a gen'ral in charge here?" Jeff queried.

The sergeant looked down his nose in distaste at their ignorance; this made no impression at all because all three men were taller than he. "General Walter Waters," he said with exasperation. "He is in command of the B.E.F."

"Someone is actually organizing this mayhem," Fessor commented. "This may prove even more interesting than I thought."

General Walter Waters was a man on a crusade. An unemployed car salesman, Waters fancied himself the equal in strength of character and leadership ability to the American hero of the Great War, General John J. Pershing. And he thought himself even more handsome than Black Jack Pershing. More than six feet tall, with a mane of dark blond hair waving above his high forehead, Waters saw the Bonus March as the perfect opportunity to firmly establish his reputation as a leader of men. Thirty-four years of age, he had left his wife and two children behind in Portland, Oregon, and led a ragtag group of veterans all the way to the Midwest.

Despite the very unmilitary surroundings of the East St. Louis Hooverville, Waters wore a khaki shirt, tight riding breeches, and tall black boots. He carried a walking stick in place of a riding crop as a badge of his authority.

"New recruits, I see. Good, good," Waters intoned when Sergeant Butcher introduced Birch, Jeff, and Fessor. "Now, men, we will be moving out in a very few days. We are waiting for contingents from

Texas and Montana to arrive, then we will push on for Washington. As you may know, the vote on the Patman Bill to authorize early payment of our bonus is expected by mid-June. The earlier our arrival in force, the greater the influence we will have on Congress. Very well, Sergeant. Assign these men to mess number six. Carry on."

Waters raised the tip of his mahogany stick to the corner of his eyebrow. There was a brief delay, but Birch returned the salute, and Jeff and Fessor complied as well. Birch noticed a slight smile on Fessor's face as he did so.

The tent to which the newcomers were assigned was surplus from the war. It was missing the shade flap over the doorway and had a large rent next to the center pole. But as Jeff remarked, after the long dry spell and the unspeakable grime acquired from riding under a train, the prospect of getting rained on was not at all unwelcome.

The lone man already in the tent when Birch first thrust his head inside introduced himself as Montgomery Freeman, also known as Monkey. Like his namesake, Freeman had long arms and a slight body, and a face often contorted into a mocking grin. "Fresh meat," he said when Birch and the others arrived. "Cut along, Butcher," he added, his pun dismissing the sergeant. "I'll see they get trimmed."

When the officious sergeant had disappeared, Monkey said, "You've already met the general and his toady. Butcher is a dull pain, but Waters is a good sort. Thinks a lot of himself, but he means well, anyway. I was in the same outfit as him. Hundred and forty-sixth field artillery."

"This camp has increased in size since I saw it last," Fessor remarked.

"You gotta hand it to Waters. He brought three hundred guys with him from Oregon, and they never once rode in the belly of the drag. Nosir! Open boxes all the way. That Waters, he has connections. Now me, I've been a flipper since before it got to be all the rage. Callie to Chi and back; that's my speed. But I never saw a layout like this. The local Sally . . ."

Birch believed that Monkey was speaking English, but he was not certain. "Come again?" he said.

"The Bible ranters. . . ."

Birch and Jeff still looked puzzled.

Monkey screwed up his face at their lack of understanding. "Sally, you know, Salvation Army? Anyhows, they feed us two squares a day on accounta Waters pitched them to it. He even has guys with clubs to police the joint; calls them MPs. No hooch, no profanity, no gambling— not so's you get caught—or out you go. 'Discharged,' he calls it."

"This doesn't sound so bad," Birch remarked to Jeff when Monkey finally paused for a moment. "I had some doubts back there under the freight, but this may really work out after all."

Monkey was eying Birch's oil-streaked face and hair and the dirt sifting out of Fessor's pockets. "Yeah, I see you guys didn't have it so cush. Come on, I'll show you where the boil-up is. By the way, you might want to hold your kind thoughts about Waters till after tomorrow morning. Butcher toots that horn at six. The general expects everybody to roll out for a little patriotic chin music, or no breakfast."

C H A P T E R   2 6

Within a few minutes after sunrise, the destruction of the cotton crop in the north field was a certainty.

As the track-building gang looked on, a single convict laborer hooked a chain onto the fence at the near corner of the forty acres. Revving the engine of the crew truck, the driver slipped the vehicle into gear and uprooted a string of posts that had stood solid for half a century.

Tom and his mother stood beneath the hickory tree in the yard and watched the devastation. "Lemme get Dad's gun, Mama!" Tom cried.

Trudy gave a single shake of her head. She stood pale and rooted to the ground, her eyes were filled with horror as the first of the trucks pulled onto the neat rows of flourishing plants. A tractor followed, churning up the soil and the dark-green cotton stalks beneath thick treads.

It was, Tom thought, something like watching a killing.

"Dad would get the gun if he was here, Mama!" Tom clutched her sleeve and cursed the men and machines that fanned out across the carefully cultivated field.

It was over that fast. Within one minute the furrows were broken, the cotton mutilated. Tom cried out as if the farm was a living thing, a member of the Tucker family being beaten before his eyes.

Trudy said nothing, but reached out to put a restraining hand on Tom's shoulder. Hopeless, helpless, defeated beyond rage, she clutched the strap of his overalls and walked slowly into the house.

The strains of reveille broke through Birch's dreams of home. "Oh, no," he groaned, rolling over in his bedroll on hard ground. "I thought I was done with that sound fourteen years ago!"

Ten minutes later, Birch, Jeff, and their tentmates stumbled out to mill around the flagpole. General Waters was already posturing on an empty apple crate, impatiently looking at his silver pocket watch and flicking away flies with his walking stick. "Dress those lines!" he ordered brusquely. "Sergeant," he shouted to Butcher, "show the new recruits where to fall in."

When the ranks had been assembled to the satisfaction of Waters, he led them in the singing of "The Star Spangled Banner." Birch noticed that the men's voices sounded strong on the first verse. On the second stanza, Birch and most of the rest dropped out or merely hummed along. Halfway through the third, only Waters himself, Jefferson, and a handful of others were still singing. There was no attempt made on verse four.

"I'm disappointed in you," Waters said. "As you know, that stirring song has been the official anthem of the army since we whipped the Hun! Shame on you who do not know it all!" He paused to frown at the assembly, but the discipline was partially undermined by the sounds of so many stomachs growling. "More to the point," he went on quickly, "that song illustrates why we will be successful in our quest for proper notice of our plight. President Hoover . . ." There was some hissing in the ranks at Hoover's name, forcing Waters to continue in a louder tone. "As I say, the president has only recently named that fine patriotic air as our national anthem, but we of the army had it first! Now, you will learn all of it, and you will be prepared to render it in Washington."

There was some grumbling about wasting time and playing at soldiering, but this was quickly silenced by the members of the camp who had been there the longest. "Knock it off!" Monkey prompted. "Or he'll keep us standing here longer!"

When the noise subsided again, Waters intoned, "Men, I have great news. Two more contingents of our force arrived during the night, and word has reached me that thousands more are on the way. So we will not delay further. We set out today for Washington!"

This unexpected information brought a cheer from the men. After the boredom of sitting around the East St. Louis Hooverville, they would finally be accomplishing something.

"Thirty minutes to grab your gear and hit the chow lines," Waters said. "Then assemble here again, ready to march!"

The row of ten railroad guards nervously paced the massed columns of three hundred veterans that had swung through the gates to the East St. Louis freight yard. Three of the guards held snarling, snapping police dogs on short chain tethers.

"Clear off, I said," repeated the captain of the group of sentries. He thumped his nightstick against the palm of his left hand to emphasize his words.

But even from three ranks back, Birch could tell the gesture was bravado. Though the May morning was cool, sweat ran down the sides of the man's face. The guard stopped waving his club to run a finger around inside the collar band of his dark blue uniform.

"But captain," General Waters said reasonably. "Surely you will cooperate. Many of us have come all the way from the Pacific coast by freight and never so much as an unkind word. These men are not vagrants or criminals. We are all ex-soldiers seeking the promised help of our government. You don't want to stand in our way."

"I got my orders," the guard said. "The B & O don't want tramps riding the rails. Now clear off!"

A low, menacing growl rippled through the ranks of men. This brought renewed snarls from the dogs, who lunged against their chains, straining to attack. Jeff remarked to Birch that the guards looked scared. "An' you cain't tell what scared men'll do," he warned. "Hope the gen'ral knows what *he's* doin'."

It was clear that Waters did not want a violent confrontation. "The Baltimore and Ohio is not as helpful as I had hoped," he said. "We did not have this difficulty with the Santa Fe. But we are law-abiding citizens. . . . All right, men. Back to camp."

"We givin' up then?" shouted Grove from the rank in front of Birch. "What kinda garbage is this? Let's just take the train!"

"Quiet in the ranks there! Sergeant, if that man speaks, I'll have him put on report," Waters ordered.

Grove turned almost purple with anger and would have shot his mouth off again if Monkey had not clapped a hand over it. In a whisper loud enough for Birch and Jeff to overhear, he said, "Pipe down, you bakehead! You want them screws to sic the bone polishers on us? The gen'ral's got another plan!"

"Aboooooout face!" Sergeant Butcher shouted. There was some shuffling and continued muttering, but the ranks reversed their direction; none refused to turn around. "Forwaaaard march!"

The man to Fessor's left in the line said something to him, then gestured for him to send the message on down the line. "Pass it on," Fessor murmured to Birch. "Plan Lux, whatever that is, will be put into operation."

Birch shot a quick glance over his shoulder. The railroad bulls had visibly relaxed, but the dogs were still pulling at the leashes, looking eager to tear into Bonus Marcher flesh.

From the row now behind Birch, Grove started singing "The Internationale" in an off-key, rasping voice.

Arise ye prisoners of starvation!
Arise ye wretched of the earth!

"None of that, either!" Waters demanded. "We'll have no Red Commie songs in this command!"

One mile east of the rail yard, the Illinois hillside beside the B & O tracks was littered with tin cans, old tires, cinders, and broken bottles. On this particular morning, however, the most conspicuous features were the milling knots of Bonus Marchers. Some of the figures were in fragments of their army uniforms; others were dressed in overalls or castoff clothes supplied by Sally.

An odd assortment of equipment added to the peculiar nature of the scene. Some men carried old paint cans full of axle grease and the stubs of worn-out brooms. Others had sagging inner tubes, which they toted on the slant over their shoulder, giving them the appearance of demented tire repairmen. Still others carted sledge hammers or pieces of timber cribbing.

"Here she comes," shouted Monkey. General Waters had assigned the nimble man to scramble aloft among the telegraph wires and watch the rails both directions.

"Take cover, men!" Waters ordered. Monkey shinnied down the pole and crouched in a clump of brush. Two hundred of the Bonus brigade sought refuge in the culverts and ditches along the tracks. The mad dash for concealment reminded Birch of the war, except that no one was shooting at them . . . yet.

A hundred more men crowded behind a pair of billboards. "Over a Million Satisfied Users—General Electric All Steel Refrigerators," one sign read. It showed a laughing baby sitting on the floor in front of an open refrigerator.

The other advertisement portrayed a kindly looking doctor and a worried man. "Constant Coughing Strains the Heart—Use Luden's Menthol Cough Drops," it advised. Jeff and Birch hid behind the cough-drop sign next to Grove and Fessor.

The freight from which the Washington-bound men had been turned away chuffed slowly up the slope toward them. Just below the refrigerator billboard, the locomotive slowed, and a brakeman alighted. He threw a lever hard over, shunting the cars onto a siding. Ponderously the train moved forward again, pulling up the grade until it filled the flanking arc of rails from General Electric to Luden's. The black bulk of the engine hissed to a stop just beside Birch's hiding place.

"We've got her now," Grove exulted. "She can't move till after the passenger train gets by."

There was a shout from the middle of the ditch on the far side of the stalled freight that was instantly repeated on the near side, then Butcher blew a ragged rendition of charge on his bugle. Men jumped up from their hiding spots and surged toward the train. Birch smiled at the absurdity of the ragtag little army attacking the stranded train.

"Hey!" bellowed the startled engineer. "What do you think—" But he got no further with his protest. Waters had detailed a pair of the biggest B.E.F. recruits to grab the man and yank him from the cab. Other teams wrestled the brakeman, the fireman, and a pair of railroad bulls to the ground and sat on them.

"Now, sonny," the general said to the engineer. "We won't hurt you or your train. Just hold still a while."

Even before the rail workers had been subdued, the rest of the assault force of Plan Lux had gone into action. With Birch carrying the bucket, Jeff swabbed the rail between the drive wheels of the engine with a liberal dose of axle grease. Grove shoved his chunk of cribbing across the tracks under a flatcar.

The dark blue and yellow of the Baltimore & Ohio passenger train screamed past on the main line. As if delighted and proud of their handiwork, many of the Bonus Marchers waved at the occupants before returning to their labors.

Fessor unslung a sloshing inner tube from across his back, careful to keep a hole in the rubber doughnut aimed skyward till he was ready. Then, turning the tube upside down and pointing it at the rails, he discharged a fragrant stream of very soapy water onto the tracks ahead of the freight. The noise of sledge hammers slapping against coupling levers mingled with the grunts and groans of men lifting the heavy links of chain from between the cars.

Soap and grease exhausted, Birch and the others stepped back to study the completion of their mission. Waters even let the engineer stand up. "You'll . . . you'll all be hanged for this," the train man sputtered.

"I don't think so," Waters replied. "By the way, you are free to go if you wish."

The engineer ran to the cab and swapped the patient panting of the steam engine for the shriek of a whistle. He threw the throttle wide open, sending a shower of greasy suds from under the rims of the eight drivers. The sound made by the wheels was a futile sizzle and a high-pitched whine. The engine lunged forward a foot, lost traction, spun frantically, and slipped backward on the slope, accompanied by the cheers of the Bonus Army. The whistle screamed over and over. To Birch it sounded angry and frustrated, as if the machine itself was infuriated at the trick that had been played on it.

"Now what, Gen'ral?" Monkey called.

"Back up with you," Waters ordered, "and keep us posted. The rest of us will just wait."

The next act of the seizure of the B & O freight was about an hour in coming. A line of five-ton trucks, painted olive drab, growled up the hill on the dirt road that paralleled the tracks. Gears howling, they pulled up the final incline, then stopped alongside the telegraph line. Birch and the others were drawn up in neat ranks of ragged men, the same as they had been in the rail yard.

The tailgates of the trucks dropped open, releasing about a hundred fresh-faced young men in uniform. Their shoulder patches identified them as members of the Illinois National Guard. Each was armed with a bolt-action rifle of Great War vintage.

"Wonder if one of them boys could be carrying the same weapon I had in France," Birch muttered to Jeff. "Wouldn't want it aimed at me."

A chubby major with flushed cheeks seemed to have command of the Guard unit. When his men were spread out in a line facing the Bonus Marchers, the major stepped forward. "Who's in charge here?" he demanded.

"I am," Waters said, as if his dress uniform and walking stick were not evidence enough. "General Waters of the Bonus Expeditionary Force. And you are?"

"Major Stone." The voice of the man squeaked, and he covered it with a cough. "Majors Stone," he repeated more forcefully. "General . . . or whoever you are, your men are trespassing on Baltimore and Ohio property and interfering with the passage of this freight train and are hereby commanded to disperse, by order of the governor."

A low, angry rumble swept through the crowd. With the armed troops in front of them and the train blocking escape behind them, Birch prayed that talking would carry the day.

"Well now, Major," Waters replied. "I don't think we are going to disperse just yet. You see, we are all American veterans, and we are on our way to Washington to lobby for passage of the Bonus Bill. Up till now, all the railway officials have been very cooperative. I don't think that the officials of the B & O understood our request, so we're just here to spell it out for them." A cheer broke from the three hundred throats of the Bonus Marchers.

"But you have to!" the major whined. "Do you want to be arrested?"

"Nope," Waters replied with a shake of his head. "But we don't mean to be stuck in Illinois, either."

"Say, Major," Monkey yelled. "I was at Compiegne. Was you in the war?"

"No, I . . ." the major stammered.

"My brother Frank was there," shouted a member of the Guard. "And he was wounded at Chateau Thierry!"

"Oh, yeah?" responded Grove. "So was I. What outfit was he with? What's his name?"

"Get back in ranks!" ordered the major. "Be quiet!"

"I was with the field artillery," Waters said, sensing the opportunity. "Many of our force here were wounded in action . . . Belleau Wood, the Argonne, the Meuse. . . . Would you shoot them down for going to Washington to claim what is owed them?"

"Ain't no way!" a young Illinois soldier replied. "My uncle was killed at Sedan. Anybody here in that battle?"

"I was," Fessor replied with a wave of his hand. "Do you want to hear about it?"

The two lines of men surged toward each other, discipline abandoned, hostility forgotten. Almost no one noticed when the major ground the gears of the last truck in the line, backing it around and roaring off down the hill. The Illinois Guard and the advance force of the Bonus Army spent an hour swapping stories and commiserating with each other about the Great Depression.

When the major returned in the olive-drab vehicle, he was followed by another line of trucks. Some of these were additional army vehicles; others were labeled Farmers' Cooperative Produce and Illinois Central Meatpacking.

Four hundred pairs of eyes watched the major with hostility and suspicion as he got out of the truck and approached Waters again. "The B & O still refuses to let your men ride," he said. The angry murmur returned, amplified by the Guard unit's angry voices. "However," he hurried to add, "the governor has arranged with several businesses to furnish food. And," he added grudgingly, "you will be permitted to use Guard equipment across the state of Illinois. They will take you all the way to Indiana. Will that be satisfactory?"

The resulting cheers were heard clear back in St. Louis.

They weren't all convicts, Trudy discovered. In fact, the majority of the workers were not convicts in prison drab, but ordinary laborers in overalls and dungarees. As if it mattered whether the men who were ripping her heart apart were convicted thieves and murderers or just men doing their jobs.

A small city of surplus army tents had been erected in the north field to shelter a construction crew of forty men—drivers, track layers, and a team of builders who set to laying a trestle across the James Fork. The foreman, Mr. Frost, was a decent enough fellow. Tall, thin, mustached, and sunburned, he spoke kindly to his men and tipped his hat and looked ashamed as Trudy, Tom, and Bobby passed him on their way to Grandma Amos's place. Tom spit into the dust, and for an instant Trudy thought he would fly into the foreman. But Tom kept walking, silent all the way to the store. Once there, he set to work cleaning the crowded chicken coops for the old woman.

Tom's job was a mercy, Trudy thought on her way back to the house alone. He would not have to stay all day within earshot of the chain saws and the coarse laughter of the men cutting down the row of birch trees one after another. It was, Trudy thought as she watched the laborers come and go, as if they had been sent to mow down her spirit along with the cotton crop and the much loved stand of birch trees.

An hour before noon, the caterers arrived. Trudy watched from the window of the bedroom as three large trucks from the Meribah Hotel and Cafe pulled onto the farm road from the main highway and then, with a roar and a lurch, rolled onto the north field to park alongside the standpipe of the well.

Trudy's eyes narrowed with resentment. "The well," she remarked simply, as if those words identified one last thing she could fight for.

Caro-line Jenson's 1930 Buick Empire followed close behind the trucks. A crew of cooks and dishwashers leapt from the backs of the trucks and began to set up long tables and wrestle out cooking equipment from beneath the canvas tarps.

Wearing a smug, satisfied smile, Caro-line stepped from behind the wheel of the Buick and surveyed the decimated acreage. Trudy saw her face turn toward the empty place where the birch trees had stood. Her head cocked a bit to the side the way a hen in the barnyard considers a bug before it dines.

Caro-line waved her hand and issued some order that made her workforce scramble to change the location of a long table. Walking to the standpipe of the artesian well, she circled it and said something to a heavyset man in a white apron. The cook retrieved a bucket and knelt to open the spigot of the well.

Something clicked inside Trudy. Her vision was reduced to a pinpoint of light. Propelled by fury, she snatched up Birch's old gun and flew out the front door.

"Hey!" she shouted at the top of her lungs. The volume of her own voice surprised her. It also turned the heads of those who were set to steal the water bubbling up from the old spring. "Get away from my water well!"

Caro-line's head snapped up. Her face hardened. She barked some unintelligible order to the cook, who scurried off around the back of the first catering truck. He returned a moment later with Mr. Frost.

Trudy's angry stride gobbled up the ground. "Get away from my water well!" she yelled again, brandishing the weapon.

Caro-line stepped back behind the open door of the Buick. "You're crazy!" she shrieked and pointed as Mr. Frost approached with the cook. "She has a gun!"

Trudy pushed past the startled catering crew and took up her place in front of the standpipe. "Get away from my well," Trudy demanded through clenched teeth.

"Your well?" Caro-line was indignant.

"My well," Trudy repeated.

"We have a court order. . . ." Caro-line began.

"You have a court order that says you have the legal right to destroy everything within the boundaries of the right-of-way. My well is not within your right."

"We'll see about that." Caro-line's voice was shrill and catlike as she challenged Trudy.

Mr. Frost stepped forward, placing himself between the two women. "Missus Tucker is right, ma'am." He addressed Caro-line as he would talk to a wild animal.

"Not have the right!" Caro-line shrieked. "How dare she! How dare this . . . farm wife . . . tell me what I may do with what is clearly and contractually mine!"

Frost's voice carried an air of amusement, as though he would enjoy seeing the two women go at each other, tooth and claw. "Missus Jenson, ma'am, y'all . . . meanin' Jenson Consolidated an' the Rock Island . . . well, ma'am . . . y'all have the right t'wreck this here fine bottomland since it suits you t' do so." He almost winced as he said it. "But ma'am, that there well is out of bounds. I got the survey in my truck. Your say-so as to what trees you want us to take out and what crops you want plowed down . . . it only goes as far as that there boulder. The water well is beyond your reach."

Caro-line's face reddened. "We'll see about that!" she shrieked. "We'll see about that!" She leapt into the automobile and threw it into reverse, churning up the soft earth beneath her tires as she left the place.

Trudy watched her go. Only after the Buick had roared onto the main highway and disappeared did Trudy's own anger abate. She lowered the barrel of the shotgun.

Mr. Frost tucked his chin, half concealing a smile behind his hand. "Thought we was gonna have a catfight right here." Then, to the astonished catering crew, he said, "Y'all gonna have t' haul in your own water."

"Haul?" belched the cook.

Frost's gaze turned steely. "It's in the Jenson Meribah Cafe contract with the Rock Island. I work for the Rock Island, not for the Jensons. What I been told an' what I seen is that you Jenson people are bound to haul us water in here. Now get your trucks away from this here well an' go get the water we was promised."

Trudy remained beside the standpipe as the Jenson trucks retreated. Mr. Frost turned to her and tipped his hat. "We ain't gonna trouble you no more 'bout your well, ma'am. I'm a farmer m'self. Know what a good well means these days."

"I suppose I should thank you." Trudy's gaze went past him to the destruction of the acreage.

"I seen y'all at the fair last autumn—that baby boy of yourn an' his chicken. How is he?"

Trudy lowered her eyes and replied very quietly, "He has passed on, Mr. Frost." She inclined her head toward the white wooden cross on the knoll.

He blanched. "My sincere regrets, ma'am." Then, "And I mean . . . for all of this. She's a mean'un, that Caro-line Jenson. The only folks who don't know that are the folks she has some use fer."

Trudy nodded. "Knowing that does not help those of us she has some power over."

"I suppose it don't, no, ma'am. Any rate, I've told the fellers your well is off-limits." He scratched his head beneath the brim of his hat. "We get a powerful thirst out here in the sun. Might want t' get that young'un of yourn out here sellin' iced tea."

"We have no ice, Mister Frost, but thank you for the suggestion."

Trudy left the well and the field and returned to the house. She fell into her rocking chair and sat through the noon hour with the shotgun across her lap. No one went near the well.

She watched the long lines of weary men form to receive the ladles of Meribah Cafe slop that passed for the noon meal. Their faces downcast and shaded beneath the brims of their hats, they seemed less than enthusiastic about their dinner.

Just regular fellows, Trudy thought as she observed them picking at the food. No doubt they felt lucky to have this terrible job, grateful even to eat the worst food in western Arkansas. They were men with families and wives at home, wives who were praying for their men as Trudy prayed for Birch. She wondered if he was eating lunch right now and if his thoughts turned to home and her cooking.

She sat and rocked and really looked at their faces and suddenly an idea came to her mind like the ringing of a firebell! "Like Birch. Just ordinary men," she murmured. "With ordinary appetites."

C H A P T E R 2 7

After eight days, six states, and a lot of cramped, bumpy miles in the back of National Guard trucks, the three hundred forty-six members of the advance party of the B.E.F. arrived in the nation's capital. Birch unfolded his stiff legs and climbed down onto the pavement of the District of Columbia, just at the Washington end of the newly opened Arlington Memorial Bridge.

Birch, Jefferson, and the others had slept in city parks, abandoned factory buildings, and in the backs of the trucks if nothing else was offered. Fed at each stop by the Salvation Army and by merchants who donated bread, pies, and sausages, the Bonus Marchers felt respected, if not exactly welcomed.

With each border crossed, the state governors had been eager to speed them on their way. Grove remarked cynically that it was because each official wanted the responsibility shifted to someone else as soon as possible.

The progress of the Bonus Expeditionary Force had even been reported state-by-state in the Washington newspapers, as if to give the Congressmen warning of its arrival. But when Birch alighted from the truck, the most immediate greeting was from the cascades of pink cherry blossoms that filled the street with a riot of color. The sidewalk opposite the line of trucks was completely overhung with masses of the rosy petals. Beneath the blooming boughs, a curious crowd of onlookers had gathered. Men in white linen summer suits and straw hats escorted stylishly dressed ladies. They and foreign diplomats in morning coats and striped trousers paused together to gawk at the newly arrived brigade of the bankrupt.

Birch looked around at the mob of his fellow Bonus Marchers who overflowed the cement walk onto the cobblestoned street. Stubble-faced, shaggy, raggedly dressed, many wearing obviously cast-off, secondhand clothing, the B.E.F. looked like a pitiful army indeed. And he saw on their faces the same humiliation that made his own face burn.

"Looks like pigs in the parlor, don't it?" Jeff murmured.

Birch shook his head sadly. "You said it! Don't look very military today, do we?"

General Waters did not seem concerned. "Fall in!" he ordered. "Form up! Lively now!" It was Waters's intention to march immediately on the Capitol. The sooner the presence of the B.E.F. was made known, he felt, the better. "I know you men are feeling concerned over your dress. Don't be! March with your heads up and your backs straight. Show them your pride despite the bad fortune you have been handed. They will appreciate your message all the more."

But every attempt to implement the general's order was defeated by the busy Washington street. Every time Birch and the others stepped from the curb, they were honked back onto the sidewalk by square-bodied Packards and twelve-cylindered Pierce-Arrows.

A convertible Graham-Paige roared past, its rumble seat packed with teenage girls. Silk scarves streaming in the breeze of the auto's speed, the young women laughed and pointed at the ragged men jumping out of the way.

A bright blue motorcycle purred up, and the weary B.E.F. once again obligingly parted their ranks to let it through. But this time the machine stopped in the middle of the group, near where Birch and Jeff were standing. The operator shut off the engine.

He was a tall man, nearly equal to Jeff in height. Slim and neatly dressed, the man pushed a pair of round-lensed goggles up onto his forehead and took off a pair of leather gloves. Walking directly up to Birch, he introduced himself as Pelham Glassford, the chief of police.

"My friends call me Happy," he said, shaking hands around in a circle. "We're glad you all arrived safely. We weren't expecting you until tomorrow, or we would have had a better greeting for you."

Birch and the rest of the Bonus Marchers squared their shoulders and stood a little taller at his words. "We thought maybe you might not be glad to see us," Birch said. "We heard tell you said for the governors not to let us through."

"I had my doubts about how well we could care for your needs," Glassford said. "But since you are here, we'll make the best of it. I'm an old soldier myself."

"Yessir, Chief Glassford, sir," exclaimed Waters, hurrying up. "I'm Walter Waters. I guess I run this outfit."

"He's sure doin' a lot of bowin' and scrapin'," Birch hissed to Fessor.

"He may call himself General Waters," Fessor replied, "but he just met the real thing. Glassford was regular army, brigadier general in France. I would imagine that Waters has decided against putting on airs . . . particularly in front of someone who could have us all run out of town."

"I expect your men are anxious for a bath and a hot meal," the police chief was saying.

Waters looked unhappy. "We had planned to march immediately."

But Glassford was already shaking his head. "Can't let you parade without a permit," he said. "But if you men will keep to the sidewalks, I'll be happy to escort you to your quarters. The Salvation Army and some other charitable organizations have agreed to give you shelter."

Grove growled in Birch's ear, "He's just splittin' us up. Mark my words, this is done to keep us down." Birch resolved that if it were possible to split away from Grove, he would happily do it.

"But General Glassford," Waters was protesting. "We are just the advance guard. There will be thousands more arriving soon. The Salvation Army can't possibly see to us all."

Glassford's pleasant face showed the first sign of unhappiness, then he shrugged. "We'll just cross that bridge when we come to it," he said. "In the meantime, a short walk and then food and clean beds. How does that sound?"

No one in the ranks of the B.E.F. could think of any objections.

But walking through the crowds of well-dressed and well-fed Washingtonians was not pleasant. In their overalls and patched denims, with shoe soles that flapped with every step, Birch and his comrades once again found it difficult to feel much pride or hold up their heads.

Birch did manage to look up enough to spot a mailbox as he passed it. He dropped in a letter to Trudy, telling her and the folks back home that he and Jeff had arrived safely.

Anacostia Flats was a dusty, vacant stretch of bottomland located across the Potomac to the southeast of the Capitol. Bookended between the Eleventh-Street Bridge and a small military airfield, the strip was used by P-12 pilots to perfect their takeoffs and landings, and Martin bombers made practice bomb runs over the bridge before returning to their base at Langley.

Soon, General Walter Waters was telling his growing army of Bonus Marchers, Anacostia Flats would be their temporary home.

Waters was correct in his prediction that thousands of veterans were on their way to Washington. On the day after Birch's arrival in Washington, three hundred more Bonus Marchers showed up, having traveled all the way from Colorado by rail. The next day two hundred from New Jersey, three hundred from Chicago, and five hundred from Texas put in their appearances. The Texas contingent even brought along a goat named Hoover as a mascot.

But even without the goat, the Salvation Army and the other charitable organizations trying to provide beds and meals for the men had quickly been taxed beyond their ability to cope. Anacostia Flats was part of the solution proposed by General Waters and Chief Glassford.

Birch, Jeff, Fessor, and the others looked out over the empty space and tried to imagine the precise, orderly rows of tents that General Waters was describing. He explained that the army would furnish canvas shelters, cots, mobile field kitchens, and provisions. Chief Glassford had sent word that contact was being made with Army Chief of Staff Douglas MacArthur that very morning. "All we have to do is furnish the labor, and there's no shortage of that, is there men?" Waters joked.

A trolley stopped at the far end of the bridge, and a khaki-clad figure in the uniform of a U.S. Army officer stepped off. The broad-shouldered man with the high forehead looked around at the river and the fields beyond, then set off toward the group of men clustered around Waters. When the officer reached Anacostia Flats, Birch could make out the oak-leaf insignia that indicated the rank of major.

"Here is the report now!" Waters said happily. "No doubt the major has news for us about when we can expect the first truckloads of equipment."

The broad face of the approaching army officer had a determined look—not at all like an expression the bearer of good news would wear. When Waters stepped forward, the general obviously expected to be saluted, but the newcomer did not oblige.

"Major Eisenhower," the officer announced crisply, "Aide to General MacArthur. Your supplies are arriving now." Major Eisenhower turned and pointed at the bridge, where a large flatbed wagon heaped with canvas and pulled by a pair of plodding draft horses was just crossing. Behind it came another horse-drawn wagon, stake-sided and carrying a mountain of straw. "Where do you want it?"

"It?" Waters snorted. "What do you mean? One wagonload of tents is not adequate. There must be some mistake."

Eisenhower shook his head. "Not tents; bed sacks, and straw to fill them. General MacArthur says he has no authority to distribute army property to civilians. The bed sacks were designated as surplus and the straw donated. Good luck." With that the major turned on his heel and started back across the river.

"Wait," Waters demanded. "Perhaps General MacArthur doesn't understand our situation. We need cooking facilities, medical care, food . . . there will be thousands camped here within the week."

Eisenhower turned again to face angry, incredulous looks. His expression softened from its official coldness. "I'm sorry," he said. "Chief Glassford made a very eloquent speech, but General MacArthur has made up his mind. No army property is to be used, no army provisions distributed, no army personnel to assist, except by direct order of the president." With that he straightened his back, saluted Waters, and pivoted sharply on his heel.

A pair of black men in overalls were throwing moth-eaten canvas bags onto the ground. Each bed sack that landed on the heap caused the ones below it to belch out billows of dust. Already the wagon was surrounded by a cloud of airborne filth. Behind them another pair of black men unloaded the heap of straw with pitchforks. It was none too clean either.

Waters bit his lip and frowned. "We'll manage anyway," he said at last. "This is only a temporary setback. We have all been living by our wits for some time; why should life come any easier now? All right, here's what we'll do: I'm off to see Chief Glassford. You men form into squads and circulate in the nearby neighborhoods. We need boards, canvas, rope, whatever they can spare. And food . . . beans . . . and pots to cook in. We'll show General High-and-Mighty MacArthur what the B.E.F. is capable of! Sergeant Butcher, take charge."

"Foraging party: Attenhhhut!" Butcher shouted. The siege of Washington had begun.

The house Birch approached to ask for donations for the B.E.F. camp was a three-story brick building with a flight of white stone steps leading up to the first-floor landing. A black wrought-iron gate enclosed the front walk, and pink roses bloomed in a tiny flower garden.

As he hammered with the brass doorknocker, his straw hat clutched in front of him, Birch reflected that he had never ever begged for anything before. Asking for handouts was so foreign to his nature that he scarcely knew what to say or where to begin.

That was precisely why he had volunteered to make the first attempt; he was determined to conquer his nervousness and get on with it. Monkey had tried to talk him into watching and learning, but Birch had insisted on going ahead. Now that he was actually on the spot, though, he was not so sure. He glanced nervously back at his three companions, who stood watching the results from outside the front gate.

He waited after knocking, but no footsteps approached the door. Birch felt a wave of relief; perhaps no one was home and he could leave. He looked longingly toward the street and raised his shoulders in question.

"Knock harder," Monkey called to him.

Taking a deep breath, Birch again raised the heavy ring and clapped it against the lion's face that was the base of the knocker. Then he stood unconsciously kneading his hat between his fingers like bread dough.

The hoped-for and dreaded footsteps sounded in the entryway. The door swung open, and Birch stood face-to-face with an austere-looking black man wearing white gloves and a dark green uniform. "Yes, what is it?" the man asked, scanning Birch's dingy clothing with obvious disdain.

"We need . . ." Birch began, but felt that he was not being polite enough. "If you could spare . . ." That was not quite right either. "You see, there's about a thousand guys . . ."

The sound of heels sharply clicking on the marble floor came from behind the butler. "Alfred," an imperious voice called, "whatever is the matter? Why are you standing there with the door open?"

The gray-haired woman who had come to the door was tall and regal looking. She stared at Birch, who wanted to melt into the stoop or run for his life.

"I am waiting for this gentleman to state his business, ma'am," the servant replied, gesturing toward Birch.

"He has *no* business here," the woman's voice pronounced categorically. "Tell him to be off, or we shall call the police." She spoke as if Birch could not hear her words himself, even though he and the woman were only a few feet apart.

"Please, ma'am," Birch said, trying to address her directly. "My friends and I just need . . ."

The smartly dressed woman looked past Birch, or through him as it seemed to him, and noticed the group waiting on the sidewalk. "Radical revolutionaries!" she said, her voice rising in tone and volume. "Vagrants!" she spat out the word with as much disgust as if she said *slime* or *filth*. "Alfred, close the door! Get the gun! I shall call the police myself. Communist rioters!"

The heavy door slammed abruptly in Birch's face, leaving him baffled and nose-to-nose with the lion-head doorknocker. "Come on!" Jeff yelled.

"She ain't kiddin' about the police," Monkey declared. "The gun neither. Let's make tracks!" Monkey swung around, the hem of the knee-length coat he wore floating around him like a cape. While not exactly running, the four wasted no time in leaving.

"Now, here's the skinny," Monkey explained after the friends had put several blocks of distance between themselves and the encounter. "With all due respect, Professor, riding them side-door Pullmans don't qualify you as no expert such as I in the finer points of being a moll buzzer."

"One who seeks contributions from women," Fessor translated for Birch and Jeff.

"Right, thanks, Fessor," Monkey agreed. "Now look here. I'm gonna give you the level so's you don't make no bonehead plays, see? When I get through learning you, everything'll be all to the mustard. Rule number one: Don't go to no front doors of high-toned joints; go to the back. Rule number two: Know what you're gonna ask before you go to the door. Rule number three: Smile big and say thank you, no matter what they say back. That way they won't call the crushers on you, see? Just sit back and watch me."

Outside a more modest brownstone home where the front stoop rose directly from the sidewalk, Monkey placed them around the corner of the house where they could hear but not be seen. "Rule number four," he said as he left them there. "Never make the citizens think you're a gang come to heist their worldly goods, lest they out with the roscoe and send little lead messages in your direction."

Birch could almost hear the sound of confident assurance in the way Monkey knocked on the selected door. "Good day, ma'am," Birch heard him say. "Do you have any chores that need done? Trash emptied, perhaps? I would be glad to oblige if you could spare a couple of eggs or a loaf of bread." Birch could not hear the reply, but an instant later he heard Monkey say, "Thank you, ma'am. Very kind, I'm sure. Pleasant day to you."

It was like knowing that a friend was returning from fishing. Birch expected to hear his story of what was caught and what got away. But Monkey, when he rounded the corner, seemed to have come up with nothing. His hands were empty, but he was whistling the "Ballad of Jesse James."

"Struck out?" Birch said. "We heard you be nice and polite, just like you said."

"What d'ya mean, stuck out? I don't call a half-pound of axle grease and a loaf of bread strikin' out."

Birch and Jeff examined the man for an unnoticed bag or parcel. "Then where you got it hid?" Jeff asked.

"You don't think I wear this coat 'cause I'm cold, do you? This here's is my foraging uniform," he said. "See these?" he asked, indicating his pockets. "They got slits inside, see?" He reached down and gently hoisted the now-drooping hem. "Butter," he said. "Bread's in the other side. It don't do to angle for provisions with your hands full already."

Monkey pointed out the next location for them to approach, then resumed humming "Jesse James." But when he started singing, he broke into a different set of words than Birch was expecting:

Oh those beans, bacon and gravy
They almost drive me crazy
I eat them till I see 'em in my dreams
But I wake up in the morning, another day is dawning
I guess I'll have another mess of beans.

As they headed down the block, Birch noticed that Fessor trailed along behind, jotting something in his notebook.

"We done seen how Monkey's way works," Jeff said as he led Birch toward his Aunt Minnie's house. "Now let's see my way." Heading northwest up Pennsylvania Avenue, the two men turned off south on Twenty-first into the neighborhood known as Foggy Bottom.

Once an industrial center, reeking from the fumes given off by coal depots and gasworks, Foggy Bottom had become the heart of the black community in the District of Columbia.

The home of Ike and Minnie Pendle was in a neat three-story brick building. Their black-painted front door was identical to the five others that shared the block, but Jeff pointed out the cheerful yellow curtains in all three sets of windows facing the street. "Mama tol' me Aunt Minnie always was partial to yella," Jeff said to Birch as the front entry flew open.

A woman a little taller than Willa Mae and every bit her equal in girth and smiles, ran down the steps and almost knocked Jeff down with the force of her embrace.

"Jefferson!" Minnie said over and over. "I is so glad to see you! Tell me all about the baby an' the twins an' Lily. An' how is your mama?"

Jeff was dumbfounded. "Hold on just a minute whilst I catch my breath, Aunt Minnie. How'd you know I was comin' today? I didn't know myself till this mornin'."

"Been watchin' for you!" Minnie declared. "Ever since your mama wrote and tol' me you was comin'. Ike heard talk in the White House 'bout the Bonus Marchers reachin' the District an' more a-comin', so I just kept settin' by the winder! Fact is, I think you is late! Where you been since you got to town?"

Jeff introduced Birch, about whom Minnie had already heard in letters from Willa Mae, and then he explained the difficulties involved in setting up the B.E.F. camp. But in the middle of his explanation, Minnie clapped her hands to her cheeks.

"An' here I keep you standin' on the stoop?" she chastised herself. "Come on in this house and set down. I bet you ain't had a decent meal since you left home. I'm gonna fix that right now, just you see if I don't.

Ike! Ike!" she hollered to her husband. "Come here and see your nephew and his friend. I gots supper to get on!"

Three plates of liver and onions later, Birch and Jeff pushed back from the Pendle table and declared themselves too stuffed to eat another bite. "Mighty fine, Missus Pendle," Birch said.

"President Hoover hisself couldn't have better," Jeff declared.

Minnie slapped her thighs and laughed. "You said it," she agreed, "an' never will. That liver come from the White House kitchen, ain't that right, Ike?"

"Missus President Hoover say she can't abide the smell," Ike Pendle agreed. "So when the butcher deliver a side of beef, she say us stewards and ushers can split it if we likes." Jeff's uncle Ike was a quiet man around Minnie, just as Hock had been around Willa Mae. But Ike's easygoing, affable manner did not mask his quick, attentive eyes. He said little, but he took in everything.

Later, in Minnie's front room, Jeff announced that he had not felt that relaxed or easy anywhere since leaving home. He pulled out the little sack of earth that was partly Pisgah and partly Shiloh and set it on the table. "Mama give me this bit of home to carry 'round with me," he explained, "but family is what matters, no matter where you is."

"What's this about the army not havin' supplies like they was 'sposed to?" Ike questioned softly. "All you men sleepin' on the ground then?"

Birch described the encounter with MacArthur's representative, then asked if Ike thought President Hoover would give the direct order that Major Eisenhower had said was required.

Ike dropped his chin and considered the matter before replying. "President Hoover is a good man," he said at last, "an' he wants to do right. But he listens to them that tell him he'll wreck the country if the government helps folks out. I'd say he ain't gonna change."

Birch looked at Jeff and shrugged. "Guess that's it, then. Tomorrow we go back to scrounging."

"What is it you mostly be needin'?" Ike asked.

"Canvas, boards, rope, and nails to build shelters," Birch replied. "And grocers to donate stale bread and such for feedin'."

"We figger ten or fifteen thousand men and their families will be coming soon," Jeff added. "That'll take a heap of scroungin'."

Ike whistled softly and Minnie murmured "Ummmm-ummm-ummm."

Then Ike said, "I guess you better give us two days to get the word out," he said. "Don't 'magine we can get things rounded up quicker'n that. Can't do it all, but when we get the church folks onto it, we can help out some of you."

"How many shelters you figger you can get material for?" Jeff asked.

Ike studied the yellow curtains. "Not as many as I wish," he said with regret. "Prob'ly no more'n for a thousand men."

Birch stared, uncertain if he'd heard correctly, then saw Jeff smile and nod. "Ike," Birch said, "that is absolutely amazing. But that'll be an awful lotta work for you and your neighbors. So I think you should know that most of the Bonus Marchers are white."

"Did you ask me for help?" Ike said fiercely. "That's all I need to know. I didn't ask you about nobody's color!" He stood up from the table and headed for his chair in the living room. "Just give us two days, an' we'll be workin' on the grocery situation, too!"

C H A P T E R   2 8

Shiloh Grammar School let out for the summer on Friday. On Saturday morning, Tom and Bobby turned the newly grown frogs loose in the James Fork swimming hole a mile and a half from the farm. And on Sunday Trudy announced in church that she and Lily and Willa Mae were starting up a cafe.

"We're going to compete with the Jenson's catering trucks and feed those rail workers some decent meals for a change." Her voice shook a little as she added, "We really would appreciate your prayers. . . ."

The prayers must have been fervent in Shiloh that week. By the following Friday, Tom and Bobby had been put to work as cook's helpers at the Dreamland Cafe.

News of the Anacostia Flats B.E.F. camp came to Shiloh on the first day that Trudy's vision of feeding good food to hungry men became a reality. Trudy's thoughts turned toward Birch and Jefferson and the Salvation Army chow lines attempting to feed arriving thousands in Washington. But there was no time to read the newspaper account that Brother Williams brought with him when he reported for work before sunup.

Since the first prayer last Sunday, Lily and the babies had moved into Willa Mae's cabin, and Dreamland had been put in service as the cafe. The location was ideal, with progress on the track moving the clientele nearer every day. Bargains had been struck with Grandma Amos for her poultry and with Brother Williams for the use of his grills and the hard labor of butchering enough hogs and chickens to feed the Rock Island army camped in the north field.

At last the mouthwatering aroma of hickory smoke and tangy barbecue sauce filled the early morning air. As the track layers trudged slowly toward their labor, heads pivoted and lean faces displayed such yearning that Trudy felt pity for them.

"They've been living off Caro-line Jenson's swill for nearly two weeks now," Trudy remarked. "Do you think they're ready for us?"

"Tantalizin'," Brother Williams said.

"I'M HONGRY!" Boomer agreed.

"We's cookin' all mornin' long," Lily said. "An' them poor fellas over yonder is smellin' it an' jus' wishin' they could get theyselfs invited to our barbeque."

"They's invited all right," Willa Mae said. "Two bits a plate is all the invitation they needs t' eat here. Two bits for the best barbecue chicken ever!"

The complaining creak of the rocking chair on Jefferson's porch competed with the metallic squeak of the crank turning the spit on the barbecue grill. Grandma Amos, occupying the chair by reason of her age, used it as the headquarters from which she issued orders to the cooks and their helpers.

"Tom," she hollered, "move your brother t' the other side of the grill. We don't want him to broil uneven."

"I can move myself!" Bobby retorted loudly. He stood on his braced leg and, with the help of a pair of hickory limbs cut to length, stumped around to the opposite end of the cookfire. Once there he gestured imperiously for his brother to bring the chair where he sat and resumed his duty, tending the rotisserie.

Suspended above the angry orange glow of the hickory coals, a dozen chickens, lately of Shiloh General Store, delivered up sizzling fat to the fire and fragrant aroma to the Shiloh skies. Grandma Amos cackled as if supplying the broiling birds with their missing voices. "Durn things near eat me out of house and home, but they are settlin' their accounts! It'll come right now."

"It better," Brother Williams grumbled from where he and Boomer were dragging an even larger grill into position beside the first. "Shore a heap of work and cremated chickens if it don't."

"CREAMY CHICKENS!" Boomer repeated so that the sound bounced off Buggy Hill and returned to echo as if the hills were demanding "Chicken . . . chicken . . . chicken."

"Hush your mouth, Brother," Grandma ordered, whacking her cane against the six crates of live chickens awaiting execution. "You and Boomer just get a move on. We gotta have that second grill ready for the pork ribs."

"RIBS!" agreed Boomer. "Ribs . . . ribs . . . ribs," craved the canyons.

The scene outside the Dreamland cabin was an absolute wonder of activity to Tom's eyes. He would have enjoyed stopping to take it all in, but every time he stood in one spot more than five seconds, somebody thought of something else for him to do. Willa Mae ordered him to carry more gallon jugs of molasses into the cabin where she and Lily were mixing sauce. His mother had him knocking together the planks he had hauled from the barn into tables and benches. And if that were not enough, his own little brother shouted for him to bring more chunks of wood for the barbecue.

Preparations had been going on since before sunup, long before the first of the railroad crew rolled out of his tent across the north field. Grandma had insisted that the fire be kindled even before Mr. Frost blew his whistle and shouted the first of the orders to the gandy dancers.

Tom had heard his mother and Willa Mae discussing the merits of having hot food ready at breakfast. But as Willa Mae put it, "Honey, I knows how to stretch porridge with a little oats an' a lotta water. Betcha Caro-line Jenson make her cooks do worse'n that. Let them mens try to eat hog slop at breakfast; they'll be even more ready to ree-bell come lunchtime."

Sneaking away from his duties to peer toward the army of track layers, Tom wet his index finger and held it aloft. The wind was just right, coming from the southeast quarter and spiraling lazily northward, right into the line of sweating, cursing railroad men.

Tom became aware of his mother standing next to him, and he wondered if she had come to scold him for leaving some task undone. "What do your young eyes conclude, Tom?" she said, gesturing to the Jenson catering vehicles and two large kettles standing like tubs of dirty laundry at the back of each. "Underdone beans or overcooked stew?"

Before the first ten workers had taken disgusted looks at their tin platters, the aroma of the roasting chicken must have drifted over to the crew. Heads swiveled and, as Tom watched, shoulders lifted in question and fingers pointed toward Dreamland.

Three men dumped their pans on the ground and started across the field. Trudy and Tom saw Mr. Frost race after them and send them back.

Then the foreman himself came on toward the cabin, walking with a rapid, purposeful stride.

"He's rising to the bait," Trudy observed, "and we're ready to set the hook." Tom was impressed that his mother spoke like a for-real fisherman. She added, "Run and tell Willa Mae to carve one of the chickens now."

Moments later, Mr. Frost wiped his hand across his thin mustache, then removed his hat and rubbed his forehead as he stood looking in wonder at the broiling chickens outside. He started to ask Brother Williams a question, but Brother just smiled and gestured toward Trudy, who was descending grandly down the steps with a plate of succulent barbecue.

Tom watched his mother present the platter to the crew boss and invite him to try it. Frost eagerly picked up a chunk of still-steaming chicken, savored the aroma, chewed with a faraway expression on his face, and absentmindedly licked the dark red sauce from his fingers.

"Two bits a plate," Trudy said, "and tonight the pork ribs will be ready."

"There's forty of my men. The twenty convicts Jenson's brung in is gonna have t' keep eatin' Jenson's pig slop, I reckon. But those of us that ain't in irons? Reckon it'll take an act of God or some disaster t' hold my men back." Frost questioned. "Should I send 'em over in shifts? Have y'all got enough?"

"Let them all come," Trudy replied, extending her hand in a regal gesture over the long rows of empty tables and the simmering, sizzling, bubbling chickens. "We'll manage. There is plenty of barbecue for all."

"BARBECUE FOR ALL!" Boomer agreed.

The tent city that sprang up across the river from Washington, D.C., was not the only Bonus Marcher encampment in the national capital, but it was by far the largest. Birch was amazed at how fast the materials they scrounged became a suburb of twenty thousand veterans and their families. "What did the folks hereabouts do with their trash before they had us to haul it off?" he asked Jefferson. "There's another whole city here, and the old one ain't any smaller. Where'd all this stuff come from?"

Jeff acknowledged that it was a miracle. Laid out according to General Waters's plans and similar in form to the much smaller camp in East St. Louis, Anacostia Flats quickly took on the character of an army base, complete with sanitation facilities and medical care.

"Waters says we're gonna have our own policemen and fire brigades, too," Birch pointed out. "Now, constables I understand, but what's a fire department gonna do? We got no hoses and no way to pump water. If all this tar paper even sees a spark, the whole shootin' match goes up like a Fourth of July firecracker."

But the firemen were not just an idle gesture toward civilization; they quickly became a valuable part of the community. They carried out inspections of the outdoor cooking arrangements, making sure that no embers could escape to torch the dwellings and saw to it that no garbage was allowed to accumulate in dangerous places. They also strictly enforced the rule against smoking inside the shacks.

Birch was not surprised that the discipline soon brought Will Grove into conflict with the camp authorities.

"Mister Grove, this is your second warning for smoking inside a residence. One more violation and you will be expelled," Fessor intoned. He was acting in his capacity as a duly elected magistrate of the temporary township of Anacostia.

"Expelled!" Grove snorted. "You and your kangaroo court can't expel me! What kind of fascist state are you running here? Try to tell me I can't smoke in my own hut that I built with my own two hands!"

"He's at least tellin' a part truth," Birch whispered to Jefferson. "He built it with his own two hands 'cause nobody else'd bunk with him!"

"Mister Grove," Fessor said severely. "Your opinions about this court or its authority are not at issue here. No one is forcing you to remain in this compound or with this organization, for that matter. You are free to go wherever you think you will be better treated. But you are not free to endanger the lives of women and children and the property of others by your own willful carelessness. Is that clear?"

Grove muttered something under his breath. "What was that?" Fessor inquired. "The court could not hear you."

"I said just wait till the revolution comes. All you lackeys bein' bought off with bread and soup'll be cryin' to us for help, just see if you don't. You don't have to kick me out; I ain't about to stay."

Birch nudged Jeff again. "He talks like a sure-enough Commie Red. But he's just like most folks that want t' force their answers down ever'one else's throat; what he really wants is to have it all his own way. He ain't thinkin' of nobody else a'tall. The real question is, how many others are there like him?"

"Well done," applauded Police Chief Glassford, who had watched the proceedings with interest without taking part. Then he added, "You Bonus Marchers are model citizens. I only wish the District was half as responsible and law abiding."

"If the idea was to get a job," Birch argued, "why didn't we just stay in Shiloh and get a job in Hartford?"

"Because," Jeff said, "they's over twenty-five thousand B.E.F. folks needin' t' be fed now. If I gets a job, that's one less in the chow line. And, Aunt Minnie and Uncle Ike been so good to me, I wants to help them out in return. 'Sides," he added with a thoughtful glance at Birch's frowning face, "they ain't no jobs to be had in Shiloh or Hartford or Fort Smith, 'less you wants to go to bootleggin'.'"

"What makes you think there are jobs to be had here?"

"'Cause I seen a gang of men workin' yesterday up on Pennsylvania Avenue, an' I figger to join 'em."

The groundbreaking for the new Justice Department building had been delayed by the depression. Authorization had just been given for it to proceed, so now the laborers digging the trenches for the foundations were working in one-hundred-degree heat.

A plank fence had originally surrounded the construction site. But now most of the pine boards were missing, having become walls in Bonus Marcher shacks or firewood under a pot of Bonus Marcher stew. The few intact pieces of fencing that remained were plastered with pamphlets announcing the Communist-led hunger march to be held June 10 or covered with scrawled epithets comparing Hoover to Emperor Nero, fiddling while Rome burned.

Birch and Jeff looked over the ground that had been cleared. A line of men, all black, sweated in the midmorning sun, wielding picks and shovels. On one side of them was a heap of earth in a long line parallel to the emerging ditch. On the other side was a pitiful row of water bottles for the workers: old army canteens, chipped Mason jars with battered lids, and a dark blue china pitcher missing its handle.

The foreman, his white shirt plastered to his wide pink back, stood under a makeshift awning and shouted directions. "Carl, you better pick more'n one teeny little piece of gravel on a shovel load, or you'll be back mucking out the stalls for the cavalry again."

"Oh, my," Jeff said, whistling softly. "This look a lot like the old days."

"Which old days? Mount Pisgah and old Master Howard?"

"Look more like slave time," Jeff said. "Did I ever tell you about my great-granddaddy? He run away from . . ."

The foreman's shout interrupted Jeff's recital. "All right, Carl! I see you leanin' on that handle. Get on up here and draw your time. You're through."

The man named Carl managed to look disgusted and relieved at the same time. He said nothing, but made an elaborate show of letting the shovel fall from his hands and wiping the sweat from his forehead before climbing out of the half-dug trench. The other laborers made signs that they might secretly envy Carl, but none of them stopped or slowed their pace.

Carl snatched up a tin water jug and brushed past Birch and Jeff. The foreman watching Carl's departure saw Jeff standing there. "Hey, you!" he shouted. "You want a job?"

"I reckon," Jeff replied.

"Get on down there and pick up that shovel. The pay is fifty cents a day."

Birch made up his mind to join Jeff, even for the pitiful sum being offered. Anything was better than sitting around the Anacostia Camp day after day with nothing to do but wait for Congress to act.

"How about me?" he called to the foreman. "I could use fifty cents, and I swing a pick good as anybody."

The boss laughed as he ran a red bandanna over his flushed face and walked over to Birch. "What's the matter with you?" he asked. "You blind or somethin'? This is a nigger crew. Go on, get out of here and let me get back to work." Jeff was already in the ditch, loading full scoops of the dusty earth and flipping it expertly out alongside. The foreman nodded his approval.

"You and that nigger know each other?" the crew chief asked Birch. "You can't work here, but you can do something for him."

"Name it."

"I see he don't got a water bottle or a lunch sack with him. You could go get him some."

Birch looked around at the Washington streets. A cheap diner was only a block off Pennsylvania and a drinking fountain was on the corner just across the intersection.

The foreman saw the direction Birch was looking and answered the question before Birch raised it.

"None of the downtown restaurants serve coloreds," he said. "And that's a whites-only drinking fountain. Closest one for niggers is three blocks away."

Birch returned in twenty minutes, having spent his last nickel on a ham sandwich. He had no remaining money, so he scrounged an empty pop bottle out of an alleyway and filled it with water. Then Birch returned to the construction site and set the items down next to the growing mound of earth that already towered above Jeff's head.

"Much obliged," Jeff said, not pausing in the rhythm of his digging. "See you back at camp tonight."

Birch turned to go, but a half-heard comment from Jeff made him turn back. "What about your great-granddaddy?"

"I just said that he made six dollars a day in his shovelin' days," Jeff said. "That was back in 1863."

CHAPTER 29

Stacks of nickels, dimes, and quarters filled the ring of light that illuminated the kitchen table. Trudy finished counting the final heap of coins, then raised her eyes to the figures gathered expectantly in the shadows. She smiled.

"Our first week. One hundred forty dollars and twenty-five cents."

Grandma Amos smacked her hands together and gave a shriek as if she had discovered a Yankee hiding in her closet. Boomer staggered back and yodeled, thumping his chest with both hands.

Willa Mae and Lily cried in simultaneous joy, "Thank You, Jeeesus!"

Brother Williams breathed a low whistle, scratched his cheek in wonder, and said, "I once won nearly this much in a poker game in Kansas City. Lost it by the end of the night, though."

"We're rich," Bobby muttered.

"Rich," Tom echoed.

"Five hundred sixty-one meals, twenty-five cents each, all in one week," Trudy whispered.

Brother sniffed and stared at the kitty. "There's only forty guys eatin' lunch an' dinner. So how come we to get that extra two bits?"

Willa Mae replied, "That boss man? Mister Frost? He come back for more ribs."

Then the group gathered around the fortune in the Tucker kitchen began to laugh with a wild cackle that rivaled the cries of a whole flock of Guinea hens. Tears ran down the cheeks of Willa Mae. Lily danced around the kitchen with her baby on her hip. Brother Williams clutched his sides and hollered that if he laughed any more he would bust.

Boomer generated war whoops reminiscent of his role in the Penny Auction Rebellion. Tom and Bobby lay on the plank floor and guffawed until they were hoarse. Eventually the uproar died into the whimper of contented and exhausted sighs.

Trudy thought how wonderful it all was, and to complete her happiness, she had gotten a letter from Birch, saying that she could write to him care of Jeff's Aunt Minnie.

The take was divided as agreed. One-third to Grandma Amos, who had provided the poultry and fixin's; one-hird to Brother and Boomer, and one-third to Trudy, Willa Mae, and Lily. Lily had already shown Trudy the place in Dreamland's old rock fireplace where a stone could be removed, revealing a space big enough to hide her cash. The unexpected quarter was presented to Tom and Bobby, who began to plan what they would do with their windfall.

"More'n forty dollars each in one week," Brother Williams exclaimed. "That's better'n six dollar a day. I ain't made six dollars in a single day since 1929."

"ME NEITHER!" Boomer hollered, sticking his hand beneath Brother's nose to collect his wages. "GOT ME A DOLLAR ONCE."

"Boomer? When did you ever make a whole dollar?" Brother asked skeptically.

"NINETEEN AND TWENTY-NINE!" Boomer shouted.

"Dollar seems fair to me," Grandma remarked to Brother Williams. "Boomer done plenty of work out there today."

"NINETEEN AND TWENTY-NINE!" Boomer interjected.

Brother sniffed with resentment as every head in the room pivoted expectantly.

"Highway robbery." Brother separated four quarters from his stack and presented the fortune to Boomer.

Boomer cocked an eye at the coins in his grimy palm, whooped and rushed out of the house.

"Where's he goin'?" Lily asked with alarm. Boomer always had an unsettling effect on Lily.

"Just out. He does that when he's real happy." Brother Williams pocketed his booty. "Since the Penny Auction, Boomer's taken to wanderin' around in the night. Jumps out from behind things and rattles trace chains at unsuspectin' folks."

Lily shuddered and her eyes got wide. "Lawd! I ain't goin' out there alone till someone collars that man."

Brother nodded. "He's likely t' get hisself shot if'n he rattles chains at any of them gandy dancer railroad men. I best go after him." He left the kitchen.

Now Trudy asked the question that had been on everybody's mind at various times as the track-laying crew crowded into the Dreamland chow line. "Have we got enough poultry to keep this up?"

"Lawd!" Grandma Amos clapped her hands and raked her pile of coins into her apron. "I got enough chickens out behind that store to last us into next September."

Lily remarked, "Them gandy dancers eat like they ain' had decent vittles in a year."

Willa Mae nodded vigorously. "They prob'ly ain't if the railroad's been servin' up slop like Caro-line Jenson an' her . . ."

A sharp rap sounded against the front door, and then a second. The women exchanged questioning glances. It was nearly nine-thirty, way past the time of evening when folks were out.

"I'll get it. Somebody probably got hold of Boomer and is bringin' him back." Tom pulled himself upright and went through the parlor to answer the insistent knock. The door swung back to reveal the smiling face of Caro-line Jenson on the other side of the screen. It was a thin smile, and her eyes were devoid of any warmth.

"Good evening, little boy." Her tone of voice was too high, too sweet, the way folks talked when addressing a very small child or a dumb animal.

"Evenin'," Tom replied, but he did not step aside or ask her in.

Was she alone? Her Buick was in the yard. The headlamps were on and the motor idled. There was no one else in sight.

"May I talk to your mommy?" she asked.

He lowered his gaze lest she see his resentment. "I reckon so, ma'am. I'll go see if she is able."

Trudy interjected in a regal tone, "Hello, Missus Jenson."

"Call me Caro-line." The smile wavered, then faded. On the other side of the screen she was a shadow, the apparition of all Tom loathed when he lay down on his bed at night and remembered how they had fallen on hard times.

Trudy was silent a moment. "It is late, Missus Jenson. May I help you with something?"

"Well yes, actually." She glanced expectantly at the knob on the screen door. Trudy did not offer to let her in. Caro-line continued. "I see." The words were clipped.

"It is very late, Missus Jenson." Trudy's chin was high. Tom wished his mother would throw Caro-line off the porch and shout at her and tell her never to come back.

"Yes. I see." Caro-line cleared her throat. "Well, I have come to make a small business proposition."

"I am aware of your sort of business. And your propositions. I am not interested."

The icy hardness, for which the woman was well known, crept back into her voice. "Since you have made it impossible for my cooks to use your well, and since that makes it more difficult for our cafe to provide meals . . ."

"Mister Frost indicated that you had promised to bring your own water."

"We had assumed that we could draw from the well in your field."

"You assumed wrongly."

"At any rate, I have come to make you a fair offer."

"Fair?"

"Jenson Consolidated will pay for the use of your water well."

Silence. Trudy shifted slightly. "Pay?"

"You heard me. We can settle this." The corner of Caro-line's mouth turned up. "I am prepared to offer you one dollar a day for the use of your well. If, that is, you will stop luring away my customers."

"Luring?"

"Field hands and workers are not accustomed to the sort of food served at a Fourth of July picnic while they are on the job."

"You are right."

"We agree then?" Caro-line smiled triumphantly.

"We agree that they are not used to having real food that they can sink their teeth into when someone like you is serving up their daily fare. Pig slop is what you produce in your steaming cauldrons, Missus Jenson. They eat it only because there is nothing else available and they are hungry."

"Well!" Her small eyes widened at the insult. "I came here in good faith. . . ."

"You came here because a few of us are doing the best with what we have to give these fellows a decent meal. And you can't stand the competition."

"Well, I never!"

"Yes. You never! We do agree on that."

"What are you implying?"

Trudy raised her head with a dignity that made Tom fill up with pride.

"I am stating, Missus Jenson, that if you will only feed people something worth eating, perhaps they will continue to frequent your establishment and will give you the honor you so crave. However, since quality is not usually on your menu, and since it is well known that you fire the cooks who put too much meat in the Jenson dishes, you should know that we intend to give you a run for your money. As for our well?" She added, "Go dig your own well, Missus Jenson. This water is a gift, not to be regarded lightly or used to fill your dishpans. You will note that it continues to flow in spite of drought and trouble. My husband and I consider this a miracle from a gracious God, and I will not . . . What is the phrase? Cast pearls before swine, perhaps? I will not pollute our well by turning even a drop of it over to you. Missus Jenson, you have proven that your forte is destroying, not nurturing. At your command the tender plants of our hard labor have been trampled. You are a despoiler of hope and joy. So, Caro-line Jenson, you have great power over the lives of many people, and I say to you on behalf of everyone you have hurt and are hurting . . . if you are thirsty, go find your own well. Ours is not for sale to the likes of you at any price."

Caro-line worked her mouth like a catfish out of water. Trudy quietly closed the door on her astonished face.

There followed a few moments of silence as Caro-line retreated down the steps. Then the stillness was shattered by the clanking of trace chains, a woman's terrified scream, and the voice of Boomer echoing across the valley, "BEWARE!"

There was no band to play Sousa marches, not even a corps of drums to mark the time. But despite these omissions, the spirits of the Bonus Expeditionary Force were as high as the temperatures on the June day. Or higher. "I ain't seen nothin' like this since we come home from France," Jefferson remarked to Birch.

The B.E.F. was preparing to demonstrate just how much pride and polish remained in the survivors of the Great War and to do it all in one parade.

"It's like we have to show who we are," Birch explained. "We earned our bonus by bein' over there, but we got to prove that we are the same men as the ones from 1918. And," he added with satisfaction, looking around at the squared shoulders and outthrust chests, "this may just do it."

Ten thousand Bonus Marchers staged themselves into units up Pennsylvania Avenue from the Capitol to hear their leader, General Walter Waters, address them. "Men," he said after Sergeant Butcher had sounded assembly on his bugle, "we have come to the crux of the matter, to the heart of the issue. We will show the reluctant politicians that we mean business and that we are strong, organized, and determined. March with pride today, and our cause is as good as won."

They cheered him then and in doing so, cheered themselves, too. Individually perhaps, the veterans were victims of the Great Depression, unable to cope with forces they neither caused nor understood. But standing shoulder to shoulder with thousands of their fellows, they felt the stirrings of hope.

"See y' after," Birch said reluctantly to Jeff. The black soldiers who had braved the same dangers in France, the black marchers who had ridden the same boxcars, were now consigned to tramp as a separate unit at the rear of the cavalcade.

Four abreast, to make the procession stretch out longer, the veterans began their display. Between the hot steel rails of the trolley tracks, they marched in step as best they were able. Many walked with a peculiar pigeon-toed gait caused by stepping gingerly on the nails that poked up through the soles of their shoes. Men who had saved their last clean white shirts for this occasion walked beside men in overalls whose only shirt was the faded flannel on their backs. Full uniforms, partial uniforms, and moth-eaten overseas caps were all considered appropriate attire.

At first the crowds shaded by the leafy elms were thin and silent, oppressed by the still heat and uncertain what to make of the array. The onlookers were neither friendly nor hostile, but merely curious. Pennsylvania Avenue was often the scene of spectacles and demonstrations, but this time the character of the marchers seemed different. They were not radicals like the Wobblies nor unswerving loyalists like the American Legion. They were not temperance supporters nor prohibition opponents nor football heroes—all of whom had paraded in Washington within the last six months.

In fact, there was only one difference between those watching the procession and those walking in it: Most of those observing from the sidewalk still had jobs.

Chief Glassford on his motorcycle and another policeman on a motorcycle with a sidecar roared past the line of the parade, clearing the route ahead and signaling the now-swelling crowd to get back out of the street. At a signal from Waters, the Bonus Marchers began to sing.

Birch wished again that he was walking next to Jeff and his strong baritone voice; the other veterans nearby could not carry a tune in a wheelbarrow.

But that fact did not keep them from belting out the words they had practiced in camp, sung to the tune of "Mademoiselle from Armentieres":

We're all the way from Oregon,
Parlez-vous.
We're all the way from Oregon,
Parlez-vous.
We're all the way from Oregon
To get some cash from Washington,
Hinky, dinky parlez-vous.

As the parade neared the White House and swung to pass by it before continuing on to Capitol Hill, the lyrics of the verse changed to: "You're going to see a better day, when Mister Hoover says okay."

Fessor, who was one of the off-key voices singing near Birch, called out to him, "This is real grassroots politics!" He waved at the Executive Mansion. "We are no different from any of the other lobbyists who come to Washington to push for a bill or project, except that they sleep in the Willard Hotel and we sleep in shacks."

"Yeah," Birch observed dryly, "and I hear they get paid just for asking for more money."

The police on duty in front of the White House and lining the avenue saluted smartly as the veterans passed. They may have been saluting the American flags that one in every ten marchers carried, but the show of respect made Birch and all the vets feel good.

The heavy wrought-iron gates to the White House driveway were closed and locked. All the curtains on the side of the Hoover residence that faced the parade route were drawn. There was no sign of activity and no suggestion that anyone inside the president's home had any interest in the Bonus Bill or its throng of unpaid lobbyists. It crossed Birch's mind that at least one person behind the pillars and the heavy brocade draperies did care: Jeff's Uncle Ike. But he doubted that Uncle Ike had much influence with President Herbert Hoover.

No matter. As Fessor had carefully explained, the Bonus Bill was up to Congress, not the president. So Birch and comrades collectively shrugged off the display of presidential indifference and continued their display of pride and solidarity. This was their day to shine.

CHAPTER 30

 It was the best news from Tom's daddy in Washington, D.C. The House of Representatives had passed the bill allowing early payment of the army bonus to the veterans of the Great War. Birch's letter arrived a week after the vote.

Addressed to Trudy first, then to everyone in Shiloh, it read:

> Those gentlemen in the House of Rep. have done right by us vets. It is not those guys we are all concerned about. Some folks in the camp are worried that our cause will not get past the Senators or President Hoover neither. If it does not pass I bet there is going to be a Roosevelt in the White House come November. Jeff and me are full of hope about it, only it sure does take a long time. We picked up your letter at Minnie and Ike Pendle's house. There are good folks every whar we go. So sorry about the cotton. But the Lord is with us. Good we did not sell them hogs back when. We sure wish we was there at Dreamland for your barbecue. . . .

Tom wished he were there, too. But in the meantime, having a rail crew work in your own backyard was an interesting proposition.

This afternoon, from the ridgeline beside the Tucker home, Tom watched the gandy dancers scurrying about their business. It was like a very complicated square dance, he thought, in which the music was supplied by the ring of the heavy sledgehammers on the spikes and the clatter of the shovels in the gravel. The turns were called by Mr. Frost yelling first for timbers and then for rails, do-si-do.

Tom also felt a twinge of guilt. He was, after all, watching the wanton destruction of their north field; he oughtn't be enjoying it. But he told himself that it was too late to change it, and he was comforted that his father would have wanted him to keep an eye on things.

Why, that very lunch hour, in fact, Tom had overheard Mr. Frost outlining the afternoon's tasks, explaining that he would be gone until later on an errand into town. Then he had driven off in the company truck, a 1924 Willys Overland. Tom believed that his father would have approved his finding out all he could about the enemy's plans.

Of course, at the speed with which the rail spur was progressing, the Rock Island men would soon enough be off Tucker land and up into the hills. Completing the trestle and doing something about the big granite boulder that stood in the way of the bridge were about all that remained. Thankfully, with miles to go before the project was complete, connecting the mines to the main line, there would still be weeks of hungry steel-driving men coming to be fed at Dreamland.

The sweltering, lazy afternoon turned even more oppressively hot; heat waves shimmered over the parched earth. Tom's eyes grew heavy, and he thought of finding a shady spot for a quick nap.

When a clash of gears roused Tom from his stupor, he believed at first that Mr. Frost was returning. But the truck that floated into view on the wavering lines of heated air was older, almost decrepit in appearance, like the skeleton of a long dead vehicle reanimated somehow to haunt the country roads. It had no hood, no roof on the cab, no sides on the bed, and its wooden-spoked wheels were more kin to horse-drawn wagons than to automobiles.

The apparition coughed and shuddered as it drew up next to the bothersome boulder. It was followed closely by the Jenson Buick. Garrick and Caro-line Jenson emerged and walked over to stand beside the granite stone. They were joined there by a figure Tom recognized as Dudley Steel, and by the driver of the aged motor vehicle.

The operator was a short, spidery man who, even at a distance, appeared to make every movement in large, elaborate gestures. Tom saw him point at the rock, then indicate Grandpa Sinnickson's water well. His hands fluttered in the air and he made cautioning signals toward the ground as if saying slow down or be careful.

The Jenson motions given in response were equally expressive. Caro-line made an emphatic slashing movement with her hand, and Garrick pointed to the back of the man's rig. Get on with your job, Garrick's gesture said. Tom saw Steel put a beefy hand on the little man's shoulder and shove him toward the truck.

The short worker resigned himself to obedience, going to the rear of the vehicle and prying open a wooden box lined with straw. The Jensons re-entered their auto and drove over to where the railroad crew was working. After a short conference with the substitute ramrod, the track-laying gang abandoned their tools and loaded into the crew vehicles.

Tom was fully awake now. It was unlike the Jensons to give anyone a break or call them away from every ounce of work that could be squeezed from them. He wondered what was up.

After watching the railroad laborers drive a short distance off and then stop again, Tom turned his attention back to the truck driver and Steel, who were now carrying bundles of something toward the boulder.

All at once the strange proceedings were horrifyingly clear. The boulder was to be destroyed by an explosion. The track layers were all a safe distance away, but not so the object of the dynamiter's concern: the artesian well.

Tom began to run down the hill even as the man was uncoiling a loop of cable and backing toward his vehicle. Tom had no thought of danger to himself. His one concern was to reach the explosives and rip out the cord before they did their destructive work.

Long before the boy reached the creek, the demolition expert had spliced his detonating cord to a spool on the back of the truck, and Steel was driving slowly away as the wire played out behind him. Tom's shouts and yells and shrill whistles went unheard above the rattling chatter of the ancient engine, his frantic waves unseen in the churning dust.

When the truck stopped again, it was below the rim of the creek bed and out of Tom's view. It came to him that they were also unable to see him and were probably even now hooking up the cable to the box of the detonator.

From the hill behind him Tom could hear his mother. She must have seen the activity around the boulder and also guessed at its intent. "No, Tom!" she cried. "Get back!"

But anger drove him on—unreasoning rage at this indignity, this violation of their home and land. His father would never have allowed it to happen. And neither would Tom.

Fifty yards from the boulder, the roar of an engine reached him, howling up from behind. Tom had an instant to wonder if the Jensons had returned and were trying to run him down. Then with a jolting bounce, the Rock Island's Overland automobile growled up beside him and Frost's wiry arm seized him around the neck and forced him onto the running board.

Tom's boots plowed two small furrows across the field. Frost steered the car and clung to the struggling boy with grim determination. He aimed the machine straight for the lip of the creek and, when they reached it, plunged over without stopping.

A giant hand seemed to hit Tom in the back, ripping him free from Frost's grasp and sending him sprawling off the running board. Before he could stand up, Frost snagged him again and threw the boy under the Willys, then dived under himself. An instant later, a meteor shower of granite rocks, some fist-sized, rained down around them. The windshield of the Overland was shattered, while the right side, turned more upward toward the sky, was pounded and punctured by the flying shards.

When the debris had settled, leaving behind a cloud of dust and acrid smoke, Tom and Mr. Frost emerged uninjured. The rail foreman shook the boy roughly. "You tryin' to get killed? How could you be so stupid?"

"The well," Tom said. "The well."

Frost set the boy down and climbed out of the ravine. A moment later, Tom joined him. The standpipe of the artesian well was shorn at the base as if severed by a pair of giant clippers. The well had tumbled in on itself, the shaft collapsed, the precious flow choked and cut off.

"They didn't need to do this," Frost muttered. "Didn't have to be done this way."

The Jenson Buick, followed by the explosives truck, motored sedately away from the scene, the plan carried through completely and thoroughly.

The letters that had arrived for Birch at Ike and Minnie Pendle's address had been full of optimism and hope. Don't worry about the cotton crop, they said. The Dreamland Cafe is practically coining money.

Of course, things were not altogether easy in Shiloh. The dust and the bills were still closing in and driving people away. Woody Woods and his family were making plans to head for California. Woody had heard there was work to be had in the fruit orchards or in the oil fields. The weather was mild; there was plenty of water and no shortage of food. It sounded like the Promised Land, flowing with milk and honey.

These notes of good prospects and confident expectations were all received before the telegram. Minnie Pendle actually telephoned the White House, something she had never ever done before, to ask her husband to locate Birch and Jeff.

Ike walked from the Executive Mansion clear to the Anacostia Camp and escorted Jeff and Birch back to his home in Foggy Bottom.

"Oh Lord," Birch said, "I pray it ain't Bobby."

Aunt Minnie waited till Birch and Jeff were inside the parlor of their home before passing the dreaded yellow envelope.

Birch took a deep breath, then ripped it open.

GRANDPA'S WELL DESTROYED, the message said. CAFE IN TROUBLE STOP ALL HERE HEALTHY STOP DETAILS FOLLOW STOP PRAYING FOR SUCCESS OF VOTE.

Jeff took the telegram from Birch's numb fingers. Both men could read the unwritten message, even though Trudy had tried to couch the news in positive terms. The string of optimism had run out; the rainbow of expectations had failed to deliver. Now they were back to relying solely and simply on a favorable outcome of the Bonus Bill. If the bonus didn't come through it was goodbye Shiloh, goodbye farm.

Birch sank into an armchair. "What do you think, Ike? Will the president change his mind since the House has voted in our favor? Will he help us with the Senate vote? Don't he know how important this is, not just to the men, but to our wives and families?"

Looking at his own wife before answering, Ike frowned and then told it straight. "President Hoover likes kids. He once risked his own life to save orphan kids in China. An' over in Europe they calls him the Great Famine Fighter. But he won't say nothin' till after the Senate votes, 'cause maybe they'll do his dirty work for him."

"But if we could just get in to see him . . . talk to him," Birch said. "Could you get us in?"

Ike shook his head. "Your Gen'ral Waters been tryin' for a month," he said. "Wouldn't do no good nohow. Talk I hear in the White House is all how the B.E.F. is a bunch of Commies and bums who was never even in the army."

"But that ain't true!" Birch retorted loudly. "We're all decent folks."

"There you've hit it," Ike said quietly. "Mister Hoover say that if the gov'ment give folks a hand, they won't be decent no more. He says it'll corrupt 'em, and there's an end on it."

Word about the Tucker well traveled fast. Doc Brown drove out to take Tom and Bobby back with him to Hartford to spend the night and perhaps take their minds off the disaster.

The next day Dreamland Cafe had a sign on the gate, CLOSED UNTIL FURTHER NOTICE. Folks in Shiloh figured that meant the place was closed for good and Trudy Tucker was finally beaten. After all, there was no water to cook with or to wash the dishes. The flow of the James Fork had dropped so low that there was barely enough to quench the thirst of the livestock.

There was only one hope left for the Tucker farm, it seemed. If the vote in favor of the early payment of the veteran's bonus did not pass the Senate, it seemed a certainty that the Tuckers and the Canfields would join the thousands of farmers forced out of their homes by foreclosure and drought.

That afternoon, Brother Williams clearly summed up the destruction of the artesian spring. "If they couldn't have the water, they didn't want nobody else to have it."

Grandma Amos sucked on her pipe and exhaled her agreement together with a cloud of smoke. "I always said them Jensons was a couple of mean dawgs in the manger. Cain't eat hay, but they bark an' growl an' bite so's the cattle cain't eat, neither." Then abruptly she said to Lily, "Walk me home, honey. I'm plumb wore out by all this." So Lily and Grandma Amos departed while Brother and Willa Mae picked up the thread of conversation.

"Mebbe we could haul us some water," Brother Williams offered, but he sounded doubtful that they could get enough to keep the Dreamland Cafe in business.

Trudy, standing on the porch of Dreamland, heard the discussion going on behind her, but it seemed like a faint echo beneath the roaring of her thoughts.

So cruel and senseless was the destruction of the artesian well by Garrick and Caro-line that the real issue was finally clear. This was not about competition in business, not about making money or owning property. The issue boiled down quite simply to power. Garrick and Caro-line were bent on the destruction of anyone who would defy or challenge their control.

The demolition of Grandpa Sinnickson's well, the shattering of the blessing that had kept hope alive for the Tucker farm and Dreamland, was the easiest route for the Jensons to regain the authority they craved. Strand by strand, the twisted tapestry of Caro-line's crippled soul became a clear picture in Trudy's mind. As for Garrick? The word *pathetic* played over and over in her mind.

Trudy gazed up toward the shorn standpipe and the rubble strewn across the field. As she did, a fresh wave of anger swept through her and tightened her grip on the porch rails. What made Trudy even more furious than losing the well was the fact that Caro-line Jenson's need for control had almost cost Tom's life.

And what had been Caro-line's response when the boy climbed out of the smoke and debris with Mr. Frost? Caro-line had smiled coolly and arched her eyebrows in surprise when Frost had called her reckless, mean-spirited, and stupid.

"The law gives us every right to do what we have done. And if this Tucker boy was fool enough to try and stop us? Well! I would say he is lucky you came along, isn't he, Mister Frost? At any rate, our rights are clearly spelled out in the contract, signed by a Tucker ten years ago. Jenson Consolidated and the Rock Island Railroad may clear the right-of-way as we see fit without interference from or further compensation for the occupants."

"It ain't the Rock Island that blow'd up this well, Missus Jenson," Frost had roared. "Y'all didn't have to do this. Y'all got a mean streak wide as this here right-of-way. This didn't need t' be done at all."

Caro-line had suggested that what was done was none of his business. He was, she had reminded him, just a hireling. Garrick Jenson had then stepped forward and assured Frost that his disrespect would be reported and that he would lose his job as sure as anything.

Throwing his hat on the ground, Mr. Frost shouted that he would have the true story told to everyone in Fort Smith and that the men in charge of the Rock Island would listen to him. Then Frost charged off in his battered vehicle. He had not returned since.

Beginning just after dawn this morning, track layers had stopped by the Tucker house to offer condolences about the well and express their hope that Dreamland Cafe would find the water needed to open again. There was a rumor among the men that Frost had been fired by the railroad company.

A good man, Trudy thought, *in a hard place.*

Brother Williams interrupted her reverie. "It's waterin' your stock concerns me now, Trudy. I'm tryin' t' think what Birch would do if'n he was here," he said, spitting a stream of tobacco juice at a troop of red ants marching across a stone. "I'd say y'all got mebbe another week 'fore the Jim Fork dries up altogether. Your house well is just about played out, an' the-nearest waterin' hole's gonna be a mile an' a half. That's three mile you'll have t' drive them mules an' your milk cow, not to mention the hogs an' chickens an' jus' keepin' your own face washed."

Trudy swallowed hard. "Such a long walk. They shall be thirsty again before I get them back home."

"That's a fact."

"Esmerelda finally went dry last week." Trudy forced herself to consider the reality of her situation. "She is no use to us."

"I was shore you'd see that." Brother coughed nervously. "I know what store you put in that leetle Jersey cow of yourn. But I cain't see keepin' her around the place when she ain't givin' milk an' all you're doin' is shovin' precious feed down her gullet."

"Point well taken." Trudy kept her eyes fixed on the shattered well. "Do you know anyone who might wish to buy a very fine milk cow?"

"That I do. I figger I can get five dollars for her anyhow, even though she's dry."

Five dollars! Trudy's senses cried out against it. Birch had paid forty dollars for her, and she had proven to be the best milk cow in Shiloh, producing an abundance of cream and good milk.

"Well, then?" Trudy replied. "Take the cow away before Doc Brown brings the boys home, if you would, Brother. It will be bad enough for me to hear her bawl all the way down the road."

Brother tipped his hat and brushed past her. Moving up the slope in long strides, he crossed the creek and headed across the hollow toward the Tucker property.

Five minutes later, as Brother disappeared into her barn, Trudy felt emotion choke her. She turned away and found Willa Mae sitting quietly behind her. How long had the old woman been watching?

Trudy sat down on the long bench. "Well, Willa Mae, it seems that someone has interfered with our dreams for Dreamland."

Willa Mae nodded slowly. "So it seem."

"Have they finished us, Willa Mae?"

"Ain't nothin' ever finished till we see Jesus, honey. Jensons ain't gonna have the last word when that day comes. Unh-uh!" She shook her head ponderously and closed her eyes as if judgment was clear before her.

"I can't wait that long."

"Only believe. Jesus a-gonna make a way for you, baby."

"I wish I could believe. But I'm afraid I'm fresh out of hope today."

"What it's gonna take t' fill you up again, gal?"

Trudy shrugged and smiled wryly. She raised her eyes to the roof of the porch in thought. "Water. Plenty of water. I think I would never doubt again if we just had enough water for us to reopen Dreamland."

Willa Mae slapped her knee and laughed easily. "Water? You don' ask overmuch of a great God, does you, honey? Sound t' me like what the Hebrew chilluns asked for in the wilderness."

"All the miracle I need right now . . ." Trudy breathed wearily. "Some little sign that God was paying attention to us down here."

Willa Mae closed her eyes and frowned as if she was listening hard for some heavenly message. She raised her arms above her head, lifting up an invisible, yet heavy, load. Then in a loud, quavering voice the old woman cried out, "Jeeeesus! Oh, Lawd! You hear what little Trudy sayin', Jesus? Uh-huh? She say she gonna trust You if'n all You does is bring us some water here. Enough water t' open up Dreamland again. I reckon that's 'bout as easy for You t' fix as . . ."

Willa Mae's prayer was interrupted by the rumble of a truck engine up by the Tucker farmhouse. Trudy turned to see a large tanker truck with the words ROCK ISLAND RAILROAD emblazoned on the side.

The brakes squealed as the truck stopped in front of the barn. Esmerelda bawled as Brother Williams led the cow out of the double doors. Brother paused for a moment to wave broadly across the hollow toward Trudy and Willa Mae, then Mr. Frost stepped out of the truck.

Brother Williams dropped Esmerelda's lead rope, and the cow retreated back toward her stall. Brother cupped his hands around his mouth to shout, "MISTER FROST HAS BRUNG . . . ENOUGH . . . AND . . ."

Trudy and Willa Mae stood expectantly on the step and strained to hear his words.

"SAY AGAIN?" Trudy called back.

Mr. Frost, impatient to have his purpose understood, jogged down the slope and across the withered pasture to the edge of the streambed. Standing on the far side of the muddy bank, he completed the shouted message. "I BRUNG Y'ALL WATER, MISSUS TUCKER! ROCK IS-LAND SENT A TANK TRUCK FULL OF WATER TO Y'ALL!"

Brother gave a holler. "IT'S MORE'N ENOUGH T' OPEN DREAM-LAND AN' TAKE CARE OF THE STOCK! I'LL PUT THE COW BACK."

CHAPTER 31

The faint breeze that funneled up the river toward Washington had the tang of salt in it and a slightly cooler feel, a pleasant change from the scorching heat that had lingered in the capital for days. It was a particular relief to the veterans and their families who covered the lawns around the Capitol building. Spread out on the turf, sidewalks, and driveways, ten thousand members of the B.E.F. were maintaining a twenty-four-hour prayer vigil as the Senate deliberated the fate of the bonus payment.

The long summer day had finally paled to light blue twilight and then deepened into night, and still no word came from the debate. The House of Representatives had passed the Bonus Bill by a margin of forty-three votes. The spontaneous celebration that had greeted that news was quickly tempered by the knowledge that the fate of the payment now shifted to the upper chamber, whose members had not been receptive to the veterans' pleas.

"Somethin's up." Jeff pointed at the policemen patrolling the Capitol grounds. Up until now, the police had made no attempt to remove the vets. They kept an eye on things, but otherwise did not interfere. "There's twice as many as they was before."

This was accurate. Everywhere Birch looked, where there had been only one man in dark blue hat and trousers and long-sleeved white shirt, now there was a pair. In a ring around the grass and the paved areas, a cordon of officers studied the veterans. Their expressions were unreadable, but none were smiling. More than one twirled a nightstick by its lanyard.

Birch looked up at the lighted dome of the Capitol building. Nothing had changed there. The brilliantly illuminated upper half gave way to the shadowed colonnade and the marble steps, but there was no clue in the impassive facade. Except for the increased presence of the patrolmen, there was no hint of any news. The conversation of the men resting on the grass increased in volume. The hum of speculation spread as more and more veterans noticed the police.

"Who will now offer another prayer?" a B.E.F. chaplain inquired.

Birch nudged Jeff, who was reclining on one elbow nearby. "Your turn," he said. "Nobody from Arkansas has prayed yet, and you're elected."

Jeff rose to his feet. Slowly, in ripples that spread out from the big man's presence, concentric rings of silence expanded over the crowd. Facing the pillars of the Capitol, but with his eyes closed and his head bowed, Jeff spoke. "Lawd," he said, "in that buildin' are the men You saw fit to have govern this land. They can do a heap of good for us and our families if they want to. Give 'em wisdom, Lawd. Let 'em see our cause and its justice. Give 'em hearts to understand that we ain't askin' for a handout; we're just tryin' to keep our homes and feed our families. Bless this land, Lawd. May all our thoughts turn to You and seek Your will, so that this terrible depression will be lifted. Hear our prayer, so's we can all have honorable work that will pay enough to provide for our loved ones. . . ."

The amplified voice of a police captain boomed, drowning Jeff's voice. "You men are ordered to disperse! The Senate has voted to turn down your request, so there's no reason for you to be here. Go on now, clear off." Birch saw the police officers hitch up their gun belts.

A low growl erupted from the crowd. Birch suddenly understood why the guards had been doubled! The senators expected that their decision would cause a violent outbreak right on their doorstep.

"Those dirty, rotten so-an'-so's," a voice near Birch complained. "Did their worst and then snuck out like rats. Sent their goons to bring us the news. Didn't even have the guts to face us themselves."

"Attention, men." The voice of General Waters was recognizable over the police megaphone, although garbled and with a metallic ring. "Men, we've lost this battle, but we have not lost the war. We won't cry like children, and we won't fuss, but we won't leave Washington either! This job isn't finished, and I for one aim to stay and see it through. We're not radicals and we won't gain anything by losing control now. We need to keep on being good soldiers. Back to your camps, and tomorrow we'll talk strategy for what comes next."

Not everyone was so easily convinced. The voice near to Birch continued grousing in the darkness, "Tomorrow! Huh! Been here a month now. Who we gonna find to even listen when all the fat cats leave town?"

Unnoticed in the hubbub that followed the announcement was Jefferson. He still stood upright in the center of the group, and he was still praying. When the amplified speaking stopped, his petition could still be heard, and once again the murmur stilled and the crowd listened. "Lawd," he was saying, "give us wisdom to trust in You, too. You done seen us through terrible times over there in France an' brought us through some mighty deep waters since. Don't let us fail this test of faith right when we need it most. We done fought for our country once. Help us to live for it now. In the mighty name of Jesus. Amen."

A scattering of amens responded. Then Jeff, in a tone that was clear and deep, began to sing,

> My country, 'tis of thee,
> Sweet land of liberty,
> Of thee I sing. . . .

Softly at first and then with gathering volume as the men stood and brushed off their clothes, the B.E.F. assembled around the Capitol became a ten-thousand-voice choir. The words bounced against the windows in the dome, vibrated around the rotunda, made the policemen remove their hats and stand at attention, and chased the departing senators in their taxis and limousines. The sweet sound overflowed the hill and washed the streets and pathways of Washington with praise and prayers.

As the last lingering echoes died away, Jeff resolutely set off walking away from the Congress. The rest of the Bonus Expeditionary Force followed his lead.

The gift of water and the loan of the tank truck by the Rock Island Railroad had put Dreamland back in business. It had also resurrected something in Trudy's heart that she thought had died with Joey.

She found the ability to hope again.

The long dry spell of her soul had finally broken.

The water truck parked beside Dreamland was perhaps, in the scope of great events, only a small miracle. But it was enough; it was Trudy's miracle.

The washtub of cutlery on Dreamland's rough plank table was almost empty. Trudy was just finishing the cleanup after another successful day; they had taken in twenty dollars. Even though the track crew had moved away into the hills, they still sent a truck down twice daily to pick up meals for forty eager appetites. The total share acquired by the Tucker-Canfield partnership was now over two hundred dollars. Trudy had written Birch to tell him to come home; they were going to make it without the bonus money, even without the cotton crop. She had prayed, with all of Shiloh, that the Bonus Bill would pass the Senate, but her life no longer hinged on the outcome of tonight's proceedings in the Senate.

Another battle had been fought and won here in Dreamland. Willa Mae and Lily had volunteered to lead the parade home to baths and bedtimes while Trudy cleaned up the aftermath of the day's conquest and prepared for tomorrow's. Grandma Amos and the others had long since departed for home.

Carried on the breeze that swirled through the open windows and front door of Dreamland, the chirping of the young frogs and the bellows of the large ones were like music. Bobby gonna walk, they had promised, and it had been so. Tonight in Trudy's ears there was even another triumphant note to their croaking. Jensons gonna flop, they laughed. Give it up, give it up.

Moonrise interrupted the bullfrog chorus. The ascent of the half-full silver disk made the croaking cease for a time before it started up again, louder and more vigorous than before. Trudy was always amazed that creatures living in ponds sometimes had more recognition of the wonder of creation than humans too busy to notice.

She washed and dried a butcher knife, tucking it into a slot on the solid oak block cutting surface, then stacked a set of tin pie pans. Grandma Amos had contributed them from the store; they worked fine as dinner plates. Just a few things to dry and put away, and then Trudy could go home also.

Busy with the toweling off and the reordering of the shelves, Trudy was unaware of anything unusual until a minute or two had passed.

Then it came to her: The frog serenade had abruptly stopped once more. Since the moon was already hanging overhead, this second halt had to be due to some intruder in frog territory. A prowling raccoon perhaps, intent on a frog-leg supper.

Hefting the sack of brown sugar, Trudy concluded that there was enough for two days of sauce before it needed refilling. She jotted herself a reminder note to ask Grandma for more. Then she turned from the counter toward the open doorway and found herself face-to-face with Dudley Steel.

The big man filled the entry, his fleshy hands gripping the frame on either side. His lumpy face peered in with undisguised delight at the alarm that registered in Trudy's eyes.

"Evenin'," he said, drawling the word for an impossibly long time. "Didn't startle ya, did I?"

Trudy squared her shoulders and vowed to show no fear. It was, she reasoned, like confronting any large, dumb, but definitely dangerous animal. Moxie was called for, chutzpah, her Bubbe would have said. "Not at all, Mister Steel, but you are too late for supper. We are closed till tomorrow."

"Didn't come for supper," he said, shaking his head ponderously from side to side.

"Where's your sheet and hood then?" Trudy challenged.

"Oh, this ain't official business," said the leader of the local night riders. "Just a friendly visit. Thought you might need a friend, seein' as how your man's been gone so long."

Trudy wished she had not stayed behind alone. If she screamed now, would anyone at home hear? And would she be causing them to race into danger if they came in answer to her yell? Her heart pounding in her throat, Trudy backed up against the worktable. She prayed Steel would not notice that her hand behind her back was anxiously trying to locate the handle of the butcher knife.

"Wasn't thoughtful of him to go off like that," Steel continued. "Leave you here with young'uns to care for, a farm to tend, and nothin' but old crones, dimwits, and niggers for comp'ny. And all for nothin'. I see you ain't heard the news from Washington then. I heard it on the radio a while ago. Senate voted it down. Your husband an' his colored boy ain't gonna get a cent of their charity payment."

The news barely registered in Trudy's mind. *Senate? Voted the Bonus Bill down? Birch will be coming home then. Oh, God! What will he find when he gets here?* Her fingers closed around the wooden handle, drew the knife slowly from the holder, held it against the small of her back. "I really must ask you to leave," she said, overcoming the catch in her throat. "I still have things to do to get ready for tomorrow's business."

"Now that's just what I come to see ya about," Steel said, grinning widely as if she were a pet that just performed a trick on cue. "Friendly advice, don'tcha see?"

Breathing a sigh of relief that was not altogether silent, Trudy braced herself up again. "Speak up then," she demanded in a firmer voice, "and let me get back to my work."

"All right then, here it is, just as plain as the nose on your purty face. It ain't right for white folks to lose money and jobs and business to niggers and them as coddles 'em. Do you take my meanin'?"

"Instantly!" Trudy snorted. "Caro-line Jenson sent you here to try and scare us into giving up our meal service. Well, it won't work."

Steel tried to put a look of aggrieved innocence on his jowled features. "This ain't got nothin' to do with . . ."

But now Trudy's ire was fully roused. "You may go back and tell Miss High-and-Mighty Jenson that neither her pouting nor her husband's conniving nor her pet bully's threats will move us. We are going to continue . . ."

"Listen!" Steel roared, advancing on her suddenly.

Trudy retreated abruptly, colliding with the edge of the counter. She fumbled the knife onto the floor, where it landed with a clatter.

Steel ignored it. "I come here to give you some neighborly counsel. I ain't the only one that thinks y'all ain't doin' right. Now stop it! You hear me? There ain't but one warnin' given!" With that he turned around and went out into the night.

Trudy scrambled after the blade, kicked it under the table, grabbed a fry pan instead, and stood trembling in the corner of the cabin farthest from the door. Even the frogs were holding their breath.

It was not until she heard the croaking choir resume that she felt safe to cross the creek bed and climb the hill to home. But she took the fry pan with her just the same.

CHAPTER 32

Even though it was only six o'clock in the morning, the air was oppressively hot and still. It was as if a giant oven had been left burning all night long, and trapped in the mouth of its wide-open door was Washington, D.C. Birch wondered if Jeff was any cooler over at his Aunt Minnie's home where he had spent the night.

Birch lay brooding on the hard ground. The straw with which his bed sack was stuffed had long since lost any springiness, but no more had been offered. Now that Congress had adjourned, the Senate having voted down the Bonus Bill and then fled, the atmosphere in the capital had changed. No longer did the veterans hear expressions of sympathy and support from the citizens. The marchers, their cause a failure, had gone back to being bums, vagrants, and tramps. Despite the declaration by General Waters that the B.E.F. would stay until the goal was achieved, no one really believed it. Congress would not reconvene until after Labor Day in the fall. The only reasons for staying on were simple: There was food here. Besides, where else was there to go?

Yesterday Birch had scanned the front page of the *Washington Evening News*. Two different front-page stories were hostile to the B.E.F. One talked about the unsanitary conditions in the encampment and claimed that a typhus epidemic had broken out. Birch knew that this was false, but nothing was more inflammatory to citizens than to suggest that twenty thousand disease carriers were in their midst.

The other article inquired editorially about how long official Washington would tolerate "Communists and red agitators" in its midst. It even suggested that the police should use force in removing "undesirables" from the streets. According to the paper, 90 percent of the Bonus Marchers were radical socialists bent on destroying American democracy; 90 percent were frauds who had never been in the military, much less overseas in the war.

Along Pennsylvania Avenue there were now two distinct fraternities. The north sidewalk was where the office workers and government employees hurried past, their eyes on the pavement. Across the cobblestones, separated by fifty feet and an enormous tear in the fabric of society, sat a double row of despondent men, their tattered cloth caps bent almost to their sagging shoulders, staring at nothing. One side of the street was purposeful, going to work or going home to family and friends; the other remained static and motionless.

The merchants who had been sending over truckloads of two-day-old bread and culled vegetables had complied with President Hoover's request not to support the marchers. Consequently, the thin, watery soup that was served in the camp grew even thinner—a bowl a day of tasteless broth with a single brown cabbage leaf floating in it.

Five or six hundred men had taken up Hoover's offer of free rail transportation home and left Washington for somewhere cooler and friendlier. Their departure left a higher proportion of men with families; the women and children were not offered train tickets and could not leave unless they walked or hitchhiked.

And no one was walking far in this heat. Sweat formed on Birch's forehead and ran down both sides of his face as he stared up at the canvas shelter. There was no point in staying in the tent. He had been awake since five and thinking about what to do. Remaining in Washington was not accomplishing anything for his folks at home in Shiloh. With the well destroyed and the Bonus March a failure, it was better to leave at once. Today Birch would find Jefferson and see if they were in agreement.

Monkey and Fessor were already outside the tent, squatting on their haunches on the shady side of the canvas. Monkey rolled a cigarette, and they spoke in quiet voices of what each would do now that the march had failed.

"I'll be moving on," Fessor was saying as Birch emerged from the shelter. "I came along to watch hope and optimism in action. If I want to observe despair, I can find it in plenty of places cooler than here. Besides, the powers that be are becoming decidedly unfriendly. They want us to represent someone else's problem for a while, and I sense that it cannot happen too soon to suit the locals."

"I'm not gonna run out," Monkey replied. "Not yet, anyways. We said we'd see it through, like in France. If we leave now, everything we said is just so much balloon juice. Here's the buzz: Waters is workin' on the military boys. We're like gate crashers, see, but the army still counts for something in this town. Once some gen'rals and admirals start speakin' up for us, things'll change."

"How about you, Birch?" Fessor asked. "Will you maintain the vigil?"

Birch shook his head. "Reckon not," he said. "I got family to think on. I can't do them no good here if I got no job. Best be pushing on somewhere else."

Sergeant Butcher, no longer the picture of military precision, hurried up to the group. The sergeant was missing both bugle and hat, and his khaki pants were wrinkled and stained. His boots were scuffed, and he wore nothing over a dirty white undershirt. Nevertheless, he still served as messenger for General Waters.

"Attention, men," he announced. "The general has an assignment for you."

"Give it a rest, will you Butcher?" Monkey moaned, "before I anoints your face with my lunchhook. This ain't the army, and no play-acting will make it be. If you want to ask for our help, do it nicelike."

Butcher raised his chin and narrowed his eyes as if he would give a belligerent reply, then sighed heavily and started over. "General Waters has been informed that some children over in the old armory have taken sick. Measles, I think. Anyways, it's too many for their folks to carry, so the general is looking for some stretcher bearers to help haul the kids to the hospital at Marshall Place. Will you guys do it?"

Birch nodded. "Count me in." Fessor and Monkey agreed to go as well.

The downtown buildings occupied by members of the B.E.F. and their families were no cooler than the Anacostia camp and more crowded. And while no breeze had been stirring across the river, between Third and Fourth Streets a breeze was not even possible. It was no wonder that the children had taken sick, Birch thought, all crammed in together with no space to play. Once again he was glad that he had not brought his family with him to Washington. At least they still had a roof over their heads back in Shiloh. For a while.

Thoughts of Trudy and the kids, Shiloh, and summer evenings sitting on the porch with a glass of lemonade made him terribly homesick. Doubts about when he would ever see Shiloh again kept him silent on the long walk across the bridge and over to Third Street.

The heat and the doubts took their toll on his companions as well. Even Monkey's normal ramblings had tapered off to a few bitter comments. "Look at them smug crushers," he said, pointing to a pair of policemen standing under a store window awning and keeping an eye on the three Bonus Marchers. "Just waitin' for us to let our dogs run on their precious grass. Got the Blue Liz wagon around the corner, no doubt."

But enforcing the rules against walking on the grass did not seem to be a high priority for the police, Birch noticed. Every corner along Third seemed to have a pair of patrolmen on duty, and all of them were facing toward the B.E.F. enclave between Pennsylvania and Missouri Avenues.

The dilapidated brick structure known as the Old Armory had been slated for destruction to make way for new federal offices. The B.E.F. had been told that the demolition would not take place before October at the earliest. Two hundred men and their families were living in the gutted interior.

When Birch, Monkey, and Fessor arrived at the building, they found it completely surrounded by blue-coated policemen. A file of Bonus Marchers exited the front of the building, between a double row of police. "And just where do you think you're going?" a lean sergeant with a black mustache asked Birch.

Birch explained about coming to help out with sick children. "We're taking them to the dispensary at Marshall Place."

"Oh, no you don't, boys," the sergeant corrected. "This whole building is being evacuated. We heard that some of you might be coming to try to hold this place. But the word is, no one else allowed in, only out."

At the top of the stairs appeared a thin, anxious-looking man. In his arms he carried a baby wrapped in a tattered blanket. A blonde-haired child walked wide-eyed by his side, one of her fists tucked into the man's coat pocket, the other was twisted into her mouth. Behind the veteran came his wife, another towheaded girl by each hand, and a meager sack of belongings wrapped in a bedsheet tied around her neck.

The look of the parents and the children put Birch in mind of something, something he had seen before. He could not exactly place where or when. He studied the officer in consternation.

"Look," he said at last, gesturing toward the frightened family being herded along the sidewalk. "Why don't you go in with me? You'll see that I'm telling the truth. Then we can get the kids and leave. These folks are scared, and they don't know where they'll go now, but they aren't making any trouble. Can't we at least make it a little easier on them?"

The sergeant looked at the pathetic scene and chewed his mustache in thought. One of the children dropped a doll made from a twisted rag with a painted-on smiling face. The little girl yanked her hand free from her mother's grip and started back after the toy. The woman made a grab for the child, and the bundle slung across her shoulders unraveled. A baby bottle fell to the pavement and smashed, and a tiny heap of clothing fluttered to the ground.

"All right," the officer growled. "Get 'em and come right out. No tricks now, see?"

Birch and the others ducked inside the building, dodging out of the way of the other evicted Bonus Marchers. Everyone they met looked stunned, disbelieving, and lost.

It was at that moment that Birch remembered where he had seen the expressions on the faces of the dispossessed: They had the same shell-shocked looks as refugees coming out of an artillery barrage.

"I know," Fessor muttered in rely to Birch's observation. "I recognize it also."

There were six children in the MacNamara family down with measles, and a woman alone trying to cope with them. "Where's your husband, ma'am?" Birch said. "We came to help you get your little ones to the doctor."

"I don't know where he is." Mrs. MacNamara groaned softly, rocking her youngest child in her arms. The other five, faces covered in red blotches, lay under a single threadbare blanket on a scrap of canvas over a concrete floor. Above their heads was a sign lettered

on the wall in red paint: CAUTION. NO SMOKING. HIGH EXPLO-
SIVES.

"He said he was going to get a doctor," the woman squeaked. "But
that was last night, and he didn't come back. He didn't come back!"
Her rhythmic rocking was so mechanical, Birch realized, that it would
have continued even if she had not been holding a child.

"Don't fret, ma'am," Birch soothed. "He must've told somebody,
'cause here we are to help. He'll find you again, you'll see."

"Mason hasn't eaten in three days," the woman said. "There wasn't
as much as before, and we divided it all amongst the little ones. Wasn't
that right? But what if he's sick and can't make it back? What'll I do?"

"Shhh," Birch warned. "Don't want to frighten the children. Come
on now, help us round up your things."

The shrill of the police whistle sounded from the front of the
building. It was immediately answered by similar shrieks from all
sides of the square. "I'll go see what's what," Monkey volunteered.
He was back an instant later, a worried frown distorting his normally
cheerful features.

"We got trouble," he reported. "The Weasels. The Reds. 'Bout thirty
or forty of them. They are headed right for the front door like they mean
to come in. Our old buddy Grove is leading them."

Birch hurried to the window to watch. Waving banners and signs
that read "Worker's Ex-Servicemen's League," "Humanity before
Property," and "Fight or Starve," the group of men moving along
Pennsylvania Avenue huddled together as they walked. The Bonus
Marchers exiting the Armory flowed around them on either side like a
stream parting around an island. Grove urged the departing veterans
to join with his force, but no one did.

Grove led the Communists up to the door of the building and found
himself face-to-face with the same police sergeant who had confronted
Birch. Birch could not hear the exchange, but he could tell from the
angry gestures and the menacing waves of the signs and banners that
it was heated.

There was no way for Birch to see from what direction the first brick
was thrown. A chunk of masonry no bigger than a man's fist arced over
the heads of the crowd. It struck the sergeant in the cheek; he staggered
back. In the next second, the mob with Grove rushed forward, intent
on seizing the opportunity to crash the police line and enter the armory.

Suddenly bottles and bricks and tin cans weighted with stones were flying into the brawl.

The opposing ranks of men dissolved into a dozen individual battles. Here a single patrolman was swarmed by four weasels, disappearing from Birch's view under their feet; there two officers with drawn nightsticks converged on a man and clubbed him to the ground.

Monkey peered around Birch at the melee. "Clubs and alley apples," he said, shaking his head. "But it won't stay that way. Come on, Birch. We gotta get these kids clear before the shooting starts."

It was already too late. A young policeman, hat knocked off by a sign that read, "We Demand Peace and Prosperity for All," was hit squarely in the forehead by a block of cobblestone. He was flung backward by the impact, windmilling both arms to grab a pillar beside the armory entrance.

When the officer reappeared in Birch's view, blood streaming down his face, he had his service weapon in his hands. From above, Birch yelled, "Don't shoot!" at the same instant that the identical words came from the police sergeant. The roar of the pistol followed before the warning was even completely uttered.

Grove clutched his chest, shrieked once, and fell face first onto the stone steps. The patrolman continued to fire. In the crowd, another Communist protester slumped to the sidewalk, yelling for help.

The front rank of the attackers panicked, turned around, and barreled into their comrades just behind, causing a pileup of struggling men. Those closest to the gun pummeled those behind in an attempt to get clear of the bullets. Two more shots were fired; two more men cried out.

Then three policemen jumped the gunman from behind and wrestled him down, pulling the pistol from his fist. The remaining Communist marchers retreated at full speed down the street, trampling veterans and their families who could not get out of the way in time. Birch, riveted by the sight, saw the family with three blonde girls split apart and knocked down in the rush, then the mob swept them out of sight around the corner. Policemen sprinted after the Weasels, bringing them down with flying tackles.

But no welcome silence succeeded the end of the shooting and the terrific screams. The air was immediately filled with the noise of sirens coming from every direction around Washington. It was as if the little square of buildings occupied by the B.E.F. and their families was drawing all the attention and all the horror of a town under siege.

Fessor tugged at Birch's sleeve. "Come on," he urged. "Monkey's right. Now is the time to leave, while we still can."

There was a back stairwell that exited the National Guard structure into the alleyway between it and some derelict shops. The ill children were too weak, too sick, and too frightened even to protest when the three men flung one over each shoulder and shoved their way down the crowded steps.

Trembling and fretting, the mother gathered the family's few possessions and followed the men down,

Birch and the others came to a heavy steel door that led outside. At first it would not budge. Then Birch set his two charges aside for a moment, put his shoulder against the door, and burst it open, sending it crashing into the brick wall. The force spilled Birch into the alley, right at the feet of a pair of policemen with upraised nightsticks. "Hold it! Wait, you mugs!"

Monkey protested. "Can't you see we're haulin' sick kids here?" His sharp warning stopped the patrolmen in midswing, but not before Birch had received two painful whacks on his legs. "Show us a quick route out of this hullabaloo," Monkey continued. "Where's a meat wagon? These kids need a doc, see?"

"What's the matter with 'em?"

"Measles," Monkey snapped. "It don't take a genius to see that we're tellin' the truth. Now are you gonna help or not?"

"There's an ambulance just pulled up at the end of the alley," one of the policemen offered. "Let's move them right now, then you three clear off."

"Glad to oblige," Fessor said earnestly. "Can't happen too soon."

When Birch, Fessor, and Monkey reached Pennsylvania Avenue and loaded the MacNamara children into the ambulance, Mrs. Mac-Namara fell on each of their necks. She hugged them, calling them saints and angels. Then the doors closed and the emergency vehicle sped away, leaving the three friends wondering if they were going to be arrested or just escorted out of the area.

But neither possibility occurred. Instead, the Washington policemen were escorted down the street by overwhelming numbers of vets. The members of the Bonus Expeditionary Force who had been lodged in the other downtown buildings had poured into the streets when the noise of the riot outside the armory was heard. Now behind improvised barricades made of overturned fruit carts, trash cans, and commandeered vehicles, eleven hundred veterans defied the police to evict them. Birch knew that everyone would have left peaceably if the Communist group had not arrived, if the rock had not been thrown, if the shots had not been fired, if only . . . if only . . .

The standoff lasted for three-quarters of an hour. Behind the impromptu ramparts, the Bonus Army strengthened its barricade, gathered bricks and bottles for defense, and tended to the wounded. Two men, including Grove, were dead; two more were seriously injured. These four had been hauled away in the ambulances along with a half-dozen bleeding policemen. The rest of the hurts were minor: cuts and bruises and broken scalps.

Then everyone sought what little shade could be found. It was a hundred and five degrees and climbing. A gallon jug of warm, stale water made the rounds of the makeshift fort. Birch took a swig, holding it in his mouth and reflecting that this was much like being back in France in the summer of '18.

No one knew what would happen next. The B.E.F., having seen the nightsticks in action, were afraid to come out. A few who surrendered were arrested, beaten, and roughly shoved into paddy wagons; this of course ensured that very few more would give themselves up.

For their part, the Washington officers were disturbed by the killings and had withdrawn their lines to a block away. Unwilling to see the riot resume if it could be avoided, the police were concentrated on containment, not attack. The sergeant repeated his demand for the veterans to evacuate the premises. When this order was again refused, he passed word to his superiors and then stood back to wait for instructions.

All this indecision gave the situation an air of unreality for Birch. The tension was extreme, and yet it was as if two sides in a football game had drawn up teams and then could not agree on how the game was to be played. Adding to the strange feel was the fact that the government offices, the shops, and the stores along Pennsylvania Avenue had discharged thousands of curious onlookers onto the sidewalks. This audience lined both sides of the broad street in ranks six to eight people deep.

The strain was finally broken by the shout of Monkey, stationed halfway up a lamppost as a lookout. "They're coming! The army is coming!"

This announcement was greeted with cheers by the veterans. Everyone knew that the military was sympathetic to the demands of the B.E.F. Fellow warriors would never let civilians push other soldiers around.

Swinging up on the base of the lamppost, Birch could see over the heads of the crowd and down the street toward the Capitol. Cavalry troopers were the vanguard of the approaching force, their dark horses prancing on the avenue, horseshoes sparking against the cobblestones. Fessor, perched on the other side of the pole, also watched the arrival of the mounted troops. "It really will be all right now," he said. "They have sent an honor guard to escort us out of this mess before anyone else gets hurt."

Someone in the B.E.F. started in on a chorus of "Over There," and the rest of the Bonus Marchers enthusiastically joined in. When they shouted the line, "Yanks were coming," the spectators cheered. Along the line of the barricade, four American flags enthusiastically waved.

This was turning out to be a better demonstration of support than the authorized parade. A rescue, a deliverance, an official recognition of the existence of the veterans and the justice of their cause. What a triumph!

"What else can you see?" Birch hollered up to Monkey.

"There's infantry swinging along behind the horse soldiers," Monkey reported after he had wiped the sweat from his face. "Maybe a coupla hundred. Wait a minute. Here's somethin' dippy. Fessor, you recollect them little tin buckets on tracks? Tanks, they call 'em? Well, there's a half-dozen of them comin' down the road."

"That doesn't sound right," Fessor said. "The cleats on those treads will tear up the streets."

Monkey took another look, shading his eyes with one hand while clinging to the pole with the other. "I'm tellin' the gospel truth," he confirmed. "Trash cans with little gun barrels pokin' out, right behind the dogfaces."

The cavalry troop had reached the position of the police line about a hundred yards from the Bonus fort. The column of twos divided and wheeled to form one rank facing north and the other south. The mounted troopers spanned an entire city block, and the police withdrew from the scene.

The spectators gave another cheer. "See," Fessor said to Birch, "they have cleared a space for us to march out of here. Both sides will retain their dignity; we have evacuated as demanded, but the army has gotten us the recognition we deserve." His words were a confident statement, but his tone sounded to Birch as if Fessor was asking for reassurance for himself.

A square-jawed major with a big nose trotted his mount down the center aisle between the two files of horses. Sunlight gleamed from his polished helmet and reflected off the pair of ivory-handled revolvers he wore. "Drawwww sabers!" he ordered.

Two hundred swords rattled free of their scabbards. It was an unpleasantly ominous sound. The light from the blades flashed painfully into the eyes of the spectators. "What's happenin'? Is that salute for us? Never seen this b'fore. We s'posed to salute back?"

"Charge!"

At the shouted command from the major, the riders of the Third Cavalry spurred their big bay horses toward the packed ranks of onlookers on the sidewalks. There was an instant of stunned disbelief, and then a collective scream went up from the crowd as the sabers arced downward. Those in the front row were slammed aside by the bodies of the horses or, unable to get out of the way, were trampled underfoot.

The next range of bystanders received punishing blows with the flats of the saber blades. Hoisting himself higher on the lamppost and staring in utter disbelief, Birch saw a trooper bat a man down, then hit another onlooker in the skull with a backhanded blow. "Clear out! Clear out!" the riders ordered witnesses. "Leave the area at once!"

The civilian bystanders did their best to comply. Fifteen people at once tried to stuff themselves back inside openings designed to admit one at a time. Those nearest the entrances were crushed against the wood and brass of the doorways. Those behind clawed and kicked to get away from the riders.

Birch saw a throng of twenty men and women crammed into the red-painted entry of a Great Atlantic and Pacific Tea Company shop. A panicked man scrambled over the backs and shoulders of those between him and safety. As he reached the top of a heap of bodies, a cavalryman plunging into the press hit him in the back with a saber. The man's forward motion was changed into airborne flight, and he smashed headfirst into the plateglass window.

During the first thirty seconds of the skirmish, the Bonus Marchers stood frozen with horror and bewilderment. So far no troopers had stormed their barricade; the furious assault had been aimed at clearing the sidewalks. Then the cavalry major yelled, "Seize those colors!" and the focus of the onslaught changed.

Mounted men swept toward the improvised fortifications. Three of the American flags were snatched back out of the way, but a furious wrestling match developed for possession of the last. A cavalryman reached over the barrier and grabbed the flagpole. He spurred his horse forward to yank the trophy free, but a swarm of Bonus Marchers clutched the staff. Birch jumped down from his perch to lend a hand.

The banner flapped in front of the horse's face, and the halyard tangled in its bridle. "Now," Birch shouted, giving the signal to pull together. The bay reared suddenly and the rider, unseated, tumbled backward to the pavement. A mass of troopers charged the struggle, sabers spinning overhead. Blades whistled past Birch's ear as he leapt aside.

Another sword was already arcing downward toward Fessor's head when Birch ran up the improvised barrier of hot-dog cart and park bench and tackled the trooper midswing. Birch and the young cavalryman crashed to the pavement together, and Birch had to duck under the belly of another prancing mount to get back to the safety of the enclosure.

The tramp of marching feet sounded as the first rank of the infantry approached. "Fixxxxx bayonets!" was the shouted command.

Another metallic clatter followed the order, and to the screams and yells on Pennsylvania Avenue was added the noise of two hundred bayonet blades clicking into place.

"What're we gonna do? We can't fight guns and pig stickers! This ain't right! They're s'posed to be on our side!" The wails of the Bonus Army intensified as six tiny but wicked-looking tanks rumbled forward, the snouts of their machine guns waving back and forth as if seeking prey.

When the cavalry troop responded to a bugle call and pivoted smartly to trot back up the avenue, the veterans had a moment to believe that someone in authority had finally come to his senses. That was before Birch and Fessor saw that the advancing foot soldiers were donning gas masks.

"We fought for this country and this flag. You want a battle? Then give us something to fight with!" Fessor yelled at the approaching men of the Thirty-Fourth Infantry. "We aren't even armed! Shame! Shame!"

The row of men behind the barricade took up the chant. "Shame! Shame! Shame!" Then the families of the Bonus Marchers who had not escaped and were still huddled inside the occupied buildings added their voices. The clerks and storekeepers and shoppers, peering cautiously around curtains and from behind shutters, echoed the chorus. "Shame! Shame!" Thousands of voices flung the rebuke at warriors too young to have known the carnage of Belleau Wood or the horrors of the Argonne or the sacrifices of the participants.

"Readyyyyy grenades!" The forward ranks of the infantry unhooked the blue canisters of tear-gas grenades from their belts.

"What are we gonna do?" Monkey asked.

"What can we do?" Fessor replied as the next command rang out and the fuses were struck. The cylinders sputtered and smoldered with heavy blue-white smoke. "Run!"

Twenty-five cans pouring out acrid, sickly sweet vapor arched over the stockade to land amid the angry veterans on Pennsylvania Avenue. Those who had experienced the mustard gas attacks of the Great War needed no reminder of how futile it was to resist the fumes without a mask. They fled down the street away from the billows of biting, stinging fog.

Those still inside the buildings were not so fortunate. The second wave of troops lit their grenades and tossed them through the windows of what only hours earlier had been the homes of Bonus Marchers and their families. The choking mist filled the halls and stairwells. More women and children were trampled underfoot as they struggled to get air.

Birch had a child under each arm. The hand of the children's father, a veteran blinded by the gas, was clamped firmly on his shoulder. Birch's eyes were streaming tears, and his voice was a barely recognizable rasp. "Look what they're doing now," he croaked as he and Fessor hurried down Third back toward the river. The soldiers were entering the evacuated buildings and tossing the meager belongings of the marchers out of the shattered windows. Moments later the first smear of a different, darker smoke puffed upward as the army set fire to the abandoned structures. Soon the whole block was ablaze.

Then, like cattle being rounded up for market, the remnants of a thousand B.E.F. veterans were herded by saber and gas grenade out of Washington and across the Eleventh Street Bridge to Anacostia Flats.

CHAPTER 33

By eight o'clock in the evening, the blistering temperature finally fell to a breathable level. The Anacostia Flats encampment was bursting its seams as Bonus Marchers—men, women, and children—were evicted from all the abandoned buildings and derelict warehouses in which they had been sheltered.

They straggled across the Eleventh Street Bridge, an army of despair and defeat. Underneath them, curious onlookers in motor yachts plied the river. Birch saw the spectators point to men with bandaged eyes and rag-wrapped head wounds. The wealthy boaters, dressed in white nautical clothing and standing on the decks of their sparkling clean pleasure ships, discussed the pathetic households trundling all their worldly goods in wheelbarrows or pulling a heap of kids, pots, pans, and clothing in a child's wagon.

The night sky over the capital was still anything but peaceful. All afternoon and into the twilight, columns of smoke had continued to rise from more and more burning buildings. "Burn down the house to kill the fleas," Monkey remarked wryly. "That's their plan."

The shriek of sirens from police cars, fire trucks, and ambulances continued to crisscross the Washington horizon. Birch wondered what the protracted fuss was about; by sundown, the retreat of the veterans had slowed to a trickle.

There was no discussion in the camp about what would happen next. Everyone was grim to the point of sullen silence, still chewing on the hard-to-swallow fact that American soldiers had attacked American veterans. A few men removed the remnants of their uniforms and, despite the summer swelter, built bonfires of the clothing.

When Sergeant Butcher reported that everything was being worked out because General Waters was meeting with MacArthur's aide, Major Eisenhower, he was roughly told to shut up. No one believed any longer that the B.E.F. could accomplish its goal or that anyone in official Washington cared to extend any help.

When there was enough energy present among the refugees for conversation at all, it was about whether to leave Washington or to remain in what was now only one more among hundreds of Hoovervilles. There was resistance to the notion of moving on. This camp was better than most; despite the makeshift construction, the orderly rows of dwellings were a source of pride. The carefully tended bits of garden that sprouted almost within the shadow of Washington's obelisk were a statement of self-respect and the intense desire to be self-sufficient again. The scores of star-spangled banners, now hanging limply from their staffs, still proclaimed that these destitute thousands were patriotic Americans, eager to rejoin the mainstream of American prosperity and culture. Their insistence on naming the dirt lanes and tending the vegetable plots broadcast to the world how much the veterans wanted to belong again to the bigger, brighter world.

"Since they have evicted us from the government buildings and away from downtown," Fessor said, "there is no reason for any further action. After all, it's not like we're any threat to the government. Now we're just one more settlement of the poor and homeless. We're back to this morning's discussion: to leave or to stay. But we won't be forced out."

As if to give the lie to Fessor's words, the noise of the sirens was supplemented by a growing rumble of engines from the direction of the bridge. The vets on the side of the camp nearest the river craned their necks and peered into the darkness to make out the source of the noise.

"There's still a flock of boats on the water," Monkey observed. "Rich folks' toys." His sharp eyes determined that the yachts were cruising in lazy circles, not steaming purposefully up or down stream. "Show's over!" he yelled. "You seen us chased across the bridge. Now clear off and leave us be!"

"That ain't it," Birch remarked. "That sound is comin' from the far bank."

A figure materialized out of the darkness. It was Jefferson. "Man, I'm glad I found you so easy," he said to Birch. "Heard what happened today. I was 'feard for you."

"Didn't have it as bad as some," Birch said, indicating those with arms in splints and gauze compresses over bayonet wounds.

"You got your things gathered up?"

Birch and Fessor heard the urgency in Jeff's question, but did not know the cause. "Not tonight," Birch protested. "We're a hound dog who come off second best to a big ol' bear, and we're just layin' here lickin' our wounds. Tomorrow'll be soon enough to head out."

Jeff shook his head with intensity, the movement exaggerated in the flaring of a campfire as yet another army blouse was added to the pyre. The light glimmered on something hanging around Jeff's neck. Birch saw that he was wearing his Legion of Honor medal. "It ain't over," Jeff said. "Soldiers is massin' 'cross the river. Ain't you heard the growlin'? They got them mechanical guns lined up all along the edge facing the camp here."

Jeff had meant his words just for Birch, Fessor, and Monkey, but they carried beyond the three men to a larger circle. "Tanks? Comin' here? They mean t' kill us all?"

The word spread throughout the encampment, and so did the argument about what to do. "I say we fight 'em. With what? Gonna throw rocks? Man, I was leavin' here anyway. But if we hang together . . . We'll all die together, you mean. No thank you, I'm gone!" All the while the controversy raged, men watched the bridge for the first sign of approaching trouble.

"There's something comin'!" Monkey warned, pointing toward the dark road. A flash of white appeared against the blackness, then resolved itself into a prancing white horse. Behind the uniformed man on horseback, marching troops filled the width of the roadway. When the soldiers arrived in Anacostia, they deployed into five columns of two files each that spread out like the fingers of a hand poised to grasp and squeeze the last B.E.F. outpost.

The weary vets, too tired to form lines, clustered around the American flags as rallying points against the inevitable. Opposing them, the figure on the white horse was planted at the foot of the river crossing as if posing for a heroic statue. "Do you know who that is?" Fessor asked bitterly. "That's General Douglas High-and-Mighty MacArthur himself!"

If there was any remaining doubt about the army's intentions, it was dispelled when the order to fix bayonets was heard again. This was followed by the shout, "Liiiiiight torches!" and suddenly the settlement was ringed by a half-circle of flames.

There was no dramatic command to charge, just a relentless sweep forward by the attacking troops. The Bonus Marchers sullenly backed away from the prodding rank of bayonet tips, eyeballing the soldiers and muttering, "Yellow! Yellow! Yellow!"

Then MacArthur's men reached the front row of shanties. The first to be set to the torch was a canvas and scrap-wood dwelling. The crackling blaze illuminated the words, "God Bless America" over the doorway, before the whole was swallowed in a sheet of orange flames.

All around the fringe of the village, cardboard shacks took off like rockets, and still there was no counterattack. It was not until an old man futilely pleaded with the soldiers not to trample his vegetable patch that something inside the hearts of vets blew wide open. Fessor ran toward the row of tomato plants being ground underfoot. He threw his lanky body onto the backs of two soldiers who were beating the gardener. Birch saw Fessor's rush carry the men to the ground, then saw him clubbed from behind and go down. There was a rush of veterans to help, and for a moment the soldiers were thrown back.

Into the battle cantered a cavalry troop, the force of their arrival brushing men aside and scattering them. The same major who had led the daytime charge against the barricade was again swinging his saber at the head of the horsemen. Birch and Monkey ran over to the garden plot just in time to save Fessor from being trampled.

Monkey leapt in front of the major's mount, causing it to shy and giving Birch a chance to drag Fessor to safety. The officer, angered by the resistance, aimed the big bay horse at Monkey and rode him down.

A dozen struggles broke out at once. Bonus Marchers menaced by bayonets responded by swinging hunks of pipe and two-by-fours. A freckle-faced private, not over eighteen years of age, thrust his torch inside the shack that belonged to a man and his son even as they were trying to throw their belongings out through a hole in the back. "Wait!" the man pleaded with the infantryman. "Gimme a minute! Thad! Where are you?"

A second soldier, wearing corporal's stripes, prodded the father in the back with his bayonet. "Get moving, you lousy bum," he menaced. Then to a torchbearer he added, "Go on. Light her up."

The frantic man waved his hands in front of the figure with the torch to keep him away from the tar paper. "Let me get my stuff and find my boy."

"I said now, you worthless piece of trash!" The move to again poke the blade into the father's back was halted by Jefferson's grip on the rifle stock.

"Leave the man get his things and his family," Jeff said firmly.

The corporal tried to wrestle his weapon free and found he could not make Jeff release his grasp. "Let go the rifle, nigger," he insisted. "You we'll hang."

"Dad, dad!" Birch heard a voice call from the other side of a row of blazing hovels. "I can't find the puppy!"

"Come here, son!"

The soldier struggling with Jeff called, "Gimme a hand!" There was a brief glimpse of a small, brown-haired dog as it streaked between the rifleman's feet and back into the shack. Right behind the frightened puppy ran a small boy.

Another bayonet point appeared in Jeff's face. "Let go, nigger," the soldier growled. Reluctantly, Jeff gave up his grip on the rifle.

"I'll get that brat," the corporal vowed, plunging into the shack. Birch jumped through the doorway right behind him.

"I just need to get my dog," the boy begged, coaxing the terrified puppy out from under a cot.

"I'll get him out," sneered the corporal, thrusting the bayonet under the bedding.

Grabbing the end of the rifle barrel, the child shouted, "No, don't hurt my dog!"

"Clear out, ya little creep!" retorted the corporal as he yanked the weapon back sharply. The movement brought a cry of pain from the boy as the blade sliced open his palm.

Birch ran into the corporal's back, knocking him headlong into the side of the shanty. "That's enough!" he yelled.

Seizing the dog in his bloody fingers, the child bolted out to find his father. The corporal whirled around, bayonet at the ready. "I'll stick you good," he said, lunging at Birch.

Birch sidestepped the vicious thrust, then closed with the noncom and delivered a fierce roundhouse blow that rocked the corporal back on his heels. The rifle flew from his hands to land with the point of the blade quivering in the dirt.

Both men jumped to retrieve the weapon. Birch got his hands on the stock first and was winning the struggle till the rifle butt hit him in the back of the head. Birch collapsed in the wreckage of the now-flaming shack and the world went black around him.

Jeff burst into the shack too late to prevent Birch from being clobbered in the skull, but his timely arrival saved Birch from being stabbed in the back.

With a fearsome growl to match the bear hug that he applied, Jeff picked up the infantryman, ripped the rifle from his hands, and flung it away. He then tossed the private face first onto the corporal, who was still dazed from Birch's blow and struggling to rise. The two soldiers collided chin to chin with a sharp crack.

The flames were licking the boards and tar paper and finding the taste very much to their liking. Jeff considered dragging all three unconscious men out by their heels, but decided there was not time. He grabbed Birch around the middle with one arm and flung him over his shoulder. Then like a circus acrobat and strong man combined, he grasped a soldier under each arm and carried all to safety just as the roof of the shanty erupted in blaze.

The mask-wearing attack forces tossed tear gas grenades into the clusters of vets defending the flags, driving the marchers away retching. The men, futilely trying to cover their mouths with bandannas, were clubbed or prodded away from the banners. The situation already looked hopeless. Jeff unceremoniously dropped the soldiers in the space between two burning tents, then, still toting Birch, he set out for the woods southeast of the encampment.

In the lurid glow from the bonfire of what had been homes only minutes before, the escaping Bonus Marchers cast long shadows on the Anacostia plain. All around Jeff there were families in flight, and the night was filled with the sounds of terror and tragedy. A mother screamed frantically, unable to locate her two missing children. Scores were burned, some terribly, trying to dash back inside a burning shack to rescue some precious bit of their life—a memento of what they longed to return to, but did not know how.

No one had much but their lives and the clothes on their backs; there had not been time. Now there were no wagons, no wheelbarrows.

Nothing remained but what could be carried by hand, and much more of this was abandoned in the stumbling flight across the field away from the flames, the tear gas, and the bayonets.

As if determined to stamp out any remaining evidence that the Bonus March had ever existed, the soldiers were systematically torching every shack, every hovel, every tent. And to ensure that the rout of the dangerous radicals was complete, the cavalry once again made an appearance, sweeping in from both flanks and riding down men, women, and children. Those who had escaped being burned or stabbed or battered with rifle butts still ran the risk of being trampled or sabered before they reached the safety of the woods.

Once inside the sheltering belt of trees, Jeff found a culvert that offered some protection and laid his friend down in the grass. Birch was still unconscious, his breath coming in ragged gasps. The lump on the back of his head was swelling to double goose-egg size, and a trickle of blood ran down his hair and over his shirt collar.

A man stumbled toward them in the dark. Jeff jumped up again, ready to resume his defense. He lashed out in the dark with a wild swing that the newcomer barely eluded by ducking under. "Hold it!" the slight figure implored, "It's me, Monkey!" Jeff explained about Birch. "Is he gonna be all right?" Monkey asked, then babbled on out of his shock and dismay. "I seen a kid bayoneted through the leg and I seen a baby killed by the tear gas and God only knows what else. Everyone's too afraid to ask for help. I mean, who you gonna ask? The police? The army? The rich folks on their yachts? They stomped on us like kickin' an anthill to make 'em run, then poured the gasoline and lit her up."

"Have you seen Fessor?" Jeff finally managed to interrupt.

"No, not since the brawl at the gardens. I don't know what happened to him. But I got this trying to get away." Monkey turned his face toward the glow from the burning camp and showed Jeff the dark gash of a saber cut on his cheek.

Then Monkey began to curse, a low, rhythmic, mechanical swearing that Jeff finally halted by laying a hand on Monkey's arm. "That ain't doin' no good," he said softly.

Monkey hung his head, and tears appeared in his eyes and voice. "The same one! I shoulda let him get kilt!"

"Who? What you talkin' 'bout?"

"It's him. I seen the major commanding the cavalry, ridin' us down," he said between shudders. "It's the same feller I got the medal for helpin' save in France! Savin' his *life*! Major George Patton hisself."

The orange glow coming into Tom and Bobby's window cast the shadow of the window frame onto their bedroom wall. It made, Tom thought drowsily, the outlines of a dozen tiny black crosses. The wavy glass in the panes made the images flicker and dance as if they were seen through a candle flame.

Flames! When the implication of that notion cracked the cocoon of sleep, Tom tossed the covers onto the floor and ran to the sill. Below the ridge, across the creek, in front of Dreamland and the Rock Island water truck was a burning cross, disturbing the night with an unholy light and fouling the air with evil-smelling smoke.

Nor was that all; Dreamland itself was on fire. Arms of flame reached out the windows and caressed the eaves at both ends of the cabin. "Fire!" Tom yelled. "Mama, wake up! Dreamland's on fire!"

"What? What?" Bobby questioned. "How'd it get on fire?"

"Just stay here," Tom ordered.

"What else can I do?" replied Bobby miserably.

But Tom had not heard his brother's lament; he was already racing out the door and down the hill.

"Tom, be careful!" Trudy shouted, hurrying off the porch in her white nightgown. "Oh, how could they do this?" she moaned when she saw the fiery cross.

The fire grew another limb that stretched out the front door. It came to the rocking chair, curled possessively up the bentwood frame, and clutched the wicker seat. The draft of hot air from the cabin entry made the rocker swing until one side weakened and the chair collapsed in a puddle of flames.

"The water truck!" Trudy shouted. "It's still half full! Turn the valve!" She grabbed the nozzle of the hose and pointed it at a window that was now a grinning mouth of combustion. The fire laughed at her, blasting into her face and driving her back choking. "Tom!" she pleaded again.

"There's no water!" he cried. "It's empty!" The ground underfoot was muddy. The men who had set the fire had also drained the only means to fight it.

"The cash box!" Trudy screamed. "All the money is still inside!" She held her arm over her face as if she was about to run into the inferno.

"No!" Tom shouted, grabbing her around the waist. "No, Mama, it's too late!" Tom dragged her back from the solid sheet of flame that now reached from the planks of the porch to the overhang above. "Come on," he said, leading her away. "We've got to get further back."

The blaze shooting out through a window touched the water truck. The paint bubbled, then flaked, then peeled away, as the knife edge of flame flayed the skin from the truck. The smell of hot oil was added to the wood smoke, the reek of kerosene, and the stench of burning feathers.

Tom and Trudy stood across the creek bed and watched as flames shot up through the roof of the cabin. While the wooden cross burned down and flickered out, the gas tank of the truck exploded with a roar, showering the field with chunks of metal and knocking a hole in the wall of Jeff and Lily's home.

It was the final wound. Dreamland collapsed, groaning, into a bonfire of unconnected timbers.

CHAPTER 34

Only the charred husk of Dreamland remained in the shadow of the scorched cross.

Brother Williams, Doc Brown, and Sheriff Potts prowled the smoking wreckage for nearly an hour. Faces set and angry, the trio returned to the Tucker farmhouse where Lily, Willa Mae, Trudy, and the children waited in the kitchen. Trudy, her face still smudged with soot, did not raise her eyes when the men came to the back door. They scraped the mud and ash from their boots and then entered the house with hardly a word of greeting.

"I made coffee." Willa Mae took up the coffeepot and poured three steaming cups of brew.

The men thanked her kindly, sipped it gingerly, and only after the first swallow did Sheriff Potts speak.

"Trudy, there is little doubt in anyone's mind who done this thing. But it'll help if y'all seen anything. Anybody."

"Just the fire," Trudy remarked in a hoarse voice as she studied the black grime beneath her nails. It would be difficult even to wash her hands now that the Rock Island water tank was destroyed. Only murky dregs remained in the domestic well beside the house.

Willa Mae interjected. "Y'all knows that white trash Kluxer Dudley Steel come by t'other night. Threatened Trudy whilst she cleaned up down at Dreamland."

"I know that." Sheriff Potts exhaled loudly. "I telephoned the constable out Meribah way. Constable says Dudley Steel was at an all-night prayer meetin' with him."

Brother slapped his hat angrily against his leg. "So the Meribah constable is in on it too!"

Potts nodded. "Along with a few other prominent Meribah citizens. The prayer meetin' was supposedly held at the Jensons' church. Preacher backed 'em up on their story."

Doc Brown put a comforting hand on Trudy's shoulder and said, "That's the way the game is played, Brother. You know that."

"Reckon I do," Brother said bitterly. He turned away to look out the window and across the little valley at the smoldering wreckage. "Looks like a war," he muttered.

Trudy did not reply, even though Brother's observation was correct. The north field destroyed, divided by a railroad berm and shiny new tracks. The birch trees mown down and timbers used in the construction of the trestle across the dry stream. The well blown up. And now the burned shell of Dreamland.

Doc Brown gave Trudy's shoulder a squeeze. "You have done noble battle here, my dear." He bowed slightly to Willa Mae and Lily. "You ladies have fought a very powerful foe. Your defiance caused Garrick and Caro-line to resort to desperate and violent acts that condemn them before all decent folks in western Arkansas.

"Thank you, Doc," Trudy replied. "But noble sentiment is not enough. The Jenson machine has beaten us. There is nothing that can be done to rectify the injustice. We are strong enough to face the truth. We have lost our homes." Her gaze locked on Lily, Trudy continued. "All the cash we made burned up with Dreamland. The Bonus March has failed. Now we must begin to think of where we will go after Birch and Jefferson get home."

There was heavy silence in the room as the truth of her statement was considered and accepted by all. They were, indeed, beaten.

"There's more," Brother Williams said just when it occurred to everyone that things could not get much worse.

"Oh Lawd, Brother!" Willa Mae threw up her hands. "What now?"

Brother pulled out a crumpled newspaper with headlines giving account of the riot in Washington, D.C.

SEVERAL KILLED, COUNTLESS INJURIES
AS ARMY FIGHTS REDS IN D.C. STREETS!

Images of Birch or Jefferson among the dead and wounded crowded every other concern from Trudy's thoughts. And then Brother dipped into his pocket and retrieved the yellow envelope of a Western Union telegram.

Lily and Willa Mae clung to one another. Willa Mae prayed for mercy.

"I couldn't see dumpin' the en-tire load on y'all all at once." Brother shrugged as if his hesitancy to present the message embarrassed him. "So I waited."

Hands trembling, Trudy took the envelope and tore it open. She scanned the contents as Willa Mae and Lily read over her shoulder.

"Is it Birch or Jeff?" Willa Mae asked.

Trudy replied by reading the wire:

BOTH OK STOP GOING WEST 4 JOB STOP WILL SEND CASH HOME LATER 4 TRAIN STOP U ALL COME 2 PROMISED LAND STOP LOVE BIRCH JEFF.

The pawnshop owner tossed the small object up and down in his hand several times, then squinted one eye and frowned at Jefferson. "How do I know it is the genuine article?" he asked.

"Look at the writin' on it," Jeff said. "And them is real little rubies 'round the edge. You think anybody gonna go to the trouble to fake that?"

The shopkeeper, a short balding man whose suspenders arched over the reach of his belly to arrive at his waistband, pursed his lips in thought.

"You do not got any tear gas grenades, do ya? I could most certainly pay somethin' for them, even was they empty. Historical interest, ya see. U.S. Army attackin' U.S. vets . . . who is gonna believe it?"

Jeff sighed with exasperation. "I tol' you already; this is all I got. No pig stickers, no billy clubs, just this."

"All right," the man said. "Two dollars."

"What?" Jeff snorted. "Talk about historic. That medal is a real French Legion of Honor outta the Great War. It was give to me in Paris, France, by Marshall Petain hisself."

"Where do ya find that it says all that?" the pawnbroker asked in a superior tone. "It do not say nothin' here 'cept honner et patrie!"

"Honor and patriotism," Jeff translated.

"Youse cannot spend either one of them things," the man said, wiping his soft, plump hand over a dome speckled with dark brown spots. "Okay, a fiver, but do not tell nobody I am such a soft touch."

Jeff thought about Birch outside, leaning against the wall with his head bandaged.

"Mister," Jeff said, "I fought in the Great War and won that medal. I come to Washington to ask for a helpin' hand and got tear gas and bayonets. Now my friend is hurt, an 'we gotta get all the way to California. So you gotta do better than a fiver."

The shopkeeper studied the ivory and emerald medallion that hung from the red silk rosette. "Okay," he said grudgingly. "Youse talked me inta it . . . sawbuck—ten dollars. But do not press me further."

"I'll take it," Jeff said.

PART III

There Is a River

God is our refuge and strength,
a very present help in trouble.
Therefore will not we fear, though the earth be
    removed,
and though the mountains be carried into the
midst of the sea. . . .
Selah.

There is a river, the streams whereof shall
make glad the city of God,
The holy place of the tabernacle of the most High.
God is in the midst of her; she shall not be moved:
God shall help her, and that right early. . . .

The Lord of hosts is with us;
the God of Jacob is our refuge.
Selah.

—Psalm 46

CHAPTER 35

August 21, 1932. Tom watched his mother circle the date on the calendar that hung on the wall beside the cookstove.

"Do you know we began the cotton harvest on this very day last year," Trudy said in a dreamy voice. "Soon it will be autumn again, Tom. Such a lovely time of year, don't you think?"

Tom did not reply. Last year seemed like someone else's memory. To compare last year with this was like comparing heaven and hell; the chasm between was too wide to cross over. The heaven of last Shiloh autumn was too distant for Tom to return to, too painful to contemplate. They had come too far ever to go back again.

It had been three weeks since Dreamland had burned and the telegram had come from Birch and Jefferson. After that, no word had come. The hoped-for letter containing cash enough to see them through had not arrived. There were, as yet, no train tickets to carry them all to the Promised Land.

"Surely they must be in California by now," Tom's mother said to him over a meager breakfast consisting of one slice of corn bread and the last of a jar of peach preserves that had been put up the previous year. There had been no more milk or butter since Esmerelda had gone dry. These days, Tom daydreamed about tall glasses of cold milk. And the canned goods in the root cellar that had sustained them through the year were finally running out. In normal times this would have been the season when canning began again. But without Grandpa's well water, Trudy's garden had shriveled to a mass of weeds and stunted survivors.

Like every other garden and field in western Arkansas, Tom thought.

The morning was oppressively hot as Tom set about his chores. A slight breath of cool air wafted up from the domestic well as he lowered the bucket into the shaft. The container came up only three-quarters filled with a dank-smelling, murky liquid. With this Tom watered the mules. The process was repeated several more times until all the stock was watered.

Each day, as the level in the well dropped, the quality of the water had worsened. The livestock seemed grateful to have it, however. They slurped it down with long, satisfied gulps morning and night. Tom and his mother knew, however, that what remained at the bottom of the house well would soon be gone.

Of the hogs, only Miss Lucy remained. The entire litter had gone to Dreamland, Willa Mae was fond of saying. As for Trudy's two dozen Rhode Island Reds, the hens still provided fresh eggs. The flock was the only lifeline for Trudy and the boys. There were eggs enough each day to provide nourishment for the noon meal. For this reason, Trudy instructed that the last of the cracked corn was to be saved for chicken feed.

Henny, the cherished pet, nested on the screened back porch away from the rest of the flock. She still laid an egg every other day while the other chickens had tapered off to one egg every three days. Henny was fed crusts of bread and allowed to pick the bugs that were consuming Trudy's withered garden. Trudy gave Henny water from the fifty-gallon barrel that held the household supply. Three times a week Trudy and Tom and Bobby drove the wagon three miles into the hills where water was still to be found. They filled the barrel one precious bucketful at a time. Then they stopped in the shade downstream and bathed in a pool between two fallen logs in the creek bed.

Now that the last of the hay was gone, Esmerelda and the mules were put out together to graze on the pathetic pasture covered with short Bermuda grass. Slim pickings. Flanks sunk in deeper every day, while ribs and hip bones protruded and long faces grew lean.

They still needed the mules, Tom told himself, to haul the water. But why did his mother keep the milk cow and the sow? He decided it was nothing more than sentiment; she still had some strange hope that the end was not at hand for everything they knew and loved in Shiloh.

His mother's hope was foolish, Tom thought bitterly. Why did she hold so dearly to her expectation of a miracle? Dad was not coming back home with a fortune to pay off the Jenson loan. They would soon be out of water and out of food.

Tom knew deep down that there were no miracles left for them. Unless he counted simple survival as a miracle. Or maybe eating enough at one meal so that he did not go to bed hungry?

The empty boxcar in which Birch and Jeff rode across the Tehachapi Mountains contained sixty other 'boes, fruit tramps, and men on the lam. Since they crossed the California border there had been three fights in the crowded space, including one in which a dispute over a nearly empty wine bottle had resulted in a man being thrown from the train.

Crushed against one wall of the car in the sweltering heat, Jeff and Birch could scarcely breathe. So when the train slowed at Mojave for its climb out of the desert and up over the pass into the San Joaquin Valley, Jeff made a suggestion. He told Birch to follow him out through the hatch to lie on top of the box in the fresh air. As he put it, "the fightin' ain't the worse part of the ride."

Birch's head was no longer wrapped in a bandage around the place where he had been clubbed, and the wound itself was mostly healed. It should be; it had taken them long enough to get this far.

They had been rousted in Chicago and sentenced to more than a week chopping weeds with other vagrants . . . lived for two days on a handful of crackers and a tin of sardines . . . seen a man knifed to death outside Denver . . . and spent days on a siding in the middle of nowhere when they had chosen the wrong car on which to pin their hopes.

But now the end was almost in sight. "Another couple hours," Birch said as they stretched out on the running board atop the car, "an' we'll see if all the tales about the Promised Land are true or not."

"Don't have to be heaven," Jeff said, shrugging, "long as there's jobs." The Santa Fe train curled through dry canyons and sagebrush-clogged draws. At times the two men had to drop back inside the car or be choked as the track plunged into dark tunnels. Birch looked around at all the arid desolation and wondered how anyone could describe this as paradise, but he refrained from voicing his opinion to Jeff.

"Reckon we can get on in the oil fields?" Birch mused.

"Don't see why not. Strong back . . ."

"And weak mind?" Birch laughed.

"Ain't nothin' more required for the cotton fields," Jeff concluded. "Should be enough for oil."

The train climbed into the brown mountains and spiraled down around the world-famous Tehachapi loop like an immense snake coiled back on itself. Birch looked out on more than a mile of flats and gondolas and reefers and still could see neither the six-engine team pulling nor the caboose bringing up the rear.

The Santa Fe freight was on the final downgrade toward the valley and free of the last of the tunnels when it finally emerged from the scrub oak–covered hills far enough to give Birch and Jeff a glimpse of their destination. "My sweet Lawd," Jeff breathed.

Stretched out before them, like a corner of Willa Mae's altar-cloth quilt, was a patchwork of fields, farms, and ranches that extended as far as they could see. Fragrant green alfalfa fields waved alongside the darker verdant shades of the cotton plantings and the pale yellow of wheat stalks. Hilltops were crowned with orchards of fruit trees and the farther hills forested with wooden and steel oil derricks. Water glistened in stock ponds and reservoirs and flowed through irrigation ditches. And the gentle slopes were carpeted with acres of vineyards, sunlight glistening on clusters of grapes as big as a man could lift.

"Look," Jeff said, pointing out the vines. "Sure 'nough Canaan land."

At the farther edge of their vision, the opposite side of the great central valley was defined by the coastal range of mountains; a far border to this crazy quilt of colorful and fertile plain. The air was so clear that even the scale of their sight was fooled; a wheat field seemed but a short distance away until they caught sight of a windmill turning beside a barn and suddenly the view jumped back several miles farther off.

"It's gonna work out," Birch said with a sigh of relief. "We can bring our families here and not hate ourselves for it. It ain't Shiloh, but it's alive and growing; . . . it's gonna work."

When the Santa Fe freight pulled into the rail yard, the hoboes surrendered their places with no more fanfare than fleas jumping from a dead dog. They simply grabbed their bedrolls and baled off into the tumbleweeds and brown dirt of Bakersfield, California. Birch and Jeff's travels had covered more than three thousand miles since Washington, but any sense of accomplishment was lost amid two practical concerns: how to eat and where to find work.

Across the tracks from the rail depot was a farmer's market. Armenians, Italians, Greeks, and Basques, previous immigrants to the Promised Land of the San Joaquin Valley, all brought their produce into town to sell. The later, poorer arrivals, who suddenly found themselves labeled Okies and Arkies, counted their pennies and counted themselves lucky to be in a place where sleeping warm at night was not a concern. A handful of coins could buy a hundredweight of potatoes, but Jeff and Birch had no money at all. They looked longingly at tomatoes and watermelon and peaches, but if the fruit had only been one Indian-head cent apiece, it still would have been too dear.

"Come on," Birch said. "No sense standin' here droolin'. Amos Grier said to cross the river to a little Hooverville on the north side and ask around for him."

The little Hooverville turned out to be a sprawling camp of tents, tar-paper-and-cardboard shacks, and regular frame houses. The settlement, standing as it did beside the Kern River, had been christened Riverview, as if a grand name could overcome its mundane reality.

"This looks an awful lot like Washington," Birch observed. "Mighty unpleasant comparison."

Birch selected men to ask for information about Amos Grier by picking out the oil-stained clothes and greasy boots common to all the oil field workers. The first had never heard of Amos, nor the second, but the third cocked his head in recognition. "Amos Grier? Yeah, I know who he is. Lives up the road there a piece."

But when Birch and Jeff followed the route the man outlined for them, they found the premises occupied by two families from Muskogee, Oklahoma. The present occupants had never even heard the name Amos Grier.

"I don't know why we thought it would be easy," Birch mused. "Who knows if he's still in this part of the country. He might've up and moved on already."

So Birch and Jeff spent their first night in California sleeping under a bridge. They had slept in worse places on their trek across the country.

The air was warm; in fact, the days were unpleasantly hot, with temperatures just over a hundred degrees.

They went to sleep hungry that evening. The next morning, they agreed to separate and go different directions with different goals in mind. Birch was to seek employment in the oil fields while Jeff sought any kind of labor that would pay enough to feed them.

Of the two, Jeff had the greater success. He walked west of Bakersfield until he came to cropland watered by canals and irrigation ditches. Inquiring at farmhouses for day labor, he soon found a rancher who wanted help bucking bales of alfalfa hay. The farmer, a man named Stockton, looked at Jeff's broad shoulders and corded, muscular arms and offered him a dollar a day plus board and said Jeff could sleep in his barn till the harvest was in.

Birch, meanwhile, walked from tin shed to brick office building looking for a job. When he cited his previous experience in Oklahoma oil production, he was told he was too old. When he sought a position with a pipeline-laying crew, he was told he lacked experience. Landing a job in California did not seem to be as simple as he had hoped.

The only way to find employment, Birch was told, was to be the first on the scene when a worker quit or was fired, and being first meant knowing someone close to the job. This made locating Amos Grier even more significant.

Fortunately for Jeff and Birch, the hay farmer was willing to employ them both if they would work for food and split the dollar. Since the meals included fresh peaches as big as Jeff's fist and all the grapes they could eat, the bargain was struck.

Rising in the predawn light, when it was cooler, the two men walked on either side of a flatbed trailer pulled by a venerable John Deere tractor. As the grower piloted the rig between rows of already baled hay, Birch and Jeff swung the steel hay hooks and bucked the one-hundred-twenty-pound cubes onto the wagon. Twelve bales made a load, which was then transported to a shed and stacked into a mountain thirty bales high and fifty yards long using an A-frame and block and tackle.

Birch sent off a postcard to let the Shiloh folks know they had arrived safely. He did not need an envelope for a letter, because there was as yet no money to enclose. He and Jeff were eating, but that was all.

The farmer was agreeable to letting them knock off in the hottest part of the day and resume stacking alfalfa in the evening. But instead of taking an afternoon siesta, as was the local custom, Birch and Jeff walked back into Bakersfield or out to Oildale in search of work in the oil patch. "At this rate," Birch groaned, "we won't ever be able to bring our families out."

Jeff cautioned him not to give up hope; something would work out when they least expected it.

CHAPTER 36

It was only a penny postcard, yet never in the memory of Grandma Amos had such a little thing caused such a great commotion.

"All the way from Californy!" Brother Williams cried as he bounded up the steps of Shiloh Store. "Ain't but a penny postcard, but it's shore 'nough word from Birch an' Jefferson!"

Trudy, Willa Mae, and Lily crowded around Brother. No one commented on the fact that whatever the message said, it had already been read by Brother Williams. No doubt everyone in Hartford already knew word for word what the two California-bound men had to say for themselves.

Tom and Bobby jostled for a place in the semicircle of Shiloh residents. An audience formed around the trio of women who stood excitedly staring at the battered leather mail pouch. Brother had slung the sack onto the counter beside the pickled pigs' feet and was heightening the drama by being slow about reaching in. A murmur of impatience rippled through the crowd of a dozen locals.

Grandma Amos reprimanded Brother's tardiness. "Well, get 'er outta the mail pouch, Brother! We all been waitin' for weeks!" The old woman clamped the cold stump of her pipe between her few teeth and muttered, "Leastwise we know they ain't dead. Is they in jail?"

"No, they ain't," Brother snapped, reaching around among the circulars and other letters for the penny postcard.

"Well, what's it say then?" Grandma demanded.

"Ain't supposed t' read mail I deliver," Brother objected, as he pulled out his package of chewing tobacco. "You know that, Gramma."

"'Course I know," Grandma retorted. "But if you ain't read it, how come you t' already know it's from Birch an' Jeff?"

"Californy postmark." Brother upended the entire contents of the bag, spilling out boiled eggs, two pocketknives, and a crescent wrench among the heap of correspondence.

The old woman's face puckered in a gotcha grin. "How come you t' know they ain't in jail, then?"

"Lawd!" Willa Mae blurted in exasperation. "Just tell us what they says, Brother! We ain't gon' report you t' no one!"

Brother grimaced and fanned the letters out among the mostly empty jars of hard candy, beef jerky, and Beeman's chewing gum.

And there it was. A white cardboard rectangle addressed to the Canfield and Tucker families. The handwriting was clearly that of Birch Tucker.

Trudy closed her eyes and breathed her thanks.

Brother held the note up. "Here 'tis. Who's a-gonna read 'er?" He lowered it and placed it into Tom's hands. "Here y'are, Possum. Read it out real loud now. Show us how good Missus Faraby done taught you in that school yonder."

Tom drew in his breath. The first words came out in a hoarse whisper. "Dearest families. . . ."

"Louder!" shouted Dan Faraby from the back row.

Tom began again. "Dearest families, God is our refuge and strength, a very present help in trouble. Therefore will we not fear. . . ."

"Lawd!" Willa Mae clapped her hands together. "Psalm forty-six. My Hock's favorite." She continued the passage: "There is a river whose streams make glad the city of God—"

"There's more," Brother interrupted.

Tom continued, his voice stronger now. "Says here, 'Job bucking hay. Camped by river. Land of milk and honey. Will send cash when able. The Lord Almighty is with us and you all! Love, Birch Tucker and Jefferson Canfield.'"

There was no room for anything else on the card. Tom held it high and let his mother scan it and then Willa Mae and Lily, both of whom wept for the joy of it.

"Jus' a penny postcard," Grandma Amos intoned. "Ain't never seen such a fuss over a penny postcard."

Governor Franklin Delano Roosevelt was campaigning for president in Connecticut. It was the start of an intense quest for votes designed to carry FDR clear across the country. President Hoover, on the other hand, was vacationing. Back in Washington, Hoover's special committee of financiers and leaders of industry came up with a new answer to the economic downturn, which Hoover had already declared to be over. Their solution: cut hours across the board and put more people back to work. Roosevelt derided the plan as replacing a million unemployed with ten million underemployed.

In Arkansas, where very few were employed at all, the temperature soared over a hundred degrees. Afternoon sunlight fell in a dirty coppery slant across the hills. Dust clung to newly washed sheets and underclothes and patched coveralls hung out to dry on the line behind the Tucker house.

From the kitchen window Tom saw his mother put a hand to her back and bend slightly to work out the kink. She picked up the empty wicker laundry basket and looked off at the odd tinge of the western sky before she came into the kitchen.

Tom's boots were on the table. The tin of Shineola polish was open and the wax applied as she had instructed him. But the leather of the old shoes, sole and upper alike, was completely worn out. There was not another day of wear in them in spite of the fact that he had gone barefoot every day but Sunday for the entire summer. Shineola was of no avail.

"It's still hot, Mama," Tom said as Trudy contemplated the beat-up lumps of leather that had carried him through the last school year. "I don't need shoes."

"School starts next week," she replied grimly, as if the opening day of school marked the absolute last day a kid could go barefoot in Shiloh.

Bobby's shoe soles now sported iron plates to keep them from wearing down. When he scraped his way across the stone walk, Mama said he sounded like a tap dancer she had once seen dance in a play on Broadway. His shoes were still good enough to wear. It was easy for Bobby to be optimistic.

Bobby offered, "Dad's letter's comin' any day now. Tom can get brand-new shoes for school when the letter and the money comes."

Trudy pursed her lips and stared at the shabby footgear as if they were her enemy, the betrayer of her fight to keep the desperation of their circumstances a secret from their neighbors.

A proud woman, Willa Mae had said about Tom's mama.

Tom thought about Sally Grier and her folks.

They were proud people, too. The faded blue dress, the wilted hair ribbon, the hand-me-down pumps that sloshed around as Sally walked.

It was clear to Tom that if he put his old shoes on his feet and went to school, everyone would know without being told that the Tuckers had come to the end of everything. He also knew that no one would care.

He studied the set to his mama's jaw. He wanted to say to her, "Everyone is in the same fix." But he held his tongue, knowing that Willa Mae was right about his mother.

"The Lord will make a way." Trudy sniffed and looked off. Some pained thought made her wince a bit. She shook it off. "I *will* believe."

Bobby uttered the words that had flashed in her mind. "Why don't we go into Meribah, Mama? Everybody in Shiloh's gone to shop at Meribah. Just sign your name for credit and. . ."

Her eyes sparked angrily at Bobby's suggestion. "Anything but that, Robert. I'd rather . . ."

Things were serious when she called Bobby by his proper name. Trudy did not finish, and Bobby ducked his head as if she might wallop him for speaking blasphemy.

Go to Meribah? Never!

Tom mentally summed up what she was thinking. Trudy Tucker would rather die than sign her name to the credit ledger in Jenson's company store. She would rather starve, rather go barefoot and face the winter in rags. In all the months since the farm had been mortgaged and the contract signed, Trudy had not made a single shopping trip into enemy territory. She would not do so now. . . .

Here was the dilemma. Grandma Amos or any shopkeeper in Hartford would have welcomed her business, been pleased to take the spoken word of Trudy Tucker as a bond that her debt would be paid.

But Trudy was no longer certain she could make good on her word, so she would not offer that verbal bond in exchange for new shoes for Tom or canned food or cornmeal or even a half-pound of salt. To give a promise to pay back her dear friends and then fail to keep her word was something akin to stealing in Trudy's mind. She had not offered her promise to the Hartford merchants in exchange for food or clothing or so much as one box of Strike Anywhere matches when the matchbox had run out.

Tom watched his mother's inward litany repeat itself again and again and then, with one final glance at the boots, he saw her resolve weaken and crumble at last.

"Meribah," she muttered.

In that one word Tom heard his mother ask herself a terrible question: *"Am I beaten?"*

Tom knew that it was one thing when his mother went to bed hungry; it was quite another when she saw that Tom and Bobby were losing weight. It was of no consequence to her, Tom knew, that her clothes were worn thin and faded from too many washings, but it pained her to the core that Tom's overalls were too short and he had no shoes for school. He could not convince her that it did not matter.

She rose stiffly from the table and picked up his boots. She swayed as she left the kitchen and the house. Tom watched her from the window as she walked slowly toward the root cellar, opened the heavy storm door, and disappeared down the dark steps.

At last Trudy emerged from the root cellar, Tom's boots still in hand. Tom and Bobby were playing on the tire swing. The wind had kicked up. The limbs of the old hickory tree groaned, and the rope supporting the tire and the brothers rocked with the motion.

Trudy squinted against the glare of daylight. She looked out toward the mountains and shielded her eyes.

"What were you doing down there?" Bobby asked. He always blurted out the question that Tom thought but did not dare to speak aloud.

"Thinking," Trudy replied absently. "Praying." Then she glanced up at the copper rooster on the roof, which whirled and crowed toward the eerie gold light. "I do not like the look of the sky, boys. Something's coming. Tom, fetch Henny and Rosey. Take them into the root cellar. I'll get the lantern."

Tom helped Bobby into the dank coolness of the shelter, then he caught the dog and Henny and guided them down the steep steps. Tom took his seat on the long bench to wait beside Bobby. It was easily twenty degrees cooler in the cellar than outside. Tom sighed with relief and thought that if the weather did not cool off he would not mind sleeping here.

The open storm doors illuminated the nearly empty storage shelves that lined the walls. White lettering on the edge of the pine planks identified where a thick forest of Ball canning jars had been last year; where the food supply for the coming months would have been if only . . .

Vegetables. Beans. Tomatoes. Okra. Spinach. Carrots. Beets. Corn. Chowchow. Fruits. Jellies. Applesauce. Apricots. Peaches. Canned Beef.

The vacant shelves over the careful labels made Tom shudder. He closed his eyes and leaned his head back against the damp brick wall.

Above them the wind began to howl. The copper rooster squawked as it spun around on its perch.

"Where is Mama?" Bobby asked and furrowed his brow as the sky darkened. The memory of the day three years before when a twister had destroyed the Tucker barn was vivid in the minds of both boys.

Tom shuddered and got up. Perhaps she needed his help with something. Maybe she had fallen. He could wait no longer.

Just then Trudy's shadow fell over the mouth of the shelter. She lowered the lantern to Tom, who hung it on a nail set in the support timber. He reached up to help her descend the steps.

"What kept you?" Bobby asked sharply as Trudy and Tom closed the storm doors and locked themselves in with a two-by-twelve-inch beam slid between the heavy iron brackets.

"I put the fire out in the stove." She sat down hard beside Bobby, her face suddenly animated and afraid as the wind rattled the door over their heads.

"Twister coming, you think?" Tom asked.

"Dust," she replied quietly, folding her hands in her lap and raising her eyes upward as if she could see through the heavy wood that separated them from the gale.

Rosey whined and slunk beneath the bench. Henny fluffed her feathers and hid her head under her wing.

"Just dust?" Bobby asked, not understanding why dust should drive them to take shelter in the cellar.

Trudy added in an awed, detached voice, "It is Oklahoma dust. I saw it . . . rising in the west. A thick, black curtain of it. Miles higher than the mountains and wider along the horizon that I could see. It is moving down towards us."

As if on cue, the storm doors banged with the violence of the tempest as the force of it arrived. The shafts of sunlight that had filtered through the cracks went suddenly and completely black.

In the same instant Trudy leapt to her feet and put her hands to her head. "My wash!" she cried. "Oh Tom! I left the laundry on the line!"

The day after the storm, Tom found his mother's laundry torn to shreds on the barbed-wire fence of the pasture. It took three days to clean up the dust that had invaded the house through every tiny crack and crevice in the wood siding and the windowsills.

But at least the roof remained intact. The barn had stood firm, and the mules had survived. The chicken coop was undamaged, and the two dozen hens began laying after the third day. The outhouse door had blown off one hinge, but structurally the Tucker farm was still sound.

On the fourth day following the dust storm, Tom was still barefoot, but the issue of shoes had been put on a back burner. That afternoon Tom, Bobby, and Trudy had gone to Grandma's store to check for the expected letter from California. Once again the Tucker pigeonhole was empty. Trudy involuntarily glanced at Tom's dusty toes, frowned, and looked quickly away.

Grandma Amos reported that Lily had not heard from Jefferson, either. The last word had been the postcard, which had been followed by a letter from Willa Mae's sister in Washington, recounting the ordeal of the riot.

"Bet them two fellers has been throw'd in jail," Grandma Amos said cheerfully. "If they's in jail, leastwise y'all won't have t' worry none 'bout 'em. They'll have vittles t' eat an' y'all can rest easy since they ain't both dead."

Encouragement from Grandma Amos was not always encouraging. Trudy bade the old woman good day, squared her shoulders, and stepped out of the store just as Arley Palmer's rattling pickup chuffed up the grade. The vehicle was laden with household goods tied to every available space. Mattresses, highboys, and chests of drawers formed the foundation. Pots and pans clanged like bells with every rut. Upside-down chairs poked out from the top and sides, their legs protruding like the spines of a riled porcupine.

Nestled among this jumble of worldly goods were the four Palmer children. Three girls were school-age, although much younger than Tom and Bobby. Then there was the little redheaded boy who had inherited all of Joey's clothes. Tom saw instantly that the child was wearing the tiny denim overalls that Mama had made for Joey. It sent a twinge through him. Trudy pretended not to notice. She drew her breath in deeply and just stood there, smiling and strong as granite, but Tom could tell she had seen. Her eyes reflected something deep and sad. Then she caught herself and, resisting memory and grief, she smiled and greeted the Palmers as Arley brought the vehicle to a shuddering halt and climbed out over the stuff tied onto the running board.

"What's all this?" Trudy asked in wonder at the sight of all the household heaped up.

Arley, looking grimy and tired, stood beside the truck and fiddled with the latch of the hood. "I could fight the fall of cotton prices. Mebbe fight the Jensons and the mortgage. For a while I figgered we could wait out the drought. But Trudy, we can't fight this dadblamed dust."

"We're headed west," Nina Palmer added. "I've got a sister in Delano, California. She has wrote and said it's real good out there, and so we're goin'."

Arley chucked his hat into the cab. "Ain't gonna be no way to pay off Jenson's nohow." He dipped his head beneath the hood and continued talking as he unscrewed the radiator cap. "Leastwise we can feed the young'uns out there. Food drippin' off the trees, I hear."

"Like paradise. I've heard it, too."

"All a feller's gotta do is go there. But I'm a-feared that ain't a certainty with this ol' heap a-carryin' us."

"This is sudden," Trudy said.

"Dust storm done it." Nina Palmer gave her head a shake. "We had flour an' cornmeal all ruined by the dust. I opened a jar of applesauce, poured it onto our plates an' it tasted like dust. We jus' cain't take another day of that."

CHAPTER 37

Former President Coolidge, entreated by Republicans to aid Hoover's reelection bid, responded by agreeing to an interview with the *New York Times*. "Hoover is safe and sound," the taciturn former chief executive had said. It did not impress readers as being an enthusiastic endorsement. It also had unfortunate overtones of what Hoover had been saying about the nation's economy ever since the Great Wall Street Crash back in '29.

"Hoover may be safe and sound," Birch quipped when he heard the quote, "but what about the rest of us? I'm voting for Roosevelt."

By the end of the second week after their arrival in the San Joaquin Valley, the haying was completed and Jeff and Birch were once again without lodging, meals, or employment. Birch was on his third visit to some of the oil company offices, still without success. He was standing at the hiring counter of Standard Oil's Monte Cristo office when a voice behind him spoke gruffly, "Heard you been askin' for me, mister. You lookin' for a fight?"

Birch ducked as he swung around, wondering who he had been mistaken for by this obviously belligerent man. Then Birch was treated to a huge laugh at the trick. Amos Grier grabbed Birch around the shoulders and invited him and Jeff home to supper.

The Griers lived in a tiny house with paper-thin walls, but Amos looked and sounded proud. He and his wife appeared better fed, if not much better clothed, than when they had left Arkansas. The girls were enrolled in school, and Amos was pleased with what he had accomplished.

"Hard work and low wages," Amos said, "but hopeful, not like back home. Difference is, out here people got jobs, and jobs give 'em hope for better."

Despite the meager surroundings, Amos explained, the families that lived in lean-tos by the river expected to be able to afford to rent half a duplex in a month and lease or even buy a four-room stucco house in a year. The Grier family had been a month in their new home, and Amos had just gotten a well-paying position on a production crew with Standard.

"New job an' a new place," Birch commented. "You've done all right, Amos."

And Amos had good news for Birch and Jeff. Since he had just landed a spot with a different outfit, he thought his former employer would take them on. "He'll be needin' to replace me," Amos said, "so you're right on the money. Show up at seven tomorrow, and don't worry about bein' Arkies." He frowned and looked at Jeff. "Or anything."

"Worry about it?"

"Yeah, some places won't hire you if you're from Oklahoma or Arkansas or . . . but anyway, Hank Correy don't care, long as you give him a day's work."

"Wish I'd known," Birch lamented. "I been tellin' ever'body right where I was from!"

Amos loaned Jeff and Birch a tent they could pitch down by the river. "Worked for us when we first come," he said. "Just bring it back when you don't need it." He also gave them a lug of some fruit that looked like dark-green warty pears.

"Avocados," Amos explained. "Guy was sellin' 'em for fifty cents a crate, so I bought two. But we cain't eat 'em all 'fore they spoil, so you take 'em and welcome."

As Birch toted the flat of unfamiliar fruit and Jeff hauled the tent, Jeff asked, "How you cook these here things.?"

"Don't know," Birch said. "Boil 'em, I guess. One of the brand new things we gotta learn out here," he concluded. "Only one of many."

Esmerelda's wide, chocolate-brown eyes blinked trustingly at Tom as he tied the rope around her neck and led her from the stall. The sweet, accepting gaze of the little Jersey cow was the only thing about her that remained unchanged, unaltered by the weeks of sparse grazing on the Bermuda-grass pasture. She had dropped at least two hundred pounds. Now she was a bony shadow of what she had been before.

At last Trudy could tolerate the terrible decline no longer. "Tie her to the back of the wagon, Tom," Trudy instructed from the spring seat of the FAMOUS wagon.

Bobby, braced legs out stiff in front of him as he sat in the bed of the wagon, leaned over and stroked Esmerelda's velvet nose as she was led past him.

"Mama, do we have to sell her?" Bobby asked. "She used to give the best milk."

Trudy jerked her head downward only once, then turned her eyes forward to the long ears of the mule team.

"But Mama—" Bobby started to argue.

"That's enough," Trudy replied sharply. "She is suffering. And I cannot bear it another day."

They were taking the little cow into Mansfield, where a government agricultural agent was buying up cattle at one dollar a head. Tom and Trudy were well aware that the intention was not to provide homes for unwanted livestock, but rather to purchase beef on the hoof to feed the soldiers stationed at Fort Chaffe. But Trudy had given Tom strict instruction that he must not tell Bobby the truth.

Brother Williams had hauled the sow away to a similar sale last Tuesday. The dollar he had obtained for Miss Lucy had purchased twenty-five pounds of flour for Trudy on the very day their supply of flour had been used up. Esmerelda was eating pasture that might have kept the mules going. She was drinking water that might have been used for the other livestock; the chickens, for instance. Thus, she became expendable.

Esmerelda might have been suffering, Tom thought as he knotted the rope, but so was every other critter between the Poteaus and Sugarloaf, including Trudy.

Tom stood beside the gentle, buckskin-colored creature. He patted Esmerelda's neck and tried not to think about the fact that she was going for her last walk down the Shiloh road.

Trudy interrupted his grim thoughts. "I will not take Esmerelda into Mansfield thirsty. We shall first walk her to the watering hole where she can drink her fill. There is no way to predict how long those government men at the sale yard will make her stand without water in the pen with a hundred other cows before—"

Trudy stopped herself. But not before Bobby frowned at the back of her head and then glanced with a horrified expression at Esmerelda.

Tom knew that the truth had come to Bobby. Tom shrugged. No matter how Trudy tried to keep it from him, Bobby knew how bad things were. How could he help but figure it out? Even little Rosey was losing weight, though Trudy always pretended to be full in order to give the hound a few remaining scraps of food from her own plate.

But taking Esmerelda to the watering hole for her last drink and then to the slaughter was something like betraying a friend, wasn't it?

Bobby stared at the Jersey for a long moment and then turned his gaze on the shattered standpipe of the well. "This wouldn't be happening if . . ."

"No use to think on that," Trudy replied quietly. "Soon everything will be all right. Your father will send for us. Jefferson will send for Lily and Willa Mae and the babies. We will all go together to. . . ."

"The Promised Land," Tom finished in a bitter voice as he took his place beside his mother.

"I'd rather stay here and have everything like it used to—"

Tom whirled around to face Bobby, "It'll never be like it used to be!" he said fiercely. "We can't stay here! We'll starve! We can't take Esmerelda with us! Nor the mules either! The chickens? They'll all go to the sale. Why do you make it harder by askin' dumb questions? Let it be, Bobby! You don't wanna know!"

Birch awoke in the tent by the river to the rhythmic groaning and squawking noise of the jack lines. Crisscrossing the low hills north of the Kern River, the jack lines were the cables that connected shallow wells to a central engine and bull wheel. The action of the wheel alternately pulling and releasing the cables pumped the oil, but the noise they made was like ten thousand giant rocking chairs swaying atop loose plank floors.

As instructed, Birch and Jeff presented themselves outside the headquarters of Superior Tank Cleaning. Reasoning that others might have heard of the opening, they arrived not at seven but at six in the morning. There was no one around. A large brass padlock secured the door to the plywood shed that passed for an office. Jeff pointed out that anyone wanting access could have just ripped the hasp, lock and all, out of the insubstantial frame.

An ancient pickup truck heaped with brooms, mops, wooden shovels, and wooden rakes, was parked next to the shed. The truck and its contents were completely covered in crude oil; in fact, it was impossible to tell if the vehicle had ever been any color than a dirty brownish-black. Inside, outside, fenders and wheels, doors and roof—all were the same uniform shade of petroleum. As the morning sun began to warm the metal, tiny drips of crude plopped onto the oil-soaked earth beneath the truck.

At five minutes before seven, a man whose whistling was punctuated by frequent pauses to spit tobacco juice strode toward the building. "Whatd'ya want?" he growled.

"Are you Correy?" Birch inquired. "Amos Grier said you might have openings."

Correy, short and built much like a fire hydrant, nodded once and clicked the dial on the combination of the lock. "You look strong enough," he said. "Amos was right, I can use both of ya. Pay is two bits an hour." He whirled around suddenly. "No smokin'," he ordered sternly. "Do ya see those shovels and rakes?" he asked, pointing at the pickup. "Wood so they don't spark. Standard Oil had three guys burn up last week. Ignorant weevil took a reg'lar shovel in the tank and ca-choom!" Correy threw both hands in the air to illustrate the resulting explosion.

"I worked on a rig back in Oklahoma," Birch protested.

"Don't mean nothin'!" Correy insisted. "You newcomers are still weevils till I say different. Now get in here and sign these papers so I know how to notify your next of kin."

Within fifteen minutes, Birch, Jeff, and two more men were loaded into the truck. Despite the oily coating on all the tools of their trade, the air was still better in the bed of the truck than in the cab, and the other employees chose to ride in back. Birch and Jeff would have done likewise, but Correy insisted that they ride up front as he drove so he could explain the job.

"Swampin' a tank ain't like muckin' out a stable," he warned. "Take a thirty-foot-diameter tank with say a foot of b.s.—that's bottom sediment—on the floor. Tank shutdown means shuttin' down the wells 'cause they got no place to put the oil. Downtime costs the company money, so I get jobs by workin' faster then anyone else, got it? Five minute break once an hour till we get her whipped."

The drive out of Riverview, past Oildale and Oil Center, took them by the cracking towers, pipes, and furnaces of a refinery, past a tank farm of squat metal drums, and into dusty rolling hills covered with derricks. The older structures were built of wooden beams, just the same as Birch had worked on back in Oklahoma. Newer than these were the frameworks made of steel girders. But either way, each derrick sat atop an oil well, and there were hundreds of the scaffolds in view.

Correy wheeled the pickup under a trio of oscillating jack lines and spiraled up a knobby mound before parking next to a silver metal tank located on its summit. In its side near the base was a two-foot-wide hatch, the only access to the interior. "Got it open an' waitin' for us," the boss said. "Good spot. Pitch the b.s. through the hatch and down the hill. Lucky all four of ya can work inside instead of havin' one outside to keep the door clear."

Jeff winked at Birch. "Lucky," he repeated.

Birch picked up a shovel and Jeff a rake. Both looked with reluctance at the small opening leading into a dark interior. Birch noticed that the other two men hesitated, also, even though they were not new to the work.

Correy caught Birch's arm just before Birch entered the steel cylinder. "Forgot somethin'," he warned. "Man goes down in there, keep clear of him. That's the rule. Don't try to help him. Once in the gunk, it's every man for himself."

The fumes coming up from the bottom sediment inside the tank rushed into Birch's nose like a dose of smelling salts. His head began a low, steady throb. When Birch climbed through the narrow hatch into the interior, he stepped down into a thick, gooey residue that reached halfway to his knees. The only light in the working area of the metallic cavern came through two small hatches in the roof, some twenty feet overhead. It was like being trapped inside a very smelly movie theater with the houselights dimmed. There was enough illumination to scoop shovels full of b.s., but nothing more.

The bottom sediment was midway between sand and grease in consistency. Heavy enough to be raked into piles, it would still ooze back down and spread out again if not immediately scooped up and tossed through the hatch.

One of the other laborers, who said his name was Jack, was also a weevil, a newcomer. A young man, no more than eighteen or twenty, he had only been shoveling for ten minutes or so when he began to complain about not being able to breathe.

Burt, the last member of the crew, was a wiry man with a permanent squint to his eyes. His hair and skin had reeked of grease even before they climbed inside, testifying to his status as an oldtimer in the tank-cleaning trade. "This ain't nothin'." He laughed at Jack. "There's tanks near Taft fulla such rotten stuff you can't shovel but five minutes without passin' out. This ain't nothin', boy."

But Birch agreed more with the younger man. The hour's work dragged on and on before the promised break ever came around, and the break was over all too quickly. Alternately shoveling and raking, the men worked out an impromptu rotation that gave each a chance to get near the entry for a breath of fresh air every few minutes or so. This routine became more and more essential as the morning wore on and the sun heated the metal skin of the tank. The fumes increased with the rise in temperature, and the atmosphere became ever more foul and unbreathable.

Gunk flowed over handles and into gloves. It crept into sleeves and shirt collars and streaked faces and hair. Birch could see yellow film over his vision. Like all the rest, he spat almost continuously, but he could still taste the sludge in his mouth.

Finally Correy stuck his head through the hatch and yelled in a grudging tone, "All right, lunch break. Thirty minutes."

Jeff, Birch, and the others wobbled some as they emerged into the daylight. Birch instinctively raised his hand to shield his eyes, but the motion was intercepted by Burt. "Don't rub 'em," he warned. "Don't even touch your fingers near your eyes, or you'll wind up like me." Then Birch saw that the permanent squint in Burt's eyes masked the fact that they were inflamed and sore. "Old tankies all get this way," he said. "Or they go blind."

Hunting a little shade, the cleaning crew went around the north side of the structure. The treeless slopes grew only creosote bushes and foxtails and offered no protection from the sun, so the men who had spent all morning working inside the belly of the steel-sided beast were forced to cuddle up against it during the break time as well.

Watching the others unwrap sandwiches and fruit and cheese and crackers, Jeff and Birch looked on hungrily. "Don't you two have any lunch?" Correy asked.

"Just these," Birch said sheepishly, pulling out a couple of avocados. "But we don't know what to do with 'em. Thought maybe we could trade for some crackers or something."

"Here," Jack said. "Let me have part of one, and I'll give you half a sandwich."

"You mean you'll eat it raw?"

"You didn't know? Try it with a little salt."

Jeff and Birch were initiated into the delights of avocados and pleased that their contribution to the meal was, in fact, worth some small trades in longhorn cheese and hard candy. For drink there was only water from a five-gallon jug on the back of the truck. "Still tastes like oil," Birch said, spitting vigorously.

"Always does," Burt observed. "Water hereabouts tastes like oil all the time—either that or sulfur. Prob'ly really good for you. Hey, Correy, what say we get out of this tank-cleaning business and just bottle Oildale water? We can sell it to rich folks back east as a tonic."

Correy did not even grin. He had been studying his watch every few minutes all during the noon meal. "Okay, time's up," he said. "Back to work."

"What's the rush?"

"Gotta big job after this one. If we finish in time, I want to move over and start it today."

CHAPTER 38

To add to the sorrow and frustration Trudy felt at having to sell the milk cow, Henny was missing! She and a hen named Taloa had both disappeared from the farmyard, probably eaten by a sneaking fox or weasel. Though there were still twenty laying hens left, Trudy felt the loss of this pair; the one because she was an old friend and the other because Trudy had worked so hard to win her over. But there was no time to think of two missing chickens today.

The wall clock in the Tucker parlor was old and ailing. Its tock was louder than its tick, and when it chimed the hour it sounded something like a child beating a dishpan with a wooden spoon. Still, it was a much loved family heirloom, brought by Trudy's forefathers from Amsterdam to London, from London to Philadelphia, and finally south to Arkansas with the Jewish migration after the Civil War.

Trudy unscrewed its brackets from the wall. She carefully lowered it to the sofa and removed the pendulum. It lay silent for the first time since Birch had hung it in its place of honor the day they moved to Shiloh.

Trudy ran her finger down one side of the smooth mahogany rectangle and tapped the wavy glass above the Roman numerals. "You are a pair of shoes for my boy," she remarked quietly as if the clock was someone worthy of an explanation.

She wrapped the clock in a crocheted afghan and carried it out to the waiting wagon. Tom stood quietly with his hand hooked onto the mule's blinder.

"You want me to drive, Mama?" Tom offered.

"You and Bobby are staying home today," she replied, carefully placing the object beneath the spring seat and climbing up to take the lines. "I have business to transact."

"Why can't we go?" Tom asked.

"Because I said you could not go, and I am the parent." She clucked her tongue, urging the team forward and onto the road to Meribah.

It took four hours of slow travel before the tall steeple of the Meribah Fellowship of Abounding Holiness came into Trudy's view. She felt no relief that the long journey was almost over. Suddenly the gravel highway became paved road. Ahead of her, trucks filled with cotton were rumbling toward the Jenson Consolidated cotton gin.

The clean brick facades of the Meribah Hotel and Cafe and the various Jenson-operated stores appeared untouched by the dust storm. Outside the meat market, a corpulent butcher was washing off the striped canvas awning that stretched across the front of his establishment. The spent water ran onto the sidewalk and then down the gutter to puddle around the tires of automobiles nosed into the curb. Such flagrant waste of something as precious as water was evidence to Trudy that all the suffering of Sebastian County had not affected the empire Garrick and Caro-line Jenson had built.

Caro-line's Buick was parked in front of the Meribah Hotel and Cafe. Trudy turned her face away as she passed the broad plate-glass windows of the establishment. She did not want to chance seeing Caro-line, not today of all days, not when Trudy had brought in her old clock to trade at the Jenson Mercantile. She had not considered offering the exchange in Hartford; her friends were already too burdened with swaps and barter.

Pulling the team down an alley where the watering troughs and hitching rails were located, Trudy whoaed up the team behind the store. She caught her reflection in the window of the back door. It pleased her that the sun and the journey had not wilted her like a bunch of flowers. The clerks of Jenson Mercantile would see her dressed in her Sunday best. The print of her dress sported cheerful red flowers on a navy-blue background. She had washed her hair this morning, and now she took out a hatbox and put on the navy-blue straw hat Birch had bought her in Oklahoma City three years before.

Climbing down carefully from the wagon, Trudy cradled the old clock in her arms and entered the store. A small bell above the door announced her arrival. A male clerk glanced up from where he was helping a prosperous-looking woman with a bolt of fabric. He wore a long white apron and visor that gave him a birdlike visage. Trudy smiled. He looked at the bundle in her arms and then went back to his business without returning her smile.

From the high ceiling came the sound of a ceiling fan ticking away. The movement of air felt good. Trudy pretended to browse, walking slowly through the stacks of denims and blue work shirts. She flipped through the pattern books and then made her way to the shelves and shelves of yellow boxes containing men's and boys' Redwing work boots.

The sight and smell of the new, tanned leather, with thick soles and shoelaces unmarred by breaking and tying and breaking again, made her almost giddy. Holding the clock in one arm, she ran her fingers over ungouged heels and smooth, unscuffed toes. She counted the metal eyes and noted that the tongues did not have a mark on them. Oh, shoes! What was an old clock compared to shoes like those on display! And there, between the MENS 7 and MENS 9, was Tom's size. Enough to give him growing room for the coming year!

"Mens 8!" she said aloud.

"May I help you, ma'am?" The clerk's expression was amused.

"My boy wears a size-eight boot. I have made a pattern of his foot to be certain." She fumbled in her pocket for the outline she had traced.

The clerk measured it against his stick and made a noise as if he was clearing his throat. "A bit less than a size seven by my reckoning. To buy him larger might hurt his feet."

Trudy was firm. "He needs growing room. I see you have an eight."

He nodded. It was not unusual for mothers of growing children to buy a size or two larger than needed, but the clerk had been instructed not to let such frugal spending habits go unchallenged.

"As you wish, ma'am." He removed the box and checked the contents for proper size and shoelaces and the like. "These are four dollars."

It was more than in the Sears and Roebuck, but mail order would not accept trade for a clock. Trudy nodded hesitantly, then unwrapped the timepiece. "Would you accept this in exchange?"

The expression beneath the visor turned suspicious. "We don't take trades in Meribah, ma'am. Cash or credit account's the way Jensons do business."

The reply was so absolute that Trudy did not attempt to argue. As she folded the afghan over the clock face, something snapped in her. "Ah. Yes. I see."

"You're not from 'round here, are you?"

"Shiloh."

"Oh!" he scoffed. "You're one of those Shiloh people! I thought I'd seen 'em all straggle through here. You're a new face."

"Not in Shiloh, I'm not." She raised her head regally. "We have an account here." She wanted those boots for Tom. Did it matter if she put her name to a Jenson charge she could not pay since Garrick and Caro-line were about to steal the Tucker farm anyway?

"You have an account?"

"Tucker," she replied and took the shoebox from him. "Check your ledger if you like."

He nodded, held up one finger, and told her he would just be a moment. Retreating to the curtained alcove behind the counter, he placed a telephone call.

Trudy heard him clearly.

"Meribah Cafe? . . . Right. . . . Missus Jenson, please. . . ."

Trudy felt her face flush with shame. She looked at the shoebox, then caught her reflection in the dark mirror by the display of hats.

"Afternoon, Missus Jenson. This is Malcolm down at the Mercantile. . . . I got me one of those Shiloh people here in the store; never seen her before. . . . Brought a beat-up old clock in. . . . She says her name is Tucker. . . ."

Trudy frowned and bit her lower lip as she considered the new shoes and the old clock.

"I told her we don't take trades. . . . She says she's got an account. . . ."

Trudy replaced the boot box among the other size eights. Tom would have to do without new shoes. Trudy walked to the back door, paused an instant more to listen.

"Tucker. She doesn't look so bad off as the rest of them Shiloh hillbillies, but she brought this clock to trade, and you know what that means, so I figgered . . ."

The bell over the door rang loudly as Trudy left the establishment, replaced the old clock under the spring seat, took off her hat and returned it to its box, and left Meribah behind.

Had the letter come from Birch and Jefferson while Trudy had been off in Meribah? Trudy was left with no hope but that.

Grandma Amos's store was closed by the time Trudy reached Shiloh. No possibility of checking the post-office box. Willa Mae and Lily would know if something had arrived.

It was after sundown, but the mules plodded on, heedless of the encroaching darkness. They knew the way home and protested the stop at Willa Mae's cabin by shaking their heads and stamping their big feet.

Lamplight glowed from the window of the Canfield cabin. Fireflies bobbed in the juniper bushes beside the house. Trudy clearly heard the singsong of Willa Mae's voice as she called, "Who's that out yonder?"

"Trudy Tucker," came the reply, as if there was any other Trudy in all of Shiloh. "I have some to see . . ."

"Why Trudy! Chil'! Is 'at you? How come you out so late on the road an' it after dark?" The planks of the porch groaned as the old woman stepped out. Framed in the doorway with the light behind her, she beckoned for Trudy to get down and come in the house.

"I only stopped to see if the letter had come."

"No. No letter. I'll take a switch t' that Jefferson when we catches up to him. He oughta have writ us a letter. An' I'll pass you the switch t' use on Birch when I is done with my boy."

"It will be appreciated," Trudy said without amusement in her voice.

Willa Mae laughed. "'Course mebbe they ain't got a penny t' pay for a penny postcard. I reckon they gon' write home when they can."

"I have been to Meribah," Trudy admitted, "to trade my old wall clock for shoes." This statement of fact was an admission of desperation.

Willa Mae chewed on the surprising information for a long moment, then said, "Lily's gone off to the schoolhouse to help Missus Faraby get the place in order on account of school startin' in the mornin'. Skeeters is real bad t'night, honey. Come on in here b'fore they eats you alive."

Only then did Trudy notice the hum beside her ear. She brushed it away and climbed from the wagon like an obedient child.

Inside the cabin, she gratefully accepted a glass of iced tea.

"Got no ice nor sugar neither," admitted Willa Mae, "but it's wet like iced tea oughta be." Willa Mae seated Trudy in the ladder-backed chair beside the old steamer trunk and took a chair opposite her. The flicker of the kerosene lantern glowed on Willa Mae's ebony skin.

Only after the proprieties of hospitality had been offered did the old woman level a compassionate gaze on Trudy. "Meribah, huh? Things as bad as all that, honey?"

The whole truth spilled out of Trudy one sip of tea at a time, how the clock had been rejected and how the clerk had phoned Caro-line Jenson and how Trudy had left the place humiliated and ashamed.

Trudy finished the tale: "To top it all off, my dear little Henny has vanished with another hen. A fox, perhaps."

"That do happen. And I is sorry. I know what store you laid by Joey's chicken."

"A silly thing, I suppose. There are the others in the coop. We eat because my hens keep laying eggs."

"I gots me some extra cornmeal." Willa Mae started to rise, but Trudy stopped her with a hand on her forearm.

"Please. No. I could not. You all are having as hard a time as we."

"You's a proud woman, Trudy Tucker. Too proud for your own good." She looked down at Trudy's hand. "I'll trade cornmeal for eggs. Eggs be good t' eat for a change."

Trudy managed a smile. "Of course."

"I'll throw in a little m'lasses. Y'all can eat hoecakes for breakfast 'fore school t'morrow."

"That is kind of you."

"Only wish I could help with them shoes. I knows what store you set in havin' them young'uns wearin' a new pair of brogans when the school year commences."

Trudy nodded. Silence between the two women. "I suppose I *am* too proud in that regard." She looked away anxiously. "I wish I had never gone to Meribah."

"Tom wouldn't wear no Meribah shoes nohow, I'm figgerin'." Willa Mae leaned back in her chair. "Tom's made a good man, Trudy. He don't need no Meribah shoes t' make him better. I'd hold that barefoot boy up against any grow'd man in boots. There ain't none better than your Tom, nor stronger hearted. Nawsir." The old woman exhaled slowly and shook her head.

"I want the best for him."

"Shoes ain't what he needs mos'."

"They need so much."

"Right now Tom needs him a mama who ain't et up with worry. Honey, the only thing worth anything that you can give your young'uns is a heart that believes God is gonna make a way through the wilderness. If you believe it, God will do it and they will see it. Then someday when hard times come for them . . . an' hard times surely come for ever' mother's chil' one day . . . then your babies, all grow'd up, will remember they had a prayin' mama! They will remember a God that answered! Thank You Jeeesus!"

"Tom still needs shoes."

Willa Mae shrugged. It was a small request for a great God to fill, was it not? "God ain't gonna shoot no brogans down from heaven, but He will make a way if you ask Him where there is a cobbler who will make that chil' some shoes an' sell 'em for what you can pay."

"I can pay one old clock."

"Reckon God didn't want you payin' them Jenson Philistines even one minute hand."

Trudy felt herself redden with renewed shame. "I should not have gone."

"No, you shouldn't of. But now that's done an' over. So start thinkin' on what's real. Worries ain't real. Worries is like a little ol' bullfrog that puffs hisself up so big he finally blows up an' jus' leaves the mess behind." She smacked her hands together. "Only one thing real that I know. Only one thing to count on, an' that is that God is faithful." She held her hands palm up and raised her eyes to the rafters as if some message was written there. Her old voice quavered as she got filled with the Holy Ghost. "Hold on! Hold on! I got me a word of knowledge a-comin'!" She closed her eyes and hummed a bit, then began to speak. "Trudy, Trudy, *Trudy!* Honey! Lawd say . . . He gonna make a way where you cain't see nothin' but briars an' brambles! He gonna pro-vide for y'all when you look out your winder an' see nothin' but locusts eatin' ever'thing you counted on! Oh, Jesus! *Jeeesus!* Amen and *Amen!* Glooory an' praise be!"

With that, the vision came to an end. It was a short vision and did not provide all the information Trudy hoped for.

Trudy, who had not seen or heard anything in the rafters, merely blinked at Willa Mae. "Anything about Birch?"

Willa Mae sucked in her breath and held it as if she might hear another little word about Birch and Jefferson. "Nope." She exhaled loudly. "They ain't in this vision, but they'll be seein' stars an' angels floatin' 'round after I lay hold of 'em."

"Is that . . . everything?" Trudy asked.

Willa Mae lowered her eyes and clasped Trudy's hands. The old woman grinned, puckering her lips around almost toothless gums. "No, it ain't entirely all, honey. This here is a word from me. . . . Go home an' put that ol' clock back on the wall. Feed them boys scrambled eggs, an' thank Jesus y'all gots eggs an' hens t' lay 'em. Put them young'uns t' bed. Then stay up an' pray all night if you has to. Pray your problems through till you has peace. Then . . . well, as the Good Book say, Joy cometh in the mornin'!"

Trudy returned the old clock to the faded rectangle on the wall. Tom did not ask where she had been or why she had returned with the clock. When Bobby opened his mouth to ask, Trudy saw Tom nudge his brother hard in the ribs. The failed trip to Meribah remained unexplained.

Yet another supper of scrambled eggs on thin toast was eaten in silence. Surely tomorrow the letter would come. Tomorrow there would be real food on the table, shoes for Tom's first day of school. To save on kerosene, the boys went to bed immediately after eating. They prayed for Birch and for Jefferson and for the letter to come.

Trudy sat in the dark parlor and listened to their soft, excited voices as they talked in low tones about the wonders of California. Could it be that they did not know how desperate the situation had become? No letter from Birch could mean only that something was terribly wrong.

At last the boys drifted off, and the sound of their conversation was replaced by the black clouds of worry and doubt that filled Trudy's mind.

Birch. Jefferson. California. These larger concerns receded as every thought came back to the issue of simply surviving until Birch sent for them. Trudy considered the meager supply of feed left for the laying hens. Without feed there would be no eggs. And there was still the problem of Tom's shoes. Tomorrow was the first day of the school year.

She had not found an answer in Meribah; only humiliation. What was left? She thought of Willa Mae's advice.

Trudy clasped her hands and tried to pray. But her words seemed fragile things that bounced back from the ceiling and shattered all around her until at last her requests dissolved into an angry accusation.

"You created the whole world! You sent us water when I needed a miracle. But shoes for my boy are too much to ask?"

Silence. The old clock tocked from the wall. The breathing of Tom and Bobby filled the empty spaces. No answer came to tell her where school shoes could be found between tonight and tomorrow morning.

The clock chimed two A.M. Trudy lay on the horsehair sofa and dozed. "Shoes," she murmured.

And then she was walking between heaps of beautiful brogans all size eight. There were shelves of open yellow shoe boxes and stacks of smooth new leather stored in the tack room and smelling like saddle soap and freshly oiled harness. Birch and Tom were there, working to repair a broken headstall.

Tom looked up in frustration. "You can do it better."

Birch said, "I'm not gonna do this for you, Tom. You can do it yourself."

Her own voice spoke, "A good father will not do for you what you can do yourself. He will only show you how."

She awoke to the single stroke of the quarter hour. How long had she been sleeping? Lighting the lampwick with an ember from the cookstove, Trudy held the light aloft, illuminating the clock face. Two-fifteen. And she had been dreaming. What was it? Somehow it seemed important. She closed her eyes and willed herself to remember the images.

The pictures in her dream were clear in her mind. The shoes had not been in the mercantile store in Meribah, but heaped up in a corner of the tack room right in the Tucker barn.

Trudy hurried from the house, following the path to the lean-to at the side of the barn where the tack was stored. The hinges groaned as she pushed back the door. Light fell on Birch's saddles, which sat astride an oak barrel in the corner. Harness and bridles dripped from the rafters. The clean, warm smell of saddle soap filled her senses as she sank to her knees in front of Birch's scuffed green tack box. She pried open the latch and threw back the lid, revealing a tray of brushes, tins of leather polish, saddle soap, a razor-edged cutting tool, a leather punch, an awl, and a roll of heavy waxed thread for stitching damaged tack. Lifting the tray, she discovered a bundle of thick new leather, tanned to a dark, smooth chestnut color. Tucked beneath the hide was the metal shoe last upon which the brogans of young Birch Tucker had once been made.

With a wondering look, Trudy held the roll of hide up in the light.

"I will be the cobbler," she whispered. "And You will show me how."

Wearing new brogans as fine as any shoes he had ever owned, Tom pulled Bobby in the handcart to Shiloh School.

"Where'd she get 'em?" Bobby stared at Tom's finely clad feet.

Tom suspected his mama had bought them in Meribah. "Hartford, where else? The dry-goods store."

The leather was thick yet soft, like the boots worn by the president of the Rock Island Railroad when he came out to Shiloh to view the opening of the rail spur to the Jenson mine.

"Don't look like any old brogans I ever saw in the dry-goods. Bet she—"

"Probably ordered them from the Sears and Roebuck," Tom finished, not allowing Bobby to complete the thought that their mama might have set foot in enemy territory.

Bobby shrugged, then shouted his howdy to Squirrel and Pigpen, who waited for them at the gate of the Hocott farm.

"Hey, Possum!" Squirrel gave a wave, hefted his rucksack over his shoulder, and jogged toward them. He was always overly excited on the first day of every school year.

Barney remained rooted in the dry, brittle grass beside the road.

So similar were the boys in looks and dress that they might have all four come from the same house. Last year's bib overalls were patched on the knees and backside. Shirts were newly laundered and ironed. Haircuts were back-porch jobs. In spite of the cut in Dee Brown's prices, it had been a long time since anyone had been able to sit tall and proud at the barbershop. Shiloh haircuts now consisted of boys perched on barrels, mixing bowls perched on heads, and a pair of scissors wielded by mothers determined to save every possible penny.

There was only one difference, in fact, between Tom and Bobby Tucker and their neighbors: Squirrel and Barney Hocott were barefoot. Catfish Pierce, running across the flat, dried-up pasture joined the group. He, too, had no footgear.

Squirrel stared openly at the beautiful new brogans on Tom's feet. His eyebrows went up questioningly. He exchanged looks with Barney, who shrugged and looked away.

It was Catfish who finally broached the subject.

"Never saw shoes like that before." He gave a low whistle. "'Cept mebbe in the wish book. Rich man's shoes."

The comment embarrassed Tom. He could not think of a reply. Nor could he admit that he thought his mother had purchased the shoes on credit in Meribah.

Squirrel remarked in an injured tone, "My pa says y'all done right good with the Dreamland Cafe."

Bobby chirped, "Real good. Goin' swell until the night riders burned it down. Don't make no difference though. We're set. Ham and bacon left over in the smokehouse and . . ."

"Shut up, Mutt," Tom muttered to Bobby.

Bobby continued, "We're gonna get new denims soon's we can get into town."

Tom flushed at the lie. He wished he was barefoot like the other Shiloh kids. What was it his dad always used to say? Never count your money in front of a poor man. Since there was no money in the Tucker wallet, maybe that advice also went for wearing shoes when everyone else was barefoot.

"I ain't never saw shoes like that b'fore," Catfish repeated "I gotta wear last year's boots, an' Mama's got those put up till cold weather. I purely do admire them brogans."

Bobby fell deeper into his folly: "Dad sent 'em from California."

Tom turned and shot his brother a hard look of warning. He jerked the tongue of the handcart, bouncing the front end up in the air and letting the rear wheels drop into a deep rut.

"Must have a real good job." Catfish gave his head a shake.

"The best," Bobby bragged, oblivious to Tom's disapproval. "Not like here."

Barney Hocott challenged Bobby. "My mom just got a letter from Ida Grier. Missus Grier says they met up with your pa an' Jefferson Canfield too."

Tom halted. "My dad?"

Barney sneered. "They rode out to California with a buncha bums. Et supper at the Grier house. Didn't have no job nor money neither. They're camped out down on the riverbank."

Bobby stammered, "That . . . that was before . . ."

"Before?" Barney scoffed. "Before they got the worst jobs in the oil fields? Even ol' Amos Grier left the job your daddy's got! Cleanin' muck outta the bottom of oil tanks. That's a fine Californy job for you!"

Tom stayed put while his friends walked on. Bobby kicked his braces against the wooden side of the cart in protest.

"We'll be late. . . ."

"Shut up," Tom menaced in a low voice. "Shut up, or I'll tell 'em what a liar you are."

Bobby bit his lip and looked away. "They ate at the Griers'. Griers was the poorest folks in the whole county."

"They ain't anymore," Tom spat out. "We are."

Squirrel turned and called for him to come. But Tom told them to go ahead, said his new shoes were hurting his feet and he wanted to wade in the creek for a few minutes. When the other boys had rounded the bend, Tom slipped off the new brogans and put them into his rucksack before starting off again for school.

Barefoot and downcast, Tom returned from school. As he entered the kitchen where his mother ironed the laundry, the expression on her face told him that there was still no later word from Birch or Jefferson.

In a joyless voice he told her about the letter from Ida Grier to Mrs. Hocott, about the fact that Jefferson and Dad had taken the worst job in the oil fields. Trudy hung her head and wept.

"They're happy tears," she explained.

Only then did she notice his bare feet.

"Did the shoes hurt?" she asked.

"Bobby told the fellers that Dad sent them from California. I figgered you got them in Meribah. Mama, not one other kid in Shiloh's got new shoes. It's not right I got such fine shoes an' the others don't. Lemme go barefooted till the weather turns off cold. But I want you to know I don't like it that you made some deal with those Meribah pirates."

More tears.

Tom did not know if these were happy or sad.

"I'm proud of you for that, Tom," Trudy said.

So these were proud tears. After explaining to him about her prayer and the dream and the all-night struggle with leather and a cobbler's last, he was relieved.

"I wouldn't ever wear them if you got them from Meribah."

"Not Meribah. Your brogans were intended to be a new seat for your father's saddle, Tom. It is fine of you to consider the feelings of your friends. I was too proud. Of course, you may wait and wear your shoes when the weather is cold."

Neither of them mentioned their hope that they might be in California by the time cold weather set in.

There was, of course, the matter of Bobby's deception to deal with.

Trudy allowed Tom to put off his after-school chores. Bobby, braced and captive in the handcart, was transported by Trudy and Tom to the Hocott farm. As Bobby blushed and fidgeted, Trudy explained to Mrs. Hocott in front of the Hocott brothers that neither she nor Willa Mae nor Lily had heard any word at all from their men beyond a single penny postcard announcing their arrival in California and their promise to send funds home. She asked to see the letter from Ida Grier.

Bobby's humiliation was absolute; the lesson successful.

As Barney and Othar glared derisively at him, Trudy read aloud the paragraph that related the Griers' encounter with Birch and Jefferson. Trudy copied down the Grier address, then left to carry the news on to Lily and Willa Mae at Grandma Amos's store. Now, at least, they could write to the Griers. Perhaps Amos would track down Birch and Jefferson, telling them that the folks back home needed some word.

Bobby was fed and put to bed before the sun was down.

In the soft pastels of dusk, Trudy scattered the chicken feed on the floor of the coop while Tom cleaned the straw in the nesting boxes. The hens gathered around Trudy as she called them each by name. Tom tried not to think about what would happen when the chicken feed ran out in another week. If the California letter did not come by then, they would be forced to sell off the household furniture piece by piece, for whatever price they could get, in order to survive. It had come to that. Perhaps Bobby was unaware of the desperation of their circumstances, but the burden of it had settled heavily on Tom's shoulders.

Trudy knelt and held out a handful of grain to a reticent hen named Nellie, who hung back while the others rushed in to grab up the feed. "Nellie is not laying like she used to." There was implied in this comment that Nellie might have to be put to other use.

"She'll be all right when we're feeding like we used to."

"I do hope so. When your father's letter comes . . ." Her voice trailed off.

Tom took up the slack. "Persimmons are nearly ripe."

"We have no sugar left, or I would make a pudding."

"Possums'll be in the persimmon patch. I was thinking that me and Rosey could go hunting, bring home a possum. It's still two bits for the hide at Brother Williams's, and fresh meat on the table for us."

"The possum will not like it much, but Nellie would be grateful, Tom." The chicken pecked every last particle of grain from Trudy's hand, then clucked contentedly as if she somehow understood that the conversation concerned her. Trudy added, "You have grown up into a man this year, Tom. I would not have wished it on you so young, but I want you to know I am glad you have done it so well. I cannot imagine how we would have managed without you."

He did not know how to respond, so he dug into the nesting boxes with renewed vigor.

The throaty grumble of an automobile engine broke the pleasant silence between mother and son. Tom recognized the sound of Caroline Jenson's Buick before it turned onto the drive. It was followed by two other cars, one of which bore the official gold-star emblem of the Meribah constable.

"What could she want with us now?" Trudy asked wearily, shaking the seed hulls from her apron. She started out to meet the vehicles. "Quickly Tom, run put on your new brogans."

He obeyed her, dashing into the kitchen and slipping on the fine new leather shoes. He was at her side again before another thought came to him. "Let me get the gun. They won't bother us."

"There is nothing left to protect from them, Tom. They as much as own this farm, but they can't touch our souls, can they? We are not the land or the house or the barn. They cannot steal who we are inside unless we let their meanness rob our joy." She looked up at the hills and then at the copper rooster on the roof.

Tom knew the farm was as good as gone. Another few weeks, and the note was due. What more could Caro-line want? What more could the Jensons do than they had already done?

Tom saw Trudy glance down the hill at the ashes of Dreamland and the small white crosses on either side of the creek. She put her hands on her hips, and Tom stood beside her, the pitchfork in his hands.

"Dream burners," Trudy remarked with detachment to the approaching vehicles.

Tom remembered the vagrant family turned out of the Sully Faulk house, the torches thrown through the windows and the place burned down so no one could ever use it again. "Why do they do it?" Tom asked.

Trudy smiled a Cheshire-cat smile, as though she knew some great secret about Garrick and Caro-line Jenson that would explain everything. "This is not about property. It never was."

The small caravan of cars pulled up in front of the house. Caro-line, her face set in a hard, angry squint, looked directly at Trudy, then looked away again with an expression of cool disgust. She climbed from her vehicle and motioned to the Meribah constable and his deputy, who hitched up their trousers and strode in identical swaggers of self-importance to stand beside her. No greeting or as much as a nod of the head to Trudy and Tom, who still stood beside the chicken coop.

The third vehicle held two men in business suits. They carried clipboards and looked at the buildings and scribbled as they walked toward Caro-line.

"Why are they here?" Tom whispered.

Caro-line's head jerked up. "I can answer that, young man. Your mother was trying to sell or trade household goods in exchange for merchandise. Boots was it? Size eight."

Tom took a step forward. He longed to rush at the woman and knock her down, or plunge the pitchfork into her icy heart.

Trudy put a restraining hand on his shoulder. "Dignity, Tom," she said in a soothing voice.

Caro-line gestured toward the new brogans. "I see you succeeded in finding someone who wanted to trade shoes for my property."

Tom spat, "Tell her the truth about my brogans, Mama! Tell her where they came from!"

Trudy's cat smile returned. "Truth is not an issue that matters to Missus Jenson."

Caro-line's lip curled in a sneer. "This is truth enough for any court. The contract your husband signed states that everything but the clothes on your back is collateral to our loan, clearly Jenson property. To sell or trade anything away before you meet the obligations of this note is strictly unlawful according to our agreement. Breach of contract requires that all sums owed to Jenson Consolidated become immediately due and payable."

Caro-line nodded at the constable, who removed a folded document from his chest pocket and approached Trudy with it. "This is to give y'all notice. Strictly legal. Auction of all household furnishings and etcetera a week from next Saturday. Y'all have thirty days after that to vacate the property. We're just here to make an inventory."

Trudy accepted the document with a slight inclination of her head. "I have seen how it works. Other farms. No need to explain further." She stepped aside and let the itemization proceed, with one small exception. To Tom she whispered, "Go to the back porch. Take Rosey and tie her up in the outhouse."

The inventory was completed before the sun set. Trudy and Tom watched in silence as the Jenson vehicles drove back the way they had come.

Tom said solemnly, "We had fun here before they wrecked it, didn't we?"

"California, Tom! Think of it! A lovely new place . . ."

Tom recalled the words of Catfish Pierce as the outcast family had rolled unsteadily away from the smoke of the Sully Faulk house: *Folks like that don't have any place to go; they just go from place to place.*

"We have a place to go," he said.

"We have one another, Tom. Your dad, me, you, Bobby. And everything else? Would I trade you for anything?"

Tom understood that his mother's mourning had finally come to an end. Her hope had turned to the Promised Land, and now she was just waiting to say farewell to the Shiloh autumn. As for Garrick and Caro-line Jenson, when Trudy considered them at all, Tom sensed that her emotion was simply pity.

They were the vagrants, the ones with nowhere to go. They were nothing but pathetic souls, moving from place to place, crushing the life out of whatever came within their grasp.

C H A P T E R   3 9

With less than two months to go till election day, Franklin Delano Roosevelt was touring the western states. He was on a grueling schedule of speeches and whistle-stops, having spent two days each in Colorado and Utah and aiming now for Washington and Oregon. President Hoover, meanwhile, was said to be planning his campaign—an effort that might take him as far west as Ohio.

Hank Correy's tank-cleaning crews laughed when they heard the comparison of strategies. As Birch said, "Maybe it's just as well Hoover ain't comin'. He don't know he's already lost!"

Two weeks had passed since Jeff and Birch had gone to work for Superior Tank Cleaning. After sixteen steel tanks and uncounted tons of sludge, gunk, and b.s., it was finally payday . . . the first real payday since their arrival in California.

"When we get paid tonight," Birch calculated, "even after takin' out what Mister Correy advanced us to buy grub, we'll still be up nineteen dollars. What say we keep on eatin' our own cookin' and send our families twelve of that?"

"Make it fourteen," Jeff amended. "I don't mind beans. Just don't make me never look at no avocado."

After finding out that the fruit could be eaten raw, the two men had peeled and consumed the entire lug of alligator pears in one day, with predictable consequences. "Made me feel green," Jeff concluded, "and that ain't no lie."

"Made you *look* green," Birch corrected, "and that ain't no small trick! All right, no avocados. But we eat on the cheap till next payday, and we send fourteen dollars home after work today."

The tank waiting to be mucked out was the largest yet undertaken by Correy's workforce since Birch and Jeff signed on. Eighty thousand gallons in capacity, it was half again larger than the biggest they had yet cleaned. Nor was its size its worst feature.

"They let this go way too long," Correy complained. "It's all silted up. Look in there; there's a good two feet of b.s. on that floor. This calls for the tractor."

"You got a tractor to work in the tank?" Birch asked with astonishment. "How's it get inside?"

"Don't let him get your hopes up," Burt admonished. "What he means is we shovel a load onto this board, see? The rope knotted through that hole in the plank goes out to Correy's bumper. He revs up that old fossil of a truck and pulls the load over to the hatch. He calls it a tractor 'cause he thinks it sounds more pro-fesh-unal."

"That'll be enough outta you, Burt," Correy warned. "'Less you'd rather be totin' the b.s. clear across the tank one shovelful at a time."

"Not me! Let's get the tractor up and goin'!"

The morning shift went smoothly enough. The men took turns working in pairs, one team loading the improvised sled and the other scraping the material out through the hatch. Given the size of the undertaking, Correy did not even gripe at them to hurry or berate them for resting in between trips of the tractor.

About two o'clock the outside temperature reached ninety degrees, and this pushed the inside heat to well over a hundred and ten. The extra depth of the gunk through which the crew had to slog added to the exhaustion they all felt. Birch and Jack were the team loading the sled, while Jeff and Burt stood near the entry to unload it.

Birch accidentally bumped into the younger man. He apologized, but Jack made no response. When Birch looked more closely, he saw that Jack was standing motionless, leaning heavily on the rake and swaying. "You all right?" he asked.

"Feel . . . sick . . . need air," Jack gasped, gulping in between words to keep from retching.

"Just let us get that pile unloaded," Burt called, "then you can trade us places. Stand clear of the board. Okay," he yelled to Correy outside in the truck, "take her away."

Birch saw, too late, that Jack's foot still rested on a corner of the sled. He shouted a warning, but the truck was already in gear and pulling the load forward.

Jack fought to keep his balance, trying to catch himself on the greasy rake handle, which shot out of his grasp. He fell, sprawling face first into the sludge.

Immediately he floundered like a drowning man, flinging his arms around and kicking wildly as he attempted to get his feet back under him on the slippery surface. His hands tore wildly at the grease that filled his mouth, but the same motion pushed the sediment up into his nose.

Jack made a choking, strangling sound, his eyes wide with fright. He really was drowning, unable to draw breath through either mouth or nostrils. "Get clear away from him!" Burt bellowed. "He'll drag you down, too! Correy, Correy! We got a mud sucker!" With that Burt jumped out through the opening.

Paying no heed to the warning, Birch grabbed the struggling worker by the arms and tried to lift him upright. As Burt had predicted, the terrified man seized Birch around the neck, and the two men toppled over together.

Seeing what was happening, Jeff plunged deeper into the tank. It took all his strength to pull Birch free of Jack's frenzied clutch, even though all three men were greased up to their shoulders. Birch's mouth was clogged with sludge, but his nose was not, and he was able to keep from panicking. A moment later Jack's eyes rolled back in his head and he fell down again, unconscious.

Jeff and Birch took an arm apiece and dragged Jack to the hatch, where Birch stepped out to receive the limp form that Jeff passed to him. Once out in the air, Birch set about sponging Jack's face with rags soaked in gasoline to cut through the gunk while Jeff pumped his chest.

For what seemed like an endless amount of time there was no response. Then Jack's chest heaved, and he coughed and gagged. His arms waved feebly, still trying to fight his way back to life. Birch switched rags to some soaked in the warm, sour water. He wiped the boy's eyes and helped him wash out his mouth.

When Birch and Jeff looked up from reviving Jack, they saw Correy standing with his hands on his hips. "I told you if a man goes down to get away from him," he remarked coldly.

"He would've died."

"He mighta taken both of you with him, too," Correy said. "Draw your time," he added. "All three of you are through."

Even though he had fired them, Hank Correy still gave Birch, Jeff, and Jack a ride out of the oil fields to Oildale. Burt refused to go back into the superheated air of the tank if it meant working alone, so there was no more to be done until Superior Tank Cleaning hired replacements. Halfway back to town, Correy regretted his rashness and told Birch and Jeff they could keep their jobs, but they refused.

Burt had already told Jeff about an opening over at Pegasus Oil and said he was certain Jeff and Birch could catch on there. When asked why he did not leave tank cleaning behind and take a new spot himself, Burt got an amused look on his face and said that there were worse things than mucking out tanks. Further explanation he declined to give. Birch declared that nothing could possibly be worse than what they had been doing for the past two weeks. Besides, he refused to work for someone who would fire a man for saving another's life.

Back at the one-room shed of Superior's headquarters, Mr. Correy counted out their pay and dismissed them. "You know," Jeff concluded, "I feel better already. Let's go get us another job, then mail the money home to our gals."

They set off walking toward Oil Center and the offices of Pegasus Oil. Unlike Superior Tank Cleaning, Pegasus was a production company, and its business involved more than one specialty operation. Pegasus operated drilling crews, pulling crews, pipeline repair teams, and other squads of men. Pegasus was involved with all aspects of getting petroleum from the depths of the earth and transporting it to refineries, where the big dealers like Standard Oil took over the process.

Pegasus even maintained a separate office for each of its divisions; a grand way of saying that each crew had a foreman and each foreman had his own ten-by-twelve slope-roofed shed in which to do his paperwork.

The main street of Oil Center was three parched miles out in the countryside. Birch and Jeff walked there on dirt road flanked by sheds and Quonset huts and abandoned tanks that had been cut up and turned into storehouses. Jeff remarked that he could tell when they had reached the town because the gravel had been sprayed with road oil to keep down the dust. This was laughable since the thousands of acres surrounding the cluster of shacks was all dust; oiling one strip of road did not seem to have made much difference.

They were directed to the accounting office, another one-room wooden building mounted on skids so it could be moved as the need arose. Behind the single window in the front wall sat the chief clerk of Pegasus Oil's Kern River Field operation. In charge of hiring, firing, and seeing that daily work schedules were drawn up and followed, Perry James was a boyish-faced man who looked even younger than his thirty years. His neatly trimmed blond hair and polished shoes looked out of place in an oil company office, but part of the time he was required to report to the general manager of Pegasus Oil, whose suite was located in a four-story brick building in Bakersfield.

"What can I do for you gentlemen?" James said cheerfully, looking up from a column of figures on a hand-cranked adding machine. "Are you here about the call for shooters?"

Birch looked at Jeff. Neither had any idea what a shooter was or did in oil field parlance; neither cared. That the work would be hot, dirty, and dangerous was a given; every aspect of oil-field life was. "Reckon we are," Birch said. "What's it pay?"

"That depends," James said, a touch primly. "Do you have experience?"

"Worked on a rig back in Oklahoma," Birch replied, "and we been swampin' tanks here for Superior till we heard about this openin'."

James frowned. "But no real experience handling explosives? Well, that's all right in the transport end of the work. The foreman, Harlan Sleeves, is very knowledgeable. I'll take you over to meet him. Unless he disapproves, you'll start tomorrow at thirty cents an hour."

Explosives? This was not anything Birch and Jeff wanted to mess with, but thirty cents an hour was an increase over the two bits Correy had paid. Jeff nudged Birch on the elbow. "Get us out of the tent and get the gals out here that much quicker," he said softly. "Let's do it."

"Can we meet the boss right now?" Birch asked. "Then we gotta get back to the post office before it closes."

"Writing home?" James asked agreeably. "Maybe I can save you a trip and some money, too. Here, use this notepad if you like. The last mail collection at my office is not for another hour. You can even use a company envelope," he volunteered, reaching in a drawer of the flat-topped oak desk. "It's already got the postage on it."

"That is mighty nice of you," Birch said, drawing the pad toward him and licking the end of the pencil. "Dear Trudy and All," he wrote, "Here is the first of the cash. We got a better paying job, so you can get your train tickets paid for that much sooner. . . ."

"Call me Red," the head shooter urged. "Red Sleeves, get me? There was a 'Pache chief name of Mangas Colorado, which is Mexican for Red Sleeves. An' that's funny 'cause I'm part Indian myself, only Cherokee. What'd you say your names was?"

Harlan "Red" Sleeves was an older man, probably in his early fifties. His cheeks were lined with deep wrinkles that creased his long, narrow face on both sides, accenting his long, thin nose. He smiled easily, and when talking, which was almost continuously, he tugged at a graying lock of black hair that hung in the center of his forehead.

"I'll leave you with Mister Sleeves then," said Perry James, escaping from Red's prattle by heading back toward the Pegasus office. "He'll fill you in on the job. Don't worry about your letter. I'll take care of it for you."

Red's headquarters was not in the line of one-room shacks back on the road through Oil Center. He was located about half a mile farther out in the sagebrush and tumbleweeds. The windowless building, half sunken in the sand, was built of telephone poles stacked up in the fashion of a log cabin. The air behind the solid-steel door was cooler than the surroundings but pungent with the sharp smell of acid.

"Just mixin' up a new batch of soup," Red explained. "I always do this job myself, till I get to know my crew real well. Either of you ever cooked nitro before?"

"No. No," Birch and Jeff said, fending off with outstretched palms any thought that they might know how to concoct the explosive mixture. They looked with cautious interest at the wooden shelves holding rows of ten-quart copper cans and the enamel-lined vat full of smelly, oily yellow fluid.

"Well, it's real easy. Five to one is what does it, get me? Five pounds of acid brew to one of the glycerin. Pour it slow, and it won't blow, that's my motto. I usually mix up enough for one job at a time."

"How much is that?" Birch asked. "One job's worth?"

"Oh, figger about six hundred pounds," Red replied with no more drama than if he had been speaking of a single firecracker. "Say, you fellers really are brand new, ain'tcha?"

Birch and Jeff nodded.

"All right, here's the ticket," Red explained. "Say a drilling crew finds good indications at four thousand feet, but the well only pumps ten barrels a day. That's when they send for us, get me? The charge cracks little channels in the formation for the oil to flow, ups the ante to fifty, maybe seventy-five barrels from the same well."

"And it takes six hundred pounds of nitro to do that?" Jeff asked. "Seems like a whole lot."

"Oh that's just your average charge," Red continued. "Soup is funny stuff. That amount does the trick down in the shale. But up here, on top of the ground, why shoot fire, sonny, if that amount right there in my mixing tub went off, my front door would land in the Pegasus office in downtown Bakersfield and they'd find your earlobe over in Shafter—that's twenty miles or so—if they found anything left at all."

"You don't mean to say we are s'posed to know how to set off this stuff?" Birch demanded.

"Oh no, sonny, I do the shootin'. You're just my assistants."

Birch looked relieved.

"What's that mean 'xactly?" Jeff asked with suspicion.

"Didn't Perry tell ya? You two load the truck with the cans of soup and drive it out to the well, then you load the torpedo before we lower it down. Just remember," he added, "there's old shooters, and there's careless shooters, but there ain't no old, careless shooters. Get me?"

Tom wandered from pile to pile of belongings sorted and stacked in the front yard: treadle sewing machine, sewing basket, pinking shears, and a bolt of cloth in one heap; saddle, bridle, headstall, mule collars in another; and so on, till all the Tucker worldly goods lay open for display, categorized and labeled. The antique clock sat in a rocking chair beside the front porch as if presiding over the dismemberment of the home.

Some things were so commonplace as to revive no special memories in Tom: butcher knives ground and sharpened so many times that they were slender shadows of what they had been when new, a saw with a broken handle, a washboard.

But other items, though just as undistinguished, caused him to alternate between great pain and anger. Tom clenched his fists when he came to a pile of Trudy's books, ruthlessly pulled from their neatly ordered shelves and dumped in the dust. He remembered a time when he had been reprimanded for carelessly tearing a single page. Now here they lay like used straw from the barn.

Stopping in front of a small wooden chair with a wicker seat, Tom recalled that it had been his when he was very small. Of course, it had been passed along to Bobby and later Joey. Still, it had been Tom's first, back in Oklahoma, before they had ever moved to Shiloh. There was no way to take it away and hide it. And anyway, what good was it to any of them now?

But it was at the stack of garden implements that his feelings welled up and overflowed the stern self-control Trudy had demanded of him. In with the spades and the rakes and the wicker gathering baskets was a single dirt-covered spoon. It had been Joey's radish planting and watering tool. In a second Tom had stooped and seized the tarnished silver object with the bent handle and stuffed it into his pocket.

Doc Brown put his hand on Tom's shoulder, making the boy jump. "Joey's?" he asked softly.

"Yes," Tom said with an edge of defiance in his tone.

Doc shook his head and patted Tom's back. "Take it," he said. "It's not a possession; it's a memory. And they can't auction your memories."

There were three arrays of people at the Tucker place, and they did not mingle at all. Standing in sorrowful support, gathered around Trudy and Bobby in the space between the house and the barn, were all their friends from Shiloh and Hartford: the Brown brothers, Willa Mae and Lily, Brother Williams and Boomer. Tom could not help but notice how much smaller this group was now than at the time of the Penny Auction Rebellion. The Griers were gone, as were the Palmers and the Woods.

Still present, but with downturned pessimistic faces were the Faraby clan and the Hocotts.

A second crew also stood and watched: the Jensons and their cronies. Garrick stood, arms folded, the place where his chin should have been pointing skyward in evident satisfaction. Caro-line, her mouth puckered in a frown, scanned from side to side, never looking at people, always inspecting things. Nearby stood the two Meribah constables and the pair of clerks who would tally the bloodletting lest a single drop escape collection.

Finally there were the buyers. Wandering through the accumulation of a family's life were the people Tom thought of as vultures, faceless men from outside the Shiloh circle who pretended to sneer at the plow and cultivator, hard-eyed women who pulled open desk drawers and inspected teacups with critical eyes.

That the rules of fair play and neighborliness did not extend to the forced sale at the Tucker's was underscored by the identity of the auctioneer: Dudley Steel. "What am I bid for this parlor table?" he intoned.

"One dollar," Doc said.

"Two dollars," raised a rail-thin woman from Little Rock.

"Two twenty-five," said Doc.

"Three," retorted the woman.

"Three ten," Doc offered.

"Five," said a little round man from Tulsa.

"Sold," concluded Steel.

The morning and the afternoon went on in this fashion. The Sebastian County neighbors tried to repeat the success of the Penny Auction, but it could not be done. There had been no way to prevent thirty interested buyers from following the Jenson advertising and arriving at the Tucker farm, no way to intimidate this auctioneer. And nobody had much money left to bid in the first place.

"These here books," Steel said with disdain, "I'm gonna let 'em go by the dozen. The first lot includes some fool versifyin' by Walt some-body and a lot of nonsense called the Count of Monday Crispo. Who'll make it a dollar?"

"A DOLLAR!" shouted Boomer.

"What'er you doin', Boomer?" Brother asked in alarm. "You don't even read."

"MIZ TRUDY ALWAYS READ ME SOME PURTY WORDS WHEN SHE COME TO THE LIVERY," Boomer retorted. "AN' IT'S MY DOLLAR!"

"His only dollar," Brother mused aloud.

"Dollar twenty-five," said an oily-looking wholesaler from Fort Smith.

Despite the lack of ice, Trudy moved regally through the crowd, dispensing tea to her friends. She held her head erect and moved with grace and dignity. Tom was proud of her. Caro-line Jenson gestured angrily at the pitcher, and Steel literally took it from Trudy's hands to be auctioned.

Trudy finished pouring the rest of the contents into Dan Faraby's glass before surrendering the container. "Here you are," she said loftily.

Tom gave her a thumb's-up sign.

"How about that weathervane?" yelled the Fort-Smith dealer, gesturing at the copper rooster still up on the roof. He hooked his thumbs in his paisley suspenders as he leaned, as if to keep the weight of his slicked-down hair from pulling him over backward.

"ONE DOLLAR!" Boomer yelled.

"I'll give five," responded the paisley suspenders.

"It's not for sale," Caro-line Jenson asserted.

"It has to be!" Doc roared. "The terms of the court document specify everything."

"Very well then," Caro-line replied coldly. "Ten dollars."

"I'm sorry, honey," Willa Mae said, showing a handful of coins to Trudy. "We tried to raise enough to save that rooster for you, but the most we could get was nine and some change."

"How about these fine laying hens?" Steel said, gesturing toward the chickens, who squawked unhappily at being confined in a small coop.

Tom thought about the two missing hens and was secretly glad that they were gone. Even being eaten by a fox seemed preferable, more honorable somehow, to being sold into slavery after having been family. The thought made him especially relieved that Rosey was safely hidden at Willa Mae's.

Delbert Simpson's butcher father, Charles, waved his hand. "Ten dollars for the lot."

"Ten and four bits," put in Brother Williams.

"Eleven," replied the butcher.

"Eleven an' . . . an' . . . dog take it." Brother groaned. "He's raised me out."

Tom watched his mother's face as the hens were sold, but her expression never wavered.

The family heirloom clock was nearly the last item brought to the block. Tom saw Willa Mae circulating among the crowd in one direction, Lily carrying the baby in the other. Mrs. Faraby nudged Dan, who dug into his pocket and handed something to Lily. Willa Mae was met by Dee Brown, who pressed something into her hands. Doc tapped on Mr. Hocott's shoulder, received a quarter, then bent to receive a penny from Squirrel's hands.

The thin-as-a-fence-post woman offered five dollars.

"Five fifty," responded Willa Mae.

"Eight," said the secondhand furniture merchant from Tulsa.

"Nine," proposed the dealer from Fort Smith.

"Twelve dollars and thirty-five cents," proclaimed Willa Mae. There was no further bidding.

"Goin' once, goin'. . ."

"SOLD!" Boomer yelled, snatching the clock from Steel's hands and presenting it to Trudy, who smiled and nodded to all her friends. Tom could see that she did not trust herself to speak.

Moments later, the auction concluded with the sale of the mules. To his own surprise, Brother Williams held the winning offer for one of the pair. "You gotta have some transport for Bobby," he said kindly. "All by hisself, that ol' mule will be just fine on Bermudy-grass pasture, till you don't need him no more."

"I'll take good care of him for you," Trudy acknowledged. Tom could see that the strain of the day held his mother in its talons, but she had not broken, had not given the Jensons the satisfaction of seeing their power cause pain.

A terrified squawk came from the row of parked cars. It was suddenly and sharply cut off, only to be followed by another and another. Charles Simpson had taken possession of his property, the twenty laying hens. Methodically, studying the birds with a practiced eye, he was picking up each hen and calmly wringing its neck. Delbert, pressed into service in the butcher shop since losing his job at Hartford Federal Bank, was furiously plucking each corpse until a small cloud of feathers filled the air.

Trudy looked once, then walked rapidly into the now-bare house. She gazed neither to right nor left, and the crowd parted for her, forming an aisle that led to the front door. Tom followed right behind her. She made no sound, no noise, no comment, until shutting the bedroom door firmly behind her.

Then Tom heard her sob.

CHAPTER 40

The explosives truck Birch and Jeff were allotted to haul the nitroglycerin out to the wells was actually a 1923 Studebaker Big Six four-seater Speedster. Of course, the rag top had long since disintegrated, and the rear seat had been removed to accommodate a large wooden crate. In fact, the wooden frame that had been added to hold the explosive soup was in better shape than the rest of the vehicle. It was lined three inches thick on sides and bottom with felt, and all the fittings were copper to minimize the chance of a spark. In contrast to the passengers in the decrepit automobile, who were bounced and jostled as the car rattled its way around the oil fields, the nitro cans rested securely in rubber fittings called boots, which cushioned the ride.

The back of the soup wagon held precisely twenty ten-quart cans, or the amount of Red's average load. On the two remaining doors of the jalopy large red-lettered signs proclaimed: DANGEROUS EXPLOSIVES.

Hanging from a pipe rack on the passenger side were the torpedoes, ten-foot-long steel cylinders designed to hold the liquid explosive and be lowered into the well.

"Now, this morning's first chore is to transfer the new batch of soup into the cans," Red instructed, "and carry them out to the truck."

Jeff and Birch set to work, gingerly ladling nitro out of the vat and into the copper canisters. At one point the tiniest drip splashed onto the outside of a container and clung there. Birch made as if to pick up the can anyway and take it out. "Hold it!" Red ordered. "Don't never leave even one teensy drop like that. Soup won't evaporate, get me? It'll just hang there till somethin' either wipes it off or . . . sets it off."

Birch and Jeff were very thorough thereafter at cleaning every single spot of the explosive brew, but their increased caution did not stop Red from repeating every horror story he knew. "Seen a guy once let a drip ride on the can like that. He didn't have no felt, either, and that little spot rode right there till he went to pull the cans out of the boots. Then just one little rub, and up she went. . . . Friction, get me? Set off that little drop, which let off the whole load. Left a smokin' hole in the ground and four mule shoes right where the mule was standin' and nothin' else."

"Wait a minute," Jeff said. "If there wasn't nothin' left, how d'you know what caused it?"

"Why shoot fire, sonny, what else could it be?"

Jeff had no answer for that.

Red saw that all the soup was packed correctly, then he gave Jeff and Birch directions to the well site before he drove ahead of them to talk to the gang pusher. Birch and Jeff tossed a coin and Birch lost, so he slipped behind the wheel.

"They's sure a lot of folks behind of us," Jeff remarked before they had driven a mile. A pulling rig with an A-frame–mounted gin-pole, a pair of welding trucks, another truck hauling a load of pipe, and Hank Correy's pickup and tank-cleaning crew were all stacked up behind the soup wagon.

"Must be 'cause we're only doin' five miles an hour," Birch said, hunched over the steering wheel and sweating. "I'll pull over and let 'em get by."

The well was one of the older wooden derricks, pumped by an oil-fired steam engine that ran a huge wooden walking beam. The gang pusher had cleared the floor of his men and equipment and was waiting for the shooters to get on with it.

"This is a recovery shot," Red explained. "This ol' well ain't been doin' so good since they drilled other holes around it, so we come along to fix it up. Like a dose of castor oil, get me? Now, this is a shallow well, 'bout nine hundred feet deep is all, so I'm only gonna put ten torpedoes down her. Your job," he said to Jeff and Birch, "is to move the soup from the truck to the floor and pour it in one torpedo at a time."

Birch noticed that as soon as Red said he was ready to commence working, the well crew loaded the gang truck and took off. It did not make him feel confident to watch them roar away in a cloud of dust and whirring gravel.

"Okay, Birch," Red called. "Quit wishin' you had a dull, borin' job and bring the first can."

Birch set the copper container of nitroglycerin down on the wooden timbers next to where the first torpedo hung swaying slightly from a cable suspended over the hole. Carefully pulling the cork, Birch poured the thick, oily liquid into the cylinder. Jeff and Birch took turns carrying and pouring until all ten long, slender rods had been filled and lowered into the hole. "Now I put in the clock an' batt'ry," Red said, loading a small box with protruding wires on top of the last tube. "A reg'lar time bomb, get me? I set it for, oh, an hour should be plenty, and then down she goes."

"Now we get out of here, too, right?" Birch inquired.

"Oh no, not yet, sonny! You two still gonna shovel that pile of pete gravel down the throat. Otherwise the shot blows straight back up thisaway instead of gettin' the job done."

"You want us to stand over the hole and scrape rocks down on top of nitroglycerin?" Birch asked, certain that he was missing something.

"You got it," Red confirmed. "Don't worry; there's a cave catcher. . . you seen that upside-down-umbrella-lookin' thing? . . . over the timer to hold the gravel. Just don't take more'n," the head shooter looked at his pocket watch, "fifty-five minutes to get the job done."

Birch tried to shovel gently and rapidly at the same time. It was a tough one to figure, but eventually the urgency for speed overcame the sense of caution. Forty-two minutes later the gravel overflowed the top of the casing and Birch and Jeff joined Red on the running board of the Studebaker about a hundred yards from the well.

A deep rumble came from below their feet, and then an arcing stream of rocks, dirt, and oil shot up through the scaffolding of the derrick, even topping the crown block sixty feet overhead. "That's the ticket," Red said, pleased with the result of his calculations. "Well, c'mon then, only two more to shoot today."

President Hoover's campaign was finally getting into gear. He had studied the farm situation, he said, and decided that wheat growers were in need of a subsidy. It was widely commented on around Shiloh that wheat was mostly grown in Republican states. The president had made no mention of helping cotton farmers, who lived in the Democratic South.

Of course, it was all idle discussion around the Tucker farm. Neither wheat nor cotton was growing there. In fact, there were no early morning chores left to do: no cotton to hoe, no chickens to feed, no cow to milk nor stalls to muck out. This being the case, Trudy had let the boys sleep in until six o'clock every morning since the auction.

Tom woke at five A.M. out of habit, then spent the next hour thinking of California and his father, wondering where Birch was and what he was doing.

This morning Bobby, who was also awake, asked, "What're you thinkin' about?"

"Wonderin' about Dad," Tom admitted. "You know. What he's doin'."

"He's sleepin'. It is three hours earlier in California; Missus Faraby said so. It's the middle of the night. He's sleepin'. Snorin' as loud as a hog," Bobby remarked dreamily. "Like Miss Lucy used to."

The certainty that his father was snoring at that exact moment was somehow comforting to Tom.

The feather mattress in the Tucker brothers' bedroom was on the floor; there was no frame or headboard. Rosey dreamed and twitched on the planks beside it, only her head resting on the lumpy padding. Beneath the sheets the mattress was lettered with the name *Hocott*. Of course, most everything in the Tucker house now bore some other family's name as protection against having the item seized by the Jensons. The parlor chairs, no two of which matched, were labeled *Amos*, *Winters*, and *Faraby*. The highbacked oak bench with the turned spindles did not have a name stenciled on it, but then it could not fail to be recognized as having come from Doc Brown's waiting room.

No one had brought a dining table, so meals were eaten on a card table furnished by Pop Lyle and labeled *Property of Hartford Bijou*. It was just as well that no formality was attached to eating; meals were odd to say the least. When Trudy examined the cupboard, she found as strange an assortment of donated canned goods as the house's borrowed furnishings. Pickled beets occupied too prominent a place next to apple butter and sauerkraut.

Tom closed his eyes and remembered cold buttermilk and hot biscuits, corn bread and ham and scrambled eggs and pork chops.

Then he heard the noise of a truck engine out front.

Bobby groaned and sat up, stepping into his brace. "How come every mornin' we get to sleep in, but I gotta use the outhouse at the same time as when we didn't used to sleep in?" With his nightshirt flapping over the iron-framed leg, Bobby reminded Tom of the Tin man of Oz.

"Now who's comin'?" Tom got up. "We got nothin' left to buy or steal."

Bobby blew his nose. "Someone else bringin' head cheese or quince preserves."

Then Tom heard Jim Brown's voice on the porch. The blacksmith, Tom's partner from the great possum hunt and the provider of Bobby's brace, was someone Tom would always be glad to see. That thought brought him up short; how much longer would it be before he left all his Shiloh friends behind forever? He helped Bobby up from the mattress and they both went to answer the door.

"Your truck looks like it is riding awfully low," Bobby observed, pointing to a mass of iron railings in the back of the pickup. The weight pushed the rear of the vehicle down onto the axle and tilted the hood skyward. Tom wondered if Jim had difficulty seeing over the nose to drive.

Jim glanced over his shoulder and answered Bobby's query as well as Tom's unspoken one. "Yep, it is a load," he acknowledged. "You boys heard from your daddy yet?"

Bobby shook his head once, as if to say that it was not a worry, then returned immediately to studying the truck. "But what is it you got there anyhow?"

"New brace for you." Jim laughed. "And a pound of real coffee beans for your mama."

"I could use a cup of coffee," Trudy said. "They forgot to auction the grinder, and I've got a coffeepot borrowed from Grandma Amos."

"Fire her up." Jim brought the bag and extended it to Trudy. She opened it, inhaled, and then shared the rich aroma with Tom. A pang of hunger went through his stomach. Had anything ever smelled so good?

"Looks like you have a load to deliver," Trudy said. "Have you time for a cup?"

"Always got time for a cup of coffee." Then Jim shuffled his feet like an awkward little boy. He blurted, "You want to see?" To cover his embarrassment, he hurried to the truck and removed a six-foot-long section of finely wrought iron fence railing. It was four feet high and topped with blunt spikes. At the center of the panel was a curlicue decoration that sprayed out among the uprights like a metallic pine bough.

"It is very fine workmanship," Trudy said. "Who is it for?"

"Well, Trudy, ma'am," Jim stuttered. "It's for you." He turned his head to stare pointedly in the direction of Joey's grave. "I know you . . . leaving behind . . ." Taking a deep breath so he could finish with a rush, he said, "I've been thinking about it some, and I know it must trouble you. It will put your mind at ease knowing Joey's place is marked properly and fenced. I got one fixed up for Hock Canfield, too. I'll come every year and paint 'em." Then Jim stopped, perhaps surprised that he had gotten it all said.

Trudy set the bag of coffee beans on the porch rail and joined Jim beside the truck. She ran her hands over the pine bough worked into the metal. "It is so fine," she said. "But how can I . . ." Her voice faltered. She breathed deeply and managed to regain her composure. "We will send payment from California as soon as we are able, Jim."

Jim was already shaking his head. "No, ma'am," he said. "I just had some extra scraps of metal going to waste is all. It pleasured me to do it. I couldn't take anything for this little bit of fence." Then as if to change the subject as quickly as possible, he asked, "Bobby, I know I promised you'd be chasin' possums before winter." Jim reached into the cab of the truck. "Maybe this will help." He extended a new leg brace. Made of shiny polished metal that gleamed silver in the morning sun, it featured an adjustable hinge on the foot clamp to make walking smoother, just as Jim had imagined months before.

Bobby sat down hard on the step. His mouth moved, but no words came out.

"Put it on. I want to see it work." Jim scratched his head. "Only one thing troubles me. I don't know if they have possums for you to hunt in California."

CHAPTER 41

Since Pegasus Oil paid its employees weekly, Jeff and Birch made a regular Friday-afternoon pilgrimage to the office of Perry James. The pay was so good and the work so steady that they were dispatching thirty dollars back to Shiloh every seven days. By remaining in the tent, refusing to accompany the other roughnecks to after-work drinking bouts and, as Jeff said, "eating their own cooking," they contrived to live on the few dollars a week that remained.

By Wednesday of the third week's employment with Red Sleeves, working around nitroglycerin had become routine, if not exactly mundane. That afternoon, Birch was using his left hand to steady a torpedo hanging over the wellhead and pouring soup into the tube with his right hand. When the metal cylinder began to slip upward through his grasp, he yelled at Red to cut it out, certain that the shooter was playing a trick and hoisting up the cable. Then he noticed that heavy, black crude was oozing out of the collar and pooling around his feet.

"Red," he yelled, quickly setting down the can of nitro so he could grab the torpedo with both hands, "it's pushin' out!"

"Hang on to it," Red yelled over his shoulder as he ran away from the well. "Put all your weight on it and hold on!"

Jeff, back at the soup wagon for another can, saw the danger and sprinted toward the derrick, only to be tackled around the knees and tripped by Red. "What're you doin'?" Jeff demanded, struggling to free himself from Red's wiry arms. "He needs help."

"No, he don't," Red insisted. "If just one of those tubes gets pushed up free of the hole and goes to bangin' on the steel, it'll set off the lot, sure as Christmas, get me? Kill us all if we don't keep down. This is one mule he's gotta ride hisself."

Deep within the earth, a pocket of natural gas had found its way to the bottom of the well. Rising slowly through the heavy crude, the bubble was lifting the oil in the casing and pushing the string of nitro cylinders upward.

Birch fought to keep the tube in the hole, to force the upwelling oil to flow around the obstruction until the gas subsided. He clung to it fiercely and for a few seconds fought the pressure to a standstill. Then, as if the underground forces suddenly perceived the puny strength of the human opposing them, the torpedo shot through Birch's grip and slid upward another three feet.

Out on the cleared ground around the well, Jeff was fighting a different kind of battle. "Lemme go," he demanded, yanking loose one of Red's hands, only to find the other still clamped on his ankle. "Lemme go!"

"Do you wanta get kilt, too?"

"I can help him! I can take up the slack in the line so the tubes don't flop around!" Jeff kicked Red in the arm and scrambled to his feet. Racing to the winch, Jeff engaged the drive, and the drum began to retrieve the loop of cable now sagging over Birch's head. As more of the tube rose up in Birch's gloved hands, the top wobbled dangerously, almost as if seeking a piece of steel with which to collide and spark.

Jeff knew he did not dare take up the cordage too quickly. Too much throttle, and the torpedo string would shoot up out of the hole, creating the same disaster he was trying to avoid. He forced himself to reel it in slowly, winding up only as much line as the rising pocket of gas coughed out of the well.

Oil was spouting from the wellhead, issuing in a gooey fountain two feet above the top of the collar. Waist-high on Birch's desperately clinging form, the rising crude threatened to wash him away from the torpedo, and yet still he hung on, knowing that Jeff's life as well as his own was now in danger.

Then, just as suddenly as it had begun, the upward strain receded. The oil ceased overflowing the wellhead and settled back down the tubing. The weight of the torpedo, precariously balanced by Birch as he fought the pressure, dropped back to hanging from the cable. Birch gratefully let his arms sag to his sides. When he stopped shaking, his very first thought was how glad he was that in all the letters home, he had never told Trudy exactly what kind of work he and Jeff were doing.

Thinking about Trudy and the boys made Birch miss them even worse than ever, so after work he went to Perry James's office even though it was not payday. "Any letter come for me or for Jeff?" he asked.

"Not a thing," Perry said. "Were you expecting something?"

"I can't understand it," Birch said. "I told my wife she could write back to us care of this office. She should've got my letter at least two weeks ago an' had time to write back."

"Well, you know how tough things are," Perry said. "Just give it time, I'm sure you'll hear something soon."

What was that noise? Tom heard a soft, dry rustle coming from across the field, off in the direction of the Rock Island spur. It sounded to Tom like a whole forest of bare trees in a high wind, branches rubbing together. But that was not quite right, either; it was more of a cross between a faint click and a whirring.

Tom picked up the halter and lead rope from the back stoop and slung them over his shoulder, then walked to the gate of the pasture. It was time to take Old Jake, the mule, to the watering hole a mile and a half away.

At least Old Jake was cooperative. Unlike his departed teammate Bob, Jake enjoyed human company and would come when called. At least usually he did. But this afternoon Jake stood on the far side of the thinly covered Bermuda-grass pasture, stomping and snorting.

Tom called him again, wondering if the poor feed and the loss of his partner had somehow upset the animal's agreeable disposition. "Jake," Tom called in a more demanding tone, "Get on over here!"

What was the mule up to? He would put his nose down to graze, nibble gingerly as if his gums were sore or his teeth hurt, then throw his neck back sharply, shaking his ears. As Tom watched from across the field, no good explanation presented itself. Old Jake pawed the ground some and snorted, but did not strike with his hooves as he would have if the problem were a cottonmouth or some other snake. What could it be?

The odd faint clicking sound persisted; in fact, it was stronger than before. Tom looked at the trees on the far side of the pasture. None of their tops were swaying. There was no breeze at all. Then Tom dropped his gaze to study the mule once more. Fretful, Tom's dad would have said; Jake was uneasy about something down on the ground. There was no brush tall enough to hide a predator. The stunted grass barely reached three inches in height and was even shorter in places where Jake had cropped it with his yellow teeth.

Hopping the fence, Tom walked toward the animal. He had not covered much of the hundred yards before he saw something else odd: The earth around the mule's hooves seemed to be in motion. The light tan of the field appeared to be flowing toward him.

Then sunlight glinted on a pair of glistening wings, and the truth became immediately apparent. Grasshoppers! An enormous swarm of the insects was crawling across the pasture. Old Jake would rip up a few sparse heads of Bermuda, then the incoming tide of grasshoppers would engulf his muzzle, making him toss his head and trot a couple of yards away.

Some of the crawly things were goaded into flight, but mostly they advanced in unperturbed and inexorable fashion. And as they came, they eliminated the grass in the path of their progress, leaving bare earth behind.

What to do? The Bermuda was all that was left to feed Jake. If the pasture disappeared, they could not keep the mule. Tom turned and ran toward the barn. His father would fight the critters with a kerosene burner, drive them out of the field and away from the remaining grass.

Tom jumped to the top of the fence and vaulted clear before he remembered: no kerosene, no burner, no tools. They had all been taken in the auction. He ran to the house anyway calling for his mother, then recalled that she and Bobby had gone to Grandma Amos's place to once again ask about a letter from Birch.

Throwing open the screen door with a bang, Tom seized a lamp from the card table in the front room and an old rag from under the kitchen sink. Back outside, he tied the rag to a stick, soaked the makeshift torch with lamp oil, and lit it with a match. The lamp oil smoked and smoldered, throwing off greasy fumes as he hurried back to the field.

There he found Old Jake, his nose stuck in a corner of the pasture, his heels lashing out at the swarm of grasshoppers. In the distance, up the spur toward the mountains and the strip mine, Tom could hear the wail of an approaching coal train.

Waving his smoking scrap of cloth, Tom drove the insects away from the gate. A cloud of bugs, disturbed by the heat and the fumes, whirred into the air around his head. They flew blindly in the smoke, blundering into Tom's face and hair and crawling inside his shirt collar. Their prickly legs scratched his cheeks and bare arms. If Tom moved forward, they jumped up onto him. If he stood still, they crawled over his bare feet and up his pants legs. He wished he had his brogans!

By revolving in place, stomping, brandishing the burning rag, and slapping himself with his free hand, Tom managed to drive the insects back.

He cleared a circle about ten feet across by swirling the smoldering brand, then advanced farther into the field. Grasshoppers caught by the flames cracked like burning sticks; those that flew into the smoke dropped stunned to the ground. Jake brayed, pawed, and kicked, crushing hundreds under his feet.

The whistle of the Rock Island engine shrilled again, getting closer. Tom waved his brand in angry circles, putting more of the insects to flight. He reached up and plucked three from his hair and shook three more from out of his shirt.

The coal freight chugged into view around a curve, howled again for a crossing, swept across the north field. The wheels ground thousands of grasshopper bodies into green, slimy pulp, and thousands more rose in a buzzing cloud that darkened the sky.

Then the train was gone, and the insects were crossing the tracks in renewed numbers. When Tom turned to inspect the area he had cleared, he found that only a small space right around the flame was free of the creatures; as soon as he walked on, they filled the gap he had just left.

Opening the gate, Tom followed the mule as Old Jake ran up toward the barn. The boy raced around inside the house, slamming doors and windows, crushing grasshoppers in the frames. It was all there was left for him to do.

Mr. Frost's B-model pickup was parked outside Shiloh General Store next to Brother Williams's Model-T when Trudy, Tom, and Bobby arrived. Trudy was pulling Bobby in the handcart and Tom leading the mule.

Trudy could tell from Brother's long face that there was still no letter from Birch. "Y'all know how far it is to Californy," Brother said. "Mail can be mighty uncertain from camps and boomtowns, ain't that right, Gramma? Why, sometimes they cobble together a whole city where there weren't but dirt the day before. Takes a while for the post office to catch up."

"Months?" Trudy asked in a clipped tone, her face drawn with worry. Then shaking her head as if to dispel her fears, she said matter-of-factly, "We want to thank you for the use of Jake, but we no longer have pasture left or other means to feed him."

"I heared about what the grasshoppers done at your place," Brother acknowledged.

"Like the plagues of Egypt," Grandma observed. "'Deed it is. Locusts."

"I'm sorry to hear about your troubles," Mr. Frost said. "Those ribs you fixed was surely the best I ever did eat. Maybe you oughta open another cafe somewheres else."

"I don't as yet know what we will do," Trudy said. "We cannot stay here, and we have nowhere else to go. But most of all, Lily and I need to find out what has happened to our husbands. And that's something I hope this letter will accomplish," she added, extending an envelope to Brother. "I have written to the Griers to ask if they have any later word of Birch and Jefferson."

"Surely it will come tomorrow." Trudy whispered her hope that Brother Williams would bring Birch's letter in the next mail delivery. It had to come tomorrow, because after tonight there would be nothing in the house left to eat. Even a few dollars would feed them and perhaps buy them lodging at Mrs. Brown's boardinghouse in Hartford, where the plague of insects was not so overwhelming.

"Joy will come in the morning." That would be a miracle. And it seemed that there could be no other miracle but a letter from Birch. Trudy told herself firmly that they had been cared for in the past and would be cared for again. Yet throughout the day, small doubts crept into her mind. It was, she thought, similar to the way the grasshoppers managed to sneak through small crevices between the floor planks and then into the house.

She whispered over and over again, "Please, help me believe."

The flour sack lay crumpled beside the borrowed kneading trough. The tin saltbox was empty. The final double handful of flour and pinch of salt would make one small loaf of bread. There would be nothing else for supper tonight when Tom and Bobby came home from school.

Sleeves rolled up, hands coated with flour, Trudy kneaded the dough and gazed out the kitchen window at the tribe of grasshoppers crawling on the upright posts of the pasture gate. The Bermuda grass consumed, the insects were now attacking the weeds and brambles of the parched acreage.

What was it Willa Mae had said about the Lord making a way in spite of a plague of locusts? Trudy recalled reading a National Geographic report about groups of nomadic people indigenous to central Africa who considered fried grasshoppers a delicacy. Also termites, grubs, and beetles. The author had tried them and found they had a distinctively nutty flavor. This thought was not comforting. Besides, Trudy thought wryly, she had no lard in which to fry them.

The ground beyond the fence swarmed with the odious creatures. Lunch for an entire tribe.

Brother Williams had poured a circle of coal oil around the base of the house to keep the insects out. This measure of prevention had met with some success, but it was still impossible to walk from one room to the other without feeling the crunch of a grasshopper underfoot. Tom now wore his brogans everywhere except to bed. This morning when he slipped into his shoes, he had given a yell and dumped out three grasshoppers from each.

How had they gotten into the house?

It was as if the dust was alive, Trudy thought, as two insects flicked up over the coal-oil boundary and latched onto the window screen, seeking some path to the inside.

The house was stifling with the heat from the cookstove, but Trudy only dared to open the windows that had screens. Yesterday the locusts had chewed holes in the laundry that had been hung outside to dry, so today the interior of the kitchen was festooned with underclothes, shirts, socks, and sheets.

She slid the bread into the warmer and sat down to wait for the dough to rise.

Darning tiny insect holes in Tom's socks took nearly an hour. For that time her thoughts shut out the unremitting whir of the insect wings outside.

Leaning her head back on the headrest of Willa Mae's rocking chair, Trudy longed to hold a good book in her hands, to read a bit and escape the reality of her desperation. All her books but one were gone now, perhaps for sale at ten cents a volume in some Fort Smith secondhand shop. The only book remaining was her Bible. Old and battered, it fell open to the ninety-first psalm when she placed it on her lap.

"He that dwelleth in the secret place of the Most High shall abide under the shadow of the Almighty. . . ."

Abide. That meant rest. And how Trudy longed for rest. She closed her eyes and wondered how it would be possible to go on trusting if Birch's letter and the money did not come.

The old clock tocked from the wall. After a long time she looked down at the rumpled page and resumed reading as if she were debating an enemy:

"He shall cover thee with his feathers, and under his wings shall thou trust: his truth shall be thy shield and buckler."

Trudy remembered baby chicks in the henhouse hiding beneath and behind the wings of their mothers, little heads poking out from behind the shield of feathers for a peek at the world. Could she be like them? Protected by the promises of a great and loving God?

"Thou shalt not be afraid for the . . . pestilence that walketh in darkness; nor for the destruction that wasteth at noonday."

She had read these same words a hundred times. And yet only now did it occur to her that the passage did not say pestilence and destruction would not come. The words simply stated that she should not be afraid when they crouched on her doorstep.

Since last autumn the plagues had arrived, one after another. The destruction was ongoing. There seemed reason to be frightened.

What will we eat tomorrow?

For weeks she had been telling everyone she was taking the boys to California to join Birch. But how would they get there?

Where was Birch? If he was able, surely he would get word to them. Had something happened to him? Was he still alive?

She rose slowly and went into the kitchen to check the loaf of bread. It had doubled in size. She punched it down again, covered it, and put it back in the warmer.

The last.

She stood at the dry sink and looked again at the undulating field of locusts. Then she noticed something larger moving slowly across the center of the pasture, heading for the gate.

She squinted into the glare. What was it? Did she dare to trust what her eyes were telling her was true?

In the center of the dun-colored pasture, in the midst of the swarms of creatures, bright sunlight glinted on a spot of red and then another. It was the auburn wings of a hen, a Rhode Island Red. Unmistakable! There was the long-lost Henny pecking a path through the pasture. Behind her at a distance of twenty feet was a second hen. So Henny had brought Taloa back with her. But where had the two hens been for so many weeks?

"Henny!" Trudy cried, overturning the water pitcher. Trudy fumbled to retrieve it, and only when she looked again did she see that the little Rhode Island Red hen was being followed, no, not merely followed but surrounded, by an entire flock of Guinea chicks! They were pecking their way through the plague of locusts, bobbing their heads with delight at the abundance of food that had overrun the briars and brambles of the field.

Heedless of the grasshoppers, Trudy burst out the door. She rushed to the pasture gate and, brushing the insects from the latch, swung it back wide.

"Henny!" Trudy called out in high falsetto. The Guinea chicks raised their downy heads in fright at the sound of her voice. They ran around in circles and clustered beneath the feathers of their two adopted mamas. Henny, wings extended, shielded her little flock from the perceived danger but continued her progress toward Trudy.

Trudy estimated that between the two hens were fifty small Guinea chicks. In the long weeks since the hen's disappearance, Henny and Taloa had evidently raided the nests and gathered the chicks of the wild

Guinea hens that roosted far up the James Fork. Now Henny was bringing her flock of Guinea hatchlings home.

Each chick was double the size of Trudy's fist. It would take two to make a meal, Trudy figured as she opened the door to the decimated garden, knowing that Henny would lead them there. The Guineas would all dine happily on the locusts. They would thrive and grow in the garden. They would provide food for Trudy and the boys.

C H A P T E R   4 2

There was still no letter or word from Birch. But even though eviction day approached, Trudy was no longer afraid. On their last day on the farm, Trudy calculated that the last Guinea chick would be eaten.

Two by two, the wild Guinea chicks fed the Tuckers. Day by day, the chicks grew and grazed happily inside the garden. By the end of the first week they were plump and succulent, and there was enough left over for Tom and Bobby to take some to school for lunch.

The Guineas maintained a sensible fear of all things human. Trudy noted to Willa Mae and Grandma Amos that whenever anyone attempted to get near them they shrieked like women fighting over linens at a Macy's white sale. No one in Shiloh General Store understood the comparison, but they agreed that there were not many critters who could raise a racket like a bunch of Guineas gone crazy.

Come twilight, the entire flock obediently trailed after the two Rhode Island Red hens to roost, not in the chicken coop, but under it. It was only after dark that Trudy dared to tiptoe out, sneak into the pen, reach under the building, and nab two of the sleeping Guineas by their legs. As instructed, she carried them upside down, which kept them relatively quiet. Their Guinea siblings, dreaming perhaps of foxes and Guinea-eating monsters, slept on, never suspecting that a human had come calling. By the time the sun came up and the others awoke, the dirty deed had been accomplished and the Guineas were already prepared for breakfast, lunch, and dinner at the Tucker house.

It was Willa Mae who told Trudy how to sneak up and grab whichever fowls were sleeping on the very end of the roost. Willa Mae took special delight in the recitation of each night's foray. And everyone in Shiloh took an active interest in the story of the wild Guinea chicks. After all, the sudden reappearance of Joey's chicken with fifty chicks was considered a miracle on par with the parting of the Red Sea. Willa Mae and Grandma Amos swapped stories for days about critters they had known who had heard the voices of angels and done miraculous things. Pop Lyle of the Hartford Bijou declared that Henny's story was a regular Biblical extravaganza worthy of an epic film by Cecil B. DeMille.

Twice, Trudy nabbed an extra Guinea, cooked it up, and took it down to share with Willa Mae, Lily, and Grandma Amos at the store. In return for her generosity, Trudy was presented with a sack of flour and a poke of salt. Tucker meals that followed included Guinea-and-dumplings, Guinea-and-biscuits, Guinea-and-bread, and Guinea pot-pie.

It tasted just like chicken.

Tonight there were twenty-five Guineas left sleeping on the perch beside Henny and Taloa. Thanks to the abundance of grasshoppers, they were now big enough that Trudy was only cooking one per day.

The harvest moon was big and orange like a pumpkin glowing in the sky above the Poteaus. Grasshoppers crunched beneath her shoes as she left the house. All was silent in the coop when she reached the gate of the wire pen.

Quietly, Trudy swung back the gate. She paused a moment to listen, hopeful that the howling of a dog across the swale had not disturbed her flock.

It was then that she heard footsteps behind her.

"Is that you, Tom?" she whispered hoarsely.

A man's voice replied also in a whisper, "No, ma'am."

Trudy gasped and closed the gate. The skin on her neck tingled with fear as she imagined Dudley Steele or worse. "Who? . . ."

"Don't be scared, Missus Tucker," the quiet voice replied. "It's just me, Mister Frost."

Trudy could see the tall, lean man's features in the moonlight. He tipped his hat to her and bowed slightly.

"Mister . . . Frost . . . yes. Good evening." Trudy remained rooted where she was, her back against the wire of the fence. "You're out . . . late. On foot?"

"Yes'm. My truck is broke down. Just on the road yonder."

"We have no telephone, Mister Frost. As you know."

"I know that, Missus Tucker. That weren't why I come."

"Oh? Well, then. I . . . it is late. I have no coffee. . . ."

"Why are we whisperin'?"

"So we do not wake the Guinea chicks sleeping beneath the coop."

He scratched his head and considered the information before he continued in a low voice, "Is your husband comin' back, ma'am?"

"We are to be evicted, Mister Frost. I thought you knew that."

"I heard it. Awful shame." He stepped nearer and took his hat off. He worked it with his hands and cleared his throat as if he was trying to speak, but could not find the words.

Trudy raised her voice to a normal volume, causing a stirring on the braces of the henhouse behind her. "Mister Frost, I really must . . . my boys are waiting up. . . ."

He blurted, "Wait, Missus Tucker. Like I said, my truck is broke down just out there on the highway beside y'all's gate. And as I was a-walkin', it come t' me that if your man ain't comin' back, well . . . you cook as fine as any woman I ever . . ."

"Mister Frost, I love my husband, and I thank you for thinking of me so kindly, but I must go in the house now."

He continued, "What I mean is, I'd like y'all t' go out t' California with me."

"I could not dream of doing any such thing."

"What I'm tryin' t' say is, I need a cook. Two weeks' work for a ride out west for you an' your boys."

Trudy drew her breath in sharply. There was safety in numbers. Perhaps it could work out if . . . "I cannot leave without Willa Mae and Lily and the Canfield babies."

"Fine, fine," he said, slapping his hat back on his head. "That Willa Mae sure can make a pineapple upside-down cake. Never tasted the like of it. I been livin' on railroad slop too long. I'll be leavin' next Friday evenin', ma'am, if y'all are so inclined. Ask Willa Mae an' Lily then. Leave word at Gramma Amos's store in the next day or so if y'all wanna come along."

It was Thursday night. Birch was stretched out on a tarp beside the tent, sucking on an orange. He listened to some neighbors singing. The song went,

You've all heard the story
Of old Sunny Cal,
The place where it never rains,
They say it don't know how.
They say, "Come on, you Okies,
Work is easy found,
Bring along your cotton pack,
You can pick the whole year round."

The strongest voice was a half-tone flat, and the three adults and three children in the group were living out of a 1925 Brewster station wagon, but the voices were cheerful and upbeat.

Jeff was using a short-handled shovel to uncover a dutch oven buried on top of hot coals underneath a layer of Kern River sand. When the cast-iron lid appeared, he carefully blew the remaining grains of grit from the top and used a hay hook to lift the lid. A cloud of fragrant steam rose from the pot of stew.

Birch roused himself and sat up. Amos Grier was walking along the trail that led from the encampment to Chester Avenue. Birch gave him a big howdy and hollered for Amos to come to supper.

But Amos had other things on his mind. "Mighty glad I found you home," he said to Birch in an anxious tone. "I got a letter for you from your missus . . . you too, Jeff," he added. He extended a pair of envelopes to the men.

Still not certain why Amos sounded upset, Birch asked, "Everything all right, Amos?" Then a thought struck him. "Wonder how come Trudy came to be writin' us at your place. I told her she could send us mail care of Pegasus."

"That's just it," Amos replied, frowning and shaking his index finger in agitation. "In the letter to Missus Grier, Trudy wrote that she ain't heard from y'all since you first got here . . . didn't know what had become of you."

"That's not possible," Birch said. "I been writin' reg'lar; sendin' home our pay every week!"

"Look here what she says," Amos instructed. Birch and Jeff crowded around to look over his shoulder. Birch recognized Trudy's handwriting. "No letters, she says, an' no money! Nothin'! Not a word!"

Birch ripped open his letter. "My dearest Birch," he read. "If this reaches you, you must know how anxious we have been about your safety. We have heard nothing from you in weeks. Birch, we are down to very little in the cupboards. . . ." The letter went on to mention the forced sale of the Tucker possessions and the plague of grasshoppers. Though it was calm and unafraid in tone, Birch could read the desperation behind the emotionless words. Lily's letter, though brief and painstakingly scrawled, told a similar tale.

"But how could that happen?" Birch wondered again. "Every Friday since we got on with Pegasus . . . even before we got on, in fact . . . we been goin' into the office and—"

"An' Mister Perry James been watchin' us put money in them envelopes before we hands 'em to him," Jeff concluded.

"Wait," Birch cautioned. "I know what it looks like, but we can't rush in and call him a thief. We'll have to catch him at it. Tomorrow."

"That's so," Jeff agreed. "And we gots us a telegram to send back home."

"That ain't even good enough," Birch objected. "We gotta find a telephone. We gotta call Gramma Amos! But we can't do either one till we get paid tomorrow, and by then we'll know the truth!"

Friday's work felt like it lasted a whole year. On the way to the first job of the day, Birch and Jeff encountered Perry James outside the Pegasus office. Both Arkansas men forced themselves to smile and nod to the grinning, boyish supervisor, though both were seething inside.

It was a dangerous shift. Once Red had to caution Birch to wipe a drop of the explosive liquid off the outside of a can, a mistake not made since their very first experience with nitro. Jeff, in a similar moment of distraction, caught his glove in the cable as the torpedoes were being lowered into the well and nearly lost a thumb before the winch was halted.

Finally the last well was shot and the work came to an end. In an elaborate show of normality, Jeff and Birch entered Perry James's office and asked him politely if he could once again spare an envelope for them to write home.

"Absolutely," James replied with a smile. "And I'll see that it gets mailed, same as always."

Birch scribbled a hasty note. Then, taking a fistful of bills from Jeff, he tucked the letter and money into the envelope and addressed it. He handed it over to Perry James with a thank-you.

Once outside the door, Birch and Jeff walked slowly till they were out of the view from the office front window. Then Jeff took up a position where he could intercept others heading for the building while Birch, bent low, crept around the side and rose cautiously up to the bottom corner of the front window.

James's back was to him, but there was no question about what was going on. The oil field manager was counting a handful of dollars. As Birch watched, the man crumpled a piece of paper into a very small wad and tossed it into the trash can under his desk.

Birch burst into the room. James whirled around, frantically trying to stuff the money into his shirt. A button popped, and a five-dollar bill escaped from the stack to flutter to the floor. "Tucker," Perry stuttered. "Did . . . did you forget something?"

"I'll say I did," Birch agreed, reaching across the desk to grasp James by the throat. "I forgot that some folks' smiles are not to be trusted."

Perry James made a strangled noise as he still tried to protest his innocence. "What are . . . why . . . help!" he called.

"I'll give you all the help you're goin' get," Birch growled as he dragged the man bodily over the desk top. Perry's shoes scrabbled against the oak surface, kicking papers in all directions.

The door to the office slammed open again. "What's going on here?" bellowed a voice. Mr. Creedmore, general manager of Pegasus Oil, had arrived for his monthly inspection. He stormed into the office, despite Jeff's attempt to head him off. "Let go of him at once," Creedmore demanded. "What is all this?"

Birch dropped James to the top of the desk, where he lay panting and rubbing his windpipe before he slipped off to stand wobbling next to his chair.

"I'm trying to tell you," Jeff said.

"You be quiet!" Creedmore shouted. "Attacking the manager? You're fired, both of you."

"Wait," Birch protested. "The money. Our money."

"That's it," James said in a rasping voice. "They were trying to rob me. See?" He pointed to the five laying on the floor.

"Then call the sheriff," Creedmore proposed.

In a reasonable but unyielding voice Jeff suggested, "Ask him what he done with our letter."

"I don't know anything about . . ." James exclaimed, nudging the wastebasket farther under his desk with his toe.

"Look for yourself," Birch said, pointing to the square metal bin. "See if there ain't a letter from me all wadded up there. See if it don't talk about thirty-five dollars, and then see if that ain't exactly the amount this man has on him."

Frowning, Creedmore did as Birch and Jeff suggested and, over the protests of Perry James, examined the crumpled letter in the basket. "It seems I owe you men an apology," he said. "And it is still a matter for the sheriff."

James bolted for the doorway, trying to dodge under the grasp of Jeff. He succeeded in ducking right into Jeff's fist, which landed squarely on the point of his jaw. James flew backward, smacking into the desk again and this time falling flat on his back atop it. He did not stir for a while.

"I don't think we'll need to restrain him while we wait for the deputies," Creedmore said dryly. "He won't be going anywhere."

Birch blurted, "We been thinkin' our wives were gettin' our pay for food and for train tickets. Times are real hard . . . and they ain't received a dime! Lord, Mister Creedmore, we gotta make a call back to Arkansas!"

The superintendent indicated the phone on the desk. "Use this one," he said. "The call will be on Mister James."

The spicy, sweet aroma of candied yams cooked up with plenty of sugar and cinnamon competed with the scent of Willa Mae's corn bread hot from the oven. Tom's stomach growled, and he looked around quickly to see if anyone had heard. Right next to him, Jim Brown's midsection gave a rumble like the passage of the Rock Island freight. "Good Lord," Jim said. "Did you ever smell anything so good?"

Brother Williams came into the Tucker house with Boomer close behind. They let in a pair of grasshoppers, but no one minded. A dozen more insects were clinging to the outside of the screen door, so only letting in a couple seemed like an achievement.

The Tucker home, though empty of furnishings, was full of friends and food. Everyone had brought something, from the stick candy furnished by Mister Winters to the apples from Doc Brown's tree. The pie that Trudy had concocted from Doc's fruit was likewise a community effort: flour from the Farabys, lard from Sheriff Potts, and sugar donated by Grandma Amos.

The Guinea chicks, half grown now and each big enough for a man-sized meal, furnished the main course. Tom watched Bobby sitting in the corner of the room with Catfish Pierce. Both younger boys had a plate heaped with food sitting beside them on the floor, but their attention was focused on Catfish's school copybook. Stopping to lick the pencil, Bobby was laboriously transcribing the Griers' address in California so his friend could write to him.

Sally Grier was in Oildale, in the same town where Tom would be before long. He was surprised that he got a funny feeling in his chest at the same time he thought of her. He put it down to having sampled too many of the candied yams.

Grandma's quavery voice started singing. It was an old hymn, "Bringing in the Sheaves." Tom was not certain whether the others joined out of enthusiasm, politeness, or just to drown out Grandma's tremulous, off-key warble, but everybody sang.

"BRINGIN' IN THE SHEEPS!" Boomer contributed.

Jim Brown motioned for Tom to join him on the floor in another corner of the room. The blacksmith carefully brushed a few grasshoppers aside before sitting down. He reached into his jacket pocket and brought out a small object wrapped in a handkerchief. "Want you to take this," he said.

"What is it?" Tom asked, untying the knotted corner of the cloth. A moment later Birch's pocket watch lay in Tom's hand.

"Nobody can take that from you now that you're leaving," Jim said. "Take it to your dad. But you can tell him from me that if he decides to let you keep it for your own, you've earned it."

"I'll fly away," Grandma sang. "O glory, I'll fly away."

"WHEN I DIE, HALLELUJAH, BY AND BY," Boomer sang happily. "I'LL FLY AWAY." To everyone's surprise, he got all the words exactly right.

"Me an' Boomer's goin' on the radio," Grandma said, thumping her cane on the floor to get everyone's attention. "If we practice ever' day, Mister McClung of the Hartford Music Company will put us on the radio, just see if he don't."

"GONNA BE ON THE RADIO!" Boomer pledged.

"Yep," Grandma said. "Tom, you an' Bobby an' your mama and Willa Mae and Lily, you listen to the radio out in Californy. Y'all will hear us singin' from back here in Shiloh."

When the last of the meal of fried Guinea hens had been packed for the journey, tearful farewells were made, and everyone went home carrying away feather mattresses, linens, chairs, pots, and pans. Willa Mae and Lily returned to their cabin with Mr. Frost to pack the Canfield household onto the back of his B-Model pickup. They were leaving that very night, soon, in fact, in order to beat the heat of traveling by day. In less than twenty-four hours they would be hundreds of miles away.

Tom joined Bobby at the porch rail. In the golden slant of late afternoon sunlight, the boys watched their mother carrying a pine bough toward the wrought-iron fence and the cross on the knoll.

"Help me, Tom," Bobby said. "I want to say goodbye to him."

Tom nodded. He stepped off the porch, allowing Bobby to climb onto his back. He carried Bobby down the hill to join Trudy.

The gate enclosure was open. The pine bough lay across the mound of earth. The slender sprig of a lilac tree had sprouted at the foot of the grave. *Had Mama planted it there,* Tom wondered? *Or did it grow at the command of Joey's angel, who had nothing else to do now but keep watch and wait until Joey woke up one day?*

Trudy spoke quietly. "Look. There is a lilac growing here." Her expression was filled with peace.

So it was Joey's angel planted it, Tom thought, and he smiled.

Bobby gripped the corner of the iron fence. In a halting voice he whispered, "There is rust on the bars already." Tom knew by this that Bobby was worried that no one would look after Joey's grave once they were gone.

Trudy replied in a matter-of-fact way, "Jim Brown has promised to paint it. Once a year he said he would paint the fence."

"The marker is only wood," Bobby said. "It will rot away."

Trudy also had an answer to this concern. "I have spoken to Hubert Smith about a nice stone. I told him we will send him payment from California. He has agreed happily and will see to it on our behalf. The stone will have Joey's name and his dates. Below that will be the words, 'Beloved son of Trudy and Birch and brother of Tom and Bobby.' So you see, our names will stay with him. It will be a fine memorial. But I think he will like this lilac best of all."

"I wish we could carve the whole story of how his Henny brought the Guineas to feed us," Bobby said.

Trudy replied, "There is not room on a single stone to tell such a miracle. We shall have to carry the story in our hearts. Perhaps you will tell it to your children one day. However, Mister Smith will see to it that a rooster is carved into the granite like the one on Joey's weathervane . . . crowing to welcome the new day."

This seemed to satisfy Bobby. He jerked his head down once in acceptance.

"Someday I'll come back here." Bobby's words were tinged with bitterness. "I'll pay them back for what they've done."

Trudy put her arm around his shoulder. Tom could see plainly that Bobby was shaking with renewed anger and grief.

"Carry away the best of what we had here, Bobby. Leave the rest behind. Let it go."

"After what they have done . . . How can you say that?" he asked. Bobby always asked the questions that were on Tom's mind.

Trudy rubbed her fingers over a single spot of rust that dulled the shine of the new iron fence. "Bitterness is like a speck of rust." She displayed the orange tinge on her thumb. "Left alone, it will eat away the metal of your soul. It will weaken the blade of a plow until it shatters on the first small stone. It will consume the strongest sword. I cannot face my future battles if I let the past eat away my strength." She turned her eyes skyward. A flock of crows cawed and wheeled in lazy circles above the bright colors of the mountains.

"It is autumn again," Trudy said without regret. "And from last autumn to this, I have learned a thing or two."

Fifteen rings.
Sixteen rings.
Seventeen rings.

"Willa Mae!" Grandma Amos croaked. "Ain't you gonna answer that thang? Might be Memphis callin'."

Eighteen rings.

"Willa Mae! . . . Naw, she's gone to Californy." The old woman hobbled toward the instrument shrilling in the alcove. "Sounds like a pig stuck under a grate," she muttered.

Nineteen rings. "Howdy! Grandma here. Who is that speakin'? What? You'll have to speak louder than that. Birch Tucker. No, he ain't here. He ain't been here in a long time. And I'd hate to be him when his wife catches up with him. He ain't written, ain't sent no . . . what's that?"

Grandma took the earpiece away and scrubbed it vigorously with the corner of an empty Pillsbury flour sack, missing a minute's worth of conversation. "There now, that's better. You say you want Trudy Tucker? Well, why didn't you say so? Gotta be clear on these telephone thangs or folks cain't take your meanin'. Now, what about Trudy? No, she ain't here."

The words, "Can somebody get her?" bellowed out of the receiver.

"You don't need to yell so; I ain't deaf. No, nobody can get her."

"Why not?" roared the phone.

"Ain't I been tryin' to tell you? She's gone . . . gone to Californy. Her and the boys and Willa Mae Canfield and Lily and the babies. They're all gone."

"How? When?"

"Why, with Mister Frost of course, what do y' think? They didn't have no automobile, nor train tickets, nor wagon, nor mule. You think they was gonna walk all the way to Californy? What? Well, how should I know when they's gonna get there? It's a long way, ain't it? Had us a fine covered-dish supper to give 'em a send-off, too." The old woman cackled a dry, wheezing laugh. "Good thing it was a covered supper, too, or them grasshoppers woulda been in the mashed 'taters! But ever'body's gone. Up and left, yessir, up and left. Whole place is busted flat. Brother Williams cain't even afford to feed Boomer no more. Boomer is workin' for me now, startin' tomorrow."

The flow of Grandma's monologue stopped abruptly as she suddenly recalled that she had Boomer coming in the morning. She held the receiver away from her ear so the obnoxious questions rattling from the other end would not disturb her recollection of some chore she needed to remember. Then it came to her: Boomer was going to live in Willa Mae's cabin and help out around the store, and it was the cabin that reminded her of something undone. "Well, I gotta go now," she said, cutting off the inquiry. "I gotta go find a blanket and some towels for Boomer to use in the cabin. Sure glad you called," she said. "Call again."

Hanging up the receiver cut off an anguished "Wait!"

Grandma bustled over to a stack of blankets, digging down till she found one a little more dusty than she could sell easily. It only had a few small grasshopper-eaten holes in it.

"I wonder who that was," she mused. "Acted like he knowed me."

CHAPTER 43

Two weeks had passed, and Jeff and Birch had still received no word of Trudy, Willa Mae, or Lily. Standing on the fingerboard up in the derrick of the new well Pegasus Oil was drilling, Jeff was not aware of the lunch break until the driller shut down the engine. That was his signal to unhook his safety line and climb down the ladder.

Birch, the floorman on the job, was already shucking his gloves and waiting for Jeff to join him. Since the discovery of Perry James's theft and the altercation in the accounting office, Mr. Creedmore had tried to make things right by getting Birch and Jeff better jobs. They were away from the nitro gang, roughnecking on a drilling crew. The pay was fifty cents an hour, with the prospect of making driller someday and receiving the lofty salary of ten dollars a shift.

But all these encouraging developments were spoiled by worry about their families. Even another costly phone call in which Birch had succeeded in reaching Doc Brown had not revealed any later news. Trudy and the rest were somewhere between Arkansas and California; that was all.

Birch and Jeff had counted the days, figured the miles, allowed for flat tires, dust storms, and miscellaneous breakdowns. They even calculated in rest stops, and still their conclusion was the same: Their families should have been there already. Being unable to make further reasonable provision made Birch think of more dire explanations: accidents, illness brought on by bad weather, missing children, and a thousand other possibilities that their worst imaginations conjured up.

"Where do you figger they are?" Birch asked Jeff for the thousandth time. Then without waiting for Jeff's answer, Birch continued, "How did I expect them to find us? California is such a big place. What if it weren't clear? Or what if they come through here already, didn't find us, and moved on? How'll we catch up to them?"

Jeff replied, the same as he always did, that Oildale had not moved, nor had the two men. "If'n they drives straight west, they cain't miss California less'n they runs into the ocean. That'll whoa 'em up, and then they'll come here," he concluded. "Just gotta keep trustin'," he added.

Birch asked the driller, a stocky man with a German surname and a guttural way of talking, if he would please keep his eyes and ears open for news of anyone asking around for Birch or Jeff. The driller agreed readily enough, as he had already done a half-dozen times before. "But joost one thing, Burch," he growled. "Day after tomorrow ve leaf for Ventura. Pegasus iss opening a new field, unt ve vill be dere first crew."

It was the worst thing possible. Ventura was on the coast, more than a hundred miles away. In one more day Jeff and Birch would have to choose between giving up their highly prized new positions or becoming almost impossible for Trudy and the others to find.

It was so vast. The great central valley of California lay sprawled across the highway in front of the B-model pickup like a giant horn-of-plenty spilling its load on the ground. This mountain pass was four thousand feet above the surface of the world. Tom had never been so high up before in his entire life. From the hills of Arkansas, they had traveled for two weeks across Texas and the southwest, and never, ever, had there been a view this grand.

"Ocean's acrost them mountains," Mr. Frost exclaimed, waving his arm out the window to the west. "Ones on the other side go up higher than you can imagine. More'n two miles, some of 'em."

Everyone was riding in the back of the truck, leaving Mr. Frost to pilot around the hairpin turns with only Rosey and a coop with Henny and Taloa inside for company. No one wanted to be crammed inside the cab when the views in the narrow canyon all seemed to be vertical.

"The backbone of the earth," Willa Mae announced, looking over the upthrust plates of rock that jutted in tortured folds from beside the road.

"Earthquake fault," Mr. Frost called back over his shoulder.

Tom, Bobby, Trudy, and Willa Mae all stood upright, craning their necks and peering over the top of the cab. Only Lily and the babies were down among the bedrolls, packing crates, and Willa Mae's trunk.

Tom could smell the rich, sweet aroma of alfalfa hay. It made him hungry. They had eaten very little the last few days.

Trudy's pocketbook had one dime remaining. She had not shared this news with anyone; Tom had watched without her knowing as she inspected the Mercury-head coin by the light of last night's campfire.

"It's so big," Tom said. "How're we ever gonna find Dad and Jeff?"

"We will," Trudy said simply. Her voice had never lost its calm assurance, even though Tom's anxiety had grown the farther away from Shiloh they had traveled.

"Don't you worry 'bout nothin', honey," Willa Mae soothed. "The Lawd is with us, truly He is. 'We've come this far by faith, leanin' on the Lawd,'" she quoted from a hymn.

It had seemed true up till now. Even the old rattletrap truck had hung together. The only engine trouble on the way had been a clogged fuel line back in Texas. Tom had cleared it himself, laughing as he blew out the dirt that they had seen the last dust of Arkansas.

But now his doubts were back, stronger than ever. How would they locate his dad in such a huge place?

Mr. Frost was prattling on about how this particular highway was nicknamed The Grapevine, when the truck rounded another curve, the downgrade steepened suddenly, and the hot, rubbery smell of burning brakes overwhelmed the scent of hay and oranges. Mr. Frost ground the gears of the truck and fought it onto the shoulder of the road.

"We got a problem," he said. "The brakes is burned up. I'll take it down on the gears, but I think y'all would be safer walkin'."

The truck did not become a runaway, but that was partly because Tom and Trudy held fast to a length of rope tied to the rear axle. The little cavalcade was overtaken repeatedly by other vehicles speeding down into the valley. Chrysler Imperials, Model-A Fords, and boxy Plymouth sedans roared past. A passenger in a yellow-bodied Peerless touring car with white sidewall tires leaned out the window and yelled, "Darn Okies! Go home!" as it flashed by.

"Pay no mind," Willa Mae instructed. "His mama and daddy come here from someplace else, too."

Four arduous hours later, they reached the foot of El Tejon Pass. At last they were able to scramble back aboard and ride again.

The vast sky arched from east to west like a canopy of cobalt blue. Mile after mile after endless mile stretched out before Tom's vision as if the valley had no northern boundary at all; it just went on forever.

"It's so big," Tom worried again. The narrow defile had given way to a long gentle slope. The chaparral was replaced by big stretches of barbed wire where cattle grazed among the tumbleweeds. These were followed by fields of recently mown hay, some with greenish bales still drying in the sun. "But where are the houses and the people?" Trudy wondered.

Frost laughed. "Farms out here are called ranches," he said, "and they are bigger than anything you ever saw. Might be thousands of acres before you come to the house."

"Children of Israel didn't have no more glorious sight lookin' 'crost the Jordan than this," Willa Mae exulted. "Promised Land, flowin' with milk an' honey."

West of the road a range of low hills studded with oil derricks sprang into focus. "Look, Mama," Tom gestured. "Mebbe that's where Dad and Jeff are."

Even though Mr. Frost tried to sound cheerful, his words were not encouraging. "There's oil all over this end of the valley," he said. "From Taft, Maricopa over where you're pointin', clean back up into the hills thataway."

Trudy said resolutely, "We will start with what we know and work from there."

Willa Mae agreed. "There is a river," she intoned, quoting both Psalm forty-six and Birch's penny-postcard message. "This might be more like heaven than any other place on earth," she said. "But yonder is the river, sure enough." She gestured toward a wavy green line of cottonwoods and willowsthat snaked down out of the mountains to the east and crossed the route ahead of them some twenty-five miles farther on.

The moist, honeyed aroma of sweet corn ready for harvest competed with the mellow smell of alfalfa and the hot, dusty odor of cotton. Could Birch be laboring in one of the fields they passed? But no, Ida Grier's letter had said he and Jeff were working in the worst job in oil. Tom raised his nose into the dry wind and sniffed the air as if he could locate Birch by the faint whiff of petroleum.

It was the longest twenty-five miles of the trip. They reached the outskirts of Bakersfield at five o'clock. Quitting time. Company cars and trucks poured onto the two-lane highway, slowing their progress even further. On either side of the road soared tall, thin-barked trees whose long, pointed leaves gave off a sharp, pungent smell. "Eucalyptus," Mr. Frost commented.

Tom peered into every car that passed; looked into the face of every man in oily clothes. He would never miss his father if Birch were anywhere nearby. Across the river to the north, Tom saw more hillsides sprouting oil derricks like giant pincushions.

Withdrawing a paper with the Griers' address on it, Trudy studied it, but looked uncertain where to begin. Bobby, holding himself upright by his grip on the slats of the stakebed, waved his free hand at a gang truck full of oil workers that had reached the intersection on their right. "There's oil men, Mama!" Bobby exulted. "Ask 'em! Ask 'em where Dad is!"

Tom did it instead. "Any of you ever heard of Birch Tucker?" he called.

"Birch? Yeah, I know him," replied a darkly tanned man wearing a shiny steel hard hat tipped back from his face. There was a line of oil streaked across his forehead from the sweatband of the helmet. "He was camped down by the river, just across the bridge. But I hear he got transferred to somewhere on the coast."

The sand around the tent was gouged with concentric rings of footprints. When Jeff sat down to think, Birch took over the pacing, as if a let-up in the fretting circles would ruin any chance they had of arriving at a solution to their dilemma. Dozens of others encamped in the crowded Hooverville looked on with a mix of amusement and sympathy.

"We cain't afford to walk out on no drilling job," Jeff said. "The good Lawd give us that chance, and we'd be wrong to give it away."

"I know," Birch agreed miserably. "But how will the gals ever find us if we go off to Ventura? How? I don't even know where it is myself."

Jeff studied on the situation some more. "How 'bout this?" he said. "Tomorra we gotta take the tent back to Amos Grier anyhow. When we do, we'll leave word with him where we're gonna be. When the womenfolk make it here and don't find us, they'll think to hunt up Amos. and he'll put 'em on to our whereabouts."

"I dunno," Birch replied, shaking his head with doubt. "Purty chancy. What if they don't find Amos? What if *he* gets moved somewheres else? What if they don't have no way of comin' on to Ventura?"

"Lawd," Jeff said prayerfully. "We don't mean to sound ungrateful for all You've did for us. But please, Sir, if'n You could spare one more little look our way, we'd be much obliged. We is powerful worried about our folks, and needs us an answer."

Away from the river bank, too far off to be distinct, an unfamiliar male voice called someone's name. How Birch wished it was Trudy calling for him. The stranger asked again for someone, received a negative reply, then inquired once more and came closer to the tent.

"Birch Tucker?" asked the newcomer. "Anyone here by that name? Birch Tucker? Jeff Canfield?"

"Over here," Jeff and Birch yelled as one man. Birch's heart started pounding and he did not know why.

The stranger walked up out of the afternoon sun. His features were shadowed by the glare as Birch and Jeff faced him. "I'm Tucker, an' this is Jeff Canfield," Birch said. "You lookin' for us?"

"Name's Frost," the unknown man said, breaking into a grin. "There's some folks come a long way to find you. It looked a mite rough down here, so they is waitin' up by my truck."

This was not entirely true. By some instinct, Trudy had followed the sound of Mr. Frost calling out Birch's name, even before Birch had answered. When Birch pushed past Frost, headed for the road, there she was, silhouetted against the sun. Birch did not recall covering the intervening fifty feet, but suddenly Trudy was in his arms, right where she belonged.

Birch and Trudy were still locked in an embrace. So were Jeff and Lily. Rosey yipped and danced around the couples, licking them and licking Tom as if she had not seen him for months.

Mr. Frost mopped his brow at the sight of the reunion and then stoically turned away and directed his attention to the few Canfield possessions and the crate of chickens in his truck. He motioned for Tom to climb up and help unload Willa Mae's steamer trunk.

"Where are you headed to now, Mister Frost?" Tom asked.

"Fresno," came the reply. "And I wanna get on the road before dark." The railroad man cocked his head to one side and squinted off down the rutted lane that passed for Riverview Road. "Y'all know them folks a'comin' yonder? They sure look like they know y'all."

A basket of linens in his arms, Tom turned to follow Frost's gaze. His heart jumped into his throat as the sun glinted on the shiny gold hair of Sally Grier. She was walking between her mother, who carried a wicker food hamper, and her father, who hefted a large wooden box on his shoulder.

"Howdy, Possum!" At the sight of Tom, Sally skipped and gave a wave.

Bobby answered for Tom, who could not find his voice. "Hey, Sally! You look swell!"

She was eight months taller than the last time Tom had seen her across the Rock Island tracks on the day Bobby had come home from the hospital. She was prettier than ever. Smiling broadly, she wore her hair in French braids tied with red ribbons. Her red-checked dress was new, Tom thought; at least he had never seen it before. Her shoes fit her feet.

Tom stood rooted and gawking in the pickup bed. Mister Frost took the basket from his hands and passed it down to Willa Mae.

"Nobody's any use at'all, Willa Mae." Frost sniffed and spat into the dirt.

"We jus' ain't seen one another for a spell." Willa Mae reached up for the load. "Give 'em a while."

Frost intoned, "Gotta get t' Fresno 'fore mornin'. My daughter's birthday tomorrow. Jus' gotta get movin' on."

Tom jumped from the tailgate as Sally rushed up to greet him. She had grown two inches taller than he, and other things about her were subtly different.

"You're big," he blurted.

She laughed and took his hand. "It's all this California food." Jerking her thumb back toward her father, she remarked brightly. "My pa is bringing y'all a whole crate of oranges."

Bobby gave a low whistle. "A crate? How many in a whole crate?"

Sally shrugged as if the number was insignificant. "Few dozen or so, I suppose. A lot."

Amos Grier shouted his hellos to all in the camp and lowered the wooden box onto a tree stump.

"Brung these for y'all." Amos looked proud as his gift finally caught the attention of Trudy and Lily.

Holding the hands of Birch and Jefferson, the two women pulled the menfolk closer to the crate to gaze in wonder at the dozens of California oranges all together in one box. A treasure.

Tom stared down at the crate. There were more of the juicy things than he had ever seen before in one place in his entire life. He remembered the single fruit he had received last Christmas, how he had hoarded that treasure until it had grown soft before finally taking it to school and splitting it with Sally.

"For us?" Bobby asked in an awed voice.

"All y'all can eat," Amos Grier exclaimed.

Sally, looking steadily into Tom's eyes, replied in a quiet voice. "Remember how you shared your Christmas orange with me?"

"It was all mushy," Tom said, feeling embarrassed as Bobby made a rubber face at him and gave him an exaggerated wink.

Sally pressed a cool, firm orange into Tom's hand. "I never tasted anything so good as that orange. Used to dream about it. It ain't no dream no more. Reckon you can have one all to yourself now, Possum. You can have as many as you want, and when this is gone we got us a whole tree full right in our backyard."

Willa Mae Canfield raised her eyes heavenward and cried in a joyful voice, "'Tis the River Jordan we done cross over this day! 'Tis the Promise Land we come to, sure as the Lawd lives! Jesus! Oh, Jesus! We is home at last!"

About the Authors

With twenty-four novels to their credit, over six million books in print and seven ECPA gold Medallion awards, Bodie and Brock Thoene have taken their works of historical fiction to the top of the best-seller charts and to the hearts of their readers.

Bodie is the storyteller, weaving plotlines and characters into stunning re-creations of bygone eras.

Broke provides the foundation for Bodie's tales. His meticulous research and attention to historical detail ensure that the books are both informative and entertaining.

The Thoenes' collaboration receives critical acclaim as well as high praise from their appreciative audience.